ROGER STEVENSON
NOV., 1993

LOOKING
FORWARD

LOOKING FORWARD

ISADORE ROSSMAN, M.D., Ph.D.

Medical Director, Home Health Agency, Montefiore
Hospital and Medical Center, New York City
Professor Emeritus, Albert Einstein College of Medicine

E. P. DUTTON  NEW YORK

Published in the United States by E. P. Dutton,
a division of Penguin Books USA Inc.,
2 Park Avenue, New York, N.Y. 10016.

Published simultaneously in Canada
by Fitzhenry and Whiteside, Limited, Toronto.

Library of Congress Cataloging-in-Publication Data

Rossman, Isadore, 1913–
  Looking forward: the complete medical guide to successful aging/
Isadore Rossman.—1st ed.
    p.   cm.
  Includes index.
  ISBN 0-525-24785-8
  1. Aged—Health and hygiene. 2. Aging. I. Title.
RA777.6.R67   1989
613'.0438—dc19   89-1578
                    CIP

Designed by REM Studios

10 9 8 7 6 5 4 3 2 1

First Edition

A major satisfaction in writing this book was the expectation that it would help younger members of the family—Paul, Jeanne, Lisa, Peter, and of course Jonathan—onward to successful aging.

—Grandpa Fizzy

ACKNOWLEDGMENTS

It is a pleasure to acknowledge the help of these key people in the progressive development of this book:

My literary agent—and patient—Herb Katz, who worships books and what they can do, first suggested this project.

William Proctor toiled heroically over the writing and intelligibility of the book.

Joyce Engelson, editor in chief at E. P. Dutton, contributed to a vastly improved book through her critical intelligence and thorough reading.

CONTENTS

AGING
IN STYLE

1

THE GOOD NEWS ABOUT AGING

Medically speaking, middle age is a very good time of life. Yet if you're in your forties, fifties, or sixties—and if you're at all observant—chances are you're feeling some doubts about your physical powers. Perhaps your body seems not to be as quick, strong, or durable as it once was. By a number of measurements, it's clear that you're getting older, and frankly, you'd rather not think about it.

But I urge you in your own interest to revise your thinking. First, aging is not synonymous with illness. Second, the middle years are still the great years of opportunity: opportunity to take inventory, to do some "stockpiling" of your physical assets, and especially to perform a lot of preventive maintenance.

Perhaps the most exciting fact about aging is this: At about the age of fifty, we are provided by nature with a remarkable second chance to undo some of the damage of the first fifty years of living. The human body is more resilient and powerful than most people ever imagine. The marvelous advances of modern medical knowl-edge, practice, and technology, combined with the sometimes mysterious power of the body to heal itself, have created a poten-tial to transform the remainder of life into a wonderful opportunity for improved health.

But not everyone has received this message. Often, I hear my patients' referring to illnesses they have—or *expect* to have—as "just a necessary part of getting older." But this is simply not true! *Reversibility* or *improvement*—not *inevitability*—should be your by-word.

Some have said, "I know I'm weaker than I was twenty years ago, but I guess that's to be expected." Yet weakness is *not* to be expected, at least not if you make the effort through nutrition and exercise to prevent it.

Others have said, "I used to be able to climb four flights of stairs without even thinking about it. Now, I'm huffing and puffing after one flight, but I suppose I'm just showing my age." Not true! I'm seventy-six years old, and for years I have fast-walked the three-mile distance between my apartment and my office every day, and I don't huff and puff—and if you did the same, neither would you!

Another typical attitude is that of a fifty-year-old female pa-tient of mine who told me, "A lot of the older women in our family have curved spines. So I imagine I should get ready for the same problem when I'm ten or twenty years older."

In the early years of my practice, I might have reluctantly agreed with her, but only because, like other doctors at the time, I didn't know what could be done about this bone condition, often called "dowager's hump." In fact, we know now that drug and hormonal treatments such as estrogen-replacement therapy, along with exercise and dietary adjustments, can keep an older woman's spine straight and healthy. Even more important, these preventive measures can diminish the risk of fractures.

Prevention can take many forms. After examining one fifty-year-old man, I concluded, "On the whole, you're in good health. Your electrocardiogram, for example, says you're normal. I can find nothing wrong with you, except a slightly elevated total cho-lesterol level.

"Still, I'm somewhat uneasy about you. For one thing, you have a family history that's positive for cardiovascular disease—in your father and an uncle. Not only that, you smoke cigarettes. And you're on what I call the all-American diet: You're consuming too much fat! The chances are, if you continue to smoke and eat as you're doing, you're going to run into major health problems."

"Is there really any point to changing my habits now?" he asked. "I've been doing these things all my life. Besides, I'm past my prime, Doc!"

"You're *not* past your prime!" I replied. "There's plenty you can do that will reverse the course you're on, and quickly and noticeably improve your health. Let's take a look at your opportunities!"

Specifically, I pointed out to him the well-known fact that 50 percent of *older* smokers eventually develop heart disease, and 10 percent develop lung cancer. Also, high saturated fat consumption promotes increased cholesterol levels and contributes to clogging of the arteries. "You have a major opportunity to escape these outcomes if you'll act now to stop smoking and change your diet," I said.

In my more than forty-five years of medical practice, I've diagnosed medical problems in thousands of middle-aged and elderly patients. I've prescribed medicines and behavioral changes for them, painstakingly cared for them, and often been in regular touch with them over months, years, and even decades.

In the course of this lifelong practice, I've been repeatedly impressed with the ability of the human body to repair itself, and this includes the bodies of those who feel they are past their physical prime. In fact, with life expectancies increasing steadily, you'll probably *never* be past medical redemption unless you think you are, and unless you fail to take appropriate steps to control the course of your health in the future. To some extent, we can all anticipate the direction of our health, and with this anticipation comes the power to change the course of our lives.

In my practice, I've discovered that I can often predict where a person of age fifty will be, physically and emotionally, at age seventy-five or eighty. Of course, this is not to say that the future course of your health is in any way fixed or predetermined. But family history and genetics, *plus* personal health habits, do play a decisive role in predisposing us for certain diseases or degenerative tendencies as we get older.

On the other hand, many diseases are preventable for those

who use their heads and make up their minds to act. Forty years ago, one of my hospital colleagues was doing some of the early research on cholesterol, a subject he was interested in because of a bad family history of coronaries. At the start, he decided that milk, eggs, and saturated fat were the repository of all evil. From then on, it was low-fat, low-cholesterol foods for him, and that meant no eggs as a separate dish at meals or even as a hidden ingredient in other recipes.

As a kind of living reminder of the validity of his nutritional theories, this doctor has made it to a ripe old age and has never had a heart problem. His only concession to prevailing dietary habits was that once a year, on his birthday, he celebrated his continuing good health by having an omelette. He also survived to see his preliminary research and predictions about cholesterol and heart disease confirmed by solid scientific studies decades later.

I'm certainly not advocating that everyone embark on a radical dietary regimen or become some sort of health fanatic. Despite my colleague's experience of good cardiovascular health, I seriously doubt that anyone is going to be struck down for eating an egg for breakfast a little more often than once a year. If you're on a trip somewhere and can't get a decent egg-free breakfast or skim milk for your cereal, go ahead and enjoy the meal, completely free of any twinges of guilt.

I'm more interested in what a person eats day in and day out, year in and year out, than in what he or she eats on special occasions. Certainly, there are some people with very serious cholesterol problems who should be careful never to violate a strict low-fat, low-cholesterol diet. But for most people—whether the problem is cholesterol or some other health consideration—the key to control is the usual daily routine, not what is done on unusual occasions.

Of course, there are limits to how far a nonphysician can manage his own health or engage in self-treatment. I've had patients walk into my office shaking with fright because they have noticed some blood in their urine. After looking up this symptom in a popular medical book, they've decided the blood may be a sign of cancer. Then, they may talk to a friend or relative who remembers somebody with this same symptom *and* a malignant tumor. As far as the patient is concerned, that clinches the dire diagnosis.

But the medical facts are usually considerably different from these ad hoc, uninformed evaluations. Typically, a woman with blood in the urine has an infection of the bladder that can be cleared up quickly and efficiently with a prescription of antibiotics. For a man, such symptoms are most often due to a benign enlargement of the prostate, again, a condition that can be taken care of successfully by a number of treatments. There are two guidelines to keep in mind here: (1) a dramatic symptom may nevertheless have a nonmalignant cause; and (2) it's important to see your doctor so that he can uncover the true facts.

Still—if you can avoid the traps of self-treatment and self-evaluation—it's important to have a general understanding of common health problems among people your age. With such knowledge, you can discern some typical signs and symptoms of illness and be ready to alert your physician to the possibility of a problem. The sooner you seek treatment, the more likely it is that you'll escape the occasionally dire consequences of neglect and worry and go on enjoying your entire life to the fullest.

Perhaps the best way to achieve many of these goals is to develop a genuine partnership with your physician. My own thinking on how a physician can help patients become more informed and assertive has changed gradually, but significantly, over the years.

For example, I used to write prescriptions in Latin, as was the custom among many of my colleagues a few decades ago. But I soon gave up this approach because I discovered that most of my patients couldn't begin to understand what the labels on the drugs meant! And after all, they, not I or the pharmacist, were the ones taking the medications!

I also found that when I visited my patients at their homes, sometimes I couldn't identify the medications in their medicine cabinets because they were inadequately labeled. If I couldn't figure them out, how could I possibly expect others with less training to keep them straight! Consequently, I started asking the pharmacists I worked with to write the purpose of the pills on the label, along with the name of the drug.

One patient of mine, for instance, had high blood pressure. So I prescribed a calcium channel blocker for this problem. To make the nature of the drug and the instructions for taking it completely clear, I had the pharmacist write on the container, "HIGH BLOOD PRESSURE PILL—ONE WITH BREAKFAST."

But I also knew that this woman had a tendency to experience swelling in her legs as a result of the water retention that was connected with the channel blocker. So I gave her a prescription for another high blood pressure medication, a diuretic, that would counter this problem. In a further effort to make things easy and understandable for the patient, I instructed the pharmacist to write this on the diuretic label: "WATER PILL—ONE FOR ANKLE-SWELLING, WHEN NEEDED. NO MORE THAN ONE A DAY."

Overall, I deplore the tendency among many doctors to distance themselves from setting up such lines of communication, which can help them immensely in establishing real relationships with their patients. Granted, life is much more complicated than it was several decades ago, and physicians today are exceptionally busy. But there's something about the custom of the heart-to-heart chat, the house call—or even the follow-up telephone call—that can do wonders for supporting the doctor-patient relationship and also for hastening the process of healing.

I still surprise many of my own patients when I call them up to ask how they are feeling and whether the medication I've prescribed is working.

"Dr. Rossman, I didn't know that doctors call patients this way!" one woman said to me the other day when I checked in with her.

I was rather taken aback at her comment, so I didn't have much of a response at the time. But after thinking about her observation, I thought, Why not? Why shouldn't doctors make an effort to keep in touch, even in this impersonal, fast-moving day and age?

After all, a short phone call takes so little time. And being sure that a patient is on the right treatment track can save a lot of trouble for everyone concerned. A quick conversation can prevent misunderstandings and mistakes as the person begins to put into effect the advice and instructions of the doctor. But we still have a long way to go, in part, because doctor-patient relationships, including the old-fashioned bedside manner, haven't been highlighted in the medical education of many modern physicians.

In the following pages, I want to provide you with a medical strategy for the middle-aged years and beyond, a strategy that will give you a foundation for making more intelligent choices and for communicating better with your physician. In developing such a comprehensive personal medical plan, you should keep in mind certain key considerations:

- Identify the special health challenges that confront those who are middle-aged and older.
- Understand what preventive steps you must take *now* to lower various risks to your own health.
- Learn how to work with your doctor in finding and effecting the best avenues of prevention and treatment.
- Know the pros and cons of selecting medications, surgery, or other types of treatment for specific illnesses and complaints.

To help you plan intelligently for the physical and emotional changes that may await you in the future, I've focused on the major health problems that confront individuals after age fifty. Here is a sampling of some of the topics we'll be considering:

- Changes you can expect in your face, skin, and vital organs as you age, and what can be done to retard the loss of youthful health, looks, and vitality
- The latest word on the possibilities of sexual performance in the later years
- How to combat insomnia, bowel disturbances, feelings of weakness, and similar complaints, which often accompany aging
- A protection plan against atherosclerosis, the "hardening of the arteries" that is the central concern of most life-threatening cardiovascular disease
- How to guard against the threat of depression
- What you should know about Alzheimer's disease
- Typical mental and personality changes that occur with age
- A program for limiting the decline of physical strength
- Sensible nutrition in the later years, including sample diets and food lists
- Winning the fight against hypertension and stroke
- Dealing with diabetes
- Reducing the pain of arthritis, both "naturally" and with medications or surgery
- How specific vitamins can help pave the way to healthier aging
- The myths and realities of prostate problems

- Special concerns about—and ways to care for—the senses of hearing, touch (especially sensitivity to cold), taste, sight, and smell
- Sensible, nonjudgmental approaches to prescription and nonprescription drugs
- Special gynecological concerns—and a great deal more

Over the past fifty years, I have watched medicine make gigantic strides forward, strides that have changed all previous notions about aging, illness, and prolongation of a high quality of life. As a result of this extended period of observation, I've become acutely aware that much of the good news about aging is still not widely known by the public.

In my own office, I constantly encounter middle-aged people who still cannot distinguish between illness and aging. I've written this book with them in mind. It is both possible and increasingly common to age well and retain significant physical and mental powers. The middle years are the years of golden opportunity, the years of your second major chance to live long and well. Seize them! Read on.

2

YOUR WONDERFULLY RESILIENT BODY

At every age, the human body is incredibly resilient and thoroughly programmed for self-preservation and self-repair.

One of my patients, a sixty-six-year-old woman, underwent a hysterectomy recently, and she was amazed how fast she returned to "full duty." She was released from the hospital in just a few days, and in less than a month, she was engaging at full tilt in all her preoperative activities.

"I can't believe how fast I bounced back!" she told me. "And at my age!"

"I *can* believe it!" I replied. "After all, you're in fine health and good physical condition. So there's every reason to expect high performance from your body."

This woman's case is not unusual. At any age, our bodies are far stronger and possess greater potential for good health and recovery from illness than we often anticipate.

When you're injured, blood-clotting mechanisms and other

healing forces immediately go to work to repair the wound. When disease strikes, antibodies and cells of the immune system rush to the site of the invasion and set up a defense against the harmful intruder. And when you age, your physical and emotional powers gradually change, and your body proceeds to play out its genetic potential.

As far as aging is concerned, neglect or abuse of the body can sometimes hasten or aggravate unwanted change. Fortunately, however, there are also some active steps you can take to enhance your body's natural resilience. You can actually slow down physical deterioration and reduce health problems that are often confused with aging.

To get a better idea of how all this works, let's take a closer look at some of the natural changes that will probably occur in your body with aging—and also consider briefly what you may be able to do about them. NOTE: We'll go into each of these concerns in greater depth later.

1. You'll age at a genetically directed rate, but you can exert significant influence over your future

Everyone has an individual biological rhythm or pace for aging, a pace that is directed by those biological units of inheritance called *genes*. I'm sure you know some families whose members seem to be unusually long-lived, and others who are characterized by relatively early deaths.

In my own medical files I can identify a number of family groupings that include blood relatives who seem to age at a slower rate and also live considerably longer than most of my other patients. There are many instances of sisters who all live well into their nineties. For that matter, brothers from such families have also lived this long, though fewer males than females generally reach very advanced years.

What such patients illustrate is a slower rate of aging than the general population. Through their seventies, many of these people look as if they are in their sixties, or even fifties. One widow I know who just passed seventy-two doesn't look a day over fifty-two. She even dates men who are in their late forties and early fifties! When such people reach their eighties, they often continue to look much younger than their chronological age, primarily because they are the heirs of a slower aging rate than that of their peers.

In some instances, deviant processes may also cause a jerky progression of aging changes, rather than the smooth aging course to which most of us are accustomed. For example, one sixty-four-year-old, highly energetic executive experienced an unaccountable twelve-pound weight loss over the course of one year. He also looked older to friends and relatives. But the man said he felt fine, and he certainly worked as hard as he ever had. Also, he played tennis several times a week, just as he always had, and he had no physical complaints or symptoms.

For a doctor, diagnosing this kind of case is always a great challenge. I tested the man for all the usual causes of weight loss, including cancer, diabetes, chronic infections such as tuberculosis, malabsorption (a failure to digest and assimilate food properly), and problems with major glands such as the thyroid. But I came up with nothing.

Then I had him keep track of his temperature over a long period of time, took blood for many additional tests, and had him checked by various other medical specialists. But still, nothing.

Finally, it became evident that my patient had no identifiable disease. A number of years went by with no further weight loss or gain, and also with no appearance of any disease. As a result, I concluded that this man had perhaps undergone a genetically influenced spurt in his rate of aging during the year when he had lost so much weight.

Genes play a big role in determining our maximum potential life spans and aging rates. But as important as genes and family heritage are, the course of the aging process is by no means inevitable. In fact, the evidence I've collected over the years suggests strongly that by taking certain preventive measures and monitoring your health closely, *you can actually prolong your life expectancy.*

How long can the average person who follows good health practices expect to live? I believe that when proper care and attention are exercised, *the maximum average age for people living today in the world's most advanced nations should be at least ninety years.* And as further advances are made against various diseases, that maximum age could increase significantly in the near future.

At the present time, the most rapidly increasing age-group in the United States is not the young or the middle-aged, but women over eighty-five! In fact, the number of people in this category more than doubled between 1970 and 1984. Currently an American woman aged seventy-five has greater life expectancy than any similar woman anywhere else in the world! The growth of this group seems to have resulted mainly from such factors as better health care, improved nutrition, and increased preventive maintenance. In line with these developments, I have attempted in this book to describe the steps necessary to help you slow your aging rate and increase your life expectancy.

2. Your vision will change, but you can usually retain much of your eye power

For all of us, the lens in the eye gets thicker at a slow rate as we grow older. To compensate for this change, glasses or contact lenses become necessary.

There are a few exceptions, of course, such as the rare eighty-year-old who has 20/20 vision and no need for reading glasses. But the large majority of people past age forty encounter increasing thickness and decreasing elasticity in the lens of the eye, which make it harder and harder for them to focus on close-up objects. These changes actually begin during the first ten years of life, although few are aware that the lens of the eye can signal a significant aging change in elementary school children!

This need for eyeglasses can even be a rather depressing experience for some people. One such "young" forty-one-year-old man gravely assured me that his need for reading glasses represented "the beginning of the end" of his life. As I peered at him through my trifocals, I said, "Young man, take it from me: I'm a geriatrician, and this change in your eyes is simply an encouraging sign of oncoming maturity!"

As it turned out, this man managed to have it both ways. He went out and bought some tinted bifocal glasses with frames that made him look like a Hollywood mogul. Then, that same night, he went out to a party that didn't break up until the wee hours, and the new glasses were a big hit with all his friends.

The next day, however, he saw that he had a price to pay. As he gazed at himself in the mirror, he was depressed to observe that his eyes were puffy and red. To his way of thinking, he looked five or ten years older than he was.

But then he reached for his new glasses and discovered that he could remove the marks of aging in the blink of an eye: The frames and lightly tinted anti-ultraviolet B lenses completely covered the facial aftereffects of the night before!

Certainly, the advent of maturity can be depressing if, like Peter Pan, you never want to grow up. But, my patient discovered, there are plenty of ways to maintain your youth as you get older. And besides, who wants to be Peter Pan?

3. Your hair will change, but you have many options

The most obvious changes that occur with aging happen on the top of our heads. When pressed, most people past thirty express some dissatisfaction if not dismay with what's happening to their hair.

More than one woman in her thirties or forties has moaned, "Dr. Rossman, why do I have to be the one who is getting prematurely gray?" And more than one man has asked my opinion of the best medical response to hairlines that are receding, or bald spots that are appearing at the crown of the head.

Certainly, there are many cosmetic steps that can be taken to reduce or eliminate the impact of these transformations. But my usual first response is to point out what a common occurrence they are. In fact, your "premature" graying or "early" baldness is usually something that millions of other people your age are also experiencing, even though it seems to you that you're the first person to undergo a particular modification of your hair.

What are the norms? In both men and women, the hairs of the head begin to become gray in the late twenties and thirties. Almost everyone has some gray hairs by age forty, although, as with every other aspect of aging, there are distinct variations within family and ethnic groups.

In Irish males, for instance, a gray forelock may appear by age thirty. In members of the black and Asian races, graying typically occurs at a later age than in whites. One rule of thumb that seems to hold fairly firm is that by age fifty, 50 percent of Caucasians are 50 percent gray. Those of other races tend to experience more of a delay in this graying process.

So what are your options for responding to this change in the color of your hair?

One possibility is to dye your hair with one of the safe, vegetable-based dyes or rinses now on the market. I prefer these to the aniline- (coal tar) based dyes, which in some studies have been linked, though only after years of usage, to a slight statistical increment in bladder cancer or leukemia. But hardly anything we do in life is risk-free, and you'll have to make your own decision about issues such as this.

Other people prefer to "go natural" by letting their hair change hues without any help from the cosmetic industry. If you feel more comfortable with this approach, that's fine too. With many faces and complexions, a gradual graying or mixing of colors may be more attractive than a dye. The aging process in some people produces a fascinating mixture of grays, whites, and even yellows, a distinctive color that we sometimes see in older people.

Or I may run into people who are content with having their hair become completely white. One of my better-known patients kept telling me how much he deplored the increasing and widespread rejection of aging. He considered that his gray hair was the result of natural processes and that the gift of a long life should be celebrated. I might also note that for this patient, the late actor Cary Grant, white hair was really a kind of beauty accent, as it produced a dramatic frame for his tanned skin and handsome features.

In addition to this graying process, there are many other changes that may take place with our body hair. A minority of men are subject to male-pattern baldness, which may make them increasingly bald in their twenties or thirties. The tendency toward this type of hair loss is passed on genetically from mother to son. It occurs in the son because of his production of testosterone, the male sex hormone.

Typically male-pattern baldness begins at the hairline on the forehead, at the crown of the head, or in both places. Gradually, the hair loss increases until, in those most affected, all or much of the hair on the top of the head is gone.

Another type of baldness occurs in most men and many women later in life, after the graying process is well under way. Beyond age sixty, especially, the hairs over most of the head may become thinner.

What can you do about this loss of hair? There are a number of possibilities. For example, certain hair-restoration products—including minoxidil, which is also used to control high blood pressure—have recently become available. Also, as we'll see later, various surgical and implant procedures have recently come into vogue.

Changes also occur with age in the "hidden" hairs on our bodies, such as those under the arms and in the pubic areas. In one study of men and women over sixty years of age, one-sixth of the men and one-half of the women had lost most or all of their underarm hairs. Also, one-fifth of the males and one-third of the females had lost significant amounts of pubic hair. And hairs on other parts of the body, such as the legs or eyebrows, tend to fall out or change with advancing years. As we become older, the remaining hairs tend to be thinner, less kinky, and grayer than in youth.

I suspect many of my readers have lost (or in some cases, gained) hairs in different places on their bodies. Or they have increasing numbers of hairs that are turning gray. Yet so often, when such changes take place, there may be a tendency to become anxious or depressed because these changes are happening to *you.* But I want to let you know in clear terms that *you are not alone!*

Just remember, you're in an age-group that is increasing so rapidly that you'll soon be part of the majority! In this regard, consider a few facts:

• Twenty percent of all Americans of working age are now at least sixty-two years old, and 11 percent of the whole population is over sixty-five.

• Nearly 30 percent of all adult Americans, or about 51 million people, are now fifty-five years old or older.

• Demographers predict that by the year 2030, 20 percent of the entire population will be sixty-five or older.

• The number of people eighty or older—perhaps the fastest-growing segment of the population—will soar from 6.2 million today to 12.1 million in 2010.

4. Your skin and face will change, but these changes can often be modified

For many people, the fear of aging (what I call "gerophobia"), which grips so many people, often finds its main symbolic expression in the appearance of new wrinkles and creases on the face or elsewhere on the body.

"Will you look at this, Dr. Rossman!" one forty-seven-year-old woman said to me as she pointed at the outside edge of her eyes. "I don't know how I missed these, but look—two new wrinkles."

"That's because you're such a happy person!" I replied. "I'd be more concerned if you had extra frown lines between your eyes!"

Such changes are certainly nothing to panic over or be depressed about. Negative attitudes toward alterations in the skin depend much more on irrational cultural biases than they do on the reality of the health of our bodies and minds.

What constitutes a healthy, well-balanced attitude toward the skin changes of aging? In brief, let me introduce you to part of my "skin strategy," which has helped ease the anxieties of many who are middle-aged or older.

First, it's important to recognize that no one is immune to gradual wrinkling and creasing of the skin. If you're lucky enough to grow old, this change comes with the territory. Certainly, some people have naturally tougher or more elastic skin than others, and they may find the onset of wrinkling somewhat delayed. But eventually, the wrinkles will come, so accept this change and recognize it as a sign that you're making it past another major milepost of life.

In fact, with the older part of the population growing larger and more dominant every year, the old ideal of clear, wrinkle-free skin is fast vanishing as the norm for physical appearance. A more mature look is now "in," and you're a part of this new image!

Second, from a relatively early age, wrinkles and creases in the skin tell the world who we are. They reveal important information about personality and character—as they did about the forty-seven-year-old woman who complained about her new wrinkles. An animated person, who smiles frequently, mugs for the camera, or otherwise projects a scintillating personality, will find that these lines become etched on the face.

The outdoors aficionado may have a few more wrinkles as a result of exposure to sun, wind, and weather. Also, the lean, well-conditioned sportsperson, or the individual who has been watching his or her diet closely in middle age, may begin to see a few more creases and lines because of a reduction of fat deposits just under the skin. We will all get various skin lines eventually, but the timing and configurations will be different, depending on our interests, temperaments, and activities.

What are some of the common changes that affect almost everyone's skin with aging? Here's what you can expect: typically, the first wrinkles appear on the forehead in the twenties. These become deeper and more pronounced in the thirties and forties. At the same time, radiating wrinkles show up at the corners of the eyes, a phenomenon commonly called "crow's-feet," but which I prefer to call "laugh lines." The dominant middle line is usually referred to as the "over-forty line," though I like "prime-of-life line" better.

Farther down, on the cheeks just to each side of the corners of the mouth, frequent smilers may develop crescent-shaped lines that reflect their chronic happiness. On the other hand, frowners tend to get two vertical or comma-shaped lines on either side of the top of the nose to reflect this side of their personality.

Other natural and harmless changes on the face may include:

• The appearance of a number of tiny red nodules, which are small clumps of blood vessels that have no known cause and no impact on your health.

• A whitish deposit around the cornea of the eye, called *arcus senilis,* which some people begin to develop in their fifties. This discoloration may expand to form a thin, complete circle around the cornea.

Still, it's nothing at all to worry about. Although almost all older people have this discoloration to some degree, it doesn't interfere with sight, nor does it signal the presence of some disease. (NOTE: In the past, however, some have tried unsuccessfully to link it to atherosclerosis, or clogging of the arteries.) Finally, the term *senilis* is probably a misnomer for this change: that word suggests old age, but the same whitish discoloration may appear in young people as well.

• A decrease in the distance between the tip of the nose and the chin. The cause: a slight elongation of the nose and some shrinking in the bones of the lower face. The final result for many people is a more interesting and wiser appearance than they had in their younger years.

• Increasingly pale skin, which arises from a decrease in the networks of capillaries or tiny blood vessels in various parts of the body.

What can you do to ward off this tendency toward pallor? Certainly, regular exercise, including some facial massage and exercises, will improve your circulation and give your skin a healthy glow.

Also, if you want to avoid overexposure to the rays of the sun, a sensible attitude for reducing the possibility of skin cancer, you may try a little bronzer. Bronzers are beauty products for men or women designed to give you a safe, realistic, and quick semblance of a suntan.

The outlook for the development of "beauty products" that will help cover wrinkles or add the blush of youth seems unlimited. Most striking has been the recent development of a vitamin A–related agent, Retin-A. Applied to the skin over the course of months, it increases the blood supply (hence, the flush that may result from its use). Also, the product thickens aging skin, which generally tends to be thin. Observations under the microscope indicate that Retin-A may actually be capable of reversing some aspects of aging, a rather comforting thought. The substance even seems capable of normalizing damaged skin, thus slowing the early changes of skin cancer.

On the other hand, the original formulation of Retin-A turned out to be too strong for many people, and it produced an irritative overreaction. This led the manufacturer to bring out a weaker cream with the caution that only a pea-size amount is to be used at any given time. Other possible drawbacks, such as increased skin sensitivity, are still being explored. So it's important to consult with your doctor before using Retin-A.

In any event, most of the changes in the face and skin that occur with aging are natural and normal and nothing to worry about. But if you become dissatisfied with the way you look and you want to "help" nature along a little bit, there are a number of medical possibilities, such as cosmetic surgery (I've devoted a section to this subject in Chapter 29). As I recently told one of my patients, "These days, the *safe* possibilities for changing the way you look are almost as numerous as the hairs on your head"—and that was quite a statement because even though this man was over sixty, he had quite a full head of hair!

5. You'll develop new body contours, but can retain your looks and body tone

There's no reason to settle for a soft, obese, or increasingly feeble body as you get older. It's quite possible for people in their fifties, sixties, and seventies to maintain significant levels of physical strength and endurance, even levels comparable to those in their twenties and thirties. The response to unattractive body contours or a decline in power levels centers on a sound, systematic program of exercise and nutrition.

Still, no matter how much you diet or work out, you may experience a certain amount of thickening around the middle in middle age. This is quite a common development, especially from the late forties through the seventies.

Many middle-aged men who come into my office are an inch or more larger around the stomach than when they were twenty years younger, and women tend to be larger around the hips. Also, the women often put on pounds in the middle of the abdomen, the upper arms, and the pubic region, though breasts may become less firm. Frequently fatty deposits accumulate around the side of the waist in both sexes.

Furthermore, as some individuals age, they may notice that formerly firm, well-rounded muscles and curves begin to be more angular or less firm. A sharpness may appear around the shoulders, ribs, and arches of the feet, and along the backbone.

One of the reasons the contours of the body may change in these ways is that our subcutaneous fat, deposited below the skin, shifts as we grow older. As men and women in their forties and fifties put on weight around the abdomen and hips, they may lose it in their faces and shoulders.

Finally, the total weight of most people tends to rise with age, peaks somewhere between ages sixty-five and seventy-four, and then begins to decline.

But these are just *typical* changes, and they don't necessarily have to affect you at the same speed or in the same way that they do other people. Unlike some of the other changes of aging, alterations in your body contours as you get older derive from factors that you can influence. Well-planned exercise, proper eating, and other preventive measures can keep your body looking youthful well beyond the middle years.

One sixty-nine-year-old woman, who had been my patient for more than twenty years, had a body that hardly seemed to age at all. During the entire time I knew her, she kept the same flat stomach and trim waist, firm legs and arms, well-toned muscles, and perfect posture.

"I know I'm a pretty good doctor, but I must admit, not all my patients manage to stay as healthy or look as good as you do," I told her one day. "What's your secret?"

"Walking every time I get a chance, swimming a half mile three times a week, doing daily calisthenics, and having a balanced, low-fat diet," she said without a moment's hesitation. Obviously, she had a well thought out strategy for staying in shape and was disciplined enough to follow it religiously.

"That's it?" I asked.

"That's it. Nothing weird or hard to understand. I just give a priority to those four things, and they work."

6. Your bones may lose some mass, but you can keep them strong

Whether the name is Iz Rossman, Susan Smith, or John Jones, we all face a similar phenomenon inside our bodies: After we reach our thirties, the density, or mass, of our bones reaches its peak. And after the forties, bone mass begins to decline.

What are the implications of this development? Most older people can expect some loss of height, as the disks between the vertebrae become thinner and bone loss occurs in the spine. The average man or woman loses one to three inches or even more in height, from the midthirties to the mideighties. At the same time, the span of arms and length of legs stays about the same because the bones in these areas remain the same length.

For those who do nothing to reduce their levels of bone loss—and especially for small-boned, blond women or others with a predisposition toward the bone-loss disease osteoporosis—the consequences can be more serious. In the worst cases, spontaneous fractures of the bones may occur.

But there are steps you can take to prevent or reduce this loss of bone mass, and I'll go into this subject in much more detail in Chapter 21.

7. Your heart and circulatory system and other organs will grow older, but you can keep them powerful and healthy

Some of the most visible signs of aging, such as skin and hair changes, may have symbolic or emotional significance, but as far as your basic health and potential for longevity are concerned, what goes on inside your body is much more important. In particular, alterations in your blood vessels and major organs can make all the difference in the length and quality of your life as you move past middle age.

The main killer in the United States today is cardiovascular disease, and cancer is the strong runner-up. I've examined men and women who appeared youthful at first glance. But then, I've found in too many cases they were suffering from serious vessel disease or other internal ailments.

One of my fifty-nine-year-old patients looked as if he might be in his early forties. There was hardly a line on his face, his full head of hair retained most of its youthful brown color, and he was quite trim and fit looking.

Yet when he came in for his first medical exam in about eight years, I had to give him some very bad news: His resting electrocardiogram (ECG) showed significant changes from an ECG that had been performed on him eight years earlier. Apparently, he had suffered at least one silent heart attack. There was also evidence of other significant difficulties with his cardiovascular system, including an exceptionally high cholesterol level.

After a battery of additional tests, including an arteriogram, which involved taking pictures of his blood vessels, we found the source of the problem. One of this man's coronary arteries, the vessels that pumped blood into his heart muscle, was almost totally blocked by fatty deposits. His life was literally hanging by a thread!

He underwent bypass surgery, and now he has fully recovered and is on a better, low-fat diet and medications that are lowering his cholesterol levels. Also, he now has medical exams more than once a year. In short, he is pursuing a lifesaving preventive medicine program that no one would have thought he needed, just from an exceptionally youthful appearance.

8. Your brain will alter with age, but some mental abilities may increase

Some people worry that their mental powers may decline as they grow older, but in fact, for certain capacities, research suggests that even the opposite may be true. Here are the facts:

As happens with other tissues, the size and weight of the brain do decrease with age. Brain tissues may decline by 100 to 150 grams (g) over a life span. By actual count, the neurons in the human brain may decrease by 30 percent from the time a person is in his twenties until he reaches age ninety.

But despite the ongoing decrease in the size of the brain, there may actually be an improvement in some types of performance. It's true that some scientific findings indicate that we don't process new information as easily after we pass the teenage years, but an important study of older males at the National Institute of Mental Health showed that on intelligence subtests relating to vocabulary and picture arrangement, the participants actually *improved* their test performances as they grew older. In conducting this study, researchers first tested the men when they were an average age of seventy, and again at an average age of eighty-one.

Furthermore, these men performed about the same as they grew older on tests for information, comprehension, recognition of similarity items, block designs, and completion of pictures.

As I've indicated, other tests show that there are declines with age in some abilities, such as the capacity to process new information quickly (that is, *fluid intelligence*). But as long as no premium is placed on fast problem solving or rapid assimilation of new material, older people do quite well.

Thus, tests comparing the ability of educationally matched young and older people to solve problems have revealed that their capacities are similar. The one exception is that the older people need more time to arrive at their answers.

Specifically, there is no decline in what is called *crystallized intelligence.* This concept refers to the person's learned ability to use his basic native intellectual endowments effectively. Among other things, evidence of crystallized intelligence includes making wise decisions on the basis of one's education and life experiences. This is why U.S. Supreme Court justices function well at advanced ages!

Certainly, there are serious mental problems, such as Alzheimer's disease, that afflict some elderly people. But such illnesses have *nothing* to do with normal aging. The average person who has moved well past middle age can still expect to enjoy most of the same intellectual capacities and satisfactions that were available decades before.

You can expect your body to remain resilient and capable of significant self-repair even after you reach a relatively advanced age.

What is required is that you pay *reasonable* attention to monitoring your health and observing the basics of preventing unnecessary disease and deterioration.

  Living a long and energetic life is a real possibility for many of us. But we need more information about our bodies and minds, and also some amount of personal discipline to apply what we know. In the following pages, I hope to provide you with the means to realize your potential for long, satisfying life.

A GUIDE
TO GOOD
NUTRITION

3

ARE YOU
WHAT YOU EAT?

When I first began practicing medicine, there was a great deal we
didn't understand about nutrition. Most doctors—and I number
myself among them—were skeptical of anything that smacked of
the avant garde in this area. We weren't comfortable with people
like Adele Davis who sometimes recommended dietary strategies,
such as the use of mineral and vitamin supplements, that hadn't
been confirmed completely by scientific research.

But I've since learned that advocates of what seemed to be
unusual nutritional concepts may have intuitively hit on ideas that
will eventually be recognized as correct. So if there seems to be a
good chance that taking extra dosages of a certain vitamin or other
nutrient *may* protect me against some illness—and also, if it seems
fairly clear that it *won't* hurt me!—I'll go ahead and indulge.

Take vitamins, for example. As I said, I was skeptical at first.
But now, even though all the evidence isn't yet in on vitamins, I'm
a firm believer in taking 1,000 milligrams (mg) of vitamin C each

day, in two separate 500-mg doses. Also, three times a week I take 30 milligrams of beta-carotene, a nutrient found in such foods as carrots, spinach, and broccoli. Carotene can be converted into vitamin A in the body.

Why do I take these supplements? Preliminary studies indicate that vitamin C, an antioxidant, helps prevent gastric cancer. The carotenoids have also been shown to inhibit cancers and tumors in various animals. The jury may indeed still be out on these and other vitamins and nutrients, but my attitude is this: Why should I wait twenty years or more to take a substance that won't harm me, and could very well do me a lot of good?

Despite our lack of knowledge about nutrition, it's absolutely clear that diet can play a major role in a great many of the important diseases of mankind: cancer, heart disease, stroke, softening of the bones, arthritis, and many, many other health problems. At the same time, it's understandable that many doctors have downgraded the study of nutrition because some food faddists have spread misleading and even dangerous advice and information.

I can still remember the heartbroken dismay among a number of my own patients when Adele Davis died of cancer. Her demise shook their faith in the belief that if you eat right, you'll keep fit and escape disease. Also, they found themselves in a quandary, because now, where could they turn to get nutritional help for the prevention of disease? Many had looked to Davis because, unlike the medical community, she had been willing to discuss the relationship between food and health. Furthermore, she had provided explicit, practical guidelines to the general public.

Certainly, many food faddists have gone too far in attributing all health and well-being to questionable food strategies. But at the same time, many people in the medical community have gone overboard in the other direction. What you eat *is* important, and in many ways it *does* determine who you are. In this regard, I've found over the years that I have to keep at least three fundamental points in mind whenever I consider the role of nutrition in my own health, or in the health of my patients.

Three Fundamentals of Food

1. Although diet is important and can never be disregarded in any assessment of your health, nutrition can't stand alone.

For example, other factors may interact with the food you eat, or even overwhelm the significance of the food. In families with elevated blood cholesterol levels (called *familial hypercholesterolemia*), for instance, drugs must supplement the diet. In fact, in this case drugs are more important than diet in lowering the cholesterol level.

2. Too much of a good thing can cause injury.

Some diet enthusiasts become a little annoyed when they hear me make this point, but I confront them with the facts anyway. One woman in her midsixties complained of feeling weak, and blood tests showed she had experienced large declines in the salt content of her blood. As it turned out, the main reason was that she was drinking too much water: She averaged about twenty-eight 8-ounce glasses a day!

She protested, "How can this be? What could be more healthy for you than good, pure water?"

Now it's true, I told her, that eight glasses a day is healthful. But water in the amounts she was drinking—even the "pure," "all-natural" high-priced variety you can buy in health-food stores—is too much. Chronic overdoses of water by mouth can injure kidney function, produce weakness and confusion, and lead to what's known as "water intoxication." Indeed, as I often observe in the hospital, older persons are more susceptible to this threat.

Recently, another older patient complained to me of increased swelling of her feet. She wondered whether she had heart or kidney disease. These ailments ran in her family, she said, and being a very health-oriented person, she was quite concerned about taking preventive steps to avert any possible problem.

My examination of her revealed no evidence of heart problems, and her urinalysis test result was normal. But the blood tests revealed a striking decline in the albumin component of her blood, to a level at which swelling in the tissues can occur.

TYPES OF EDEMA (FLUID IN TISSUES, SWELLING)

- *Dependent.* The most common type of edema. Occurs as a result of relative inactivity, with legs dangling most of the time. Swelling of the legs and feet appears. Harmless but a nuisance.
- *Venous edema.* Often follows clotting in a larger vein with obstruction of blood flow. Most often in a lower extremity, and frequently asymmetrical.
- *Cardiac.* In cardiac failure swelling of legs generally is symmetrical. May extend above the knees and become more generalized: That is, it may move over other parts of the body such as the sacrum, abdomen, or scrotum.
- *Kidney (renal).* Follows loss of protein into the urine in kidney disease. As protein level of blood falls, swelling of tissues follows. Often, the swelling is generalized to include face, eyelids, extremities, and trunk.
- *Lymphatic.* The lymphatics conduct fluid away from the tissues. Injury or obstruction to these vessels and lymph nodes produces a back-up edema. Seen most commonly after surgery or irradiation (as after a breast operation).
- *Nutritional.* In association with subnutrition or starvation: for example, "war edema." Generalized, though most likely to appear in the legs first.

It turned out that because she was concerned about a history of mental illness in her background, she had been taking large amounts of nicotinic acid (also known as *niacin,* and a member of the B-complex vitamin family) in an attempt to prevent mental illness in herself. As a matter of fact, she had taken this step as a result of advice she had read by some food-and-supplement "expert." As a result, the overdose of nicotinic acid had injured her liver cells and impaired the liver's manufacture of albumin.

Fortunately, this woman followed my advice to "cease and desist" from taking the megadoses of vitamins. Within a few weeks, the swelling disappeared, and her blood albumin rose back to normal levels.

Of course, this vitamin does have some important medical uses. We recommend nicotinic acid (niacin) in some patients in large doses, perhaps as much as 2 to 6 g daily, to lower elevated cholesterol. In these cases, the vitamin impairs the ability of the liver cells to make cholesterol. In other words, here we have an example of using a vitamin in very large dosages in a good, medically sound manner. WARNING: Niacin, especially in such large doses, can damage the liver and should *always* be taken *only* under close medical supervision.

In effect, then, taking such megadoses of nicotinic acid, certain other vitamins, and a variety of other "natural substances" is the same as taking drugs. These substances actually *act* as powerful drugs when they are used in these amounts, even though they don't have to be obtained by a prescription. So always check with your doctor before you begin to treat yourself with vitamins or anything else. Don't allow yourself to begin "practicing medicine without a license"! Otherwise, you may find that a substance you thought was beneficial has actually become a two-edged sword that undercuts your health.

3. Although there's a lot of helpful information on nutrition available these days, there's also plenty of *bad* information. So it's important to use good judgment, even as you experiment with food strategies and supplements that are on the cutting edge of current research.

While standing in line recently at a natural-food store, waiting to buy some oatmeal bran (because I believe this food also has cholesterol-lowering capabilities), I was alternately bemused and shocked by the stream of question-and-answer conversation I overheard between a flow of inquiring customers and the proprietor:

A middle-aged man asked: "What's good for prostate problems?"

Answer: "Take two or three zinc tablets after each meal."

A fiftyish woman: "Have you any pills for blood pressure?"

She didn't specify whether the blood pressure was high, very high, low, or somewhere in between. Still, she got her answer: "Try garlic tablets with each meal."

A man who looked as if he were in his sixties: "I think I have low blood sugar."

Answer: "Don't use any white sugar—brown sugar or honey only."

The shop owner's answers came unhesitatingly, and his quick responses were almost invariably dead wrong, or at least highly questionable. If the questions had been put to me, I would have had to pause, reflect, and ask a few more questions. Sometimes, my approach to treatment might have focused on nutrition, and sometimes I probably would have chosen a nonnutritional tack.

The important, point, though, is this: Feel free to follow an unusual diet *if* you're sure it's well balanced and healthy. If you allow yourself to be seduced by food fads and gurus of misinformation, you may very well find that your diet is doing you more harm than good. Over the years, you certainly will "become what you eat," but you won't be very satisfied with the result!

The Antidote for a Host of Health Concerns

Over the years, I've realized that many of the physical and some of the emotional complaints of patients have a nutritional base. Sometimes, the problems are relatively mild and transient. An amazing number of people, for example, begin to feel tired, grouchy, or otherwise "out of sorts" simply because they have eaten too much of the wrong food, such as rich or fatty meals in the middle of the day. Or they may not be eating enough of the right food, such as fruits or other complex carbohydrates. These are especially important late in the afternoon, when blood sugar levels may dwindle and produce tiredness and grumpiness.

As far as this last point is concerned, I can still vividly recall the solution that the wife of one of my sixty-four-year-old male patients found for the tremendous fatigue and irascibility that her husband often experienced just before the evening meal. When he came home about 4:30 or 5:00 P.M., he often seemed almost unable to walk, he was so tired. Also, the most innocuous comments she made to him could easily "set him off" on an angry tirade, after which he would collapse exhausted into his favorite chair.

Her antidote? She frequently met him at the door with a piece of fruit or a glass of orange juice, which she sometimes almost had to force into his mouth! Invariably, after he had assimilated some of the quick energy from the ingestion of carbohydrates, the husband would seem to become a different person. He shook off his fatigue, became much more energetic, and—most important of all for the wife—his mood improved dramatically.

Late morning and late afternoon drops in blood sugar are more likely to occur after stress, exercise, or exposure to cold. Perhaps this fact explains the British invention of four o'clock tea and the custom of a "second breakfast" among many Germans.

In fact, I've discovered in my practice that many people feel much better and more energetic when they have five or six small feedings per day instead of the traditional three meals. So I frequently suggest that they arrange their meal schedules accordingly. As you'll see in Chapter 11, I've designed menus for weight reduction with this principle in mind.

Because good nutrition is primarily a *preventive* measure, both doctors and patients often overlook its significance. Physicians tend to focus on symptoms. Because of their time constraints and other considerations, they are more concerned with curing a disease or condition after it has already appeared than they are with heading it off before it occurs. Similarly, patients tend to be concerned about their health only after it deteriorates. They are typically too busy or preoccupied with other matters to take appropriate steps before the onset of illness, though such preventive measures as a healthy diet could lower their risk for many health problems.

The requirements of good nutrition are generally the same throughout adult life. But some special concerns and problems may arise as you move into the second half of life, and one of the most insidious of these is a loss of appetite.

What's Wrong with a Tiny Appetite?

Most people, from youth to middle age, seem to worry about having too many pounds on their bodies. But many older people have the opposite problem, and their nutrition problems often begin with a loss of appetite. Foods that once could make the mouth water now begin to seem uninteresting and less tasty.

Some younger people who are on the heavy side may dream of losing interest in food, but the condition can pose serious, health-threatening problems for the elderly. They may experience a dangerous loss of bone and muscle mass, a loss of energy, and serious deficiencies of essential vitamins, minerals, and other nutrients.

A number of studies have revealed that the average person's weight tends to peak in the midforties. Then, the weight often plateaus for a number of years and generally begins a steady decline after age sixty to seventy.

In one thirty-year longitudinal study of men aged sixty-five to ninety-seven years old, the percentage of overweight males decreased from about 30 percent initially to only 10 percent of the total group. At the same time, the number of underweight men increased from 20 to 50 percent of the group.

The women in the sixty-five to ninety-seven-year age range experienced similar weight shifts: The percentage of overweight females decreased from 40 to 10 percent, while that of underweight women increased from 20 to 55 percent.

Clearly, there is a tendency for many older people to become leaner and even undernourished with advancing age. And all too often, one of the reasons that weight and nutrient consumption decline is a decrease in appetite.

Why You May Lose Your Appetite as You Age

Here are a number of factors, one or more of which may be responsible for loss of appetite during aging.

1. First of all, the *papillae* of the tongue—the small projections that contain your taste buds—often shrink with age. In the 1948 through 1972 Michigan Longitudinal Study, two-thirds of the surviving women who came in for clinical evaluations showed some degree of wasting away of these papillae. Along with this deterioration comes a declining ability to distinguish among various sweet, salty, or sharp tastes.

Why does this decline in the taste buds occur? The experts aren't completely sure, although several explanations have been offered: (a) the taste buds, like other elements of the nervous system, deteriorate with age in many people; (b) those with fewer taste buds also tend to have lower intakes of vitamin C; and (c) those with greater atrophy of the taste buds often wear dentures.

2. Appetite may also decline as the sense of smell deteriorates with age. Why should this be? By some estimates, the ability to distinguish the odors of foods accounts for about 80 percent of flavor sensations.

3. Tooth and gum problems increase with age, and these difficulties can lessen the enjoyment of food. For some people, it's painful or unpleasant to chew on teeth or gums that are giving them trouble. Others have dentures that may not fit quite right and thus may make it hard to chew.

4. Others who live alone may eat poorly because they lack the self-imposed discipline of having another person for whom they have to prepare balanced meals. Also, the lack of the companionship and conviviality that often accompany shared meals may remove zest and enjoyment—and mutual commitment to nutritional balance—from the eating experience.

5. A decrease in the efficiency of the secretions and organs in the aging body, along with the presence of certain diseases or drugs, may cause a loss of appetite.

For example, the inability of the aging stomach to produce the usual level of acid in the digestive process may cause discomfort—such as gas, cramps, or a "heavy" feeling—after the consumption of certain foods. I frequently find that my older patients dislike eating beef and other meats because of the unpleasant aftereffects.

Also, the declining levels of the lactase enzyme with age may result in "lactose intolerance." This leads to gas, cramps, and diarrhea reactions to the sugar in milk and in some other dairy products.

CAUTION: As we'll see in Chapter 21, it *is* necessary for older people, both men and women, to take in adequate amounts of calcium, and that means at least the Recommended Dietary Allowance (RDA) amount of 800 mg a day, and preferably more than 1,000 mg a day. Calcium is essential to reduce the inevitable loss in bone mass that occurs in all of us as we move past our forties.

KEY FACTS

SOME DIETARY CONTRIBUTORS TO GAS

Milk and dairy products, in persons with a lactase deficiency
Candy sucking
Gum chewing
Air swallowing
Beans
Peas
Cabbage
Brussels sprouts
Cauliflower
High-fiber foods
Fruit juices: apple, grape, prune
Broccoli
Turnips
Onions
Raw fruits
Yogurt
Starches
Inadequate carbohydrate absorption (Healthy people may experience an inefficient breakdown in the colon of 20 percent of the carbohydrates they consume. These malabsorbed carbohydrates then are fermented by bacteria in the large intestine to produce gases such as carbon dioxide, hydrogen, methane, and oxygen.)

To achieve a sufficient level of calcium intake, milk products or calcium supplements are almost always necessary.

Some older women may develop anorexia, or a lack of desire for food, because of gastritis, which involves an atrophy or chronic inflammation of the stomach lining. One form of this atrophy is associated with pernicious anemia, due to an inability to absorb vitamin B_{12}. Others may be reacting to long-term use of sedatives or digitalis preparations.

This form of anorexia, by the way, should be distinguished from *anorexia nervosa,* which is virtually unknown among the elderly. Anorexia nervosa is primarily a psychological problem that afflicts young women who starve themselves for a variety of psychological reasons.

Usually, anorexia nervosa and related problems such as *bulimia* (forced vomiting, often after a meal) involve some secrecy in avoiding or getting rid of food. In contrast, anorexia among the elderly is usually quite open: The person just refuses food outright, or spits it out immediately after it's placed in the mouth.

Finally, patients with serious physical diseases or emotional disturbances may lose their appetites. Those who have had a partial *gastrectomy* (surgical removal of the stomach) often complain of a lack of interest in food. Parkinson's disease is well known to cause impairment of the appetite. Also, declining efficiency or failure of the kidneys and liver may undercut one's desire for food.

Furthermore, a loss or decrease in appetite can signal the presence of a tumor or cancer in the digestive tract. In addition, an early warning of depression can be a person's complaint of a loss of interest in food.

Obviously, some of these problems, such as underlying physical diseases or serious emotional disturbances, have to be treated by measures that are not purely nutritional. As we'll see later in Chapter 19, which discusses the digestive tract, and Chapter 27, which discusses depression, surgery or drugs may be required if the problem is a malignancy or a failing organ. Antidepressant drugs may be in order for those with depression.

But if the problem is primarily a decline in interest in food associated with the aging process, the first line of attack should be to encourage the person to eat a well-balanced diet. One way to achieve this is through multiple small meals. I'll include a sample program based on this multiple-meal approach later, and I'll also give you the basic nutritional strategies you need to ensure that you'll be eating a balanced diet, no matter what your age (see chapters 11, 12).

6. Swallowing difficulties, a common problem among the elderly, contribute to diminished appetite and lack of proper nutrition. Some medications can also promote swallowing problems.

In the condition known as *dysphagia*, there may be a sticking of solid food at some point in the throat, an event that may even be painful. Some people with this problem may be able to swallow liquids easily. Others have trouble swallowing anything; still others may swallow, but then almost immediately regurgitate what has gone down the throat.

Some individuals may chew on something for long periods of time, but then they seem to lack the courage or the will even to try to swallow the food, perhaps because they have choked on other things in the past. It's quite common, for example, for older people to fail to chew up foods adequately, especially if they wear poorly fitted dentures. This occasionally allows bones or other large objects to slip into their throats, with alarming and painful consequences.

Sometimes, swallowing difficulties may result from a malignancy, such as a cancer of the esophagus. Frequently, this problem may be a residue of a stroke that has affected the throat. A hiatus hernia, at the opening where the esophagus passes through the diaphragm and meets the stomach, may be the source of the swallowing trouble.

Swallowing difficulties also arise from physical alterations with aging. As we get older, there's a tendency for the esophagus—the "food pipe" in our bodies that runs from the back of the mouth and the throat to the stomach—to become less coordinated in the way it works.

The proper swallowing mechanism can be likened to a smooth wave that requires considerable coordination of the nerves and muscles. Normally, the process of swallowing takes place automatically and involuntarily after we get it started in our mouths and upper throats. When you're young, you take a gulp of food or liquid, and this action sets into motion a series of pushing and relaxing movements. An extensive area of the esophagus relaxes while the area just above it tightens and pushes the food on down into the stomach.

It's fascinating to watch the forceful drive of the swallowing action through a fluoroscope, as the smooth, propulsive contractions push that food down from the upper throat to the stomach. In fact, when the esophagus is working properly, this drive can even work while you're doing a handstand! It's always struck me as rather remarkable that a person who is capable of performing a handstand can swallow something in that position—and still have it go *upward* into his stomach.

But as you get older, say seventy or more, the smooth propulsion of this swallowing mechanism may decrease. Sometimes, the wave action from throat to stomach just doesn't operate as smoothly as it once did. The movements may become so uncoordinated that a kind of corkscrew effect occurs. This phenomenon, known as the *corkscrew esophagus*, involves the contraction of smaller areas of the esophagus at times and in places that are inappropriate to a smooth swallow. In other words, too much of the esophagus is tightening up, and too little is relaxing. Sometimes, the corkscrew effect may become so pronounced that it actually causes pain, in addition to inhibiting the swallowing process.

The spasms that occur with this swallowing problem can often be controlled by certain drugs, such as the so-called calcium channel blocking agents. Although these drugs are often used to treat angina pains in the heart and high blood pressure, they can also be quite helpful for controlling spasms in the esophagus. In addition, a physician may prescribe antispasmodic drugs, such as Pro-Banthīne.

Another problem that may develop as a person ages is a constriction or closing-down that may occur in the sphincter ("cardiac sphincter") muscle that joins the stomach and the esophagus. In a procedure that can be performed in the doctor's office, a specialist can insert a weighted catheter down the patient's throat, push it through the constricted sphincter, and open up the esophagus. The procedure may be accompanied by some discomfort, but the benefits in enhancing swallowing are well worth it.

Swallowing difficulties may also come on with age because of impingements on the esophagus from the spine or vertebral column, against which the esophagus rests. The vertebral column may become bent or may thicken at some points because of arthritis. As a result, the bones may press on the esophagus so that there are bumps and ridges at various points that are supposed to be smooth, as the food goes past them and on to the stomach.

Another possible cause of swallowing problems in the elderly is the development of a pouch of the esophagus, called a *diverticulum*. Usually, a single pouch develops in the neck area, and when the person swallows food, some gets caught there. Sometimes, if the pouches are relatively large, unpleasant smells may develop because of the decomposing food that is trapped in them. Surgery can correct this condition.

Some of these problems can be corrected or at least relieved with the drugs or medical procedures I've mentioned. But some people may find that they have to live with a degree of swallowing difficulty. The best solution that many older people have found to this problem is to choose diets with softer foods, which go down the aging esophagus more easily. Certainly, it's better to turn to a softer-food menu, which can easily provide sufficient nutrition, than settle for too little food, which can lead to all sorts of nutrition-related problems!

7. Inactivity may contribute to a loss of appetite. A number of studies have shown that older people increasingly take in fewer calories than their younger counterparts. One reason for this is that our metabolism begins to slow gradually after about age twenty-five. The "hot blood" of youth begins to cool, so that by some estimates, we need less food fuel to maintain our normal weight.

It's been estimated that for each decade after age twenty-five, the number of calories the average person requires to maintain a given weight drops by at least 2 percent. This means that by age sixty-five, you need 8 percent fewer calories than you did at age twenty-five.

In fact, the drop in calorie consumption may be even more dramatic as you get older. One twenty-four-year longitudinal study done on Michigan women revealed that those alive at the end of the study were consuming 25 percent fewer calories than they did at the beginning of the study. Specifically, the intake of calories dropped from 1,683 in 1948 when the average age of the women was fifty-one, to 1,297 calories in 1972, when their average age was seventy-five.

With this decline in metabolism comes a decrease in overall muscle mass and also a decrease in the maximum breathing capacity of the lungs by an estimated 30 to 50 percent. The combination of less muscle and less lung capacity means less ability to use calories, in either strength or endurance activities.

Most experts agree that regular exercise and a concerted effort to avoid a sedentary life-style can retard much of this decline in physical capacity. Not only that, but if you keep active and exercise regularly, your appetite will be better and you'll be more likely to take in the essential nutrients you need in your diet.

Unfortunately, some people do become partially or wholly physically incapacitated as they get older, and so it isn't possible for everyone to exercise in order to increase the appetite. But a significant number of older people *are* capable of exercising regularly, and they should exercise, for enhanced appetite and for a number of other reasons that we'll discuss in Chapter 4. Even if the exercise is limited, it's still valuable.

Now you have some ideas about how a loss of appetite may occur, and also some suggestions on what you can do about it if you confront this problem. But sometimes, you may find that an unavoidable decrease in the function of your taste buds, or a decline in your sense of smell, or some other factor may be taking the edge off your desire for food. If this is the case, what can you do?

Some Tips to Make Food Tastier

Try experimenting with various foods to see whether you can't find something that will satisfy. For example, if some foods cause you discomfort, juggle your menus to eliminate them and substitute more acceptable dishes. I've found that chicken and fish suit my stomach and intestines much better than beef, and in many ways they are better foods anyhow!

On the other hand, if your problem is a diminishing sense of taste, try increasing the spicy foods you eat. You may find that peppers or other seasonings that seemed unpleasant years ago are now just the thing to make your mouth water. In some cases, older people may find that the textures of certain foods are more interesting than they ever realized. For this reason, some prefer a potpourri of soft and crunchy foods that may be bland to the taste but feel fascinating and satisfying to the mouth.

Those who have no objection to imbibing a little alcohol may find that a small dose of wine can stimulate the appetite quite nicely. But let me emphasize the "small" aspect of this advice. As you get older, your brain becomes more sensitive to alcohol, and the efficiency of your liver may decrease. As a result, alcohol will stay in the body's systems longer, and this means that older people become tipsy sooner and should drink less.

In any case, it's important to be flexible as you deal with your appetite problem. I remember one seventy-year-old woman who was practically wasting away because she refused to eat any of the food that was put before her.

"I can't stand any of it!" she told me. "It all looks like too much work!"

As I began to question her about what she *could* stand, I learned that, contrary to the experience of many older people, she liked thick, cold milk shakes! The milk apparently gave her no problem with the gas and cramps that accompany lactose intolerance. Also, she had quite low levels of cholesterol and other blood lipids, so she really had no worries about cardiovascular risks from this dietary source.

But she had avoided making any shakes for herself because she thought they were "kid stuff." Also, she was prejudiced against them because they were supposedly "unhealthy sweets" and "fattening."

But then I pointed out to her that she wasn't getting anywhere near enough calories or nutrients to maintain good health, normal weight, or adequate energy levels. She was usually so fatigued that she just sat around her house and had given up many of her normal activities with friends.

"There are a number of ways you can make nutritious milk-shake-like drinks," I told her, and I proceeded to give her several ideas.

One recipe I suggested involved using about a cup of skim milk and two scoops of medium-fat ice cream. Then, all she had to do was stir the ice cream vigorously into the milk with a spoon (or a blender, if she liked), and in seconds, she would have a tasty milk shake. In her case, she probably could have used a very rich ice cream with 20 percent fat. But to minimize the saturated fat intake, I decided to suggest the medium-fat variety, which has less than 10 percent fat.

NOTE: A person with cholesterol concerns or other blood lipid problems should probably *not* try a drink like this. But over the short run, where calorie increases are important, I often put aside the usual fat guidelines. In geriatric practice, flexibility is important: You do what works! Incidentally, preparing various foods, including meats and vegetables, with a blender may be the only way to coax some persons back to good nutrition.

In the case of this particular patient, there was an overriding need for more calories and nutrition. So she took my advice, and when I saw her a month later, she had gained four pounds and appeared radiant!

Obviously, you can't live just on milk shakes. But this woman, by being flexible about her menus, at least had found a way to begin to recoup much of her energy and to return to a more nutritious diet.

Other older people find that they like to eat only breakfast foods at each meal. Again, there's nothing wrong with this preference, so long as the daily diet includes other necessary foods. If you prefer, it's quite all right to have hot cereals morning, noon, and night. But they should be supplemented with foods containing the vitamins, minerals, and other nutrients that your body needs to function properly.

What constitutes a well-balanced diet for people over fifty? In general, the best diet for you is the same as the best diet for younger people: Every day, your meals should comprise foods that provide you with calories in these percentages:

• Complex carbohydrates (such as vegetables, fruits, and grain products) should constitute about 50 to 60 percent of the calories in your daily diet.
• Protein (such as chicken, fish, and beef) should account for about 15 to 20 percent of your daily calorie intake.
• Fats (such as butter, fat in whole-milk products, and salad dressings) should amount to less than 30 percent of your total daily calories.

NOTE: The average American consumes about 40 percent of total daily calories as fats; in this area, it is better to be below the national average!

Also, it's important to distinguish between different types of fats: Saturated fats (found in butter, whole milk, various animal products, and a few vegetable oils such as palm oil and coconut oil) should be limited to no more than 33 percent of your daily fat intake, or less than 10 percent of your daily calories. The reason? As we'll see in chapters 10, 11, and 12 on the relationship between diet and cardiovascular disease, and also in discussions in chapters 17 and 18 on the link between diet and cancer, saturated fats can promote clogging of the arteries, as well as development of malignancies.

A diet balanced in accordance with these concepts will help to provide you with defenses against a number of the health problems that typically plague people who have made it to the second half of life. The only way to look forward to your later years with a sense of excitement and anticipation is from the vantage point of good health firmly rooted in the best nutrition. But without a healthful diet, you'll open yourself up to a host of nutrition-related problems that impair or threaten the quality of life, which is why you should take steps to correct them.

4

NUTRITION AND AGING

Good food and good health always go hand in hand, but the nature of this friendly relationship becomes more complex the older we get. When you're young, you may be able to bolt your food, skip meals with abandon or eat anything that's put before you, with few or no aftereffects. But after my patients pass age fifty, I begin to hear more complaints like these:

- "I eat too much."
- "I eat too fast."
- "I suspect I haven't been eating a balanced diet."
- "I *knew* I shouldn't have eaten that dish last night!"

In this chapter, I want to highlight a few of the most common problems associated with poor or unwise nutrition among older people. But let me offer a couple of words of caution at the outset.

First, this list is by no means exhaustive. There are many other problems that may arise as a result of an unbalanced diet. So it will be up to you and your physician to sort through the possibilities and identify the source of the difficulties you may be facing.

Second, the health problems I'll describe here *may* stem from poor nutrition. But then again, they may not. Practically every disease or other aspect of poor health has more than one contributing factor, and treatments often involve attacking the problem on several fronts simultaneously.

So now, with these qualifications in mind, let's look at a few of the common nutrition-related problems of aging.

Constipation

Constipation, which often becomes a problem as a person gets older, is often defined with two characteristics in mind: This involves (1) a condition in which stool, or fecal matter in the intestines, is hard to pass in an attempted bowel movement, and also (2) a dissatisfaction with the size and adequacy of the bowel movements.

Many times, constipation is thought of with only the physical problems in mind. So, we may focus on the facts that the feces in constipated bowels tend to be smaller and drier than usual, and that one person may go to the bathroom less frequently than normal. But "regularity" is a relative concept. Some people are having healthy, regular bowel movements if they take two trips to the toilet each day. Others are regular if they go every other day or even every three days.

In any case, your feelings about your bowels are important because only you know what sort of bowel pattern makes you feel satisfied and relaxed. Sometimes, those who have "regular" daily bowel movements may still suffer from a form of constipation! The reason for this is that the rectum may not be completely emptied after a bowel movement because of the presence of hard or dry fecal matter. If a relatively large amount of feces remains in your intestines, you may still feel "slow," sluggish, uncomfortable, or out-of-sorts, even after you've had a bowel movement.

Everyone, regardless of age, has been constipated. But constipation becomes an increasing problem for many people as they get older. One reason is a disturbance in the sequence of contraction and expulsion of the stool by the colon. The stool may pile up in the lower colon (the sigmoid) and in the rectum and stay there for longer periods than earlier in life. This has been referred to as the "terminal-reservoir" phenomenon. When I perform a rectal examination on a young person, I expect to find the rectum empty. Not so in many older persons! Many of them are aware of this and complain bitterly, but they really haven't evacuated well.

Besides this change in the body, there are other contributing factors to constipation:

• *A failure to include sufficient amounts of cellulose fiber and other bulk in the diet.* Every person's diet, and especially that of those in the second half of life, should include plenty of fruits and vegetables. These foods contain plenty of bulk, or fibrous material that swells in the intestines and facilitates bowel movements. Bran cereals also contain a great deal of helpful fiber.

On the other hand, it's important not to overdo consumption of bran. Those who eat excessive amounts—which may be defined generally as more than one normal-size cereal bowl per day—may start eliminating too many important nutrients through their stools. For example, extended and excessive use of wheat bran has been shown to produce reduced levels of iron and calcium in the blood.

Also, patients who are bed-bound or who have blockages or strictures in the intestines should avoid bran and high-fiber supplements unless they use them under a doctor's close supervision. Otherwise, those with these conditions may be placed in danger of a serious intestinal obstruction and possible internal organ damage. We'll discuss this "fiber factor" in more depth a little later in this chapter.

• *A tendency to eat too many foods that cause constipation.* For some people, processed cheese may encourage hard stools. Others may respond similarly to foods that are high in animal fats, such as meats, milk and other dairy products, and eggs. The same may be true of many refined sugary foods, such as rich desserts, candies, and other sweets. Some nutritionists even talk darkly about "the sugar diseases," which may mean anything from constipation to diabetes.

The simple solution to this problem is to reduce or eliminate these foods from your diet and to substitute more high-fiber products.

• *A failure to drink enough water and other liquids.* Everyone should drink at least eight glasses of water per day, or the equivalent in easily digestible juices. In addition, I often recommend that older people who have problems with constipation drink a glass of warm to hot water in the morning, perhaps adding a little lemon juice. This liquid frequently initiates a wave of activity in the intestines that can end with satisfactory results.

• *A failure to use natural food laxatives.* Many times, in addition to bran, foods such as prunes, figs, apples, and various juices can trigger a bowel movement. You can learn best what works for you by experimenting. Many older people have learned, for example, that a small dish of prunes or glass of prune juice just before bedtime can greatly expedite bowel movements the following morning.

• *A failure to respond when the urge strikes.* When you feel that you need to have a bowel movement, that's the time to head for the bathroom! If you are delayed or procrastinate, the urge may pass, and the likelihood will increase that part of your stool will harden and create constipation problems.

• *A failure to exercise regularly.* Exercise helps combat constipation in several important ways. First, the movement of your body during exercise helps to soften and break up fecal matter in your intestines.

Second, one of the reasons that people become constipated as they grow older is that, as do other parts of the body, the muscles that are involved in bowel movements grow weaker with age. Specifically, the muscles of the diaphragm, abdominal wall, and pelvic floor lose their power to cause the expulsive force that pushes a stool out of the body.

Studies have shown that when older people are given capsules that mark the progress of the stool, the capsules tend to collect in the lower part of the colon, particularly in the rectum. This collection phenomenon doesn't occur to any extent in most young people, mainly because transit time is faster and expulsive movements are stronger when you are young than when you are older.

But a general physical-fitness regimen, with an emphasis on abdominal and midbody strengthening, stretching, and conditioning, can do wonders for maintaining the power and tone of some of the muscles that help expedite bowel movements.

• *Abuse of laxatives or enemas.* Ironically, taking too many laxatives or enemas may have the opposite effect to what is intended. To begin with, these procedures can produce diarrhea. But then, when you stop using them, the intestines and related muscles may fail to respond readily to normal stimulation. In other words, your body begins to rely on high-stimulation methods to get the bowel-movement process going. Over time, the natural bodily mechanisms for emptying waste may fail to work without the help of drugs.

A variety of other factors may also contribute to constipation, such as:

• cold or unpleasant toilet facilities;
• changes of environment;
• emotional or physical stress;
• drugs such as antidepressants, antacids containing aluminum or calcium, antihistamines, and diuretics and medications prescribed for Parkinson's disease;
• depression or mental confusion; or
• failure to develop basic bowel-movement habits at a younger age.

Many times, you can correct these problems and develop a regular, healthy routine of bowel movements with preventive measures, such as good nutrition. But in some cases, older people may need the help of drugs or other laxatives or enemas. As long as these substances or procedures aren't abused, they can be quite helpful in overcoming constipation. But any extended use of these methods should *only* be tried with a doctor's supervision.

The potential dangers associated with the misuse or abuse of these substances are many and varied. For example, mineral oil, one of the popular laxatives in many over-the-counter products, may reduce the absorption of important vitamins, such as A, D, E, and K. Mineral oil may interact and produce undesirable side effects with other drugs, such as anticoagulants given to prevent blood clots or other laxatives. Chronic use of mineral oil often results in leakages down the windpipe and into the lungs. There,

COMMON LAXATIVES AND HOW THEY OPERATE

Some of the most common laxatives, along with their popular names and modes of operation, include:

TYPE	EXAMPLES	OPERATION
Irritant	Castor oil Cascara Bisacodyl Phenolphthalein	Increases secretion of water in small intestine and decreases absorption
Stool softener	Dioctyl sodium sulfosuccinate	Increases secretion of water in small intestines and decreases absorption; hydrates (waters) and softens stool
Saline or osmotic	Magnesium sulfate Magnesium citrate Magnesium hydroxide	Increases secretion of water in small intestine and decreases transit time of feces
Lubricant	Mineral oil	Softens fecal matter and helps prevent its dehydration

it operates as a foreign body because the lungs cannot break down mineral oil.

Hemorrhoids

The appearance of the unpleasant condition known as *hemorrhoids* is often associated with straining during constipation, and by implication with an improper diet.

A hemorrhoid is simply a distended little vein covered with overlying tissue, which appears either at the anal opening or just inside the anal canal. The first is called an *external hemorrhoid*, and the second is known as an *internal hemorrhoid.*

You can easily feel external hemorrhoids, which are usually about the size of a pea. Several of them may appear together and form an encircling cluster. People usually learn they have hemorrhoids when the surface of the hemorrhoid is torn and bleeding results, or simply when pain or discomfort occurs in the anal area.

Sometimes, hemorrhoids may become so bothersome that your doctor may recommend surgical removal. When internal hemorrhoids begin to protrude, it may be possible to reduce pain by tucking them back inside the rectum.

Another possibility for treating hemorrhoids is the use of laser beams. The lasers destroy the tissue, coagulate the blood, and cause the hemorrhoids to fall off. This procedure is usually performed on an outpatient basis: The patient enters a hospital for a few hours to undergo the surgery by a specialist known as a proctologist and then is released from the hospital the same day. The laser has similarly been used for treatment of fissures (painful cracks at the anal opening) that may or may not be associated with hemorrhoids.

In most cases, however, minor hemorrhoid symptoms can be relieved simply by taking a hot sitz bath (a bath taken in around six inches of water while sitting) or by applying soothing anesthetic ointments. Many of these products can be bought over the counter.

Because constipation may trigger problems with hemorrhoids, one line of attack against this problem may be to pay more attention to your diet. Among other steps, you should consider making the dietary changes that are necessary to eliminate the constipation, and then the hemorrhoids will often take care of themselves.

But before you try to treat yourself, it's best to check with your doctor. Sometimes, hemorrhoids are associated with other disorders higher up in the rectum or colon, and only a physician can be sure that they are the result of common, less risky causes such as constipation.

Vitamin and Mineral Deficiencies

An improper diet in later life may result in a variety of problems or increased health risks related to vitamin and mineral deficiencies. Here are a few possibilities:

• Deficiencies in the vitamin B_{12} complex, including folic acid, may lead to confusion and other alterations in the way a person usually behaves. Also, inadequate folic acid may contribute to various forms of anemia.

Folic acid is involved in the formation of *heme,* which is an iron-filled protein necessary for the production of red blood cells. If there's a decline in the production of red blood cells, anemia may result.

One form of anemia called *megaloblastic anemia,* which leads to the formation of abnormally large cells in the blood, may be relieved by supplying the bone marrow with vitamin B_{12} and folic acid, as illustrated by a typical report in the *Journal of the American Medical Association* (July 31, 1972).

In this case, a sixty-nine-year-old woman with megaloblastic anemia came into a hospital looking very pale and suffering from loss of memory and excessive fatigue. But she had been given vitamin B_{12} just before entering the hospital, and she also took folic acid after her admission. She promptly became better and was soon released from the hospital. Tests made six months later showed that the megaloblastic anemia had disappeared.

Symptoms of a slowly progressing anemia may not appear at first, even with a less than normal count of red blood cells indicated by a routine blood test. But as the anemia gets worse, the person may experience shortness of breath, weakness, fatigue, constipation, abnormal skin pallor, and perhaps inability to think clearly.

Vitamin B_{12} and folic acid deficiencies may be aggravated by a lack of certain foods in the diet, such as green leafy vegetables, liver, milk products, and brewer's yeast. Important sources of folic acid include whole grains, oysters, and salmon. You can increase your intake of these vitamins, adjusting your diet by adding these foods, or by taking dietary supplements.

Although this nutrient is quite important for your health, very little vitamin B_{12}—3 micrograms (mcg) for adults—can satisfy the RDA. As for folic acid, the RDA is 400 mcg for adults, and you will need a prescription for doses higher than a 400-mcg tablet.

• Iron deficiency, the most common cause of anemia, may be due to unnoted loss of blood from the body, as well as inadequate dietary iron. With most patients, this problem can be corrected with a course of iron tablets. (The RDA for iron is 10 mg per day, but you should consult your doctor if you think you have problems with iron deficiency anemia.)

Natural sources of iron, some of which should be in your daily diet, include organ meats and other meats, eggs, fish, poultry, green leafy vegetables, and dried fruits.

• A deficiency of vitamin A—including carotene, a substance that has to be converted into vitamin A before it can be used by the body—has been associated with a shorter life-span among some older people who were studied in one California research project over a four-year period. Studies of animals have shown that vitamin A and its precursors can inhibit the formation of certain cancers.

The RDA for vitamin A is 5,000 international units (IU) for adults, and you should be able to get at least that amount by concentrating on such foods as dark green leafy vegetables, deep yellow vegetables (carrots), and fruits that contain carotenes (peaches, cantaloupes, and apricots).

Supplements may also be helpful if you find you simply can't get enough vitamin A through your ordinary diet. But if you use supplements, be sure you don't overdose! Those without a vitamin deficiency who ingest 50,000 IU or more may find themselves becoming poisoned by vitamin A. Signs of toxicity may include diarrhea, vomiting, nausea, dry skin, hair loss, appetite decline, or headache.

• Vitamin C has been the subject of many unproven claims, such as relief of the symptoms of the common cold. But don't let the uncertain track record for this vitamin put you off. In fact, even though a great deal remains unknown about exactly what healthful influences vitamin C can have on your body, many physicians still recommend that their patients get plenty of it, for a number of possibly beneficial reasons.

First, let's return to anemia for a moment. As you get older, your stomach tends to become less acidic, and this change may decrease the ability of your body to absorb iron. But if you add a little extra vitamin C to your diet, this may increase your stomach acidity and enhance your ability to absorb iron.

Like vitamin A, vitamin C used in higher amounts in the diet of older people has been associated with a longer life, though it's certainly not known whether vitamin A or C itself helps increase longevity. In addition, animal experiments have shown that vitamin C (also known as *ascorbic acid*) can help prevent certain stomach cancers in those animals. Currently, though, there's no convincing evidence that this vitamin helps with established cancer in humans.

HEALTH REPORT

HOW MUCH VITAMIN C?

For reasons that are currently unknown, human beings, a few primates, guinea pigs, and Indian fruit bats are unable to synthesize their own ascorbic acid (vitamin C).

In man, the minimum daily requirement of vitamin C that prevents scurvy has been known since around 1753. But the author of a 1986 article in *The New England Journal of Medicine* seriously questions whether this minimum level—roughly the RDA of 60 mg—is necessarily the optimum amount.

It's true that 60 mg of ascorbate per day will maintain a body pool of 1,500 mg and protect against scurvy for at least 30 days, even if there is no other ascorbate in the diet. As a result, the RDA has been set at that amount. But researchers have found that in volunteers taking 200 mg per day, the body pool of vitamin C can be expanded to 2,300 to 2,800 mg, and perhaps this amount may be better for our health.

Animals capable of making their own ascorbic acid do so at a higher level than the RDA level, and they also maintain a high body pool of the substance.

Stress increases the need for ascorbate.

Pending the final word on many of these issues, it is still not possible to affirm what the optimum dosage should be. But there seems little doubt that the optimum is greater than the RDA.

H. Levine, "New Concepts in the Biology and Biochemistry of Ascorbic Acid," *The New England Journal of Medicine* 314 (1986): 892.

The minimum daily requirement of vitamin C is 60 mg, but in light of the trend of scientific studies, I think there is justification for older people to take as much as 500 to 1,000 mg per day. More than that probably won't do much good; too much—say above 5 g a day—may result in toxic symptoms, such as a burning sensation during urination, diarrhea, or skin rash.

Rich natural sources of vitamin C include citrus fruits, dark green leafy vegetables, cantaloupe, strawberries, broccoli, green peppers, and tomatoes.

Hypertension

Diet is also sometimes deeply involved in problems with hypertension or high blood pressure (see Chapter 15). We'll deal in more detail with hypertension later, but for now, consider some of its nutrition-related aspects.

Blood pressure that rises above about 140/90 may call for some form of treatment, and one of the first that many physicians turn to is an adjustment in the diet. First, obesity can contribute to high blood pressure, so attempts should be made immediately to get rid of any excess weight. To this end, you may want to consider embarking on the weight-loss program outlined in Chapter 11.

Second, reducing the intake of salt can help lower blood pressure for many people. A great number of studies have associated the sodium in salt with high blood pressure. As a result, I'd suggest that if you have problems with hypertension or consider yourself potentially to be at risk by personal or family history you should avoid adding salt to your foods, either during cooking or during meals.

In particular, avoid the following foods: potato chips, pretzels, salted crackers, biscuits, pancakes, pastries or cakes made from self-rising flour mixes, pickles, sauerkraut, soy sauce, catsup, olives, commercially prepared soups or stews, bouillon, ham, sausages, frankfurters, smoked meats or fish, sardines, canned tomato juice, frozen lima beans, frozen peas, canned spinach, canned carrots, various cheeses, and fast foods.

In addition to these two measures—losing weight and reducing salt intake—a person with high blood pressure may be able to improve his condition by increasing his level of endurance exercises. But a person with hypertension should *always* check first with his physician before engaging in strenuous physical activity.

If none of these "natural" approaches works, a physician may prescribe one of the many effective drugs that are now commonly used to control high blood pressure. We'll go into this subject in much more detail later in Chapter 15.

Diabetes

As you get older, your "glucose intolerance" rises. That is, the sugar levels in your blood, as reflected in the rises following administered glucose or food, tend to increase. If the glucose levels in your blood get too high—and especially if they rise into or above the range of 140 mg (after fasting) to 200 mg per deciliter (after eating), then you may have developed *diabetes mellitus.*

Diabetes mellitus is a condition in which the body cells can't properly take up the glucose made chiefly by the liver. Usually, when a person eats sugars or starches, the body changes these foods into a sugar called *glucose,* which is an energy-producing fuel in the bloodstream. In diabetes, the body can't deal normally with the amount of glucose in the blood. As a result, the glucose increases to dangerous levels with accompanying symptoms such as fatigue and weakness, frequent urination, weight loss, blurred vision, skin infections and itching, and unusual thirst. Eventually, other disturbances associated with the out-of-control glucose level may begin to damage the body's organs. Among frequent late complications, diabetes may lead to stroke, heart and kidney problems, impaired leg circulation, and nerve damage.

This increase in glucose occurs for one of two reasons: (1) the body doesn't have enough *insulin,* which is the hormone that regulates the glucose levels in the blood (as in type I diabetes, generally found in the young); or (2) the insulin doesn't operate properly in the body (as in type II adult-onset diabetes).

Although diabetes cannot be cured, it can be controlled by close attention to diet, exercise, weight loss, and use of appropriate drugs, including a number of prescription pills or insulin.

Describing the details of a proper diet for diabetes mellitus is beyond the scope of this book. But the information is available from the American Diabetes Association, which has chapters or phone numbers in most cities.

In brief, though, I can say this about your diet if you have diabetes or are at risk for it:

- You should lose weight if you're overweight. Lowering total body fat usually lowers levels of glucose in the bloodstream.
- Pay attention to including adequate amounts of protein in your diet. Specifically, you should eat a minimum of slightly less than half a gram of protein for each pound of your body weight. This means if you weigh one hundred and thirty pounds, you should be eating 60 to 65 g of protein each day. You can figure out the approximate amount of protein in your food by examining the list and amounts of nutrients on food labels.

Rich sources of protein include whole-grain products, milk and milk products, soybean foods, meats, fish, poultry, and whites of eggs.

- Restrict the intake of sucrose, or simple sugars (simple carbohydrates), in your diet. This may mean cutting or eliminating desserts, candies, and other such foods from your daily consumption.
- Focus more on complex carbohydrates, such as whole-grain cereals and breads, vegetables, rice, and noodles.

NOTE: You should only alter your intake of carbohydrates after consulting with your doctor. Including the usually recommended 50 to 60 percent of your daily calories as carbohydrates may work well with those who have the *mild* diabetes that appears with advancing age. In this case, such a diet has been associated with improved glucose tolerance. On the other hand, when a person has more serious signs of diabetes, such as a fasting blood glucose level above 200 mg per deciliter, a high-carbohydrate diet may worsen the levels of blood glucose.

It's always advisable to keep in close touch with your physician when you're designing any diet, whether for a diabetic condition or for another purpose. You may be able to resolve many health concerns or manage them quite well with diet or weight loss alone. But nutrition is a very individual matter, and measures other than dietary adjustment may be required. For example, the only way to take care of certain diabetic problems is to turn to medications such as the oral hypoglycemic drugs or insulin. Only a qualified physician can make this kind of determination.

COMMON ACHES, PAINS, AND OTHER COMPLAINTS

5

SURMOUNTING INSOMNIA

I've been a rotten sleeper for thirty years. In the first place, when I fail to take the steps I know are necessary to relieve the problem, I have trouble falling asleep. Then, after I've been asleep for three or four hours, I typically wake up and begin to toss and turn.

Some of my colleagues say, "I just get up and do some work if I find I can't sleep."

But that doesn't help me. Even when I find I can't get back to sleep, I have a lot of trouble dragging myself out of bed. My eyes burn, my vision is blurred, and I simply can't get my mind in gear.

Furthermore, I'm not the only older person *or* the only doctor who has faced this problem. A number of years ago, I polled a number of physicians, middle aged and older, in the New York area about their sleeping habits. And I discovered that about one-fourth of them had some sort of sleeping problem, such as trouble with falling asleep, or tossing and turning during the night, or waking up too early. I also wrote an article titled, "Does Your

Doctor Take Sleeping Pills?" And the answer was yes, for some physicians.

The problem with insomnia is particularly acute among older people. By some estimates, as many as half of those over sixty-five may "frequently" use sleeping pills, including over-the-counter medications. One recent study revealed that although only about 14 percent of the population was considered "elderly," the elderly group received one-third of all "hypnotic" prescription medications for insomnia. Other studies in California and Florida have reported that between 25 and 40 percent of people over the age of sixty have complaints about their sleep habits.

So I—and perhaps you, as well—am part of a rather sizable group with sleep problems. But there is hope for all of us! As you'll see during our discussions in this chapter, I've found some ways to deal with my insomnia, and the chances are you can too. But to understand this problem better, and to decide what you can do to surmount insomnia in your own life, it's important first to identify exactly what kind of sleeplessness it is that may be plaguing you.

What Are the Main Types of Insomnia?

Those of us who are in the second half of life typically wrestle with one or more of these three main types of insomnia:

Hit-and-Run Insomnia

Sometimes called *transient insomnia,* the "hit-and-run" type may result from such fleeting events as a reaction to jet lag, change of sleeping locations, strange beds, or hospitalization. Usually, this kind of sleeplessness "hits" and then "runs away," and it's usually nothing to worry about.

Transient insomnia usually doesn't provide sufficient justification for taking sleeping pills or other medications. But as we'll see shortly, there are some measures short of medication you can take to minimize this type of insomnia. This problem can bother young people as well as those who are older, and it has little to do with the aging process.

Situational Insomnia

Situational insomnia is a kind of sleeplessness, typically lasting for a couple of days up to about three weeks, that often arises as a result of an anxiety-producing event. Sometimes, the event may have already occurred, but it may continue to stay on your mind, particularly at night as you try to go to sleep. Other times, you may find yourself anticipating the event, playing through possible scenarios, and worrying about the outcomes.

I know that periodically this type of insomnia has troubled me, as well as many of my patients. There's no doubt that we live in an "age of anxiety," as various pundits have suggested. Specifically, concerns about the economy (including the impact on our personal investments!), family relationships, jobs, or the loss of a loved one can impair the ability to sleep.

I've discovered in my practice that many times the tendency to worry about the pressures of daily situations—hence, "situational insomnia"—can be a particular problem among the elderly. Too often, as people get older, their feelings of powerlessness increase. Their problems with health, personal finances, and bereavement may escalate. In such cases, the worries that cause insomnia may not be far behind.

All of us who live and work in an urban society are especially prone to this type of insomnia, and the elderly may be especially at risk. If you're a particularly intelligent older person with extra free time on your hands, your susceptibility to situational insomnia may intensify. Some French physicians have called this problem *cerebral insomnia* because it's a sleeplessness caused by thoughts whirling around and around in your mind.

Sometimes, medical intervention is advisable for situational insomnia, especially if it occurs on a regular basis. We'll consider ways to overcome this and other forms of sleeplessness shortly.

Chronic Insomnia

Sleeplessness among older people may occur periodically or frequently for a month or much longer, and there may be no clear-cut factor you can identify as the cause. In this case, you may be experiencing a result of the aging process that is called by such names as *chronic* or *long-term insomnia*.

Some people have this problem all their lives. But for most of us, chronic insomnia doesn't appear until we are middle-aged or older. As for me, I know some of my sleeplessness is "situational": that is, it can be attributed to thinking and worrying too much about my work or other matters at bedtime. But I am also aware that on many occasions, I can't isolate a particular cause of my insomnia. At those times, I seem to be suffering from the chronic or long-term variety of this condition.

As I've said earlier, nearly half of those over sixty have some complaints about their sleep, and at least one-third say they regularly wake up feeling unrefreshed. Also, I've discovered that the older people get, the worse the problem becomes. One sixty-six-year-old woman who came into my office recently typifies the condition.

"It takes me about an hour to fall asleep, but then I wake up two hours later," she complained. "I'm certainly not wide awake when my sleep is interrupted, but still, I can't go right back to sleep. I feel restless, fidgety. When I do finally fall asleep again, I invariably wake up earlier than I want to.

"My daughter says, 'Why don't you just stop worrying about sleeping and try to relax! Then, you'd drop right off to sleep again!' But I *can't* relax! She just doesn't understand my problem."

But I *do* understand this frustration because I've experienced it. It's quite true that you often can't simply "relax" on command. And the problem seems to escalate over the years as a physiologic, age-related phenomenon. So if you find you have insomnia more often as you get older, you're by no means alone. Many people have the same problem, and for many of us it's a natural consequence of getting older.

William C. Dement, a neuropsychiatrist from Stanford University who has done a great deal of research on sleep among the elderly, has found that many older people may wake as often as 150 times during the night, whereas younger people may not wake up at all! He learned this by checking the brain waves of various subjects during sleep with an electroencephalogram.

Usually, older people with this problem wake up for only a few seconds during their multiple awakenings, and they have no memory of the arousals. But the result is a fragmented, disordered sleep experience that can leave them tired and irritable during the day.

Another factor that can affect sleep as you get older is the tendency for the overall sleep rhythms in your body to change. According to various well-documented studies, elderly people spend about as much time in bed as any age-group, but they also usually *need* less sleep than their younger counterparts. In general, although total sleep at night decreases with age, many older people *expect* to sleep longer. So they spend many unnecessary hours tossing and turning.

In part, the decrease in nighttime sleep may be the result of a more sedentary way of life among older people. There also seems to be a natural change in sleep patterns as a person gets older: There's a tendency to fall asleep earlier than in youth and wake up earlier. Some sleep experts have suggested that this change in patterns may be caused by a shortening of the inner sleep-wake mechanisms that are thought to control the times we prefer to retire and arise.

Other studies have revealed that, along with a shortening of the sleep-wake cycles and a fragmentation of sleeping patterns with age, older people tend to take more naps. So even though an older person may be getting less sleep at night, the *total* amount of sleep during the entire day may be close to what he or she normally had at a younger age.

One thing that all this says to me, as I compare the scientific findings with my daily medical practice, is that most people need to change their expectations about sleep as they grow older. Many times, the main problem with fatigue and sleep can be traced to the anxiety that arises from being unable to sleep the way we think we should!

So it's not always necessary to get concerned or upset if you're not sleeping exactly as you used to when you were younger. Instead, take a look at your whole sleep experience, and see whether it's possible to accept many of the changes that are occurring as an inevitable part of getting older. With a more positive attitude toward your evolving sleep patterns, you may well find that your fretting disappears and your old energy returns!

On the other hand, there are many sleep problems that can't be eliminated simply by changing your expectations and getting a better perspective on those hours you spend in bed. If you seem to have a persistent problem with sleep that you can't trace to a definite cause or factor, you may be confronting a genuine chronic insomnia. And this type of insomnia is certainly the most difficult to overcome.

HEALTH REPORT

DEPRESSION AND SLEEP

In a longitudinal study published in 1988 in the *Journal of Gerontology,* 264 people, aged 62 to 90, were followed for a three-year period. During this time, they were interviewed eight times about their sleep, depression, general health, medications, and activities.

The researchers reported that depressed feelings were positively related to sleep disturbances, and especially to early morning awakenings. This finding is in agreement with other studies that have shown early morning awakening to be an important symptom of depression in the elderly.

J. Rodin, G. McAvary, C. Timko," A Longitudinal Study of Depressed Mood and Sleep Disturbances in Elderly Adults," *Journal of Gerontology* 43 (1988): 45.

In confronting chronic insomnia, by the way, one should also think of the possibility of a depression. Depressions in old age are not like those in earlier years, as you'll see in Chapter 27. Although it is true that one cardinal sign of depression at any age is taking to bed and escaping by the sleep route, another signal may be insomnia.

Agitation is often a key feature in depression, hence, the term *agitated depression.* This agitation may be the component that prevents people from falling asleep. Depressive insomnia responds to an antidepressant, and as the depression improves, so does the sleep.

I have also seen persons with mild depressions sleep much better with an antidepressant. This observation taught me that the impact of this group of drugs is more far-ranging and complex than one might anticipate. Small doses of antidepressants certainly seem to have a salutary effect on people with age-related chronic insomnia.

Another example of a reversible medical condition that can produce sleep difficulty is mild congestive heart failure. When the heart starts to fail in its pump function, fluid leaks out into tissues. The most familiar site for this to occur is in the legs.

HEALTH REPORT

HOW DEPRESSION IS LINKED TO INSOMNIA

In a random sample of 1,023 elderly people, 38 percent of those interviewed reported problems with insomnia at least "sometimes."

Specifically, in the sixty-five- to seventy-four-year age group, these percentages said they had problems sleeping:

- 15 percent: "sometimes"
- 10 percent: "often"
- 11 percent: "all the time"

For those who were seventy-five years or older, the figures in each category were slightly higher.

As far as medication was concerned, 30 percent of those who said they had problems sleeping often or all the time were using sleeping pills.

A key point for our discussion of depression: Psychological evaluations indicated that sleep problems were more common in those with some depression or anxiety. The authors of this study concluded that in addition to the irreversible age-related changes in sleep patterns, insomnia in the elderly may be treatable by intervening to correct physical and psychological disorders.

K. Morgan, H. Dalosso, S. Ebrahim, et al., "Characteristics of Subjective Insomnia in the Elderly Living at Home," *Age and Ageing* 17 (1988): 1.

But the leakage may also occur in the lungs, and when this happens, we speak of *pulmonary congestion,* a problem that may come on at night. The person typically wakes up with some shortness of breath, malaise, and even bad dreams. The episodes may even be blamed on the bad dreams. But everything clears up with a few diuretic pills.

In the dramatic forms of congestive heart failure, the short-ness of breath is severe, and the disorder is easy to diagnose as *paroxysmal nocturnal dyspnea.* But mild forms—and congestive heart failure in the elderly *is* often mild—may escape diagnosis for a long time. Clues to its detection are the frequent association with high blood pressure, the relief obtained from sleeping on extra pillows, and the report of increasing shortness of breath on exertion.

As you may realize, insomnia is a symptom, a complaint, but not a disease entity. It's important to figure out what's causing it before attributing it solely to age-related impairment of the sleep cycle.

But chronic insomnia, like other types of sleeplessness, *can* be overcome, if you approach it with your doctor in the step-by-step fashion I've outlined in the next section.

How to Overcome Insomnia

What causes insomnia? As I've already indicated, chronic insomnia may not seem to have a readily identifiable cause, other than the natural aging process. But many times, the patients I deal with *can* put their finger on a specific cause, especially when there's a partic-ular situation that they know is provoking worry or concern.

To help you track down the possible cause for your insomnia, I've provided the list on the facing page.

I find a list like this, with the causes of insomnia clearly out-lined in black and white, to be quite helpful in eliminating certain easily identified factors. In my own case, if I'm having trouble sleeping, at first I may think, "Well, I'm just getting older." But then, I go over this list in my mind, and suddenly I may realize that the *real* problem is a nagging pain from a pulled muscle . . . or worry about an article for a medical journal that hasn't been fin-ished . . . or noisy construction that has recently been going on outside my window.

It's often possible to overcome insomnia, both the chronic and the situational insomnia that intensify as we get older, by some simple procedures and techniques that don't involve medical inter-vention. Here are a few that have been tried with varying degrees of success by different individuals over the years:

● *Changing your sleeping habits to conform with the changing body and sleep patterns of aging.* As I've already mentioned, our sleeping patterns tend to change as we get older. Spend a few minutes now

---

POSSIBLE CAUSES OF INSOMNIA AMONG OLDER PEOPLE

LIFE-STYLE AND ENVIRONMENT
Sedentary life-style/too little exercise
Noise
Uncomfortable bed or bedroom situation
Recent change of sleeping location, including hospital stay

PHYSICAL AND PSYCHOLOGICAL
Chronic anxiety
Worry about a particular problem, situation, or event
Depression
Physical sickness that causes discomfort or restlessness
Muscle twitching during sleep
Difficulty in breathing (including "sleep apnea")
Pain or other discomfort
Gastric or intestinal problems resulting from the diet (gas or cramps that may arise from an inability to digest milk or other dairy products)

DRUGS AND MEDICATIONS
Alcoholic drinks (excess may cause insomnia)
Beta-blockers (may interfere with sleep and cause bad dreams)
Reserpine (may trigger nightmares)
Diuretics (often taken for hypertension) (may necessitate waking during the night to urinate)
Stimulant drugs or other substances (including sympathomimetics, such as amphetamines and decongestants, and xanthines, such as caffeine)
Withdrawal from drugs or other substances (including alcoholic beverages, barbiturates, benzodiazepines, and tricyclic antidepressants)

thinking about the way you seem to sleep most naturally, under normal conditions in your own bedroom. After some reflection, you may well find that it's most natural for you to go to bed earlier, arise earlier, and, in general, sleep fewer hours at night than you did when you were younger.

If you find that this is happening, conform your sleep habits to fit the changing pattern in your body and mind. In other words, don't force yourself to stay up to watch the late movie on TV just because you used to do this in your thirties or forties. Instead, go on to bed when you feel sleepy, even if it's only 9:30 or 10:00 P.M.

Then, if you wake up at 4:30 or 5:00 A.M., don't lie around in bed, especially if you find yourself getting frustrated just because you can't go back to sleep. Instead, arise and get a head start on the day.

If you find yourself running out of steam in the afternoon— and you determine your problem isn't the result of poor nutrition or some other non-sleep-related factor—try setting aside an hour or so for a nap.

Some experts have proposed that the most natural way for many older people to sleep is by taking multiple naps during the day, rather than just one block of sleep at night. The argument is that certain parts of the brain change their sleep-timing mechanisms as we age. Our mental faculties are no longer saying, "Go to sleep tonight for eight hours." Instead, the message we may be getting is, "Sleep tonight for five hours, and then take two one-hour naps during the day."

In general, it's best first to determine your natural sleep cycle at your present age. Then, in accordance with that determination, set a fixed time to go to bed and get up.

According to one method that is currently used among sleep experts working with older people, you may find it useful to keep a sleep diary for a couple of weeks. In this diary, you should write down the amount of time you spend in bed each night and the approximate amount of time you think you spend in actual sleep. Then, find both your average time in bed and your average time sleeping over the fourteen-day period. Finally, schedule your sleeping times at night so that you spend only slightly more time in bed than you actually sleep. The same procedure can be used to schedule any naps you may need during the day.

In any event, whatever approach you settle upon, routine is important so that you can be sure you're getting the right amount of rest on a regular basis.

• *Performance of monotonous tasks or exposure to monotonous events.* This time-honored technique for tackling insomnia may include the classic case of counting sheep—though I must say, so far I haven't encountered one insomniac who has actually tried this!

A related technique has been used successfully by the stress expert Dr. Herbert Benson of the Harvard Medical School. In his books *Beyond the Relaxation Response* and *Your Maximum Mind,* he suggests first lying down and relaxing every muscle. Then, he recommends repeating a "focus word" or phrase over and over again to yourself as you exhale. Preferably, the focus word should be rooted in your value system or religious faith. For example, you might try the Hebrew word for peace, *shalom,* or the New Testament phrase "God is love." But Dr. Benson says that any word or short phrase will do so long as you repeat it silently for ten to twenty minutes.

Any distracting thoughts or influences should be gently pushed aside so that your attention is consumed by the focus word. Most people who continue with this exercise for ten to twenty minutes fall asleep, he says.

As an alternative, you might try reading a relatively slow-paced book or listening to soothing, soporific music.

• *Muscle relaxation methods.* It's been established that too much stimulation from the muscles along the spinal column in the trunk and neck can bombard the "wakefulness centers" in the brain and keep you awake. Conversely, interrupting the stimulation by soothing tight muscles that lead to the spinal area can induce sleep.

Some means that have been suggested to achieve this result without medications are gentle massage, tepid baths, and progressive muscle relaxing exercises. One technique for the latter method is to start tensing and then relaxing each set of muscles in your body. You begin with your toes and feet and work up progressively until you get to your head and the tips of your fingers.

• *Diversion.* If your problem is worrying or thinking incessantly in bed about some particular issue, you might try an approach taken by an elderly British physician. He had suffered from chronic insomnia until he discovered the trick of playing two or three rounds of imaginary golf in his mind as he lay in bed.

He reported that after a few minutes, "bogies and birdies follow one another in bewildering and impossible profusion—and suddenly the early morning tea arrives!"

This method is especially recommended for golfers, though chess, tennis, or any other favorite activity should work as well. A personal variation: I've dozed off quite nicely listening to tapes of medical lectures!

Many other nonmedical antidotes to insomnia have been advocated by doctors and lay people alike. These include such techniques as:

- avoiding heavy meals just before bedtime;
- engaging in exercise, but no later than three hours or more before bedtime;
- having a warm drink (preferably milk) just before retiring;
- taking a little wine; and
- using special mattresses or other sleeping gear.

As far as this last suggestion is concerned, I've discovered a major antidote to my own sleeping problems in a couple of great inventions: the "egg-crate mattress" and the contour pillow. Hospitals introduced these devices years ago, but they've only recently become more popular among those who aren't hospitalized or bed-bound.

The egg-crate mattress is a foamlike pad with a corrugated surface that fits on top of your regular mattress. When you lie on the corrugated surface to sleep, the weight of your body tends to be distributed more diffusely than on a regular mattress surface. As a result, there's less pressure on any given spot, including angular bones, sore joints, or other sensitive areas.

The contour pillow comes in various sizes and shapes, and you can choose the one that best fits the flexibility and shape of your head and neck. I prefer a relatively thin pillow with a dip in the center, but other people, including many of my patients, choose larger sizes and different shapes.

Both the pillow and the mattress can be purchased in most

medical supply stores. Also, ordinary department stores have begun to carry them.

Why are the egg-crate mattress and contour pillows often useful solutions for older people with sleep problems?

There are several reasons. The older we get, the stiffer and less flexible our joints and tissues become. Elderly people also often have increasing problems with arthritis, or painful swelling or inflammation of the joints. As a result, when they fall asleep, they may begin to feel pain or discomfort, especially when they turn over or rest too long on one part of the body.

Unfortunately, when any pain signal reaches the brain, the person is roused. Then, he may fall asleep again. But before long there's another feeling of pain or discomfort, and once again, he's awake. Perhaps for this reason, aspirin and similar drugs help some people sleep.

The traditional wisdom has always been that older people, like those who are younger, should sleep on a flat, firm mattress. But I've never been comfortable on a flat, hard mattress, and I've discovered that many of my older patients have the same reaction I do. Arms, shoulders, hips, and legs may simply not "fit" well onto a regular hard mattress. The egg-crate mattress is often a great alternative.

The contour pillow can also work quite well when the flexibility of the neck or upper back begins to decrease with age.

CAUTION: None of these suggestions should be accepted as providing a generally applicable panacea for insomnia. In fact, every nonmedical recommendation for overcoming insomnia has to be evaluated in terms of your own personal experience and responses.

Some people, for example, sleep soundly after a warm bath; others become wide awake after any bath and can't possibly go to sleep. Some sleep quite well after a warm glass of milk; others, with a lactose intolerance, get cramps or gas that prevents them from sleeping. I've also run into a number of individuals who can automatically drop off to sleep when they read any kind of book in bed; others can only count on sleeping when they read dense, fact-packed books.

One British expert on sleep has recommended reading the novels of Anthony Trollope in bed. On the other hand, another physician, who suggested "Ten Commandments for Good Sleeping" back in the 1950s, laid down this rule in no uncertain terms: "Never, positively *never,* read in bed!"

Obviously, if you have sleep problems and are looking for solutions that do not involve drugs, you may have to try several approaches until you find the one that works well for you. Of course, you may not find the answer among these suggestions because your problems may require more serious medical intervention.

Should You Try a Sleeping Medication?

Sometimes, no matter how many nonmedicinal methods you try, you may still not be able to get to sleep. You try all my suggestions, but *still* you find that you can't get to sleep quickly, or you wake up several times during the night, or you wake up feeling unrefreshed before you want to rise.

You may be facing insomnia that's simply related to the aging process. In other words, your sleep mechanism may be more impaired than it was when you were younger. You may also be waking up briefly many times during the night when you're not even aware of it, as we've seen from Dr. William Dement's research.

Under these circumstances, there's nothing wrong with an intelligent use of sleeping medications, so long as you are careful and remain under the care of a competent physician. I've found that I, as well as many of my patients, occasionally need some help from medication to get a good night's sleep.

So if you decide to try this approach, what medications should you use?

To get an idea of the possibilities, consider the accompanying list of medications, which in one way or another may help you sleep more soundly. Some of these can be bought over the counter, whereas others can be purchased only with a doctor's prescription.

Clearly, there are many drug options from which you can choose as you plan a strategy to overcome your insomnia. In the last analysis, the ultimate decision will be yours and your physician's. But let me provide you with a few thoughts and principles that may help you arrive at a final conclusion.

<table>

KEY FACTS

Sleeping Medications for the Elderly

MEDICATION	DOSE	HOW TO USE
Aspirin	1–2 325-mg tablets	Take just before bedtime to relieve pain or discomfort from arthritis or other joint or muscle soreness. The ibuprofen group (Advil, Nuprin, Medipren) may similarly help. Some patients report aspirin induces sleep apart from pain relief. Those with gastric problems, including past or present ulcers, should not use aspirin. But equivalent medications, such as acetaminophen (for example, Tylenol), are acceptable.
Benzodiazepines: Regular sleeping medications Triazolam (Halcion)	0.125–0.25 mg	Effects wear off relatively quickly. Low doses best for older people. May produce insomnia after long-term use.

</table>

MEDICATION	DOSE	HOW TO USE
Benzodiazepines: Regular sleeping: 　medications (cont.) 　Flurazepam 　(Dalmane)	15 mg	Has long-term, cumulative effects. More effective on second and third nights after it's taken, than on the first. May produce sluggishness, drowsy feelings, or mental confusion during day. Also, possible loss of coordination. Low doses best for older people. Little production of secondary insomnia.
Temazepam (Restoril)	15–30 mg	Not usually the drug of choice. Acts after some delay. Not for those who have trouble falling asleep, though may be helpful for those who wake up early. Side effects: drowsiness, mental dullness, lack of coordination are often apparent at 30-mg doses.
Mild tranquilizers: 　Meprobamates 　(Miltown, Equanil); 　Benzodiazepines 　(Valium, Librium)	Slightly higher dosage than for tranquilizing effect; follow instructions of your physician!	For mild insomnia. Usually none of usual side effects or withdrawal symptoms.

MEDICATION	DOSE	HOW TO USE
Antihistamines: Pyrilamine, Doxylamine, Diphenhydramine	25–50 mg	Many over-the-counter drugs contain antihistamines. Helpful if you have trouble falling asleep, though there may be side effects in older people: constipation, retention of urine, dry mouth, and blurred vision. Also, daytime drowsiness, lack of muscle coordination, dullness of thought processes.
Chloral hydrate Noctec	0.5–2 gm	An older drug that has become increasingly popular in recent years. Acts quickly to help those who have trouble falling asleep. Also, significant effects last up to 12 hours to promote a good night's sleep. Relatively inexpensive. Has adverse interactions with alcohol and the drug warfarin. Few other side effects, other than occasional gastrointestinal discomfort or feelings of agitation. Objectionable taste in liquid form (but capsules are available).

MEDICATION	DOSE	HOW TO USE
Barbiturates: Pentobarbital (Nembutal), Secobarbital (Seconal) Phenobarbital	50–100 mg	These drugs, which must be obtained by prescription, "hang on" in the body's systems long after they have been taken, with significant effects that may last up to one week. Side effects include hangovers and drowsiness. Overdoses can prove fatal. When taken over a long period, may produce withdrawal insomnia. Also, adverse interactions with many other drugs.

Some Basic Principles for Using Sleeping Pills

First, use the minimum amount of medication to get the desired amount of sleep. Second, in consultation with your doctor, you may want to rotate medications to prevent any cumulative impact or other undesirable side effect that they may have on your body.

Where should you start? If you know that pain, stiffness, or physical discomfort from arthritis or another source is at least part of your problem, aspirin may be the first medication to try. As indicated in the table, however, be sure you have no physical condition, such as stomach sensitivity, that makes aspirin unacceptable.

No matter what medication you use, be sure to monitor yourself closely for side effects. Sometimes, if you're not alert, you can be fooled into thinking that something other than the medication is at the root of the problem.

For example, when older people come into my office complaining of dizziness, they may offer a variety of possible guesses about their difficulty, from tumors to nutrition. But one of the first questions I ask is "What medications are you taking?"

Many times, the problem can be traced to the time when they began to take a sleeping pill. One woman told me she was taking the benzodiazepine medication Dalmane, which often does a good job of inducing sleep but has a tendency to accumulate in the body. The *half-life* of Dalmane (generic name flurazepam) is about ninety-six hours. This means that if you take a single capsule when you go to sleep, half of the medication is still in your body ninety-six hours later.

In fact, this woman had been taking one every night for several weeks, and the medication had literally overwhelmed her system. As a result, she began to feel dizzy and light-headed. By finding a shorter-acting equivalent, she was able to prevent the dizziness and still get a reasonable amount of sleep.

On another occasion, a seventy-year-old man was referred to me because his family feared he had Alzheimer's disease. Most mornings, they told me, he just didn't seem to be "with it." He was frequently confused, his memory was poor, and he didn't seem quite in touch with what was going on around him.

"He just can't put two and two together," his son told me.

But when I interviewed him and the family and began to put two and two together myself, I discovered that the problem wasn't Alzheimer's disease at all. Significantly, he didn't have mental troubles throughout the day. Rather, his impairment was worse in the mornings, and he tended to get better in the afternoons.

As it turned out, the man had been taking the barbiturate Seconal to fall asleep. The medication had been accumulating in his system for weeks and was producing side effects that made his family think he was losing his wits. So I discontinued the Seconal and substituted another sleeping medication, and his condition improved immediately.

Some of the most popular and widely prescribed sleeping pills at the present time are the benzodiazepines, but even these may produce strange reactions. One elderly woman came into my office afraid that she was losing her mind on the basis of a disturbing incident of a couple of nights earlier. She had awakened at about 3:00 A.M. as a result of an alarming nightmare-hallucination.

"Although I don't remember everything, my family members

do!" she told me. "I screamed out the window, 'What are the police doing here? Why are they taking over our house?' That didn't make me too popular with my family *or* with the neighbors."

Her outburst didn't sound to me as if it had anything to do with normal aging. So I questioned her in some depth and learned that she had been taking the benzodiazepine Halcion (generic name triazolam).

Normally, this medication is quite effective and helpful for those with sleeping problems. Most people take it at bedtime, say 10:30 or 11:00 P.M., and then they go right to sleep. Furthermore, they can expect most of it to be out of their system by the time they get up in the morning, with no ill effects. But this woman was an exception, and so I took her off Halcion and substituted chloral hydrate, which worked well without the side effects.

Before we leave this topic, I want to deal with a special age-related problem that may have important implications for medications, the peculiar condition called *sleep apnea.*

Controlling Sleep Apnea

As you get older, the chances increase that you'll experience to some degree a condition known as sleep apnea. To show you what this is all about, consider with me for a few moments some of the things that happen in your body to cause this condition.

At the base of the brain, there is a remarkable group of cells that control your breathing throughout your lifetime. They are known as the *respiratory center.* These are the cells that keep your chest muscles and diaphragm contracting and relaxing at rates dictated by the body's needs: much faster when you exercise, much slower when you are asleep.

Breathing rates are generally even and regular at around twenty times a minute when we are awake and resting. Fortunately, they're also entirely automatic.

There's also a voluntary "override" on this mechanism. In other words, you can take a deep breath or two, or sigh to express an emotion, or breathe more rapidly at a physician's request during a medical examination. Voluntary rapid breathing, by the way, may produce light-headedness.

KEY FACTS

BREATHING PATTERNS AND SLEEP DISORDERS

Researchers who made a study of sleep-disordered breathing among older people reached these conclusions:

- Sleep-disordered breathing is common among healthy elderly people.
- Breathing problems during sleep in general had no impact on the daytime sleepiness or behavior of elderly people.
- Sleep-disordered breathing and frequent arousals during the night, which are quite abnormal in young people, are common in the elderly.

In this report, 29 healthy older people were studied in a sleep lab with technology designed to measure brain waves, eye muscle movement, and electrocardiograms. Also, there were devices for measuring airflow through the nose and mouth.

The researchers arranged for in-depth psychological assessment of the participants, plus an evaluation of their daytime sleepiness and behavior. Here are some of the results in the mean (average) times or number of incidents for certain types of behavior, and also the ranges for those types in all the participants.

BEHAVIOR	MEAN	RANGES
Time in bed (minutes)	368	282–434
Total sleep time (minutes)	254	118–390
Number of arousals	53	2–134
Number of awakenings	21	2–51
Number of apneas	17	0–139

D. T. R. Berry, B. A. Phillips, Y. R. Cook, et al., "Sleep-Disordered Breathing in Healthy Aged Persons," *Journal of Gerontology* 42 (1987): 620.

But there are also departures from the smooth, predictable, automatic action of breathing that occur during sleep, especially as we age. Involuntary interruptions are called *apnea,* which literally means "no breathing." The most common form is known as *obstructive apnea.*

This obstructive apnea problem apparently results from the shrinkage of the muscles in the throat area or other anatomical changes in the support structures in the throat. As a result, when the person falls asleep, structures around the back of the throat seem to collapse together during the intake phase of the breathing process. Air cannot get into the throat and lungs, and so the person snorts and wakes up briefly to clear his throat. Then, he goes back to sleep until the breath obstruction occurs a few minutes or seconds later.

This phenomenon is more likely to occur when you sleep on your back. Those who have experienced apnea soon learn to sleep on one or the other side to escape the difficulty. Sleeping in a more upright position, propped up with pillows, may also work.

In some instances, the apnea seems to be due to problems with the respiratory center, which loses its sensitivity to accumulating carbon dioxide. But mixtures of the forms of apnea are common.

In most cases, sleep apnea is mild and poses no particular danger. On the other hand, if the condition is severe, oxygen flow to the brain and other organs may be impeded for too long, and organ damage may occur. Whether mild or serious, multiple breathing interruptions can wreak havoc with a decent night's sleep.

According to various studies, this particular disorder is widely prevalent among the elderly. It's been estimated that some degree of sleep apnea may afflict anywhere from 28 to 37 percent of the senior population.

Typical symptoms include loud snoring, shallow breathing, or struggling to breathe. Also, the sufferer may engage in frequent sleep talking and assume unusual positions during sleep. How often this is occurring can sometimes be evaluated only by what a spouse reports, or better yet, by a sleep lab.

So what can you do about this problem?

It is important *not* to use any of the benzodiazepine group of drugs, which as we've already discussed are now quite popular sleep medications. Taking one of these drugs can exacerbate the problem and even prove dangerous if the patient falls so soundly asleep that she fails to be aroused quickly by the lack of airflow into her body.

Because most cases of sleep apnea are relatively mild, however, your physician may just say, "Don't worry about it unless it gets worse." He may suggest raising the head of the bed or using more pillows, but nothing major. In short, *nonintervention* is a frequent treatment for the variable, less serious forms of apnea.

Or he may suggest that you try to change your sleep positions, and he may encourage your spouse to help you with this alteration in bedtime habits. It's been found, for example, that the supine position, or lying down on your back with the face upward, aggravates sleep apnea, whereas lying prone, on your stomach, can relieve the condition. Also, your doctor will probably suggest weight loss if you happen to be overweight because obesity can contribute significantly to this condition.

But you may find that none of these conservative life-style solutions works. Suppose that you are constantly quite tired during the day, or you otherwise find that your functioning is significantly impaired because of a lack of sleep due to sleep apnea. After confirmation by a sleep lab, your doctor has several other more serious avenues of treatment that he can choose or suggest. These include:

- permanent tracheostomy, which is a surgical incision into the windpipe;
- surgery on the throat and palate;
- surgical lengthening of the lower jawbone;
- application of pressure on the nasal airways with various mechanical devices; or
- administration of oxygen under pressure to support the upper airway during sleep.

Before you face any such serious medical intervention, however, your physician will perform a battery of tests to determine just how severe your sleep apnea is.

Insomnia, clearly, is a problem with many facets and implications. I've covered a wide range of sleep problems in this section, including some that may turn out to be quite serious. But the chances are that if you have trouble with sleep, your difficulty is relatively simple to understand, *and* probably simple to relieve. I would just urge you to develop a systematic strategy to surmount your insomnia that is measured and cautious. If, keeping in touch with your doctor, you move step by step—from making changes in life-style and environment to taking doctor-monitored medications, if necessary—you'll find that you're on safe ground. And most likely, you'll begin to sleep *almost* like a baby again!

6

ACHES, PAINS, AND MINOR COMPLAINTS

One fifty-five-year-old woman came to me complaining of a pain and sense of stiffness in her knee. "I guess my mother's arthritis is finally hitting me," she said in a resigned tone of voice. But in fact, as I began to examine her, I discovered that the root of her problem had nothing to do with classic arthritis.

Arthritis is an inflammation in the joints and an accompanying pain in that area. We'll go into the subject of *real* arthritis in Chapter 22. But many times, as in this woman's case, the pain may be in the general area of the joint, but not in the joint itself. So the proper diagnosis can't be arthritis.

This woman's knee wasn't swollen and it didn't have any other indications of internal inflammation. As a matter of fact, her real problem was located just to the *side* of her knee.

After some discussion, I determined that the woman's real difficulty was that she had apparently pulled or strained a tendon that ran down to her knee. It seems that she had twisted her knee, either when she was walking or when she was asleep. After this injury, the pain had begun, and she had automatically misdiagnosed her malady: "It must be arthritis—just like my mother's!"

It Must Be Arthritis!

We all become more susceptible to pulled tendons and muscles as we get older. Also, certain aches, pains, and other complaints become more frequent or bothersome: a response that's quite common and within normal experience.

Unfortunately, many people become overly concerned and some even panic when an unusual pain or feeling of discomfort appears. When they feel an ache in the back or a shoulder, the first thought that comes to mind may be: "Uh, oh! Aunt Gladys had arthritis, and now I'm getting it too!"

But there's no reason to overreact this way. There's no reason to be fooled by the common aches and pains of long life, which may masquerade as something more serious. One of the main reasons that older people come to my office is that they have observed some change or felt some pain in their bodies. But then they make a diagnosis that is really a *misdiagnosis* and rush in to me in a state of near-hysteria, driven by the expectation that they're on their last legs.

In fact, one of the most common of these misdiagnoses arises from the problem I've already referred to, a fear of arthritis. On another occasion, a sixty-two-year-old man came in complaining of an ache in his hip, and the very first words out of his mouth reflected the common fear: "Do you think it's arthritis? Or maybe osteoporosis?"

No, I answered. Neither of those. In his case, the problem was just a common joint pain that we call *arthralgia.* As you grow older—or even when you're relatively young—a slight trauma to a joint, such as a twist or an undue strain, may result in an injury to structures around the joint, which causes pain for a day or two or even longer. Again, however, this is not arthritis. It's just a common pain in the joint region that will soon go away after the damaged or bruised tissues have healed.

This tendency to misdiagnose an ache or pain—and even to

confuse it with arthritis—may also focus on one of the most common complaints of aging, the backache.

The Garden-Variety Backache

A patient of mine was quite worried because of what she had been told after some X rays at a walk-in clinic. She had been experiencing some lower-back pain, and the X rays had shown what the attending physician at the clinic had described as "degenerative changes in the joints."

"There, you see, there are these little growths on your bones in your spine," he had said. "That's called arthritis: *osteoarthritis.* Those little bone projections are called *osteophytes.*"

The woman had immediately assumed that her back pain was due entirely to those degenerative changes in her spine, and the doctor she was talking to was apparently too busy to explain the true implications of her situation. So she left the examination thoroughly disheartened and close to panic.

But as we talked, I told her that those little bone projections that she could see on the X rays were common occurrences in most people as they get older.

"In fact," I said, "you can almost 'guesstimate' the age of a person by the degree of degenerative changes in the joints or in the spine. But those changes don't necessarily mean you're going to get a backache." In her case, I said, it was by no means certain that the back pain she was experiencing had any relation to those projections she was seeing on the X rays.

Indeed, further examination and the passage of time revealed that the back pain apparently had resulted from a heavy load she had tried to lift. Even though the pain hadn't hit her immediately, it did occur soon afterward. But somehow, she hadn't associated the onset of the pain or the continuing discomfort over a period of a couple of weeks with that unfortunate lifting experience.

So I simply prescribed bed rest with a heating pad and reduced activity for a week. At the end of that time, the pain had subsided significantly.

In fact, many people with a history of recurrent backache over a lifetime experience *less* of it in their older years, so in some respects, aging changes may stabilize the back. On the other hand, many of the supportive structures around the joints, the so-called connective tissues, become stiffer and more vulnerable to stress and pain with aging.

In many cases, these aches and pains of aging are taken care of by a process that is sometimes known by the mouthful term *vis medicatrix naturae,* meaning "the healing force of nature," which usually works in favor of the doctor and the patient. Often, it's just necessary to rest the painful or injured part of the body for a few days, and then improvement, including a lessening of the pain, will begin.

If I can't find some other apparent cause of back pain, I often prescribe one of the common over-the-counter painkillers such as aspirin or acetaminophen (Tylenol), in addition to plenty of "get-off-your-feet" behavior and rest. If after about a week to ten days the pain is still there, or if there hasn't at least been significant improvement, we begin a battery of more extensive tests.

A major point I want to get across to you in this discussion of backaches and other joint and body pains is that they often do not indicate major disease processes. If they occurred to you when you were young, you wouldn't automatically think, "Arthritis!" As a matter of fact, many of the common complaints of people in the second half of life are unrelated to aging! They happen to all people, regardless of age.

True, after a certain age, usually beginning in the thirties, we tend to get injured more easily, for instance, by pulling or straining muscles. Flexibility typically decreases with age, and as a result, it's easy to overextend muscles and put undue pressure on bones and joints. But in many cases these aches are attributable to the gradual weakening and stiffening of the body with age, and they involve only minor discomforts. Also, remember that much of the natural decline in our flexibility, strength, and endurance with age can be slowed significantly *if* we just keep active and pursue a regular program of exercise. For suggestions about how to do this, see the exercise programs described in Chapter 13.

In any event, it's a big mistake to assume that every little pain is a signal of some major health problem. But it's easy to fall into this trap if you forget what your health was like when you were younger.

Your Health History

As we get older, we frequently forget our earlier health history, and this can make us much more inclined to hypochondria. I recall one seventy-year-old man who came to me because of a backache. After we had chatted for a while, however, it became apparent that the problem he was describing hadn't by any means started recently. Rather, he had been suffering from periodic backaches ever since he had been in his thirties.

Furthermore, he told me that the backaches usually began after he had been under a particular period of stress. When he was younger, a particularly pressure-packed day at the office or some great problem bearing down on him at home had been sufficient to trigger an attack.

Now that he was older, the same sequence of events tended to happen: In this most recent situation, he had been trying to resolve a difficult problem between a couple of his children and had been forced to make a couple of long plane trips to straighten out the problem. The backache had begun just after one of those journeys.

"So you see," I said, "this is nothing new. Part of your health history has been backaches, and really, as far as I can tell, they're no worse now than they were earlier. Perhaps they *seem* worse because you're extremely tired of having them, and maybe you even think that it's unfair for you to have to wrestle with bothersome pains at this stage in your life. But in fact, you're the same person in many ways that you were thirty years ago, and so don't be surprised if some of the problems you experienced earlier continue to stay with you."

The best antidote in his case was to take some aspirin, spend more time for the next few days loafing and resting in bed, and avoid all heavy or stressful activity for at least a week. He called at the end of that time and said, "I'm much better!"

I advised him that if he wanted to *stay* better, he should try to do something about future stress. That way, he could perhaps prevent the onset of these backaches by changing the patterns that had been part of his makeup since he had been a young man.

Some Key Types of Back Pain

The backaches we've been discussing are among the most common physical complaints: More than 80 million Americans have already suffered some sort of backache; about 2 million of these people experience chronic pain; and an estimated 8 million new cases of backache occur each year.

But what exactly causes backache, and what can you do about it? You've already been introduced to some of the possibilities in the illustrations involving some of my own patients. Now, to understand these and other causes, and their remedies, here's an overview of the most common types of backache.

Common Low-Back Pain

Low-back pain typically arises when a section of the lower back, the so-called facet joint, is twisted slightly and triggers muscle spasms.

For example, one of my patients recently complained that his "back had gone out" when he had reached over to pick up his shoe that morning. He was particularly annoyed that his lower back was hurting after such a seemingly simple and innocuous movement.

"I bent over very slowly and leaned a little to one side to get the shoe," he explained. "But then as I straightened up, this pain shot through my lower back. I immediately lay back on the bed, and I found I had a lot of trouble getting up again. I could hardly move!"

After examining him, I determined that this was a classic example of a problem with the facet joint. As this man indicated, the movement that triggers the problem may seem far too gentle or easy for the painful result it produces. But that's part of the nature of the difficulty. It usually doesn't take much to produce a facet-joint pain, just a bend and a slight twist of the body.

The treatment for this man was the same as for almost any simple backache: I encouraged him to rest as much as possible during the next few days; specifically, it was most helpful for him to lie down and elevate his legs and knees a few inches.

Also, I told him to apply heat pads regularly to the injured part of the back. Other physicians might recommend the application of cold packs—either ice that has been wrapped in a watertight bag or one of the frozen plastic packs you can buy in most drugstores. These heat and cold treatments aren't necessarily inconsistent with each other, though I feel with this particular injury, the heat works better to relax the muscles and eliminate the spasms.

Finally, to reduce the pain and discomfort, I recommended that he take the usual adult dose of two coated aspirin tablets every four hours.

Muscle Strains or Pulls in the Back

Unlike the injury described previously, a pulled or strained muscle may result from excessive physical work, such as lifting a relatively heavy piece of household equipment.

In this case, rest and an over-the-counter painkiller such as aspirin or Tylenol may also be in order. But because of the nature of the injury—usually a tear of some sort in a muscle or ligament—cold may do more good than heat. Treatment involves application of ice to the injured area, preferably every ten to twenty minutes for several hours (some physicians recommend continuing the treatments for up to forty-eight hours). The cold serves a couple of important functions: Acting as a kind of local anesthetic, it numbs the area that's in pain. Also, the cold helps reduce internal bleeding and promotes faster blood clotting and healing.

In any event, before you launch any extensive self-treatment plans for such an injury, it's important to check first with your doctor. He will be able to identify the precise type of back problem you have and recommend the most appropriate remedy.

More Serious Back Injuries

The most serious back problems include degenerative disk disease, which is discussed in the upcoming section, "When You Should Worry About Your Back"; back problems related to bone loss (osteoporosis), which are dealt with in Chapter 21; and other chronic back problems, such as inherited or congenital conditions, which your physician must diagnose and treat.

With most back problems, including even the most serious ones, it's often possible to minimize the pain and danger to your back by paying close attention to your life-style and fitness habits.

How to Care for Your Back

In general, I tell my patients that there are two main ways to take care of your back and prevent back injuries: (1) do a simple set of body-trunk exercises every day; and (2) pay close attention to your body positions and movements.

The Exercise Solution

The key to a healthy back is strong, firm abdominal muscles. These muscles provide important support for the spine and trunk of the body. When the stomach begins to get weak and flabby, the back is placed at increasing risk for injury.

To guard against this possibility, I recommend several rather easy, quick exercises, which should be performed daily or, at a minimum, four times a week:

• *Leg raises.* This exercise, which helps strengthen the lower abdominal area, can be done the first thing in the morning, while you're still lying on your back in bed.

To begin, raise the left leg slowly off the bed with the knee slightly bent. Continue to bend the knee and move the upper part of the leg up as close to the chest as possible. Then, lower the leg back to the bed.

Do ten to twenty repetitions (or fewer if you can't manage that many), and repeat the exercise with the right leg.

Finally, raise both legs, with bent knees, up to your chest and return them to the bed. Repeat ten to twenty times, or fewer if necessary.

• *Bent-leg sit-ups.* Lie flat on your back on a soft rug or mat, with your feet flat on the ground and your knees bent at about a forty-five-degree angle. If you like, you can put the insteps of your feet under something solid, like the bed, or have a companion hold your feet down.

Next, with your arms folded across your chest, raise your upper body slowly to a sitting position; then slowly lower your upper body again to the floor. Repeat ten times, or as often as you can comfortably manage. Your goal should be to work up to three sets of ten repetitions, with a brief rest of about ten to fifteen seconds between each set.

• *Lower-back extensions.* As a variation on what is sometimes called the "Williams exercises," these extensions help to remove the stress and strain from your lower back.

Begin by lying flat on your back on a soft surface on the floor. Then, tuck in your buttocks and force the small of your back to lie flat against the floor. Hold this position for about ten seconds. Then, repeat the motion ten times.

Next, lying flat on the floor, bend your left leg up toward your chest until your left knee almost touches your chest. Grasp your left knee and shin with your hands, and pull your leg even closer into your chest. Hold this position for thirty seconds.

Repeat this motion with your right leg.

Finally, pull *both* your knees up against your chest and hold this position for thirty seconds.

As simple and easy as these movements may seem, they can work wonders for a tired, tense, hurting back, and they can help protect against strains and pulls.

Body Positions and Movements

The exercises I've just described will help strengthen and tone up the muscles that support and surround your back. But you can protect yourself even further by being careful about way you sit, sleep, stand, and move. Here are some suggestions I frequently pass on to my patients:

• *Sitting* can put more stress on your back than standing, so follow these guidelines to reduce the pressure and risk of injury:

You should choose a chair that allows you to keep your feet flat on the floor, with knees slightly elevated above the hips. If a chair doesn't allow this, try to put something firm under your feet so that your knees will be elevated.

Your seat cushion should be firm so that you don't sink far down into it. Also, it's best for the chair to have a relatively straight back, with a section that supports your lower back.

Finally, don't sit still for long periods of time. Get up and walk about every twenty to thirty minutes, at least.

• *Standing and walking* should be done with good posture. This means keeping your upper body straight and your buttocks tucked in to reduce the arch or "sway" in your lower back. In this way, you'll reduce unnecessary pressure on your lower spine.

• When *sleeping,* avoid lying on your stomach: that position puts the most stress on your spine. Instead, sleep on your side, with your knees bent up toward your body. As an alternative, you might sleep on your back. On the other hand, if you're one of those people who must sleep on his or her stomach, get an extra pillow and place it under your hips or the lower part of one of your legs, so as to reduce the arch in your lower back. Most likely, you'll have to experiment with pillow supports to find the position that suits you best.

• When *reaching, bending, or lifting,* keep these guidelines in mind:

Always bend at the knees and use your *legs* to lift any object from the ground. *Don't* bend over from the waist and allow your back to do the lifting.

When you bend down, move in a straight, up-and-down motion. *Don't twist,* even slightly. REMEMBER: That facet joint in the lower back can cause muscle spasms at the slightest provocation.

Don't carry heavy loads, such as groceries, in a bag in front of you. It's always best to use a cart of some sort. Second best is to distribute the load between two bags and carry them in each hand at your sides. If you must wrestle with one bag, hold it very close to your body and as low as possible in front of you.

Avoid excessive reaching for objects. Take the extra second or two to get close to the object or place where you're trying to reach.

If you follow these basic guidelines for moving and positioning your body—and you work regularly at strengthening your back-related muscles—you should greatly lower your risk of back injury as you get older.

When You Should Worry About Your Back

Sometimes the back pains that we experience as we get older—as well as those among younger people—are the result of quite serious problems, such as a herniated disk. With advancing age, the fibrous cartilage between the vertebrae becomes more rigid and shrinks, with the result that there's a loss of height. The age-related deterioration of this tissue may cause the centers of this cartilage (the *nucleus pulposus*) to break out of their normal position and protrude from the vertebral column.

KEY FACTS

IMPORTANT POINTS ON BACK PAIN AND SCIATICA

A 1988 *New England Journal of Medicine* article mentioned the following important facts about back pain and sciatica:

- Over a lifetime, 60 to 90 percent of us will experience significant bouts with low-back pain.

- The annual incidence of low-back pain involves 5 percent of the population, and over an average lifetime, sciatica—involving pain in the lower back and legs—occurs in 40 percent of the population.

- Risk factors for lower-back pain and sciatica include (1) repetitive lifting by bending forward from the waist and twisting the body as the lift is executed, (2) vibrations of vehicles or machinery, and (3) cigarette smoking.

- Osteoporosis—progressive loss of bone mass that typically occurs after about age forty—may account for the fact that elderly women have more low-back symptoms than elderly men.

- Low-back pain is generally self-limiting, and 50 percent of patients with sciatica recover within a month.

- Basic treatment for acute low-back pain is bed rest, which has been shown to cut the time to recovery in half. Other treatments include heat or cold, pain pills, traction, physiotherapy and exercise programs (such as those described in this text).

- Manipulative treatment (that is, osteopathic or chiropractic manipulations) may temporarily decrease pain and improve back function, but it has little or no lasting benefit. There is no convincing evidence that it corrects spinal malalignment.

- In 10 percent of patients, low-back pain persists for more than six weeks, though the cause may still be elusive.
- With sciatica, the most important cause is pressure from a herniated disk. Nonsurgical treatment includes bed rest, medication, injection of steroids around the nerve, and braces.
- About 5 to 10 percent of patients with unrelenting sciatica may require an operation.

J. W. Frymoyer, "Back Pain and Sciatica," *The New England Journal of Medicine* 318 (1988): 291.

When one of these disks presses against a nerve, the pain can be excruciating, and medical intervention will be in order. Among other consequences, a person with this problem may have *sciatica,* a pain down the longest nerve in the body, the sciatic nerve, which runs from the lumbar spine down into the lower limbs. Patients with sciatica may have disabling pains down past the hip and into the legs.

But a slipped or herniated disk is not the only cause of sciatica. Sometimes, this kind of back pain may result from bony thickening around the opening through which the nerve emerges. Infrequently, it may result from the condition known as *shingles,* a viral disease affecting the nerve and its endings in the skin and resulting in blisters and a crusting of the skin. With shingles, the affected nerves are often quite painful. If the sciatic nerve is involved, you may have sciatica, but of course, this shingles pain has nothing to do with a herniated disk.

One of my patients was certain that she had a major disk problem one weekend when her sciatic nerve began to hurt. But I told her to rest a day or two and come in for an exam. When she returned to my office, it became evident that a herniated disk wasn't the problem at all. Instead, a classic shingles eruption had broken out. As a result, I began to treat her for the real problem, shingles, with prescriptions of corticosteroid drugs. The medication diminished the inflammation within a few days, the pain subsided, and we soon tapered her off the steroids. NOTE: Shingles is rare before age sixty.

Another problem I hear about just as often as back pain in my older patients is an increasing sensitivity to heat and cold.

Too Cold . . . or Too Hot?

As you get older, your body typically becomes more sensitive to both heat and cold (although some older people have the opposite reaction: they lose their sensitivity to temperature changes). One reason for any increase in sensitivity to heat or cold is that many people tend to lose body fat, especially from the skin tissues, a process that reduces the body's natural insulation. Older people also typically experience a lowering of their body's metabolism and decreased circulation to the hands and feet, which may be the result of a less active, more sedentary way of life.

Cold

When it gets cold outside, one response that I've seen among a number of my patients is the cold-weather solution that the Russian people often use all winter: They pile one garment on top of the other until they seem twice as large as they are in summertime! On examining an individual who dresses like this, I've sometimes found four, five, or even more layers of clothing confronting me before I finally get down to the heart or lungs, my target for examination.

Even on relatively warm days, some of my older patients—say those in their seventies or older—wear a sweater or two. On the other hand, in warm climates, older people may feel the heat more than younger people, particularly when external temperatures rise above body temperature. They may become less energetic and have much less zip, again because they lack the efficient compensations and other physical mechanisms to bear up well under the heat.

Of course, not all older people have this problem. But for those who do, the sensitivity to cold or heat doesn't present any insurmountable problem. You just dress more warmly than younger people when the temperature is low, or you reduce the level of your activity on very hot days so that you are not "done in" by the heat.

Still, it's important to be careful and realize that your increased sensitivity to heat and cold does provide an important signal to prevent you from suffering serious injury when the temperature drops or rises precipitously. For example, one major problem in cold weather that may wreak havoc with an older person's health is *hypothermia,* or a drop in internal body temperature that can be life-threatening if it's not identified and treated right away.

Hypothermia is a condition that arises from a below-normal body temperature, typically ninety-five degrees Fahrenheit (F) (thirty-five degrees Celsius [C]) or less. Anybody of any age can suffer from hypothermia in very cold weather. But some older people who have particular problems with body metabolism or activity may experience this after exposure to relatively moderate cold. Elderly people most likely to develop accidental hypothermia include

- the chronically ill, especially those who are bedridden;
- the poor who can't afford heating fuel;
- those who don't have the foresight to dress warmly;
- those whose internal heat regulation in the body is severely impaired; and
- those who have lost much of their sensitivity to cold and fail to shiver (shivering raises the level of body heat). REMEMBER: Most older people become more sensitive to heat or cold.

Also, those who are feeble or susceptible to falls may fall down on the ice or cold ground, and if they're not soon picked up, they may quickly become hypothermic. For that matter, the fall may occur in a cold bedroom, where the elderly person may lie for a long time before being discovered. It's even possible for an older person to develop hypothermia while lying in bed under the covers. Most people have experienced being in a bed under one set of covers but still being cold because the blankets aren't warm enough. Multiply that feeling by several times, and you'll get a sense of what older people with a sensitivity to cold may feel when they're not properly wrapped up and "tucked away" in bed.

Hypothermia is especially dangerous in the elderly because it may have such effects as pneumonia, pancreatitis, heart attacks, and occasionally even gangrene. Obviously, in severe cases, death is a possibility.

Usually, things don't go this far with an older person who is sensitive to cold. In most cases, the problem can be identified and corrected early simply by getting warm. But the first order of business is to ascertain that there's a problem; then you can take steps to correct it. Signs that may indicate the onset of hypothermia include the following:

• An unusual change in appearance or behavior during cold weather
   • Slow and sometimes irregular heartbeats
   • Slurred speech
   • Shallow, very slow breathing
   • Sluggishness
   • Mental confusion

If the symptoms are severe and sustained, the warming up should be done under a doctor's supervision, and the best place to do this may be in a hospital.

Of course, the best approach, before the situation becomes this serious, is to take intelligent preventive measures to protect yourself from the cold. To this end, the temperatures in your living areas should be set at least at 65 degrees F (18.3°C). Those who are particularly sensitive to cold or who are sick or unusually inactive may need higher room temperatures.

Also, to prevent suffering from hypothermia by accident, you should

• dress warmly, even when you're indoors;
   • wear layers of clothing, an approach that enhances warmth and also allows you to remove or add to your dress as needed;
   • eat plenty of food;
   • stay as physically active as possible—and that means regular aerobic exercises such as walking;
   • stay warm in bed by wearing sufficiently heavy pajamas and socks;
   • use plenty of blankets, including electric blankets or pads;
   • check on the possible impact of your medicines (drugs to treat anxiety, depression, nervousness, or nausea, such as the phenothiazines and antidepressants, may depress body reactions to low temperatures);

• ask a friend or relative to check on you once or twice a day, especially when the weather is cold. As an alternative, you might find out whether your community has a telephone check-in or personal visitation service for the elderly or housebound.

For further information on problems with cold, you might write for the National Institute on Aging's brochure *A Winter Hazard for the Old: Accidental Hypothermia*, National Institute on Aging/Hypo, Building 31, Room 5C35, Bethesda, Maryland 20892.

Heat

The other side of the coin is that older people also become quite sensitive to hot and humid temperatures. As a result, they become more subject than younger people to problems of heat prostration when temperatures rise toward 100 degrees F.

In part, the problem with heat stems from the gradual impairment of the sweating mechanism as we become older. Elderly people who are diabetic or who have problems with atherosclerosis (clogging or "hardening" of the arteries) may have more difficulties with hot weather.

It's not necessary to be exposed directly to the sun, by the way, to have a problem with heat. In one situation that I personally observed, twelve of about three hundred elderly patients residing in various nursing homes developed serious heat-related problems—but none had been outdoors. The attacks occurred one summer after a series of days when temperatures had exceeded 38 degrees C (100°F) in non-air-conditioned facilities.

These nursing home residents first became apathetic, weak, faint, and headachy. Then, some of them developed high fevers, heart problems, and dryness of skin. There was even one death in the group, though most responded promptly to ice packs and intravenous fluids.

During hot or humid weather, body heat can build up and trigger one of the two most common heat-related dangers, heatstroke or heat exhaustion:

• *Heatstroke.* This is the most serious heat-provoked problem and requires immediate medical attention. The symptoms include faintness, dizziness, headaches, nausea, loss of consciousness, body temperature of 104 degrees F (40°C) or higher (measured rectally), rapid pulse rates, and flushed skin.

Treatment includes plunging the victim into a cold bath or tub filled with ice to lower the body temperature as quickly as possible.

● *Heat exhaustion.* Heat exhaustion usually develops over a longer period of time than heatstroke, which often hits like a lightning bolt. Heat exhaustion results from a loss of body water and salt. The symptoms include weakness, heavy sweating, nausea, and giddiness. Common treatments involve resting in bed away from the heat and drinking plenty of cool liquids containing salt, potassium, and other minerals.

But there's no reason to allow these problems with heat to go this far! Older people with a particular sensitivity to heat or susceptibility to heat problems should stay inside in an air-conditined room during hot weather. Or if you don't have air-conditioning at home, you might spend most of your time during the hot part of the day in a cool public place, such as a library, a movie theater, or a store.

Here are a few other good ways that I advise my patients to stay cool on those hot days:

- take cool baths or showers;
- put ice bags or wet towels on the body;
- use wet towels on arms and legs;
- place several electric fans around the house;
- stay away from direct sunlight and avoid strenuous activity;
- wear lightweight, light-colored, loose-fitting clothing that allows your sweat to evaporate;
- drink plenty of liquids, such as water and fruit and vegetable juices; and
- avoid alcoholic beverages or fluids that contain excess salt.

Common Cramps, Itching, and Minor Foot Trouble

Cramps

As you get older, you may experience a variety of muscle cramps that you never had, or never noticed, when you were younger. Don't worry! This sort of thing is not all that abnormal. Furthermore, there are often steps you can take at home to reduce or remove the problems.

For example, sometimes patients who take diuretic drugs, such as those used for hypertension, may experience cramps in the leg muscles because of a rapid loss of fluids, salt, and other minerals from the body. Among other symptoms, patients using these drugs may suffer from a pain in one or both calf muscles as they walk.

How do you take care of this problem? Consult your doctor to see whether he can change your medication. If he can't, you can usually relieve the problem simply by resting more often and using your muscles less strenuously.

Sometimes, a peculiar and troublesome form of cramp may hit older people at night. I recall one woman who was often awakened frequently by sudden, agonizing spasms in her calf muscle and sometimes in her toes. Because these attacks seemed to her to be occurring at an accelerating rate, she became worried and came to me for advice.

I explained that these stiff, painful contractions were really nothing to worry about because apparently they weren't producing any long-term debilitation. She confirmed that indeed, they lasted only for seconds, not minutes, and then she felt all right. But oh, those terrible seconds!

The best way to respond to these attacks, I told her, is to press manually against your toes or foot in the opposite direction to that in which the spasm or cramp is occurring. Usually, this remedy, or, as an alternative, some sort of massage in the affected area, seems to take care of the problem.

"Another good approach is to get out of bed and start walking around," I told her. "Walking involves an alternating contraction and relaxation of your muscles in a regular rhythm, and that's often what you need to undo those cramps."

Upon trying these approaches, she found that her problem became much less severe and bothersome.

It's not always clear what causes these contractions that lead to such painful cramping, but I've developed an idea over the years that the pressure of sheets and blankets on the feet in bed may play a role. You can correct this situation by not tucking in your bed too tightly or by using a footboard, which allows the sheets and blankets to rest loosely at the foot of the bed.

In some cases, cramps or spasms may occur when you over-work your muscles, and this is a problem that may increase as you reach middle age and your muscle power decreases.

For example, if you are in your fifties and aren't used to playing volleyball, basketball, or another sport that requires a great deal of jumping, don't assume that you can just run out on the court and behave like a teenager.

Probably, your leg muscles, and especially your calves, will soon become tight and fatigued, in part because of the buildup of lactic acid in the tissues. This lactic acid is formed as part of the final part of the sugar metabolism in the body. If an excessive amount of this substance accumulates in your muscles, you'll most likely suffer cramps and perhaps even more serious injuries.

One of my fifty-year-old patients was laid up for four days after a particularly rigorous volleyball game! In his case, the remedy was as follows: First, ice packs were applied to the area of the calf where the cramps were occurring for about fifteen to twenty minutes. Then, the patient applied ice periodically to the affected area for the next twenty-four hours and took it *very* easy. He walked about as little as possible and got plenty of sleep. For the next few days, he avoided walking as much as possible and of course stayed away from all forms of exercise. Gradually, the cramping subsided, and his leg returned to normal by the fourth day.

Painful muscular cramps are more likely to occur in people with low blood calcium levels, though most people who complain of this problem have normal levels. Apparently, as with other problems related to calcium deficiency, such as osteoporosis, the calcium lack doesn't show up in the blood.

Because of this possible calcium connection, another remedy to the cramping problem may be to drink a cup of hot milk before retiring at night. Also, if severe cramping remains a problem, your doctor may be able to prescribe a muscle-relaxing drug.

Itching

As you get older, your skin becomes thinner and also drier as a result of diminished secretions. One result of this change may be recurrent itching sensations, especially during the winter ("winter itch"), when the skin is driest. In some older people the skin may appear normal, except for some dryness, slight roughness, and scratch marks.

One medical response to itching may be drugs such as sedatives, antihistamines, or a medication called Periactin. But when the main problem seems to be dryness of the skin, many of the over-the-counter lubricants can be useful. You can add these to your bath or massage them into your skin after you bathe.

Sometimes, itching of the skin may signal an underlying disease, such as chronic renal (kidney) failure. Diabetics may complain of itching if their sugar metabolism has gone out of control. There are other underlying health disturbances that may cause itching, and your physician will be in the best position to determine whether one of these causes applies to you.

But again, don't panic just because you feel an increased need to scratch! If the itching persists over a period of a week or more, you should certainly see your doctor. Ointments containing cortisone are astonishingly effective for itching in some areas, including the ears. But most likely, your doctor won't find anything wrong with you, other than the fact that you're getting a little older and drier. Or maybe he'll tell you to stop overusing soap!

In some cases, the itching may occur in the anal area (*pruritus ani*) or genital area. Occasionally, the cause may be a yeast infection that can arise from unrecognized diabetes, or a malfunction in the body's immune system may be the cause. Much more likely, the itching is a temporary aggravation of unknown cause, worsened by the itch-scratch cycle, which will soon pass away if you can just "wait it out."

Sometimes, though, a cause of anal or genital itching can be found and corrected. For example, itching in these areas may arise from hygiene problems. Elderly people who have problems with continence, for instance, may experience itching sensations that can quickly be eliminated when they clean the troublesome area.

If you have this problem, you should wipe with moistened paper after each bowel movement or use a bidet or sitz bath. In addition, many people have found that glycerin-soaked pads, such as Tucks, work better than dry toilet paper.

On the other hand, wipes containing alcohol may burn, and soap may aggravate itching if the skin has become irritated or abraded as a result of scratching. Overly vigorous wiping with toilet tissue can also be abrasive and may rub in any residue of fecal material or urine, a process that will cause irritation. Finally, a failure to clean the anal area thoroughly may aggravate itching caused by hemorrhoids.

Minor Foot Trouble

Many times, minor foot problems give us the most daily trouble, and it's understandable when you think of the workout we give our feet over the course of a lifetime.

For example, just cutting toenails may present special challenges for elderly people. Some nails can become so thick that they resemble a parrot's beak. In fact, the medical term for this condition, *onychogryphosis,* actually means "parrot's beak" in Greek. Considerable care and skill are required to cut and treat such nails, and for those who can't bend over far enough or see well enough to do the job, that usually means a trained friend or relative or a medical worker has to be available to help out.

Also, the cracking due to athlete's foot may serve as a dangerous gateway for the entry of an infection. Washing the feet with a good antibacterial soap and dusting with an antifungal powder are good routines to prevent a new infection and spread of the present fungal infection.

Another special problem that affects many aging feet involves the loss of the fat pads from the soles of the feet. This process occurs in older people along with the general loss of fat from the body.

When these sole cushions are gone, the heads of the metatarsal bones, which form the prominent part of the foot arch and carry the body's weight, are more susceptible to damage and injury. As a result, it may be quite painful just to walk down the street! Calluses and even ulcerations may occur on the soles of the feet as the bones press harder on the skin.

What can you do about this problem? Sometimes, a cushioning for the sole of the foot can be fashioned by a podiatrist and then fitted inside the shoe. Another simple and often quite practical solution that makes up for the loss of those natural fat pads is just to wear sneakers. In fact, nice-looking sneakers or soft walking shoes should now be regarded as basic footgear for those who are aging, as well as for ardent young athletes!

Several common foot problems may intensify with the aging process:

- *Various fungal and bacterial conditions.* I've already mentioned athlete's foot, which is in this category. The reason this sort of problem develops is that your feet are usually enclosed in dark, damp, warm shoes, which are ideal homes for fungi and bacteria. Infections may be a particular danger in those with diabetes. Such infections can cause bad smells, redness, blisters, peeling, or itching. Unless the infection is treated promptly, it can become very hard to cure.

Rather than focusing on the cure, however, I'd suggest that you concentrate on prevention. Keep your feet, especially the between-the-toe areas, clean and dry. Soap and water and foot powder are the main tools to use. Also, expose your feet to sun and air whenever you can.

- *Dry skin.* A problem we talked about previously—dry skin— may also cause itching and burning sensations in the feet. To counter this difficulty, you might apply body lotions to your legs and feet every day. You can also use fatty soaps, such as those that contain cold cream.

The best moisturizers are those that contain petrolatum or lanolin. In general, soaps can cause the skin to dry out if used too often. So it's best to use them sparingly on dry skin, especially in winter.

Finally, even though bath oils may feel good when you apply them, they should not be added to your bath water because they can make your feet and bathtub very slippery. In other words, the cure for dry feet may be worse than the problem if you end up falling down and hurting yourself!

- *Corns and calluses.* These tough overlays of skin may appear on the feet as a response to repeated friction and pressure from your shoes. Some corns and calluses are symptoms of more serious conditions, such as bone deformities, but it shouldn't be up to you to diagnose such problems. Your family doctor will be able to tell you what these tough patches of skin really mean. Eventually, it may be wise to consult a specialist, such as a dermatologist (who concentrates on the skin) or a podiatrist (who specializes in the care of the feet).

CAUTION: Treating corns and calluses by yourself may be harmful, especially for those who have diabetes or poor circulation. Also, over-the-counter medicines that are advertised as "cures" for corns may contain acids that destroy your skin tissue but do not treat the underlying cause. Still, when such medications are used under proper medical supervision, they may eliminate the need for surgery.

• *Warts.* These skin growths are caused by viruses and may be quite painful if they're left untreated. Also, they may spread to other parts of the body.

Over-the-counter preparations rarely cure warts, so it's usually best to seek professional care. Your doctor may apply medicines to dry up the warts; he may remove them surgically; or he may use anesthesia to burn or freeze them off.

• *Bunions.* A bunion is a swelling produced by a bony deformity and involves the skin and fatty tissue, generally on the inner side of the big toe at the joint. (A similar change at the base of the *little* toe is called a "bunionette"!) These may appear when the toe joints are out of line and are subjected to friction and walking stress. Bunions may be caused by the pressure of ill-fitting shoes on the joint, and perhaps also by an inherited weakness of the foot structure.

If a bunion is not severe, wearing shoes that are wide at the instep and toes may provide relief. Protective pads can be used to cushion a painful area.

As for treatment, the application or injection of certain drugs into the area may be effective. Whirlpool baths can also help. In addition, bunions that are especially painful can sometimes be corrected surgically by a procedure called *bunionectomy,* but only if the circulation is adequate.

Surgery, however, is a last resort. This procedure requires cutting out a portion of the protruding bone on the side of the foot so that the big toe returns to a straighter position. The postoperative recovery phase of the surgery usually takes weeks, requires significant restriction of movement, and can be quite uncomfortable or even painful.

One of my neighbors who had a bunionectomy found that she

was unable to bear weight on her foot for a number of weeks. She remarked, "They didn't tell me that I wouldn't be able to walk for so long!"

Furthermore, the hoped-for cosmetic improvement on the foot is sometimes disappointing to the patient.

● *Diabetes.* This disease, which involves the inability of the body to burn up or store sugars usually furnished by the diet, can make an individual susceptible to sores and infections of the feet. One reason for this is that diabetes may impair the sense of feeling in the feet. As a result, any foot injuries may be exacerbated because the person isn't aware of pain that might signal that he should rest or tend to the injury.

Any cuts on a diabetic's foot should receive immediate medical attention because diabetics tend to heal slowly. Even minor infections may take months to heal, and their complications may in some cases necessitate surgery. Diabetics should also be careful to avoid extremely hot or cold bath water, to keep their feet clean and dry, and to avoid stepping on sharp objects or dirty surfaces with bare feet.

Many of these problems can be prevented entirely by some simple techniques:

● *Increasing circulation to the feet* through exercise or massage. Walking, stretching exercises, even just standing can help. Warm foot baths (of about 95°F or 35°C) may enhance circulation.

● *Avoiding those situations or habits that decrease circulation to the feet.* For example, circulation may be impaired by being exposed to cold temperatures, wading or bathing in cold water, putting pressure on the feet with tight shoes, sitting or resting for long periods of time, and, especially, smoking. In addition, sitting with the legs crossed or wearing tight, elastic garters or socks can impair circulation.

● *Choosing shoes carefully.* The upper part of your shoe should be made of a soft, flexible material that will allow the shoe to conform to the shape of the foot. The soles should provide solid footing and should not be slippery. Low-heeled shoes are less damaging to the feet than those with high heels. Shoes made of leather allow the feet to "breathe" more and can reduce the possibility of skin irritation.

KEY FACTS

FOOT-CARE INSTRUCTIONS
FOR THOSE WITH DIABETES OR PERIPHERAL
VASCULAR DISEASE (PVD)

NOTE: *Peripheral vascular disease* is a disease of the blood vessels at a distance from the heart, such as those in the legs. Usually, this disease involves the clogging of the arteries known as *atherosclerosis,* which reduces the circulation of blood to outlying areas.

• Inspect feet (including areas between toes) daily for blisters, cuts, calluses, bruises, and so on. A mirror can help you see the soles.

• If vision is impaired, ask a family member to inspect the feet and trim the nails.

• Wash feet daily, using mild soap. Dry carefully, especially between toes. Do not rub.

• After bathing, use a moderate amount of moisturizing cream on feet (except between toes) and on legs.

• Avoid temperature extremes. Test water before bathing.

• If feet are cold at night, wear socks. Never apply hot water bottles or heating pads to the lower extremities (though application to the abdomen is acceptable) or soak feet in hot water.

• Cut toenails straight across. Don't cut calluses or corns or treat them with chemicals.

• Wear properly fitted stockings (cotton or wool). White is preferable. Avoid wearing mended stockings or those with seams, and avoid garters. Change stockings daily.

• Shoes must be comfortable when purchased and should be broken in gradually.

• Inspect shoes daily for foreign objects, nail points and torn linings.

• *Never* wear shoes without stockings or sandals with thongs between the toes or walk barefooted.

• See your physician regularly. Tell your podiatrist you are a diabetic.

For more information on foot care, write to the American Podiatry Association, 20 Chevy Chase Circle, N.W., Washington, D.C. 20015.

Good News! Fewer Headaches!

If you are in your sixties or seventies or older, perhaps you're still having as many headaches as you did when you were younger. But most physicians who work with the elderly find that headache complaints become less common as people grow older, though no one knows exactly why.

One possible reason for the decrease in headaches may be that some of the tensions of life that afflict many younger people, such as family worries or job pressures, abate with age. It may be that those pressures that produce headaches are no longer as dominant. Some doctors even feel that those who have suffered with migraine headaches all their lives can expect a lessening of this devastating pain as they grow older.

On the other hand, many older people do continue to have migraines or other severe headaches, just as they always did. And some may have *more* headaches with age. So it is not possible to make any absolute generalizations.

Specifically, some elderly people suffer muscle-tension headaches, often when they stoop or incline forward, thereby putting extra strains on the muscles and ligaments in the back and neck.

Other older people may develop chronic headaches that rise through the neck and into the head, perhaps as a result of arthritis or stress on the ligaments in the neck region.

There's also a classic headache known as the "cluster headache," which often begins in the middle years and may continue on into older age. This pain frequently starts at night and can be quite disabling for a relatively long period of time. Typically, it may cause pain for some hours, subside for a time, and then return the next day. The result is a series of painful waves or "clusters" of headaches, hence the name. These cluster headaches may last for a week or two, or even longer, before disappearing.

No one knows exactly what causes many of the age-related headaches, but more important than identifying the cause is the question, What can you do about them? Here are several suggestions that various doctors have offered:

- As you might expect, the old standard remedies may do the job as well as anything: For example, I often just prescribe coated aspirin tablets or acetaminophen (for example, Tylenol), and more often than not, one of these medications helps reduce pain for the milder varieties of headache.
- In addition, the nonsteroidal anti-inflammatory drug (NSAID) group has become quite popular recently. These include prescription drugs (for example, Motrin) and over-the-counter medications (Nuprin and Advil).
- For migraine headaches, doctors may prescribe drugs like the calcium channel blocking agents and a number of drugs used to control hypertension. These include propranolol (Inderal). (For a list of these medications, see Chapter 15.)
- Avoid alcohol under all circumstances when you have a headache. Liquor in any form will just make the situation worse for most people.
- An older drug, Fiorinal, which was developed at the headache clinic at Montefiore Hospital in New York City, has been found to be useful for a variety of headaches, including migraines.
- A variety of strong prescription painkillers, such as codeine or other narcotic drugs, may help with headaches. But of course, these must be provided by a physician and pharmacist as a part of supervised medical care. A number of these are included in the listing of drugs for arthritic pain in Chapter 23.
- Some people find cold packs applied to the forehead to be helpful in reducing headache discomfort. In general, the application of heat doesn't help except when the focus of the pain is at the back of the neck. In that case, hot cloths may reduce neck tension and cut down on any pain that may be radiating up into the head.
- Various people have also found that relaxation techniques, such as forms of meditation or visualization, can reduce headache pains that are attributable primarily to stress.

NOTE: Contrary to popular opinion, ordinary levels of high blood pressure do not cause headache.

Most of the time, headaches are relatively minor concerns. But still, whenever I encounter an older person with severe headaches, I always perform a thorough examination because, in many cases, there may be serious underlying health problems. Severe periodic headaches can arise from a lesion within the skull or from a circulatory disorder. Severe headaches or facial pains may also be the sign of a form of *arteritis* (an inflammation of the arteries in the head). These sorts of problem are quite serious and should be treated by a physician promptly.

Fortunately, most headaches are usually just part of being human and reacting to the stresses and pressures of daily life. As I've said, they often decrease in frequency with age. But like other "minor complaints," they should be monitored: Determine just how unusual they are, given your past health history. Note how long they last, and how painful they feel. Then, if you perceive something out of the ordinary about them, don't hesitate to consult your doctor.

The relatively minor problems that we've discussed in this chapter—including backaches, sensitivity to cold and heat, cramping, itching, foot trouble, and headaches—provide you with a general introduction to some common complaints that may be voiced by older people.

KEY FACTS

HOW COMMON ARE COMMON COMPLAINTS AMONG THE ELDERLY?

The most common complaints of 1,927 women and 1,140 men, of a mean age of about seventy-five years, were reported recently in the *Journal of the American Geriatrics Society*. Here are some of the results:

MOST COMMON SYMPTOMS IN WOMEN

- Getting up at night to urinate (80 percent)
- Swollen feet (30 percent)

- Cold feet (29 percent)
- Irregular heartbeat (23 percent)

MOST COMMON SYMPTOMS IN MEN

- Getting up at night to urinate (80 percent)
- Irregular heartbeat (25 percent)
- Cold feet, cold legs, or both (24 percent)
- Tinnitus (buzzing in the ears) (23 percent)

OTHER COMMON COMPLAINTS

- Constipation
- Pain in the calves when walking (intermittent claudication)
- Chest discomfort when walking (angina pains)
- Transient numbness in the arms or legs
- Dizziness
- Blacking out
- Frequent headaches (though they decreased with aging)
- Problems in swallowing
- Recurrent cough

As might be expected, those who reported the greater number of medical conditions also had the most symptoms and used the largest amount of drugs. Some observers have raised the objection that medications may produce some of these complaints as side effects. But the researchers respond that many of the common complaints reported are clearly not medication-related. Consequently, it may be unwise to stop a useful medication in the hope that the complaints will decrease.

W. E. Hale, L. L. Perkins, F. E. May, et al., "Symptom Prevalence in the Elderly," *Journal of the American Geriatrics Society* 34 (1986): 333.

In general, these difficulties are usually nothing to get too concerned about. And many times, just by taking certain simple preventive steps you can prevent them altogether or reduce the discomfort they give you.

Still, in some cases a particular pain or discomfort may be signaling an underlying problem that should be tended to immediately. So if you have any question about what's wrong with you, don't try to play doctor on yourself or a family member. Check out the situation with your physician, and then you'll be in a much stronger position to carry through by yourself on the best approach to prevention or self-treatment.

7

WEAKNESS, DIZZINESS, FALLS, AND FAINTS

"I always seem to be very weak and tired," a seventy-nine-year-old patient complained.

She also seemed unable to overcome her problem by following my standard suggestions about increasing exercise or engaging in more interesting activities.

For one thing, she had never been particularly athletic in her earlier life. So she felt it would be too much for her to begin a regular walking program or exercise regimen at her age (though I still think she could have embarked on such a program if she had really wanted to).

As for interesting activities, she was already involved in an active social service club, and she liked the people and projects. But she said she often felt too tired to do the things that she really enjoyed.

As a result, I prescribed a small twice-a-day dose of Ritalin for her, and almost immediately she perked up. When she came in to see me the next week, she said, "It's as if I'm a different person! Now, I'm able to participate completely in the service projects my club sponsors. We have a feed-the-hungry program, and before, I often didn't even feel like even *beginning* to serve food to people. But now, I can stick with the serving lines we've set up until all the food is gone!"

But then, she asked a curious question: "You don't think I'm hyperactive, do you?" she said.

"No, why?" I responded in surprise.

"Because I think the medicine you're giving me is the same thing my grandson had to take for hyperactivity. Is that possible?"

In fact, as I explained to her, it *was* possible. It's paradoxical that Ritalin, the same drug that can be used to pep up older people, can also be prescribed to calm down youngsters. Exactly why these different reactions should occur in children and in older people isn't clear, but the fact remains that the same drug is quite helpful in both cases.

As you get older, there may be a tendency to become somewhat less stable on your feet, and also to feel light-headed or fatigued more often. Sometimes, I have patients, mostly in the over-seventy-five age bracket, who complain of episodes of weakness, dizziness, and faintness. Sometimes, an "unexpected" drug like Ritalin may work, but other times, benign neglect may be the best prescription.

Transient light-headedness and dizziness on standing up or turning the head are nothing to worry about. Indeed, these symptoms may occur in young persons who have blood pressures in the lower range. In older people, they're generally part of the impaired reflexes and compensations that accompany age. There may be nothing much that we can do about them, except to get up slowly and turn cautiously. But there are times when there may be legitimate cause for concern and good reason to seek medical attention, as when these symptoms accompany the use of medications.

To help you evaluate the level of seriousness of these common experiences when they happen to you or a family member, let's take a closer look at several typical problems and see what you can do about them.

Weakness

One of the most common complaints that I hear from my older patients is "I'm so weak much of the time. Can't you give me something to pep me up?"

When I hear this complaint, I first check to be sure that there aren't any serious underlying health problems, such as anemia, a thyroid disorder, diabetes, depression, or a heart condition. Or the weakness may be caused by a sedentary life-style, a factor that can be corrected by increased activity and exercise.

If I find no definite cause for weakness or fatigue in an older person, I usually assume that the problem is rooted in the various changes in the muscles and nervous system that accompany aging. In fact, men lose a third of their muscle mass over their life span, and women lose somewhat less. The loss of strength and endurance can certainly be annoying and deflating to one's sense of confidence and self-esteem. But it's possible to counter this tendency by paying close attention to good nutrition and exercise.

On the other hand, no matter how many preventive measures you try, getting a little weaker or less active with age is inevitable. And the process may serve a useful purpose: It's probably important to begin to limit activities that might otherwise result in serious injuries. I'm reminded of one fifty-six-year-old man who thought he could continue to ski with reckless abandon down the most dangerous slopes in Colorado, until he failed to negotiate a difficult turn on one vacation and broke one of his legs.

"I always could make that turn in the past!" he protested while lying flat on his back in the hospital.

"Yes, but in the past you were younger and stronger," his doctor replied. "You're still strong, but maybe the time has come to recognize that there are some things you did when you were younger that you can't or shouldn't do now."

Those who are even older than this man and have become rather unstable or who have significant thinning of the bones have to be more careful because a fall might produce more serious fractures, or even death. So if you find it harder to go rock climbing or hang gliding, that may be all for the best!

But having said this, I don't want to leave the impression that we necessarily have to expect a precipitous decline in our strength and endurance as we get older. There's plenty that can be done about the problem of weakness or fatigue.

Two Easy-to-Apply Antidotes to Weakness and Fatigue

One of the main reasons that older people feel weak is that they slip into a *sedentary life-style* or allow themselves to be trapped by boredom. But there are some easily applied antidotes to these enemies of high-energy living.

● *Develop strategies to combat sedentary living.* With inadequate physical activity, muscles begin to lose strength, and they tend to feel weaker and weaker. As we've seen in the previous chapter and as will become even clearer in later chapters, exercise is one of the best available strategies to counter this decline in muscle strength and endurance. Many times, more exercise is exactly what I prescribe. You can embark at any age on a program to build up your muscles and increase your aerobic lung capacity. The more exercise you do, the more likely you are to increase the energy and "zip" in your life.

● *Learn creative ways to combat boredom.* Another common cause of weakness and fatigue in older people is boredom. Many of the people who come to me with these complaints have retired and lack a regular daily schedule or activities to keep them interested and involved in life. As a result, they begin to feel useless and may start suffering from depression. A chronic sense of weakness or fatigue is a natural consequence of this process.

I've long believed that compulsory—and unwilling—retirement is one of the great geriatric threats in our society. For many people, stopping work sets the stage for diminishing brain stimulation and loss of muscle strength.

As I told one sixty-eight-year-old male retiree, who consulted me about constant fatigue: "The best cure for your problem would be a part-time job of some sort. You should work a few hours each day, just to keep your mind and body active. I can almost guarantee you that if you do this, your feelings of fatigue will disappear."

I later learned that he had taken me up on the suggestion and had been hired for a part-time position. As a matter of fact, I never heard directly from him again. But it turned out he had become too busy to keep in touch! From all appearances, much of the energy and purpose in his life had returned with the new employment.

Of course, I don't want to suggest that overcoming fatigue as you age is always solvable by simple, straightforward responses or strategies. Many times, it isn't enough just to go out and get a job, begin an exercise program, or otherwise increase your involvement in productive or stimulating activities.

The Chemical Component of Fatigue

Many factors may combine to produce greater fatigue as we age, and some of these are probably related to changes that take place in our brains. For example, there's an enzyme in the brain called *monoamine oxidase* (MAO) that often increases in our brains as we age. The problem is that MAO reduces some of the chemicals or neurotransmitters in the brain, the *catecholamines,* which at proper levels help keep us alert and sharp. The more MAO in the brain, then, the fewer "pick-me-up" neurotransmitters we have at our disposal, and the more fatigued we may feel.

Obviously, not everybody has exactly the same trouble with this aging increase in MAO or with other brain changes. But many older people do seem to experience this difficulty, and the result can be an increase in feelings of weakness or fatigue.

What can you do about these lethargic reactions if exercise, an increase in interesting activities, or other such steps don't work?

One answer, if there is also some depression present, is that your physician may prescribe drugs that inhibit the MAO or otherwise alter neurotransmitter balance. With these, the neurotransmitters in your brain rise and your energy levels may increase.

Many physicians give small doses of antidepressant pills or

psychostimulants to patients who complain of constant fatigue, and it may be that all these drugs work to increase the presence of stimulating neurotransmitters. Psychostimulants that may be prescribed for this purpose include small doses of amphetamines, and the drug that I prefer, methylphenidate (brand name Ritalin).

What Does It Mean If You Are Short of Breath?

A physical symptom that may accompany feelings of weakness or fatigue is shortness of breath, or *dyspnea,* as the condition is called by doctors.

Of course, a major reason that people of any age become short of breath is exertion while in poor physical condition. Most sedentary people, regardless of how old they are, begin to huff and puff after jogging or walking fast for a few hundred yards. At the same time, trained athletes at almost any age level can often run for miles without entering a state of "oxygen debt," or breathlessness. In this condition, a person is using more oxygen through exercise than he's able to take in through his breathing. As a result, he begins to gulp or gasp for extra air, a typical sign of being "out of breath."

If you frequently feel breathless after climbing a flight of stairs or otherwise exerting yourself, your problem may simply be that you're out of shape. And even if you're quite old, you can probably improve your stamina dramatically by embarking on an aerobic exercise program, such as the systematic approach to walking I describe in Chapter 13, relating to the prevention of cardiovascular disease.

But sometimes, breathlessness can signal a more serious condition than just being out of shape. That's why it's important to check with your physician if shortness of breath is an ongoing problem. In general, there are two major concerns, other than simply a lack of endurance: underlying heart disease or lung problems.

One woman in her sixties consulted me about shortness of breath, and I immediately put her through a thorough physical exam. She was expecting me to tell her that she was just out of shape. In fact, she had even gone out to buy an athletic outfit to use in a light aerobics program that some of her neighbors attended.

"No, I'm afraid this exercise program isn't the thing for you, at least not until we've corrected a problem with your heart I've discovered," I replied.

My examination had revealed that this woman was suffering from deficiency in the pumping action of her heart as a result of a condition called *mitral valve prolapse.* In simple terms, I explained to her that the mitral valve on the left side of her heart, between the chambers called the *atrium* and the *ventricle,* had fallen away from its proper position. As a result, the blood wasn't being ejected properly by the heart. The major outward symptoms were her sense of weakness and shortness of breath.

We finally decided that it would be best to schedule surgery and a mitral valve replacement. The operation was a great success, and after a period of recuperation, this woman was able to start a graduated exercise program. Surgery had been absolutely essential to correct her breathlessness and weakness.

A second serious reason for breathlessness may be an underlying lung problem. One possibility is *emphysema,* a condition often associated with smoking that involves the enlargement of air spaces in the lungs. As the spaces increase in size, it becomes harder to breathe, and eventual damage to the heart may result. Besides smoking, asthma and chronic bronchitis may contribute to emphysema.

With emphysema, chronic bronchitis, and other serious lung problems, the first line of treatment for smokers is to discontinue use of tobacco. Also, a series of other measures, including using oxygen at home and paying strict attention to keeping the body's airways clear of pollutants and mucus, may help.

We'll deal in more detail with these and other serious lung problems in Chapter 24. For now, it's just important to understand that breathlessness may signal more than a lack of conditioning. In any event, your physician is in the best position to diagnose and treat the problem.

Dizziness

Another common problem that arises as people get older is a tendency to feel light-headed and to experience a sensation of instability. One Boston neurologist has called this complaint the "wobbly-giddies," and I think that term quite accurately describes the symptoms of a seventy-two-year-old man who told me that many times, he felt as if he were walking along the deck of a rolling ship.

"Occasionally, I feel that I'm lurching about and that my body is completely out of control," he said. "Also, I may get a little dizzy and even feel mildly nauseous, though that's not a common reaction for me."

I put him through a battery of tests, but didn't find anything in particular wrong with him. His blood pressure seemed normal, and his reflexes were all right. A thorough exam of his ears, nose, and throat revealed no problems. In addition, he wasn't taking any drugs that could have produced these symptoms.

Finally, we determined that the problem was related to transient drops in his blood pressure when he shifted position, stood up quickly, or got out of bed abruptly in the morning.

"As we get older, there's a tendency for our blood pressure to drop more when we stand up or move about after being in one position for a period of time," I explained. "If you move too quickly, you may feel dizzy or unstable."

So at my advice, this man began to be more careful about the way he changed his bodily positions. He moved more slowly as he stood up and bent over, and he made it a point to sit for a few seconds in bed before he finally stood up. These changes in his movement patterns took care of most of the problems he had been experiencing with the "wobbly-giddies."

Sometimes, dizziness or vertigo can be linked to other conditions, some of which you can correct yourself, and some of which will require medical assistance. Here, then, are a few of the major causes of dizziness among older people:

• *Viral infections.* When the infection has been cleared up, the dizziness usually disappears.

- *Great fatigue or lack of sleep.* The antidote: more rest!
- *Abuse of tobacco.* The best treatment here is to stop smoking.
- *Depression.* Treating depression can be an extended, complex affair that involves considerable medical intervention and the use of prescription drugs. See my description of depression and its treatment in chapters 26 and 27.
- *Meniere's disease.* This problem, which is fairly common in elderly patients, may be traced to a disturbance in the labyrinths of the inner ear. The condition results in such dizziness that there is often a sense that the world is "spinning about." Consequently, the sufferer is usually immobilized until the attack has passed. Nausea and vomiting may accompany this problem. Sometimes, eliminating salt from the diet or using diuretics may diminish recurrences. Patients are told to rest and take motion sickness or antinausea medications.
- *Progressive anemia.* Iron deficiency, vitamin B_{12} deficiency, kidney disease, and other causes of anemia have to be identified in a medical examination.
- *Gastrointestinal bleeding.* This is not always recognized at the time it occurs, but hospitalization or close medical supervision is required.
- *Hypertension.* Various diuretics or other drugs designed to lower blood pressure can reduce the feelings of dizziness associated with markedly elevated blood pressures.
- *Changes in the rhythm of the heartbeat.* This condition may involve such symptoms as too rapid a heart rate or too many skipped beats. Again, ongoing medical supervision is necessary.
- *Heart attacks.* Dizziness, along with a feeling of weakness, may signal the onset of a *myocardial infarction,* or heart attack.
- *Circulatory problems in the head.* Any insufficiency of blood to the brain, including mild strokes, can cause vertigo.
- *An accumulation of wax in the ears.* Cleaning by a physician or properly trained technician can quickly remedy this problem.
- *Diseases of the middle ear.* Antibiotics or other medications may help, but the most important first step is to see your physician.
- *A tumor in the ear region.*
- *Acute labyrinthitis.* This condition involves an inflammation of the inner ear, which can cause dizziness and a loss of the sense of balance.
- *Side effects of certain drugs.* High dosages of drugs such as

salicylates and quinidine and ordinary dosages of barbiturates and antihypertensive medications may be a source of dizziness.

One classic study on the status of older people in Wolverhampton, England, reported that more than half of those studied said they had some problems with vertigo or dizziness. Sometimes, the causes for these feelings could be identified and treated. But on many other occasions, the source of the symptoms remained a mystery. In general, however, as we get older, changes that we may not be able to control begin to occur in our circulatory system and in our brain centers. As these changes take place, some form of the wobbly-giddies may result.

HEALTH REPORT

X RAYS OF THE NECK CANNOT PREDICT DIZZINESS

A study in the journal *Age and Ageing* acknowledged that transient attacks of dizziness, perhaps accompanied by a fall, may occur in the elderly because of diminished circulation to the back part of the brain and the brain stem. In technical terms, this is known as *vertebrobasilar insufficiency.* The underlying reason for this problem may be arthritic changes in the neck vertebrae, causing them to press against the arteries.

The researchers in this study compared the X rays of the neck in older persons having dizziness with those of a group who were free of dizziness and falls. They found no X-ray differences between the two groups. Some older people with mild osteoarthritic changes had the dizziness symptoms, but some with severe changes had no symptoms. Their conclusion: X rays of the neck shed no light on the problem of dizziness.

[NOTE: I've often observed that X rays of the neck in the elderly cannot distinguish between those with such complaints as stiffness and neck pain, and those free of these complaints. Hence, I don't usually order such X rays as part of my evaluation.]

K. Adams, M. W. Young, M. Lye, G. H. Whithouse, "Are Cervical Spine Radiographs of Value in Elderly Patients with Vertebrobasilar Insufficiency?" *Age and Ageing* 15 (1986): 57.

If you and your physician can't identify any particular factor as the cause of your dizziness and if symptoms persist, you may find you have to learn to live with the problem. In this regard, it's important to keep your movements slow and deliberate, especially when you stand up or change positions. Quick rotation or raising of the body can sometimes aggravate the symptoms. It may also be wise to carry a cane or other stabilizing instrument to help you maintain your balance and to prevent a fall.

Fainting, "Drop Attacks," and Fits

Fainting

An eighty-two-year-old man began to experience what he called "fainting spells" when he woke up at night and walked into the bathroom to urinate. Typically, he said, he felt fine as he entered the bathroom. But when he stood still before the toilet, he sometimes began to get dizzy and lose consciousness. On two occasions, he had managed to sit down on the edge of the bathtub until his head cleared. But once he had actually blacked out, fallen to the floor, and bruised himself. It was after that incident that he decided to seek medical help.

My initial approach to this man's problem was to conduct a thorough physical exam to see whether he was suffering from any underlying problems that might be causing the fainting. I tested him for various possibilities:

- Drops in blood pressure in different positions
- Internal bleeding
- Evidence of unusual changes in his heart rate
- The Stokes-Adams attack, which is associated with a transient pause or similar alteration in the heartbeat

If there had been a problem with the rhythm of his heartbeat, I might have prescribed certain heart-regulating medications for him. Or I might even have recommended the installation of a cardiac pacemaker, a mechanical device that stimulates the heartbeat.

As it happened, the man was suffering from none of these problems. He apparently had trouble with a form of dizziness that appeared to be linked to relatively low blood pressure. This condition was more likely to result in a complete fainting spell at night when he was standing up half asleep and his body's compensatory mechanisms were at a low point than it was at other times of the day.

So I recommended that he do one of two things: (1) use a bedside urinal to relieve himself at night or (2) ask his wife, who was several years younger and in good health, to accompany him to the bathroom, just to be sure that he didn't injure himself. As it turned out, his wife was happy to help him, and so his problem was solved.

Other older people may complain of faintness or even loss of consciousness when they extend their necks while reaching up toward high shelves or when they reach up to shut windows. The reason for this is that the blood vessels that run vertically, paralleling the neck bones, may already be partially obstructed by the buildup of plaque or by other changes in the vascular system. The course of the vessels in this area may become more twisty and winding as a person grows older and may even receive pressure from bony projections arising from the spine.

HEALTH REPORT

COMMON CAUSES OF FAINTING IN OLDER PEOPLE

In a 1987 report in *Geriatrics,* the authors note that faints (*syncope*) that result in falls are among the great banes of old age. One institutionalized group experienced a 6 percent incidence per year of faints, with a substantial repeat rate.

Fainting can make some persons lose their sense of independence and become housebound. So it's imperative to identify the causes of fainting and try to do something about them. Here are a few common causes:

• *Blood pressure disorders.* One common form is the faint that occurs upon drawing blood or receiving a painful injection. It's more often seen in younger than older persons.

• *Drops in blood pressure* in the standing position. Known as *orthostatic hypotension,* this condition may be worsened by certain drugs, such as antidepressants, and overtreatments with diuretics.

• *Carotid sinus hypersensitivity.* The carotid sinus is a special area in the carotid artery, which runs up the neck to nourish the head and brain. The carotid sinus contains special nerve endings that regulate blood pressure. Sometimes, a tight collar or a turning of the head may affect this mechanism with a resultant blood pressure drop.

• *Cardiac disorders,* such as obstruction to the outflow of blood from the heart. These may be caused by narrowing of the heart's openings onto the large artery leading from the heart, the aorta *(aortic stenosis).*

• *Cardiac rhythm disorders,* as when the beats become too slow or too fast.

• *Seizures,* often originating in some part of the brain when circulation is inadequate.

• *Situational syncope* (fainting in specific situations) associated with such events as coughing or urination.

A physician may be able to make a diagnosis and identify a clear cause of fainting after taking a patient's history and doing a physical exam. But in about half the cases, the cause of the fainting remains unclear.

C. Whiteside-Yim, "Syncope in the Elderly: A Clinical Approach," *Geriatrics* 42 (1987): 37.

When the circulatory system is changing in these ways, it may only take a slight amount of extra pressure, as from a reaching-up motion, to impinge on the blood vessels and produce a blackout. Older people who find they have a tendency toward this disorder should be especially careful in making upward movements that tilt the neck and put extra pressure on the blood vessels there.

"Drop Attacks"

A special form of fainting that typically occurs in older people is known as the "drop attack." Although physicians don't understand exactly what causes these attacks, they do have many good descriptions of what happens to individual patients.

One seventy-four-year-old woman told me that as she was

standing in her kitchen to prepare some food, her knees suddenly gave way and she collapsed on the floor. As she lay on the floor for close to a minute, her leg muscles seemed to have no power whatsoever. Finally, she had to call her daughter to help her get back on her feet.

"It was the most helpless feeling I've ever experienced," she said. "I thought some dread disease had stricken me and I'd never walk again!"

But after only a couple of minutes, the strength returned to her legs and she was able to walk about as if nothing had happened.

Worried that she might indeed be contracting some serious sickness, she came in to see me for a checkup. From her description, I was able to identify the phenomenon as a drop attack.

As I told her, these attacks may strike only once or twice and seldom occur repeatedly in older people. Apparently, they are caused by fleeting changes in those brain cells that control the muscles that hold us upright in a firm, steady state.

Fortunately, this woman hadn't hurt herself as a result of the fall, even though it had been unexpected and unpredictable. I warned her not to go out alone in the cold weather until we had a better feel for her particular situation.

"Sometimes, drop attacks may be responsible for falls outside, and overexposure on the cold ground may result when the person can't get back to her feet again," I said.

The loss of muscle power may last for only a few seconds or minutes, but it can go on longer. So it's best to be cautious.

I also informed her about a useful technique that often works to restore strength to the legs of those who have suffered drop attacks: Usually, if the person can place the soles of her feet against a firm object and give a push, the muscle strength in the legs returns immediately.

With this information in hand, the woman was prepared to deal with any future drop attacks. And fortunately, up to now, she hasn't had a recurrence of the first incident.

Fits and Other Attacks

A few persons begin to suffer epileptic attacks for the first time in their lives as they get older. Such attacks may occur weeks or

---

HEALTH REPORT

WHAT CAUSES DROP ATTACKS?

Drop attacks, which are unique in being limited to older people, are characterized by a sudden "drop" to the floor or ground, without loss of consciousness. They have been described by victims as coming without warning. The muscles that keep one upright seem to have been suddenly "turned off."

What causes drop attacks? In the 108 patients described in a study reported in 1986 in *Neurology,* 66 percent had no identifiable cause. In the remainder of the patients, these factors were pinpointed as at least contributing to the attacks:

- Heart problems in 12 percent
- Altered brain circulation in 8 percent
- Combinations of heart problems and brain circulation in 7 percent
- Seizures in 5 percent
- Inner ear disturbances in 3 percent

There is no treatment for drop attacks, only treatment for associated conditions, such as heart or circulation problems. Often the attacks don't recur, and the study also found that there is no associated shortening of the life span or increase in the incidence of stroke.

I. Meissner, D. O. Wiebers, J. W. Swanson, et al., "The Natural History of Drop Attacks," *Neurology* 36 (1986): 1029.

---

months after the person has suffered a stroke or had a head injury. It may occur with a heart attack or follow other problems involving loss of blood and oxygen to the brain. Brain tumors may announce themselves this way. Because the possible causes of epileptic seizures among older people are potentially serious, it's essential for those with this problem to be examined immediately by a physician.

Older people also may experience hysterical fits, which may involve twitching, shaking of their beds, trembling, falling on the floor, and even having temper tantrums. Sometimes, these reactions may stem from the patient's desire to control the situation or care givers who are trying to persuade him to do something.

For example, one elderly woman lapsed into hysteria, including uncontrolled crying and trembling, when she was told she would have to leave her home and enter a hospital for treatment. She desperately wanted to stay at home, but her children and the nurses who had been assigned to her were insisting that she go to the hospital. In fact, it was essential to her health that she be hospitalized.

But she was impervious to rational persuasion. Lacking the power to respond in any other way, she retreated into a hysterical condition. Her reaction was probably the result of both a voluntary decision to resist and an involuntary lashing out in the face of a sense of powerlessness.

With these fits and attacks of hysteria, it's important for care givers to respond firmly and try to restore an atmosphere of calmness, even as they move to take those actions that are in the patient's best interest. As much as possible, the person who is experiencing the hysteria should be given authority and control over his life and choices. At the same time, care givers should also recognize that there may be a component of control or manipulation in the behavior of the patient. So it may be necessary to act counter to the patient's stated wishes if such action clearly seems in his or her best interests.

How to Face the Possibility of a Fall

George Bernard Shaw once remarked, "The trouble with old age is you keep falling down." And I must say, I've too often observed the truth of his observation in my practice.

Some types of falls, such as drop attacks, usually do not involve serious injury. Apparently when one collapses to the floor in a drop attack, the muscles are relaxed enough and the fall is sudden enough that the body rolls safely to the floor, much as happens with a falling infant or toddler.

KEY FACTS

THE FACTS ABOUT FALLS

Of the 200,000 annual hip fractures, 84 percent occur in those sixty-five years of age or older.

Fall-related deaths increase with advancing age and at least double with each decade in the older years.

Contributory factors to falling include declines in vision, balance, reaction time, muscle strength, and cardiovascular reflexes. The increasing incidence of faints leads to more falls.

Falls may also result from the condition known as *senile gait disorder.* This is characterized by stooped posture, diminished arm swing, small steps, and stiffness in turning. Some of these features are found in exaggerated form in Parkinson's disease, in which the center of gravity is displaced forward. There may be a "freezing" of walking, with the feet coming to a halt, even though the body is still moving forward.

Other gait problems may be present in victims of stroke, cerebellar (hindbrain) disease and other neurologic disorders.

Falls increase in those with dementia or depression and with the use of multiple drugs (especially tranquilizers, sleeping pills, and diuretics).

The bathroom and the bedroom are the two most common locales for falls. The hazards in the environment (such as loose rugs, poor lighting, glare, low toilet seats, slippery or inconvenient bathtubs, and low chairs) should be evaluated as to whether they may contribute to falls.

R. Tideiksaar, "Falls in the Elderly," *Bulletin of the New York Academy of Medicine* 64 (1988): 145.

On the other hand, falls can result in serious injury. Therefore, it is important to take certain precautions if you think you or a family member faces this danger.

Falling Out of Bed

Falling out of bed is very common at home and even in the best-run hospitals. If you have this problem anywhere, you should order side rails. These are metal railings attached alongside the bed to prevent the person from rolling over onto the floor at night. They can be purchased at any medical supply store.

But even with side rails, there may be a problem if the older person becomes confused and starts climbing over them. In fact, injuries can be even more serious if the individual falls from a greater height, at the top of the side rails. So be sensitive and alert to see whether the problem is simply a tendency to roll over onto the floor, or whether something else—such as fear, anxiety, or pain—is involved. If the only difficulty is restlessness or disorientation with trouble staying in bed, simply lining up chairs alongside the edge of the mattress may be helpful in preventing a rollover onto the floor.

Standing or Walking

Older people often find that when they lose their balance, they have trouble recovering their equilibrium. Slippery surfaces present a special danger: The individual may simply be unable to catch himself when his feet start to go out from under him.

One seventy-eight-year-old man who had experienced a couple of falls but still hadn't broken any bones asked for my advice about safety precautions because he was very worried he might fall down and break a hip. So I provided him with the following tips:

• Avoid all slippery surfaces. Or, when this isn't possible, have someone or something (such as a railing) at hand to steady you.
• Always move more slowly and carefully over surfaces that you think *may* be slippery.
• Remove all the scatter rugs in your home.
• If you feel you can't remove an area rug (for instance, a favorite Oriental carpet), be sure it sits on a good nonskid pad backing.
• Never have a high-wax shine on your floors.
• Avoid stairs whenever possible, and always use handrails when you have to climb them.

HEALTH REPORT

FALLS AND FRACTURES OF THE WRIST

Fractures of the wrist (Colles' fracture) become increasingly common with age, particularly in women who have passed through menopause. By age sixty 5 percent of women have had such a fracture, and by age eighty, 15 percent. Throughout much of this age range, men have fewer falls.

But there's an interesting twist behind these statistics: Despite the fact that they have fewer wrist fractures than older people, middle-aged people are still at relatively high risk of this injury when they fall. Why is this? In part, it's because the middle-aged seem more likely to tumble down on the outstretched hand. The elderly, in contrast, seem to be less likely to stretch out an arm to break a fall. Thus, middle-aged fallers (especially women) are likely to fracture a wrist when they fall. Older fallers of both sexes are likely to fracture a hip.

But why do older people fall? The righting reflexes, which enable one to compensate quickly for a lack of balance, deteriorate with age. Older people often report knowing they were falling, but feeling helpless to do anything about it.

The authors of the 1987 article in *Age and Ageing*, from which this information comes, describe a delicate sway apparatus that registers the slight sway that individuals exhibit while standing immobile. The degree of sway increases with aging. It is also more marked in middle-aged women who have fallen and experienced a wrist fracture than in those who have not. The increased sway reflects an impairment that may be a risk factor for a fall.

R. G. Crilly, L. D. Richardson, J. H. Roth, et al., "Postural Stability and Colles' Fracture," *Age and Ageing* 16 (1987): 133.

When a Cane or Walker Becomes Necessary

Finally, I recommend that when a person gets too wobbly to walk around without a serious danger of falling, he or she should begin to use a walker, a cane, or a wheelchair. Obviously, these devices are a wise alternative to painful falls and fractures, and in the later

years, they can greatly enhance a person's ability to move about
safely and efficiently.

There are many movement-assisting devices that are now
available, and if you're thinking about trying one, here are some
guidelines to keep in mind:

• Many people prefer to try a cane first, particularly if they
have one side that has become weak as a result of an injury, stroke,
or other physical difficulty. An ordinary single-ended cane may be
adequate, but I strongly suggest that you buy one with an adjust-
able length or be fitted by an expert dealer. A proper cane should
be long enough that you can lean on it with your arm almost fully
extended.

There are many alternative cane products now on the market,
some constructed with an eye to style, and some with more focus
on function. For example, a number of particularly attractive canes
are made of transparent lucite. They are so unobtrusive that I
hardly notice them when one of my patients carries one into my
office.

• Another important variety of cane for those with extra stability problems is the "quad" type, which rests on four props,
rather than the single end. I always recommend this sort of cane
for those who are especially worried about or in danger of falling,
but who do not need a walker.

• Walkers have a solid, curved rest for the hands at the top
and four long legs, which may end at the floor in canelike projections or in small wheels. The best ones are made of sturdy but
lightweight metal or plastic.

Many people have an image of a person with a walker as one
who is "on his last legs." In my practice, I've encountered many
people who see a walker as a symbol of a major decline in personal
abilities. There's an image of the walker user as one who is particularly impaired and feeble.

But in fact, the people I know who use walkers are generally
quite lively and competent. It's just that they have lost the complete use of one part of their bodies, their legs. On the whole, their
minds and other faculties are as sharp and adequate as ever.

As I told one of my patients who was confronting the decision of having to use a walker, "If I were in your shoes, with an instability and uncertainty about my gait, the first thing I would ask for would be a walker. It's much safer than a cane. You can still get around. And it's certainly preferable to lying in bed with a fracture."

8

WHY CAN'T I HEAR?

Al, a sixty-one-year-old businessman, walked into my examining room and sat down before my desk with an extremely glum expression on his face. He looked like a person who had been physically pushed and pulled into the doctor's office, and in fact, he *had* been bullied into seeing me.

"My wife and children insist I have a hearing problem, but I think it's their imagination," he said. "As far as I can tell—and I've checked this out with other friends of mine—I think I have a family of mumblers. To satisfy them, though, I decided to come in to see you."

That was a challenge if I've ever heard one! But Al wasn't by any means the only person I've run into with this attitude. In daring me to find that he had a hearing problem, he was echoing what I've heard many times from patients who feel that their hearing problem lies not in their own ears, but in the failure of others to speak clearly or loudly enough.

In any event, I took up the gauntlet Al had thrown at me and put him through a series of tests and interviews to determine just what sort of hearing he had. As it turned out, Al had suffered some hearing loss over the years. In part this had resulted from a common deterioration in the inner ear, a common condition called *presbycusis.*

In addition, Al had done a great deal of target shooting and hunting when he was a boy. He had also served in the infantry, where he had spent a great deal of time on firing ranges and in training exercises without always wearing protective devices on his ears. These loud rifle and gun sounds had apparently injured his hearing as well.

When Al saw the results of his hearing tests from an audio-gram printout, he finally acknowledged that he really did have a problem. In his case, the prescription of a hearing aid was in order, and that was the next step that we took.

Often, I find that older people can go for years denying they have a hearing problem because they seem to perceive it as a major inferiority, a defect that reflects badly on them. I've often asked myself why a reasonably intelligent older person persists in the denial. In the last analysis, even though a decline in hearing ability is a natural concomitant of aging, many individuals simply cannot face this particular decrease in their physical abilities.

But this denial can postpone the correction of a problem that prevents large numbers of older people from really enjoying life to the fullest. In fact, it's been estimated that about 30 percent of adults aged sixty-five through seventy-four and 50 percent of those aged seventy-five through seventy-nine have some degree of hearing loss. In the United States, more than 10 million older people are hearing-impaired, according to a report from the National Institutes of Health.

Men seem to develop hearing problems more often than women, and in most cases, those with hearing loss first notice the problem because they keep missing out on low-level conversation. They can't hear the higher tones of voices or musical instruments. As the auditory nerves deteriorate with age, one ear may be affected more than the other. So an older person may prefer to use one ear more than the other to talk over the telephone. Or he may cock his head so that he can pick up sounds and voices better with his good ear.

In any event, there's no need to feel alone if you have a problem with your hearing. Most people experience some hearing loss over the years. In fact, many presidents and elder statesmen wear hearing aids. So you're in good company when you acknowledge *now* that you're facing a common problem of aging and take steps to do something about it!

What can you do? First, you have to admit that you really do have a problem. Then, you and your physician will have to determine the kind of deafness or hearing loss you have. Finally, you'll find there are a number of effective treatments or responses that are available to help you, a number of which are described later in this chapter.

How Can You Tell Whether You Have a Hearing Problem?

There are a number of signals that may indicate you have a problem with your hearing. These include:

- an inability to understand conversation that others seem to have no difficulty understanding;
- a sense that many people are talking with slurred speech or in a mumbling manner;
- a need to strain to hear words or sounds because they often seem rather faint;
- an inability to hear high notes of musical instruments, or sharp, staccato sounds such as the dripping of a faucet;
- the presence of a constant ringing or hissing sound in your ears;
- an inability to follow what's being said or played in movies, concerts, television presentations, or other cultural or social events; or
- recurrent suggestions by friends or relatives that you may have a problem with your hearing.

If you have encountered any of these situations, feelings, or symptoms, you may very well have a problem with your hearing. So the next appropriate step is to check it out with your doctor and find out whether you indeed have hearing loss, and if so, what type.

How to Identify
Your Specific Hearing Problem

To learn exactly what's wrong with your hearing, you'll have to undergo tests by a physician, and you may be able to get all the guidance you need from your family doctor. Occasionally, a significant element of the hearing loss is due to wax accumulation, and if that happens to be the situation with you, you're in good luck! On the other hand, your doctor may want you to have a further exam, which may involve a check-up by a hearing specialist called an *otologist* or *otolaryngologist.*

In addition, you may be referred to an *audiologist,* who specializes in the testing of hearing with an instrument called an *audiometer.* Those tested with an audiometer enter a special closetlike sound booth, put on earphones, and respond by pressing a button every time they hear sounds at various ranges. The patient's responses in the sound booth enable the audiologist to determine the exact level of hearing loss. An audiologist can also advise you about the prevention and management of hearing problems, including information you need to have about hearing aids. But he is not licensed to prescribe drugs or perform surgery.

After you've undergone the appropriate tests, your physician will be in a better position to tell you what's wrong with your hearing. Probably, he'll identify your difficulty as being in one of three general categories: (1) presbycusis, (2) conduction deafness, or (3) central deafness.

Presbycusis: The Most Common Age-Related Hearing Loss

Most hearing loss that occurs with age results from changes in tissue structure, a deterioration of special cells in the inner ear. This form of deterioration, which is known as *presbycusis,* makes sounds fainter and may cause older people to have difficulty understanding speech. Ironically, the condition may also make them more sensitive to loud noises. The problem involving my patient

Al, mentioned at the beginning of this chapter is a typical example of presbycusis.

HEALTH REPORT

SOME PRACTICAL TIPS ON PRESBYCUSIS

Impaired hearing in the elderly (presbycusis), a problem that is increasing in our society, is a condition that affects 30 to 60 percent of those past age sixty, say two authors of a 1986 report in *Journal of General Internal Medicine.* Of those eighty years and older, half consider hearing loss the greatest obstacle to a good life.

The senior author, a well-known internist, confesses, "during my early sixties, I began to notice, with some annoyance, that many people mumbled."

Two audiologists correctly diagnosed sensorineural deafness (the usual type in the elderly). But "they did not discuss what to expect or what else might help," the author continued. "Unlike the blind and the paralyzed, who elicit consideration and sympathy, people with poor hearing commonly encounter impatience and exasperation. I think sometimes people wondered whether I was inattentive, stupid, confused, or perhaps becoming demented."

The authors note that half of such patients can get considerable help from a proper hearing aid. But much energy, persuasion, and support may be necessary before the hearing-impaired older person masters the device and profits by it.

There are a considerable number of useful devices, including telephone amplifiers, headphones to plug into TV and radios, and speech-reading groups.

Hospital charts should have on their cover "POOR HEARING." A similar sign on the bed might also enhance communication between doctor and patient.

M. Lipkin and M. E. Williams, "Presbycusis and Communication," *Journal of General Internal Medicine* 1 (1986): 399.

Most of us begin to lose hearing ability bit by bit after about age fifty as a result of this deteriorative process. Presbycusis may be aggravated by exposure to loud noises, by certain drugs, by improper diet, or by genetic factors. The hearing loss associated with presbycusis can be worse in those suffering from such disorders as thyroid disease, diabetes, atherosclerosis (hardening or clogging of the arteries), and hypertension.

Only your physician or a hearing specialist will be able to sort through all the possible contributing factors to your hearing loss and prescribe appropriate treatment. Some of the possible treatments that have been prescribed for presbycusis have included vasodilators, B-complex vitamins, nicotinic acid (one of the B-complex vitamins) alone, and a variety of drugs and other preparations. But unfortunately, these approaches usually don't work. At the present time there's no really effective way to treat presbycusis medically or surgically. The only recognized approach that may help significantly is a hearing aid, a mechanical device that we'll be discussing in more detail later in this chapter.

Conduction Deafness—and the Virtue of Clean Ears!

A distraught fifty-six-year-old man rushed up to me one day and cried, "Dr. Rossman, I can't believe I'm really going deaf at my age! But it must be true because I know for a fact that I can't hear as well as most other people!"

When I had calmed him, he began to describe his problem in more detail, and that allowed me to identify the source of his complaint more precisely. In fact, he *was* experiencing some hearing problems, but they weren't quite what he thought they were.

According to his descriptions, his hearing of outside sounds, including conversations, seemed muffled. However, when he spoke, his own voice seemed to reverberate so much that he thought he was shouting.

"Obviously, there's something seriously wrong with my hearing mechanism, Doc," he said. "Go ahead. Give me the bad news."

"I have *good* news, unless you think an accumulation of wax in your ears is bad news," I replied.

His problem was that over a period of months, and perhaps years, wax had built up in his ears to the extent that he might as well have been wearing earplugs! Like many men, he had exceptionally hairy external ear canals, which prevented the wax from falling out of his ears naturally. By a simple procedure in my office,

I irrigated his ears with lukewarm water from a syringe. Within a few seconds, all the wax had been cleaned out, and he could hear clearly once again.

Unfortunately, the treatment isn't always this simple for those with obstructions in their ears. Sometimes, it's not possible to remove a wax buildup with a simple syringe-and-water procedure because the patient may have a damaged *tympanic membrane,* or eardrum. Also, if there is an infection in the ear or similar problem, antibiotics and other medications, or even surgery, may be necessary. In addition, some people have bony protrusions in the ear canals that aggravate wax buildup. Maneuvering around these obstructions may require more complex treatment procedures.

Central Deafness

One middle-aged daughter brought her eighty-four-year-old mother in for an exam because she had noticed that the older woman seemed to have trouble following conversations.

"She's always been quite alert, and in the past she's participated in discussions around the house as much as anybody," the daughter said. "But in the last few months, I've noticed that she doesn't seem to hear or understand what's being said. I'm hoping it's only a hearing problem, but I'm worried that her mind may be going."

After a number of hearing tests and a computerized tomography (CT) scan, I discovered that the woman's problem was related to hearing, but the difficulty didn't lie in her ears. Instead, one of the hearing centers in her brain had apparently been damaged by a mild stroke, which had somehow gone undetected.

Sometimes, the auditory nerves and the hearing centers in the brain can be damaged by infections, lengthy exposure to loud noises, use of certain drugs, head injuries, circulatory problems, or tumors. But in this woman's case, the source of the problem seemed to lie in a limited stroke that she had suffered in the recent past without anyone's really being aware of it. As a result, she could hear sounds as well as anyone. But she couldn't decipher what they meant.

"You mean her problem has nothing to do with the volume of sound?" the daughter asked.

"No, nothing," I replied. "It's all in the way she understands things. She can't translate what she's hearing. It's as if she has been transplanted to a foreign country, and she doesn't know the language."

There was nothing that could be done medically or surgically to treat this woman's problem. But she was able to be retrained in the other ways of understanding the English language. Consequently, her family enlisted a speech therapist to help her by teaching her lipreading, and gradually, the woman began to recover some capacity to translate the words that were being spoken around her.

Should I Get a Hearing Aid?

Hearing aids have been becoming more and more sophisticated in recent years, so much so that the space-age devices that President Ronald Reagan has used have been getting feature coverage in the national press. His hearing aids, which cost hundreds of dollars and may be priced beyond the level of the average person, are not only able to magnify sounds; they can also filter out background noises that may interfere with efficient hearing.

But even if you have some problem with your hearing, that's not a sure sign that you need a hearing aid. Many older people with some hearing difficulties in the fifteen- to twenty-decibel ranges have been sold hearing devices, even though they don't really need them. In fact, a hearing aid for mild hearing loss may confuse, upset, or simply bother the user more than it helps.

In general, if you have only a slight hearing loss, you should first try functioning as well as you can by such strategies as:

● Watching closely the lips of those who are speaking to see whether by a combination of visual and auditory means you can pick up the conversation. If you can, you probably don't need a hearing aid. (Classes in lipreading are available in many communities, and facility in this skill can be very helpful if hearing continues to deteriorate.)

- Using an amplified telephone bell or door buzzer. Obviously, you don't want devices with such high volumes that they disturb others. But slightly increasing the sound levels may enable you to function normally without bothering anybody else.
- Using radio and TV earphones. Some people with normal hearing prefer to use these instruments, so there's certainly nothing unusual about their use by those with slight hearing loss.
- Being particularly alert during group conversations, and relaxing rather than becoming tense or anxious when you fail to pick up every word that's said. Often, by remaining calm and attentive, you can get the gist of most conversations as well as or even better than those with better hearing.
- Feeling free to ask people to repeat what they've said. Rather than trying to "fake it" in one-to-one conversations with friends and acquaintances, it's usually best to say politely, "I'm afraid I didn't quite understand you. Could you repeat that?"
- Limiting background noise, such as radio and television sounds, that may interfere with your ability to hear discussions clearly.
- Simply telling people you have a little trouble hearing and asking them to speak somewhat more loudly than normal.

Of course, at some point, when a person's hearing deteriorates too much, these strategies won't work well. At that time, it may be advisable to get mechanical assistance through a hearing device.

What You Should Know About Hearing Aids

Before you can get a hearing aid, you have to do one of two things: (1) get a written statement from your doctor saying that your hearing has been evaluated medically and that you'll benefit from a hearing aid, or (2) sign a waiver that you don't want a medical exam for your hearing.

If you decide to get a hearing aid, you should comparison-shop for one, just as you would for any other consumer product. There are many types of mechanical hearing devices, at widely varying prices and levels of electronic sophistication. Some may fit your needs and personality quite well; others may not.

Also, note the quality of the service being offered with the hearing aid. It's important for you to be fitted properly and also for you to be informed and counseled about the maintenance and use of the device.

In addition, remember that the most expensive device may not be the best for your needs. You should buy an aid that has only the features you require. There's no need to get a high-powered, complicated device if you only need a simple one that is able to boost your hearing up toward normal.

The controls for hearing devices tend to be quite small, and as a result they can be hard to manipulate. Some miniature controls can be virtually impossible for those with arthritis or vision problems to operate alone. So try out the device several times before you purchase it, just to be sure you can use it easily.

In general, it's wise to do a thorough "test run" with every control movement you feel you'll have to make with the device, including changing the batteries, adjusting the volume, and manipulating any other switches or controls. Even after you buy a hearing device, it may take several days or weeks for you to ascertain whether or not you can really use it effectively.

To facilitate such consumer testing, many dealers offer trial purchases, such as a thirty-day period during which you can return the device if you find it's not working properly for you. REMEMBER: This trial period has been provided to make sure you're completely happy. So if you decide you're not satisfied within the trial period, don't hesitate to take the device back! After all, you'll probably have to live with the hearing aid for years. You should be as certain as possible that it's right for you.

For outside advice on hearing aids and other assistance for the hearing impaired, you might want to contact one or both of these organizations: The American Speech-Language-Hearing Association, 10801 Rockville Pike, Dept. AP, Rockville, Maryland 20852, or The National Association for Hearing and Speech Action, at 1-800-638-8255.

What Causes Those Noises in My Ears?

"Dr. Rossman, I hear a constant roaring sound in my head," one seventy-year-old man complained to me. "It sounds as if I'm at the seashore, or as if I have my ear stuck in a conch shell. Am I going crazy or what?"

In his case, a brief examination revealed our old problem, earwax, which had collected against the eardrum. After I had removed the wax, the roaring sounds, which are known as *tinnitus,* disappeared.

But tinnitus usually cannot be disposed of this simply. Some of us may have a temporary introduction to this problem at one time or another. Anyone who sits quietly in a silent location, insulated from outside noises, begins to "hear things" inside his ears or head. The beating of the heart, with the resulting pulse past the middle and inner ear, or other internal activity in our bodies produces sounds that are not normally heard because they are masked by outside sounds. But when everything around us is very quiet— as in a special sound booth or in bed on a very quiet night—those inner sounds become more apparent.

As one gets older, these inner sounds may increase in intensity so that they resemble a hissing or rushing water sound, or a constant roaring, ringing, or similar noise. Most of the time, and at lower levels, tinnitus is an annoyance that occurs in a substantial minority of our population as they grow older: The sounds are nothing to worry about, they may not impair hearing, and, many times, there's nothing we can do about them.

Still, you should always assume that tinnitus may be a symptom of something, just to play it safe. It's best to mention it to your physician so that he can examine you. Although the noises you are hearing may only be part of an aging process, on occasion tinnitus may signal a significant underlying health problem.

Here are a few of the possibilities, both serious and not so serious, that tinnitus may indicate:

• Tinnitus may be the first symptom of a tumor of the auditory nerve or some adjacent part of the hearing mechanism.

- It may be the first symptom of *otosclerosis*, a type of deafness in aging persons characterized by an excessive growth of bone within the hearing mechanism.
- It may signal a *glomus tumor* in the jugular vein in the neck.
- Tinnitus may indicate a *lesion*, or a change due to disease or injury, in the skull.
- Hearing loss of many types can be accompanied by noises in the ear. Tinnitus may result from hearing loss due to exposure to loud noises. These inner ear sounds may also increase with the normal deterioration of the auditory nerve, the condition noted earlier of *presbycusis*, which often accompanies aging. In short, tinnitus may be an indication that your doctor should check your hearing ability.
- *Meniere's disease*, an inner ear problem that involves both vertigo (dizziness) and hearing loss, may also include tinnitus.

Most of the time, the sounds you hear in your head are "subjective," in that they cannot be heard by your doctor with any of his instruments. Rarely, the tinnitus may be "objective": that is, your physician may be able to hear the noises with a stethoscope or other instrument. This sound is known in medical terms as a *bruit*.

Usually, these objective sounds of tinnitus occur when the noise you hear is coming from someplace in your head, other than in your ears. That is, the tinnitus is said to be *cranial* (in the head), rather than *aural* (in the ear).

This much rarer cranial type of tinnitus, which your doctor may be able to hear along with you, is typically described as a "roaring" or "rushing" sound, and from your perspective, it's not limited to the ear region. It seems to be coming from the head in a generalized way, rather than just from the ear.

The causes of this form of tinnitus may include:

- *anemia*, or an insufficiency in the quantity of red blood cells;
- *hypertension*, or high blood pressure;
- *hypotension*, or low blood pressure; and
- *polycythemia*, or an excess of red blood cells, sometimes accompanied by an enlarged spleen or overactive bone marrow.

What Can You Do About Tinnitus?

Many times, there's no specific treatment that can be prescribed for tinnitus. Those who hear this roaring or ringing in their ears as they get older may just have to learn to live with it.

But still, there are sometimes things we can do to manage or mask the annoying sounds. For example:

• You may be able just to "wait out" the condition. In many cases, a problem in the inner ear, such as an infection or lesion, may appear and then gradually heal and disappear. When the problem goes, the tinnitus may go with it.

• Hearing aids can sometimes help reduce ear noise or mask the tinnitus. A properly fitted hearing device may let in just enough background noise from the environment to overcome the tinnitus sounds. In most cases, hearing devices reduce rather than aggravate problems with tinnitus.

• Small doses of certain sedative drugs, such as tranquilizers or phenobarbital, may help reduce the annoyance of internal ear noises. These drugs may be especially helpful at night, when our surroundings are quieter and the tendency to hear tinnitus increases. But if you take drugs for this problem you should use them only for short periods of time and probably alternate the medications. In this way, the side effects and tendency to become dependent on them are minimized.

• There's no such thing as surgery specifically designed to eliminate tinnitus. But if the ear noises are caused by some underlying condition such as a tumor, surgery for that condition may help eliminate the inner noise.

Relating to Those
with Hearing Problems

No matter what treatments or other steps may be taken by physicians, therapists, or other health experts, an older person may still experience hearing problems. Even the most advanced hearing aids may not restore full auditory abilities in those whose hearing is very severely impaired. So some people will have to be reconciled to hearing that is impaired to some degree.

But friends and relatives can make the lives of those with hearing problems much easier if they just follow a few simple rules. These guidelines are based on observations I've made in my own practice, on reports by the National Institutes of Health, and on other sources.

- Don't remove yourself from the sight of a hearing-impaired person in an effort to speak directly into his ear. It's important for those with hearing difficulties to be able to *see* you, including your lips and gestures, so that they can put those visual aids together with what they are able to hear.
- Talk in front of the person at a distance of no more than six feet. Be sure that your features are well-lighted. If you are arranging a discussion with several people, observe the six-foot and good-lighting guidelines for all the participants. That is, no person should be more than six feet from any other person.
- If you're setting up a meeting where you know some hearing-impaired people will be present, alert the speaker to the fact that some in the audience do not hear well. Tell him to speak as loudly and clearly as possible, and use a sound system if one is available.
- Avoid mumbling, eating, or chewing while you speak or any other practice or obstruction that may make it difficult for others to hear you.
- If you're the speaker at a meeting, make an announcement at the beginning of your talk that you want people to raise their hands if they can't hear you. Put the onus on yourself by saying something like "Sometimes my voice drops, so let me know if you can't hear." That way, you may help remove some of the self-consciousness that the hard-of-hearing may feel.
- If someone indicates he hasn't heard what you've said, be quick to repeat your words in simple, clear language.
- When you talk to those who do not hear well, speak *slightly* more loudly than you normally would. If you raise the volume of your voice too much, the sounds may be distorted and you may become more difficult to hear.

- When you talk to the hearing-impaired, speak relatively slowly, but maintain a normal rhythm and pacing to your speech. Otherwise, you will interrupt the flow of normal communication and may make it harder to be understood.
- Above all, do not ignore a person who is hard-of-hearing during a group discussion. If you have to repeat yourself for her, do so patiently. In this way, you'll draw the person into the discussion and solicit opinions and insights that might otherwise be lost.

If you want other information on helping those who are hearing-impaired, you might get in contact with one or more of these organizations:

- The American Academy of Otolaryngologists (Head and Neck Surgery), Inc., 1101 Vermont Ave., N.W., Washington, D.C. 20005.
- The Office of Scientific and Health Reports, National Institute of Neurological and Communicative Disorders and Stroke, Building 31, Room 8A06, Bethesda, Maryland 20205. (NOTE: You might ask for the institute's pamphlet *Hearing Loss: Hope Through Research.*)
- Self Help for Hard of Hearing People (SHHH), 4848 Battery Land, Dept. E, Bethesda, Maryland 20814.

9
TO SAVE YOUR SIGHT

Barbara was driving down a country road in the Northwest when suddenly she noticed something like a veil flopping around in front of her. For a second, she thought a piece of paper or cloth was flying about inside the car. But then, she realized that whatever was obscuring her vision was *inside* her right eye.

Barbara was puzzled because in her sixty-seven years, she had never before experienced anything quite like this. Still, she paid no attention at first to the problem. But the next day, the situation was worse, and the day after that, she could hardly see out of the eye at all. So she sought the help of an eye specialist.

As it happened, it was fortunate that she had gone to the doctor because her problem was a detached retina. If she had waited too long, she might have become totally blind in that eye. But since she underwent an exam without too much delay, the doctor was able to perform an operation that restored most of her vision.

The *retina,* the sensory covering tissue at the back of the eye, may tear loose in people of any age. But the problem is more common in older patients, especially those who have undergone cataract surgery. When the retina begins to loosen, the individual may notice a shadow from the side, which approaches the center of the line of vision. As we've seen, Barbara described what she saw as a kind of "veil." Dark flakes may also seem to float around in the eye, and there may be unusual flashes of light.

If the detached retina is detected and diagnosed soon enough, as Barbara's was, a physician can often perform an operation known as *scleral buckling.* This procedure involves placing the retina against the back of the eye, where it reattaches itself.

One lesson in this story is that eye problems are not something you can ignore. If anything out of the ordinary seems to be happening with your vision, it's wise to check with your physician immediately. Otherwise, a delay may cause irreparable damage.

On the other hand, eye problems are increasingly common as we grow older, and most are not serious threats to our vision. In many cases, the difficulties can be corrected with simple treatments. Hundreds of thousands of eye operations, such as cataract surgery, are performed without a glitch every year. In fact, there are more than 300,000 cataract operations in the United States annually, and virtually every one is successful!

Some of the more common eye complaints that I hear in my office on a regular basis may include some that have bothered you.

Common Eye Complaints

• *Reading problems.* As we grow older, most of us find it harder to focus on objects or words that are near us. This problem is known as *presbyopia.*

REMEDY: Prescription glasses or contact lenses usually can restore close vision to perfect focus.

• *Reduced night vision.* As you probably know, the average person's eyes usually take from ten to thirty minutes to adjust to moderate degrees of darkness. After that period, most people can usually see well enough to make their way about without extra lights. But as we get older, this ability to see in the dark diminishes.

SUGGESTION: Keep your eyeglass prescription up-to-date. Many times, vision problems at night or at dusk are simply an extension of an inability to see clearly in the light. In any event, it's wise to have your eyes checked if you notice persistent night vision problems, and to be more cautious as you move about in the dark!

• *An increase in "floaters."* Floaters are the small flakes, spots, and threads you sometimes see when you look up at the sky or at anything with a light-colored background. We all have these specks, and, like occasional flashes of light in the eye, they are usually nothing to worry about. But if you notice a sudden increase in floaters, or if you find they are accompanied by flashes of light, this condition may signal a possible detached retina. So if it occurs, you should have an eye examination immediately.

• *Watery eyes.* If your eyes tend to tear often, you may be experiencing eye irritation as a result of excessive fatigue or exposure to water (as in swimming). In addition, tearing can be caused by irritation from light, wind, or dust.

REMEDY: Rest, or wear protection over the eyes, such as sunglasses or goggles. Eyedrops may also help relieve these symptoms, but, in most cases, you should use such medications only after consulting with your physician.

Watery eyes may also occur as a result of infections, allergies, or blocked tear ducts. These problems can usually be dealt with by a physician.

• *Dry eyes.* When your tear glands produce too few tears, your eyes may become excessively dry. Consequently, your vision may become blurred, or you may experience an itching or burning sensation in your eyes. Medical specialists can usually prescribe eyedrop medications to remedy this difficulty. The most effective medications include artificial tear solutions and afford considerable relief.

Unfortunately, not all eye problems are as easily treated as these common complaints. But even with more serious eye concerns, swift and effective treatment by a specialist can often take care of the ailment. Some of those that we'll be dealing with in the following sections are cataracts, glaucoma, retinal problems, special diabetic concerns, and brain problems that have important implications for your vision.

If You Are Concerned About Cataracts

"I've noticed that things appear to be rather blurry, with some double vision in one of my eyes," Paul, a seventy-five-year-old retired executive, said. "Also, bright lights often seem to hurt my eyes and may even give me a headache. But it's strange, because I'm also finding I need more light on my books to read properly."

On questioning Paul further, I found that other than the bothersome effect of bright lights, his eyes didn't hurt him. Then, on physical examination of his eyes, I discovered what I had begun to suspect was his problem: Paul had cataracts.

Cataracts, the most common cause of visual problems among older people, often develop over a number of years. They are cloudy or opaque areas covering part or all of the lens of the eye. The lens is situated just behind the pupil, and it's normally entirely transparent. The function of the lens is to help the eye project images onto the retina at the back of the eye. The retina, in turn, transmits these images to the brain, and sight is the final result.

Obviously, if the lens is not transmitting light properly—if it is clouded or otherwise fogged or obscured by a cataract—there are going to be difficulties with sight.

What causes cataracts? There's little doubt at this time that cataracts result from age-associated chemical changes in the lens proteins. Also, these factors may contribute to cataracts:

- Eye infections
- High blood sugar, as in diabetes
- Irradiation
- Overexposure to light

In addition, cataracts may arise from lengthy treatment with steroid drugs. BUT NOTE: Steroid medications may be unavoidable when a person has a serious disease that can be controlled only through them.

The symptoms of cataracts, some of which were present in Paul's case, may include:

- blurry vision;
- double vision;
- ghost images;
- the sense that there's a film over the eye;
- the impression that bright light is bothersome;
- the impression that artificial or natural lighting, which others may regard as normal, isn't bright enough for reading or other close-up work;
- frequent changes in the prescriptions of your eyeglasses; and
- the development of a milky or yellowish spot in your normally black pupil (this discoloration can be seen from the outside by others).

After a cataract develops over a period of months or years, it may intefere with vision so much that something has to be done about it. The usual answer is surgery, a safe procedure that is entirely successful in more than ninety-five out of one hundred cases. Surgery was the decision in Paul's case, and he was one of the great majority of people who have had their vision corrected quite effectively.

There are several surgical techniques that are currently available. First of all, the cataracts can simply be removed, and the patient can begin to wear special cataract glasses or contact lenses. These operate more or less like a magnifying glass, and they replace the natural magnifying power of the lens. Usually, it takes at least six weeks for a person to be able to use these glasses in his routine activities.

Another possibility is placement of an artificial intraocular lens implant in the eye during surgery. This implant is a plastic lens that is inserted where the natural clouded lens used to be. After about two months, the patient is able to see distant objects more clearly. In some cases, he may need a further mild correction in his vision with glasses, for instance, for reading.

Older patients who cannot handle inserting contact lenses every day, or who do not want to be bothered with them, may elect this latter approach. Paul chose the lens implant route, and now he usually gets along without any glasses at all!

The Threat of Glaucoma

Sonya, an otherwise healthy sixty-nine-year-old, experienced an acute, sudden burst of pain and redness in her eye. She even found herself becoming nauseous.

Because she had a history of occasional migraines, she at first thought her problem was just another version of those bad headaches. But something seemed strange about this particular attack. So she got in touch with me immediately—fortunately. Her problem was *glaucoma,* an eye disease that is the most common cause of blindness among those over forty years of age.

What is glaucoma? The fluid content of the eye is usually maintained at a low and fairly steady pressure. But sometimes, this fluid pressure may rise, either intermittently or steadily. Above a certain level, the fluid pressure constitutes a major threat to vision as it presses against the optic nerve at the back of the eye. The prevalence of the disease increases with age, rising from a relatively low rate among young adults to as high as 5 to 10 percent among those who have reached their eighth decade of life.

It had been years since Sonya had seen a doctor, and that was one reason why her first indications of glaucoma had come to her attention in such dramatic fashion. Usually, glaucoma develops stealthily, over a period of years. In most cases, there are no early symptoms, though sometimes a patient may complain of seeing halos around lights. More obvious symptoms, such as pain, redness of the eye, nausea, and occasionally vomiting, occur after the disease has progressed fairly far.

First of all, I placed the index finger of each hand onto each of Sonya's eyeballs while she had her eyes closed. Her eyes felt firm to the touch, considerably harder than normal eyes. Usually, the eye has a little bit of "give" when you press against it, but there was no "give" at all in Sonya's case. This hardness can be a useful indication of glaucoma.

Then, I arranged to perform two routine, painless tests on Sonya, tonometry and ophthalmoscopy. These procedures gave us a fairly certain indication that she had glaucoma.

• *Tonometry* involves putting drops into the eye to numb it, and then measuring the eye pressure with a device known as a *tonometer*.

• *Ophthalmoscopy* involves using an instrument to look directly into the eye through the pupil, from a very short distance away from the surface of the eye. The physician using the ophthalmo-scope can examine the optic nerve and evaluate whether or not it seems to be damaged.

If these tests suggest there is a problem, the doctor may then order one or two additional tests: perimetry and gonioscopy.

• *Perimetry* involves mapping the area of vision of the eye by asking the patient at what point she observes a light slowly moved from the periphery of her vision in various directions.

Everyone has a small "blind spot" in the eye where the optic nerve enters the back of the eye, and this spot shows up on the vision map. But if a person has glaucoma, as Sonya did, the area of blindness is much larger than normal. This test may take several minutes to perform, but it is painless.

• *Gonioscopy* is a procedure that enables the doctor to observe the angle at which the iris meets the cornea. The *iris*, by the way, is the colored part of the eye that twists open and shut, to regulate the amount of light that enters the eye. The *cornea* is the clear part of the eye in front of the iris, which allows light to enter the eye.

This test is performed first by putting drops into the eye to numb it. Then, the doctor places a contact lens gently onto the surface of the eye and examines the angle between the iris and cornea. This measurement enables him to evaluate the type and severity of the glaucoma.

These tests showed that Sonya's glaucoma was relatively se-vere. As a result, we prescribed medications that increased the drainage of the fluids out of her eyes, thereby lowering the danger-ous pressure against her optic nerve. Because she is experiencing some side effects, such as headaches, she would like to discontinue the medications entirely.

So she is now being evaluated for surgery, which could open up the drainage canals in her eyes and perhaps permanently re-lieve the pressures.

KEY FACTS

COMMON DRUGS PRESCRIBED FOR GLAUCOMA AND THEIR UNCOMMON SIDE EFFECTS

MEDICATIONS	SIDE EFFECTS
Meiotics Pilocarpine	Can cause headaches, excessive sweating, salivation, and diarrhea
Cholinesterase inhibitors Phospholine iodide	Shouldn't be used with succinylcholine during general anesthesia because prolonged apnea (stoppage of breathing) may occur
Beta-adrenergic blockers Timolol maleate	May cause congestive heart failure, also may lead to respiratory problems in patients with asthma or emphysema; concurrent use of epinephrine may aggravate angina or hypertension

Carbonic anhydrase inhibitors
  (orally administered)
  Acetazolamide; methazolamide
	May cause malaise, fatigue, anorexia, weight loss, or gastrointestinal disturbances; occasionally may result in kidney stones; concurrent use with thiazide diuretic for hypertension can cause severe hypokalemia (too little potassium in the blood)

Possible surgical procedures that Sonya could undergo include two:

• *Laser surgery.* With this technique, a narrow beam of light is focused on the area of the eye, such as the drainage canals that need to be opened. Then, the laser is used to cut a small hole in the desired area. This new approach is still regarded as quasi-experimental by some in the medical community. But it's quick, it's painless, and it can be quite successful, though there are still questions about the permanency of the improvement.

• *Microsurgery.* This type of operation involves removing a piece of the iris and then making a tiny opening in the white part of the eye. Finally, the surgeon creates a new drainage canal to relieve the fluid pressure on the eye.

Usually performed with a local anesthetic, this operation requires several days of recuperation. Microsurgery is often successful in cases of severe glaucoma, but it may have to be repeated if the new drainage canals become clogged.

Remedies for the Retina

As we've already seen from the example of a detached retina, problems with that part of the eye can present serious threats to vision for older people. The retina, you'll recall, is the thin lining at the back of the eye, which consists of nerve cells that receive visual images and pass them on to the brain through the optic nerve.

But a retinal detachment is only one possible problem. Two others, which can involve just as much danger to the eye, are a condition known as *age-related macular degeneration* (AMD) and another called *diabetic retinopathy.*

Age-Related Macular Degeneration (AMD)

Age-related macular degeneration, as obscure-sounding as it is, can involve some very practical and personal implications for people over fifty years of age, the group that faces the greatest risk of AMD. Although AMD usually does not result in complete blindness, it can cause serious problems for reading, sewing, driving a car, or performing other activities that require relatively precise and fine vision.

What exactly is AMD? It is a degenerative disease that causes a wasting away of a small area of the eye tissue called the *macula,* which lies in the center of the retina. This part of the retina is responsible for producing sharp, central (as opposed to peripheral) vision. The cause of AMD may be atherosclerosis (clogging of the arteries as a result of the buildup of plaque), heredity, a blow or other trauma to the eye, or other conditions that are not now fully understood.

HEALTH REPORT

THE OUTLOOK FOR REATTACHMENT OF THE RETINA

The problem of detachment of the retina may begin when the rather solid, clear gel in the back of the eye (the *vitreous*) shrinks away from the *retina*, the light-sensitive layer at the back of the eye. This shrinkage is more likely to occur in those who are nearsighted and may be a complication of an eye injury or a cataract extraction if vitreous fluid is lost.

Subsequent to these initial problems, the retina may become detached from the back of the eye. If bleeding occurs with this detachment, the person may note a sudden shower of black spots. Initially, there is usually a small defect in the visual field on the periphery of vision. But then, the loss of sight may progress rapidly.

Before modern surgical advances, this process could culminate in blindness. But now, a 95 percent reattachment rate can be expected. The outcome with respect to central vision (including the ability to read well) depends on the extent of damage to the *macula*, the fine-vision center of the retina.

A number of successful procedures for reattachment have been developed, according to the author of a 1987 report in the *British Medical Journal*. But he emphasizes that to enhance the chances for success, a speedy response to a detached retina, including prompt referral into a hospital, is extremely important. This medical attention should be initiated within twenty-four hours of the first symptoms, the author says.

A. H. Chignelli, "Retinal Detachment," *British Medical Journal* 294 (1987): 661.

The symptoms of macular degeneration include:

• the blurring of words or type;
• a distortion of vertical lines, such as the curving of telephone poles;
• a dark spot at the center of vision, or the point of focus of vision (typically, the dark spot blots out the image);

- a distortion of an image in which the center of the image seems smaller than the surrounding scene; or
- the appearance of small white spots, called *drusen,* which a physician may notice in your eye (these spots contain waste material but do not interfere with sight).

If you have regular eye examinations, your physician or ophthalmologist will quickly pick up any signs of AMD and begin to treat them. On the other hand, even if you do not have your eyes checked regularly, you can still take some steps to monitor your own condition.

If you notice any of the symptoms listed here, you should see your physician immediately. Also, you might try testing yourself with the Amsler Grid Test for Macular Degeneration, which I've reproduced on the next page from materials provided by the National Society to Prevent Blindness, 500 E. Remington Road, Schaumburg, Illinois 60173.

In checking your vision with this chart, simply look at the dot in the middle of the grid while keeping one eye covered. Be sure to test each of your eyes separately. If the lines near the dot appear wavy or distorted, this could be a symptom of AMD or other visual problem.

Is there a remedy for age-related macular degeneration?

At the present, no generally effective medication is available to treat the disease. But magnifying glasses and other vision aids may help. It's sometimes comforting to remember that there will not be a total loss of vision with AMD, just a loss of fine and reading vision.

Research continues in this area, including some recent work reporting that zinc tablets taken orally may inhibit the progression of macular degeneration. There are limits to this approach because some people cannot tolerate zinc: Among other reactions, they may develop indigestion or stomach cramps. It is also unclear from the present state of research just how much zinc may be required and what percentage of people can be expected to benefit from this treatment. In any case, it's important to check first with your physician before you try zinc tablets.

Another possibility for dealing with macular degeneration is laser surgery, but fewer than 10 percent of those with AMD may be treated successfully with this procedure. Ralph, a fifty-eight-

HEALTH REPORT

AMSLER GRID TEXT FOR MACULAR DEGENERATION

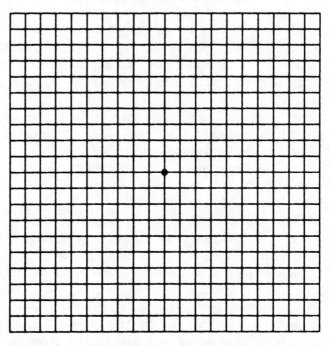

INSTRUCTIONS: (1) Place the grid on the wall at eye level. (2) View it from 12 inches. (3) If you wear glasses for reading, you should wear them for the test. (4) Test one eye at a time. (5) Look at the center dot. (6) Tell your doctor if you can't see all the lines, or if some lines appear wavy.

Reprinted with the permission of the National Society to Prevent Blindness.

year-old engineer, was a typical candidate for this type of treatment. He had what's known as "wet" AMD in one eye. The "wet" form of the disease is caused by leaking blood vessels that produce fluid that distorts the vision.

SOLAR RADIATION AND AGE-RELATED MACULAR DEGENERATION

A considerable number of experimental studies have shown that light may damage the retina, according to a 1988 article in the *Survey of Ophthalmology*. The macula, that portion of the retina concerned with close, sharp vision, is particularly vulnerable.

A striking example were the thirty-five hundred persons who suffered macular damage viewing the 1912 solar eclipse. There is also evidence that far less intense sunlight over the lifetime can accelerate or call forth damage. NOTE: Brunettes with more protective pigment in their eyes may fare better than light-skinned persons.

There is evidence also that photochemical damage may be inhibited or repaired better with antioxidants, such as vitamin C, tocopherol (vitamin E), and beta-carotene, none of which is manufactured in the human body. These substances are available through adequate diet or supplement.

Furthermore, the author recommends protective lenses when exposure to significant sunlight is to occur. He notes that ordinary sunglasses may not successfully screen out the blue portion of the light that is most damaging. But an increasing number of manufacturers are producing glasses with good filtration for the ultraviolet part of the light spectrum. CAUTION: Check with your optometrist for specific recommendations.

R. W. Young, "Solar Radiation and Age-Related Macular Degeneration," *Survey of Ophthalmology* 32 (1988): 252.

Because Ralph's condition was identified at an early stage, he was scheduled for laser surgery, which is designed to stop the leaking of the blood vessels in the eye. After the surgery, which was successful, Ralph's leaking blood vessels were sealed off, and he resumed a normal life, with much better vision. The laser operation had been performed painlessly in a short procedure in his doctor's office, and no hospitalization was required.

Diabetic Retinopathy

Sometimes, retinal problems may develop in those with diabetes. The condition known as *diabetic retinopathy* arises when small blood vessels that nourish the retina weaken and break down or become blocked.

The retina, as you know, is necessary to vision, and it acts somewhat like the film of a camera: It receives an image from the front of the eye that has to be transmitted through the optic nerve into the brain. There, the image is in effect "developed."

The delicate nerves in the retina, which are highly sensitive to light, are supplied with oxygen and other nutrients by tiny blood vessels. But in retinopathy, these vessels may begin to bulge out in the form of an aneurysm. They may also leak fluids and bleed, thus producing distorted vision. In later stages of the disease, weak little branches may grow out from the main vessels, and then these branches may rupture and release blood into the eye's inner "vitreous" section, a condition that clouds the vision. The retina may also become detached as a result of this condition.

It's been estimated that more than 40 percent of people who have had diabetes for fifteen or more years have some amount of damage to the retinal blood vessels. On the other hand, some diabetics develop retinopathy as a first or early symptom of the disease.

What guidelines should be kept in mind for prevention and treatment of this problem? Here are a few suggestions:

• Have regular eye exams if you have diabetes; once a year is recommended as a routine.
• Seek early treatment if there are signs of retinopathy; if you act quickly, you may save your sight.
• Be especially alert if you're a diabetic with hypertension.
• Stop smoking.

Also, if the retinopathy condition is far advanced, you should explore the possibility of laser surgery to seal the damaged blood vessels in the eye. Not all people respond to this treatment, however, so it will be up to you and your doctor to decide whether your situation warrants such surgery.

Finally, you might consider *vitrectomy,* a delicate technique by which the blood deposits and scar tissues in the gel *(vitreous)* behind the lens are broken up. Then, these deposits and tissues, along with the jellylike vitreous fluid, are removed by suction. Finally, a clear salt solution is injected into the eye to replace the vitreous.

Your personal physician should be able to refer you to a specialist who can outline the pros and cons of these alternatives for your individual situation.

Extraocular Causes of Vision Loss

One seventy-six-year-old woman complained of a loss in vision in one of her eyes, which she said "reminded me of having somebody pull a shade down in front of my face."

As it turned out, the cause of her vision problems didn't lie in the eye. Rather, she had suffered a *transient ischemic attack* (TIA), which involves a sudden and temporary loss of circulation to the vision center of the brain.

Sometimes, TIAs may result from a narrowing or roughness in the carotid arteries in the neck. The underlying cause may be clogging of the arteries as a result of atherosclerosis, plugging due to aggregation of platelets, or some other circulation-inhibiting factor, including drastic drops in blood pressure.

After examining a number of possibilities, this woman's physicians concluded that a narrowing of the carotid artery was the source of her problem. So they placed her on aspirin, which is an antiplatelet agent. That is, it helps reverse platelet clumps—or "thin the blood out"—and thus prevents clotting.

Also—and perhaps most important—the doctors discovered she was a smoker. Because smoking is a major risk factor in TIAs, they urged her to quit.

This patient has not suffered any further transient ischemic attacks, and she's not alone: many people who have one never experience another. On the other hand, a TIA can be a harbinger of a later tendency toward a full-blown stroke. So it's essential for those who have a TIA to take it as a signal that there probably are habits they should change or medications they should use to reduce their level of risk.

The transient ischemic attack is just one example of a non-eye-related vision problem. Given the number of possibilities within the eye itself, as well as the potential for problems outside the eye, it should be obvious by now that any change in your vision is a cause for concern.

So monitor yourself and take reasonable precautions in caring for your eyes. If you notice something unusual, such as any of the various symptoms I've discussed so far, see your physician without delay. Fortunately, most eye problems can be corrected, or at least managed successfully, if they are discovered and treated at an early stage.

Some Final Thoughts on Eye Care

Here are a few basic guidelines on eye care for older people that I've found helpful in preventing many vision problems, or at least enabling individuals to discover potentially dangerous conditions at an early stage. These tips come from the National Institutes of Health, the National Society to Prevent Blindness, the American Foundation for the Blind, The Lighthouse–The New York Association for the Blind, as well as my own observations in medical practice.

• Have your eyes checked by your family physician every year, and have a complete eye exam by an eye doctor every other year. Those with diabetes or a family or personal history of eye disease should be checked more often, preferably at least once a year.

• See the doctor even if you're healthy. The best time to catch eye problems is when they're in an early stage, without obvious symptoms.

• See a doctor *immediately* if you experience symptoms such as dimming or blurring of vision, redness in the eye, double vision, pain in the eye, increase in "floaters," or any of the other signs we've discussed in this chapter.

• Learn as much as you can about eye problems that occur with aging, especially if you have a personal or family history involving a particular disease.

To this end, you might write to one or more of the following organizations and ask them for brochures, pamphlets, and other information:

1. Office of Scientific Reporting, The National Eye Institute (National Institutes of Health), Building 31, Room 6A32, Bethesda, Maryland 20892. Ask for free brochures on eye disorders.

2. The National Society to Prevent Blindness, 79 Madison Ave., New York, New York 10016. They have a number of free pamphlets and also a Home Eye Test for Adults, which costs $1.00.

3. The American Foundation for the Blind, 15 West Sixteenth Street, New York, New York 10011. Ask for free publications. They have a helpful brochure titled *Products for People with Vision Problems.*

4. Vision Foundation, 2 Mt. Auburn Street, Watertown, Massachusetts 02172. Ask for the list of special products and services for those who have impaired vision.

5. The American Optometric Association, Communications Division, 243 North Lindbergh Boulevard, St. Louis, Missouri 63141.

6. The American Academy of Ophthalmology, 655 Beach Street, San Francisco, California 94105-1336.

7. The Food and Drug Administration, 5600 Fishers Lane, Rockville, Maryland 20857. Ask for their article "Keeping an Eye on Glaucoma," from the *FDA Consumer.*

8. The Public Citizen's Health Research Group, 2000 P ST., N.W., Suite 708, Washington, D.C. 20036. They have a $3.50 book called *Cataracts: A Consumer's Guide to Choosing the Best Treatment.*

9. The Lighthouse–The New York Association for the Blind, 111 East Fifty-ninth Street, New York, New York 10022. They provide information on such aids to vision as:

• reading glasses, including special half-glasses, high-powered bifocals, and reading telescopes;
• hand magnifiers;
• stand magnifiers, both illuminated and nonilluminated;
• telescopes for distance vision, including both hand-held and spectacle-mounted versions;

- video magnifiers, including enlargers for reading and large-print computer terminals;
- special lamps for those with vision problems;
- fiber-tip pens and large-print books and magazines;
- accessory devices, such as "talking books," audio tapes, and reading stands;
- free cassette recorders and other helpful aids through the Library of Congress. Check your local library for information.

TAKING THE BEST CARE OF YOUR BODY

10

A USER'S GUIDE TO THE HEART

Shortly after I had launched my medical practice, I was told by an older—and, I thought, wiser—physician, "Heart disease is the 'doctor's disease.' Most of us develop a problem with our coronary arteries by the time we reach our fifties, so you should play your life accordingly!"

Without questioning this sage further, I provisionally accepted the prediction and began to assume that I, too, would develop a cardiovascular problem, and probably have a heart attack, by that age.

In fact, this man *did* die before he reached sixty. Yet here I am, in my midseventies, with no sign of cardiovascular trouble! What happened? There are at least three good reasons why my colleague erred in his prophecy about me, and why he succumbed himself.

In the first place, he was a cigarette smoker all his life, and I quit back in the 1950s. As we know now, smoking is a major risk factor for the development of heart disease.

In the second place, he consistently ate a diet that was rich in saturated fats and cholesterol. Eggs, fatty beef and pork dishes, ice cream, and gooey desserts were his standard fare.

As for me, for most of my life I've eaten more poultry and fish than beef, pork, or other domesticated animal meats. At first, the motivation for my choice of diet was more a matter of family economics than anything else. When I was a boy, beef was a luxury we couldn't afford often. Fish was for the poor, and so we ate it. The family cat and I were both fond of herring.

Even when I began to earn enough to afford richer foods such as beef, I *still* stayed away from them, mainly because of the findings of a prescient medical expert, Dr. Norman Jolliffe of the New York City Department of Health. Forty years ago, before present-day approaches to diet were at all popular, he designed a low-fat, low-cholesterol diet, the "Prudent Diet." This regimen was designed to provide a well-balanced way to good nutrition and also to reduce the danger of heart disease.

In fact, his efforts were so well regarded that the people who founded Weight Watchers adopted some of his theories and food techniques. Certainly, Jolliffe impressed me, and I ended up sticking with eating patterns close to my traditional family diet that had emphasized fish and fowl and deemphasized beef, pork, and other such meats.

In the third place, I probably have avoided heart disease in part because of genetic factors. Somehow, the inherited tendencies that caused cardiovascular problems in some of my ancestors have not become part of my own makeup.

So by general good luck and "clean living"—which I freely admit I didn't fully understand when I made those early choices about diet and life-style—I've managed to steer clear of any heart problems. And as it turns out, I'm in good and growing company.

An increasingly large group of Americans have succeeded in preventing the ravages of cardiovascular problems in recent years. To be sure, heart disease is still the nation's number-one killer, as it takes the lives of more than a half million people each year. But since 1968, mortality from coronary heart disease has fallen by more than 30 percent, a decline that has resulted in the saving of more than 800,000 lives.

HEALTH REPORT

WHAT HEART ATTACK SIGNALS CAN YOU EXPECT IN OLDER PEOPLE?

A study published in 1987 compared heart attack symptoms in one hundred very old people (eighty-five years or older) with a group of younger individuals (sixty-five to eighty-four years). In the very old group, symptoms were often unlike those of the usual heart attack. In fact, in twenty-seven individuals a heart attack wasn't suspected at all at first.

Specifically, only forty-one of the very old people complained of chest pain, which is generally thought to be a characteristic symptom of heart attack. Also, in twenty-two cases, confusion was reported as the major finding; seventeen fainted; and forty-two had shortness of breath.

The younger people, in contrast, experienced more typical symptoms of a heart attack, such as uncomfortable pressure or pain in the center of the chest and a spreading of the pain to the shoulder, neck, or arms.

The investigators made the point that very old persons become more and more atypical when they have a heart attack as compared with younger age groups. Thus, the possibility of heart attack when an old person suddenly becomes confused, faints, or becomes weak should be borne in mind.

J. J. Day, A. J. Bayer, M. S. J. Pathy, and J. S. Chadha, "Acute Myocardial Infarction: Diagnostic Difficulties and Outcome in Advanced Old Age," *Age and Ageing* 16 (1987): 239.

What have been the reasons for this decline in heart disease deaths? Most medical experts cite these developments, which in part, at least, reflect my own personal situation:

- Decreased cigarette smoking
- Wider acceptance of low-fat, low-cholesterol diets
- Increased exercise
- Better control of hypertension
- Improved methods of medical treatment

HEALTH REPORT

WHAT TO EXPECT FROM THE OLDER HEART

Contributors to a medical textbook on geriatric medicine note that by ages fifty-one to sixty, almost a fourth of the population have significant coronary disease. Some may have anginal pains (which reflect "obvious disease"), but a majority of those with the disease are still free of symptoms. Physicians can often detect the presence of coronary disease (called "latent disease") in those without angina through stress testing or special scans.

When you exclude these people with "obvious" and "latent" disease, it becomes clear that there is no decline in cardiac performance with normal aging. In other words, if a person's heart and arteries have stayed in relatively good shape into middle age and later—either through good genes or an effective program of prevention or both—there's every reason to think the cardiovascular system will continue to do well.

For example, older subjects (aged sixty-five to seventy-nine) have the same cardiac output on bicycle testing as do younger people (aged twenty-five to forty-four). The older people compensate for a slower heart rate by increased filling and ejection of blood per stroke of the heart. But the progressive inroads of coronary disease diminish the percentage of these older people with healthy hearts in the latter decades.

The authors conclude: "the greatest promise [is] that by the optimization of life-style variables such as diet, tobacco use and exercise, a large proportion of cardiovascular disease will never be allowed to develop."

J. L. Fleg and E. G. Lakatta, "Cardiovascular Disease in Old Age," in I. Rossman, ed., *Clinical Geriatrics*, 3d ed. (New York: J. B. Lippincott Company, 1986): 169–96.

But if you have passed, or are passing, successfully through your fifties or sixties, this is not necessarily the time to begin to sigh with relief or cheer that you've "made it" past the major killer. It's still important to consider exactly what heart disease involves in the later years and to explore what you can do to achieve *continued* protection.

The Signals of a Heart Attack, and How You Should Respond

A number of my older patients, aware that they have some degree of occlusion or closing of their coronary arteries, have two overriding concerns:

1. How do I recognize a heart attack when it begins?
2. What should I do to counter the impact of the attack?

I tell them first of all that a heart attack, or myocardial infarction, usually occurs as a result of atherosclerosis, or "hardening of the arteries," though other problems such as a sudden abnormality in the heart's rhythmic beating may also trigger an attack. Typically, a clot builds up in one of the coronary arteries that supply blood to the heart until there's a total blockage of circulation. At this point, the heart muscle starts to die.

The possible signals of a heart attack include the following, which are highlighted in many communications of the American Heart Association:

- An uncomfortable pressure, fullness, squeezing, or pain occurs in the center of the chest for two minutes or longer.
- The pain may steadily worsen.
- The pain may spread to the entire chest.
- The pain may travel down the left arm and sometimes even down the right arm.
- The pain may spread to the shoulders, neck, and jaw.
- The victim may experience sweating, nausea, vomiting, faintness, dizziness, weakness, palpitations of the heart, or shortness of breath.
- The person may feel pressure in the stomach and interpret the sensation as indigestion.

NOTE: Generally speaking, sharp, stabbing pains are usually not signals of a heart attack. Furthermore, chest pains brought on by breathing or movement do not constitute such signals.

If you or a family member experience any of these symptoms, you should call your doctor or hospital immediately for an ambulance. On the other hand, if you can get to the hospital emergency room faster by car, have someone drive you. But don't drive yourself!

Above all, don't delay! Minutes and even seconds can count in this situation. The faster you can receive medical attention, the better your chances of recovery will be.

What should you do if a friend or loved one is experiencing these symptoms? Over the years, I've found the tips advocated by my own hospital, the Montefiore Medical Center, to be helpful in advising patients:

- Stay calm.
- Loosen the heart-attack victim's clothing around the neck and midriff.
- Call the doctor or an ambulance.
- If help isn't available immediately, take the person to a hospital emergency room without delay.
- If possible, take someone with you in the car who knows how to administer cardiopulmonary resuscitation (CPR). If the victim loses consciousness and there is no pulse or if breathing stops, CPR should be started and continued until medical help arrives.
- Don't allow the victim to walk from the car to the emergency room. Instead, carry the person or run into the hospital and ask for a stretcher or wheelchair.

What Is the Connection Between Angina and Heart Disease?

I'm often asked by my patients who have cardiovascular problems, "What does it mean when I have angina pain? Is that a signal that a heart attack is coming on?"

First of all, I tell them, angina is not the same as a heart attack. There may be similarities between angina pain and the pain that precedes a myocardial infarction, or heart attack. But if you have had angina before, you soon find you can recognize when that particular pain is occurring.

On the other hand, if you haven't had angina before, and you think the pain may be the signal of the onset of a heart attack, be cautious: Assume you're really having a heart attack. In other words, call your doctor, head for the hospital, and take other measures to protect yourself. It's better to take a false alarm seriously than to assume the real thing is only a false alarm.

Angina, also called "angina pectoris," is a recurring, uncomfortable, dull pain in the chest that occurs when the supply of blood to a part of the heart muscle is insufficient. Usually, the anginal pain appears because the coronary arteries are occluded, or partially closed down, as a result of atherosclerosis. But an anginal attack doesn't necessarily indicate damage to the heart muscle, as happens with a heart attack.

Usually, anginal pains last only a few minutes and are characterized by a sense of heaviness, tightness, burning, squeezing, or pressure. The discomfort or pain typically strikes just behind the breastbone.

What can you do about angina? To counter an attack, your physician may prescribe nitroglycerin pills or some other medication. Also, you can help prevent attacks by limiting or managing certain activities that have been pinpointed by the American Heart Association as culprits in triggering angina. Specifically, you should try:

- controlling your physical activity;
- avoiding emotionally upsetting situations;
- adopting good eating habits, such as a low-fat, low-cholesterol, high-fiber diet that can prevent and may even reverse the development of atherosclerosis;
- checking with your doctor about your use of alcohol; and
- avoiding cigarette smoking.

KEY FACTS

FIVE COMMON STEPS
IN THE DEVELOPMENT OF CARDIOVASCULAR
DISEASE

1. *Coronary atherosclerosis.* This term refers to the fatty deposits that commonly develop over the lifetime in human arteries, and specifically in the coronary arteries, which carry life-sustaining blood to the heart muscle.

2. *Coronary occlusion.* This term refers to the degree of narrowing or closing of the coronary arteries resulting from atherosclerosis. Many people may be walking about with as much as 50 to 60 percent occlusion, though they are free of symptoms.

3. *Ischemic heart disease.* When the occlusion or closing of the coronary arteries to the heart passes the 50 to 60 percent level, a person may begin to show signs of *ischemia.* This condition involves a lack of blood flow, including oxygen, to a part of the body, in this case, the heart. Sometimes, a spasm may result in a further reduction of the blood supply to the heart. Typically, this condition shows up on an electrocardiogram.

4. *Angina pectoris.* Also known simply as "angina," this condition involves pain in the center of the chest, which is a common sequel to the narrowing of a coronary artery. The pain, which signals inadequate circulation to the heart muscle, may be brought on by physical effort and usually subsides after rest or administration of nitroglycerin. *Note:* Not everyone with atherosclerosis or coronary occlusion has angina.

5. *Myocardial infarction.* This event, which is commonly called a "heart attack," is the last step in the progressive closing-off of the circulation of blood to the heart. With myocardial infarction, the circulation is actually shut off for a sufficient time to jeopardize or destroy a portion of the heart muscle. Usually, an infarction occurs when a blood clot *(thrombosis)* totally closes off the flow of blood through the narrowed coronary arteries.

Atherosclerosis: The Major Villain in Cardiovascular Disease

Most heart disease, including heart attacks, can be traced back to the condition that we doctors call *atherosclerosis,* popularly known as "hardening of the arteries."

In brief, atherosclerosis involves a gradual, progressive buildup of fatty deposits, called *plaque,* in the body's arteries. This process often begins quite early in life and is caused by the sticking in the artery walls of cholesterol and of a protein known as *apolipoprotein B,* which is attached to the cholesterol. The presence of this cholesterol and its companion protein in the blood derives from two major sources: (1) a diet that includes saturated fats and cholesterol, and (2) the internal production of cholesterol by the liver.

The Cholesterol Connection

It used to be that hardening of the arteries was regarded as an inevitable development in some people. As I've already mentioned, I was told that heart disease was the "doctor's disease." For that matter, well before my time, Sir Arthur Conan Doyle suggested in his Sherlock Holmes mystery *The Hound of the Baskervilles* that a possible murder victim might have died as a result of an inevitable tendency toward hardening of the arteries that ran in his family. (In fact, Holmes proved later that the cause of death was *not* the "inevitable" familial atherosclerosis, but the work of a diabolical murderer.)

Today, our attitude toward atherosclerosis has changed considerably. We not only refuse to accept as inevitable the loss of health and perhaps even of life from hardening of the arteries; we've also identified the management of blood cholesterol as a major factor in combating the disease.

What exactly is cholesterol?

It's an odorless, white, waxy, powdery substance that you can't taste or see in the foods you eat. But it's there! Cholesterol is found in all foods of animal origin; in fact, it's an essential part of every animal cell. High on the list of cholesterol usage is its finding in such key body substances as cell walls and hormones.

HEALTH REPORT

LOWER CHOLESTEROL LEVELS MEAN LOWER DEATH RATES

In a British study published in 1986, the cholesterol levels of 17,718 civil servants, aged forty to sixty-four, were measured and followed up over a ten-year period. Of the participants, 703 died of heart attacks.

The researchers found a direct correlation between rising levels of cholesterol and coronary death rate. The lower the total cholesterol, the lower the death rate.

Specifically, those in the study who were in the lowest 10 percent of cholesterol levels did better than the next higher 10 percent, and so on. The authors calculated that lowering cholesterol levels by 8 percent for the entire population would lower the death rate by 8 percent over a ten-year period.

G. Rose and M. Shipley, "Plasma Cholesterol Concentration and Death from Coronary Heart Disease: 10 Year Results of the Whitehall Study," *British Medical Journal* 293 (1986): 306.

About three-fourths of the cholesterol in our bodies is produced internally by the liver. The rest comes in through our diets, either directly in the cholesterol-containing foods we eat, or indirectly, by the interaction of the saturated fats in foods with the body's chemistry. Many experts believe that our intake of saturated fats is even more important in raising our cholesterol levels than is our consumption of cholesterol itself.

● *"Good" and "bad" cholesterol.* Years of medical research have revealed that there are two types of cholesterol-bearing lipoproteins that apparently have quite different impacts on the development of atherosclerosis.

The first type of lipoprotein, low-density lipoprotein (LDL), is known popularly as "bad" cholesterol because it's been linked to the development of atherosclerosis. It's the LDL and a companion protein, apolipoprotein B, that stick in the artery walls and promote the formation of plaque. This plaque, in turn, narrows those artery walls over the years and may eventually be a factor in a total blockage in the coronary arteries, and a heart attack. LDLs make up most of the total cholesterol count reflected in the results of a blood test.

In contrast, the high-density lipoprotein (HDL) is often called the "good" cholesterol because higher levels of HDLs in the blood have been strongly associated with lower levels of coronary artery disease. One theory on the beneficial effects of HDLs is that they act as a kind of "garbage removal service" in the bloodstream: They clean out the extra LDLs and apolipoprotein Bs and thus help prevent the clogging of the arteries through atherosclerosis.

To prevent the development of atherosclerosis, what should your cholesterol levels be?

I realize that a number of popular and comprehensive books and studies on this subject for all age groups are currently in circulation. Some of these contain detailed risk-factor charts at various age levels. But let me suggest the set of simplified cholesterol guidelines for both men and women over fifty shown below. These ranges, which represent my own conclusions about the cholesterol question, are based in part on recommendations by the National Institutes of Health.

In addition to these three figures—the total cholesterol, LDL cholesterol, and HDL cholesterol—many experts also believe that any determination of risk should take into account the ratio of your total cholesterol to HDL cholesterol. In other words, if your total cholesterol is 200 milligrams per deciliter (mg/dl) and your HDL

THE RISK OF DIFFERENT CHOLESTEROL LEVELS

DESIRABLE (MG/DL)	BORDERLINE-HIGH (MG/DL)	HIGH (MG/DL)
Total cholesterol: Less than 200	200–239	240+
LDL ("bad") cholesterol: Less than 130	130–159	160+
HDL ("good") cholesterol: 55 and above	35– 54	Below 35

cholesterol is 50, you have a ratio of 4.0 (200 divided by 50).
Generally speaking, men over 50 years of age should try to keep
their ratios below 4.5, and women over 50 should strive to maintain ratios below 4.0.

So far, I've focused mostly on what can happen if clogging occurs
in the coronary arteries that bring blood to the heart. But there is
also a serious set of problems that may develop when atherosclerosis strikes the "peripheral" vascular system, including the arteries
in the legs and other parts of the body.

   The complaints of one of my patients illustrates how this
condition may come to light. He found he was able to walk shorter
and shorter distances, and for a while, he just assumed that he was
"getting old." But when he described his problems to me, it became evident that he was suffering from *peripheral vascular disease*
(PVD), or atherosclerosis affecting arteries at the periphery of his
body, namely, those in his legs.

   Specifically, this man said, "I can walk about a block, but then
this pain hits my leg and I have to stop. If I wait a minute or two,
then the pain gets better and I can walk for about another block."

   The onset of pain with exercise and its subsidence with rest,
known as *intermittent claudication,* is a typical indication of peripheral vascular disease. It is important to diagnose and treat this
condition early through changes in diet and life-style, or drugs and
surgery if necessary.

HEALTH REPORT

CLOGGING OF THE ARTERIES OUTSIDE THE
HEART

The classic symptom of diminished circulation to the lower
extremities is *intermittent claudication,* a cramplike pain in the
calf that comes on with walking and improves with resting.
These symptoms are a signal of the presence of *peripheral
vascular disease* (PVD).

   But don't jump to any conclusions until you see your
doctor: A similar set of symptoms may occur with an unrelated condition known as *spinal stenosis,* in which there is a
thickening of the long canal where the spinal cord or its
emerging nerves run.

According to a study reported in 1987, one set of findings that point to true PVD is the following:

- In the supine position (lying on one's back), elevation of the legs to a sixty- to seventy-five-degree angle produces pallor and coolness of the skin of the legs.

- Jiggling the ankle twenty to thirty times, as one would in pumping a gas pedal, should lead to pinkness and warmth in the healthy foot. Coolness and pallor indicate peripheral vascular disease.

- Normally, shifting from the supine position to a position where the legs dangle off the side of a table or bed should restore color to the legs within ten seconds, and filling of the veins in about fifteen seconds. If it takes more than thirty-five to forty seconds for this to happen, there may be inadequate circulation in the leg.

Doppler flow studies and other lab findings related to the circulation can confirm the diagnosis and may indicate the level of obstruction.

There are no effective medications for peripheral vascular disease. Exercise is helpful in developing collateral vessels (other vessels that can carry the blood supply) and improving the circulation. Surgical alternatives include bypass operations, cleaning out the clogged artery (endarterectomy), and balloon angioplasty, in which the obstructed area is forcibly dilated.

J. L. Halperin, "Peripheral Vascular Disease: Medical Evaluation and Treatment," *Geriatrics* 42 (1987): 47.

In about a third of the cases of peripheral vascular disease, there is also coronary artery disease. Also, those with PVD are at increased risk for a stroke. PVD pain in the legs may thus forewarn a patient of other, more serious problems.

Are You at Risk for Heart Disease?

As a result of many clinical studies, population surveys, and other scientific investigations, representatives of the American Heart Association and other medical experts have identified a number of personal characteristics that serve as danger signals for the development of heart disease.

KEY FACTS

RISK FACTORS FOR CARDIOVASCULAR DISEASE

- Aging
- Elevated blood cholesterol
- Cigarette smoking
- Family history of heart disease
- Diabetes mellitus
- Hypertension
- Obesity
- Male sex
- Lack of exercise, sedentary life-style
- Early menopause

These signals, called *risk factors,* indicate how likely it is that a given person will eventually suffer from heart disease. Because the risk factors are rooted in statistical analysis, there's no guarantee that a *particular* individual with few risk factors will escape heart disease. Nor is there any guarantee that a particular person with many risk factors will suffer from heart disease. But the *probabilities* are that those with many risk factors will confront cardiovascular problems, and that those without risk factors won't.

Sometimes a risk factor, such as a high blood cholesterol level, may be changed by the individual through diet or other alterations in life-style. Other times, however, risk factors such as a family history of heart disease are "givens": That is, they can't be changed, though the impact of such factors may be reduced by altering other risk factors.

In other parts of this section on cardiovascular problems, I've gone into some detail on how to deal with certain of the coronary risk factors, such as cholesterol levels, hypertension, and sedentary living. But at this point, I want to highlight several of the other key risk factors, namely, smoking, diabetes mellitus, and obesity.

HEALTH REPORT

IS THE EARLOBE CREASE A SIGNAL OF CORONARY ARTERY DISEASE?

The earlobe crease is a wrinkle in the lobe of the ear that may become quite prominent in older people. Wrinkles appearing on the forehead or radiating from the corners of the eyes are clearly associated with emotions or expressions. But these factors can play no part in the development of the earlobe crease, which is located in an immobile part of the body. For these and other reasons, this crease can be regarded as a clear-cut aging change.

But is there something more to the earlobe crease than meets the eye?

Over the past seventeen years, a number of studies suggesting that the earlobe crease is a marker for coronary artery disease have appeared. In effect, if this is true, the crease would be a case of guilt by association: A wrinkle of this sort has no connection with the process that produces narrowing of the arteries through the deposit of fats.

In a study published in 1987, a number of researchers examined various groups with and without coronary artery disease by using angiography (a process involving injecting dye into the arteries and then taking pictures of the vessels). At the same time, the investigators noted whether or not the participants had the earlobe crease.

Their conclusion: There is no valid correlation between the earlobe crease and coronary artery disease. To put this another way, individuals with coronary artery disease may or may not have such a crease.

[COMMENT: I have had an earlobe crease for more than twenty years, and nothing's happened yet! By the way, I often look for the crease in seemingly young entertainers who have had cosmetic surgery, because plastic surgeons typically do not operate on this part of the body. If a person has the crease, you know he may be older than he looks because it's quite rare before age fifty.]

P. M. Brady, M. A. Zire, R. J. Goldgery, et al., "A New Wrinkle to the Earlobe Crease," *Archives of Internal Medicine* 147 (1987): 65.

Smoking

Smoking may contribute to heart disease in a number of ways:

- It reduces the levels of HDL, the "good" cholesterol in the blood.
- It may hasten the progress of atherosclerosis, perhaps by injuring the artery walls and thus allowing more cholesterol and apolipoprotein B to be deposited.
- It may cause coronary thrombosis, or blood clotting that can block the blood flow to the heart muscle.
- It may disturb the rhythmic beating of the heart and, as a result, cause sudden death.

According to various studies, cigarette smokers have a coronary heart disease death rate that is 70 percent greater than that of nonsmokers. Those who smoke two or more packs of cigarettes a day have two to three times the risk of death from heart disease.

Furthermore, smoking *compounds* the danger that accompanies other coronary risk factors. For example, a smoker has double the risk of coronary heart disease of a person who has no major risk factors. But if a person both smokes *and* has another risk factor, such as high cholesterol level or hypertension, his risk of heart disease is multiplied fourfold.

But there is considerable hope for controlling this risk factor. According to the United States surgeon general, if you quit smoking, you lower your risk of heart disease substantially.

According to one study conducted over six years by the National Institutes of Health, those who quit smoking lowered their heart disease risk to half that of the individuals who continued to smoke. Other studies have shown that by five to ten years after quitting, the coronary heart disease death rate for former smokers who had consumed less than one pack of cigarettes daily was virtually the same as that of lifelong nonsmokers. For former smokers who had used more than a pack a day, the risk was also significantly lower than for smokers.

Diabetes Mellitus

I've already dealt in some detail with the problem of diabetes mellitus, a condition characterized by an abnormally high blood sugar level, in the section dealing with nutrition. But it's important at least to refer to it again here as a specific risk factor for cardio-vascular disease.

The adult-onset type of diabetes may appear later in life, and if this problem runs in your family, the chances increase that you may suffer from it yourself. The main problem as far as coronary artery disease is concerned is that diabetes can produce abnormalities in the lipoproteins in the blood, and this process may hasten the development of atherosclerosis.

HEALTH REPORT

AMERICAN ACTIVISM: AN INTERNATIONAL EXAMPLE FOR REDUCING CORONARY RISK

There is a decided contrast between the active U.S. attitude toward coronary artery disease and the attitude prevalent until recently in Britain, according to Dr. J. T. Hart.

"Nowhere has the Atlantic been wider than in professional attitudes to coronary prevention," Dr. Hart says.

In the United States, the word started to spread twenty to thirty years ago with the first work on risk factors. In a remarkably brief time, results were evident:

In American men aged thirty-five to seventy-four, coronary death rates fell from 800 per 100,000 in 1968 to 500 per 100,000 in 1979. In women, rates plunged from 330 to 180.

The 1987 British Cardiac Society's endorsement of a national campaign to lower coronary artery disease expresses some reservations about the American consensus views, noting that the coagulation system in the blood may be as much involved in the disease as cholesterol levels. But Hart cautions that any doubt about this shouldn't be used to justify inertia.

[NOTE: There can be no doubt that the U.S. work on risk factors has been most instructive to the rest of the world. High-risk countries such as Finland, which have put into operation the dietary basics and other practices advocated in the United States, have already experienced striking declines in mortality from heart disease.]

J. T. Hart, "Coronary Prevention in Britain: Action at Last?" *British Medical Journal* 294 (1987): 725.

Many people who have the adult version of diabetes mellitus are overweight, and an effective way to counter the effects of this risk factor is simply to take off those extra pounds. The loss of extra fat can reduce the glucose (sugar) in your blood and may even cure the disease.

But the importance of weight loss as a way of reducing your risk of coronary artery disease isn't by any means limited to diabetes, as we'll see in the following chapter.

11

OBESITY: A CONTROLLABLE CORONARY RISK FACTOR

A rotund husband and wife, both in their late seventies, had managed to live to a relatively old age, apparently because they had good genes. But they weren't enjoying themselves very much, primarily because of weight-related health problems. Increasingly, the husband found himself facing the fact that if he didn't take some sort of countermeasures quite soon, he could be facing a threat to his very life.

This man had already undergone two coronary bypass operations, and his high cholesterol levels and high-calorie, high-fat diet portended ongoing cardiovascular disease. The woman had been wrestling with hypertension for several years, and gradually, she had found she was having to cut down on social activities she loved.

She said, "I just don't feel that well a lot of the time. And I lack the energy to do the things I used to do quite easily."

Their main problem? Poor nutrition, which was wreaking havoc with their health in a number of ways, especially in promoting that important coronary risk factor, obesity. My advice: "You have to change your diets! If you don't, your health will worsen, and you may well shorten your lives."

HEALTH REPORT

WEIGHT AND LONGEVITY

In the respected Framingham Heart Study, a population of sixty-five-year-old nonsmokers was singled out and followed for about twenty-three years. The heaviest 30 percent of those studied had a distinctly increased mortality rate when compared with the lightest 10 to 30 percent. The main causes of death were cardiovascular disease and cancer. This increased risk associated with overweight could not be ascribed to cholesterol or sugar levels. The findings indicate that in those past sixty-five, obesity is indeed a definite risk factor, even in a nonsmoking group.

Still, the thinnest 10 percent in the study suffered the greatest mortality, especially in the first four years of the follow-up. The reason? Apparently, many of those who were *very* thin were already suffering from a disease process. On the other hand, the researchers indicated that those who have been thin all their lives may not exhibit this increased risk.

T. Harris, E. F. Cook, R. Garrison, et al., "Body Mass Index and Mortality Among Nonsmoking Older Persons: The Framingham Heart Study," *The Journal of the American Medical Association* 259 (1988): 1520.

As we've seen earlier, many older people tend to lose weight. But some manage to retain a voracious appetite well into old age, though in most cases, that means extra pounds and deteriorating health. In particular, overweight people—those with too much fatty tissue—are at greater than normal risk for coronary artery disease. Why the increased risk? Some of the known factors are the following:

• Obesity raises the levels of blood fats (or lipids), such as cholesterol, and triglycerides, which are often associated with cardiovascular disease.

• Obesity aggravates diabetes mellitus, which is also a coronary risk factor.

• Obesity raises blood pressure.

HEALTH REPORT

OVERWEIGHT AND SUDDEN DEATH

A new study on the relationship between overweight and sudden death begins with this two-thousand-year-old observation by Hippocrates: "Sudden death is more common in those who are naturally fat than in the lean."

The obese people in this study were 150 percent above their ideal weight, and those classified as lean subjects were less than 105 percent of their ideal weight, as measured by the Metropolitan Life Insurance Company's tables. All the participants were apparently free of coronary disease and were not using antihypertensive drugs.

After continuous tracings of an electrocardiograph were performed for 24 hours on the participants, half of the obese people were shown to have thickening of the wall of the heart. There were many more electrocardiographic abnormalities in the obese subjects, especially premature ventricular contractions (PVCs). PVCs are regarded as evidence of irritability of the heart muscle and are often found when there is evidence of inadequate circulation to the muscle.

The authors also noted that the obese persons who are put on a high-protein, low-carbohydrate diet, with a resultant excessive weight loss, may encounter serious health problems. Specifically, they may exhibit increased electrocardiographic abnormalities, rapid heart rate, and, occasionally, sudden death.

"Clearly, this dire complication must be considered before obese patients are allowed to embark on a weight reduction program without medical supervision," the researchers said.

F. H. Messerli, B. D. Nunez, H. O. Ventura, and D. W. Snyder, "Overweight and Sudden Death," *Archives of Internal Medicine* 147 (1987): 1725.

In addition to these factors, obesity, all by itself, is increasingly being recognized as an independent risk factor for cardiovascular trouble. The Framingham Study, for example, has reported that if everyone could maintain an optimal weight, there would be 25 percent less coronary heart disease and 35 percent less cardiac failure or strokes in the general population.

Obesity is a condition that begins to emerge as a problem when more than about 22 percent of a man's or 24 percent of a woman's body weight consists of fatty tissue. The more those percentages increase, the greater the risk of incurring a variety of health problems.

According to other definitions of obesity, the condition begins to be serious when a person is thirty to forty pounds overweight, or perhaps when actual weight exceeds ideal body weight by 10 to 15 percent. Usually, "ideal body weight" is determined by classifying the person as having a light, medium, or heavy build and then comparing the weight with those of others of the same sex and height. The Metropolitan Life Insurance Company has published standard charts showing these figures.

Obesity has been identified by a number of experts as an independent risk factor for diabetes, for hypertension, for higher cholesterol levels—and perhaps even for a shortened life span.

Sometimes, overeaters concentrate on sweets or other foods that have few essential nutrients. As a result, they may consume too many calories, but too few key vitamins and minerals. Usually, however, those who overload on food are simply getting too much of a good thing. They need to worry more about cutting unnecessary calories, rather than upping their intake of the right nutrients.

So what can you do to lose those unwanted pounds?

Obviously, people have a variety of ideas about losing weight, and they have written countless best-selling books to promote their theories. But I'd like to share with you an approach that has worked for many of my own patients, without requiring them to turn their lives upside down or embark on a completely weird and unfamiliar eating and cooking regimen. Instead, this weight-loss program is what I call my "Supersimple Rules for Weight Reduction."

Supersimple Rules for Weight Reduction

First, if you want to lose weight, remember the Law of the Calorie: Fat comes from extra calories; it diminishes with lessened calories. There are no waivers or exceptions to this law! So I'd suggest that you reduce your intake of calories to about one thousand per day. If you can't function on that amount of food, at least try to keep your intake below fourteen hundred calories.

Second, when you begin to cut calories, *do not* reduce your level of physical activity. In fact, if you've been sedentary, it's a good idea to exercise more. Various studies have shown that long-term weight loss is best achieved when you combine exercise with dietary calorie cutting. Among other things, exercise helps you burn up those extra calories (walking one mile burns up nearly one hundred calories!).

Third, eat your food each day in *six* meals instead of the usual three. In that way, you'll be more likely to cut your appetite—and the temptations to snack—by always keeping some food in your stomach. Now, here's a sample one-day, six-meal menu for a 1,000-calorie diet, which includes a healthy balance among the essential food groups. Calories are indicated in parentheses.

SPECIAL NOTES: Fruit juice includes orange, grapefruit, and tomato.

All meat, fish, or fowl must be broiled, boiled, or roasted. Only lean cuts of beef, lamb, or veal should be served.

Egg substitutes may include 4 tablespoons of cottage cheese or ½ cup of cold cereal with 3 ounces of fat-free milk.

Coffee and tea may be served as you desire and in the amounts you can tolerate, but without cream or sugar. You can also drink sodas that contain no or minimal calories.

If you have special dietary requirements, such as a need for an extremely low fat or low cholesterol intake, you'll have to make adjustments in consultation with your doctor or a nutritionist. Keep in mind that items such as canned soup may be high in salt. If you are on a salt-restricted diet, check the labels.

Fruits include the following:

½ Cantaloupe
Melon wedge
Small orange
Medium peach
Pineapple slice
1 Cup of strawberries
½ Slice watermelon
Small apple
3 Medium apricots
½ Cup blueberries
½ Cup cherries
½ Pear

Canned soups include 7-ounce portions of the following:

Beef noodle
Beef broth
Chicken vegetable
Chicken gumbo
Chicken with rice
Onion
Cream of asparagus
Cream of celery
Manhattan clam chowder

Vegetables include ½ cup portions of the following:

Asparagus
Beet greens
Broccoli
Cauliflower
Celery
Cucumber
Mushrooms
Radishes
Sauerkraut
Spinach
Squash
String beans
Beets

Cabbage
Green pepper
Turnips

Finally, if you want to increase the calories in this diet from 1,000 to 1,400 per day, you can begin to double the portions of desired foods, beginning with the vegetables and fruits. If you need extra protein, you can double the portions of meat, poultry, and fish until you reach the 1,400-calorie limit.

Now, here are the sample menus; calories are indicated in parentheses.

Breakfast
3 Ounces fruit juice (40)
1 Egg or egg substitute (75)
½ Slice wheat bread (30)

Midmorning
2 Ounces fat-free milk (50)
1 Slice wheat bread (60)

Lunch
1 Cup soup (60)
1 Medium tomato and ¼ head lettuce (40)
4 Tablespoons cottage cheese (or 1 egg) (60)
1 Serving fruit (50)

Here's an alternative lunch
½ Cup soup (30)
2 Ounces hamburger (130)
1 Serving fruit (50)

Midafternoon
3 Ounces gelatin or Jell-O (50)
4 Ounces fat-free milk (50)

Supper
2 Cubes bouillon (5)
1 3-Ounce serving meat, or ½ small chicken, or
   4 ounces fish or turkey (195)
2 Servings vegetables (40)
½ Serving pat corn oil margarine (25)
1 Slice wheat bread or 1 serving fruit (50)

Bedtime
8 Ounces buttermilk, or 1 6-ounce cup plain
yogurt with fruit, or repeat midmorning or
midafternoon meal (110)

Finally, I make no promises about the rate at which this diet will take off the pounds. But I do guarantee that if you stick with it and follow the simple rules I've included here, you will lose weight, and probably much more quickly than you ever expected!

HEALTH REPORT

WEIGHT LOSS: A MUST FOR OBESE DIABETICS

The difficulty overweight diabetic patients face in achieving normal weight is well known, but if they can lose weight, they show significant improvement in their health.

A study reported in the *Archives of Internal Medicine* evaluated the effect of modest weight losses in 114 diabetics who were enrolled in a behavioral weight-control program. The patients were followed by monitoring the glycosylated hemoglobin of the blood (hb A_1c), a good test for overall control of the diabetes.

The results? The average weight loss of the participants was about twelve pounds. One person lost thirty-seven pounds. The findings showed that the greater the weight loss, the greater the improvement in the diabetes. Blood fat and cholesterol levels also improved with weight loss.

All patients who lost as much as twenty-two pounds, even those who remained above their ideal weight, showed significant improvement in their diabetes. But those who lost fifteen pounds or less had no significant improvement. The patients with the greater losses were generally able to discontinue use of their antidiabetes medications.

R. R. Wing, R. Kieske, L. H. Epstein, et al., "Long-Term Effects of Modest Weight Loss in Type II Diabetic Patients," *Archives of Internal Medicine* 147 (1987): 1749.

Now, let's move on to a nutrition-related topic that is relevant to weight loss and has been gaining popularity in recent years: what I call the trend toward adopting a "subnutrition strategy."

Should You Try "Subnutrition"?

Years ago, one of Mahatma Gandhi's physicians, a bright-eyed, energetic Indian woman, paid me a visit after the death of the great Hindu nationalist leader and social reformer. The reason for her visit, she said, was that she knew I was interested in the way the diets of different ethnic and national groups had influenced their health.

This woman had become increasingly aware that the only patients she had been seeing with the typical Western European and American disorders of hypertension and heart attacks were the upper-class Hindus, most of whom had adopted Western diets. The subnourished masses, she had noted, usually escaped cardio-vascular diseases.

As it happened, her patient Mahatma Gandhi ate the "poor person's" diet, and he had enjoyed good health and high energy levels all his life, up to the time he was assassinated. So this physician thought I might be interested in some "inside information" about the impact of Gandhi's personal nutritional habits.

Furthermore, this woman said that although she had come from a middle-class Hindu family, she had been attracted to Gandhi and his doctrines; as a matter of fact, she had even adopted his diet. As we talked, she reminded me that the Gandhi diet was exceedingly sparse. It was a very strict vegetarian regimen, with many special roots and plants you'd never find in a typical Western grocery store.

"At first, when I began to follow this diet, I experienced a peculiar light-headed sensation," she told me. "I really didn't feel too well. But then, this feeling disappeared, and I felt better than I had ever felt before. My head got very clear. I realized that up until that point, I had mostly been a great big digestive machine!"

She said that before converting to Gandhi's style of diet, she sat down three times a day and typically ate until she was sated. But then, rumblings and distension in her digestive tract typically caused her to feel uncomfortable, and she often became quite sleepy just after a meal. The sleepiness arose from the fact that after a big meal, much of her circulation was being diverted to the operation of her digestive system.

HEALTH REPORT

SUBNUTRITION AND MAXIMUM LIFE SPAN

Maximum life span (MLS) is the age attained by the oldest person in a population. In humans, this is 110 to 115 years.

The *average* life span has been extended over recent decades to around 74 years, chiefly by the abolition of important infections and, more recently, improvements in cardiovascular mortality rate. To attain *maximum* life span, however, an alteration in the *rate* of aging is necessary.

Dr. R. L. Walford, an expert on geriatric immunology and also subnutrition, believes that attaining MLS is feasible by the nutritional route: specifically, by a drastic reduction in caloric intake. To achieve subnutrition and prevent malnutrition, a 50 percent reduction in calories, with appropriate additions of vitamins, minerals, and other nutrients, has to be achieved.

Walford notes that the maximum life span achieved by mice when eating normally is less than forty-four months. But calorically restricted mice regularly live past fifty-four months. Citing this finding and studies in other species, Walford believes the case for prolongation of life by subnutrition has been clearly proved.

He notes that on the Japanese island of Okinawa, people consume a high-quality diet that is substantially lower in calories than the diet of other Japanese. The Okinawans are somewhat shorter, but not genetically different. Yet they exhibit a lesser incidence and later onset of the "diseases of aging." There are fifteen to forty times more centenarians on Okinawa than elsewhere in Japan!

R. L. Walford, "The Extension of Maximum Life Span," *Clinics in Geriatric Medicine* 1 (1985): 29.

But everything changed after she began to practice on Gandhi's diet. She remained wide awake throughout the day and felt much more energetic than in the past. She also lost about eighteen pounds of extra fat.

I mostly listened during this meeting, and I continued to ponder what this woman had told me long after she left. She reenforced my conviction that we Americans—and that included me!—were the cardiovascular victims of diets too rich in meats, fats, and calories. That was forty years ago, and yet much subsequent research has borne out the truth of these ideas. The more I considered the problems of my patients and other older people whom I knew, the more convinced I became that some suitable variations of Gandhi's "poor man's diet" would prevent disease in most of us. Perhaps all this seems too simple to be true, but it *is* true, nonetheless.

A Strategy for Limiting Your Calories

The basic guideline for developing any wise subnutrition strategy is this: You may decide to limit your calories more as you get older, but *do not* limit your necessary nutrients. If you begin to cut the vitamins and minerals your body and mind need for good health, any benefits you may achieve from subnutrition will quickly evaporate. Now, with these basic thoughts in mind, let's consider some of the evidence that favors the limitation of calories.

Is there much scientific basis for limiting calories in this way? Indeed, all the animal studies suggest that a careful restriction of calories may retard the aging process. In studies made a half century ago, Clive M. McCay demonstrated that the life span of the rat could be virtually doubled if the animal's daily intake of calories were cut by 30 percent. The reproductive functions of these animals continued far longer than those of ordinary rats, and the animals suffered fewer spontaneous tumors, degenerative disorders, and chronic infectious diseases. Overall, the subnourished rats maintained the capacities of their immune systems longer than the rats who ate more. All succeeding animal studies have confirmed the McCay experiment. At present, calorie restriction remains the only known way to achieve a major extension of life span.

Furthermore, many researchers feel that the same should be true of humans. But when you look at the many different human societies with their vastly differing food intakes, there is no clear-cut evidence indicating that subnutrition is associated with increased longevity. The trouble is that human subnutrition is usually *involuntary* and is commonly associated with many other aspects of poor nutrition, poor hygiene, and poor medical care: all of which shorten the life span and cancel the benefits of caloric limitation.

Solid scientific studies of the effect of subnutrition on human beings remain to be done. But there are encouraging signs from a number of quarters. For example, in a twenty-four-year longitudinal study of women in California, the women who lived longest, with an average age of seventy-five, had decreased their intake of calories over the twenty-four-year period by 25 percent.

BUT NOTE: Although the surviving women in the study cut their calories by reducing their intake of fat and carbohydrates, they maintained and in some cases (as with vitamin C, niacin, and proteins) *increased* their intake of important nutrients.

"The findings on nutrient intake would seem to indicate that such patterns may contribute to the maintenance of good health in later life," concluded Dr. Eleanor D. Schlenker of the University of Vermont, who reported on this study for the National Institute on Aging in Baltimore.

Before you decide to decrease your calorie intake, however, a few words of caution are in order:

First, the studies on the effect of subnutrition are not always consistent. The Baltimore Longitudinal Aging Study, for instance, reported that the men in the study who lived longest were not the thinnest ones, but rather, the modestly overweight! Of course, excessive obesity has been associated with heart disease and other serious health problems, and so I certainly wouldn't suggest that you accept this finding as a basis for adding extra pounds. But still, the Baltimore Study suggests that a great deal more work needs to be done in this area before we can reach any hard-and-fast conclusions.

In my practice, I've followed some people through their sixties and seventies who have been gaining weight to some degree, year after year. These patients seem to be unusually good "agers." They remain lively, energetic, and youthful in many ways. It's possible that their bounciness, good appetites, and steady weight gains are good markers for successful aging. But I also ask myself this question: What would have been the outcome in their health if they had curbed their caloric intake and not gained the extra weight? They might possibly live longer and also be freer of disease. But no such study has ever been done, and I don't see any in the offing.

Second, even those who advocate restricting calories disagree on such points as the effect of limiting protein consumption. Dr. Barrows of the National Institute on Aging found that up to a point, reducing protein consumption in animals can increase their life span. But when you limit their protein too much, their longevity decreases.

In practical terms, what can we conclude from all this?

On the whole, I think there is a great deal to be said for those who argue that cutting calories can increase clarity of thinking, energy levels, and perhaps even life expectancy. But in the same breath, I also must emphasize a series of caveats:

First, before you try to make any adjustments in your diet, consult your physician. More harm has been done to people's health by fad diets than perhaps any other single factor.

Second, be sure that if you do cut calories, you *do not* cut out those foods that supply you with important vitamins and minerals.

For example, as we've already seen, too many older people avoid high-calcium foods such as milk either because they don't like them or because they cause gas, cramps, or other discomforts. Typically, these problems occur because of lactose intolerance, an inability to digest milk sugars properly. But if you avoid these foods, you probably will not be getting enough calcium, and calcium is absolutely essential to enable both men and women to ward off the brittle bones of osteoporosis that become an increasing threat with age. A possible solution, if recommended by your doctor, is to add lactase, sold at many drugstores, to the milk. It "digests" the offending lactose. Some supermarkets now sell milk that has been so treated.

Third, if you cut calories, focus on those foods that contain the "empty" or "hollow" calories: the sugary desserts, candies, and junk foods that add pounds without supplying necessary body-strengthening nutrients such as vitamins and minerals. You should also eliminate the saturated fats and high-cholesterol foods, such as eggs.

NOTE: You can keep your intake of calcium up and at the same time reduce your intake of saturated fats and cholesterol if you drink skim milk rather than whole milk. In fact, skim milk contains slightly more calcium than whole milk!

Finally, monitor your feelings and energy levels after you reduce your calorie intake. If after a week or so you find that you feel more fatigued or run-down, especially just before a scheduled meal, you may not be consuming enough calories to maintain your necessary energy levels. In such a case, feel free to increase your intake of high-energy, nutritious foods, even though this means an increase in your calorie levels.

In the last analysis, just remember this: You will not help your health—or your enjoyment of your later years—by restricting your diet so much that you do not feel up to performing as your old energetic and active self. As you get older, you should certainly avoid eating too much. But at the same time, it is absolutely essential that you eat enough! Probably the best rule of thumb is "neither too thin nor too fat!"

This, then, is a brief introduction to some of the basic principles of fighting obesity. If you have a tendency to become overweight, it's essential that you find an intelligent strategy for limiting your calories, while still being sure that you get all the necessary nutrients. In this way, you'll be much more likely to stay healthy and happy and eliminate what is perhaps the most controllable coronary risk factor from your life.

12

LOWERING YOUR CHOLESTEROL RISK THROUGH YOUR DIET

When fifty-eight-year-old Will came to me for a comprehensive checkup, I welcomed him with open arms because I had been trying to get him in for a complete exam for years. He would see me when something went wrong, such as an infection or a persistent cough that was keeping him awake at night or some other ailment that he didn't feel he could handle himself. But in general, he was a "do-it-yourself" type, who harbored a deep distrust of doctors and adhered to a personal health philosophy of "if-it-ain't-broke-don't-fix-it."

Unfortunately, however, a person does not always know whether his body is "broke" or not—at least not until a medical problem has progressed so far that it becomes a serious threat to health and even life. Many dangers to our physical well-being lie hidden for years, and when they finally emerge in the form of some symptom, it may be too late by that time to act effectively.

Fortunately for Will, his exam revealed a major problem with his cholesterol level *before* the appearance of any serious symptoms such as a heart attack or sudden death. Specifically, his cholesterol reading was 265 mg/dl, a result that placed him well within the high-risk category.

My response? I placed him on a low-saturated-fat, low-cholesterol diet, but *without* any cholesterol-lowering medications. I also directed him to report to me in three months for another blood test, to find out whether the diet was working. If it did not seem to be lowering his cholesterol significantly, then I planned to put him on medications.

Will, I should mention, did *not* look like the kind of person who needed a diet. He regularly played tennis and jogged; his body fat was less than 20 percent of his total body weight. In fact, when I proposed the dietary approach, he protested: "Doc, if I tell my wife I'm going on a diet, she'll think I'm crazy! And she'll think *you're* crazy too! She's always trying to fatten me up!"

But I told him that apart from being relatively unconcerned about what his wife thought about my mental state, the purpose of this diet had nothing to do with weight. If Will had been obese, I would have recommended a weight-loss diet of the type outlined in Chapter 11. His problem, though dietary, really had no relation to calories: The problem was saturated fats and cholesterol.

"I expect you to continue to eat about as many calories as you're eating now," I told him. "The only difference is that what you'll be eating will be quite different."

Among other things, I explained, he would be eliminating those two eggs and the bacon he had been consuming for breakfast every morning, and the hamburgers and french fries for lunch, and the rich French foods and pastries his gourmet-cooking spouse frequently provided to "fatten him up." I handed him a list of low-fat, low-cholesterol foods and explained the other basics of this diet, which emphasized balanced nutrition along with the cholesterol-lowering principles.

Will grudgingly accepted what I was telling him, but I must say, I was somewhat pessimistic about his prospects for following the regimen I had outlined. I had seen too many people, including those who were obviously much more convinced than Will, start off with good intentions but then fall by the wayside in their low-fat, low-cholesterol dietary objectives. As a matter of fact, I had more or less consigned Will to that category of people who would have to use medications.

When he returned to see me three months later, I gave him another blood test and was surprised by the result almost to the point of being speechless. His total cholesterol level was now down to 195!

"I don't believe this!" I exclaimed. "This is amazing!"

"What's so amazing?" Will asked matter-of-factly. "You said this diet would work, and it did. So what's the big surprise?"

I didn't see much point in laboring the fact that many people who are prescribed one of these diets do not stay on it. Certainly, I didn't want to encourage him to change the successful track he was on. My surprise, I should emphasize again, was not that the diet principles worked: They usually do if a person adheres to them faithfully. Instead, I was amazed that Will was one of those disciplined, committed people who saw a threat to his health early because of the cholesterol risk factor and then resolved to act decisively.

What exactly did I tell Will about how to lower his cholesterol successfully? In the following pages, I will outline the major nutritional principles and foods that we discussed. I have also included a list of the fat contents of various foods, which you can use in your daily menus.

If you are a person who also has a cholesterol problem—and if you can make a solid commitment to changing your way of eating—these guidelines should be as helpful for you as they were for Will.

The Basics of a Balanced Cholesterol-Lowering Diet

One of the first questions many people ask me when I suggest a cholesterol-lowering diet is "How many calories am I supposed to consume each day?"

The answer to this question is a very individual matter because each person's metabolism, including the rate at which he or she

HEALTH REPORT

THE IMPACT OF NUTRITION
ON CARDIOVASCULAR DISEASE IN THE ELDERLY

William B. Kannel, the director of the highly respected Framingham Study, has pointed out in a recent medical article that many cardiovascular risk factors in older people can be improved by dietary modification and weight control.

He notes that hypertension, elevated cholesterol, impaired glucose (sugar) tolerance, and obesity are all responsive to diet. Some suggestions:

- Cut excess calories.
- Reduce saturated fats.
- Cut cholesterol.
- Reduce salt.
- Increase potassium.
- Increase calcium.
- Increase magnesium.
- Add fiber.
- Add polyunsaturated fats.
- Add vegetable proteins.

Kannel notes that in the Oslo diet modification study, middle-aged high-risk men experienced a 47 percent reduction in coronary heart disease and in deaths related to coronary heart disease. These men lowered their serum (blood) cholesterol level by an average of 13 percent.

Kannel also says that although consumption of a little alcohol may be beneficial, a higher level of use seems to be responsible for 10 percent of the hypertension in men, and 1 percent of that in women.

Furthermore, it is helpful to cut calories derived from fats: In Japan, only 10 to 15 percent of calories consumed are fat-derived, and life expectancy exceeds that in the United States for individuals of all ages, including the elderly.

"A low sodium, low fat, high fiber diet may be as effective as a diuretic for mild hypertension," Kannel observed.

W. B. Kannel, "Nutritional Contributors to Cardiovascular Disease in the Elderly," *Journal of the American Geriatrics Society* 34 (1986): 27.

burns up calories, is different. On average, however, I recommend that moderately active older women limit their intake of calories each day to fourteen hundred to sixteen hundred. Moderately active older men should consume two thousand to twenty-five hundred calories per day.

On the other hand, if you are quite active—for example, if you engage in vigorous exercise regularly—you may well find you have to consume more calories to maintain your weight and energy levels. If you need to lose weight, you will want to consume fewer. You'll note that in Chapter 11 I've included some guidelines for helping older people design a weight-reduction diet.

In addition to these calorie considerations, I tell my high-cholesterol patients to follow the suggestions about balanced diets put out by the American Heart Association and other recognized organizations and experts. In general, I sum up these key dietary principles for them this way: Older people on a cholesterol-lowering diet should strive for balance in their nutrition, much as those who are not following a special diet should. Specifically, the healthiest low-fat diets usually contain the following elements:

Protein

About 10 to 20 percent of your total calories each day should come from protein.

Protein is the fundamental substance that makes up the various parts of our bodies, including muscles, bones, brain, skin, blood, and various organs. The protein in your body is especially important because it is a key factor in helping your body's cells to grow and repair themselves. Protein also helps form the antibodies that resist diseases.

Unlike fats and carbohydrates, proteins cannot be stored in your body. On a protein-deficient diet, the body will be driven to breaking down its own cells, such as those in the muscles.

What foods contain protein? What we call "complete" proteins can be found in meat, fish, chicken, dairy products, and eggs. They contain all eleven *essential amino acids,* the irreplaceable nutrients that compose protein and are the basic building blocks of life.

Plants also contain proteins, though some are considered "incomplete" because they do not have all the essential amino acids.

Corn, for example, lacks the essential amino acid tryptophan. Still, when you combine these plant proteins with animal foods that have complete proteins, the plant protein can then become complete.

KEY FACTS

OUR UP-TO-DATE UNDERSTANDING OF CAFFEINE

A 1987 review in the *British Medical Journal,* discussing caffeine as "probably the world's most popular drug," makes these points:

One study has suggested that boiled but not filtered coffee may raise the blood cholesterol.

There is no evidence that clearly indicates a relationship of coffee to heart attacks, but caffeine may cause arrhythmias (irregular heartbeats).

One important study showed no relation between coffee intake and any major cause of death.

In moderate doses, caffeine can elevate a person's mood and intellectual performance. Larger doses may produce anxiety, insomnia, headache, irritability, tremor, or gastrointestinal upset.

Prudence in using caffeine is advised for those with heart disease, elevated blood cholesterol, anxiety, and psychiatric disorders.

NOTE: Coffee intake has also been linked to an increased incidence of cysts in the breast in some women.

C. H. Ashton, "Caffeine and Health," *British Medical Journal* 275 (1987): 1293.

Foods that provide protein carry a kind of "fringe benefit" in that they are often the major sources of essential vitamins and minerals that your body needs. But again, plant proteins may not measure up: Strict vegetarians, for instance, may be on B_{12}-deficient diets; this vitamin is not made by the human body and is very difficult to get in sufficient quantities from sources other than fish, pork, eggs, organ meats, milk and dairy products, or vitamin supplements.

Carbohydrates

For the most balanced low-cholesterol diet, it is advisable that at least 50 to 60 percent of your total calories each day consist of carbohydrates.

But it is also *very* important to remember there are two types of carbohydrates: complex and simple. The first, *complex carbohydrates,* are good for your body; the second, *simple carbohydrates,* are not so good and should be strictly limited or eliminated entirely.

Complex carbohydrates include the starches that can be found in whole-grain cereals, legumes, grains, potatoes, and other vegetables. Fruits and milk also contain complex carbohydrates. As with protein, these foods can supply necessary vitamins, minerals, and fiber, in addition to the calories required for energy.

In contrast, simple carbohydrates—which are found in sugar-loaded foods such as desserts, candy, honey, and pastries—contain empty calories, with few additional nutrients. So it is best to cut down on sweets and increase fruits, vegetables, and other complex carbohydrates.

I am sometimes asked how breads and high-fiber foods fit into this carbohydrate scenario. In brief, breads and cereals are better for you if they are made from whole-grain products. These include whole wheat and rye breads, crackers, and cereals. Other common foods are bran cereals and muffins, oatmeal, barley, and brown rice.

Recent studies have suggested that water-soluble fibers such as oat bran can act independently to help lower cholesterol. Here are a few of the findings:

• At the University of Kentucky, participants in a study lowered their cholesterol by an average of 13 percent in only ten days by adding 3.5 ounces of oat bran to their diets. They made no other changes in their diets. One of the participants in this study even lowered his cholesterol level by 30 percent during the ten-day period.

• In a Northwestern University study, one group of people with average cholesterol levels of about 210 mg/dl added 2 ounces of oat bran each day to a diet recommended by the American Heart Association (AHA). Another group only adhered to the AHA diet, without adding the oat bran. The results: Those with the oat bran lowered their cholesterol levels an additional 5 percent below those who did not use the oat bran.

HEALTH REPORT

FIBER LOWERS CHOLESTEROL

In a 1988 study reported in *Archives of Internal Medicine,* twenty-six men with mild to moderate elevations of blood cholesterol were treated with the drug psyllium mucilloid (Metamucil), which operates in the body much as food fiber does. The results: On average, they experienced a decrease of 14.8 percent in their total cholesterol, and of 20 percent in their low-density lipoproteins (LDLs, the "bad cholesterol" associated with the development of coronary artery disease).

The mechanism for this improvement in the men's blood profiles is unknown. But it may be due to an absorption of bile acids and possibly to binding of some cholesterol. Because the diet of most people is inadequate in fiber, the drug used in this test, psyllium mucilloid, may be regarded as an acceptable substitute.

NOTE: Researcher Sir Dennis Burkitt's original hypothesis was that many of the diseases of Western people—including colon cancer, diverticulosis, and cardiovascular disease—are due to the abandonment of fiber as an important component of the diet.

J. W. Anderson, N. Zettwoch, T. Feldman, et al., *Archives of Internal Medicine* 148 (1988): 292.

A number of other studies, including one by the Quaker Oats Company, have come up with similar results: an indication that consuming water-soluble fiber, such as that contained in oat bran, may be advisable for those with high cholesterol.

Fats

The fats in your diet should constitute *no more* than 30 percent of your total calories, and preferably much less. For a person like

Will, whose case we discussed earlier in this chapter, I recommend that fats be kept below 20 percent of total calories.

It is also important for those trying to lower their cholesterol levels to limit the saturated fats in the diet: that is, the ones that come from animal fats and from certain nonanimal sources such as cottonseed, palm, and coconut oils.

Fats are certainly an important part of our diets because they provide needed fatty acids and also make our foods tastier. But the typical American diet is far too high in fats: Recent studies have shown that the average person consumes at least 40 percent of his or her calories each day in the form of fats.

What exactly is wrong with too much fat? For one thing, you get many additional, unnecessary calories through fat, and that will put on unwanted pounds. Just as important, saturated fats often contain high concentrations of cholesterol and also have the capacity to promote the production of extra cholesterol in your body.

IMPORTANT NOTE: Saturated fats can increase the cholesterol levels in your blood even if they do not contain cholesterol themselves! Many experts feel that it is as important to focus on limiting saturated fats as on limiting cholesterol.

Polyunsaturated fats, which commonly come from corn oil and other vegetable sources, are generally good substitutes for saturated fats. Monounsaturated fats, such as those found in olive oil, have also been associated with lower levels of heart disease. And as we'll see later, some other oils (omega-3) found in certain deep-water fish such as mackerel may be the best of all.

Now, to assist you in choosing those foods that are low in saturated fats and cholesterol, on the following pages are some tables from the U.S. Department of Health and Human Services, which indicate the fat and cholesterol content and composition of common foods, fats, and oils.

Do You Need Extra Vitamins or Supplements?

If you eat a well-balanced diet, one that emphasizes foods low in saturated fats and cholesterol, the chances are that you will get most of the nutrients you need to age gracefully and energetically.

FATTY COMPOSITION OF COMMON FATS AND OILS

VEGETABLE OILS AND SHORTENING	POLYUNSATURATED FATTY ACIDS*	MONOUNSATURATED FATTY ACIDS*	TOTAL UNSATURATED FATTY ACIDS**	SATURATED FATTY ACIDS*
Safflower oil	75%	12%	86%	9%
Sunflower oil	66%	20%	86%	10%
Corn oil	59%	24%	83%	13%
Soybean oil	58%	23%	81%	14%
Cottonseed oil	52%	18%	70%	26%
Canola oil	33%	55%	88%	7%
Olive oil	8%	74%	82%	13%
Peanut oil	32%	46%	78%	17%
Soft tub margarine***	31%	47%	78%	18%
Stick margarine***	18%	59%	77%	19%
Household vegetable shortening***	14%	51%	65%	31%
Palm oil	9%	37%	46%	49%
Coconut oil	2%	6%	8%	86%
Palm kernel oil	2%	11%	13%	81%

FATTY COMPOSITION OF COMMON FATS AND OILS (*continued*)

VEGETABLE OILS AND SHORTENING	POLYUNSATURATED FATTY ACIDS*	MONOUNSATURATED FATTY ACIDS*	TOTAL UNSATURATED FATTY ACIDS**	SATURATED FATTY ACIDS*
ANIMAL FATS				
Tuna fat****	37%	26%	63%	27%
Chicken fat	21%	45%	66%	30%
Lard	11%	45%	56%	40%
Mutton fat	8%	41%	49%	47%
Beef fat	4%	42%	46%	50%
Butter fat	4%	29%	33%	62%

*Values are given as percentage of total fat.

**Total unsaturated fatty acids = polyunsaturated fatty acids + monounsaturated fatty acids. The sum of total unsaturated fatty acids + saturated fatty acids does not equal 100 percent because each item has a small amount of other fatty substances that are neither saturated nor unsaturated. The size of the "other" category varies.

***Made with hydrogenated soybean oil + hydrogenated cottonseed oil.

****Fat from white tuna, canned in water, drained solids.

SOURCE: U.S. Department of Health and Human Services.

FAT AND CHOLESTEROL COMPOSITION OF COMMON FOODS

EXAMPLE OF	ITEM	SATURATED FATTY ACIDS (G)	TOTAL FAT (G)	CHOLESTEROL (MG)
BEEF 100 g (3½ oz)	Top round, lean only, broiled	2.2	6.2	84
	Ground lean, broiled medium	7.3	18.5	87
	Beef prime rib, meat, lean and fat, broiled	14.9	35.2	86
PROCESSED MEATS 100 g (3½ oz)	Dutch loaf, pork and beef	6.4	17.8	47
	Sausage smoked, link, beef and pork	10.6	30.3	71
	Bologna, beef	11.7	28.4	56
	Frankfurter, beef	12.0	29.4	48
	Salami, dry or hard, pork, beef	12.2	34.4	79
PORK 100 g (3½ oz)	Ham steak, extra lean	1.4	4.2	45
	Pork, center loin, lean only, braised	4.7	13.7	111
	Pork, spareribs, lean and fat, braised	11.8	30.3	121
POULTRY 100 g (3½ oz)	Chicken broilers or fryers, roasted:			
	● Light meat without skin	1.3	4.5	85
	● Light meat with skin	3.1	10.9	84
	● Dark meat without skin	2.7	9.7	93
	● Dark meat with skin	4.4	15.8	91
	● Chicken skin	11.4	40.7	83

FAT AND CHOLESTEROL COMPOSITION OF COMMON FOODS (*continued*)

EXAMPLE OF	ITEM	SATURATED FATTY ACIDS (G)	TOTAL FAT (G)	CHOLESTEROL (MG)
FIN FISH				
100 g (3½ oz)	Cod, Atlantic, dry-heat cooked	0.1	0.7	58
	Perch, mixed species, dry-heat cooked	0.2	1.2	115
	Snapper, mixed species, dry-heat cooked	0.4	1.7	47
	Rockfish, Pacific, mixed species, dry-heat cooked	0.5	2.0	44
	Tuna, bluefin, dry-heat cooked	1.6	6.3	49
	Mackerel, Atlantic, dry-heat cooked	4.2	17.8	75
MOLLUSKS				
100 g (3½ oz)	Clam, mixed species, moist-heat cooked	0.2	2.0	67
	Mussel, blue, moist-heat cooked	0.9	4.5	56
	Oyster, eastern, moist-heat cooked	1.3	5.0	109
CRUSTACEANS				
100 g (3½ oz)	Crab, blue, moist-heat cooked	0.2	1.8	100
	Lobster, northern, moist-heat cooked	0.1	0.6	72
	Shrimp, mixed species, moist-heat cooked	0.3	1.1	195
LIVER AND ORGAN MEATS				
100 g (3½ oz)	Chicken liver, cooked, simmered	1.8	5.5	631
	Beef liver, braised	1.9	4.9	389
	Pork brains, cooked	2.2	9.5	2,552
EGGS				
(1 yolk = 17 g)	Egg yolk, chicken, raw	1.7	5.6	272
(1 white = 33 g)	Egg white, chicken, raw	0	trace	0
(1 whole = 50 g)	Egg, whole, chicken, raw	1.7	5.6	272

FAT AND CHOLESTEROL COMPOSITION OF COMMON FOODS *(continued)*

ITEM	SATURATED FATTY ACIDS (G)	TOTAL FAT (G)	CHOLESTEROL (MG)
NUTS AND SEEDS 100 g (3½ oz)			
Chestnuts, European, roasted	0.4	2.2	0
Almonds, dry roasted	4.9	51.6	0
Sunflower seed kernels, dry roasted	5.2	49.8	0
Pecans, dry roasted	5.2	64.6	0
Walnuts, English, dried	5.6	61.9	0
Pistachio nuts, dried	6.1	48.4	0
Peanut kernels, dried	6.8	49.2	0
Cashew nuts, dry roasted	9.2	46.4	0
Brazil nuts, dried	16.2	66.2	0
FRUITS 100 g (3½ oz)			
Peaches, raw	0.010	0.09	0
Oranges, raw	0.015	0.12	0
Strawberries, raw	0.020	0.37	0
Apples, with skin, raw	0.058	0.36	0

FAT AND CHOLESTEROL COMPOSITION OF COMMON FOODS (continued)

ITEM	SATURATED FATTY ACIDS (G)	TOTAL FAT (G)	CHOLESTEROL (MG)
VEGETABLES			
100 g (3½ oz)			
Cooked, boiled, drained:			
• Potato, without skin	0.026	0.10	0
• Carrots	0.034	0.18	0
• Spinach	0.042	0.26	0
• Broccoli	0.043	0.28	0
• Beans, green and yellow	0.064	0.28	0
• Squash, yellow, crookneck	0.064	0.31	0
• Corn	0.197	1.28	0
Avocado, raw, without skin or seed:			
• Florida origin	1.74	8.86	0
• California origin	2.60	17.34	0
GRAINS AND LEGUMES			
100 g (3½ oz)			
Split peas, cooked, boiled	0.054	0.39	0
Red kidney beans, cooked, boiled	0.07	0.5	0
Oatmeal, cooked	0.19	1.0	0
MILK AND CREAM			
1 cup (8 fluid oz)			
Skim milk	0.3	0.4	4
Buttermilk (0.9% fat)	1.3	2.2	9
Low-fat milk (1% fat)	1.6	2.6	10
Whole milk (3.7% fat)	5.6	8.9	35
Light cream	28.8	46.3	159
Heavy whipping cream	54.8	88.1	326

FAT AND CHOLESTEROL COMPOSITION OF COMMON FOODS (*continued*)

EXAMPLE OF	ITEM	SATURATED FATTY ACIDS (G)	TOTAL FAT (G)	CHOLESTEROL (MG)
YOGURT AND SOUR CREAM				
1 cup (8 fluid oz)	Plain yogurt, skim milk	0.3	0.4	4
	Plain yogurt, low fat (1.6%)	2.3	3.5	14
	Plain yogurt, whole milk	4.8	7.4	29
	Sour cream	30.0	48.2	102
SOFT CHEESES				
1 cup (8 fluid oz)	Cottage cheese, low fat (1% fat)	1.5	2.3	10
	Cottage cheese, creamed	6.0	9.5	31
	Ricotta, part skim	12.1	19.5	76
	Ricotta, whole milk	18.8	29.5	116
	American processed spread	30.2	48.1	125
	Cream cheese	49.9	79.2	250
HARD CHEESES				
(8 oz)	Mozzarella, part skim	22.9	36.1	132
	Mozzarella, whole milk	29.7	49.0	177
	Provolone	38.8	60.4	157
	Swiss	40.4	62.4	209
	Blue	42.4	65.1	170
	Brick	42.7	67.4	213
	Muenster	43.4	68.1	218
	American processed	44.7	71.1	213
	Cheddar	47.9	75.1	238

FAT AND CHOLESTEROL COMPOSITION OF COMMON FOODS (continued)

EXAMPLE OF	ITEM	SATURATED FATTY ACIDS (G)	TOTAL FAT (G)	CHOLESTEROL (MG)
VEGETABLE OILS AND SHORTENING	Canola oil	14.8	218.0	0
1 cup (8 fluid oz)	Safflower oil	19.8	218.0	0
	Sunflower oil	22.5	218.0	0
	Corn oil	27.7	218.0	0
	Olive oil	29.2	216.0	0
	Soybean oil	31.4	218.0	0
	Margarine, regular soft tub*	32.2	182.6	0
	Margarine, stick or brick*	34.2	182.6	0
	Peanut oil	36.4	216.0	0
	Household vegetable shortening*	51.2	205.0	0
	Cottonseed oil	56.4	218.0	0
	Palm oil	107.4	218.0	0
	Coconut oil	188.5	218.0	0
	Palm kernel oil	177.4	218.0	0
ANIMAL FATS	Chicken fat	61.2	205.0	174
1 cup (8 fluid oz)	Lard	80.4	205.0	195
	Mutton fat	96.9	205.0	209
	Beef fat	102.1	205.0	223
	Butter	114.4	183.9	496

*Made with hydrogenated soybean oil + hydrogenated cottonseed oil.

Contrary to many popular notions, you really do not need to overload on vitamin and mineral supplements, although you may want to supplement your diet to some extent with these substances. In addition to a regular diet, I do recommend added vitamin C and carotenoids for their potential anticancer effects. Adding vitamin E may have a useful antioxidant impact.

The fat-soluble vitamins A, D, E, and K are absorbed right along with the fat from the various foods you need. Furthermore, these vitamins will be *stored* in your body for use later, in case you fail to include them in a future meal.

The water-soluble vitamins, such as the various B vitamins and vitamin C, are not stored in the body, however. They have to be supplied regularly in your daily diet through such foods as citrus fruits and juices; whole-grain products; meats, fish, and poultry; legumes (such as peas and beans); and root vegetables.

A well-balanced diet will usually provide you with all the important minerals you need: phosphorus, iron, iodine, magnesium, zinc, and calcium. But sometimes, older people need to give special emphasis to certain nutrients and certain strategies for designing their diets, just to be certain they are getting everything they need. Your physician can advise you about your particular nutritional needs.

But some generalizations can be made. So let me conclude this section by highlighting once more, and in a somewhat different way, the most important piece of broadly applicable advice for older people who embark on cholesterol-lowering diets:

If you are over fifty, it is especially important to limit your foods that come from animal products, and when you do eat animal foods, to make them fish or fowl.

There are several good reasons—some related to cholesterol and some not—for everyone to keep eggs, dairy products, and animal meats to a minimum. For example:

• Many people find that as they get older, they cannot digest meats such as beef easily.

The fats and other products in these foods may cause a "heavy" feeling and produce bloating, gas, or other intestinal symptoms. Fat, by the way, is known to slow the emptying process in the stomach. In part, the problems may result from an alteration with age of the way fat is processed in the stomach and intestines.

• Recent research suggests that certain types of fish oils, specifically a fatty acid known as "omega-3," may lower the risk of coronary heart disease.

In particular, studies have shown that fish of the type eaten by Greenland Eskimos may have this effect. These include mackerel, herring, common salmon, whitefish, Chinook salmon, sardines, and halibut.

• Beef, pork, eggs, whole milk, and other animal products contain higher amounts of undesirable saturated fats and cholesterol than other foods.

REMEMBER: Cholesterol in the bloodstream has been associated with the buildup of plaque and clogging of arteries known as *atherosclerosis* (a form of arteriosclerosis). Specifically, recent studies suggest that, statistically speaking, cholesterol levels higher than 200 milligrams per deciliter (mg/dl) can increase the risk of heart disease. One important research project has concluded that a drop of 1 percent in cholesterol levels above the 200 mg/dl level can result in a 2 percent drop in risk of coronary heart disease.

Some older people have resisted lowering their intake of saturated fats and cholesterol because of a false message of hope they have read about in magazines or newspapers: A number of studies have shown that average cholesterol levels begin to decline steadily shortly after age sixty. In the Baltimore Longitudinal Study of Aging, for instance, an analysis done between 1963 and 1971 showed that average cholesterol levels peaked at just under 250 mg/dl when people were in their late fifties. Then, the levels decreased steadily to less than 230 mg/dl for those in their late seventies.

Why the decline in cholesterol with age? Some have suggested that people with higher cholesterol levels tend to die at younger ages of atherosclerosis. Then, as the population ages, the survivors have lower cholesterol levels—and they bring the average cholesterol measurements down. Other researchers have disputed this conclusion, but without offering any decisive alternative explanation.

Whatever the reasons, the tendency of older people to have lower cholesterol levels should not lead to complacency. If your cholesterol is above 200 mg/dl, your risk of coronary heart disease is higher, and it is essential that you take steps to bring that cholesterol down.

To sum up, then: Cholesterol in the blood is directly influenced both by the body's internal production systems and by diet. So you will probably go a long way toward improving the cholesterol level in your blood if you limit or eliminate your intake of eggs, fatty dairy foods, and beef and other meats high in saturated fats.

Of course, if this dietary approach doesn't work—as it doesn't for some people—you'll have to check with your doctor whether cholesterol-lowering drugs such as niacin (vitamin B_3) are in order. We'll delve into the question of medications in Chapter 14, but first, let's take a look at one more "natural" way to reduce your risk of heart disease: the exercise antidote.

13

EXERCISE: THE ANTIDOTE TO THE SEDENTARY RISK FACTOR

Like most people, I am not and never have been an Olympic athlete. Furthermore, I do not spend my free time training for marathons, playing tennis or squash on a rigorous club tournament circuit, or otherwise following a high-performance physical fitness regimen.

On the other hand, because I know that sedentary living is a risk factor for the development of cardiovascular disease, I *do* believe in regular exercise, and I also get plenty of it almost every day. My main physical-fitness activity? Walking.

Although when pressed I may drive from my apartment to my office or to a hospital where I am seeing a patient or doing other work, I still have to spend a great deal of time on my feet. In fact, I estimate that in the course of my regular work around the city, I walk at least four or five miles a day. And I used to boast about all my house calls in Bronx walk-up apartment houses.

On the weekends or in the evenings, I sometimes walk even more intensively than I do during the day. New York City is a "walking city," and Manhattan, where I live, is the "walkingest" part of New York. So when I go to a play, a movie, or a restaurant, I usually plan to travel a good part of the way to my destination by foot.

When I entertain friends from out of town, one of the first things they notice is how much I walk! And they are not always enthusiastic about following me on one of my treks. In fact, one couple, about two decades my junior, who fancied themselves to be in top-notch physical condition, complained about sore legs for two or three days after an outing we had together in Manhattan. This walking way of life seems so natural to me that I sometimes simply forget that many people do not spend as much time on their feet as I do.

Walking is generally recognized as one of the best *aerobic* exercises: that is, exercises that promote endurance and cardiovascular fitness. So when I advise older people about embarking on an exercise program, I usually recommend walking as the basic component of any program. And that means, at a minimum, working up to the point where you can walk vigorously two to three miles a day, three to four days a week. Or, to put this in terms of time, you should walk a minimum of about twenty-five to thirty minutes a day, three to four days a week.

Generally speaking, those who are in good health and who check regularly with their physicians can begin a walking program without any other special preliminary examinations. But if you plan on starting a more strenuous program of exercise, such as jogging, it is important that you have a stress test and a thorough physical exam designed to ascertain whether you are ready for demanding athletic activity.

At this point, however, you may say, "Hold on, Doc, you're getting ahead of yourself! You're already getting me started on a exercise program when I'm not even sure I need one! All this fitness business sometimes seems to be just a fad that interests some people, but is exercise really necessary for everybody who's getting older? What exactly is the problem you're trying to solve?"

What Is the Problem That Exercise Can Help Solve?

As a geriatrician, I see many older patients, and invariably, those who are the least active seem to age the fastest. The sedentary person begins to go downhill faster than his or her more active contemporaries, beginning as early as the late thirties and forties. By the time such inactive people have passed through their fifties, sixties, and seventies, the ravages of old age have often overtaken them. Muscles become weaker and stringier, shoulders become bowed, skin loses vibrancy, and energy levels plummet.

Various studies reported in the *Lancet,* a British medical journal, put my clinical observations in more precise statistical terms:

- Aerobic power (that is, endurance) and muscle strength decline at a rate of approximately 1 percent a year in the later years. To put this another way, in the absence of an aerobic exercise program, the strength of the heart and cardiovascular system declines markedly with age.

- For the average seventy- to seventy-five-year-old woman, walking at slightly more than three miles per hour is a *maximum* aerobic exercise!

- An average eighty-year-old woman has to make *maximum* contractions of her thigh muscles to get up from a low, armless chair.

- The average eighty-year-old woman is unable to negotiate a forty-centimeter step without support.

- Only one healthy seventy-nine-year-old woman in three can walk fast enough to cross a thirty-meter road so that she is fully protected by the timing of the signals at a pedestrian crossing.

For the average person, aging results in a significant decline in the ability of the heart to pump forcefully. Blood pressure tends to rise, often to levels where some sort of prescription medication is required. This deterioration in the body increases the risk of cardiovascular disease.

In addition, bones begin to lose their mass: In men, bone loss takes place at an annual rate of about 0.4 percent, beginning around age forty. Women begin to experience bone loss at an even more rapid rate at about thirty-five years of age. They lose their bone density at about 1 percent a year at first, and then the rate of loss accelerates to 2 to 3 percent annually after menopause. Finally, after about age sixty to sixty-five, a woman's rate of bone loss decreases back to about 1 percent a year.

HEALTH REPORT

EXERCISE IS ESSENTIAL TO SUCCESSFUL AGING

To maintain mobility and independence as you get older, physical conditioning from regular exercise is essential, say the authors of a 1987 report in the *Archives of Internal Medicine.*

The conditioning effects of even moderate forms of exercise are important for all older people, including those who are just embarking on a fitness program after years of sedentary living. The goal in such exercise is to *prolong active life expectancy,* rather than settle for a long disabled existence.

By several measurements, the rate of decline in *functional age*—the physical and mental level at which you actually operate, regardless of your age in years—is greater in sedentary older persons than in those who exercise.

The authors also review the hazards of exercise, from heart attack to exhaustion. They recommend medically supervised programs for some people, including those who are in some way disabled or who have cardiovascular problems or other health difficulties.

In general, walking seems to be the best exercise for older people, because it is relatively safe and produces an adequate training effect. Still, the best overall exercise program for an aging society has yet to be determined, the authors say.

E. G. Larson and R. A. Bruce, "Health Benefits of Exercise in an Aging Society," *Archives of Internal Medicine* 147 (1987): 353.

Muscles also deteriorate with age in the average person. Beginning in middle age, there is a 3 to 5 percent loss of muscle tissue every ten years. The muscles of the legs and torso are particularly vulnerable to this problem.

Finally, the body's flexibility tends to decline with age. The reason for this is that muscles get shorter, and certain components of the connective tissue also shrink with disuse.

But is this deterioration really necessary?

Certainly, we all have to expect some physical decline as we age. But increasingly, scientific research is demonstrating that much of the so-called inevitable physical decline of age can be retarded, at least to some extent. And one of the most important antidotes to the aging process is turning out to be exercise.

Exercise: A Major Antidote to the Aging Process

What exactly can regular exercise do for you? Again I return to some studies summarized in *Lancet:*

• Up to age seventy, *oxygen uptake* (the ability of the body to process oxygen) can be improved by 10 to 25 percent through endurance exercise training. This improvement is the key to the development and maintenance of a strong heart and cardiovascular system.

• Exercise can readily improve the strength of the quadriceps muscles (thigh muscles) of seventy-year-old men by 10 to 20 percent.

• Glucose (body sugar) tolerance, a prime factor in preventing diabetes, can be improved with exercise in older people.

• Osteoporosis, the bone loss that occurs with aging, can be retarded by weight-bearing exercises, such as walking.

Although cardiovascular function tends to decline with age, one study done at the Washington University School of Medicine at St. Louis showed that the opposite may be possible with athletic activity. A group of healthy men and women, aged sixty-one to sixty-seven, experienced improvements of 25 to 30 percent in their cardiovascular function after twelve months of endurance exercise.

HEALTH REPORT

BENEFITS AND RISKS OF EXERCISE
FOR THOSE WITH CORONARY ARTERY DISEASE

It's generally agreed that if it is possible and safe for the patient, exercise is desirable for those with coronary artery disease (CAD), according to a 1988 report in *The Journal of the American Medical Association.*

What are the benefits? Exercise increases the rate of coronary artery blood flow, increases the efficiency of utilization of oxygen, and leads to a slower, more efficient resting heart rate.

The overall message of a number of studies is that there may be as much as a 19 percent reduction in mortality (deaths) in exercise-treated individuals who have had a previous heart attack. Furthermore, the risk of exercise is small: Studies show there will be one cardiac arrest for every 112,-000 patient exercise hours, one heart attack for every 294,000 exercise hours, and one death for every 784,000 exercise hours. In addition, 85 percent of those who suffer a cardiac arrest are successfully resuscitated if the problem occurred in medically supervised programs.

The authors conclude that progressive physical activity should be encouraged in most patients with chronic coronary artery disease. The recommended program is the American Heart Association's walking program, which begins with a ten-minute walk two weeks after the heart attack or the coronary bypass operation. Then the program progresses with five minutes of additional walking each week.

P. D. Thompson, "The Benefits and Risks of Exercise Training in Patients with Chronic Coronary Artery Disease," *The Journal of the American Medical Association* 259 (1988): 1537.

Muscle strength can also increase and need not deteriorate as you get older, if you concentrate on strength conditioning. A study of seventy-year-old men at the University of Southern California in Los Angeles revealed greater muscle strength in the participants after only eight weeks of strength training. Similarly, women aged fifty to sixty-three had significant improvements in their muscle strength after six months of aerobic dancing or walking at a project conducted by West Virginia University.

In addition to these benefits of regular exercise, various research projects have revealed that physically active, well-conditioned older people are less vulnerable to injuries from falls. Some studies have also concluded that moderate exercise can help relieve mild to moderate depression and otherwise improve a person's emotional state.

Another major benefit of exercise for older people who have a tendency to put on extra pounds in fatty tissue is the fact that physical activity is one of the best weight-reduction secrets known to man (or woman)! There is evidence that it may reset the *appestat,* the appetite center in the brain, at a better balance, thus diminishing eating that goes on to overweight. And remember: Because obesity is a major risk factor for heart disease, an exercise program that reduces obesity will go a long way toward eliminating this particular risk.

To get an idea of the possibilities of exercise as a weight-reduction tool, the table on the next page shows the way a number of activities can burn up calories.*

Perhaps most encouraging of all, exercise may prove to be the ultimate antidote to aging because it seems to be able to prolong life. In a frequently cited study of Harvard University alumni by Dr. Ralph S. Paffenbarger and his colleagues that was reported in 1986 by the prestigious *New England Journal of Medicine,* mortality rates were significantly lower among physically active men. Furthermore, by age eighty, an extra one to two years of life could be attributed to regular, adequate exercise, the researchers said.

These, then, are some of the facts. And I must say, they seem to support overwhelmingly the proposition that we should all get up out of our easy chairs and start getting into condition. But in practical terms, how do you go about it?

*From S. M. Fox, J. P. Naughton, and T. A. Gorman, "Physical Activity and Cardiovascular Health," Part 3, *Modern Concepts in Cardiovascular Disease* 41 (June 1972): 25–30.

CALORIES BURNED PER HOUR IN ROUTINE ACTIVITIES

ACTIVITY	CALORIES BURNED
Lying down/sleeping	80
Sitting	100
Driving an auto	120
Standing	140
Domestic work	180
Walking/2.5 mph	210
Bicycling/5.5 mph	210
Gardening	220
Golf	250
Lawn mowing/power mower	250
Bowling	270
Walking/3.75 mph	300
Swimming/0.25 mph	300
Square dancing	350
Volleyball	350
Roller skating	350
Badminton	350
Table tennis	360
Wood chopping/sawing	400
Ice skating/10 mph	400
Tennis	420
Waterskiing	480
Cross-country skiing/10 mph	600
Squash/handball	600
Bicycling/13 mph	660
Running/10 mph	900

SOURCE: Raymond Harris, M.D., President of the Center for the Study of Aging, Albany, New York.

How to Get Started

As I said earlier, it's important to check with your doctor before you start on an exercise program, and this procedure becomes especially important if you plan to engage in rigorous exercise.

It is also essential for anyone who wants to embark on a fairly strenuous sport such as jogging, cycling, or swimming to have a stress test. The stress test, which usually takes place on a treadmill or a specially designed stationary bicycle, is important because it indicates how your heart will react under exercise conditions. An electrocardiogram (ECG) taken while you are resting may suggest that your heart is just fine. But an ECG taken as part of a stress test may signal serious blockages of the arteries leading to your heart or other abnormalities, any of which might lead to serious problems with exercise.

In general, I recommend that most older people—and especially those who have been sedentary—limit themselves to a walking program and perhaps some light calisthenics. You can get all the endurance conditioning you need to benefit your heart and circulatory system with brisk walking, and you can do it without many of the risks of a more strenuous fitness program.

After you've had your medical checkup, the next thing you should do is to plan your walking program in three stages: the warm-up; the main exercise period; and the cool-down. You should also set aside three to four days a week for this program, with one day in between each session to give you an opportunity to rest and recover.

The warm-up, which can consist of slow walking and perhaps some light stretching exercises, should help your body ease gradually into the more vigorous main exercise phase. This way, you'll be less prone to pull a muscle or otherwise injure yourself. In general, I recommend about five minutes for this first phase of the program.

Next, after you are warmed up, you are ready to start *walking*—and that means moving out at a brisk pace. If you're just beginning, you should limit this part of your exercise to fifteen minutes, and many people will prefer to spend ten minutes or less.

The goal is to increase your heart rate during this entire exercise period up to what's called your *target heart rate:* the number of heartbeats per minute that will give you optimum cardiovascular conditioning and serve as a major antidote to the sedentary risk factor.

The target heart rate is a figure that is considerably higher than your resting pulse rate. But it is lower than your maximum heart rate, which usually occurs just as you reach your maximum level of endurance and become exhausted.

How do you determine your target heart rate? There are formulas you can use to calculate it. But I find it easier just to use the following table, from Dr. Raymond Harris, president of the Center for the Study of Aging:

TARGET HEART RATE AND AVERAGE MAXIMUM HEART RATE,
BY AGE

AGE	TARGET HEART RATE	AVERAGE MAXIMUM HEART RATE
40	108–135	180
45	105–131	175
50	102–127	170
55	99–123	165
60	96–126	160
65	93–116	155
70	90–113	150

SOURCE: Raymond Harris, M.D., President of the Center for the Study of Aging, Albany, New York.

You can determine your heart rate during exercise by stopping for a moment to take your pulse, either at the wrist or at one of your carotid arteries, which are located on either side of your neck close to the Adam's apple. You determine the rate by counting the pulse beats for ten seconds and then multiplying by 6 to get the rate per minute.

CAUTION: If you take your pulse at the neck, do not press hard. A light touch should be sufficient to feel the beat. The touch should be on only one side of the neck, not both. Too much pressure on the carotid artery can produce unconsciousness.

Although you should begin this exercise portion of your walking workout with relatively short sessions of fifteen minutes or less, your goal should be more like twenty-five to thirty minutes of brisk walking. And as I said, you should be exercising at this level at least three to four days a week, with a day of rest in between each exercise day.

Finally, the last part of the exercise routine is the cool-down, which should take about five to ten minutes. The harder you have worked during the exercise portion, the more time you should take to cool down. Many exercise experts have cautioned that this cool-down phase is particularly important to protect you against dizziness, fainting, or even heart problems that can occur if you try to stop vigorous exercise too abruptly.

The idea here is just to slow the pace of your walking so that your metabolism and heart rate can return gradually to normal. It can also help to swing your arms about and perhaps do some very light stretching exercises. As an added benefit, you will also minimize the possibility that you will experience stiffness and soreness in your muscles the following day.

One good walking program, which has been approved by the American Heart Association and the National Heart, Lung, and Blood Institute, has impressed me as being quite appropriate for older people who are just getting started with exercise. This particular program works like this:

Week 1 (three sessions)
Warm-up: Walk slowly for five minutes.
Target-zone exercise: Walk briskly for five minutes.
Cool-down: Walk slowly for five minutes.
Total time: Fifteen minutes.

Week 2 (three sessions)
Warm-up: Walk slowly for five minutes.
Target-zone exercise: Walk briskly for seven minutes.
Cool-down: Walk slowly for five minutes.
Total time: Seventeen minutes.

Week 3 (three sessions)
Warm-up: Walk slowly for five minutes.
Target-zone exercise: Walk briskly for nine minutes.
Cool-down: Walk slowly for five minutes.
Total time: Nineteen minutes.

Week 4 (three sessions)
Warm-up: Walk slowly for five minutes.
Target-zone exercise: Walk briskly for eleven minutes.
Cool-down: Walk slowly for five minutes.
Total time: Twenty-one minutes.

Week 5 (three sessions)
Warm-up: Walk slowly for five minutes.
Target-zone exercise: Walk briskly for thirteen minutes.
Cool-down: Walk slowly for five minutes.
Total time: Twenty-three minutes.

Week 6 (three sessions)
Warm-up: Walk slowly for five minutes.
Target-zone exercise: Walk briskly for fifteen minutes.
Cool-down: Walk slowly for five minutes.
Total time: Twenty-five minutes.

Week 7 (three sessions)
Warm-up: Walk slowly for five minutes.
Target-zone exercise: Walk briskly for eighteen
  minutes.
Cool-down: Walk slowly for five minutes.
Total time: Twenty-eight minutes.

Week 8 (three sessions)
Warm-up: Walk slowly for five minutes.
Target-zone exercise: Walk briskly for twenty minutes.
Cool-down: Walk slowly for five minutes.
Total time: Thirty minutes.

Week 9 (three sessions)
Warm-up: Walk slowly for five minutes.
Target-zone exercise: Walk briskly for twenty-three
  minutes.
Cool-down: Walk slowly for five minutes.
Total time: Thirty-three minutes.

Week 10 (three sessions)
Warm-up: Walk slowly for five minutes.
Target-zone exercise: Walk briskly for twenty-six
  minutes.
Cool-down: Walk slowly for five minutes.
Total time: Thirty-six minutes.

Week 11 (three sessions)
Warm-up: Walk slowly for five minutes.
Target-zone exercise: Walk briskly for twenty-eight
  minutes.
Cool-down: Walk slowly for five minutes.
Total time: Thirty-eight minutes.

Week 12 (three sessions)
Warm-up: Walk slowly for five minutes.
Target-zone exercise: Walk briskly for thirty minutes.

Cool-down: Walk slowly for five minutes.
Total time: Forty minutes.

Week 13 on (three sessions per week)

As you continue to exercise, check your pulse periodically to determine whether you are exercising within your target zone. As you get into better shape, your pulse rate will probably drop, and so you may have to increase the intensity of your exercise to get the full cardiovascular benefits. You might also try increasing your exercise sessions each week from three to four.

Sometimes older people, especially those who have already been involved in a regular aerobic exercise program, may be able to go on to more demanding activities, such as jogging. Others, however, may not feel they are able to handle even this relatively mild, graduated walking program just outlined. But, in fact, there are almost always plenty of exercise possibilities, even for those who are particularly weak, disabled, or otherwise unable to walk regularly.

Exercises for Those Who Think They Cannot Exercise

One eighty-six-year-old woman, who had been house-bound for several months after breaking her ankle, complained, "I seem to get weaker by the day. Most of the time, I don't even feel like getting out of bed in the morning."

On further questioning, I learned that she had become an elderly version of the "couch potato." She sat around most days watching television or engaging in other sedentary activities. She might go for days on end without even walking out of her front door except to check on the mail. When she did walk, she relied on a cane that she had started using after her ankle injury.

A complete medical examination revealed that there was nothing physically wrong with her, except a continuing weakness in her injured ankle. In fact, she was in quite good health. Her main problem was that she was simply too inactive. Because she was almost entirely sedentary, she was at higher risk for heart disease than if she had been more active.

So I suggested that she try some very light exercise to tone up her muscles and increase her energy levels. But she replied, "I'm too old to exercise! Besides, I'm a cripple! I can barely walk around the house."

This woman's main problem was that her expectations of her own abilities and her concept of exercise were inaccurate. In fact, everything you do with your body can be classified as a form of exercise. Furthermore, practically everybody, regardless of physical condition, can begin an exercise program and increase strength and energy levels. It is just a matter of knowing what kind of exercise to select and how to structure a personal program that is suitable for you personally.

Here are some exercises, a number of which finally worked for my resisting female patient and could work for you as well if you have been particularly inactive.

Exercises for Those with Physical Limitations

The first step in starting an exercise program if you have physical limitations is to check with your doctor, just to be sure that an increased level of activity is safe for you. If he gives you the go-ahead, then you should begin to increase your level of exertion in the normal activities of life. Here are a few suggestions, which involve exercises which should be done at least five or six days a week:

Sitting and Rising from a Chair

Do you normally sit down and get up from a chair once an hour? If so, try doing it twice an hour for a couple of days. Then, a few days later, try sitting down and getting up four times an hour. Next, a few days later, make it six times an hour, and so on. You will soon discover your leg muscles and endurance will increase significantly, and you will also feel much less cramped and sluggish.

This sitting-and-rising routine should be followed no matter what you're doing, watching television, sewing, or chatting on the phone. Whenever you engage in some otherwise sedentary pursuit, resolve to make that activity truly *active!*

NOTE: It is important to do your sitting in a safe way. Many older people have slipped and fallen as they have tried to get seated. Here are a few safety tips:

• Drop whatever you're carrying to the floor before you try to sit. You should always have both your hands free to catch yourself if necessary.

• Back up to the chair, sofa, or bench on which you plan to sit so that you actually feel the back of your legs against it. This way, you'll be less likely to misjudge where you are in relation to the seat.

• Edge your feet up against or under the seat.

• Next, execute these motions together: Slowly bend your knees; bend your body forward at the waist; thrust your buttocks back toward the chair; and grasp the arms of the chair (if it has arms) with both hands. If there is only one armrest, grasp that with your nearer hand. At the same time, keep your chin and head up. (If your head sinks below the level of your heart, you may become dizzy.)

• Finally, lower yourself into the seat, all the while using your hands and arms to guide and support your weight.

House Walking

If you can walk at all, then this exercise can be quite beneficial in increasing your strength and endurance. The main idea is just to increase the amount of walking you do around the house, even as you are increasing your sitting and rising.

One approach that has worked for a number of older people—especially those who, for whatever reason, feel they cannot walk outside—is to do "living-room laps." You begin by walking around and around the outer edge of your living room, or through several rooms and hallways if that seems more interesting. Start off with one or two minutes of easy, slow walking, using a cane, walker, or other device to stabilize yourself if necessary. If you get overly tired or something starts hurting and the pain does not immediately disappear, stop for the day. If the pain persists, check with your physician.

From week to week, increase the amount of walking you do around the house by a minute or two, or more if you feel comfortable increasing the amount of exercise. Eventually, you may well find that this "house-walking" workout will prepare you to embark on the regular walking program described previously.

Smooth Moves

To increase your strength, warm up your body, and increase your stamina, it is important to put your legs, arms, and other parts of your body into motion as much as possible during the day. But for most people, it is essential to establish a definite program to keep in shape. Otherwise, if you are like most other relatively sedentary people, the chances are that you will not move about enough to maintain adequate muscle tone and endurance in your major muscle groups.

Here are a few suggestions that will work even for those who cannot walk, who have suffered a stroke, or who are otherwise incapacitated. If you cannot move an arm or leg, do the exercises only with your good arm or leg. Then, if possible, use your good arm to move your incapacitated arm or leg as much as possible in accordance with the suggested motions. In my experience, the more you move injured limbs—as long as those movements are smooth and cautious—the more likely you are to experience some degree of rehabilitation.

In every case, it is advisable to move slowly and smoothly as you do the exercises—no jerky motions—to prevent strain.

• Sit down in a straight-backed chair. Grasp your right leg under the knee with both hands, and pull your leg up as far as you can toward your chest. Use both your leg and your arm muscles to raise the leg. When your right knee is as close to your chest as you can comfortably get it, extend your right foot upward, again as far as you can comfortably move it. Then, lower the foot, and lower the entire leg back to the floor.

Repeat the entire sequence with the left leg. Alternate these movements with the right and left legs until you feel pleasantly tired.

• Sit in a straight-backed chair. Raise your right foot off the floor and wiggle it about in a rotational movement until you begin to "feel" the muscles on the top of your thigh or elsewhere in your body. Then, lower the right foot to the floor and repeat the exercise with the left leg.

Continue with the exercise, alternating right and left legs, until you are pleasantly tired.

• Shrug your shoulders and move your head around in nodding and shaking motions for ten or fifteen seconds, or as long as you feel comfortable.

• Keeping your arms straight at the elbows, raise and lower them from your sides to a position straight up over your head. Then return to the starting position. Repeat as many times as possible without becoming too tired.

• Hold both your hands in front of you with your arms bent at the elbows. Then, as if you were raising your hand to ask a question in a class, raise your right hand over your head until your arm is fully extended. Finally, lower your arm.

Repeat the movement with your left arm and alternate this right-up, left-up pumping action of your arms until you are pleasantly tired.

Obviously there are many other types of "smooth moves" that you can do to increase your strength and stamina. For example, if you are bedridden, you might just try raising your arms alternately from beside you on the bed to a position above your chest, with arms extended and straight at the elbows. Or you might bend your legs at the knees, then lower them back to the bed, and repeat with each leg as many times as you can.

The primary principle here is just to *keep your body active!* With only a little thought and planning, practically anyone can develop a sound exercise program that can restore tired or debilitated limbs and body parts and make the aging process a lot more productive and enjoyable! REMEMBER: The more active you stay in every aspect of your life, the more you will reduce the impact of the sedentary risk factor for heart disease.

But at whatever stage you're exercising—whether you're incapacitated or quite healthy for your age, whether you're a rank beginner or a seasoned older athlete—it is important always to keep certain safety precautions at the forefront of your mind.

Better Safe than Sorry

As I have said many times before, you should begin with a thorough medical examination. But even if you have an adequate medical exam before you launch your exercise program, it is still important to be careful and "listen to your body," as the old saying goes. Some of the warning symptoms or signs that you may be engaging in excessive exercise are the following:

- dizziness,
- fainting,
- nausea,
- excessive shortness of breath,
- severe leg pain,
- tendency to stagger,
- persistent lack of coordination,
- excessive fatigue,
- fatigue lasting more than several hours,
- severe distress of any type,
- significant rise or fall in blood pressure,
- wheezing or other abnormal sounds during breathing, or
- irregular heartbeats.

If you experience any of these symptoms, stop exercising immediately, and seek medical help or advice.

In general, injuries or other problems occur during or after exercise when you have gone to an extreme in your workout. Most of the time, if you stick to a graduated, moderate program, you can avoid any difficulties.

Still, as you get older you will become more vulnerable to injuries and other physical problems as you work out. So it is important to take certain preventive precautions to minimize the possibility of any danger. Here are a few safety tips that I recommend to my patients:

- Be aware of your personal physical weaknesses. Respect them. If you have a history of arthritis, for example, do not choose an exercise activity that will aggravate the problem.

KEY FACTS

EXERCISE FOR ELDERLY CORONARY PATIENTS

A 1987 report in the *Journal of the American Geriatrics Society* examined the conditioning effects of a supervised medical program on groups of younger (middle-aged) and older patients, all of whom had suffered heart attacks or undergone a coronary artery bypass operation.

Their findings: Both younger and older groups showed similar degrees of improvement in exercise capacity. They were measured by such criteria as the rise in heart rate and blood pressure during treadmill or bicycle exercise.

The researchers reported that there was no increased incidence of heart problems as a result of the exercise.

Their conclusion: Older cardiac patients can safely participate in a supervised conditioning program and can make substantial gains in their exercise capacity.

But one sobering fact emerged from the study: Despite the recruitment efforts of the researchers, only 19 percent of older patients, as opposed to 57 percent of the middle-aged ones, took up the offered program. One of the reasons for the reluctance of the older people may have been the greater acceptance of the sedentary way of life by the elderly, the researchers concluded.

P. A. Ades, J. S. Hanson, P. G. S. Gunther, and R. P. Tonino, "Exercise Conditioning in the Elderly Coronary Patient," *Journal of the American Geriatrics Society* 35 (1987): 121.

• Select a sound basic sports wardrobe. Proper clothing, footwear, and equipment are essential to ensure safe exercise, my friend Dr. Raymond Harris reminds us. Proper shoes, for example, can help prevent injuries for serious walkers. Walkers, by the way, should wear comfortable, lightweight, well-built walking shoes.

Generally, they should have heavy rubber or crepe soles to provide the feet with good cushioning. A firm heel support that cups the heel will prevent sliding and blistering. Walking shoes should also have a slightly elevated heel and a wide and comfortable arch support. The upper part of the shoe should be made of leather or nylon mesh that allows the feet to "breathe."

Finally, your walking shoes should have a good width at the toes, with about one-quarter to one-half inch between the longest toe and the front of the shoe.

• Pay attention to the weather. Older people need to pay particular attention to weather conditions. On hot, humid days, it is best to exercise during the cooler parts of the day, as in the early morning or early evening. You may also want to exercise less than you normally do until your body becomes adapted to the heat.

It is essential during hot weather to drink plenty of fluids, especially water. You do not need extra salt because you ordinarily get plenty of salt through your diet. The better-conditioned your body becomes, the more efficiently you will be able to conserve salt.

I'd suggest that you avoid rubberized or plastic suits or any other attire that will make you perspire excessively. The best thing to wear is light, loose-fitting clothing that keeps you as cool as possible.

NOTE: You will not lose any extra body fat by sweating a lot. You will just lose fluids from your body.

Finally, it is especially important during hot weather to look out for signs of heatstroke or heat exhaustion. If you feel dizzy, weak, light-headed, or excessively tired, stop exercising immediately, move into the shade, and begin to drink fluids. You may be suffering from some form of heat exhaustion.

Heatstroke is more serious. Signs of this problem are failure to sweat; hot, dry skin; and rising body temperature. If these symptoms appear, get into some cool or cold water, or apply ice to your body.

Older people may become particularly sensitive to cold, so it is also important to be careful if you're exercising outside on a cold day. In that case, you should typically wear one less layer of clothing than you would if you were outside and *not* exercising. It is also best to wear several layers of clothing rather than one heavy layer.

To protect your hands, you might wear old mittens, gloves, or even cotton socks. You should also wear some sort of hat or cap. Up to 40 percent of your body heat is lost through your neck and head.

On rainy or snowy days, be aware that you are less visible than you are in good weather. So watch closely for cars and drivers who may not see you. Be especially careful about slippery ground conditions that may cause you to fall. Remember: Broken bones are among the most insidious enemies of active, healthy older people.

- Stop exercising if you feel any pain or discomfort.

Pains in the joints or bones may signal the beginning of an injury that you can minimize if you just stop, avoid exercise for a few days, and allow the problem to heal. If you try to "run through it," or otherwise ignore the pain, you may be seriously hurt and have to miss weeks or months of your fitness program.

- If possible, exercise in the company of other people, or under expert supervision.

It just stands to reason that if you have other people around you while you exercise, you will be more likely to get help quickly if something goes wrong. Supervised programs also typically have ready access to medical help or first aid. Besides, it is usually much more fun to work out with one or more companions than it is to do so by yourself!

Most local communities have centers or facilities with specially designed exercise classes and programs for older people. For example, you might check with such organizations as

> churches,
> synagogues,
> civic centers,
> community colleges,
> park or recreational associations,
> senior citizens' centers,
> Area Jewish Community Centers,
> YMCAs,
> YWCAs, or
> YMHAs.

These organizations and centers may offer formal exercise programs, or they may provide access to exercise-related programs such as nature walks, social dancing, or other such activities. To get more information on exercise programs and opportunities

for older people, you can write to the following address and ask
for a list of resources:

Exercise
National Institute on Aging
Building 31, Room 5C35
Bethesda, Maryland 20205

In general, the main idea behind all these tips is just to use
good common sense. You should know your body as well as anyone. After all, you have spent decades getting to know yourself and
your responses. If you just listen closely to what your body is trying
to tell you, you will know when to stop or alter your exercise
routine.

The Ultimate Possibilities of Exercise

Up to this point, we have been talking about the usual approach
to exercise that is appropriate for most people—and I include
myself in this category. At the same time, however, I'm always
fascinated and encouraged when I consider what various "super-
athletes" of advanced ages have been able to do.

In one recent New York City Marathon, for example, of the
18,000 runners who were competing, there were a substantial
number of older athletes, including

- 4,719 people in their forties,
- 1,302 in their fifties,
- 217 in their sixties,
- 19 over seventy, including one eighty-five-year-old man
who had traveled all the way from San Diego.

It is surprising even to me that so many people in the second
half of life can get out there and run more than twenty-six straight
miles in that event.

But the New York contest is just one example. Many people
were even more impressed when a fifty-four-year-old Dominican
nun named Marion Irvine qualified for the 1984 Olympic trials.

She did not make the team, but the fact that at her age she qualified to compete says something important to me about the potential of the older human body.

In the sport of rowing, Stuyvesant Pell, a New York insurance man, found he was able to row faster times at age fifty-three than he could when he was a member of the Princeton University crew thirty years earlier.

A forty-eight-year-old swimmer, David Costill, found himself working out more vigorously in middle age than he had when he was a competitive swimmer at Ohio University. Furthermore, he developed into a championship-caliber butterfly and freestyle swimmer in the forty-five- to forty-nine-year-old age bracket.

There seems to be no end to these stories about the possibilities of the older body. Obviously, some of these people have the genetic capability to perform at extremely high athletic levels well beyond what is possible for the average person. But in many cases, the key to achieving athletic prowess at a relatively advanced age seems mostly the result of exercise and training.

In the final analysis, I would certainly point to some of the super older athletes as inspirations for the rest of us. But I would not necessarily hold them up as role models, at least not unless you have aspirations to compete on their level. For most people, a good, steady, sane and safe fitness program is all that's needed to provide an antidote to the sedentary risk factor. So concentrate on your walking—and live long and well!

14

THE MEDICAL MANAGEMENT OF CARDIOVASCULAR DISEASE

When I examined Alice, a sixty-three-year-old professional woman, I discovered some disturbing facts:

She had a very high total cholesterol level of 316 (the count should ideally be less than 200). She also had relatively low levels of "good" cholesterol (HDLs, or high-density lipoproteins). Specifically, her HDLs were 45 mg/dl, when they should have been 55 or higher.

She had an abnormal electrocardiogram, an indication that the coronary arteries leading to her heart were significantly blocked by fatty deposits. Furthermore, rapid walking gave her a sense of pressure in her chest. A further special procedure, an arteriogram that involved taking X-ray pictures of her arteries, revealed that one branch of her coronary arteries was about 90 percent blocked. Another was about 80 percent closed off, and a third, about 75 percent blocked.

For about a year, Alice had been trying to reduce her cholesterol levels through her diet. The only drug she had been taking was low doses of aspirin, about 100 mg per day. NOTE: Research has shown that aspirin can prevent blood platelets from sticking together to form clots. Even on one "baby aspirin" a day, there is less of a chance that a clot will form in one of the coronary arteries narrowed as a result of atherosclerosis.

But except for occasional dips into the 270 to 280 range, Alice had experienced almost no success with her approach. In other words, the "natural," dietary, non-prescription-drug approaches simply had not worked, and now, she was a clear candidate for more serious medical intervention.

Eventually, Alice underwent a three-vessel bypass operation. I also placed her on a drug program involving a combination of colestipol and nicotinic acid (also known as niacin, one of the B-complex vitamins, B_3). The colestipol is designed to lower total cholesterol levels, especially the "bad" LDL (low-density lipoprotein) cholesterol. The nicotinic acid also tends to lower total cholesterol, including LDLs. Furthermore, it helps to raise the good HDL cholesterol.

The medications worked in Alice's case just as they were supposed to. Her total cholesterol level dropped to around 200, and her HDLs rose to 60: levels that placed her in a low-risk category. She also continued the low doses of aspirin.

Sometimes people in Alice's position find they have to turn to medications or special medical procedures, such as bypass surgery, to manage their cardiovascular problems effectively. Fortunately, modern science continues to provide us with an impressive array of drugs and special procedures to deal with this problem.

It All Begins with Aspirin

For years, many physicians have suspected that taking small doses of aspirin regularly can help prevent heart attacks, strokes, and other dangerous cardiovascular events. Just recently, these suspicions have been confirmed as leading American and British medical journals have reported on studies that demonstrate the power of aspirin to reduce the incidence of heart disease and stroke.

A GLOSSARY OF CARDIOVASCULAR PROCEDURES

- *Electrocardiogram.* Also known as an "ECG" or "EKG," this procedure produces a graph-paper visualization of the electrical impulses emitted by the beating heart. Those undergoing this test typically have a number of electrodes attached to the chest.

  This exam may be done as a "resting ECG," during which the patient lies on his or her back, or as part of a stress test. In a *stress test,* the patient raises his heartbeat to a high level through exercise, usually on a treadmill or stationary bicycle. The reason for taking a stress test, as well as a resting ECG, is that certain abnormalities of the heart may be revealed only when the heart is working hard, but not when it is at rest.

- *Sonogram.* A visualization of the heart and its valves in action, created by a sound wave recording.

- *Angiogram (also arteriogram).* An X-ray visualization of blood vessels or heart chambers produced by injecting a dye into the bloodstream.

- *Thallium scan.* A visualization of the beating heart produced by the heart's uptake of a radioactive isotope (thallium). If the scan shows areas of poor uptake or poor motion, that generally indicates an inadequate blood supply.

- *Angioplasty.* A dilation of an artery produced by passing a balloon catheter into it.

- *Valvuloplasty.* A similar procedure to angioplasty, generally designed to open an area with narrowed valves.

- *Coronary artery bypass graft (CABG).* Also known as "open heart surgery," this is a surgical procedure in which narrowed areas of coronary arteries are bypassed with segments of veins or arteries. The number of such bypasses are also referred to in describing the operation: triple (three areas bypassed), quadruple (four areas), or quintuple (five segments). There are rarely more than five arterial segments that are bypassed, though there are occasionally fewer than three.

HEALTH REPORT

HOW ASPIRIN TREATMENTS CAN REDUCE STROKE AND HEART ATTACK

In a 1988 report in the *British Medical Journal,* researchers who studied twenty-nine-thousand patients reported that treatments with aspirin, which were designed to prevent clotting of the blood, reduced stroke and heart attack by 30 percent.

The researchers explained that one way to inhibit the clotting of blood is with agents that prevent the blood platelets from "clumping" together. Treatments that involve this prevention of blood clotting among certain high-risk groups are referred to as *secondary prevention.*

The high-risk individuals on whom this study focused included people who had suffered heart attacks and certain forms of angina or who were regarded as vulnerable to stroke.

One ordinary aspirin a day did as well in reducing the likelihood of stroke and heart attack as did higher doses of aspirin or some other medication.

"Antiplatelet Trialist's Collaboration: Secondary Prevention of Vascular Disease by Prolonged Antiplatelet Treatment," *British Medical Journal* 296 (1988): 320.

I myself have developed the habit of taking a 325-mg dose of aspirin every other day because I have been a believer in the validity of the physicians' study, the results of which were reported in *The New England Journal of Medicine* in 1988. As for my patients who may be at risk for cardiovascular disease, I generally recommend that they take smaller doses, say 80 to 100 mg, on a daily basis.

By taking small doses, you minimize any stomach difficulties, such as bleeding or nausea. The studies have also shown that small doses do as much good as large doses. In fact, smaller doses may be better: An overly large dose of aspirin can actually counteract the benefits of the anticlotting mechanism that low doses of aspirin produce.

HEALTH REPORT

HOW MUCH ASPIRIN DO OLDER PATIENTS NEED?

Recent clinical trials have demonstrated aspirin to be safe and effective in preventing coronary attacks and strokes in high-risk persons. Aspirin clearly prevents a second heart attack and diminishes the threat of heart attack in those with unstable angina. People who have had a transient ischemic attack (TIA), a phenomenon in which reversible brain changes occur that is often the forerunner of a stroke, have a diminished risk of stroke with aspirin.

How much aspirin is necessary to achieve adequate prevention? Some of the first trials used much higher doses than were necessary. One aspirin a day (325 mg), and perhaps as little as one-third of an ordinary aspirin per day, seems entirely effective. Moreover, on the lower doses, the risk of stomach irritation or bleeding is markedly reduced. In fact, the risk of such stomach problems is about the same as that for a placebo, or sugar pill.

NOTE: The diminished risk of heart attack in some eleven thousand physicians has been demonstrated in studies using one aspirin tablet, three times a week. Even more recently, it has been shown that aspirin taken at the time of a heart attack cuts the damage to the heart and the death rate.

J. Hirsh, "Aspirin as an Antithrombotic Agent in the Geriatric Patient," *Geriatric Medicine Today* 6 (1987): 67.

How exactly does aspirin reduce your cardiovascular risk? Here is some of the essential background we need to answer this question:

A thrombosis, or blood clot, is usually a major factor in myocardial infarctions, or heart attacks. Typically, the clot blocks off a *coronary artery,* the channel for blood flow to the heart. Blood clots usually form as a result of an aggregation of blood *platelets,* small colorless disks that circulate in the bloodstream.

Clotting is inhibited by the *endothelium,* which is the cellular lining of the blood vessels. The endothelium works against clotting both by the production of prostacyclin, an antiplatelet substance, and by the resistance of its surface to the clumping of platelets. On the other hand, if the endothelial cell lining of a vessel is damaged, blood platelets may clump together and initiate a *thrombosis,* or clot.

Aspirin steps into the scenario this way: When the aspirin enters your bloodstream, it acts directly on the platelets to reduce clotting. For example, a 100-mg dose of aspirin produces a reduction in the clumping together of platelets for up to seven days.

But large doses of aspirin may have a *reverse* effect on clotting: For all the good it does, aspirin also tends to counter the production of prostacyclin, which is an anticlotting agent. Some studies have indicated that in humans massive doses would be necessary to have significant effect on the prostacyclin. Still, *any* negative impact on the prostacyclin could partially neutralize the anticlotting impact of aspirin. Hence, I believe it is wise to keep those doses of aspirin quite low: at about 325 mg every other day, or about 100 mg daily.

HEALTH REPORT

ASPIRIN WORKS FOR DOCTORS

A 1988 article in the prestigious *New England Journal of Medicine* reported on an aspirin study involving 22,071 male physicians, aged forty to eighty-four. Half of these doctors had been on one aspirin tablet (5 grains, 325 mg) taken every other day. The other half were on a similar-appearing, but inactive tablet (a placebo). None of the participants had any previous history of cardiovascular illness.

The results? Before the first five-year period had ended, it became clear that the incidence of heart attack had decreased by almost half in those taking the aspirin. There were eighteen fatal heart attacks in those using the placebo, compared with only five in those on aspirin. No such protective effect on stroke was seen: the numbers involving stroke were small and the differences not significant.

"Preliminary Report: Findings from the Aspirin Component of the Ongoing Physicians' Health Study," *The New England Journal of Medicine* 318 (1988): 262.

Finally, here's an important WORD OF CAUTION about aspirin: You should take aspirin regularly *only* under the supervision of your doctor. As I have already indicated, some people may have adverse gastrointestinal reactions to aspirin, such as stomach bleeding or ulcers. More seriously, others with a family history of stroke may find their risk of suffering stroke increases with regular doses of aspirin, particularly in the presence of hypertension.

REMEMBER: Even though you can buy aspirin in unlimited quantities over the counter, it is a drug—and a powerful one, at that. As a result, medical consultation for regular or unusual use of aspirin is absolutely necessary for your safety.

Medications That Can Reduce Your Cholesterol Risk

I usually recommend that a patient with high cholesterol or other blood fat levels, such as high triglycerides, first try a dietary approach before turning to drugs. But if diet fails to bring total cholesterol below about 240 mg/dl, or triglycerides (another blood fat) below about 250 mg/dl, I consider prescribing one of the many effective lipid-lowering drugs that are available.

Obviously, your doctor is the one who must make the decision about when to use a certain drug, and which one to prescribe. But I find it helpful to inform my patients about some of the options, characteristics, side effects, and combination treatments that are available. They know what to expect from the medications and are in a better position to give me feedback and interact with me about future drug strategies.

Here are some of the possibilities, including the purpose and expected action of the drugs, the side effects, and the typical doses:

• *Niacin (nicotinic acid).* This over-the-counter product of the vitamin B complex (B$_3$) lowers triglycerides significantly and lowers LDL cholesterol and total cholesterol to some extent. And it may raise HDL levels. Typically, doctors start you off at about 100 to 200 mg a day, and then work up to large doses of 1 to 2 g, two to three times a day (or a total daily dose of 2 to 6 g).

WARNING: Do *not* rush out, buy niacin, and take it without a doctor's close supervision! The negative side effects can be quite serious in some patients: bad flushing of the body, dry skin, gastrointestinal disorders, and damage to the liver.

• *Gemfibrozil.* A prescription drug that lowers triglycerides and raises HDL levels significantly. It also acts to lower total cholesterol and LDL levels. The typical dose is 600 mg, once or twice a day.

Possible side effects: Diarrhea, abdominal pains, nausea, vomiting, interaction with anticoagulant drugs.

• *Cholestyramine.* Lowers total cholesterol and LDL cholesterol significantly and may raise triglycerides. Dose is 9 g, one to six times a day.

Possible side effects: Constipation, bloating, nausea, inhibition of the absorption of fat-soluble vitamins, including vitamins A, D, and K.

• *Colestipol.* Lowers cholesterol and LDL levels significantly but may raise triglycerides. Dose is 15 to 30 g a day.

Possible side effects: Constipation, nausea, bloating, reduction in absorption of vitamins A, D, and K.

• *Clofibrate.* Significantly lowers triglycerides and may also lower total cholesterol and raise HDL levels. Dose is 1 to 2 g daily.

Possible side effects: Gastrointestinal problems, diarrhea, nausea, interaction with anticoagulant drugs, muscle pain.

• *Probucol:* Significantly lowers cholesterol and LDL levels but also lowers HDL levels. Dose is 250 to 1,000 mg daily.

Possible side effects: Headaches, body rashes, diarrhea, nausea, abdominal pains.

• *Lovastatin:* Lowers total cholesterol and LDL levels significantly, with no adverse impact on HDL levels. Dose is 40 to 60 mg daily.

Possible side effects: Few known, except some slight but reversible alterations in liver enzymes, and in some cases a thickening of the lens of the eye.

HEALTH REPORT

HOW A DRUG CAN HELP CONTROL CHOLESTEROL

A group of men who were studied for seven to ten years were treated in one of two ways: (1) with the drug cholestyramine (Questran) and a low-fat diet or (2) with a placebo and a low-fat diet. The researchers also identified certain *endpoints* for the study, such as a heart attack or a death ascribable to coronary artery disease.

The results? For every 1-mg rise in HDL cholesterol ("good" cholesterol), there was a 5.5 percent decline in the coronary endpoints (heart attacks or death from coronary artery disease). Even the men taking placebos who experienced a rise in their HDL cholesterol enjoyed better cardiovascular health, with fewer endpoints.

The men being treated with the drug plus diet had a significant decline in their LDL ("bad") cholesterol. In fact, the statistical analysis by the researchers revealed that the decline in the LDLs that occurred with the cholestyramine treatment was even more beneficial to the men's cardiovascular health than the rise in the HDLs.

D. J. Gordon, J. Knoke, and J. L. Probstfield, "High-Density Lipoprotein Cholesterol and Coronary Heart Disease," *Circulation* 74 (1986): 1217.

The Estrogen-Progesterone Factor

In the last few years I've noticed increasing numbers of women coming in for medical treatment who have just passed through menopause. My personal observations reflect an ongoing shift in the American population: Now, an estimated 35 million women in the United States, about 30 percent of the female population, are fifty years old or older. Furthermore, most of those in this older group have passed through menopause.

When a woman goes through menopause and menstruation ceases, a number of important physical changes take place, including a marked decline in the ability of the body to produce estrogen.

This loss of estrogen may result in a number of health problems: a tendency toward osteoporosis, or thinning of the bones; atrophy of urinary and genital organs; and flushing. Various scientific studies show that the lack of estrogen after menopause can significantly increase a woman's risk of cardiovascular disease.

HEALTH REPORT

THE PROMISE OF LOVASTATIN

The Journal of the American Medical Association reported in 1987 on a study from the National Heart, Lung and Blood Institute of four different drugs that inhibit the body's manufacture of cholesterol. These include lovastatin (Mevacor), which has been heralded as a potential wonder drug for lowering cholesterol levels.

Specifically, these drugs lower the levels of total cholesterol and LDL ("bad") cholesterol by 20 to 40 percent. As a result, they are considered the most potent agents currently available for this purpose. When combined with other medications—such as nicotinic acid, bile acid sequestrants (such as colestipol) or a low-fat diet—they may produce a drop of as much as 50 percent in LDL levels.

The side effects of these drugs, although still not completely certain, are apparently mild. The drugs are notably free of discomfort, although a few subjects have complained of muscle tenderness. There is also an unknown potential for possible changes in the lens of the eye.

Lovastatin has already been released, and the other drugs are almost ready for release. If they prove to be safe, these drugs may become as widely used as any of the more common cholesterol-controlling drugs, and they may also have a great impact on cardiovascular disease.

J. M. Joeg and B. Brewer, "3-Hydroxy-3 Methylglutaryl-Coenzyme A Reductase Inhibitors in the Treatment of Hypercholesterolemia," *The Journal of the American Medical Association* 258 (1987): 3532.

For example, the Framingham Study in Massachusetts has shown that *post*menopausal women have twice as much cardiovascular disease as women who are *pre*menopausal. Younger women who have had their ovaries surgically removed—and who thus lose their ability to produce estrogen, much like older postmenopausal women—have more heart disease than do normal premenopausal women.

One answer to the threat of heart problems posed by menopause is estrogen-replacement therapy. A number of recent studies have concluded that women who receive this supplemental estrogen may have a reduced risk of heart disease. How might this cardiovascular protection from estrogen work? One way is that supplemental estrogen tends to lower the levels of "bad" LDL cholesterol in postmenopausal women and raise the levels of "good" HDL cholesterol.

But there are some dangers that have been associated with estrogen therapy. These include an increased incidence of endometrial cancer (cancer of the lining of the uterus), high blood pressure, and gallbladder disease. To counter the possibility of endometrial cancer and related problems, doctors typically prescribe the hormone progesterone along with estrogen. In some cases, however, the progesterone counteracts the beneficial cardiovascular effects of the estrogen by raising LDLs or lowering HDLs.

So where do we stand on estrogens and heart disease in women? Certainly, the evidence that estrogen therapy can help protect postmenopausal women from heart disease is growing stronger, but the final word has not yet been written on this issue. So the best advice I can give you is this: If you and your physician decide to try this route, you should monitor your levels of cholesterol very closely and see what effect, if any, the treatment has on the lipids in your blood. That way, you'll be much more likely to find the right blend of an estrogen-progesterone balance that may lower your risk of cardiovascular disease, without increasing the risk for other health problems.

Are You a Candidate for Bypass Surgery?

After one of my patients has heard that he or she apparently has some degree of coronary artery disease, a common question I hear is "Do I have to undergo surgery?"

In most cases, the answer is no. Typically, occluded coronary arteries, which have been partially blocked by the buildup of fatty deposits of LDL ("bad") cholesterol and apolipoprotein B, can be dealt with by changes in diet, exercise, or the use of drugs. But sometimes, a cardiologist (heart specialist) decides that coronary artery bypass surgery is in order.

What exactly is this bypass surgery?

To answer this question you have to understand a little about one of my professional specialties, anatomy, specifically, the anatomy of the heart. In a sense, the heart "feeds itself" by pumping blood and oxygen to the heart muscle through vessels that we call *coronary arteries.* There are two of these arteries, the right and left, and the left one is divided again into two arteries, the *left anterior descending artery* and the *circumflex artery.*

In other words, there are really *three* main arteries that convey blood to the heart muscle. And these in turn branch out to supply life-sustaining fluid to the whole heart. If any of these becomes blocked through atherosclerosis, the part of the heart that that vessel "feeds" becomes damaged and may die.

If your doctor decides that bypass surgery is necessary to promote better blood flow to the heart, the surgical procedure will be done this way:

The purpose of a bypass is to establish an extra vessel pathway to the heart muscle. In other words, the surgeon builds a "bypass" around the blocked or partially blocked vessel. To achieve this result, he typically takes a vein from the leg and attaches one end of it to the preblock segment and the other end to a point on the blocked coronary artery beyond the obstruction. Another method to achieve a bypass is to redirect an artery from the chest directly to the heart muscle.

The typical bypass operation is performed by making an incision in the chest, hence, the term *open heart surgery* for the procedure. The surgeon stops the heart from beating during the operation by dousing the organ in a solution that suspends its function. The operation usually lasts several hours, and during this period, the operating team sets up an artificial pump to supply blood to the body.

Those whom many physicians consider candidates for coronary artery bypass surgery include the following:

● Patients with angina pains and also those with unstable angina

- Patients who continue to have chest pains after suffering from a heart attack
- People who have undergone a coronary angioplasty procedure
- Those who experience chest pains that seem to worsen with time or who have suffered several heart attacks.*

The ultimate benefits of coronary artery bypass surgery have been the subject of a degree of controversy. Some experts would argue that this procedure will alleviate chest pains to a significant extent in 95 percent of patients. Also, they say, the operation *may* prolong life and *may* cut the risk of heart attacks. Certain enhancements to the quality of life—increased physical capacity, lessening of shortness of breath, increased ability to work—are all frequent pluses.

On the other hand, death does occur during the operation in up to 2 percent of the patients. A heart attack may occur in up to 10 percent, either during or just after the operation.

A July 1988 report in *The Journal of the American Medical Association* warned further that almost half (44 percent) of the patients who had undergone heart bypass operations in three hospitals in the western United States either shouldn't have had the operations or might have fared as well without them.

The researchers in this study, who were from the RAND Corporation, also noted that their findings raise some questions about whether these results warrant the number or cost of the bypass operations. In 1987, for example, nearly a quarter million bypass operations were performed in the United States at a total cost of $6 billion. The average individual heart bypass operation costs about $30,000.

I'm frequently asked, "Dr. Rossman, how do *you* feel about the bypass procedure?"

Certainly, I think it is warranted in some cases, such as those in which the coronary arteries are so obstructed that the patient seems in imminent danger of a heart attack. But in general, I exhaust every other avenue of treatment, including diet and drugs, before I turn to surgery. The operation is too expensive and too risky, and the benefits too uncertain to justify the frequency with which some doctors have chosen this procedure in past years.

*See David Vorcheimer and David Tepper, "A Patient's Guide to Coronary Artery Bypass Graft Surgery," *Cardiovascular Reviews and Reports* 8, no. 3 (March 1987): 69ff.

I can still remember attending a lecture on bypass surgery by one of the nation's most prominent open heart surgeons early in the history of its development.

"Any middle-aged man with the onset of angina should be immediately operated on," the lecturer said. "Otherwise, he may have a coronary, a massive coronary. He may die. It's malpractice to sit around and watch him decline. As for me, I don't watch them—I cure them!"

That shook me up. After all, I had been successfully (I thought) treating many patients with angina, and I had been following them for many years, watching them survive on the medical programs I had devised. But had I been wrong? Was this approach passé? Had surgery come onto the scene and displaced all of my cherished programs?

Then, only a few years later, the pendulum swung the other way. The new conclusion: We were overdoing surgery. No one had really evaluated it scientifically. The surgical advocates were not mentioning the operative mortality, or the mortality within the first couple of months of the surgery, or the closing off of the bypasses, which returned the patient to the condition he had been in before. In short, no one was comparing the surgically treated with the medically treated patient.

Does medical treatment work? You bet it does. Time and time again, I have taken the anginal patient, made him lose weight, lowered his blood cholesterol, screamed at him so that he stopped smoking, and then watched with satisfaction as his angina disappeared. Despite the great surgeon's exhortations, I was not sending that kind of patient in for surgery!

As you can see from *The Journal of the American Medical Association* findings, perhaps 44 percent of cardiac surgery was not really necessary. Doubtless some of the remainder of the operations were life-saving, however. So how does one decide on medical versus surgical approaches?

I think of surgery when these conditions are present:

• The patient's angina and disability are progressive and seriously damaging to the quality of life.
• The patient wants a more active life-style than his damaged coronary arteries permit. One patient, an active and enthusiastic skier, said, "I'm not giving up my skiing. I'm not willing to sit

around worrying about sexual intercourse, even though some say it's better to worry than to have surgery. So operate!"

- There is a severe obstruction to the left anterior descending artery, a main artery sometimes dubbed "the artery of sudden death."
- The patient's angina suddenly becomes unstable or unpredictable in its relation to the degree of effort expended. This is especially a problem if the angina wakes the person from a sound sleep. Such a disturbance is a warning that a heart attack may be in the offing.

On the other hand, the situation is different if the angina is what we call *chronic stable angina.* This is long-standing angina that may have been present for many months, that occurs predictably with a certain level of effort and then subsides, and that is responsive to the medical measures I've mentioned. In these cases, I'm willing to treat the problem medically, an approach that involves employing such means as

- prophylactic aspirin,
- beta-blockers (a group of medicines known to diminish *second* heart attacks—and, I'm quite certain, *first* attacks as well), and
- drastic lowering of blood cholesterol levels, which has been shown to diminish the extent of the plaque obstruction in some people's coronary arteries.

So, in weighing medical and surgical approaches, remember that for many persons, *there is a choice.* It is not as simple as saying that if you survive the surgery, the problem is solved. And it is not as clear-cut as some surgical proponents may make it out to be.

In any case, remember that even after surgery, *the medical treatment has to be continued.* That means lower the cholesterol, take aspirin to keep arteries and grafts open, exercise (with caution), and avoid psychic stress.

Coronary Angioplasty: An Alternative to a Bypass

"Doctor Rossman," one of my seventy-year-old patients said one day, "I understand that I may have to undergo a bypass operation before too long if my disease gets worse. But isn't there another way? I really don't want to undergo a major operation at my age."

HEALTH REPORT

HOW ASPIRIN CAN HELP WITH A BYPASS

In a study reported in 1984 in the British medical journal *Lancet,* one group of patients who had just undergone bypass surgery were given low (100-mg) doses of aspirin daily. Another group of patients who had also undergone the bypass procedure were put on a placebo. The researchers reviewed the status of the patients two weeks and also four months after their operations.

The results: Irregular heartbeats increased more after surgery among those patients on the placebo than among those on the aspirin. Also, a 100-mg dose daily of aspirin effectively blocked the formation of blood clots. None of the patients reported any side effects.

R. L. Lorenz et al., "Improved Aortocoronary Bypass Patency by Low-Dose Aspirin (100 mg. Daily)," *Lancet* (June 9, 1984): 1261.

Yes, I responded, there often *is* "another way" for a growing number of people with cardiovascular problems, and especially those who are older. To open up clogged coronary arteries, physicians are increasingly turning to the procedure known as *coronary angioplasty* as an alternative to the bypass operation.

It is comforting to know that there are now nearly 150,000 angioplasty operations performed each year, a figure that represents more than half the number of bypasses. The great majority of those angioplasty procedures, about 90 percent, are quite successful. In fact, the success rate is approximately the same as the rate for the bypass operation.

How does coronary angioplasty work?

The physicians who specialize in this procedure introduce a catheter (a long, thin tube) through a peripheral artery, such as one in the groin. The catheter, which contains a tiny, inflatable balloon, is then moved up through the blood vessels until it reaches an artery that has been clogged with fatty plaque by atherosclerosis. In coronary angioplasty, the clogged arteries involved are one or more of the coronary arteries that feed blood to

---

HEALTH REPORT

A BALLOON FOR YOUR HEART?

The aorta, which is roughly the size of a garden hose, is the largest artery in the body. It conveys oxygenated blood from the heart to the head, trunk, and extremities.

At the originating point of the aorta is a valve that opens with each heartbeat and then closes off between beats, thus preventing blood from running back into the heart. A narrowing of the area around the aortic valve, known as a *stenosis,* may occur in some older people and is a process that is often associated with calcium deposits. Hence, doctors may refer to this narrowing as *calcific aortic stenosis.*

As the narrowing of the aorta progresses, the heart is put under a burden to do extra work. Before long, the heart muscle thickens and may eventually fail. Because of the stenosis, or closing-down of the artery, less blood is pumped out to the rest of the body, and this lack may cause fainting or even sudden death.

Up until about 1986, it was not feasible to do anything to correct this heart condition, other than perform an operation to replace the aortic valve, a high-risk, difficult operation. But then, medical experts found that passing a special catheter up into the aorta and blowing up a balloon that was attached to it could satisfactorily open up the stenosis.

Researchers from England reported in 1988 on the results of using this procedure, which is called *valvuloplasty,* on thirty-two patients, aged sixty-five to eighty-six years. With these individuals, there were only four significant complications, and more than half of all the participants showed improvement for three months or longer. The dilation procedure could be repeated as often as needed.

D. C. Springings, J. B. Chamers, and G. Jackson, "Balloon Valvuloplasty of Aortic Stenosis in the Elderly," *Geriatric Medicine Today* 7 (1988): 84.

the heart muscle. Of course, the patient is under anesthesia during this procedure.

When the end of the catheter reaches the clogged part of the artery, the physician performing the procedure inflates the little balloon for about twenty to ninety seconds so as to stretch and open up the obstructed vessel. In the process, the soft to firm fatty plaque that is blocking the vessel breaks up. As a result, blood can flow through the coronary artery more freely.

An angioplasty is considered successful if it produces at least a 20 percent increase in the inside of the artery, and if it also lowers the blood pressure differential across the clogged section to less than 20 millimeters of mercury (mm Hg).*

Generally speaking, most coronary angioplasty involves people with one-vessel disease, but the procedure is also being used for those who have more than one clogged coronary artery. On the other hand, those with extensive hardening of many arteries and vessels usually are not candidates for the procedure.

There are risks that accompany angioplasty: For example, in an estimated 5 percent of the cases, a heart attack occurs, usually during or just after the procedure. In as many as 4 percent of the cases, an emergency bypass operation may be necessary. Also, in up to 3 percent, the artery that the physician is trying to open may close down completely. But death occurs less than 1 percent of the time during the hospital procedure. Because of the relative safety of the procedure, elderly people and those who are otherwise considered unsuitable risks for more serious bypass surgery are often candidates for angioplasty.

Will the vessel or vessels opened through this procedure stay open?

One of the main problems with angioplasty is the tendency of the cleared vessel to become clogged again. This occurs in about one-third of the patients who undergo this procedure. But there are things a patient can do to reduce this risk. The most important ways to control the controllable risk factors include these:

- *Stop smoking cigarettes.*
- *Control diabetes mellitus.*
- *Balance cholesterol and other blood fats.*

*See David P. Faxon, "Current Status of Coronary Angioplasty," *Hospital Practice* 22 (1987): 59.

HEALTH REPORT

WHAT KIND OF SUCCESS CAN YOU EXPECT FROM MULTIPLE-VESSEL CORONARY ANGIOPLASTY?

In a 1985 report of the short-term and long-term results of coronary angioplasty of multiple vessels, medical experts came to the following conclusions:

The immediate results of a procedure performed on 100 patients were rather dramatic: 95 percent experienced at least some improvement in their clinical exams and angiograms; 84 percent experienced success in clearing more than one vessel; and 79 percent had success with all their blocked vessels.

On the other hand, there were a number of short-term problems: 11 percent had some sort of medical complications; 4 percent had to undergo emergency bypass surgery; and 4 percent had myocardial infarctions (heart attacks).

In the long term, there were some encouraging signs. When follow-up exams were conducted more than one year after the operation, 64 percent showed improvement, and 48 percent had no symptoms of disease whatsoever.

On the negative side, 34 percent showed recurrence of clogging of their cleared arteries; 18 percent underwent bypass surgery; and smaller percentages underwent additional angioplasty or other medical therapy. One of the patients had a heart attack, but none died.

The researchers concluded, "These short- and long-term follow-up results suggest that [coronary angioplasty] of multiple vessels is a safe and effective therapy in selected patients with multivessel coronary artery disease."

M. J. Cowley, G. W. Vetrovec, G. DiSciascio, et al., "Coronary Angioplasty of Multiple Vessels: Short-Term Outcome and Long-Term Results," *Circulation* 72 (1985): 1314.

In short, if you can reduce your risk of cardiovascular disease in the way I've described in Chapters 11 and 12, you can also reduce the risk that vessels opened through angioplasty will become clogged again.

A peek at the future. A very recent development in angioplasty is the use of a small laser with the balloon to clear clogged vessels. In the methods currently being employed, the laser melts or vaporizes a channel through the plaque. Then, the balloon, which has been deflated up to this point, is pushed through the cleared path in the plaque and inflated.

So far, this laser approach has been employed only sparingly on the coronary arteries of patients. But as the technique gets better, the use of the laser will almost certainly increase.

How About Using the Balloon Treatment in Your Peripheral Arteries?

You may remember the patient I mentioned in Chapter 10 who experienced pain in his legs after he walked for a block. Then, the pain would subside after a short period of rest, and he would begin to walk again, only to feel that pain in his legs once more.

He thought he was just "getting old," but as I pointed out to him, that was not the problem at all. Instead, he was experiencing periodic, painful intermittent claudication from clogged vessels in his legs. In some ways, these pains are the leg's version of angina pectoris.

There really are no good drugs to relieve this condition; the best of the lot, pentoxifylline, has had only limited acceptance in the medical community. A much more promising approach is what's called *peripheral vascular angioplasty,* another use of our old friend, the little balloon that expands clogged vessels.

This procedure is faster, less expensive, and less risky than surgical alternatives, and its popularity is growing by leaps and bounds among physicians. Like its coronary counterpart, peripheral angioplasty requires the insertion of a catheter with a tiny balloon attached into the obstructed artery. Then, the balloon is inflated, thus stretching and opening up the narrowed artery.

The reported success rate is even better than that for coronary angioplasty. In the hands of an expert, this procedure can result in dilation of practically all clogged peripheral arteries, except for those with lesions (tissue changes from serious disease) that are longer than 10 centimeters (cm). Furthermore, the recurrence rate of clogging is a reported 5 to 15 percent of vessels that have been cleared, a rate that is lower than that associated with coronary angioplasty.*

Medical developments are moving quite swiftly in the realm of peripheral angioplasty, with physicians from different specialties vying to establish themselves as the premier wielders of the new techniques. Cardiologists, radiologists, and vascular surgeons are learning how to perform traditional catheter-and-balloon peripheral angioplasty. There is also considerable interest in acquiring skills for the new laser techniques that have been more commonly applied to the peripheral vessels than to the coronary arteries that feed the heart. So if your physician determines that you are a candidate for this procedure, it would be wise to work closely with him to find a specialist who has a long, established track record in helping patients with your particular problem.

*Medical World News, December 14, 1987:34.

15

COMBATING HYPERTENSION

Marilyn, who was in her early sixties, episodically had slightly elevated blood pressure, so I had recommended that she come in to see me more than once a year for a checkup. But I had not performed a medical exam on her in about three years because she said she had just been too busy; she had been unable to set aside the time. Unfortunately, in the interim her blood pressure had risen to a level that required more serious treatment.

When she had been in for previous checkups, her blood pressure readings had hovered at about 140/88 millimeters of mercury (mm Hg), which was within the normal range for her age. But on several occasions, the pressure had registered as high as 160/95, a level that indicated some sort of treatment was in order. NOTE: In general, most experts feel that blood pressure above 140/90 should receive some sort of treatment.

Because her blood pressure had not remained consistently at an elevated level in previous years, I had not prescribed any drugs.

Instead, I had recommended that Marilyn lose weight: She was about twenty pounds above her ideal body weight. Also, I had placed her on a low-salt diet and a regular exercise program.

But as I learned when she came in for her latest exam, she had not lost any weight at all; in fact, she had put on about four pounds! She admitted she hadn't been following the low-salt diet or exercise regimen that I had prescribed. The results on her blood pressure were telling: A series of blood pressure readings showed that her pressure was now consistently in the 190/110 range, and that meant we had to turn to drugs to get it down.

"I don't understand how I can have high blood pressure," Marilyn protested. "I know I haven't been on the diet you gave me, or been doing the other things you told me to do. But I *feel* just fine! I certainly don't seem to have any symptoms."

"There usually aren't any symptoms for high blood pressure, at least not until the readings get extremely high," I responded. "But even asymptomatic hypertension can silently erode your health and put you at greater risk for serious cardiovascular disease, including strokes and heart attacks. So we have to take some definite steps to bring your blood pressure back to normal."

I've frequently had patients who had systolic readings of 200 or more. (The *systolic* reading is the first of the two blood-pressure numbers that are quoted.) Yet even at that high level, they often do not report any symptoms at all.

On the other hand, some patients with persistently high readings *may* experience some symptoms, such as throbbing morning headaches, a feeling that one's head is "full," giddiness, dimness of vision or other visual disturbances.

In Marilyn's case, I prescribed a diuretic drug. This medication increases urinary excretion of salt and, by this and other mechanisms, lowers blood pressure. Within a few days her blood pressure dropped to 175/100. Then, we followed a slow, low-dose technique using a further medication (a beta-blocker). This approach was designed to prevent undesirable side effects. On this combination of drugs, the side effects might include electrolyte abnormalities (such as an unhealthy drop in potassium) or hypotension (too-low blood pressure). Sometimes, if a person's blood pressure drops too quickly with these medications, the side effects can create as many problems as they solve.

HEALTH REPORT

SHOULD THE ELDERLY HYPERTENSIVE BE TREATED?

Some early studies of high blood pressure in the elderly did not clearly demonstrate a beneficial effect of treatment. As a result, some physicians became hesitant to treat older people because of the long-standing belief that higher pressure forced blood through narrowed arteries better. There was also a prevalent feeling that the elderly were more subject to adverse effects of medications.

But contrary to this older view, this review of the pertinent investigations comes out very positively in favor of treatment. In the Framingham Study and the European Working Party Study, elderly persons whose blood pressures were successfully treated had a lower rate of strokes than a nontreated group of controls.

Beneficial results were noted both in persons with only one component of the blood pressure elevated and in those with both components elevated. That is, there were benefits to those with both systolic and diastolic hypertension. The analysis covered eight major studies.

In one larger study, the evidence of side effects such as impotence, depression, inordinate drop in blood pressure, dizziness, drowsiness, and weakness was less in the sixty- to sixty-nine-year-old group than in those up to thirty years younger.

R. A. Davidson and G. J. Caranasos, "Should the Elderly Hypertensive Be Treated?" *Archives of Internal Medicine* 147 (1987): 1933.

I also encouraged Marilyn in even stronger terms than before to lose weight and decrease her salt intake. This time, sufficiently concerned about her health, she complied. Gradually, over a period of about a year, we got her readings down to the 150/90 range, which was much safer.

A Silent but Prevalent Problem

Luckily for Marilyn, a medical exam revealed her hypertension before any serious damage had been done. But her case is only one example of a silent, prevalent problem that does not always end so happily.

According to various estimates, about 58 to 60 million Americans have some form of high blood pressure (a term that is synonymous with hypertension). For these purposes, a person with *high blood pressure* has been defined as one who has a systolic (upper) reading above 140, who has a diastolic (lower) reading above 90, or who is taking an antihypertensive medication.

To put this in other terms, approximately 40 percent of whites and 50 percent of blacks above the age of sixty-five have some form of high blood pressure. Furthermore, from a statistical viewpoint, the problem gets worse as people get older: Many experts expect that about two-thirds of people from sixty-five to seventy-four years old will develop high blood pressure by this definition. And an even higher proportion—an estimated three-fourths—of those seventy-five and older will suffer from hypertension.

Because most hypertension develops without any symptoms, only an estimated 54 percent with this problem actually know about it. And even fewer—one-third of all hypertensive individuals—are receiving any medications.

The consequences of allowing this silent destroyer to roam freely among us, without sufficient medical attention, are fearful to contemplate. High blood pressure is a major player in a variety of cardiovascular ills and other health problems. Consider this ominous list of ills that are often tied in to hypertension:

- *The 1.5 million heart attacks* that hit Americans annually (more than a half million of which are fatal)
- *The 0.5 million strokes* (175,000 of which are fatal)
- *Kidney failure*
- *Congestive heart failure*
- *Clogging of peripheral vessels,* such as those in the legs, through atherosclerosis

• *Aneurysm* (a dilatation or ballooning outward of the vessel wall) of the aorta, the large artery leading from the heart

---

KEY FACTS

SYMPTOMS OFTEN MISTAKENLY ATTRIBUTED TO HYPERTENSION

The following symptoms are common complaints *both* in people who are under treatment for hypertension *and* in those whose blood pressures are normal. So do not push the panic button before you check your condition with your physician!
- Headache
- Dizziness
- "Full" sensation in the head
- "Tight" sensation in the neck
- Eyestrain symptoms
- Fatigue
- Light-headedness
- Nosebleed
- Flushing
- Wobbliness when standing up

With so many health difficulties linked to hypertension and so many people unaware of their need for treatment, it is essential for everyone over fifty to become better informed about this pervasive disorder. So now, let's consider in more detail exactly what hypertension is, and what you can do about it.

The Basics of Blood Pressure

After a thorough examination, one of my older patients was informed that the only health problem he faced was hypertension. "Well, at least I don't have high blood pressure anymore!" he replied.

I had to begin at square one with him! It's best to get your terminology straight if you hope to carry on a meaningful conversation with your doctor. So remember: Hypertension and high blood pressure are the same thing.

But what exactly is hypertension?

To answer this question it is important to understand something about the basics of blood pressure. As blood flows out of the heart to the blood vessels, the current creates pressure against the blood vessel walls. The blood pressure readings that measure this vessel pressure are expressed in two numbers, one on top of the other. The upper reading, called *systolic pressure,* reveals the maximum amount of pressure exerted on your arteries while your heart is pumping blood. The lower reading, the *diastolic pressure,* reflects the minimum pressure on your arteries, when the heart is "resting" between beats and filling with blood before the next beat.

Some Tips on Taking Blood Pressure

A blood pressure reading is taken with a cuff-and-meter device (called a *sphygmomanometer*) that is strapped around the upper arm. To determine your actual blood pressure, your physician should take several blood pressure readings on several different days. Blood pressure levels may change from day to day and from circumstance to circumstance, so to get a true picture, a number of such readings are necessary.

When your blood pressure is being taken, you should avoid any positions or postures that cause your body to tense. Although hypertension does not imply that you are necessarily a "tense" person, being in a tense body position when you're measured *can* drive up your readings. In general, you should avoid sitting on the edge of a chair or table, and you should also be sure that the arm on which the measurement device is cuffed is relaxed and supported. A relaxed sitting position with your "cuff arm" resting comfortably on a solid surface is usually best.

Many times, when a person goes into a doctor's office for a blood pressure check or when a doctor walks into his hospital room for a measurement, the blood pressure shoots up. This is sometimes called the "cuff syndrome" or "white coat hypertension," and is a common response that should be kept in mind when blood pressure is being evaluated. Tense, jumpy patients are more susceptible to this problem. To get a truer reading, they should be asked by their physicians to take their blood pressure readings at home, where the negative presence of the doctor is not a factor.

HEALTH REPORT

HOW YOUR DOCTOR'S PRESENCE CAN INCREASE YOUR BLOOD PRESSURE

In a study reported in a 1987 issue of the British medical journal *Lancet,* researchers investigated the impact of doctors' presence on blood pressure readings.

In almost all of the forty-eight normal and hypertensive patients tested, the arrival of the doctor at the bedside caused immediate rises in both systolic and diastolic blood pressures. The blood pressure readings typically peaked within one to four minutes of the doctor's arrival.

Large differences were noted between how much the blood pressure readings increased in the various patients. The range involved an increase of 4 to 75 mm Hg for systolic (upper) readings and 1 to 36 mm Hg for the diastolic (lower) pressure. The researchers also observed an increased incidence of rapid heartbeats, though this response was only slightly correlated with the rises in blood pressure.

After the peak response, the blood pressure in the patients declined, and at the end of the doctor's visit it was only slightly higher than the previsit level. A second visit by the same doctor did not change the average size of the increase in blood pressure or the rate of its decline.

G. Mancia, G. Bertinieri, G. Grassi, et al., "Effects of Blood-Pressure Measurement by the Doctor on Patient's Blood Pressure and Heart Rate," *Lancet* 2 (1983): 695.

I am convinced some patients being treated for hypertension are in fact normal outside the office. More than once, I have had the experience of paying a house call on patients with apparent high blood pressure, only to find them well within the normal range at home.

What Is Normal?

The average blood pressure reading for adults is about 120/80, but a reading that is somewhat lower or higher is still considered normal and safe, or *normotensive,* to use the medical term. Readings in lower ranges—down to about 110/70—are acceptable, but anything lower may be regarded as *hypotensive,* or below normal.

Hypotension: The Opposite of Hypertension

The symptoms of hypotension include fatigue, limpness, dizziness, and sometimes a tendency to faint upon standing. This latter finding, termed *postural hypotension,* increases in the aged. This is a reversal of the situation found in younger individuals, in whom blood pressures taken when standing are generally higher than those taken while sitting. Finally, others with severe hypotension may feel sick when they even try to sit up.

What causes hypotension? As a sudden new finding, it may be brought on in older people by a serious hemorrhage in the digestive tract, by a heart attack, or by a shutoff of blood (infarction) in the lungs caused by a blood clot. More often, low blood pressure can result from the excessive use of antihypertensive drugs. As I've mentioned earlier in Chapter 7, hypotension is a major cause of falls and fainting in older people.

How High Is Too High?

As far as higher readings are concerned, blood pressures below 140/90 in older people are generally safe and require no special treatment. But a systolic (upper) or diastolic (lower) reading higher than that is considered hypertensive and may necessitate treatment, according to the current thinking of hypertension experts.

This view on safe blood pressure readings in the upper ranges represents a change in medical thinking. It used to be said that a systolic reading equal to "100 plus your age" was acceptable. So, if a person was sixty years old, a systolic pressure of 160 was all right. In fact, until just a few years ago, most physicians did not regard readings of up to 160/95 as indicative of hypertension. But now, the prevailing opinion is that readings above 140/90 are at least borderline hypertension and should be treated in some way.

Generally, physicians first try to deal with borderline hypertension through nonprescription means, such as changes in diet (including a reduction of salt intake), weight loss, and exercise. If these approaches do not work—and especially if the patient persistently experiences blood pressure readings of 160/95 or higher—drugs may be in order.

What Causes Hypertension?

In the large majority of cases of hypertension—at least 90 percent—no cause for the condition can be identified. These cases are known as *primary* or *essential hypertension.*

In the other 10 percent of cases, known as *secondary hypertension,* a definite cause *can* be identified. These causes include such factors as the following:

- *Kidney-related problems*
- *Overactive adrenal glands* (for example, in Cushing's disease)
- *Various tumors* that secrete pressor substances (those that raise blood pressure)
- *Oral contraceptives*
- *Pregnancy*

Even though the causes of hypertension cannot be precisely identified in most cases, medical experts do have a good idea about the factors that contribute to this problem. For example, high blood pressure is more common in blacks than in whites, and the disease also tends to be more severe in blacks. There are strong indications that obesity (body weight that is 20 percent or more above the person's ideal body weight) and diets high in salt help trigger hypertension.

According to the American Heart Association, other factors may contribute to the problem.

- *Heredity.* The propensity toward high blood pressure often seems to run in families. So, if your parents or other close blood relatives had high blood pressure, you're more likely to develop it than is someone with a family history of normal blood pressure. If other family members have suffered strokes or heart attacks at an early age, you and your family members should have your blood pressure checked regularly.

• *Sex.* Men are more likely to develop high blood pressure than women. But after menopause, a woman's risk of hypertension increases and exceeds the incidence in men.

• *Age.* High blood pressure occurs most often in those over age thirty-five. Men seem to experience hypertension most often between thirty-five and fifty; women are more likely to develop it after menopause. In general, the older a person gets, the greater the chance that he or she will develop high blood pressure.

• *Sodium sensitivity.* Heavy sodium consumption increases blood pressure in some people more than in others, mainly because their blood pressure regulators are more reactive to sodium. Consequently, many who are disgnosed as hypertensive are routinely put on a sodium-restricted diet.

• *Alcohol.* A number of studies have shown that heavy, regular consumption of alcohol can increase blood pressure dramatically.

• *Combined risk factors, such as oral contraceptives with smoking.* The risk of developing high blood pressure increases by several times when women who take oral contraceptives also smoke cigarettes. The risk also increases when an overweight person smokes.

• *Sedentary life-style.* A lack of exercise contributes to hypertension by promoting obesity and poor circulation.

But exercise caution! Moderate exercise may help those with relatively mild hypertension. On the other hand, overexertion can be dangerous and, in some cases, may not be advisable. Patients whose blood pressures stay higher than about 170/105, even when taking medications, should avoid exercise entirely.

In any case, an aspiring exerciser with high blood pressure should always check first with his or her physician to plan a safe program of activity.

Some of the factors that may contribute to or help cause hypertension are controllable, and some are not. The important thing is to focus not on what you cannot change, but on what you can. Obviously, you cannot change your family history, or your natural tendency to be sensitive to sodium, or the fact that you're a man or woman, black or white.

HEALTH REPORT

HOW EXERCISE CAN HELP MILD HYPERTENSION

In a study of fifty-six patients at the Institute for Aerobics Research in Dallas, researchers report that they were able to achieve significant reductions in diastolic and systolic blood pressures through a sixteen-week program of aerobic exercise.

Specifically, the average systolic pressure of the patients dropped from 146.3 to 133.9 mm Hg, and diastolic pressure dropped from 94.3 to 87.2 mm Hg. None of the patients was on any antihypertensive medication during the evaluation.

The exercise involved three one-hour sessions per week: After a ten- to fifteen-minute warm-up, the participants walked and jogged so as to elevate their heartrate to 70 to 80 percent of their maximal heartrate. Then, they had a ten-minute cool-down period. As the program progressed, the patients gradually decreased their walking and increased their jogging.

John J. Duncan, J. E. Farr, S. J. Upton, et al., "Effects of Exercise in Mild Hypertension," *The Journal of the American Medical Association* 254 (1985): 2609.

But you *can* influence the relative impact of many of these factors. For example, by making certain key dietary changes, many people can reduce or even eliminate their problems with hypertension.

How to Control Hypertension Through Your Diet

When John came in for a medical exam, he was thirty pounds overweight and, by my calculations, he was consuming about 8 g of salt per day. His blood pressure was 150/95, a reading that placed him in a mild or borderline hypertensive category. It was clear that he had to do something to bring that blood pressure down, and his diet seemed clearly to be the first line of attack.

As I pointed out to him, various statistical studies have revealed that many people who have high blood pressure are also overweight, and John definitely needed to lose quite a few pounds. So I gave him a weight loss diet similar to the one outlined in Chapter 11.

Also, I recommended that he reduce or, if possible, eliminate his consumption of alcohol, which amounted to about 4 ounces a day in the form of hard liquor. I explained to him that alcohol adds pounds and in quantity has been shown in many medical studies to raise blood pressure readings.

Another important part of his dietary strategy was to reduce his intake of fat, and especially saturated fat, which at the time of his exam was about at the national average of 40 percent of his total daily calories. High consumption of saturated fats has been associated with hypertension, I said, and so we set a moderate goal in accordance with American Heart Association guidelines: He was to keep his total consumption of fats at less than 30 percent of his total daily calories, and his consumption of saturated fats—including those in animal meats and butter and dairy products—at less than 10 percent of his daily calories.

Next, I recommended that he increase the fiber in his diet. This meant eating more whole grains, bran, and vegetables. Again, I was trying to stack his diet in favor of lowering his blood pressure: At least one study has shown that increasing fiber in the diet will lower blood pressure readings.

One of the most important points I made was to emphasize the necessity of cutting down on his high sodium intake: "You have to get rid of that extra salt in your diet!" I said. "You may very well be one of those sodium-sensitive people whose blood pressure is influenced by a salty diet."

I set a goal for him of only 2 g of salt a day, or one-fourth of what he had been consuming. As I explained, this meant staying away from foods that are obviously high in salt, reducing the amount of salt used in cooking at home, and eliminating the use of table salt when he prepared to eat.

"Also, educate yourself by reading the labels on the foods you eat, and choose those that are low in salt," I advised. "And you might try experimenting with nonsalty spices and seasonings, such as lemon juice or various herbs."

The foods I recommended emphasized fruits and vegetables and embodied the various goals of low salt, high fiber, and low saturated fat. They also contained relatively high amounts of potassium, a mineral that may help lower blood pressure in some people and also often has to be supplemented for those on diuretic medications. Some of the antihypertensive foods I suggested, which are part of the program promoted by the American Heart Association for those with hypertension, included the following:

- *Fruits.* Apples, apricots, avocados, bananas, cantaloupes, dates, grapefruits, honeydew melons, nectarines, prunes, raisins, watermelons
- *Juices.* Apple, grapefruit, prune, orange
- *Vegetables.* Asparagus, white or green beans, broccoli, brussels sprouts, cooked cabbage, cooked cauliflower, corn on the cob, cooked eggplant, fresh and cooked lima beans, fresh and cooked green peas, peppers, baked or boiled potatoes, radishes, cooked summer or winter squash
- *Meats.* Chicken stripped of all visible fat, fish, and lean meats are acceptable, but they should be cooked with little or no salt and served without any table salt.

Finally, it is advisable to avoid foods that are high in potassium but also high in sodium or salt. These include the following: potato chips, pretzels, salted crackers, biscuits, pancakes, pastries or cakes made from self-rising flour mixes, pickles, soy sauce, olives, commercially prepared soups, ham, sausages, frankfurters, smoked meats or fish, canned tomato juice, raw clams, sardines, frozen lima beans, frozen peas, canned spinach, canned carrots.

The Relaxation Strategy

A number of studies have shown that the use of certain relaxation or biofeedback techniques may help to lower blood pressure.

In general, these techniques involve first a systematic relaxation of the muscles in every part of the body, from the toes to the head. Then, the hypertensive begins to breathe regularly and simultaneously concentrates on the breathing mechanism, or on a particular word, phrase, or sound for a period of ten to twenty minutes, twice a day. The technique must be pursued in a low-key but focused fashion, with full attention being paid to the exercise for the prescribed ten to twenty minutes, twice daily.

In a number of cases, those practicing these techniques regularly over a period of several weeks have found that their blood pressure readings decrease, sometimes to the point where they no longer need medications. But there are several keys to success with these methods:

First, this approach seems to work best with milder forms of hypertension.

Second, some people are naturally more successful with these relaxation strategies than others. The minds and bodies of some people seem more genetically tuned to this approach, and if such is the case with you, great! If not, you will have to turn to other methods of combating your hypertension.

Third, it is necessary to be regular and consistent in practicing the techniques. If you lay off for several days at a time, the relaxation strategy probably will not work for you.

The Pros and Cons of the Antihypertensive Drugs

If changes in diet, embarking on an exercise program, relaxation techniques, or losing weight does not lower your blood pressure sufficiently, you and your physician may decide to try one of the many effective antihypertension drugs.

My patient Marilyn, whose situation was described at the beginning of this chapter, was one of those people who could not keep her blood pressure at a normal level with a nondrug approach, and so I prescribed a diuretic for her. In general, as was the case with Marilyn, I believe that drugs should be considered seriously if these "natural" means do not keep blood pressure below about 150/95.

KEY FACTS

DRUGS FOR THE TREATMENT OF HIGH BLOOD PRESSURE *(brand names in parentheses)*

I. DIURETICS
   Hydrochlorothiazide (HCTZ) (HydroDIURIL, Esidrix)
   Chlorthalidone (Hygroton)
   Indapamide (Lozol)
   Metolazone (Zaroxolyn)
   Furosemide (Lasix)
   Bumetaride (Bumex)

COMBINATIONS:
   Hydrochlorothiazide 25 mg and triamterene 50 mg (Dyazide)
   HCTZ 50 mg and triamterene 75 mg (also in half-strength) (Maxzide)
   HCTZ 50 mg plus amiloride 5 mg (Moduretic)

II. BETA-BLOCKING AGENTS
   Atenolol (Tenormin)
   Metoprolol (Lopressor)
   Nadolol (Corgard)
   Pindol (Visken)
   Labetalol (Trandate, Normodyne)
   Propranolol (Inderal)
   Timolol (Blocadren)

III. DRUGS ACTING ON BRAINSTEM (VASOMOTOR CENTER)
   Clonidine (Catapres)
   Guanabenz (Wytensin)
   Methyldopa (Aldomet)
   Guanfacine (Tenex)

IV. ANGIOTENSIN CONVERTING ENZYME INHIBITORS (ACE)
   Captopril (Capoten)
   Enalapril (Vasotec)
   Lisinopril (Zestril)

V. DILATORS
   Hydralazine (Apresoline)
   Minoxidil (Loniten)

VI. CALCIUM CHANNEL BLOCKERS
   Nifedipine (Procardia, Adalat)
   Diltiazem (Cardizem)
   Verapamil (Isoptin, Calan)

THE CASE OF THE MYSTERIOUS COUGH

Medical researcher Dr. W. B. Strum describes the case of a seventy-six-year-old woman with a complicated cardiac history and on a variety of medications including digoxin, metaclopramide (Reglan), ranitidine (Zantac), warfarin (Coumadin), and enalapril (Vasotech).

Her main problem: She had developed an intractable cough, day and night, sitting and supine, and was coughing up around a cup of watery mucus every twenty-four hours.

After a complete cardiac "workup," she was advised to try discontinuing the antihypertensive drug enalapril. She did stop the drug, and the cough abated and then disappeared within five days. Furthermore, it was established that the cough had begun a few weeks after she had started the medication.

Dr. Strum notes that a cough may be a side effect of the group of valuable drugs known as the angiotensin converting enzyme (ACE) inhibitors, which are used for the treatment of hypertension and congestive heart failure. NOTE: The cough is a not uncommon side effect that has only recently been recognized, and the precise physical mechanism is unknown.

W. B. Strum, "The Case of the Constant Cough," *Hospital Practice* 23 (1988): 153.

What are the options for hypertensive drugs? You can see the spectrum of various medications and their manner of operation in the Key Facts on page 283. But in addition, let me provide you with an overview of the major drug categories and also some of the side effects. Of course, all drugs have side effects, but in general, they are tolerable. Otherwise, the drug would be abandoned. With any such drug, the question is whether the side effects are acceptable and worth the returns that are positive, especially normalization of the blood pressure. Because there are now so many medications, we are in a better position to pick and choose.

The Diuretics

The diuretics, including such drugs as the thiazides, lower blood pressure by reducing the volume of blood, and by other mechanisms still not fully understood. The volume of fluid in the body's system decreases as the diuretics promote greater urination and loss of salt through the kidneys.

HEALTH REPORT

TREATING HYPERTENSION IN DIABETICS

The coexistence of hypertension and diabetes is fairly common, especially in an older population. Treatment of the two conditions can be complex and illustrates some of the general problems of the use of multiple drugs and their interactions in a given patient.

Some examples:

Commonly used diuretics may increase the blood fats, which are already often elevated, in the diabetic.

The beta-blocking agents may worsen the blood sugar level or conceal the fact that it may have dropped too low.

Long continued use of diuretics has been reported to raise the blood sugar level of some patients into the diabetic range. This process may be reversed by discontinuing use of the drug.

None of these negative effects occurs with the use of calcium channel blockers or ACE inhibitors, two classes of drugs that may therefore be preferable. Of course, for some illnesses a diuretic may be mandatory in either the diabetic or the nondiabetic, but side effects must be monitored.

P. Raskin, "How to Treat Hypertension in Diabetic Patients," *Postgraduate Medicine* 83 (1988): 213.

But there are a number of possible side effects: leg cramps, fatigue, and weakness are common, especially as the body loses sodium and potassium through increased urination. There may also be a decrease in the male sex drive, attacks of gout in a few patients, and increases in the blood sugar levels in latent diabetics.

The Sympathetic Nervous System Inhibitors

Sympathetic nervous system inhibitors, a broad class of drugs, that includes the beta-blockers, alpha-blockers, and related medications, lower blood pressure by inhibiting the activity of the sympathetic nervous system. The *sympathetic nervous system* is that part of the nervous system that controls such automatic bodily functions as heart rate, blood vessel contraction, and perspiration. Through various means, including the release or blocking of different transmitters, these drugs operate to relax the smooth muscles that keep small arteries at a certain level of tautness or "tone."

It is important to keep the possible side effects of some of these drugs in mind:

• *Reserpine* may cause minor discomforts such as diarrhea, feelings of indigestion, or a stuffy nose. More serious side effects, such as insomnia, depression, or nightmares, call for a physician's attention.

• *Beta-blockers* may produce cold hands and feet, insomnia, fatigue, depression, or a slow heartbeat. They may also trigger asthma symptoms. In some cases, impotence may be a problem. Diabetics on insulin should be examined regularly by their physician.

• *Alpha-methyldopa* (Aldomet) may cause feelings of weakness or faintness, especially during standing or walking. There may also be sleepiness, sluggishness, dryness of the mouth, anemia, or fever. Impotence may be a problem for men taking this drug.

• *Guanethidine* (Ismelin) may lead to diarrhea, light-headedness, and feelings of weakness when one stands up suddenly. Dizziness or faintness may be a particular problem when patients on this drug get out of bed, so it is important to move slowly and carefully to prevent fainting. Again, impotence may result in males taking this drug.

• *Clonidine* (Catapres) may cause dryness of the mouth, sleepiness, or constipation.

• *Prazosin* (Minipress), an alpha-blocker, may result in tiredness or a sudden fall in blood pressure when it is used initially.

• *Guanabenz* (Wytensin) may produce dryness of the mouth, tiredness, or sleepiness.

The Vasodilators

Drugs that operate as vasodilators open up the small vessels, called *arterioles,* that branch out from arteries. These arterioles are instrumental in regulating blood pressure.

KEY FACTS

DRUGS THAT MAY PRODUCE SEXUAL DYSFUNCTION

The following drugs may interfere with normal sexual functioning:
- Drugs used to control hypertension, including beta-blockers and diuretics
- Tranquilizers
- Mood-altering drugs, including amphetamines
- Antidepressants
- Anticonvulsants
- Opiates

One image that I like to use in explaining how the arterioles work is the nozzle of a hose. If you open the nozzle up or take it off the hose, the water flows out relatively slowly under reduced pressure. But if you close the nozzle down, the water pressure inside the hose builds up and the water shoots out in a harder, narrower stream.

Similarly, if the arterioles become narrower, the blood is forced through them under greater pressure. As a result, blood pressure rises. These vasodilators, in various ways, help to keep those arterioles more open, or dilated, so that the blood pressure stays lower. Sometimes, the vasodilators act directly on the arterioles; sometimes they block calcium from entering the vessels; and sometimes they inhibit enzymes that constrict the vessels.

Here are a few examples of these drugs, with their side effects:

- *Hydralazine* (Apresoline) may produce swelling around the eyes, pounding heartbeats, headaches, or painful joints. Usually, these problems disappear on reduction of the dose or after a few weeks on the drug, but if they continue, you should consult your doctor.

• *Minoxidil* (Loniten) is a powerful medication that is generally used only when other drugs fail. Side effects include retention of fluids and extra hair growth, a characteristic that has made this drug popular recently among bald or balding men.

• *Captopril* (Capoten) is one of the angiotensin converting enzyme (ACE) inhibitors. These drugs are increasingly being prescribed as first- or second-line drugs, and they *may* be quite free of side effects for some people. Some have the convenience of once-a-day dosage. They do not affect the blood salts, fats, or sugars in the body. *Possible side effects* are skin rash, loss of taste, weakness, cough, and, in a few cases, kidney problems.

Obviously, these are only a few of the drug options available to those with hypertension. Probably, if your physician prescribes medication for you, the drug will fit into one of these categories. But it is important for you to question your doctor closely about possible side effects. Then, when you know what *may* happen in your body as you take the medication, you'll be prepared to monitor the actual results of the drug. If you find that the side effects are severe or in some other way unacceptable, notify your doctor and work with him to find a more suitable drug, or to alter the administration of the one you are taking.

It is also important to keep in mind the variety of strategies that are possible in taking antihypertensive medications. Many times, a patient moves from one medication (such as a diuretic) to another (for instance, a beta-blocker) because the effects of the second have a less severe impact on the person's physical responses or life-style. In choosing such a strategy, the physician usually works closely with the patient to monitor the benefits and side effects of a particular drug.

Also, the amount of a medication a physician prescribes in lowering blood pressure may vary, depending on how quickly the medication acts. With older patients, in particular, it is important to lower blood pressure *gradually*, so as to prevent such potentially dangerous responses as postural hypotension (low blood pressure on standing or getting out of bed suddenly).

The latest thinking on the gradual reduction of high blood pressure follows.

WHY IT MAY BE IMPORTANT FOR OLDER PEOPLE TO LOWER THEIR BLOOD PRESSURE GRADUALLY

In a review of hypertensive medications in a 1986 report in *Hospital Practice,* Dr. F. H. Messerli notes that there are a number of problems in treating the elderly with traditional antihypertensive medications:

- Diuretics may increase the risk of *hyponatremia* (too little sodium in the blood), which can lead to weakness and confusion and other abnormalities in the body's electrolytes, such as potassium.
- Diuretics may worsen glucose intolerance.
- Diuretics may aggravate a tendency toward hyperuricemia, or excess uric acid in the blood (a condition that characterizes gout).
- Diuretics may decrease blood flow through the kidneys.
- Beta-blockers decrease kidney blood flow and filtration.
- Beta-blockers increase resistance in the peripheral blood vessels, thus restricting blood flow and increasing the tendency of the extremities to become colder.

Because of the possible negative impact of some of the drugs on older people, Messerli advocates his own version of the "start low, go slow" philosophy of administering antihypertensive medications. If he has a patient with a blood pressure reading of 200/120, he tries to bring the person down to 180/100 within a few days. Then, he keeps the patient at that level for six months to assess any side effects.

Next, he tries to reduce the person's blood pressure to 170/95, and then to 160/90, always operating within the same six-month time interval as he moves from one level to the next. The main objective is first preservation of healthy blood flow and organ function and only then, reduction of blood pressure.

F. H. Messerli, "The Age Factor in Hypertension," *Hospital Practice* 21 (1986): 103–12.

16

WHAT YOU SHOULD KNOW ABOUT STROKES

A sixty-nine-year-old man walked unannounced into my office one morning and said, "Something's wrong with my arm. When I woke up this morning, my hand was weak and it seemed floppy. Now I can't move my left hand at all."

My examination revealed he had suffered a stroke as a consequence of a clot in a brain vessel. His speech had not been affected, however: There is only one brain center for speech, which is located on the dominant side; because he was right-handed, he escaped speech loss.

But large areas of the human brain are devoted to the hands, and that is the reason stroke damage often involves them. This man was able to walk into the office and tell me what was wrong, but he was unable to grasp my fingers with his left hand.

Stroke is an event that strikes about 400,000 Americans each year. It is generally due to a rupture or clotting in a blood vessel, either within the neck (*carotid stroke*) or within the skull itself. The result may be partial paralysis, as my patient experienced; loss of consciousness; or even death.

Many strokes and heart attacks occur between about 6:00 A.M. and 10:00 A.M., perhaps because of the tendency of the blood to slow down and clot during those early morning hours. This man's experience fitted right in with this early-morning pattern.

Fortunately for my patient, the stroke was relatively mild, and the outlook for recovery was bright. As a matter of fact, he recovered almost completely by the next day, an improvement that indicated that he had experienced something like a transient ischemic attack (TIA). This is a "ministroke" that almost always involves full recovery but is a strong signal that a major stroke may occur in the near future.

Just how fortunate my "unfortunate" patient was is shown by other statistics: About 160,000 people who have a stroke die immediately or shortly after the event. Many are very old, and the stroke is a final blow.

Furthermore, the problem of stroke may be becoming worse, though for several decades, this health problem seemed to be in retreat. For a number of years, the death rate for stroke declined in the United States, from 88 per 100,000 population in 1950 to 35 per 100,000 in 1983. That represented a 1 percent drop each year until 1972, and after that an even greater decline of about 5 percent a year.

But very recent studies have indicated that the rate may be rising again. For example, experts at the Mayo Clinic have identified an increased stroke rate of 15 percent in one representative area, Rochester, Minnesota. One of the Mayo experts explained that this rise in reported strokes may be the result of both an aging population and better methods of detecting the occurrence of strokes. Indeed, with our new machines, such as the computerized tomography CT scanner, we now find evidence of tiny strokes that never could be identified before.

What Are Strokes?

In general, a *stroke* may be defined as one kind of cardiovascular disease, in which there is blockage of blood flow—including oxy-

gen and various nutrients—to the brain. As a result of the shut-off
of oxygen and nutrients, the part of the brain that the occluded
vessel feeds begins to die.

There are several types of strokes, which may be lumped into
two basic categories: (1) those caused by blood clots and (2) those
caused by *hemorrhaging,* or bleeding in the brain. It is important for
physicians to diagnose the exact type of stroke that has occurred
because treatment varies, depending on the nature of the stroke.

Strokes Caused by Blood Clots

Strokes caused by blood clots may occur when a clot forms inside
an artery leading to the brain and then blocks the blood flow. This
type of clot may also appear in a vessel in the brain (called a *cerebral
thrombosis*). Blood clots form most often in arteries damaged by
atherosclerosis, the hardening of the arteries that results from the
buildup of fatty deposits and plaque.

In addition to this type of clot, a stroke may be caused by one
that moves through the bloodstream from another part of the body
and then lodges in an artery leading to the brain, or in the brain
itself. This type of stroke is known as a *cerebral embolism.*

Thus, a small clot formed in the heart after an arrhythmia
(irregular heartbeat) or heart attack may be propelled out of the
heart into the brain. This is why I check every stroke victim for a
possible heart attack. More than one patient has told me, "First,
I had severe chest pain and palpitations. A little later, the paralysis
came on." The sequence here is heart attack, drop in blood pressure, clot within the brain, and, finally, stroke.

When strokes are caused by this kind of clot blockage, physicians may prescribe anticoagulant drugs, such as warfarin and
heparin, which help prevent the clots from growing bigger. Recently, for some patients, we have also been experimentally resort-
ing to tissue plasminogen activator (TPA), the same clot dissolver
being used for heart attacks. But if the stroke is caused by something other than a clot, such as hemorrhaging, this treatment could
be fatal: hence, the need to establish whether the source of the
problem is a clot. Here, the CT scan or magnetic resonance imag-
ing (MRI) test can be very helpful.

NOTE: About two-thirds of all strokes result from various kinds
of clots. Hemorrhages account for the rest.

Strokes Caused by Hemorrhaging

More serious strokes may result from a ruptured blood vessel in or around the brain. These occurrences are especially dangerous because of two factors: (1) the part of the brain fed by the blood vessel may die; and (2) the spreading of the blood from the rupture may damage other parts of the brain tissue.

Sometimes, the hemorrhage is caused by a head injury, which breaks or damages a blood vessel. These strokes may result from an aneurysm that bursts. Aneurysms are blood-filled pouches that balloon out from weak spots in the artery wall. Some of these are congenital, but in many cases, they develop and break because of the presence of high blood pressure. This fact helps to explain the great decline in stroke when the modern blood pressure drugs came along.

As with clot-caused strokes, those resulting from hemorrhaging also require special approaches to treatment. Typically, physicians dealing with this type of stroke prescribe drugs that prevent further bleeding, reduce swelling in the brain, or lower blood pressure.

What Are the Warning Signs of a Stroke?

It is helpful for everyone over age fifty to have a general knowledge of the danger signals for the onset of a stroke. If you know what to look for—and act quickly enough—you may save your health or even your life.

Some of the warning signs that I look for, and that are highlighted by the American Heart Association, are the following:

- Sudden weakness or numbness of the face, arm, or leg on one side of the body
- Loss of speech or difficulty in talking or understanding speech
- Dimness or loss of vision, particularly when in only one eye
- Unexplained dizziness, unsteadiness, or sudden falls

About 10 percent of major strokes are preceded by what might be called "little strokes," or, in more precise medical language, transient ischemic attacks (TIAs). These are the types of reversible episodes that my patient described at the beginning of this chapter had experienced. These ministrokes signal that the blood flow to the brain has been temporarily interrupted (a process called *ischemia*). They may occur days, weeks, or even years before a major stroke. Usually, the cause of the TIA is the temporary plugging of

---

HEALTH REPORT

WHAT IS A TIA, AND WHAT CAN BE DONE ABOUT IT?

A transient ischemic attack (TIA) is a reversible ministroke. The symptoms of weakness and impaired speech or visual difficulty may last for minutes or hours, but by definition, no more than a day. After this short period, everything pretty much returns to the status quo.

TIAs have troublesome implications: they may recur; they may be a warning of a bigger stroke; and they have been associated with an increase in heart attacks.

Some arise from a narrowed or ulcerated area in the carotid artery, the major artery in the neck that conducts blood to the head and brain. Occasionally, such a narrowed area can be operated on successfully. Often, however, the platelets clump or a small clot arises from the heart, so that a carotid operation does not solve the problem.

As an alternative treatment, aspirin may inhibit the clumping of platelets that can occur in such a carotid artery and decrease the risk.

This study showed that palpitations (heavy heartbeats) or angina (chest pain) before the TIA point to a heart-related origin, as does the common disorder of heart rhythm called *atrial fibrillation*. In contrast, a murmur over the carotid artery in the neck and marked narrowing of the artery revealed by X ray or similar technique points to the artery as the cause of the TIA.

J. Bogousslavisky, V. C. Hachinski, D. R. Bougliner, et al., "Cardiac and Arterial Lesions in Carotid Transient Ischemic Attacks," *Archives of Neurology* 43 (1986): 223.

the vessel by tiny platelet clumps or blood clots, called *emboli*, which may break off from plaque areas in the heart or neck arteries.

The symptoms are similar to those of a full-fledged stroke, except for the fact that they typically last only twenty-four hours or less. In fact, attacks often last for less than thirty minutes, with a complete recovery. The symptoms may include blindness in one eye (described often as a "blackout" or "whiteout" of vision), difficulty speaking or writing, or numbness or weakness of the face, arm, or leg on one side of the body.

Do not ignore a TIA, even if it lasts only a few minutes and then you feel as normal as ever! About one-third of those who have a TIA can expect a real stroke within five years. Put in other terms, a person who has had a TIA is 9.5 times more likely to have a stroke than another person of the same age and sex who has not had one.

So it is essential for those who think they have experienced a TIA to contact their doctor immediately for a checkup. For that matter, it is equally important for everyone over fifty to reduce or eliminate the risk factors in life that may eventually lead to a stroke.

What Is Your Risk of Having a Stroke?

Whenever possible, I always try to provide my patients with information they can use to evaluate their level of risk for various health concerns. Fortunately, stroke is one problem that we can be forewarned about through the presence of certain established risk factors.

When advising my patients, I like to follow the practice of dividing these risk factors into those that cannot be changed and those that can. But remember: Even though it is not possible to change some things, it is possible to limit or reduce the risk associated with them by making alterations elsewhere in your life pattern.

Certain risk factors *cannot* be changed:

• *Age.* Even though stroke can occur to anyone, regardless of age, the danger does increase with age. Studies show that 80 percent of strokes occur in people who are sixty-five years old or older.

KEY FACTS

RISK FACTORS FOR STROKE

Eighteen hundred residents of Rochester, Minnesota, aged fifty or more, were followed at the Mayo Clinic for thirteen years. Among other procedures, the researchers made an analysis of the strokes that occurred in this group. Their study revealed that the following risk factors, in descending order of importance, were most often associated with stroke:

- Hypertension
- Heart disease
- Male gender
- Diabetes
- Aging

Hypertension, then, is the major villain on the stroke scene. Note also that having heart disease or diabetes greatly increases the risk. Finally, even in the absence of all other diseases, aging alone increases the risk.

P. H. Davis, J. M. Dambrosia, B. S. Schoenberg, et al., "Risk Factors for Ischemic Stroke," *Annals of Neurology* 22 (1987): 319.

- *Family history.* Stroke victims often have a parent or parents who have also had strokes. One piece of evidence of the genetic link to stroke: Several studies have shown that high blood pressure and diseases of the blood vessels in the brain occur more frequently among identical twins than among fraternal twins of the same sex. NOTE: Identical twins have exactly the same genes; fraternal twins do not.
- *Sex.* Men are more likely to have a stroke than women up to age seventy-five. After seventy-five, the incidence is about the same for men as for women.
- *Race.* Blacks in the thirty-five- to seventy-five-year age-group have fatal strokes almost twice as often as whites. Probably the major factor in strokes among blacks is the greater incidence of high blood pressure in this group. Sickle cell anemia, which occurs almost exclusively in blacks, often causes strokes through blood clots.

• *A personal history of stroke.* People who have had one stroke and survived it are at greater risk to have another stroke. In the Framingham Study, a study of nearly 5,000 residents of a Massachusetts city that has been going on since 1949, researchers found that of 198 men and 196 women who had strokes, 84 had second strokes and 27 had third strokes.

• *Diabetes mellitus.* I include this condition among problems that cannot be changed because you are born with a tendency toward diabetes. On the other hand, diabetes can be controlled through diet, weight loss, and other measures. So do not assume if you have diabetes, that you have to give up on reducing the impact of this disease as a stroke risk factor!

Those who have too much sugar in the blood run almost double the risk of stroke. The reason? One possibility is that the excessive blood sugar that results from diabetes not only damages blood vessels, but also interferes with the normal breakdown of *fibrin,* a plasma protein that holds blood clots together.

There are several risk factors that you *can* influence:

• *High blood pressure.* This may be the most serious risk factor for stroke. Strokes occur two to four times more often in those with high blood pressure than in those with normal blood pressure. Here, high blood pressure would be defined as a reading of 160/95 or higher. REMEMBER: The newest definitions require that blood pressure higher than 140/90 be treated in some fashion.

As blood pressure—and especially systolic pressure (the upper number in the blood pressure reading)—increases, the chance of stroke increases as well.

• *Heart disease.* Blood clots may develop and become stuck in narrowed arteries of those with atherosclerosis, or hardening of the arteries. If the clot blocks off blood to the brain, a stroke may occur.

Blood clots may also form in those who have heart valve defects and after heart attacks or certain bacterial infections, such as in rheumatic valves. In addition, heart surgery and artificial hearts may cause clots to appear.

• *Transient ischemic attacks (TIAs).* From our previous discussions of TIAs, you already know that these "ministrokes" can signal the possibility of later strokes in many people.

• *A high number of red blood cells.* In a disease known as *polycythemia,* the body manufactures too many red blood cells, thus causing the blood to become thick and sludgelike. The flow of this "thick" blood to the brain is slower than that of normal blood, and the tendency for clots to form increases. Clots in vessels leading to the brain, as you know, are a major factor in the development of many strokes.

This problem can be relieved by systematic bleeding under a physician's supervision so that the number of red blood cells is reduced.

• *Smoking.* In the Framingham Study, cigarette smoking was shown to be a risk factor for stroke, especially in men under sixty-five. A 1988 study at Harvard University and the Brigham and Women's Hospital in Boston also reported that women who smoke increase their risk of stroke substantially.

The researchers found that women up to fifty-five years old who smoked as few as fourteen cigarettes a day had a risk of developing a stroke 2.2 times greater than that of nonsmokers. Those who smoked twenty-five or more cigarettes a day had a 3.7 times greater risk of stroke. Fatal strokes were almost 6 times more common among smokers than nonsmokers.

• *Alcohol.* Those who drink heavily are at a greater risk of stroke.

I was appalled several years ago to read of the numerous admissions to Swedish hospitals of men under forty with the diagnosis of stroke. Investigation showed that most of them had a history of major weekend bouts of drinking. This was indeed *heavy* drinking: say, up to a fifth a day for several days. Such imbibing produces rising blood pressure and dehydration, with possible blood clots or hemorrhaging within the brain.

An early insight on this issue, which has seldom been mentioned, was made clear to me more than forty years ago in work by one of my colleagues, Melvin H. Kniseley, at the University of Chicago. Kniseley had been making microscopic observations on the blood flow through the smaller vessels in the eyelid and nail bed. He noted the effect of heat, cold, excitement, and other events in these areas.

In the course of his work, he stumbled onto the fact that after a single alcoholic drink, the red blood cells no longer flowed along as individual cells; instead, they became clumped together. Furthermore, as the amount of alcohol consumption increased, the blood cell clumps grew larger. Blood flow slowed so much that the circulation became slow and very abnormal.

Kniseley made some calculations that convinced him that in the small vessels of the brain, these abnormalities would cut down on the oxygen supply. Then, the clumping could lead to clotting. His observations and calculations so appalled him that he swore off liquor and became a teetotaler!

I looked down the same microscope at the evidence that Kniseley had viewed, and I can vouch for the red blood cell clumping. So when the reports came out of Sweden, I gasped, "Mel was right!"

HEALTH REPORT

CIGARETTE SMOKING AS A RISK FACTOR FOR STROKE

Over a twelve-year period of observation, the risk of stroke in male smokers studied was two to three times greater than that in nonsmokers. In the men who stopped smoking, the risk dropped close to that of the nonsmokers.*

In the Framingham Study of 4,255 men and women, ages thirty-six to sixty-eight years, there were 459 strokes over a twenty-six-year follow-up period. The results:

Regardless of smoking status in either sex, there was twice as much stroke in those with hypertension.

The risk of stroke increased as cigarette consumption increased. The relative risk in heavy smokers (two or more packs per day) was twice that of light smokers. In those who quit, risk decreased significantly after two years and came down to the level of the nonsmoker by five years after smoking had ceased.†

*R. D. Abbott, Y. Yin, D. M. Reed, et al., "Risk of Stroke in Male Cigarette Smokers," *The New England Journal of Medicine* 315 (1986); 717.
†P. A. Wolf, R. B. D'Agostino, W. B. Kannel, et al., "Cigarette Smoking as a Risk Factor for Stroke—The Framingham Study," *The Journal of the American Medical Association* 259 (1988): 1025.

In weighing the pros and cons—after all, a drink a day does raise the HDLs, the "good cholesterol"—I came to this conclusion: Humans, being social animals, can certainly have one cocktail per day. But they should never have more, and it would be wise to skip some days altogether. There is no evidence that social

---

HEALTH REPORT

THE LINK BETWEEN ALCOHOL AND STROKE

The following are highlights from a 1988 review article on alcohol and stroke:

A 1974 Kaiser-Permanente study concluded that moderate drinking might lower coronary artery disease. This "happy possibility" has been repeatedly reexamined since then. Most studies have concluded that light drinking *does* seem to lower coronary artery risk and that this reduction may take place because of a beneficial effect of alcohol on cholesterol fractions of the blood.

The author of the review points out, however, that moderate drinkers are likely to have moderate life patterns and that their overall life behavior may be the reason for their better coronary mortality. It is also entirely clear that *heavy* drinking *is* a risk factor for heart disease. Furthermore, heavy drinking materially increases the risk of stroke.

On the other hand, there is a possibility that light drinking may be protective against stroke: In one study, stroke risk was only half as high in very light drinkers (3 ounces or less per week) as in nondrinkers. But heavier drinkers (10 ounces or more per week) had four times the risk of nondrinkers.

In another study of stroke due to hemorrhage, the incidence of stroke per 100 men was 4.6 for nondrinkers, 10.0 for light drinkers, 13.2 for moderate drinkers, and 21.2 for heavy drinkers. Conclusion: There can be no doubt that heavy drinking is a risk factor for both coronary artery disease and stroke.

E. R. Eichner, "Alcohol, Stroke and Coronary Artery Disease," *American Family Physician* 37 (1988): 217.

drinking, say one or two cocktails per day, has a harmful impact on the cardiovascular system. But heavy drinking? That's definitely a bad idea.

• *Drug abuse.* A stroke may be brought on by the injection of amphetamines, cocaine, pentazocine, or tripelennamine. Heroin and LSD use has also been linked to stroke.

What About Surgery
to Prevent or Treat Stroke?

Many times, after a person has suffered a "ministroke" or TIA, an examination reveals that one of his or her *carotid arteries* (the large arteries on each side of the neck) has become narrowed or blocked with fatty deposits. In fact, it has been estimated that disease of these arteries accounts for up to 50 percent of all strokes.

Because of the role that clogging of the carotid arteries often plays in stroke, surgeons have frequently recommended an operation known as a *carotid endarterectomy* to clean out the fatty deposits in these vessels. Who might be a candidate for this surgery?

Sometimes, in an effort to prevent the onset of a major stroke, the operation is performed on those who have experienced TIAs. On other occasions, patients who have already had a major stroke undergo the procedure to increase blood flow to the head. Some people who have shown no symptoms may still be recommended for this surgery if an arteriogram or other such test shows that they have significant blockages in a carotid artery.

The popularity of this operation peaked in 1985, when doctors performed carotid endarterectomies on 107,000 people in the United States. But then, criticisms began to mount that perhaps too much of this type of surgery was being performed. The number of operations dropped to 83,000 in 1986.

A study conducted at the RAND Corporation in Santa Monica, California, and published in 1988 in *The New England Journal of Medicine,* revealed that 10 percent of the elderly Americans who undergo this surgery either die or suffer strokes as a direct result of the operation. The report charged that two-thirds of the operations are done for inappropriate or questionable reasons.

On the other hand, the researchers said, the rate of major complications was much lower—about 3 percent—at major medical centers.

Should you have this surgery? I would suggest you consider certain guidelines, namely, that you should only undergo this procedure if

- you have suffered warning symptoms, such as a TIA;
- you have significant clogging of your carotid arteries;
- you are in good enough health to withstand the operation; and
- you can secure the services of a surgeon who has a good track record for this type of operation, including few or no complications in his previous cases.

The Outlook for Rehabilitation

In addition to surgery, there are a number of other approaches to treatment or rehabilitation after a stroke has occurred. Successful rehabilitation depends on the extent of brain damage, the attitude of the patient, the skill of the specialists managing the rehabilitation, and the cooperation of family and friends. An effective rehabilitation program takes all these factors into consideration.

The first key to success is quick action. In general, physical and mental improvement decreases considerably after about six weeks, with little further improvement six months after the stroke occurs.

One fast-action plan for getting rehabilitation started quickly goes like this:

First day: The patient, if conscious, should be sitting up in a chair.

Second day: He or she should try some balancing exercises on the end of the bed or in a chair.

Third day: The patient should stand on his feet with the support of the medical staff.

After this, the stroke victim should engage in various physical activities, such as walking and moving the arms and legs. He should also return home as soon as possible to help lift his spirits.

HEALTH REPORT

TRAVEL RECOMMENDATIONS FOR STROKE PATIENTS WITH URINARY INCONTINENCE

The "Questions and Answers" section of *The Journal of the American Medical Association* is a useful doctor-to-doctor exchange with much practical information. One questioner writing in this section described an elderly wheelchair-bound stroke victim who was generally able to control an otherwise urgent bladder, but who, on failure to use a toilet, experienced occasional urinary incontinence every four hours in a home setting.

But now, the woman is faced with a a real challenge: a six- to seven-hour flight. She has also been informed that the plane's toilets are not wide enough for a wheelchair.

The medical expert answering this question advises against the use of a catheter but does suggest one or both of the following approaches:

• Use of drugs to cut down on bladder activity, one of which is imipramine (Elavil). This drug alone may do the job.

• Cease all liquid intake for twelve hours before departure; void in a wheelchair-accessible bathroom in the airport just before departure; and wear an adult-type diaper as further precaution.

D. D. Cardenas, "The Stroke Patient with Urinary Incontinence: Recommendations for Travel," *The Journal of the American Medical Association* 257 (1987): 244.

Because depression often follows a stroke, a physician may prescribe antidepressants after the attack. In one study at the Cleveland Metropolitan General and Highland View Hospital, the drug doxepin was given to eleven men and women, aged seventy to eighty-three, who had suffered a stroke. The medication significantly reduced their depressive symptoms.

17

AN INTRODUCTION
TO THE CHALLENGE
OF CANCER

Forty years ago, I was a two-pack-a-day cigarette smoker. But then, I started hearing about research developments that were linking smoking to lung cancer. All the evidence was not in at the time, but I was impressed with the preliminary findings. The arguments the medical researchers were making convinced me that I had nothing to lose and probably a lot to gain by giving up cigarettes forever.

It was difficult. I had tried several times, and I knew I was addicted. But I finally resolved to act decisively, primarily on a gut feeling that I was probably harming my health: I quit smoking completely in 1952 and advised my patients to do the same. As it has turned out, I have lived to see the solid evidence that smoking causes not only lung cancer, but other types of cancers and also heart disease.

Not all my colleagues were so lucky. I remember, when I was about to give up smoking in 1952, that I got into a discussion with the chief of the cancer division of my hospital. During our talk, I referred to a study I had just read on an association that had been noted between smoking and lung cancer.

Holding a cigarette and blowing smoke not far from my face, he said, "Yes, I've seen that study. I think the evidence is kind of weak. It's just an association. Besides, I know plenty of older people who are lifelong smokers but who don't have cancer of the lung."

Many scientists feel they *have* to be in possession of definitive evidence on a subject before they can commit themselves to some sort of action. But I am not that way: If everything points in a certain direction—and it's clear that going in that direction will not damage my health or that of my patients—I move ahead on the basis of the evidence at hand.

But my cancer chief wasn't of this frame of mind. He had to know *definitely,* or he wouldn't act. So he continued to smoke during the ensuing years, even as the evidence piled up on the unhealthy effects of smoking.

Finally, in 1962, the United States surgeon general reported that cancers outside the lung were also related to smoking. Of these, cancers of the kidney, bladder, and brain were among the most serious. But by then, it was too late for my colleague. He had already died, presumably of a smoking-related brain tumor.

I tell this story not to suggest that I was smarter than my friend and therefore I am the one now alive. Rather, I want to emphasize that point about the importance of acting decisively in some circumstances on the evidence at hand, without necessarily waiting for the final word. Waiting for presumptive evidence to turn into certainty may be risky, or even lethal.

As far as cancer is concerned, there is plenty of solid evidence, as well as some strong indicators that haven't quite reached the level of evidence, that making certain changes in your life may well help you prevent the onset of cancer. You should also know about how to detect it early, when effective steps can be taken to treat it. To understand what is now known about cancer, and what you may be able to do about it, it is important first to have a grasp of the basic concepts of the disease.

What Is Cancer?

Cancer is the second greatest killer disease in our society, with only heart disease claiming more victims.

About 75 million Americans who are now alive, or 30 percent of the population, will eventually suffer from some form of cancer. Cancer strikes more often as people get older. Nearly a half million people a year die from cancer, with lung cancer, the bane of the smoker, the major cause of death.

What exactly is cancer? It is a disease characterized by an uncontrolled growth and spread of abnormal cells. Usually, the cells that make up the various parts of the body reproduce so that growth, replacement of worn-out tissues, and repair of physical injuries proceed in an orderly fashion.

On occasion, however, a cell may careen out of control and multiply into a mass of tissue called a *tumor.* Even in that event, the problem may be minor: some tumors are benign, or noncancerous. They may grow too large and become an annoyance or interfere with some bodily function. But they do not invade other tissues in the body, and they usually do not threaten a person's life. The typical way of dealing with a benign tumor that causes discomfort is to have it removed surgically.

But other tumors are malignant, or cancerous. They invade and destroy other bodily tissues. Cancerous cells also may break away from their original locations through a process called *metastasis.* When this happens, they spread through the blood and lymph systems to other parts of the body, where they create new cancer colonies.

This spread of cancer may occur quickly, or it may take years. But the result, in the absence of effective treatment, will often be death.

What Can Be Done to Prevent Cancer?

Understanding cancer well enough to take steps to prevent it is not always an easy task.

One of the last lectures I heard as I was leaving the University of Chicago Medical School in 1942 was by Leo Loeb, the distinguished research scientist from St. Louis. The problem that he had devoted countless hours to studying was that of metastasis (spread of cancer from its original site to a more distant location). It has always been a challenging problem to try to determine why some cancers slip into the blood vessels or lymphatic vessels and then reappear at distant places in the body.

The most-favored "distant destinations" for cancerous cells in the bloodstream are the liver, the lungs, and the bone marrow. Nearby or distant lymph nodes may also be involved in the transport of metastasis because the lymphatic vessels form a complete system throughout the body, much like the blood (vascular) system.

But not all cancers are "traveling" diseases. Some tumors that look quite malignant under the microscope multiply in place and never spread to a distant location. Obviously they lend themselves to removal and cure much more readily.

The goal that Dr. Loeb had set for himself was to elucidate the difference between tumors that spread and tumors that do not spread. Among other things, he thought that with study and observation of tumors in animals, he would be able to resolve this problem.

In the course of his lecture, he showed us a lot of interesting slides of tumors invading blood vessels, as against tumors that were pushed away by the vessel wall. In the end, though, he confessed that he was unable to make out the reasons for this basic difference.

As I sat listening to Dr. Loeb, I thought to myself, "By the time I get to his age, we will have worked that one out!"

But here we are, some forty-seven years later, and in many fields of cancer study, we do not seem to have made much progress at all. As far as metastasis is concerned, we are *still* very far from understanding why certain body cells go astray and start multiplying haphazardly and invasively, encroaching on nearby and distant tissues.

On the other hand, we *have* made a considerable amount of progress in some ways, and that progress has given us a foundation for beginning to develop useful plans for cancer prevention. An important reason for the headway in the war against cancer has been the work of the National Cancer Institute, which for years has been giving out about a billion dollars per annum in research grants.

As a result of this work, our understanding of cancer has increased in a number of important areas, such as:

- *The genetic connection.* We know much more today than we did in Dr. Loeb's time that cancer operates through genetic changes, the changes in the chromosomes of the cell nucleus, which turn on the closed spigot of cell reproduction.

  Among other advances, we have a far greater understanding of carcinogenic substances, which alter the deoxyribonucleic acid (DNA), the genetic material of the cell, and then proceed to initiate or promote cancer. For some cancers and leukemias, the precise gene responsible for uncontrolled growth has been identified.

HEALTH REPORT

DOES HAIR DYE CAUSE CANCER?

A number of studies over the past decade have indicated that beauticians and cosmetologists handling hair dyes in their work are at increased risk for cancers of the urinary tract and of the blood cell manufacturing system (for example, leukemia and lymphoma).

This study, emanating from the National Cancer Institute, also finds an increase in cancer of the lymphatic cell line in individuals to whom the hair dye is applied. The risk is approximately double that of persons who do not use hair coloring agents. Duration of use seems to increase risk. Which of the dyes and coloring agents are riskier remains for further research to determine.

K. P. Cantor, A. Blair, G. Everett, et al., "Hair Dye Use and Risk of Leukemia and Lymphoma," *American Journal of Public Health* 78 (1988): 570.

- *The role of carcinogenic substances.* We have mastered a considerable amount of information about cancer-promoting substances

---

HEALTH REPORT

DIET, SMOKING, AND LUNG CANCER

The question of why some smokers escape lung cancer has stimulated studies of diets in a search for protective factors.

One large Japanese study found a lower risk of lung cancer for both smokers and nonsmokers who had a higher green and yellow vegetable intake. A Norwegian study confirmed this decrease for current and former smokers by identifying the importance of a higher vitamin A intake.

In an American Cancer Society study, a strong protective effect was ascribed to green salads, fruits, and fruit juice consumed five to seven times a week. Still other studies have pointed to beta-carotene, a precursor to vitamin A, as an important protective agent.

Selenium has also been demonstrated statistically to exert a similar protective effect, but no major influence has been unearthed for vitamin E or C.

The authors observe that, by far, the best protection against lung cancer is to be a nonsmoker.

G. A. Colditz, M. J. Stampfer, and W. C. Willett, "Diet and Lung Cancer," *Archives of Internal Medicine* 147 (1987): 157.

---

such as those in tobacco, for instance, whore role was unknown when I was a cigarette-smoking medical student.

• *The similarity between certain cancers.* We know, for example, that there is a parallel incidence of certain cancers such as those of the breast and colon. Contrary trends may also be found: For instance, while the incidence of cancer of the stomach has decreased by more than half over the last thirty years, that of colon cancer has risen. This points to entirely different causations, including perhaps dietary changes.

• *The multiple-factor issue.* We appreciate far more that there are multiple factors involved in causing or promoting cancer. In other words, cancer is not a single disease, but one of many origins.

• *The variability of cancer among different populations.* Cancer has a strikingly different distribution in different populations.

HEALTH REPORT

WHAT IF NOBODY SMOKED?

Cigarette smoking causes more premature deaths than all of the following together: auto accident, homicide and suicide, fire, drug abuse (including alcohol), and acquired immune deficiency syndrome (AIDS). In a tobacco-free United States, the life expectancy gain would be comparable to what it would be if all forms of cancer disappeared.

The economic implications of a tobacco-free United States are almost innumerable. For example:

• There would be economic damage to the manufacturers of shellac, an additive in cigarettes.

• There would be a short-term boom for apparel manufacturers because of weight gain in former smokers, but this boom would be balanced by a loss of sales due to burns in clothing.

• There are 710,000 jobs in tobacco-related industries, and these would be placed in jeopardy if no one smoked. But 350,000 people die each year as a result of using tobacco; each of these victims loses an average of fifteen years of life. The tobacco industry calls attention to the first figure and is silent about the second one.

K. E. Warner, "Health and Economic Implications of a Tobacco-Free Society," *The Journal of the American Medical Association* 258 (1987): 2080.

For example, we know that cancer of the colon, now the number-one cancer in the elderly of both sexes, is fourteen times more common in most advanced societies of Western Europe and the United States than it is in Third World countries, with poorer standards of living.

We also know that Japanese women have a far lower incidence of breast cancer in Japan than they have after they migrate to Hawaii or to the United States. This certainly suggests that some-

---

HEALTH REPORT

COLON DISEASE IN THE ELDERLY

A few highlights from the cancer section of an informative 1985 review:

Colon cancer is an important cancer because of its high incidence in old age and its successful surgical cure rate.

Benign tumors (adenomas) are found in 5 to 10 percent of the population over forty. Adenomas can turn into cancers over a ten- to fifteen-year period. The incidence is slightly higher in those whose gallbladders have been removed. This is attributable to changes in the bile acids, which are known to be elevated in patients with colon cancer and to be lower in low-risk groups, such as vegetarians.

Other studies have linked increased incidence of colon cancer to high-meat diets.

In animal experiments, fiber has been shown to exert a protective effect, as does calcium, which may act by turning the bile acids and free fatty acids into insoluble calcium soaps.

Rates of colon cancer are three times as high in the United States, Canada, Belgium, and Ireland as in Japan. Screening procedures, such as stool tests for blood and proctosigmoidoscopy, are of value in detecting earlier cases of colon adenomas and cancers.

J. C. Brocklehurst, "Colonic Disease in the Elderly," *Clinics in Gastroenterology* 14, no. 9 (1985): 725.

---

thing in the environment is cancer-inciting, with the best probability that it is something in the diet.

KEY FACTS

LIMITING CANCER-INDUCING SUBSTANCES IN YOUR DIET

In a landmark contribution, the discoverer of a rapid test for mutagens reviewed the large number of known cancer-inciting and mutagenic (gene-changing) substances of natural origin. The following are some of the sixteen examples of carcinogens that he describes:

• *Safrole,* found in many edible plants and present in "natural" sarsaparilla root beer and in black pepper.

• *Hydrazines,* found in many edible mushrooms.

• *Psoralen derivatives,* found in celery, parsnips, figs, and parsley.

• *Allyl isothiocyanate,* in mustard and horseradish.

• *Gossypol,* found in cottonseed and its oil. (NOTE: This substance is being tested as a male contraceptive in China because it destroys sperm!)

• *Mold carcinogens,* present in mold-contaminated corn, grain, nuts, peanut butter, cheese, fruit, and apple juice.

• *Nitrites,* found in beets, celery, lettuce, spinach, radishes, and often in well water.

Products such as burned food, rancid fats, coffee, and high-fat foods have also been associated with cancers of the colon and breast.

Obviously, we cannot completely avoid all these foods, and we should not. Many of them are a necessary part of our diets. Yet what can protect us from all these potentially cancer-inciting substances? To put this another way, what may be the *anti*carcinogens in our diet?

They may include vitamin E, beta-carotene (found in carrots), selenium, ascorbic acid (vitamin C), glutathione, and plants such as the cabbages, which are known to inhibit cancer in certain experimental animals.

Ames indicates that all living forms have had to grapple with cancer-producing substances in the course of their development. The key seems to be gaining knowledge of what may contribute to cancer and then limiting or avoiding it. But this approach *does not* mean we should become obsessed about remaining completely pure or separated from all these substances, because that's just not possible. The cancer-fighting agents in a good diet should overcome the moderate amounts of natural carcinogens to which most of us are exposed.

B. N. Ames, "Dietary Carcinogens and Anticarcinogens," *Science* 221 (1983): 1256.

- *The cause of lung cancer.* It is an absolute certainty that cancer of the lung is at least 90 percent attributable to smoking.
- *The cause of skin cancer.* Cancers of the skin occur almost exclusively in some exposed areas of the body. The disease results from mutagenic changes in the skin cells produced by ultraviolet light.

HEALTH REPORT

SKIN PROBLEMS AMONG THE FIFTY-PLUS, INCLUDING SKIN CANCER

In this 1988 study, sixty-eight persons aged fifty to ninety-one years residing in a community in the northeastern United States (average age seventy-four) were evaluated by questionnaires and complete examination.

Sixty-six percent of the group and more than 80 percent of the octogenarians had concerns with their skin, most of them itching. Important findings included the following: xerosis (dryness), 85 percent; seborrheic keratoses (benign, slightly elevated pigmented areas), 61 percent; cherry angiomas (benign, tiny cherry red growths), 54 percent; actinic keratoses (sun-damaged areas, generally considered to be premalignant), 18 percent; athlete's foot, 18 percent; skin cancer, 4 percent.

Most sufferers from dry skin used a moisturizer regularly. Frequency of bathing was only slightly less in those over eighty (5.4 baths or showers per week) than in those younger (6.1). Sixty percent regularly shaved some part of the body. Six of the eight men and ten of the sixty women shaved in the beard area, and seven more women tweezed or depilated facial hair.

The authors note that in the oldest age-group (sixty-five to seventy-four) of the national health survey 40 percent were judged to have "significant skin pathology" by the examining dermatologist, with 18 percent having benign or malignant skin tumors. A majority had not sought medical attention for the skin.

S. Beauregard and B. A. Gilchrest, "A Survey of Skin Problems and Skin Care Regimens in the Elderly," *Archives of Dermatology* 123 (1988): 1638.

The accumulation of such facts increases the probability of preventing cancer from a hope to a certainty, at least at some point in the future. In the meantime, we still face the stark reality that as people grow older, the incidence of various cancers increases. Why should this be?

Why Cancer Risk Increases with Age

Recently, a number of interesting studies have focused on the body's immune system, with its defense mechanisms against cancer. Although scientists have found some ways to stimulate these defenses, we are still very far from being able to prevent cancer at the cellular level. The statistics speak for themselves about our success, or lack thereof: It is still true that 25 percent of all deaths can be ascribed to cancer, so clearly we have a long way to go.

One reason for the persistently high mortality rate for cancer is that the disease doubles in incidence for every decade past age thirty. The older people get, the more likely they are to get cancer.

What are the reasons for this? There are some who point out that the body's immune system, which enables it to fight off many threats, shows a decline with aging.

An example of this phenomenon is the disease shingles. After an attack of chicken pox in childhood, the chicken pox virus remains latent in the body, generally "sleeping" in the nerve cells of the spinal cord for many decades.

But with aging, the virus reasserts itself in the form of that unpleasant, painful disease called *shingles.* This is a disease of the endings of the nerves, with such symptoms as crusts on the skin, blisters, and pain in the nerve. Obviously, the virus has been held in check for half a century or more. But at some point, the immune balance in the body has been altered, and the viral infection has flared up again.

By analogy, many scientists feel that the ability to fight off cells that have turned malignant may also be impaired with aging.

Still another important age-related point is the fact that it takes many years for an agent known to incite cancer actually to do its work. A good example is tobacco, which is known to be "weakly carcinogenic," that is to say, weakly cancer-producing.

HEALTH REPORT

DOES THE PROGRESS OF CANCER SLOW WITH AGE?

It has been generally thought that in the very old, cancers grow at a slower rate, but that idea is *not* corroborated in a study of breast cancer in Swedish women.

The records of 57,068 cases were studied between 1960 and 1978. The best survival rate was in women aged forty-five to forty-nine. After this age, relative survival rates declined, especially for women fifty to fifty-nine at the time of diagnosis.

The worst rate was found for women over seventy-five. For premenopausal women the annual mortality rate was 1 to 2 percent, but it exceeded 5 percent for women in the oldest age-group, after corrections for other causes of death.

Virtually all the women were treated by mastectomy and without adjunct therapy, as was customary in the time period studied. Under these circumstances the study demonstrates no slowing of cancer's progress in the old as against the young.

[NOTE: Since then, it has been shown that the outlook is significantly improved by various adjunctive treatments, such as hormonal manipulation, chemotherapy, and irradiation. Specifically in the case of older women, the drug tamoxifen improves the outlook.]

H. O. Adami, B. Malker, L. Holmberg, et al., "The Relation Between Survival and Age at Diagnosis of Breast Cancer," *The New England Journal of Medicine* 315 (1986): 559.

The substances in smoke have to be applied to the lining of bronchial tubes for many years before cancer arises. Consequently, one rarely sees cancer in a smoker before some twenty years of smoking. In other smokers, thirty or forty years of smoking may elapse before the appearance of a tumor. Similarly, cancers of the skin have been related to bad sunburns in youth, though they occur predominantly in the elderly.

So for a variety of reasons, decades have to pass before cancer will become manifest. The slowness of the development of the disease may be the chief reason for the apparent link between aging and cancer.

HEALTH REPORT

ALCOHOL AND BREAST CANCER

In this 1987 study, 7,188 women, twenty-five to seventy-four years of age, were followed for more than ten years.

The findings: 121 cases of breast cancer developed. The risk at any level of drinking (beer, wine, liquor), as compared to no drinking at all, was 1.5. The increased risk was noted with as little as three drinks per week. No increased risk was noted with cigarette smoking alone.

M. D. Schatzkin, D. Y. Jones, R. N. Hoover, et al., "Alcohol Consumption and Breast Cancer," *The New England Journal of Medicine* 316 (1987): 1169.

The connection between cancer and aging is evident in virtually all forms of the disease past childhood. Breast cancer, for example, shows two appearance "spurts" in the female population: First, the incidence of this disease tends to be relatively high for women in their forties; then, there is another surge of breast cancer among women in their sixties and beyond.

Cancer of the prostate also comes on fairly late in life. It rarely emerges before a man is in his fifties, but then it rises to become perhaps the most common cancer in men in their eighties and beyond. Hence its nickname, "the old man's cancer."

Because most people want to grow older we find that we increasingly have to reckon with the cancer threat. But a well-thought-out plan of prevention can go a long way toward helping reduce the risks and enhancing the chances of victory.

A Basic Cancer-Prevention Plan

How can you go about formulating an effective approach to reduce your risk of getting cancer? I think in terms of the following three-part plan.

Avoid Risky Life Patterns

One strategy is to take steps to prevent changes in the cell's mechanisms for controlling growth. To this end, whenever possible, you must dodge the cancer-inducing agents that have been identified in our environment. This may be as simple as using protective ointments against the sun, or as complex as developing a completely new nutritional program designed to do such things as lower your fat intake and raise your consumption of fiber.

Perhaps the clearest example of avoiding unnecessary risks is quitting smoking. As you know, smoking is not only the cause of almost all cancer of the lung, a fairly lethal form of cancer; it is also involved in other forms of cancer.

Specifically, it has been clearly documented that the incidence of cancer in a variety of human organs is higher in smokers. We know, for example, that cancer-inducing agents inhaled from the cigarette smoke make their way to the kidney and are excreted in the urine. For this reason cancer of the kidney; the ureter, which conducts the urine down from the kidney to the bladder; and the bladder itself are all significantly higher in smokers. What is more, even distant cancers, such as brain tumors, are increased in smokers.

Cancers of the skin—both the common basal cell cancers and the more aggressive squamous cell cancers—are clearly related to some sun exposure. These tumors occur almost exclusively on the face, head, lip, and backs of the hands, all sun-exposed areas. They are clearly associated with other well-known ultraviolet-induced aging changes in these locations.

Thus, two life-style changes—avoiding smoking and dodging sun exposure (or using ultraviolet blockers)—can make a real contribution in the fight against cancer.

Watch What You Eat!

There can be no doubt that there are many relationships between diet and cancer. As a result, I suggest that you keep the following nutritional facts in mind:

• High-fat diets have been definitely implicated in an increased incidence of cancer of the breast and of the bowel. The calories derived from fat in the average American's diet represent

KEY FACTS

SOME FACTS ABOUT ADULT DIETS AND CANCER

In the Second National Health Survey (1976–80), the diet patterns of 11,658 adults were contrasted with the cancer dietary guidelines of the National Academy of Sciences and the American Cancer Society.

The survey revealed that the percentage of adults consuming recommended protective foods was small:

- 21 percent consumed the recommended amounts of fruits and vegetables;
- 16 percent ate enough high-fiber breads or cereals;
- 18 percent ate adequate amounts of cruciferous vegetables (the cauliflower, broccoli, and cabbage groups).

The percentages of people eating those foods that potentially add to the risk of cancer were relatively high:

- 55 percent, more than half, ate red meats.
- 43 percent ate bacon and lunch meats.

In general, the proportion of those consuming fruits and vegetables rose with increased income. Most groups reported eating more meat than poultry or fish.

Those reporting on the survey pointed out that helpful dietary changes may have occurred since 1980 because of increased publicity about healthful diets, growing popularity of salad bars, and addition of fiber to the diet.

B. H. Patterson and G. Block, "Food Choices and the Cancer Guidelines," *American Journal of Public Health* 78 (1988): 282.

40 percent of the person's total calories. This percentage should be cut to below 30 percent. In general, the less fat in your diet, the better!

- Some vitamin A components of the diet seem to lower the incidence of cancer. These nutrients are found in green leafy vegetables, fruits, and fruit juices.
- There are other foods that seem to have special protective values. Certain vegetables (cauliflower, brussels sprouts, broccoli)

have been shown to diminish the predictable incidence of cancer of the intestinal tract in animal experiments. Collateral lines of evidence indicate that this may be true for humans also.

HEALTH REPORT

THE SCOURGE OF STOMACH CANCER

Stomach cancer, though on the decline, is still the second most common fatal cancer worldwide.

Although no definite dietary causes have been identified, those with the disease regularly eat less fruit and vegetables than a control group.

Much attention has been paid to nitrates in the diet, especially levels in water, though various studies have not been in agreement on this. The European Community recommendation is that nitrates not exceed 25 mg per liter. In parts of South America, however, nitrates may exceed several hundred mg per liter, and, overall nutrition may be poor.

The author notes the possibility that despite the nitrates that may be found in vegetables, the presence of vitamin C may inhibit the chemical changes in nitrates that are thought to lead to cancerous compounds. He therefore endorses consumption of foods containing vitamin C.

He observes that there are dietary compounds that after treatment with nitrates are turned into potent direct-acting mutagens. They are found, for example, in Japanese soy sauce, in preserved fish, and in fava beans in Colombia. In both Japan and Colombia there are exceptionally high rates of stomach cancer. [NOTE: Smoked foods have also been linked to increased stomach cancer.]

D. Forman, "Gastric Cancer, Diet and Nitrate Exposure," *British Medical Journal* 294 (1987): 528.

• Obesity predisposes an individual to cancer, as well as to a variety of other diseases. So if you are carrying extra pounds around, weight reduction is in order!

• Other ingredients in the diet that have been shown to diminish the probability of cancer include adequate amounts of selenium, vitamin E, and vitamin C. The presumption is that on a good mixed diet these elements are present.

- Vegetarian diets have been shown to diminish the usual incidence of cancers in various bodily organs.

HEALTH REPORT

FAT, FIBER, CALCIUM, AND CANCER

A review of the use of nutrition to prevent cancer appeared recently in *Clinics in Geriatric Medicine.* Some highlights follow.

Half of all cancers occur in those over sixty-five years old, and the incidence at eighty years of age is double that at sixty.

An example of the importance of diet: The Seventh-Day Adventists, who are vegetarians, have half the incidence of colon cancer of the rest of the U.S. population.

Why should a vegetarian regimen be helpful? Dietary animal fats increase the content of fatty acids in the colon. Some of these acids are derived from bile, which is known to be an irritant to the cells of the lining of the colon.

Calcium in the diet combines with these fatty substances and diminishes the rate of proliferation of the irritated lining cells. High-fiber, "high-residue" foods may dilute the impact of potential cancer-inducing agents.

Also helpful in reducing dietary fats: choose leaner cuts of meat; trim all visible fat from foods; remove skin from poultry; eat low-fat dietary products; use smaller amounts of oils in dressings and cooking.

Besides calcium, vitamin C may also be of value, but ingestion of more than 1,000 mg per day may cause diarrhea, increase the possibility of kidney stones, and increase iron absorption (which may or may not be desirable, depending on your health status).

The authors believe that because cancer is a slow, multi-stage process, nutritional intervention at various points along the way may reverse it.

J. G. Guillem, M. S. Matsui, and C. A. O'Brian, "Nutrition in the Prevention of Neoplastic Disease in the Elderly," *Clinics in Geriatric Medicine* 3 (1987): 373.

• There are various lines of evidence to suggest that increasing the intake of fiber in the diet may diminish the expected incidence of cancer of the colon.

To what extent should you use *dietary supplements* as part of a cancer prevention plan? In my opinion, it is worthwhile for most people to take—in moderate doses—certain diet supplements that seem capable of inhibiting or even reversing the march toward malignancy.

One such group are the substances known as carotenoids, which are precursors of vitamin A. Carotenoids have been shown to reverse leukoplakia (white plaques that form on surfaces such as the lip and mouth), which are known to be precursors to cancer. In theory, there is no reason why the carotenoids and perhaps other supplements could not be taken by mouth, be assimilated, and be transported to unseen parts of the body, where there, too, they may reverse premalignant changes.

HEALTH REPORT

AN ATTACK ON "WHITE PLAQUE"

Leukoplakia (literally, "white plaque") is a well-recognized precursor to cancer and is found most commonly in the lining of the mouth.

The retinoids are a group of precursors of vitamin A reported to have anticancer effects. In this study 13-*cis*-retinoic acid was administered by mouth for three months.

The results: The typical white plaques shrank considerably in two-thirds of the subjects, and the abnormal appearance of the tissue under the microscope was reversed in more than half the cases. The study indicates that the early changes that lead to a cancer can be reversed.

W. K. Hong, J. Endicott, L. M. Itri, et al., "13-*cis*-Retinoic Acid in the Treatment of Oral Leukoplakia," *The New England Journal of Medicine* 315 (1986): 1501.

If you decide to take the supplement route, you'll be in good company. Many experts in cancer prevention whom I know take supplementary vitamin C up to a level of 1,000 mg per day, but not higher. There are some who lean toward taking the antioxidants: vitamin E, vitamin C, and the vitamin A precursors such as beta-carotene.

NOTE: The antioxidants have been shown to inhibit the impact of a carcinogen on the cell and to prevent the binding of the carcinogen to the cell's chromosome material. This binding is considered to be the first step in cancer formation.

Take Advantage of Cancer-Screening Procedures

Screening measures are of undoubted value in the battle against cancer. One prime example is *mammography,* an X-ray diagnostic method that allows physicians to identify small cancers of the breast before they can be felt by even the most skilled examiner.

KEY FACTS

SOME RISK FACTORS FOR BREAST CANCER

- Family history, especially breast cancer in mother, siblings
- High-fat diets, especially beef
- Alcohol
- Few or no pregnancies
- Little or no breast feeding
- Long reproductive span: early-onset menstruation, late menopause

---

Several large-scale studies have shown that women with access to mammography have better rates of survival. The reason? The tumors that are identified in their breasts and then removed are smaller, and therefore their outlook for recovery is improved.

Currently, the American Cancer Society recommends that every woman over forty should have a mammogram every couple of years and every woman over age fifty should have a mammogram every year.

Other screening measures that can form part of a cancer detection examination include the following:

● *Proctosigmoidoscopy.* In this procedure, a long, rigid or flexible, snakelike instrument with a light attached is inserted into the rectum and up into the lower portion of the colon. Because almost one-third of all colonic and rectal cancers are found within reach of this instrument, its use is recognized as a valid part of an annual physical examination

---

HEALTH REPORT

IS MAMMOGRAPHY PAINFUL?

Reports of pain or discomfort caused by mammography have been of concern to some women. In this survey of 1,847 women, the expectation of pain and the experience of pain and discomfort on examination were evaluated and categorized.

The results: 49 percent experienced no discomfort, and 39 percent mild discomfort only. Another 9 percent had moderate discomfort, and 1 percent, severe discomfort. Only 10 percent complained of moderate pain. None had pain to a degree that would lead her to refuse follow-up mammography.

Older women had no increase in discomfort, and the seventy- to eighty-nine-year groups had much less than the twenty- to twenty-nine-year group. Overall, those who anticipated discomfort had somewhat more.

P. C. Stomper, D. B. Kopans, and N. L. Sadowsky, "Is Mammography Painful?" *Archives of Internal Medicine* 148 (1988): 521.

● *The Papanicolaou test.* The Papanicolaou (Pap) test is mainly directed to finding cancer of the cervix, though cancer of the uterus above the level of the cervix may also be revealed through this method.

The test involves a scraping of cells from the cervix, the lowermost part of the uterus, and of the pool of cells in the upper vaginal vault. Then, the cells are spread out on a slide, stained, and examined under the microscope by a specially trained screener. It is possible to pick up early cancers of this area by this method. The gradual decline in the mortality from cancer of the cervix by American women has been chiefly due to Pap tests.

REMEMBER: This type of cancer increases with age, and so it is a mistake to stop performing this procedure for women past sixty. Women sometimes refuse this examination for one or another reason, and that's a major mistake. But if several consecutive tests have negative results, the interval may be lengthened to several years.

• *The Hemoccult slide test.* Another screening procedure is the Hemoccult test of the stool to detect invisible (occult) blood.

It's well known that tumors of the colon may break down or leak blood into the stool. The small amounts that are invisible can be detected in the stool specimen with this test.

Of course, bleeding from hemorrhoids and even blood swallowed from injured gums after vigorous tooth brushing may yield positive test results. On the other hand, a positive test finding will only alert the physician to consider the possibilities.

• *Other blood-test possibilities.* From time to time over my decades of practice, people have talked about the need for a blood test for cancer. Periodically, claims for such a test have arisen, but they have failed to stand up to scrutiny.

Still, there are tests with some limitations that may be of some value in certain circumstances. The carcinoembryonic antigen test (CEA), for example, is a test that may yield positive results for cancers of the colon and a few other parts of the digestive system. But this procedure suffers from an excessive number of false-negative and false-positive results.

One way this test can be useful, however, is for follow-up studies of persons who have had cancers of the colon surgically removed. A rise in the level of the CEA in the blood may call for a second look.

Another blood test that has some value in cancer detection is the so-called male Pap test, which measures the prostatic acid phosphatase, an enzyme secreted only by the prostate. When positive, this test result points to the probability of prostatic cancer.

The test is so sensitive, however, that it cannot or should not be done after a routine examination of the prostate. The reason is that prostatic massage tends to press some of the enzyme out into the bloodstream.

The fact that we do have some tests that yield positive results in the presence of cancers of the colon and of the prostate indicate that, both in theory and in practice, blood tests for the detection of cancer in different organs are feasible. There is a high probability that more acceptably accurate tests will come along in the future. Until then, a complete physical examination, use of the screening techniques mentioned, and self-examination by women of their breasts form a major part of the battle against the disease.

18

THE TREATMENT
OF CANCER

Quite naturally, the first question that a patient usually asks me on learning of the presence of cancer is "What are my chances?" And the second is "How are you going to treat it?"

These questions are closely linked because, of course, we want to choose the treatment that will provide the patient with the best chance of survival. To understand why some approaches may be chosen over others and what the outlook is for successfully limiting or curing specific forms of the disease, it is necessary to have an overview of the major treatment possibilities.

Is Surgery in Order?

The treatment of cancer has been disappointingly static for many decades, despite much research by our best brains and the outlay of huge sums of money. The oldest and still the most widely used treatment is surgical: throughout the early history of a cancerous growth, it remains localized. Hence, total removal by surgery at this stage can often cure the disease.

In fact, even if the tumor has infiltrated into the surrounding tissue or worse, has spread to nearby lymph nodes, it is often still a regional affair. So here again, surgical removal of the affected region may produce a cure, though it is apparent that with a greater spread of the disease, there is less hope that a regional removal will be sufficient.

Breast Cancer Surgery: The Ground-Breaking Field

A landmark in the history of cancer surgery was the development of the radical approach to breast surgery by the brilliant American surgeon Ward Halsted in 1894.

After studying the development of this type of cancer, Halsted concluded that with many breast tumors, the cells had already spread along lymphatic vessels running to the armpit. He also noted that spread to underlying tissues such as the breast muscles frequently was a factor. In addition, he saw that breast cancer often spread to the overlying skin, with puckering or even ulcerations that were grossly visible.

So he developed a surgical procedure to improve the chances of women with breast cancer. The Halsted operation consisted of a surgical removal of the entire breast, plus the underlying muscle and the lymph nodes in the armpit (axillary). For obvious reasons, the operation was termed a *radical mastectomy.*

An extensive body of knowledge sprang up about the radical mastectomy, which was considered to be a woman's best chance for survival. The evaluation of the axillary lymph nodes also became part of the routine of the breast examination: Perhaps twenty to twenty-five of the nodes would be examined microscopically. If none was involved with cancer, the outlook was considered good. Though there were exceptions, specialists in the Halsted method found that in general, in the absence of nodal involvement, cures were likely. But as the count of cancer-involved lymph nodes rose higher, the long-term experience indicated declining cure rates.

For some eighty years, the Halsted radical mastectomy was regarded as the gold standard in breast and cancer surgery. The theoretical base of the approach seemed secure, and the practice of Halsted's methods became entrenched. Gradually, however, voices began to be heard in opposition.

For one thing, there had always been a tendency toward troublesome disability for most women after the radical procedure, which required removal of useful muscles. There was also often chronic swelling that occurred in the arms.

Because of these drawbacks, the *simple mastectomy,* which left the pectoral muscles alone, gradually emerged as the predominant surgery. But there was still the loss of the breast to be considered.

Consequently, a new school that advocated an even more conservative surgery arose. Advocates published studies indicating that a very small excision, called a *lumpectomy,* followed by irradiation of the breast to kill off any microscopic groups of tumor cells, yielded results comparable to those of the more radical procedures.

And so the wheel turned full circle, and the gold standard of radical mastectomy collapsed. But still, the core approach remains the surgical one, especially for the most accessible breast tumors.

Cancer in the Rectum and Colon: Another Key Surgical Target

We physicians strive for a surgical cure with cancers in the rectum or colon because that is the approach most likely to "kill off" this killer disease. Consequently, we place a high priority on early detection so that surgery will have the best chance to succeed.

What colon surgeons find when they operate are tumors that exhibit varying degrees of penetration down into the bowel wall. The less the penetration, the better the outlook. But even if the tumor has spread through the wall, and even if it involves nearby lymph nodes, surgery continues to offer the best hope for cure.

In more advanced stages, the surgeon may see evidence of spread to the liver. With liver involvement, the possibility of surgical cure vanishes, though one occasionally sees reports of successful surgical removal of a part of the liver containing such a metastasis.

NOTE: The general principles discussed up to this point also hold for cancer surgery elsewhere in the body. Localized growths can usually be removed successfully, and a cure then becomes possible. But any spread of the cancer away from the original site, or extension to lymph nodes or other organs, generally makes the outlook poor.

Often, it may be feasible to add irradiation or chemotherapy to the surgery and improve the outlook. In fact, this adding of one treatment approach to another is now almost standard for breast cancer. A number of recent studies clearly indicate that outcome (measured by five- and ten-year cures) is significantly improved by routinely adding chemotherapy to surgery.

Fiascoes of "informed consent." As for my personal views about cancer surgery, they are mixed: I have always deplored surgery as a primitive procedure, applauded it as a necessary procedure, and admired the perseverance and brilliance of many career surgeons. I stand in awe of the highly skilled operative procedures that have been developed, such as those for replacing a bladder with a loop of intestine or contriving ingenious new hook-ups when a long segment of bowel is removed.

Patients are not always as fascinated about the details of surgery as doctors. They may understandably become upset when some of the specifics of cancer surgery are discussed. But they do not always have a choice about what they must hear. Full disclosure is now mandated by law: Only a fully informed patient can give the necessary *informed consent.*

Personally, I prefer to emphasize the optimistic side of an operation, rather than dwelling on the details required by informed consent. I point out to my patients that surgically produced pain and suffering will pass. The body's repair mechanisms, no matter what the degree of surgical assault, are reliable and always spring into action. Wounds heal, scars shrink, functions return, and life continues to be worth living.

I generally find patients willing to cope when the facts are set forth in a positive context. But I must admit that it may have been easier in some respects to deal with patients in the days before informed consent became law. My only quarrel with informed consent and the legal issues attached to it is that we now have to give patients a large amount of information that is not wholly digestible.

To illustrate: I walked into the room of one of my very bright patients to find her ashen and quaking with fright.

"What's wrong?" I asked.

"I've just been visited by the anesthesiologist, who told me about the anesthesia for tomorrow's operation," she replied. "He said that a tube has to be passed into my throat for an airway. He said he had to inform me that infrequently a tooth may be damaged or chipped when the tube is inserted. He added that occasionally damage can be done to the throat or the vocal cords. He also said there is a possibility of cardiac disturbances and rarely a death due to anesthesia. He then asked me to sign a consent form."

I promptly told her that all of these warnings were part of the informed consent requirement, and that all this information was so remote as to be irrelevant.

"I've never seen these complications," I said. "And that should tell you how improbable those dire events are. The trouble with informed consent is that discussing improbable events seriously seems to lift them to the level of the probable. How would you react if as you boarded an airplane, an informed consent specialist reeled off some statistics on airplane engine failure, aborted takeoffs, and the likelihood of cockpit fires?"

She saw my point and relaxed.

Of course, there *are* some risks to cancer surgery, particularly with some of the more complex procedures. To be sure, any patient can expect some postoperative discomfort. And as we all are aware, surgery is not always successful.

But for the average patient, if this is the solution to a life-threatening problem, I tell them to go for it.

"Concentrate on the goal," I tell them. "This is the only cure we have. You want a cure? You really want to be with your family months or years from now? Then you sign for the surgery."

The Outlook for Surgical Cure

More than 90 percent of those who undergo surgery of smaller breast or colon cancers are cured. But when tumors are larger, experience has taught me not to be glib in my predictions. Really accurate forecasts of the future are for the prophets, not the doctors. Medicine is not a mathematical science. One of the things I like about it is the "rule of the fortunate exception," which is good for patients, keeps the doctor modest, and can best be explained through an illustration.

Years ago, one of my colleagues told me of seeing a young man with a cancer of the testicle and an obvious metastasis in the lung. There was no chemotherapy then, and everyone despaired of the prospects for this patient.

But the young man was a fortunate exception. After surgery had been completed on the testicle, the lung was irradiated, and the tumor there disappeared. The young man went on to become a distinguished United States senator and died decades later of an unrelated illness.

The Possibilities of Irradiation

You may have noted from some of the examples quoted that irradiation may be combined with surgery successfully. On its own, irradiation treatment can score resounding successes. Tumor cells are generally sensitive to radiation, though radio-resistant tumors do occur. In the lung, for example, the most common cancer tumors, the squamous cell type, tend to be resistant to radiation, though I have seen some cures. But another type, the oat cell type, is quite sensitive and all but vanishes after a few treatments.

Similarly, tumors that arise from the lymph cell series are radiosensitive and predictably curable with X-irradiation.

The chief problem with this treatment technique is in determining how much tissue has become involved with the tumor and deciding where to deliver the tumor-killing rays.

But in general, those who practice this method are enthusiastic about the possibilities. Some X-ray specialists have deplored the primary emphasis on surgery here in the United States. They tell me their results with irradiation for such common cancers as those in the womb or prostate are just as good as the results with surgery.

A sometimes overlooked but important use of irradiation is in the control of metastasis (spread of cancer) and of pain. Pain may respond dramatically, and the patient may be freed of much anguish and the need to use narcotics. I have kept some patients functioning well for years with judicious courses of irradiation.

The Promise of Chemotherapy

In contrast to surgery and irradiation, chemotherapy is a true twentieth-century advance.

Chemotherapy relies on killing tumor cells with one or more chemicals and occasionally with hormonal agents. Elaborate combinations of agents and timing of their administration have been worked out on the basis of cooperative trials by oncologists (specialists in this field).

There is no truly selective chemotherapy. Normal cells lining the gastrointestinal tract, cells in the hair follicles, and dividing cells in the bone marrow are also hit by the chemicals. Thus, the hair may fall out, blood counts may drop, and nausea, vomiting, and diarrhea may occur.

For some leukemias in which aggressive treatment is needed, "chemo" becomes a battle to destroy the leukemic cells while trying to preserve enough normal cells to allow the patient to survive. As white blood cell counts drop, some patients become *immune compromised* and more subject to infection. Antibiotics may be given to counter this problem.

Generally, though, it is not necessary to get this close to danger. For example, there has been a growing tendency to give *courses,* or applications, of chemotherapy to premenopausal women with breast cancer. Outcome studies indicate that chances for cure are enhanced by this approach. At the usual dosage levels, lurking and unseen tumor cells can be destroyed without undue danger to the rest of the body. But hair loss is more or less inevitable, and use of a wig becomes necessary.

Chemotherapy has been both a disappointment and a hope. Initial expectations that we could develop chemical programs that would destroy all tumors or, failing that, at least a majority of them, have not panned out. But chemotherapy has proved very useful in the treatment of many tumors of the lung, ovary, and bladder, and in blood cell disorders, to cite a few of the successes.

One obvious advantage of chemotherapy is that the agents relentlessly hunt down the tumor cells, wherever they may be in the body. One exception is the brain, which often does not permit admission of chemotherapeutic agents. In the brain, light courses of irradiation may have to be added to ensure impact on leukemic cells.

There is a great deal of research going on in this field. New combinations of agents are constantly being tried out and reported on, and, fitfully, progress continues to be made. As an example, a new combination of these agents was recently reported as having produced cures in 40 percent of certain urinary tract cancers that had formerly been deemed incurable.

What Is the Outlook for Cancer Treatment?

It is apparent that fresh new approaches are badly needed. But where might they come from?

It has long been suspected that the body's immune system might be pivotal in the control of cancer. The *immune system* is a defense system that constantly monitors threats such as bacterial and viral assaults. When this system is compromised, a person is subject not only to infections but also to tumor growths.

Recently, the National Institutes of Health has developed a method of stimulating and mobilizing one element of the immune system, the natural killer cells of the blood. With this procedure, tumors of various origins showed marked shrinkage as the killer cells attacked.

Lurking on the horizon is the dazzling possibility of being able to control the abnormal growth characteristic of a tumor. It has been found that identifiable genes within every normal cell are responsible for normal growth. When these genes are shifted to new locations (the process is called *translocation*), they may escape from adjacent inhibitors and spur the altered cell into continuous abnormal growth.

The challenge is to restore the normal equilibrium that prevents the growth potential of every human cell from expressing itself in distorted ways. That sort of control, if applied to all cancer cells, could be the successful conclusion of the worldwide search to rid the human species of the cancer threat.

Past experience suggests that much long and difficult research will be necessary to attain this end. But the "rule of the fortunate exception" may hold here too: We may hit the target with an unexpected and unforeseen breakthrough, much as Sir Alexander Fleming stumbled onto penicillin.

Key Questions and Answers on Cancer

In the course of my medical practice during the past forty years, I have heard quite a few questions about cancer. The following pages contain the major queries that have been put to me, with the most practical, up-to-date responses currently available.

The information I have included in my answers comes from a variety of sources, including the American Cancer Society, the National Cancer Institute, medical journal articles, and my own clinical experience.

Q: *Is there a predisposition to cancer? Does cancer run in families?*

A: When I was a medical student back in the thirties, Maude Slye, a pathologist at our school, created quite a stir by developing a breed of mice in which *all* the females had cancer of the breast. Since then, other breeds have been developed that have regular, predictable tumors in other selected organs.

To produce all these animal tumors, inbreeding has to go on for many generations and create a special strain with a high incidence of a given tumor. It is obvious at once that this sort of inbreeding does not occur in human mating and reproduction. Still, it's conceivable, and in fact seems to be the case, that even on a random basis, resistance or predisposition to tumors can occur. And these tendencies may emerge in the context of certain cancer-prone or cancer-resistant families.

Breast cancer sometimes provides an example of a familial trend. I have in my case files numerous examples of families with breast cancer predisposition. One of my patients started to worry about her family tree during her middle years as, in succession, her mother and four maternal aunts developed breast cancer.

With the goal of early detection of possible cancer, we started to follow her closely with mammography. At around her sixtieth birthday, a minute breast cancer was detected on the mammogram and was successfully operated on.

I have since noted that in this family of afflicted women surgery was curative, as long as the cancer was detected soon enough. Many went on for twenty or more years without recurrence. Perhaps easy curability was also part of the hereditary aspect, but early treatment seems to have been just as important.

In recognition of some of these facts, the American Cancer Society took the position that there are women at higher risk because of family history. They should have mammography earlier in life and on a more rigid schedule and should certainly be taught breast self-examination.

Although I agree with this position, I also caution my patients not to adopt the doom theory. By that, I mean the notion that because a sister, mother, or maternal aunt has had the disease, the patient will also get it. The fact is that all the analyses deal with mathematical risks, not with human certainties. There are lots of sisters of breast cancer victims who never develop the disease, some of whom I have followed well into their eighties who now agree that perhaps they did worry unnecessarily when they were younger.

Still, with the incidence of breast cancer in American women now at a staggering 10 percent, it may be best to be overly cautious and do such procedures as mammograms ritually—like brushing one's teeth.

As far as the other parts of the body are concerned, we also see potential family factors in cancers of the colon and rectum. It has long been known that a disease in which many polyps grow in the lining of the colon runs in some families. Though rare, *familial colonic polyposis* (a tendency to have polyps of the colon) almost inevitably leads to colon cancer early in life. This propensity has therefore always been of research interest in teaching us how growths in the lining gradually transform into a malignant tumor.

In fact, the same sequence of events apparently occurs in the 150,000 cases of rectocolonic cancer that appear annually in the U.S. population: A small growth, called an *adenoma*, enlarges into a grape-size or larger tumor, which looks increasingly malignant under the microscope. Occasionally, there are more than one of these—called *multiple adenomata*—at several bodily sites.

Recent studies plainly indicate that in the apparently random cases of colorectal cancer, hereditary factors do play a role. Studies of the families of patients with these adenomas and cancers reveal a higher incidence of similar events in blood relatives. Thus, in married couples, who are presumably exposed to much the same environmental variables such as diet, the spouse who had the family history was more likely to contract a rectocolonic cancer.

The implication of this finding is that an individual whose parents or close relatives have developed these forms of cancer has to be doubly vigilant with regard to screening procedures. Furthermore, those at risk because of family history should be more attentive to potential dietary factors, such as the importance of consuming low-fat, high-fiber foods.

There is even some early evidence that indicates that increased dietary calcium may be of some value. Because I encourage most of my patients to take calcium supplements to protect their bones, I may also be doing the linings of their colons a lot of good—at any rate, time will tell.

Elsewhere in the body, there is little or no evidence that hereditary factors are all that significant. Often, a particular tumor, say of the ovary or lung, seems to strike a certain family member at random, with no one else's having it.

Often, it is clear that groupings of cases are due to environmental factors, and these may have a geographic background: In certain parts of China, for instance, there is a high incidence of cancer of the esophagus. In much of the Orient, there is a high incidence of liver cancer, almost certainly of viral origin.

In Japan, a grouping of leukemias has also been shown to be viral. In contrast, the incidence of breast cancer in Japan is strikingly low, almost certainly *not* because of genetic resistance, but because of low-fat diet and other life-style variables.

One can conclude that although the role of family or genetic factors is definitely operative for some forms of cancer, on an overall basis environmental factors carry by far the heaviest weight. Identifying and changing the environmental variables still remain the major hope in cancer control.

Q: *What tests are available for cancer, and how often should I have them?*

A: The latest recommendations by the American Cancer Society for the early detection of cancer in those without symptoms are outlined in the table on pages 338–39.

Q: *I sometimes get confused by all the cancer information that gets tossed about. Is there an easy-to-understand, compact checklist I can use to limit my cancer risk?*

A: Here is a brief checklist, suggested by the American Cancer Society and by various physicians who treat cancer patients. I make this information available to my own patients as a quick-and-easy guide to combat cancer in daily life.

- *Eliminate cigarette smoking.* As I have already indicated, cigarette smoking is the main cause of lung cancer: It is responsible for 83 percent of lung cancers in men and 43 percent in women, or more than 75 percent of all lung cancers.

Furthermore, cigarette smoking is the cause of 25 to 30 percent of *all* cancers, not just lung cancers.

Chewing tobacco is also a very risky practice: Those who chew have a higher incidence of mouth and throat cancer. Finally, those who smoke cigars and pipes—without inhaling the smoke—are less likely to develop lung cancer than cigarette smokers who inhale. But pipe and cigar users are at higher risk of cancers of the throat, larnyx, mouth, and esophagus.

Generally speaking, it takes a number of years for smoking and tobacco exposure to result in cancer. In medical terms, this time factor reflects the understanding that smoke contains "weak carcinogens." This means that the cancer-causing agents in smoke work very gradually, and if the offending behavior—in this case, smoking—is stopped, the risk declines and may disappear altogether.

- *Limit your exposure to the sun.* Staying out in the sun, or even outdoors on a cloudy day, may promote skin cancer. If you have to be outside, protect yourself with a suntan lotion that contains at least a number 15 sunscreen. It is also advisable to wear long sleeves, hats, or other cover-ups, especially during the middle of the day, from about 10:00 A.M. to 3:00 P.M. NOTE: If you notice a

SUMMARY OF
AMERICAN CANCER SOCIETY RECOMMENDATIONS
FOR THE EARLY DETECTION OF CANCER
IN ASYMPTOMATIC PEOPLE

| TEST OR PROCEDURE | POPULATION | | FREQUENCY |
	SEX	AGE	
Sigmoidoscopy	M & F	Over 50	After 2 negative exams 1 year apart, perform every 3–5 years.
Stool guaiac slide test	M & F	Over 50	Every year
Digital rectal examination	M & F	Over 40	Every year
Pap test	F		All women who are, or who have been, sexually active, or have reached age 18, should have an annual Pap test and pelvic examination. After a woman has had three or more consecutive satisfactory normal annual examinations, the Pap test may be performed less frequently at the discretion of her physician
Pelvic examination	F		
Endometrial tissue sample	F	At menopause, women at high risk*	At menopause
Breast self-examination	F	20 and over	Every month

SOURCE: American Cancer Society
*History of infertility, obesity, failure to ovulate, abnormal uterine bleeding, or estrogen therapy.

SUMMARY OF
AMERICAN CANCER SOCIETY RECOMMENDATIONS
FOR THE EARLY DETECTION OF CANCER
IN ASYMPTOMATIC PEOPLE (continued)

TEST OR PROCEDURE	POPULATION SEX	AGE	FREQUENCY
Breast physical examination	F	20–40	Every 3 years
		Over 40	Every year
Mammography	F	35–39	Baseline
		40–49	Every 1–2 years
		50 and over	Every year
Chest X ray			Not recommended
Sputum cytology			Not recommended
Health counseling and cancer checkup**	M & F	Over 20	Every 3 years
	M & F	Over 40	Every year

**To include examination for cancers of the thyroid, testicles, prostate, ovaries, lymph nodes, oral region, and skin.

change in your skin, such as a mole or sore that does not heal, see your doctor immediately. (See the questions on skin cancer and melanoma that follow.)

• *Reduce your dietary fat consumption, especially of saturated fat.* Various studies have linked fat intake to cancers of the prostate, breast, and colon.

High fat consumption is also often associated with obesity, another risk factor for cancer. If you are overweight, especially as much as 40 percent overweight, your risk increases for cancers of the uterus, breast, colon, and gallbladder.

The best way to avoid fats is to concentrate on menus that

emphasize fresh vegetables, lean meat, fish, skinned poultry, and low-fat or no-fat dairy products. It is desirable to stay away from pastries and sweets, which usually contain high amounts of fats and, often, empty calories.

• *Avoid foods that are smoked or cured with salt or nitrites.* Demographic studies show that cancers of the stomach and esophagus are more common in nations with foods prepared this way. In general, it is best to reduce your intake of ham, frankfurters, salt-cured fish, and bacon.

• *Limit alcoholic beverages.* Cancers of the esophagus, mouth, throat, and larynx have been associated with heavy alcohol drinking. If you smoke *and* drink, your risk of developing these cancers increases.

• *Eat more vegetables in the cabbage family.* Known as *cruciferous* vegetables, these include cabbage, broccoli, brussels sprouts, cauliflower, and kohlrabi. A number of studies have shown that high intake of these vegetables can be protective against cancers of the colon, rectum, stomach, and respiratory system.

• *Eat more high-fiber foods.* A diet high in fiber may help protect you against colon cancer. Foods high in fiber include vegetables, fruits, and whole grains. Examples are peaches, strawberries, spinach, tomatoes, potatoes, wheat and bran cereals, rice, and whole-wheat breads.

• *Eat more foods high in vitamin C.* Vitamin C may help protect us against cancers of the stomach and esophagus. Examples of these foods are oranges, grapefruits, cantaloupes, strawberries, broccoli, tomatoes, and red and green peppers.

• *Choose foods high in carotene.* Those foods that are high in beta-carotene, the precursor of vitamin A, may be protective against a number of cancers. Examples are carrots, sweet potatoes, apricots, squash, peaches, and broccoli.

• *Limit your exposure to X rays or other forms of radiation.* When X-ray exams are properly used by trained medical personnel, there is no problem. But overexposure to X rays or to byproducts of atomic energy can contribute to the development of such cancers as leukemia.

Q: *What are the signs or symptoms of cancer of the colon or rectum?*

A: There are a number of possible signs or symptoms, depending on where the cancer is located and how far it has progressed.

- Often there is an obstruction in the bowel tract.
- The closer the cancer is to the rectal area, the more likely it is that rectal bleeding will appear.
- There may be constipation or diarrhea, an increase in gas, or cramping.

Q: *Is a colorectal examination painful?*

A: The various exams used to detect colon or rectal cancer may be a little uncomfortable for some people, but they are usually not painful. The key point to keep in mind is to remain relaxed during each procedure. The more tense or rigid a person is before and during the exam, the more uncomfortable he or she is likely to be.

The types of tests used to detect this form of cancer include the following:

- A *digital-rectal exam,* in which the physician probes just inside the rectal area with a finger encased in a rubber glove.
- A *proctosigmoidoscopic exam,* or a "procto," which involves an inspection of the rectum and lower colon with a lighted tube called a *proctosigmoidoscope.* This procedure usually reveals all rectal cancers and about one-third of colon cancers.
- A *colonoscopy,* which requires the use of a longer, more flexible instrument that moves even farther up into the colon.
- A *barium enema,* which first involves the injection of liquid barium into the intestines with an enema. Then, when the intestines and colon are filled with this substance, the physician takes a picture of the entire intestinal tract to detect any abnormalities.
- A *slide test* of fecal matter, the Hemoccult test, to determine whether there is any blood in the stool. This test, which can be conducted in the privacy of your own home, involves the collection of a small amount of fecal matter on a chemically treated paper slide. The appearance of blood on the slide may indicate the presence of cancer, though there may be other causes, such as bleeding hemorrhoids.

The importance of these tests is highlighted by the rate of success in treating colorectal cancer when it is detected early: If the cancer remains localized when detected, 76 percent of patients with colon cancer are still alive five years after treatment; 73 percent of those with localized rectal cancer are still alive.

On the other hand, after the cancer has spread, only 31 percent of those with colon cancer and 23 percent of those with rectal cancer are alive after five years.

Q: *What is a colostomy?*

A: After extensive surgery, the surgeon may not be able to connect the two ends of the bowel. Consequently, an opening will have to be made in the abdominal wall, through which the patient can evacuate bodily wastes. This operation is known as a *colostomy.*

Only about 15 percent of all patients with rectal cancer have to undergo permanent colostomies. The procedure is unnecessary for almost all patients with colon cancer that has been detected at an early stage.

Q: *What women are at the highest risk of having breast cancer?*

A: Those who are over age fifty, who have already had breast cancer, who have a history of breast cancer in the immediate family, who are childless, and who have had their first child after age thirty.

Q: *Are women with large breasts at greater risk?*

A: No. But larger breasts may make breast self-examination and early detection of cancer more difficult. Mammography—an X-ray picture of the breast—is especially helpful for older women with large breasts whose glandular tissue has been replaced by fatty tissue. In any case, mammography should be performed at least annually on all women over fifty years of age.

Q: *What are some symptoms of breast cancer?*

A: A change in the shape of the breast; dimpling, scaling, or puckering of the skin around the nipple; any secretions from the nipples; a lump or thickening of the breast.

Q: *What is the best approach to breast self-examination?*

A: It is best to perform this self-exam on the same day once a month (do it in the first week following menstruation if menopause has not already occurred). The American Cancer Society recommends these steps:

• Lie down and place a pillow under your right shoulder. If your breasts are large, hold your right breast in your right hand and perform the exam with your left hand.
• Use the finger pads of your three middle fingers on your

left hand to feel for lumps. Employ a rubbing motion.

• Press hard enough so that you can feel deeply into the breast.

• Feel the entire breast and chest area. Usually, it will take at least two minutes for women with small breasts to perform this procedure on one breast, and those with larger breasts will need more time.

• Go over your entire breast systematically, from one side to the other, so that you are sure not to miss any area.

• After you have completed the examination of your right breast, use the same approach to check the left breast.

• Check your breasts in a mirror to see whether there seems to be any change in the contour of the breast or the look of the skin or nipple.

Q: *What increases a woman's risk of cancer of the uterus?*

A: Uterine cancer typically involves cancer of the cervix or of the endometrium, the lining of the uterus.

Those at highest risk for cancer of the cervix include women who have had their first intercourse when they were quite young and those who have had a number of sexual partners.

Those at high risk for endometrial cancer include women with a history of infertility, a failure to ovulate regularly, late menopause, or prolonged estrogen therapy after menopause. The dangers of estrogen can be lessened if the hormone is administered with progesterone under a doctor's close supervision.

Advancing age is also a major risk factor for uterine cancer. Cancers of the cervix typically occur in women who are fifty to fifty-nine years old; endometrial cancers most often appear in women between fifty-five and sixty-four years of age.

Q: *What are the symptoms of uterine cancer?*

A: Typical warning signs of cervical cancer are vaginal discharge and irregular bleeding, especially after sexual intercourse.

The signals for endometrial cancer include bleeding after menopause. For younger women, symptoms may include bleeding between menstrual periods and excessive bleeding during menstruation.

Q: *Are there any other ways to detect these cancers?*

A: Every woman over fifty should have a Pap test every year.

HEALTH REPORT

FEMALE SEX HORMONES AND CANCER?

There were approximately 131,000 new cases of breast cancer in the United States in 1987, but most studies find no increased risk with estrogen use even after many years, and some report a *lessened* incidence.

When progesterone is given in addition for ten to thirteen days each month, the incidence of breast cancer is *lowered:* 66.8 per 100,000 users of progesterone as against 343.5 per 100,000 nonusers in one large study. Those who used estrogen alone in this study also had less than 50 percent of the incidence of breast cancer of the nonusers. There is some evidence, however, that a progesterone deficiency before the menopause increases breast cancer risk.

As for cancer of the uterus, the evidence is clear-cut that estrogen alone increases the risk considerably. When progesterone is added, however, the risk falls to levels far below that of the nonhormone user.

The author advocates a combination of estrogen and progesterone for thirteen days per month. The only drawback is that this may lead to menstruation, but even this result can be prevented by administering a small daily dose of the progestin (progesterone).

R. D. Gambrell, "Sex Steroids and Cancer," *Obstetric and Gynecology Clinics of North America* 14 (1987): 191.

The Pap test, which helps a physician detect cervical cancer at an early stage, is 95 percent accurate.

It is also helpful in identifying endometrial cancer. But a pelvic exam is essential too because the Pap test does not always pick up evidence of endometrial disease.

Again, the key point to remember here is *act early!* When cervical cancer is diagnosed at an early stage, the survival rate for five years is 81 percent, compared with a 57 percent overall rate of survival. The five-year survival rate for endometrial cancers that are caught early is 88 percent, as compared with an overall rate of 75 percent.

Q: *What are the symptoms of prostate cancer?*

A: As men get older, problems with the prostate, including cancer, become more common. The prostate is a walnut-size gland just behind the outlet of the urinary bladder, which is necessary for transporting semen. When it is removed, a man becomes infertile, though he can still retain his ability to have an erection. More than half of American men over fifty have some degree of enlargement of the prostate gland, but most prostate enlargement is benign, and not a precursor of cancer. On the other hand, about 80 percent of all prostate cancers are found in men who are over sixty-five.

The signs of prostate cancer are subtle, if they are present at all. Symptoms are much like those of benign enlargement and may include weak or interrupted flow of urine; difficulty in beginning to urinate; need to urinate often, especially during the night; blood in the urine; or burning sensation while urinating. With spread, there may develop pains in the pelvis, back, or thighs.

Because these symptoms may also indicate other problems— or may be completely absent—every man over forty years of age should have a prostate exam as part of his annual physical. During the exam, your doctor checks the state of your prostate by a simple digital probe through the rectum.

Q: *What is the treatment for prostate cancer?*

A: Physicians may recommend surgery, irradiation therapy or hormone therapy, or a combination of these approaches. Chemotherapy is also a possibility in serious cases in which the cancer has spread. In some situations in which the cancer has spread, the female hormone estrogen may be administered to counteract the male hormone, which promotes the growth of prostate cancer. A similar result may be achieved through castration.

Most of the time, however, the treatments are less serious, and 64 percent of all prostate cancers are discovered before they spread. More than four out of five patients whose tumors are diagnosed at this early stage are still alive five years after treatment begins. The survival rate for all stages of the disease after five years is 71 percent.

Q: *Is cancer of the mouth something to worry about?*

A: There were an estimated 30,000 new cases of oral cancer in 1988, with more than twice as many men as women suffering from the disease. The problem is most frequent in men over age forty.

This type of cancer—which can strike any part of the oral cavity, including the lip, tongue, mouth, or throat—has been linked to smoking and to use of smokeless tobacco (for example, chewing tobacco). The incidence of oral cancer is higher among cigar and pipe smokers and heavy alcohol drinkers.

Q: *What are the symptoms of oral cancer?*
A: The symptoms include the following:

- sores that bleed easly and do not heal,
- a lump or thickening in the mouth area, and
- a persistent reddish or whitish patch.

Difficulty in chewing, swallowing, or moving the tongue or jaws is a late symptom of the disease.

If you notice any of these symptoms, you should see your doctor immediately. NOTE: This cancer is likely to be detected relatively early if you have regular dental checkups.

Q: *What are the treatments for oral cancer?*
A: Radiation therapy and surgery are the most common, though chemotherapy is being explored in conjunction with surgery for more advanced types of this disease.

The survival rates for oral cancer vary considerably, depending on the location of the problem. For example, there is a 32 percent survival rate for cancer of the pharynx after five years, but a 91 percent rate for cancer of the lip.

Q: *What people are at greatest risk for skin cancer?*
A: Those with fair complexions whose skin is exposed to excessive sunlight are at the greatest risk. People with dark or olive-colored skin have a lower risk because the pigment of their skin provides them with more protection against the ultraviolet rays of the sun. One study has reported that serious sunburn in childhood carries with it a greater risk of the most serious form of skin cancer, melanoma, later in life.

The incidence of skin cancer is higher in people whose occupations or life-styles expose them to pitch, coal tar, creosote, arsenic compounds, or radium.

Q: *What is the best strategy to prevent skin cancer?*

A: It is wise to follow these guidelines, which have been recommended by the American Cancer Society and other skin cancer experts:

• Avoid excessive exposure to the sun, especially between the midday hours of 10:00 A.M. and 3:00 P.M. At that time, the ultraviolet rays of the sun are strongest and most dangerous.

• If you have to be in the sun, wear protective clothing, including sun hats.

• Use a strong sunscreen, with an SPF rating of at least number 15. Reapply the sunscreen after you swim or perspire.

• Avoid sunlamps or other tanning devices.

• A beach umbrella will not necessarily protect you completely from the sun's rays. They may penetrate the umbrella or bounce toward you off the water or sand.

• Cloudy days are not sufficient protection because 70 to 80 percent of the sun's untraviolet rays penetrate the cloud covering. These rays can reach you when you are swimming three feet below the surface of the water.

• Ultraviolet rays can also penetrate to your skin through a wet T-shirt, via water droplets.

• The beach is not the only danger spot: The sun's rays are stronger in the mountains because there is less atmosphere to act as a filter. Snow can reflect up to 85 percent of the sun's rays.

• It is best to keep moving in the sun, rather than just sitting and soaking in the rays. As the American Cancer Society has said, "A moving target is harder for the rays to find than a motionless one."

• Stay away from sun reflectors because they direct the sun's rays to the most sensitive parts of the skin, such as under the chin, the eyelids, and the earlobes.

• Be especially careful if you plan to be out in the sun in southern climes. There is proportionately more skin cancer in southern and southwestern states than in other parts of the United States.

• Check your skin regularly, at least once a month, to see whether there are any unusual changes or spots on it. If you detect something unusual, notify your physician immediately.

Q: *What is the method of treatment for skin cancer?*

A: There are four approaches to treatment. Surgery is used in 90 percent of the cases. In the rest, a physician may choose radiation therapy, electrodesiccation (tissue destruction by heat), or, for early skin cancers, cryosurgery (tissue destruction by freezing).

Q: *What is melanoma?*

A: Most skin cancers are either basal cell or squamous cell cancers, which can usually be treated quite successfully and are rarely life-threatening. Malignant melanoma, a third type of skin cancer, is less common but much more serious. In fact, every year about twenty-seven thousand people in the United States develop melanoma, and more than five thousand die from it.

Melanoma consists of out-of-control *melanocytes,* skin cells that produce the dark protective pigment called *melanin.* Unlike the other forms of skin cancer, melanoma tends to spread elsewhere in the body. Then, when the cancerous cells reach other bodily organs, they become much harder to treat.

A melanoma may appear in a previously clear part of the body, or it may arise near or around an existing mole. How do you tell the difference between a melanoma and an ordinary mole or freckle? The ABCD rule is helpful:

- A—*asymmetry:* One half of the mole does not match the other half.
- B—*border irregularity:* The edges of the mole are uneven, blurred, or ragged.
- C—*color:* The color of the mole is not regular or uniform. There may be shades of brown, black, and tan. Red, white, and blue coloring may be present.
- D—*diameter* greater than 6 millimeters (mm): A sudden or gradual increase in size of the mole, especially beyond the size of an ordinary pencil eraser, is cause for concern.

As with most other forms of cancer, early detection and speed in seeking treatment can be decisive in curing melanoma. Generally, the cancer is removed by surgery; nearby lympth nodes may also be removed to present spread of the disease. The overall five-year survival rate for white patients with malignant malanoma is 80 percent, but once the melanoma has spread, the survival rate is 39 percent.

Some Strategies to Relieve
the Pain of Cancer

Pain or discomfort does not always accompany cancer, especially in the early stages of the disease. But sometimes, especially after the cancer has developed or spread, pain may become a factor. Here are some strategies for helping you deal with pains associated with cancer:

It is important to remove certain underlying factors that may exacerbate pain. For example, anxiety or depression can make it seem worse. Your doctor or psychotherapist may be able to help you relieve the emotional pressures that are causing these problems and aggravating your cancer pain.

Antidepressant drugs such as Sinequan, Elavil, or Tofranil, taken daily, can help relieve depression associated with cancer pain. Usually, these antidepressant drugs take about fourteen to twenty-one days to work.

NOTE: There may be some side effects: dry mouth, bad dreams, dizziness, or nausea. The dizziness and nausea usually end within two weeks. The dry mouth may continue but can be relieved through the techniques described later.

If anxiety or irritability is a factor in your pain, tranquilizers can help calm you. Your doctor will be able to evaluate your situation and make an appropriate prescription.

Fatigue can lessen your tolerance to pain. If you can get more sleep and rest, you will most likely find that the impact of the pain will decrease.

But even if you take care of these underlying conditions, you may still find yourself experiencing pain from cancer. So it will be necessary to turn to one of the following approaches to pain relief.

Nonprescription Pain Relievers

The two major nonprescription pain relievers used to treat cancer are aspirin and acetaminophen (brand names: Tylenol and Datril). These two drugs have roughly equal power to produce pain relief and reduce fever, but there are some important differences:

• Aspirin reduces swelling from inflammation; acetaminophen does not.

• Aspirin can reduce pain of swollen joints and other inflamed areas better than acetaminophen.

• Aspirin may cause an upset stomach or stomach bleeding; acetaminophen does not.

It's especially important to check with your doctor before you choose aspirin because of several additional factors:

• Other drugs you are taking may cause bleeding, and aspirin can aggravate this condition.

• Aspirin should not be used with steroid medications.

• Aspirin should be avoided by those who are scheduled for surgery within a week.

• Aspirin should not be used by those who are using blood-thinning medicine or who have stomach ulcers or other bleeding disorders.

• Aspirin should be avoided by patients on strong arthritis drugs or antidiabetic or antigout drugs.

How much of these nonprescription medications should you expect to take daily?

You should *always* check with your physician before embarking on any drug program. But in general, it is considered safe to take two to three tablets (325 mg each) of aspirin, three or four times a day. Eight aspirins a day is regarded as a moderate dose, and many adults can safely take twelve a day. Medical experts warn, however, that dosages in excess of twelve per day should be taken only under medical supervision.

As for acetaminophen, adults can usually safely take two to three tablets (325 mg each), three or four times a day, or a total of eight to twelve tablets a day. But be sure to read the labels to be certain that you are taking regular tablets, not extra-strength tablets. One extra-strength Tylenol, for example, is equal to 1.5 regular Tylenol tablets.

Prescription Pain Relievers

Frequently used prescription pain relievers for cancer include codeine, hydromorphone (Dilaudid), levorphanol (Levo-Dromoran), meperidine (Demerol), methadone (Dolophine), morphine, oxycodone (in Percodan), and oxymorphone (Numorphan).

These narcotic drugs, which may be obtained only with a doctor's prescription, can be taken in one or more of the following ways: by mouth, by injection, through the vein, or by rectal suppository.

Sometimes, there are side effects of these drugs that you should be aware of before you begin to take them. The most common are drowsiness, constipation, dry mouth, nausea, and vomiting.

What can you do about these side effects? Here are some ways to counteract the negative effects:

• *Drowsiness.* Usually, this effect disappears after you have used the medication for a few days, so it is wise to wait it out to see whether that helps. If it does not, see your doctor. He may adjust the prescription by reducing the amount of the drug so that your pain will still be relieved, without the attendant feelings of sleepiness or fatigue. He may also prescribe a mild stimulant, such as caffeine, an amphetamine (such as Dexedrine), or methylphenidate (Ritalin).

• *Constipation.* After checking with your physician, you may be able to relieve this problem by increasing the fiber in your diet, for instance, by adding one or two tablespoons of bran to your food. Also drink plenty of liquids: at least eight to ten eight-ounce glasses of fluid per day. In addition, you might increase your amount of exercise. Finally, your doctor may recommend a stool softener, such as docusate (Colace) or a bulk laxative, such as Metamucil.

• *Dry mouth.* Narcotics may reduce the amount of saliva in your mouth. If this happens, you should drink more water and other liquids and choose moist foods, such as nonacid fruits and ice cream. In addition, rinse your mouth with wet gauze sponges, suck on ice chips, and avoid commercial mouthwashes that contain alcohol or salt.

Your doctor may also be able to change other medications, such as antihistamines, that might be aggravating the condition. He or she may even be able to provide you with artificial saliva, which can relieve the dry-mouth problem.

• *Vomiting and nausea.* As with other discomforts related to cancer medications, vomiting and nausea may occur only for a few days and then cease. So the first line of attack is just to wait to see whether the problem decreases naturally.

If the upset stomach persists, your physician may prescribe medicines such as Compazine, Tigan, or Torecan. If you find that your nausea occurs mostly when you are up and about, you might stay in your bed for an hour or so after taking the medication. In effect, you may be experiencing a kind of motion sickness or sea-sickness from the drug.

Finally, sometimes the pain itself is the cause of the nausea, and simply taking painkilling medication will make the nausea end.

Other techniques for promoting pain relief in cancer patients, which have met with some success, include the following:

Relaxation Techniques

There are a number of effective techniques for achieving a relaxed state, which in turn reduces tension in the muscles and mitigates pain. Most involve concentration on a particular object, word, or phrase for ten to twenty minutes, twice a day.

When pursuing this technique, it is important to relax all the muscles in the body, breathe rhythmically, and gently push away intruding thoughts when they come to mind. An extensive treatment of this approach can be found in the works of Dr. Herbert Benson of Harvard Medical School, including *The Relaxation Response* and *Your Maximum Mind.*

Distraction

If you can succeed in taking your mind off your pain, you may very well find that you become completely unaware of the pain or dis-comfort, at least for limited periods of time.

Distraction can be achieved through any activity that occupies your attention. Examples are needlework, model-building, paint-ing, and reading a good book. For that matter, watching television or attending an absorbing movie can do the job.

Surgery and Local Painkillers

When pain is particularly bad, a neurosurgeon may cut a nerve close to the spinal cord or sever bundles of nerves in the spinal cord itself. This type of operation destroys the nerves that transmit

---

HEALTH REPORT

THE AGING THYROID GLAND—INCLUDING THE POSSIBILITY OF CANCER

The thyroid gland tends to become more nodular with age, especially in women. The sudden appearance of a nodule, particularly a hard one, suggests possible thyroid cancer. This development is even more suspicious in men than in women.

Each year, underfunctioning of the gland (hypothyroidism) occurs in one to two cases per thousand in middle-aged women. The symptoms are insidious and may be erroneously attributed to "aging." They may include puffy face, dry skin, cold intolerance, unsteadiness, deafness, and confusion. The symptoms respond well to taking the hormone by mouth. But this approach should be used cautiously to prevent unpleasant cardiac stimulation.

Overactivity of the gland (hyperthyroidism) may also develop insidiously, and, unlike younger patients, older people may not show the expected thyroid enlargement or heat intolerance. Furthermore, they may have a loss of, rather than increase in, appetite.

It is important to be alert to symptoms of hyperthyroidism such as weakness, palpitations of the heart, shortness of breath, "nervousness," and anxiety.

Administration of radioactive iodine is a common approach to treatment, but the patient should be watched for an associated exacerbation of symptoms, as the irradiated thyroid releases more of its hormone.

Despite some such thyroid problems, however, the overwhelming majority of older people maintain a balanced thyroid state.

S. W. Spaulding, "Age and the Thyroid," *Endocrinology and Metabolism Clinics* 16 (1987): 1013.

---

the pain and helps eliminate the pain at the root of the problem.

But there is potential danger here: After such operations, patients may sustain injuries to the numbed area but then fail to seek appropriate medical help, simply because they lack the nerves that can tell them something is wrong.

Doctors may also inject painkilling substances, such as local anesthetics, into the nerves that are transmitting the pain. This procedure can block the feelings of discomfort, at least temporarily.

Other methods of relieving pain have also been tried over the years, but many of them have limited use or are accompanied by potential dangers. These include alcohol, which may certainly provide pain relief but is also subject to abuse when the pain persists and drinking becomes heavier.

Hypnosis works on some patients, and a few have learned to hypnotize themselves fairly effectively. But in general, this approach is unpredictable as a means of pain relief.

Some patients have also been helped by various skin stimulation techniques. These include certain chemical substances that excite nerve endings on the skin and simultaneously reduce the pain elsewhere in the body.

For example, rubbing a small amount of a menthol preparation (such as Ben-Gay, Icy Hot, or Heet) may help. Or the use of a *transcutaneous electric nerve stimulation* (TENS) unit works to reduce pain in some people. These units give out tingling sensations through small electric impulses.

The application of cold through icy gel packs may numb an area of the body that is in pain. For some people, the application of heat may be a better approach.

In the last analysis, with your doctor's help, you will probably have to experiment with methods like these to find the right combination for pain relief. A number of possibilities are available, however, so resolve to keep trying until you find the most effective approach.

19

ALL ABOUT THE DIGESTIVE TRACT

Tom, a sixty-eight-year-old entrepreneur who, over the years, had bought and consumed a lot of rich, high-fat foods entertaining clients, found that his system was not responding as well now as it had in the past to that sort of diet.

"I have an uncomfortably 'full' feeling after meals more often that I used to," he told me. "Also, I seem to have more trouble digesting things like steak and other meats, and those foods have been the staple of my diet! As I was telling my wife the other day, I still like meat, but meat doesn't seem to like me!

"In fact—and I really hate to admit this—I find that I really prefer eating what amounts to two or three breakfasts a day, rather than my usual well-balanced meals at noon and in the evening. That's the way my ninety-year-old mother eats!"

What Tom was describing is a common phenomenon among many people as they get older. After you pass age fifty, it is normal to find that heavy, high-fat foods like red meat seem to "stay with you" longer than they did when you were younger. The digestive system just does not work as quickly for many people.

MANAGING INDIGESTION

In a 1988 *Lancet* article, a research group defined *dyspepsia* (including the various forms of indigestion) as feelings of pain, discomfort, heartburn, nausea, or vomiting in the upper abdominal, or *retrosternal,* area (the region behind the lower breastbone).

Dyspepsia may be an early symptom of serious illness, such as ulcers, cancer, or gallbladder trouble. But often, no organic problem or lesion can be found. The dyspepsia may be chronic or recurrent. The patient may be otherwise well but appear to be a worrier.

Some of the symptoms may suggest *reflux,* a regurgitation of stomach acid into the esophagus: These include discomfort on lying flat after large meals or on stooping. In such situations, relief may be obtained through antacids.

Other symptoms may suggest disturbances in gastrointestinal motility (movement of food): These include distension, fullness, rapid filling during meals, and nausea.

A small number of patients have ulcer symptoms: awakening at night with pain or episodic pain relieved by small meals or antacids. But still, they may not have an ulcer.

Other people with dyspepsia are air swallowers or burpers.

In general, the causes of dyspepsia are poorly understood. Furthermore, if a physician finds an abnormality, such as gallstones, that finding does not necessarily mean the abnormality is the cause of the problem.

In some cases, mild inflammation may occur in the gastrointestinal tract. In others, the disturbances seem related to delays in the emptying of the stomach. For individuals over age forty-five, a complete medical exam is necessary to exclude serious possibilities.

For those found to have reflux problems (backup of stomach acid into the esophagus), recommendations include the following: raising the head of the bed, quitting smoking, avoiding chocolate, cutting out caffeine, and making use of antacid treatments.

For motility problems—that is, disturbances of the ability of the gastrointestinal tract to move food along—drugs may be of help. These include metoclopramide (Reglan).

Some treatments must of necessity fall into the trial-and-error category because they work for some patients and not for others. These may include use of bismuth (a chemical that can be used as a protective coating for the lining of the stomach and intestines) or antispasmodics, or dietary manipulation.

"Management of Dyspepsia: Report of a Working Party," *Lancet* 1 (1988): 576.

Changes may also occur in our production of stomach and intestinal enzymes and acids, which are essential to the digestive process. For example, there is less hydrochloric acid and pepsin in the stomach. These play an important role in protein digestion, and when they are lacking, other enzymes from the pancreas, which pour into the small intestine, may have more digestive work to do. In any event, when there is too little gastric (stomach-produced) hydrochloric acid, the breakdown of foods may not occur as efficiently or as rapidly, and a "full" feeling or other discomfort may result.

In addition, the lactase enzyme of the intestine, which breaks down the special sugar in milk and dairy products, may become less and less available as we get older. As a result, many people develop what's called *lactose* (milk sugar) *intolerance.* Signs of this condition include increased production of gas, abdominal cramping, and loose stools.

Along with these changes, most older people experience a decline in their sense of taste with deterioration and loss of the taste buds, which are scattered all over the tongue. With this loss of taste, the ability to enjoy the foods of one's youth may decrease.

My advice to Tom and others with various age-related changes in their digestion: Do not worry simply because you feel less comfortable with foods you favored when you were younger. The change in taste capacity or in the ability of your gastrointestinal system to break down foods as efficiently as in youth is a pretty universal development. You simply have to experiment a little with other foods and seasonings to see what sparks your interest and produces the greatest sense of comfort.

Furthermore, you may very well find that the foods that you no longer like so much—or that you find you don't digest so easily—are the very foods that should be avoided for health. For example, as we have already seen in previous chapters, red meats and high-fat dairy products tend to have higher concentrations of cholesterol and saturated fats and are not at all good for your cardiovascular system. The fact that your body begins to react to these foods as you grow older may have survival value.

"Don't get concerned just because you want to eat more than one 'breakfast' a day!" I told Tom. "As far as I can tell, you're getting enough vegetables and other nutrients, so you're certainly eating a well-balanced diet. In fact, as long as you use skim milk on your cereal and stay away from butter and other high-fat products, you'll be consuming a healthier diet than you were before!"

To help you understand better how your digestive system works as you get older and how you can deal with certain common gastrointestinal health problems related to aging, I will now take you on a tour of your digestive system, from top to bottom.

It All Starts in the Mouth

The mouth—or as we in the medical profession call it, the *oral cavity*—is the first part of the digestive tract. This is where everything gets started, and the condition of your teeth and gums is therefore the first important concern.

A few of the basics: Your incisors are the teeth in the very front of your mouth and are used for biting into food; the molars in the rear are intended for grinding. Good teeth play a key role in good nutrition, not to mention the enjoyment of food as the years advance. After all, if you cannot chew effectively, that limits the variety of healthful things you can eat, such as the proverbial apple a day that keeps the doctor away. Pain or discomfort during chewing can discourage many older people from wanting to eat at all. It is hard to look forward to a meal that is likely to become an ordeal, rather than an occasion for satisfaction and good fellowship.

Unfortunately, the majority of people over sixty-five whom I see in my office—and they are representative of the population at large—do not have many working teeth any longer. Most need partial plates, implants, or false teeth, to one degree or another.

What causes this problem? There are two major changes, the first of which is rather obvious: Older people have had more time to accumulate *caries,* or cavities, following decay in their teeth. In most cases, they did not have the fluoridated water and other dental protections many young people enjoy these days. As a result, their teeth began to cause problems at an early age, and their lack of know-how about oral hygiene exacerbated mouth problems. One of the few aging changes that may have a value in the teeth is the progressive thickening of the dentin at the expense of the innermost sensitive pulp. This process lessens pain and may enable dental procedures to be performed without local anesthesia.

In addition to the cavities, older people commonly experience a loosening of their teeth through gingivitis (inflammation of the gums) and other gum problems. The tendency of those over fifty to have problems with osteoporosis (or loss of bone mass) may affect the bone structures in the jaw and contribute to loose teeth. In many cases, the person may develop a loosening or loss of teeth, even if he or she does not really have a problem with cavities.

I recall one seventy-five-year-old woman who came in to see me with a loose-tooth problem, though she had only one small filling in her entire mouth! Despite her good dental care and almost total lack of cavities, she was a person clearly at high risk for osteoporosis: fair-complexioned, small-boned, with a family history of the disease. She had already suffered symptoms of osteoporosis, including a fractured wrist from a relatively mild fall. The declining bone mass in her jaw was part of a much broader bone-loss problem. This woman eventually had to have many teeth pulled and a rather extensive set of plates.

What is the answer to these tooth problems? There are several possible strategies, depending on the condition of your teeth.

• It is often forgotten that gingivitis is primarily an infection. This problem should be treated with antibiotics, of which tetracycline may be the first choice. Furthermore, the antibiotics may have to be continued for weeks or even months. But I've seen remarkable cases in which firm, healthy gums finally reappeared, and loose teeth firmed.

• If your teeth are still firmly fixed in the gums and in relatively good shape, give thanks and close attention to good dental and bone care. Continue to see your dentist for cleaning and a checkup every six months. Brush your teeth after every meal (yes, this parental admonition still applies after fifty, as it applied to you when you were a youngster!). Use fluoridated toothpastes and fluoride mouthwashes, which prevent decay in exposed roots.

• Use dental floss at least once a day. By flossing between your teeth regularly, you remove food particles that can promote decay and reduce the possibility that plaque will build up between the teeth.

But now, a word of caution, especially applicable to older people: When you floss, do not push down so vigorously that your gums begin to bleed. Repeated, too-vigorous flossing may damage gums and aggravate their problems.

• If your teeth are already loose or in such bad shape that dentures seem to be in your future, consider *implants* instead. A number of my patients have chosen to have two or three implants to hang false teeth from, thus avoiding full dentures. The result is much more security in the mouth.

Here's the happy experience of one sixty-seven-year-old woman: She had three teeth that were getting quite loose, and the dental problems were interfering seriously with her eating habits. She still loved fine cuisine, and she was quite a gourmet cook. But she found herself eating very gingerly, always afraid that she would lose a tooth as she bit into some semihard piece of food.

One of this woman's options, given her entire dental condition, was to put in a complete dental plate. But dentures tend to float around in the mouth and can cause embarrassment if they come loose at the wrong moment. She was concerned that she might just be substituting one source of dental anxiety for another.

So she decided instead to try the newer implant procedure for only those three teeth. This involved having her dental specialist extract the teeth and then screw a piece of perforated titanium into the jaw. Titanium is a very neutral substance as far as the body is concerned, and so there is no immunological reaction to it.

The titanium was then allowed to sit in the jaw for some months, and the bone from the jaw grew into the holes. Finally, the dental specialist screwed single teeth into the titanium implants, and the woman had what amounted to three permanent teeth.

These implants are, in effect, a series of "partials," or partial dentures, with the major advantage that they are solidly fixed in the jaw. If this woman needs more teeth replaced later, she can either have additional implants or get a regular denture and hang it from the "permanent" implants.

One obstacle to this technique can be posed by osteoporosis. If the bone mass in the jaw has declined to a great extent, it may not be possible to fix the titanium screws and attach the substitute teeth firmly into the jawbone. But for many people, however—and I include myself in this category—the implant approach is an attractive possibility in the event that full mouth dentures appear in the offing. Implants give you something solid to hang your teeth on!

The Tongue as a Matter of Taste

Even if your teeth and gums are in good shape, you may still find as you get older that certain foods have less appeal than they had when you were younger. An exquisitely marinated fish or meat dish or a subtly seasoned sauce that once caused you to overeat without a second thought may seem flat or unappetizing. One of the main reasons for this development may be the decline over the years in the sensitivity of taste buds, which have their home on your tongue.

Beyond these personal culinary considerations, the first portion of the digestive tract that is routinely subjected to medical scrutiny is the tongue. When I ask a patient to "stick out your tongue, please," I can, at a glance, diagnose several possible diseases.

The tongue, like other parts of the oral cavity, has a remarkable resistance to infection and heals quickly if it is injured, but it can also signal certain underlying problems. For example, inflammation of the tongue, called *glossitis,* may result from excessive smoking, from one of the anemias that often strike older people, or from some vitamin deficiencies.

In pernicious anemia, for instance, the tongue has a bald, red appearance. The cells that line the tongue decrease markedly in thickness, and the papillae (the taste buds) become shrunken or disappear altogether. When there is a deficiency of vitamin B, as sometimes happens with older people who have lost their zest for food, the tongue may have a beefy red or magenta color. The patient may also complain of a burning sensation in the tongue.

The tongue is truly an amazing part of our bodies. In my graduate courses, which eventually led to a doctorate in anatomy, I was as fascinated by the tongue as by anything I studied. Let me wax eloquent for a few moments on the virtues and nature of the tongue so that you can know what to expect of it and how to care for it.

The tongue is a mass of muscles that run in all directions. As a result of their ability to contract, the front part of the tongue can thicken, flatten, curl back on itself, and move about in all parts of the mouth. And do not forget that all this occurs in the speech function, as well as in the digestive function. The back of the tongue, in contrast, remains in a fixed position. The entire muscle package that constitutes the tongue is unique. Nowhere else in the body does a mass of muscle simply dangle free as does the tongue.

What are the practical implications of the tongue's versatility? For one thing, it can act as a shovel, moving food here and there under the grinding teeth. The tongue can also pass food back into the throat as the initial act of swallowing.

The surface of the healthy tongue presents an even, pink-white appearance. Its lining consists of piled-up cells, comparable to those in the skin. Often, there may be a thick accumulation of cells and debris on the surface of the tongue, and again, this is something that doctors or savvy patients are attuned to look for. Too much of this debris, or unusual changes in color, may occur with a fever or other health disturbances.

The accumulation of matter on the tongue is usually referred to as "fur." But if you have just run to the mirror to check your own tongue and found some fur there, don't worry. A furred tongue does not necessarily indicate any disease, nor does good oral hygiene even make it mandatory that it be removed.

On the other hand, the experience of some of my patients suggests that this fur may be related to bad breath. So there are people who assiduously remove the fur on their tongues and other cell accumulations on the roof of their mouths, just to be safe. It may very well be that with some older people, bad breath can result from one or more problems in the mouth, including bad teeth, gum problems, or an excessively "furred" tongue or palate (roof of the mouth).

One way to remove the fur on the tongue is simply to brush it off lightly with a toothbrush. The palate may be brushed in the same way. Other people, notably certain Europeans, prefer to "defur" their mouths with a strip of flexible plastic, designed to be used as a tongue scraper.

On the whole, though, variations in tongue fur are nothing to be concerned about, even when they produce strange or even bizarre-looking configurations. Occasionally, the lining cells that form the surface of the tongue do not grow out at the same height all over. Their irregular proliferation may produce a number of dips and rises in the surface of the tongue, most of which are on average dime-size. These peculiar variations are known as the "geographic tongue" because of their resemblance to contour maps. They are nothing to worry about.

Another harmless variation of tongue fur results in a number of deep furrows. These give the tongue the appearance of an irregularly plowed field.

If you look carefully at your own tongue, you can see a number of little elevations all over it, resembling tiny goosebumps and other much larger mounds. It is on these elevations, which are called *papillae,* that a number of your taste buds reside. Some, called *filiform papillae,* are shaped like little fingers. Others, known as *fungiform papillae,* look like tiny mushrooms.

The most impressive of the papillae are the *circumvallate* type, which are located well toward the back of the tongue. There are eight to ten of these, and they measure about three-eighths of an inch or so in diameter. In some ways, these papillae resemble pink domes completely surrounded by circular moats.

Scattered about among these cells are specialized papillae that control different nuances in the taste sensations. Scientists have identified certain groupings of taste buds that are involved in conveying sweet, sour, salty, and bitter sensations. This explains why some substances can be tasted better on one part of the tongue than another. If, as a result of aging or some other damage or deterioration, the power of a particular set of taste buds has declined, that particular food may lose its appeal or its negative impact.

For example, sensations of bitterness can best be tasted in the cells of the circumvallate papillae, at the back of the tongue. Consequently, you are not often aware of how bitter a food is until it passes over the front of your mouth and heads toward your throat. Of course, at that time, it may be too late to prevent the food from being swallowed! But this bitterness signal may become less obvious or clear as you get older.

The tongue undergoes quite a lot of stress and use during a lifetime, including tremendous shifts from hot to cold foods. Yet it usually withstands these assaults quite unimpaired. But some decrease in the tongue's ability to convey taste sensations can occur over time, especially for those who smoke. Still, many people who stop smoking, including those beyond age fifty, have noticed improved taste perceptions within a week or two.

On the other hand, professional or amateur chefs who constantly sample very hot, spicy foods find that their taste sensibilities decrease permanently over the years.

Finally, a word about saliva: The taste buds respond only to substances that are in solution. It is generally agreed among physicians that a perfectly dry substance cannot be tasted. Hence, the importance of the salivary glands, which pour secretions into the mouth and enhance the sense of taste.

The largest of these are the *parotid glands,* located in the area between the angle of the jaws and the lower portion of the ears. These are the glands frequently attacked by the mumps virus. The other salivary glands include the *sublinqual glands,* just below the free border of the tongue, and the *submaxillary glands,* which nestle within the lower border of each jawbone, near the angles of the jaw.

A quart or more of saliva is secreted by these glands each day, though this figure is a good deal higher in gum chewers. The reason? The act of chewing stimulates secretion.

Those who truly appreciate saliva are those deprived of it. The dry mouth feels uncomfortable; talking, swallowing, and chewing one's food become difficult. In the dry mouth, the tongue has a glazed appearance and is subject to cracks and infections. Worse yet, in the absence of saliva, teeth are highly prone to decay.

The chief complaint I hear about antidepressant drugs is their drying effect on the mouth, and that is quite depressing!

There are a few conditions in medicine that lessen salivary secretion to the point of discomfort. Rheumatoid arthritis is perhaps the best known. In the combination described by the Swedish doctor Sjögren—and therefore known as *Sjögren's syndrome*—the rheumatoid patient complains of dry eyes (diminished tear production). He also has dry mouth (diminished saliva production).

Artificial tears and artificial saliva are available as replacements, but they are not up to the real thing. This syndrome can be a depressing one, both for patient and for doctor. Fortunately, however, the salivary glands keep trying so that most complaints relate to diminished rather than absent production.

Other diseases of the salivary glands are more common among older people. For example, various forms of *sialadenitis,* or inflammation of a salivary gland, may be caused by infection and result in swelling and pain in the face. Recurrent infections may necessitate an operation such as a partial or total parotidectomy, or removal of the parotid gland. Conditions that promote dry mouth (xerostomia), such as dehydration or irradiation treatments, may also contribute to inflammation of the salivary glands. One way to counter this condition is to give the patient plenty of liquids so as to keep him well hydrated.

Chronic inflammation of a salivary gland, particularly the parotid or submaxillary gland, often occurs because of the development of small stones, which block off the gland's ducts. Symptoms of this condition, known as *sialolithiasis,* include a gland enlargement that periodically increases and decreases; pain, especially during eating (or even when you are *thinking* of food!); and thick, mucuslike discharges from the glands. Your physician may treat this condition by cutting open the gland or probing for the stone.

Beyond Good Taste

Once our food moves beyond the tongue, the ability to taste declines abruptly. There is no significant taste sensation, either in the hard palate (the bony arch of the upper jaw) or in the soft palate (the soft covering for the back of the mouth and the beginning of the throat).

For this reason, as I have told a number of my patients, it is something of a misnomer to refer to a gourmet as having a "refined palate." What she really has is a refined tongue!

In fact, the remainder of the gastrointestinal tract has no sensation comparable to taste. For that matter, the tract does not experience touch, pressure, or heat and cold sensations, at least, not in the usual manner.

I mentioned to one woman who was having trouble staying on a diet: "When you're about to take a bite of something you know you should avoid, think of this: Once you've swallowed all that food, its attractiveness disappears. All the seasoning, the gourmet touches, the sweet sensations—they're finished!

"After food has departed from the back of the tongue, the joys of cooking are transformed into the ordinary facts of digestion. So try to concentrate on what that extra food is doing to your fatty contours after it's digested, rather than on what it smells or tastes like."

She was a rather cerebral person, and this suggestion enabled her to detach herself somewhat from the eating process. She even found this new idea served as a greater motivation for her dietary goals.

The Swallowing Scene

In a healthy state, swallowing takes place automatically and superbly and is taken for granted. But innumerable disorders may play havoc with the swallowing mechanism.

Once your food moves beyond the tongue and palate and enters the throat region, which is known as the *pharynx,* matters begin to get more complicated. The pharynx, as a space common to both the respiratory and digestive systems, is the scene of many air-food "traffic" problems. The food you eat must move through this area toward the stomach; the air you breathe also must be channeled through this space. All this activity makes for a lot of stop-and-go signals for the pharynx.

During most of the day, the *esophagus,* or food pipe, is closed down, and the *trachea,* or windpipe, remains open to allow you to breathe freely. Unconsciously and automatically, your *diaphragm,* the muscular wall that separates your chest and abdominal cavities, descends and causes your lungs to expand. This motion pulls air into your body, generally through your nose. The air then passes down through the pharynx, into the trachea (windpipe), and finally into your lungs. When the diaphragm moves back up and presses against your lungs, you exhale through your nose to complete the breathing cycle.

But this natural process of breathing is interrupted when you take food into your body and begin to swallow. To make swallowing a success, it's necessary for your body to manage two lines of traffic: (1) Air must come in from the back of the nose and be channeled down into the windpipe; and (2) food must be directed from the mouth down into the esophagus. Obviously, there is plenty of opportunity for collisions here.

The solution to this traffic problem has been the creation of a barrier in the pharynx, so that what we eat has the "right of way." Only one route, the one that food takes through the esophagus (the food pipe), has priority during a snack or meal. Our swallowing in effect shuts off the two incoming routes: No more food can be taken in through the mouth and no more air can be inspired. Swallowing also erects a "stop sign" up in front of the outgoing route that exhaling air takes through the windpipe. In more detail, here's how this blocking action occurs:

• The oral cavity is blocked off by the tongue, which rises upward and backward to the roof of the mouth when you swallow.

• The back opening into the nose is blocked by the elevation of the soft palate at the top of the throat.

• Finally, the trachea is blocked off as the opening to it rises up under the shelter of the base of the tongue. This is why the Adam's apple bobs up and down as you swallow.

To ensure that no foods or liquids enter the windpipe during eating, a miniature trap door known as the *epiglottis* is slammed shut over the tracheal opening. The seal produced by this movement is watertight.

With three of the four avenues into the pharynx thus cut off, the contraction of the muscles in that area during swallowing can, without obstruction, push the food into the only open channel, the esophagus, and finally down into the stomach.

Sometimes, however, this tidy process of traffic control goes awry, especially in older people. The muscles that produce good swallowing may decline somewhat in power and coordination with age, and as a result, there may be more of a danger of choking on food.

When such choking occurs, a piece of food typically gets caught in the trachea before it closes down during swallowing. As a result, the victim's breathing apparatus is plugged up, and if steps to dislodge the food are not taken quickly, the person may suffocate.

One of the most popular methods for causing the food to pop out of the windpipe is the Heimlich maneuver. I still recall the account one of my sixty-five-year-old patients gave of how he saved a friend of about the same age at a restaurant dinner table with this technique.

He stood behind his friend and wrapped his arms around the man's upper trunk, with his hands joined in a fist at a point just below the victim's sternum, high in the midline of the abdomen. Then, my patient executed the maneuver by squeezing his arms together in a hard, abrupt motion, with his fist pushing up and into his friend's lower chest. The food—a piece of steak—popped right up into the victim's mouth. Aside from a short bout of gasping and coughing, the man was able to walk out of the restaurant in good health.

Of course, this problem can plague younger people as well as older ones. But there do seem to be more reported cases of choking on food among those who are middle-aged and older. This tendency probably has some relation to a decrease in the efficiency of the swallowing mechanism. Because of the possibility of a gradually increasing danger in this area, I strongly recommend that as you get older, you pay more attention to what your mother probably taught you while you were a child: Go slowly in your eating. And chew your food thoroughly before you try to swallow. With these simple precautions, most people do not have to worry about choking on their food.

Because of the complexity of the swallowing mechanism, it is apparent that difficulty may arise if disordered nerves, muscles, growths, or inflammations appear on the swallowing scene.

A swallowing difficulty, as we noted in Chapter 3, is called *dysphagia.* This condition may result from many processes, including the following: possible cancers; disorders of the central nervous system, such as Parkinson's disease; peripheral nervous system disease, such as occurs with diabetes mellitus; thyroid problems; side effects of certain medications; nerve impairments after a stroke; or aftereffects of certain operations.

So if you have any trouble swallowing, do not simply assume, "I'm just getting older." There could be an identifiable disease. Have your doctor check it out, and be certain of the diagnosis.

The Highway of the Esophagus

After your food makes it through the pharynx, the *esophagus,* a ten-inch muscular tube less than a garden hose in diameter, takes over as a conduit or "highway" to the stomach. The muscles of the esophagus propel the food along with a moderate thrust, sufficiently strong that many healthy people can swallow while in an upside-down position!

But the transit of food through this anatomical highway isn't as rapid, or in some cases in older people, as easy as many imagine. It takes on the order of eight to ten seconds for food to traverse the ten-inch length of the esophagus. In contrast, the musculature of a dog's esophagus contracts much more rapidly, so that a dog can "wolf" its food down with such impressive speed.

In its course through the chest cavity, the esophagus passes close to such important structures as the aorta, the largest artery in the body, which arises from the heart. The esophagus also passes just behind the heart. Consequently, a doctor can detect certain forms of enlargement of the heart by having the patient swallow some barium and then X-raying him as the liquid passes through the food pipe. An enlarged heart pushes the barium-filled esophagus backward.

The esophagus has relatively few glands, and no digestion occurs in it. As a structure of the neck and chest only, it penetrates the diaphragm through an opening called the *hiatus*. Once through this aperture, the esophagus enters the abdomen and there ends in the expanded portion of the digestive tract we know as the stomach.

As you get older, the efficiency of your esophagus's transporting mechanisms may deteriorate somewhat. Specifically, those over sixty may find that their esophageal muscles do not relax, contract, and relax again as well as they once did. Contractions may be relatively weak and disordered, or spastic and close together. The latter movement produces a well-known picture on the X ray, termed the "corkscrew esophagus." It may be associated with chest pains that have been confused with cardiac disease, such as angina.

Some of the health problems that may arise in the esophagus as a result of age-related changes, as well as from other factors, include the following:

• *Esophagitis.* Esophagitis is a discomfort usually described as a "heartburn." Generally in the lower esophagus, it may be caused by a variety of events. One patient of mine who had been thriving for years on highly seasoned foods came in complaining of a sense of burning and fullness in the middle of the chest. Sometimes, the burning pain awoke him at night.

"Could this be my heart?" he asked. As it turned out, this man's problem was both his diet *and* a tendency of his highly acidic stomach juices to back up into the esophagus. This condition is referred to as *reflux.*

"The esophagus just doesn't tolerate those acid gastic juices very well," I told him. "And those spicy foods you're eating are aggravating the irritation." In addition, the glass or two of wine he liked with dinner increased stomach acids and his esophageal irritation.

The solution? I instructed him to eat bland foods and skip the wine. I also advised him to elevate the head of his bed with a couple of blocks, so that the stomach juices would stay down where they were supposed to at night. Finally, I told him to take moderate doses of a common antacid to reduce the acidity of the reflux into the esophagus. These steps relieved the irritation completely.

HEALTH REPORT

HOW TO GET RELIEF FROM ESOPHAGITIS

The *reflux,* or backup, of acid from the stomach into the lower esophagus can produce irritation, and in severe cases, ulceration. Symptoms vary from a little "heartburn" to severe pain.

An older approach to relieve this problem advocated raising the head of the bed on blocks. More recent treatments include gastric acid suppressants, such as ranitidine (Zantac).

In this study, these methods were used separately and then together. The esophagus was examined to check changes by esophagoscopy. Each of the two approaches was helpful, but the best results were obtained by using them both. Smoking and alcohol use both interfered with the healing process.

[NOTE: A more recent drug, still unreleased, which is a total acid suppressant, may be the ultimate answer to peptic esophagitis. Of course, people with any form of ulcer disease who smoke or drink should have their heads as well as their digestive systems examined!]

R. F. Harvey, N. Hadley, T. R. Gill, et al., "Effect of Sleeping with the Bed-head Raised and of Ranitidine in Patients with Severe Peptic Oesophagitis," *Lancet* 2 (1987): 1200.

Sometimes, a reflux inflammation of the esophagus can be eliminated by cutting out a specific food item. Chocolate and coffee are common causes, as are onions, peppers, and garlic. Fats and fried foods are frequent offenders also. I am often impressed by how patients can promptly tell me what gives them heartburn, and yet how frequently they continue to eat those items anyway.

Certain medications may also be involved in the problem, for example, theophylline, anticholinergics, beta-adrenergic agonists, alpha-adrenergic antagonists, dopamine, diazepam, and the calcium channel blocking agents. Your doctor may be able to change your medication and help reduce the esophageal discomfort.

KEY FACTS

WHAT DOES IT MEAN TO BE INTOLERANT?

In medical parlance, *intolerance* means your body reacts badly to certain substances, which may be taken in through the diet. Here are a few key examples:

• *Lactose intolerance.* Lactose, or milk sugar, is broken down in the digestive tract by the enzyme lactase. This enzyme often diminishes with age so that many middle-aged and older persons develop bloating, gas rumbling, and loose stools when they drink milk or eat dairy products.

• *Disaccharide intolerance.* Disaccharides are chemically composed of two sugar combinations, glucose and fructose. Lactose is a disaccharide, as is common table sugar, sucrose. After gastrointestinal upsets, some disaccharide intolerance to lactose in milk products and other sugars may develop. This problem is usually temporary and may not be recognized as distinct from the original upset.

• *Fat intolerance.* The ability to digest fats may be greatly diminished in chronic pancreatic disease. In such a case, eating fats can lead to indigestion and excretion of undigested fats in the stool, a phenomenon known as *steatorrhea.* Older people also complain of less serious forms of fat intolerance: They may experience dyspepsia (indigestion) on eating beef or other fatty foods. Perhaps this is a natural result of aging changes, but sometimes gallbladder disease may be responsible for this problem.

• *Glucose intolerance.* Glucose tolerance is tested for by instructing the patient to drink a standard test dose of glucose. With this dose, the blood sugar, which also is glucose, rises. Normally, insulin is then stimulated to emerge from the pancreas, and the glucose levels fall. But with glucose intolerance, the blood sugar levels stay high for abnormally long periods of time.

Although this test result may indicate diabetes mellitus, that is not always the case. With aging, the test levels may also rise to near-diabetic levels in some people who are not true diabetics. They may have a condition referred to as "indeterminate" glucose intolerance. Typically, these patients will be advised to adjust their diets and life-styles, including increasing the levels of their activity and exercise. But they do not necessarily have to be treated as diabetics.

• *Ulcer formation.* An *ulcer,* which may arise in many parts of the body, is a defect in the normally continuous lining of a bodily surface. Often, in areas exposed to acids, the ulcerated spot is raw and inflamed, with underlying tissue exposed. Formation of an ulcer may be the next phase of the long-term irritation of esophagitis that has gone untreated. With the development of ulcers, bleeding may also occur.

KEY FACTS

RISK FACTORS FOR ULCERS

Those with the following factors in their life are at higher risk for ulcers of the digestive tract:
  • Family history of ulcers
  • Smoking
  • Regular or excessive use of aspirin or related drugs
  • Alcoholism
  • Relatively high levels of stress

• *Liver disorders.* Only your doctor can determine through a series of tests whether your esophageal problems are related to a liver disorder. In these cases, there may be a swelling of the veins in the lower esophagus, similar to the varicose veins of the legs. Such a vein is called a *varix.* Occasionally, serious bleeding may occur from a varix.

• *Cancer of the esophagus.* Tumors of the esophagus are most common between the ages of fifty and seventy, and it is two to six times more common in men than in women. In the United States, this disease accounts for about 2 percent of all known cancers.

The symptoms include difficulty in swallowing (dysphagia). Food sometimes seems to "stick" at a particular level, usually in the middle part of the esophagus. The discomfort may be specific enough that the patient can often point to the spot that feels uncomfortable.

The causes of this problem? No one knows for certain, but a number of factors have been suggested as strong possibilities. These include tobacco use, alcohol, irritation from hot foods, and poor oral hygiene. Probably, the problem builds up from poor health habits over many years or a lifetime, much as lung cancer does.

The outlook for those with esophageal cancer is, I'm sad to say, "dismal," to quote a contributor to my textbook *Clinical Geriatrics.* The usual methods of treatment are surgical removal of the cancerous tissue and irradiation. Chemotherapy may be called for as well. Unfortunately, fewer than 50 percent of all patients with esophageal carcinoma can be successfully operated upon. Even those who are candidates for surgery face dim prospects: Only about 10 percent of those who undergo this surgery are alive apparently cancer-free after five years.

The good news, however, is that it is curable if caught early, and it does require a great deal of time to develop. So if you are attuned to changes in the way your swallowing and digestive system are working, you are in a better position to take positive, and perhaps even lifesaving, action.

The main message here: See your doctor immediately if you begin to experience any changes in your swallowing or any difficulty or discomfort in your upper digestive system.

• *Esophageal spasms and other less serious disorders.* Fortunately, most of the difficulties in swallowing or in the other behavior of the esophagus are nothing to worry about. Some require intervention.

For example, one type of spasm that may create discomfort occurs at the juncture between the esophagus and stomach. Since this area is close to the heart, it is called the *cardia,* and the spasm is sometimes referred to as a *cardiospasm.* When cardiospasm becomes chronic, considerable distention of the esophagus may occur, as food piles up instead of being passed on efficiently to the stomach. This problem can be improved or cured by a dilatation procedure performed by the doctor.

Sometimes, bouts of pain and spasm can be controlled simply by a change of diet or sleeping position, with the head raised as I recommended in the case of the previous patient. At other times, it is necessary to turn to medications that promote smooth muscle relaxation. These include nitroglycerin, long-acting nitrates, and, in some cases, the calcium channel blocking agents, nifedipine and verapamil, which are sometimes used for hypertension.

The Stomach: The Center of Digestion

The stomach, of course, is that familiar receptacle at the end of the esophagus, roughly the size and shape of a somewhat small, lop-sided football, into which we can deposit large amounts of food. When your doctor looks at your stomach through an X ray after you have swallowed barium, he generally sees an organ that appears to have a J-shape, with coarse folds running down the long axis of the J. These folds, known as *rugae,* usually flatten out as the stomach fills up.

KEY FACTS

A GLOSSARY OF GASTROINTESTINAL PROCEDURES AND TESTS

● *Upper GI series.* This test involves an X-ray visualization of the esophagus, stomach, and first part of the small intestine after drinking a glass of barium, an opaque substance that shows up on X rays.

● *Barium enema.* An X-ray visualization of the rectum and colon by administering barium through an enema tube.

● *Proctoscopy (also sigmoidoscopy).* A direct visualization of the rectum and a segment of the colon just above the rectum (the sigmoid colon). This is done by passing a rigid or flexible tube with its own light source up through the rectum.

● *Colonoscopy.* Direct visualization of the entire colon by passing an even longer, flexible tube with its light source through the rectum.

● *Esophagoscopy (gastroscopy).* A similar procedure to colonoscopy, in which the tube is passed down the throat and esophagus, and into the stomach.

The shape of the stomach may vary considerably, depending on the person's body build. I can usually take one look at my patients and predict what their stomachs will look like on the barium X ray:

In slender people, the stomach tends to be elongated and may even dip down as far as the upper part of the pelvis. On the other hand, in some short, stocky individuals, the stomach may have an almost sideways, transverse position. This produces an X-ray configuration known as the "steer-horn" stomach.

The curved upper part of the stomach, known as the *fundus,* rises up above the level at which the esophagus enters the stomach. This upper section of the stomach nestles against the diaphragm and is the place where swallowed air accumulates. It's this air that we attempt to release when we "burp the baby" or when we belch after a meal.

The major part of the stomach, the *corpus,* dips down below the fundus and contains most of the acid-secreting glands making the hydrochloric acid, which helps with digestion. The stomach then ends in a narrowed portion, the *pylorus,* that connects to the small intestine.

Here are a number of disorders that the stomach may present as you age:

The Ability to Digest Food

As I have already mentioned, the older you get, the less hydrochloric acid you tend to produce in the stomach's corpus (the large, main part of the stomach). With the passage of the decades past age fifty, the lining of the stomach wall, from which the secretions come, tends to shrink. This process is termed *atrophic gastritis.* Its cause is unknown, but the outcome is a decline in hydrochloric acid secretion and digestive enzymes.

Perhaps because of these declines in the gastric juices, the digestion of certain types of foods, such as red meats or high-fat dishes, is less efficient and rapid within the stomach.

Hiatus Hernia

Hiatus hernia is a common condition among those over fifty that occurs when a portion of the stomach penetrates the hiatus (the junction between the esophagus and stomach) and nestles alongside the esophagus, either within the hiatus opening or up into the chest itself.

Often, a hiatus hernia produces no symptoms and is picked up incidentally on X rays. On the other hand, the condition may produce heartburn, chest pain, or a "crampy" sensation and may eventually predispose one to the formation of an ulcer in the herniated portion of the stomach.

When a seventy-year-old patient came in to me complaining of chest pains, she was distraught: "Dr. Rossman, I've got angina! Am I having a heart attack?"

After calming her, I determined that she was, indeed, having pains behind the lower part of the breastbone where angina typically occurs. But a series of tests showed that the problem was not her heart: She had developed a typical hiatus hernia, a condition that afflicts approximately 5 to 10 percent of the older population. The symptoms are sometimes similar to angina, and one condition is often confused with the other until a doctor makes a definitive differential diagnosis.

The treatment? I advised her to eat small meals and avoid hard-to-digest foods that would distend her stomach. The reason for this was that the more bloated her stomach became, the more likely it was that the upper part would move up through the hiatus opening into the esophagus and give her those uncomfortable pains again. Many physicians believe that a major cause or aggravation of this hernia is that the stomach acids seep up into the esophageal opening and begin to irritate the hiatus.

In my patient's case, the recommended dietary changes meant avoiding fats, heavy meat dishes, or recipes saturated with creamy sauces. I also instructed her to cut down on the amount of soups and liquids she was taking with her meal, again, to prevent distending her stomach. Another helpful adjustment involved her sleeping habits: I advised her to raise the head of her bed when she slept so that there would be less likelihood of the stomach acids' churning up into the hiatal opening or the esophagus.

In addition to adjusting her diet and her sleeping position, this woman began to take an over-the-counter alkalinizing medication to reduce the amount of acid that was spilling over from her stomach into the hiatus. Finally, I prescribed the drug Reglan, which helped the propulsive movement in the upper part of her digestive tract. As she had grown older, this woman had experienced some trouble with swallowing. It also seemed likely that the muscular efficiency of her esophagus had declined somewhat. The drug just helped the food move along better into the stomach and the intestines.

The result of all these changes and treatments? Her "angina" pain—which, of course, was not angina at all—disappeared.

Peptic Ulcer

Peptic ulcers are formed as a result of an eating-away of the stomach or upper part of the small intestine (the duodenum) by the powerful gastric (stomach) juice, composed in part of the enzyme pepsin, plus acid.

To understand how this process works, and what your risks may be, let's spend a few more moments considering the way your stomach works. I use this brief "lecture" in discussions with many of my patients, and the information seems to give many of them a helpful tool to deal with their own gastric or duodenal ulcers.

It is important to understand one basic fact: The major digestive function of the stomach is to launch a vigorous assault on protein foods. As a matter of fact, the stomach really does not pay much attention to other items in your diet. Proteins are its main target!

The concentration on proteins is important because your body cannot assimilate or tolerate foreign proteins unless they are broken into their component parts. Each cell of every species has its own characteristic protein structures, and one species cannot use the protein of another without preparing the ingested protein for its own bodily use.

The attack the stomach makes against outside protein is made possible through the secretion of the powerful gastric juice. An examination of the lining of the stomach with a simple hand lens reveals that it is studded with minute pits. These pits mark the openings of the gastric glands. From these openings, the gastric juices, with their powerful pepsin enzyme, emerge.

Pepsin in an acid solution rapidly breaks down dietary protein, a process that can be illustrated by placing a sliver of meat in a test tube and covering it with gastric juice. I continue to be impressed by this experiment when it is performed in medical classes. The meat soon begins to develop a frayed appearance, and if you shake the solution a little, the meat breaks into fragments.

In an action that mimics this test-tube shaking, powerful churning and propulsive movements continually sweep over the stomach in the process of digestion. These waves of activity ensure a thorough mixing of the food with the gastric juice. As digestion proceeds, some of the contractions are sufficient to push the gastric contents on into the first part of the intestine (the first twelve inches of intestine we call the *duodenum*).

This phase of gastric emptying into the intestine is controlled to a large extent by the type of food we eat. Starchy foods leave the stomach rather rapidly, because they cannot be digested there. In contrast, protein and fatty foods stay in the stomach much longer. Or as the old sayings go, "meat sticks with you much longer," or "meat sticks to your ribs!"

These characteristics of protein suggest the value of high-protein diets in reducing programs because they assist in postponing the need for more food. Protein is also a key element in other special diets, such as hypoglycemia diets, which are designed to control wide fluctuations in blood sugar.

There is little absorption of nutrients through the wall of the stomach into the rest of the body, though both water and alcohol can permeate the gastric barriers. Furthermore, observant drinkers have noted that absorption of alcohol occurs much more rapidly on an empty than a full stomach. Alcohol also can stimulate the output of gastric juices. Indeed, for many years alcohol was used as a test substance to determine how well gastric juice production occurred in a patient.

A logical question that has been raised by a number of my patients: "If the stomach attacks protein foods so vigorously, why doesn't the stomach attack *itself*? After all, the stomach is made of protein, isn't it?"

The complete explanation is still not known. There is no identified substance within the stomach wall that might prevent it from undergoing self-digestion. But some protection against this danger is certainly provided by the protective coating of mucus that covers the stomach's surface. The alkalinity of the blood and tissue juices adds some protection to the living cells of the living body.

In addition, some of the agents known as *prostaglandins* are also protective. Interference with their production in the stomach wall (which may happen with drugs of the aspirin group) may contribute to ulcer.

Self-digestion *may* occur when the stomach's defense mechanisms are not working properly, and this can lead to a peptic ulcer. A peptic ulcer in the stomach wall or in the wall of the upper part of the small intestine (the duodenum) occurs at one time or another in approximately 10 percent of our population, and the disease is on the increase among the elderly segment of the population. Although duodenal ulcers occur two to three times more often than gastric ulcers, gastric ulcers are responsible for two-thirds of all ulcer-related deaths.

Many times, those with such an ulcer do not even know they have it, and the ulcer may heal before they become aware of the disease. The only sign that the stomach has "eaten itself" or the adjacent part of the small intestine is a small telltale scar. In a relatively small number of people, peptic ulcer becomes a chronic, serious, and sometimes incapacitating disease.

What causes a given individual to have a peptic ulcer?

This problem, which has been described as the "wound stripe" of civilization, seems to occur most often among modern city dwellers. It has been linked to psychosomatic disorders involving expression of emotions such as anger, which in some people seem to stimulate extra output of acidic gastric juices. In contrast, fear and anxiety may decrease movements of the stomach and its secretions, and that is a reason why it is sometimes so difficult to digest food properly in the presence of these emotions.

Some scholars have even tried to link a predisposition to ulcers to body build. And it is true in my own practice that many people with peptic ulcer tend to be tall and slender. Or, in Shakespeare's terms, "Yon Cassius hath a lean and hungry look." But there are too many stocky exceptions to this observation.

About all that we can say with certainty is that an inherent tendency to make excessively acid gastric juice may put a person at greater risk for ulcer. But to determine this innate tendency, it is more important to look at a person's family history of ulcers, rather than body build or some other outward sign.

Finally, peptic ulcer is found more often in men than women.

HEALTH REPORT

WHAT ROLE MAY BACTERIA PLAY IN ULCER FORMATION?

Evidence keeps mounting that a spiral-shaped bacterium, called *Campylobacter pyloridis,* may play an important role in ulcer of the stomach and duodenum, and also in gastritis (inflammation of the lining of the stomach).

This organism is found in a very high percentage of patients with those disorders: 70 to 100 percent, according to various studies. Accidental ingestion of the organism has led to acute gastritis and dyspepsia. Volunteers who swallow cultures of it develop the same problem. Typically, with this condition gastroscopes reveal inflammation (gastritis) in the gastrointestinal tract.

Medications such as bismuth subnitrate or metronidazole (Flagyl) clear away the organism and eliminate the inflammation. These medications also help heal the ulceration and lessen the rate of recurrence.

A. T. R. Axon, "Campylobacter pyloridis: What Role in Gastritis and Peptic Ulcer?" *British Medical Journal* 293 (1986): 772.

Other than these general considerations, older people who are at risk for peptic ulcer are those on certain drugs, especially those used in the treatment of rheumatoid and arthritic disorders. These include corticosteroids and the nonsteroidal anti-inflammatory agents, such as aspirin, indomethacin, and phenylbutazone.

What are the warning symptoms of this problem?

As I have already said, there may be no symptoms at all. Sometimes, the discomfort is disregarded as something banal: common heartburn, "acid indigestion," "viral upset," or the like. I become especially suspicious if the pain awakens the patient at night and if it recurs despite alkalinizers and food. If the person has ever had an ulcer in the past, even decades ago, beware!

HEALTH REPORT

WHAT CAN ANTI-INFLAMMATORY DRUGS DO TO YOUR STOMACH?

A certain class of drugs, the nonsteroidal anti-inflammatory drugs (NSAIDs), are used widely in the treatment of arthritis and other pain. They include such familiar prescription drugs as Motrin, Naprosyn, Clinoril, Tolectin, and Feldene. In small doses, NSAIDs can be found in over-the-counter items such as Advil, Nuprin, and Profen.

These drugs are potent and convenient alternatives to aspirin. But all of them may produce damage to the stomach lining and the duodenum, with possible gastritis, ulceration, or bleeding in some people, according to a report in the *American Journal of Medicine.* The local damage is aggravated by the stomach's acid secretions.

Thus, drugs that inhibit acid production—cimetidine (Tagamet) and ranitidine (Zantac) and the coating agent sucralfate—may be helpful in protecting against serious complications.

Those with a history of peptic ulcer or bleeding should avoid these anti-inflammatory drugs. But if they must be used, a combined treatment with a coating agent, or the use of specially coated aspirin (enteric aspirin, Ecotrin), may be appropriate.

NSAID- or aspirin-induced ulcers may not produce warning symptoms in many people. So the first sign may be bleeding, which shows up in black stools or vomiting of blood. If a patient complains of a burning stomach or indigestion, it may be wise to stop all these drugs. Acetaminophen (Tylenol) may be a good alternative painkiller.

J. F. Ivey, "Mechanisms of Nonsteroidal Anti-Inflammatory Drug-Induced Gastric Damage," *American Journal of Medicine* 84 (Supplement 2A) (1988): 41.

In older people, the first appearance of an ulcer may be in the form of gastrointestinal bleeding, which often appears as a dark stool; swallowing difficulties; or anginalike pains in the lower sternal area (the breastbone). Chronic loss of blood is more common with gastric (stomach) than with duodenal (upper intestinal) ulcers and may lead to anemia and, in turn, possibly heart irregularities or mental confusion. Significant weight loss and generally poor health may also indicate the presence of a very large stomach or intestinal ulcer, or a malignancy.

HEALTH REPORT

CAN RECURRENCE OF DUODENAL ULCERS BE PREVENTED?

Successfully treated duodenal ulcers may recur in 70 to 90 percent of patients within twelve months, according to a 1988 *Lancet* study.

The recurrent ulcer may or may not produce pain or other diagnostic symptoms. The ulcer patients in this study were treated initially with the potent antiulcer drug ranitidine (Zantac) at a daily 300-mg dose level. Then, they were placed on a maintenance dose of 150 mg.

An endoscopic examination was performed once a month on a routine basis. The results: Only 45 percent developed recurrences within the first six months, and more than half of the patients (fifteen of twenty-seven) were without symptoms.

In contrast a control group of ulcer patients *not* on maintenance treatment showed an 86 percent recurrence rate!

Because of the decreased recurrence rate on treatment and the lessened likelihood of bleeding, the authors argue for the continued use of maintenance therapy where indicated.

E. F. S. Boyd, J. G. Penston, D. A. Johnston, K. and G. Wormsley, "Does Maintenance Therapy Keep Duodenal Ulcers Healed?" *Lancet* 1 (1988): 1324.

A common treatment your physician may prescribe for a peptic ulcer is an antacid. But care must be exercised with these medications, because too much antacid medication in older people may increase the salt intake and aggravate kidney disease or congestive heart failure. There also may be undesirable changes in bowel habits, most often, some diarrhea, and with the drug Amphogel, constipation. Antacids may also interact deleteriously with other drugs.

For example, aluminum hydroxide, found in many of these agents and the sole ingredient of Amphogel, may *ad*sorb drugs such as digoxin and quinidine. In this process, the antacid compound pulls other therapeutic drugs into itself. Aluminum hydroxide may also interfere with the *ab*sorption of these drugs into the body.

The big breakthrough in recent years was the discovery of the two acid-blocking agents, cimetidine (Tagamet) and ranitidine (Zantac). These virtually abolish all acid production, a prime requisite for ulcer healing. When successful, these drugs end the agonies of chronic ulcer so well that both patient and doctor are tempted to continue them almost indefinitely. It is still uncertain what the best long-term programs for an ulcer patient should be, especially after a recurrence.

There may be side effects to the acid-blocker drugs, and especially cimetidine. The negative effects include mental confusion, depression, diminished libido, and breast enlargement.

The *anticholinergic agents*—drugs that may be used to treat peptic ulcers by blocking the passage of impulses through the autonomic nerves (those over which we have no control)—can trigger a host of problems. These include sluggishness in the functioning of the stomach and the digestive process, reduction in intestinal muscle tone, acute glaucoma, and obstruction in the urinary tract, where bladder contractions are weakened.

Finally, gastric X-irradiation is an old method, but long considered safe, to reduce the secretion of gastric juices, at least on a temporary basis. I have used it in stubborn cases that were poor surgical risks.

I mention the various side effects of the drugs, by the way, *not* to try to scare you away from taking them. It is important for you to be aware of possible discomforts and dangers so that you can alert your physician if they happen to appear.

The Intestines and Beyond

You have already been introduced to the intestinal tract through our discussion of duodenal ulcers. But there is more to be said about this important part of the digestive system, which plays a key role in successful aging.

How the Small Intestines Work

A few more words on how the small intestine works: The small intestine is composed of that portion of the digestive tract between the pyloric opening at the end of the stomach and the large intestine, or colon. We call this the "small" intestine because of its width, not its length.

The small intestine is about the same size in diameter as the esophagus, but that is the only way it is small. This part of the digestive tract is at least a dozen feet in length, and it is the major organ for absorption of food and nutrients, as well as for continued digestion. Into it are poured the secretions of the pancreas and the bile secreted by the liver. All these enter on top of digestive secretions of the intestinal cells themselves. Even in the absence of the stomach, digestion should be complete because of small intestinal activity. This is a prime example of nature's backup planning.

The small intestine is packed into all the available abdominal space not occupied by the other organs. As a result, the three major parts of this organ coil about in a somewhat complex manner.

The first portion of the small intestine, the ten-inch duodenum (where duodenal ulcers occur), is fixed in position. It derives its name from the fact that it is about twelve fingers' breadth in length, as first described by the Greek Herophilus in 344 B.C.

The C-shaped curve of the duodenum, which is sometimes referred to as the "duodenal sweep," encloses the head of the pancreas. The *pancreas* is the organ that secretes enzymes into the intestines for the digestion of food and also manufactures insulin, which is secreted into the bloodstream for the control of blood sugar. If X rays show an unusually widened duodenal sweep, that is an important finding because it may indicate a tumor of the pancreas.

In contrast to the duodenum, the rest of the small intestine is capable of some mobility. This mobility is possible because the small intestine is suspended in a loose covering membrane known as the *mesentery*.

The mesentery is a clear, double-layered film of tissue that is attached to the back body wall. Various arteries and nerves necessary to the functioning of the intestinal tract course through the mesentery tissue. Despite the many twists and turns of the small intestine, the flow of food is always in one direction: from the stomach exit to the colon entrance.

The second part of the small intestine, loops of which mainly occupy the left upper portion of the abdomen, is known as the *jejunum.* "Jejuneness" is a quality of being empty or scanty, an appropriate description for this part of the small intestine, which frequently appears to be empty. This state of relative emptiness stands in sharp contrast to the lower part of the intestinal tract, which is usually filled with fecal matter.

The remainder of the small intestine is known as the *ileum.* No sharp line distinguishes the jejunum from the ileum. Rather, there is a gradual change from a somewhat thicker-walled organ to a somewhat thinner-walled one.

There is still much to be learned about the small intestine. For example, we still wonder why the inflammatory disorder known as Crohn's disease typically attacks the ileum, rather than the jejunum. This condition, also known as "regional ileitis," became celebrated and made the headlines after it attacked President Dwight Eisenhower. An acute attack may be mistaken for appendicitis. The inflammation may then skip on to the colon, where it is known as *ileocolitis.* Unfortunately, there is no specific treatment. But the cortisone group of drugs may be of some help.

Common Concerns with the Small Intestines

The meandering course of the small intestines assumes a greater importance if you are scheduled for surgery on this particular part of your body. Suppose, for instance, you have a particularly serious duodenal ulcer—a common problem faced by older people—that, because of scarring, necessitates an operation known as a *gastrojejunostomy.* This involves making an opening on the greater curvature of the stomach and then sewing this opening to another opening made on a loop of the jejunum.

This operation is most frequently required when a duodenal ulcer has caused obstruction or marked narrowing of the duodenum (the first part of the small intestine that leads out of the stomach). The operation enables food to move from the stomach on into the jejunum and thus bypass the diseased narrowed portion of the duodenum.

As I told one of my patients who recently faced this operation, "A moment's reflection will suggest to you how important it is that the first part of the jejunum be used for this operation. If a loop of your small intestine further along the digestive tract should be used, there would be a danger of bypassing too much of your small intestine. And that might produce malnutrition."

Indeed, in one operation for severe obesity, this was deliberately done to produce maldigestion and weight loss. After some years, however, the procedure was abandoned because of malnutrition and liver problems.

My patient facing the ulcer operation asked, "Why malnutrition?" That provided me with a chance for another practical anatomy lesson.

I explained to him that all digestion ends with the transit through the small intestine. As a result, the small intestine is equipped chemically to deal with every kind of foodstuff: protein, fat, or carbohydrate. So it is important that you hold on to as much of your small intestine as possible so that the digestive process and the absorption of nutrients into the body can proceed successfully and efficiently.

Of the various types of food that enter the small intestine under normal circumstances, protein enters in partially digested condition from the stomach. But fats are not digested at all, and starchy materials may or may not have undergone some preliminary breakdown as a result of the action of the saliva in the mouth.

For these reasons, further digestive action must occur in the small intestine. So at the very gateway of the small intestine (in the duodenum), a new group of digestive secretions appears from the liver and the pancreas.

Because the small intestine is the major site for the assimilation of foods, it is structurally designed for this function. Thus, the internal lining of the small intestine contains literally millions of minute elevations known as *villi,* which give the internal surface of the organ a velvety appearance and enormously increase the surface area capable of absorption of food.

The Malabsorption Issue

In recent years, it has become increasingly clear that a distinction must be made between diseases of digestion and those of absorption. Difficulties of absorption that may create problems for older people have been grouped under the category of "malabsorption." These may be marked by such symptoms as weight loss, anemia, vitamin deficiencies, bloating, and diarrhea. The patient may also suffer from *osteomalacia* (a malformation and softening of the skeletal structure), vitamin A deficiencies, or insufficient calcium in the blood, which can produce muscle spasms *(tetany)* or, rarely, convulsions.

Frequently, an underlying cause of malabsorption is an overgrowth of certain bacteria in the upper small intestine. These bacteria then interfere with the transmission of nutrients into the body. A common treatment for this bacterial problem is the prescription of antibiotics, such as tetracycline or ampicillin.

Another similar condition of malabsorption, common in the elderly, is known as "sprue." Sprue is due to an intestinal intolerance for gluten, a protein in wheat. Symptoms such as diarrhea and others listed previously may clear up when the patient begins a gluten-free diet. But reexposure to the gluten in wheat may trigger diarrhea again. All this is entirely comparable to what is called *celiac disease* in childhood.

One way to diagnose a disease of malabsorption is by use of the *Shiner tube*. This instrument can be swallowed by the patient, moved through the entire esophagus and stomach, and passed on into the small intestine. With appropriate maneuvers by the physician, a small part of the intestinal lining can then be removed (a *biopsy specimen*), pulled out, and examined under a microscope. If the villi on the lining appear short and blunted—as opposed to having their normally long and finger-shaped look—then it is likely that a disease of malabsorption is present.

How About Anemia?

The lining of the small intestine does not absorb everything in an indiscriminate, spongelike fashion. For example, there is an intestinal barrier to the absorption of iron. Usually only a minute proportion of the iron presented to the intestinal lining gets through.

But in the presence of anemia, the barriers to iron absorption are modified. Specifically, the gates are opened a little wider, so to speak, and the small intestine permits more iron to enter the system as a corrective to the anemia.

Anemia takes various forms, but in general, the condition involves an insufficiency of the quantity or quality of red blood cells. As far as gastrointestinal-related diseases are concerned, *pernicious anemia* is one of the serious forms of the disease. This condition is linked to a lack of hydrochloric acid in the stomach, plus atrophic gastritis. Symptoms, often neurological, include weakness, sore tongue, and a burning, tingling sensation such as is common with neuritis. Researchers and practicing physicians alike have observed that people with pernicious anemia tend to turn gray early in life.

Pernicious anemia typically involves a failure of the digestive tract to absorb vitamin B_{12}. This vitamin cannot be absorbed by the small intestine unless a specific substance secreted by the stomach (known as the "intrinsic factor") is present. But the stomach sometimes fails to produce the intrinsic factor, often along with a failure to secrete hydrochloric acid. The result is a lack of vitamin B_{12} absorption, with the onset of pernicious anemia.

Many disorders in elderly people can produce these low levels of vitamin B_{12} in the blood, including bacterial overgrowth in the small intestines, insufficient secretions by the pancreas, drug-related malabsorption, and decrease in production of the intrinsic factor in the stomach.

One of the great medical advances was the development of treatment for pernicious anemia. Physicians can administer large amounts of vitamin B_{12} into the skin instead of by mouth. As a result, the vitamin can enter the body by bypassing the defective digestive tract.

Encouragement About the Small Intestine

In general, the small intestine is far less prone to disease than either the stomach or the large intestine. Usually, the problems that do arise can be easily and quickly corrected.

In addition to the more serious problems already discussed, more common complaints tend to fall into the category of *gastroenteritis,* which involves temporary inflammation of the digestive tract, accompanied by diarrhea or vomiting. Many times, such problems are produced by viruses.

More serious inflammations are rather rare, and even tumors of the small intestine are far less common that those of the stomach or colon. Why this is true is unknown. Pouches in the digestive tract, known as *diverticula,* can occur in the small intestine, but in general, they are uncommon in that location. When all is said and done, then, the most common disease of the small intestine is the one we have already considered in some detail: the duodenal ulcer.

Colon Concerns

I see many more problems related to the *colon*—or large intestine, as it is often called—than to the small intestine. As already mentioned in our consideration of cancer (Chapter 17), malignancies of the colon and rectum are a great deal more common than those of the small intestine.

How the Colon Works

To understand health problems related to the colon, it is necessary to have a grasp of the overall operation of this important organ.

The colon is readily distinguished from the small intestine because of its large size. In some ways, the large intestine bears the same relationship to the small as a warehouse does to the factory it serves. The colon warehouse is large but performs no digestive business. Other than storage, the single most important function of the colon is the absorption of fluids. Incoming wastes are gradually made more solid as fluids are absorbed into the body during the journey through the large intestine.

The bulk of the material the colon deals with involves the indigestible residues from our food. In the ordinary mixed diet, these include the mostly cellulose remnants of the vegetables and fruits we eat. A good deal of cellular debris can also be found in the stool: cast-off lining cells, various kinds of white blood cells, and variable amounts of mucous secretions. These products help determine the constituency, including the hardness or softness, of the stool.

On the other hand, the color of the stool depends on the bile that enters from the liver: Slight modifications in the chemical structure of the bile pigments produce colors ranging from green to yellow, and on to brown or various shades. All of these colors are perfectly normal. They are derived from the bile, which is initially green but then is chemically altered to other shades.

Bacteria also flourish in the large intestine in incredible numbers. One-third of the dry weight of the stool consists of bacteria! Many of these bacteria, in going through their own life cycles, perform useful functions. For example, some manufacture vitamins in significant amounts. Others act on protein residue to produce breakdown products, including small amounts of ammonia. Others, such as the lactobacillus found in sour milk, break down carbohydrate materials.

But it is also possible for the bacterial inhabitants of our bowels to become unbalanced. Sometimes, for instance, antibiotics such as tetracycline may have a marked effect on one group of bacteria and thereby upset the balance of the bacterial population.

I have had a number of patients on antibiotics complain to me about symptoms such as cramps, diarrhea, and rectal irritation. Women patients often develop a yeast vaginitis.

A reduction or change in the antibiotics can help with some of these problems. In addition, yogurt is frequently taken for vaginitis, and it seems to be helpful. Because the problem tends to repeat itself in some patients each time a given antibiotic is taken, it may be worth experimenting with different antibiotics under the supervision of your physician.

The Course of the Colon

The colon makes two fairly sharp changes in its course through the body, a pattern that can be useful in trying to determine where some discomforts arise: The ascending colon, the first part of this organ, arises in the right lower position of the abdomen and runs in a more or less straight path upward to the liver. At this point, the colon executes a sharp turn to the left known as the *hepatic flexure.*

The next portion of the colon runs more or less straight across the abdomen from right to left, but may droop downward through part of its course. This is called the *transverse colon.* In the upper left portion of the abdomen, the organ then executes another turn known as the *splenic flexure* (after the spleen).

Then, the colon runs more or less straight down the left side of the abdomen as the *descending colon.* Finally, it enters the upper portion of the pelvis, where it is sometimes referred to as the *pelvic colon.*

The first portion of the pelvic colon forms a configuration that has been compared to the Greek letter S, or *sigma.* It is therefore sometimes called the "sigmoid colon." Below the sigmoid is a relatively straight portion of the organ that we commonly call the rectum. (*Rectum* is Latin for "straight.") The rectum finally emerges at the anal opening, which is the end of the digestive system.

In terms of length, the colon is much shorter than the small intestine: The ascending colon is roughly six inches in length; the transverse, around eighteen inches; and the descending, about twelve inches. The pelvic colon, including the sigmoid, is usually under eighteen inches in length.

The much longer, though narrower, small intestine enters the colon through a valvelike slit called the ileocolic valve. Just below this entrance is a pouchlike area in the colon called the *cecum,* the home of one of the most famous of all abdominal organs, the appendix.

The Appendix in the Patient over Fifty

The *appendix,* a three- to five-inch, pencil-size projection from the cecum, performs no digestive functions. But it can certainly create big problems in older people!

Fortunately, the appendix is a relatively uncommon cause of difficulties in elderly people. In fact, appendicitis in all age brackets seems on a definite decline. But appendicitis in patients over sixty years of age does account for 6 to 8 percent of all appendectomies, so it is important to know something about this structure and about the symptoms that may arise when appendicitis strikes.

A sixty-one-year-old man called me to report the classic symptoms of appendicitis: some nausea, pain in the lower right quarter of the abdomen, localized tenderness in that area, and fever. I asked him to come in for an immediate examination, and a quick blood test revealed another indication of appendicitis: *leukocytosis,* or an increase in the number of white blood cells that may occur with serious infections. I immediately sent him in for surgery, and his diseased appendix was removed uneventfully. Early recognition is mandatory!

It is especially important to act quickly with a possible appendix problem as you get older. If you delay seeking medical care, there is a greater likelihood that you, as a person over fifty, will suffer a ruptured appendix than will those who are younger. Mortality rates among older people with a ruptured appendix can range from 7 to 9 percent. But even with rupture and considerable intra-abdominal infection, wonderful new antibiotics can prove lifesaving.

In a consideration of abdominal pain at any age, always think of acute appendicitis. Never take a laxative for abdominal pains! That may hasten a rupture.

Poisons in the Colon?

For many decades, discussions have been going on in the medical community as to whether bacterial activities in the colon—and production of many toxic substances there—may be adversely affecting people as they age.

It is clear that many of the products of colon bacteria are toxic. But fortunately, the liver has been set up as a watchdog on the large intestine. For example, one of the known toxic products in the colon is ammonia. But this poison is transported from the large intestine to the liver by way of the portal vein. In the liver, the ammonia is changed into *urea,* a nontoxic substance that is excreted by the kidney into the urine.

But certain forms of liver disease lead to an inability to handle incoming ammonia. This produces the condition known as "ammonia intoxication." The resulting high levels of ammonia in the blood may act adversely on the brain to produce drowsiness, lack of coordination, tremors, and even coma.

The treatment for ammonia intoxication is to give antibiotics designed to destroy many of the proteolytic (ammonia-producing) bacteria in the colon. A physician will usually also prescribe multiple cleansing enemas. As the bacterial population decreases with these treatments, the ammonia intoxication lessens.

Ammonia is but one example of potentially toxic substances created in the fermentation vat we call the colon. The liver recognizes and disposes of many more. These toxic substances vary, depending on diet and kinds of bacteria present in the bowel. Though the liver shrinks with aging, it seems to retain its competence over the longest lifetime.

Questions about the colon's bacteria have continually fascinated the scientific community. Years ago, the celebrated Rockefeller University bacteriologist Rene Dubos told me of raising a group of rats on a high-protein (meat) diet. A parallel group was raised on a lower-protein, higher-carbohydrate (grain) diet. On stool cultures, the groups had entirely different colonic bacteria, one predominantly proteolytic, the other predominantly carbohydrate-fermenting bacteria. This latter group were freer of disease and lived longer. Dubos told me he never published these observations.

The yogurt connection. The possible link between long life and the bacteria balance in the colon is directly related to discussions about yogurt that became intense around the turn of the century.

In those days, there was a prevalent belief that a person could keep a healthy balance of bacteria in the colon by eating relatively large amounts of yogurt. The great bacteriologist Elie Metchnikoff became impressed by the health record and longevity of a group of Bulgarian mountaineers, whose colonic bacteria had been somewhat altered by their high intake of yogurt and other soured milk products. But there were too many other variables in this group to be able to ascribe their longevity to diet alone.

For many years, Metchnikoff's ideas about changing the balance of bacteria in the colon, which he described by the term *autointoxication,* were pooh-poohed. But decades later, the discovery of ammonia intoxication came to the fore and was shown to be due to colonic bacteria. So the yogurt theory was revived.

In the final analysis, then, you may be not only what you eat, but what your bacteria are! I would not close my mind to the notion.

Right now, the jury still seems to be out on the subject. But I am inclined to recommend yogurt as part of an aging person's diet. It certainly seems to "sit better" than a fast-food hamburger. My philosophy, which I've already stated in another context, is this: It can't hurt, and it may very well help your health, including the condition of your colon. So why not try it!

Other Disorders and Diseases of the Colon

The most serious disease of the colon is cancer, a topic we've already dealt with in some detail in Chapters 17 and 18. But in addition to cancer and the other colon-related diseases discussed so far, there are a number of other health concerns that may be related to your large intestine as you get older. Here are a few of the possibilities:

- *Bacillary and amoebic dysentery.* These, as well as other infections, may produce inflammation, ulceration, and diarrhea. On diagnosis, your doctor will prescribe appropriate antibiotics or other medications.
- *Ulcerative colitis.* A chronic and recurrent disease of unknown cause, this can occur for the first time at almost any age. It produces diarrhea and bleeding, much as a chronic dysentery does. A sulfa drug (sulfasalazine), corticosteroids by mouth, and by enema are useful, but surgery is occasionally necessary.
- *Diverticulosis and diverticulitis.* Diverticulosis involves development of pouches in the colon; diverticulitis involves inflammation of one or more of these pouches.

In a considerable number of people who are fifty or older, small out-pouchings may develop on the wall of the colon. Most of these pouches are quite tiny, seldom exceeding the diameter of a cherry pit in size. But they may number in the dozens, and occasionally even in the hundreds.

Known as *diverticula,* these pouches usually produce no symptoms whatsoever. But occasionally they may become inflamed and produce disturbances in the bowel function, such as pain, tenderness, bleeding, and even obstruction.

Many times, bleeding stops spontaneously. But if it continues, physicians may prescribe a vasoconstrictor (vessel-constricting) agent, such as vasopressin. A surgical removal of part of the colon may also be necessary if bleeding continues. For diverticulitis, which involves infection, doctors usually prescribe antibiotics.

There is also an increasing trend toward prescribing a high-fiber diet for diverticular diseases. But it is still not clear whether this approach deters the further development of the disorder.

- *Constipation.* For a complete discussion, see the section in Chapter 4 that deals with this subject.
- *Reduction or cutoff in blood flow to the intestines.* When blood flow to an organ is reduced or stopped, the life-giving oxygen can no longer reach the tissues. As a result, the organ may be damaged or even die. This problem, known as *ischemia* (lack of blood sup-

ply), is most familiar to us when a coronary artery becomes blocked and blood flow to the heart is shut off, resulting in myocardial infarction (heart attack).

But the heart is not the only organ or part of the body that may be subject to ischemia. Another form of this problem is known as *acute mesenteric ischemia*. This condition results from the blocking off of blood to the intestines through one or both of the two mesenteric arteries, which supply blood to the intestines. Here are a few of the characteristics of this disease:

The problem is usually triggered by some serious cardiovascular event, such as a heart attack, congestive heart failure, irregular heartbeats, or hypotension.

1. Most of the time, older people have this problem.

2. Atherosclerosis typically accompanies the condition.

3. Those with this disease usually *appear* to be sick: For example, they may have severe pain, but rectal bleeding and diarrhea are rare until the disease has progressed fairly far. Other symptoms that develop at a late stage also include nausea, vomiting, back pain, shock, and increasing swelling of the abdomen.

It is important to head for a hospital immediately if any of these symptoms develops. Often, the patient will be checked with *angiography*, an X-ray picture of the vessels in the abdominal area. If the problem is diagnosed early enough, a vasodilating drug such as papaverine may be administered into the arteries to overcome constriction of the vessels. Physicians treating this problem frequently have to treat related cardiovascular problems, such as congestive heart failure or heart attack. In the most advanced cases, surgery to remove part of the intestine may be required.

A related problem, sometimes hard to distinguish from acute mesenteric ischemia, is *colonic ischemia*. This is regarded by many experts as the most common vascular disorder of the intestines. The condition is often associated with low blood flow to the colon because of clogging of the vessels through atherosclerosis.

Here are some of the characteristics of colonic ischemia, many of which differ from those of acute mesenteric ischemia:

1. Approximately 90 percent of patients with this problem are over sixty years of age.

2. It is unusual for there to be triggering events, such as a heart attack or congestive heart failure. In other words, colonic ischemia usually occurs on its own, without related cardiovascular problems.

3. On the other hand, in about 20 percent of the patients, there are other, noncardiovascular problems, such as cancer of the colon or diverticulitis.

THE MEANING OF EXCESSIVE GAS

Complaints of having a "gas problem" fall into three categories, according to a 1985 article by M. D. Levitt in *Hospital Practice:*

1. *Excessive belching (eructation).* A true burp is usually a single event experienced after drinking something like a carbonated beverage. Under the fluoroscope, one can see the air bubble in the stomach move up into the esophagus and out into the mouth.

Many who complain of repeated burping are under stress or are nervous about something. They may swallow air inadvertently as they talk or eat. Persuading them to concentrate on *not* swallowing the air may solve the problem.

2. *Abdominal bloating and discomfort.* This may be attributed to "too much bowel gas." Abdominal X rays and direct measures of intestinal gas can show what amounts are normal, as well as the composition of the gas. If a person does indeed have too much gas, certain drugs that increase intestinal motility may be more helpful than those that relax the intestines.

3. *Excessive rectal gas.* Many with this complaint are unaware of what is normal. Levitt reports that eight twenty-five- to thirty-five-year-old "normal" doctors kept a record of the amount of gas they passed. They found that on average they passed gas thirteen times a day, with an upper limit of twenty-one times a day.

In contrast, he said, 50 percent of the patients who have consulted him about this complaint pass gas fewer than twenty times a day. (Hence, what is "excessive" is a very personal matter and may in fact *not* be excessive in comparison with the experience of others.)

What are the most common causes of excessive gas? Levitt said that those with true excessive gas passage usually had trouble digesting carbohydrates, including the lactose sugar in dairy products. In addition to lactose problems, some had trouble attributed to the consumption of bran, vegetables, or beans. In such cases, dietary changes may be helpful.

M. D. Levitt, "Excessive Gas: Patient Perception and Reality," *Hospital Practice* 20 (1985): 143.

4. Most patients with this problem do not seem to be as ill as one would anticipate.

5. Symptoms may include some rectal bleeding, diarrhea, slight abdominal pain, and perhaps some tenderness in the abdomen.

The first test usually recommended for diagnosis is a barium enema, rather than angiography. Treatment may include antibiotics and "resting" the colon by feeding the patient intravenously.

Symptoms—such as abdominal pain, fever, diarrhea, or bleeding—that worsen or persist for two weeks may indicate that irreversible damage to the colon has occurred. In these cases, surgery is usually required to remove the diseased portion of the organ.

• *Intestinal gas.* A number of my patients, both men and women, have been concerned about an increased tendency to pass gas or belch as they get older. One woman in her sixties told me, "It really gets embarrassing sometimes because I can't always control this problem when I'm with friends, or at a social gathering. What can I do about it?"

Intestinal gas consists in large part of nitrogen derived from the air taken in through the mouth. Hydrogen, methane, and carbon dioxide are often present in gas.

Because most gas is caused by an excessive swallowing of air, I spent some time with this woman exploring how she might be taking in too much air through the mouth. We considered what steps she might take to correct the problem.

As it happened, she had developed the habit of sucking on hard candies. This kind of mouth action is tailor-made to increase air swallowing and production of gas. She had also been eating large quantities of foods that tend to produce extra gas, including high-fiber cereals, beans, peas, and brussels sprouts. I advised her to cut down on the candy and the gas-producing vegetables, and the gas problem virtually disappeared.

Of course, sometimes gas may be produced by fermentative bacteria, diseases of the bowel, mental depression, or other illnesses. So it is important for the physician to run a series of tests to eliminate these possibilities. For example, some patients may belch to relieve the uncomfortable feelings associated with a hiatal hernia, peptic ulcer, or gallbladder disease. But once these serious alternatives have been discarded, the problem can usually be taken care of by reduction of air swallowing or by diet therapy.

20

THE GALLBLADDER, PANCREAS, AND LIVER: THE SUPPORT SYSTEMS FOR DIGESTION

The joke about doctors is that they make the worst patients. I never fully understood that until I was hospitalized a number of years ago.

The occasion was an emergency gallbladder operation. But to make my experience completely clear to you, I first have to provide a little more information about the gallbladder, which is part of what I call the "support system for digestion," along with the liver and pancreas.

The gallbladder is a hollow, pearlike structure, situated under the liver in the upper right part of the abdomen. Its function is to store and concentrate bile from the liver. The chief work of bile is to render fats more soluble, much as a detergent will dissolve grease. The bile from the gallbladder pours through a duct into the duodenum, the upper part of the small intestine.

Usually, you are not aware of your gallbladder unless it develops a malfunction. But when that happens, you become very much aware. Gallbladder pain has a memorable quality to it!

So I still recall vividly, during a period of months when I was in my late fifties, suffering from a series of gallbladder-related ailments, including gallstones and an inflammation of the gallbladder. These problems resulted in extreme tenderness in the right upper quarter of my abdomen at the rib margin and occasional low-grade fevers. I also seemed to have much more trouble digesting fatty foods: They tended just to "sit" in my digestive tract.

At first a fat-free diet seemed to control the disorder. Then I experienced attacks in spite of the diet. I kept postponing the solution on the ground that I was too busy, and besides, I was a doctor, not a patient.

I was still operating as if a rule of thumb I had been taught about gallbladders were true: that to be at risk for gallbladder trouble, you had to fit within the "four F's": fair, fat, forty, and female. Because I was none of these, I decided it did not make sense that everyone was telling me I had this problem.

But my denial did not bring me any closer to proper treatment. In any event, a couple of days later, I was in the hospital, scheduled for an operation to remove the organ.

Even as I went into surgery, I was sure I would stage the fastest recovery of any patient in history. But again I was to be disappointed. They made an incision into the right upper abdomen area, and when I came out of the anesthesia, I was hurting badly.

Still, I wasn't about to be defeated. I thought I could at least be brave about it, so I refused any narcotics to kill my pain. But after twenty-four hours, I finally found that I had to throw in the towel and become like any other patient. My physician prescribed Demerol (generic name: meperidine), and the nurse who gave me the shot came over with a big smile.

I heard her say, "I hope this helps you, doctor," and that was the last thing I heard for hours.

It took me longer to recover from this operation than most patients, even those who were considerably older. And I must say, that was a blow to my image as the doctor who was going to walk right in and out of an operation. But all in all, I did gain a much better understanding of my gallbladder, and a greater appreciation about what can go wrong with it.

What Can Go Wrong with the Gallbladder

Gallbladder disease is the most common reason for abdominal surgery in those over sixty. Specifically, there is a progressive increase in the appearance of gallstones after about age twenty, so that 25 percent of those aged fifty to sixty have the problem; 40 percent aged sixty to seventy have it; and the incidence rises steadily, the older we get.

The most common problem presented by the gallbladder is that of stones. Perhaps this is related to the fact that one of the chief contributions the gallbladder makes is to concentrate the bile, which flows out of the liver. The gallbladder stores bile and makes it into a denser fluid. Then, when a fatty meal is passed on by the stomach into the small intestine, the gallbladder contracts and pours the concentrated bile out and over the food.

This is a sensible arrangement, with one drawback: The gallbladder bile is *so* concentrated that its ability to hold its constituents in solution is limited. A trace of a foreign substance, perhaps a clump of bacteria or other tissue, may become a focus for deposits of bile components, and this is the beginning of a stone.

As we know from serial X rays, tiny gallstones tend to grow slowly larger by ongoing deposits. Their constitution also varies. Some, it turns out, are virtually pure cholesterol. Others are chiefly the bile pigment; still others are a mix of chemicals, may include calcium, and are sometimes quite large.

Stones may thus vary from tiny—under a millimeter—to grape-size. Also, they come in varying shapes, including round and square. Some gallbladders contain hundreds of small stones, and others a few grape-size ones. I have known certain patients who insisted on seeing their gallbladders and stones after their operations. They have sometimes shaken their fingers or fists at the organ and said nasty things to it!

What creates this wrath is that the gallstones may move out from the gallbladder, a journey that creates pain and sometimes havoc. For example, a stone may be jammed into the cystic duct. This is the small canal that leads from the gallbladder to the main bile duct, which then runs on to the intestine. The stone obstructs the channel through which gallbladder bile is passed out. Painful distention of the gallbladder results.

But that is not the only source of discomfort: Painful contractions aimed to get the stone moving out are known as *biliary colic.* Those who have experienced gallbladder colic never forget it. An injection of a narcotic is usually required to provide relief.

Sometimes, with luck, a nitroglycerin tablet or one of the calcium channel blockers (used mostly for angina and hypertension) will relax the painful muscular contraction and afford some relief.

Repeated bouts of gallstone colic are likely to drive the sufferer to a surgeon for relief, as they drove me. Besides the pain there is also the troublesome aspect of uncertainty: One never knows when the next episode of colic may strike.

One otherwise reasonable patient of mine refused to leave the United States for a vacation trip. He explained: "I wouldn't enjoy being in a foreign city with a bout of this stuff. Who could I call on? Suppose I needed surgery: where and by whom?"

Being a fearful type, he kept postponing the recommended surgery, but he continued to suffer from the unpredictable episodes of colic.

We have learned in recent years that gallstones are extraordinarily common and may occur in up to 50 percent of older groups. What is more, these findings indicate that perhaps much of the time, gallstones may be dormant, producing no symptoms.

The problem is that once they have become symptomatic, for whatever reason, the transition from no symptoms to pain occurs. At that point, further bouts of pain are likely. How likely? This is very difficult to predict. I have nursed along some older, bad-risk patients with gallstones and been pleasantly surprised as to how well they did. They might go for many months or longer without a painful attack.

On the other hand, the situation becomes much more serious in some circumstances: if the attacks become frequent, despite low-fat diets and other precautions; or if fever and inflammation (cholecystitis) occurs; or if obstructive jaundice takes place. In such cases, our hand is forced and delay may be precarious. Generally, surgeons prefer to operate during an asymptomatic interval: The operation is easier, and the complications fewer.

Much attention has been paid recently to the possibility that, as with kidney stones, nonsurgical approaches to gallstones may become feasible. Some chemical approaches using agents capable of slowly dissolving the gallstones are being investigated. Combinations of these two types of management have also been suggested.

Overall, the situation is more complicated in the case of gallstones than with kidney stones. One must also reckon on the existence of gallbladder disease associated with or independent of the stones. Even assuming that some gallstones may be treatable by these new nonsurgical methods, questions as to how long the cure would work—that is, when the gallstones might recur—must still be answered.

Currently, there are many who believe that an asymptomatic gallbladder with stones can be left under observation. Even when a bout of gallbladder colic has occurred, one may still delay, proponents of this approach argue. But if several bouts of colic occur, most seem to agree that surgery—removal of the gallbladder—may be the best answer. NOTE: After successful surgery, there are no negative consequences to living without a gallbladder.

On to the Pancreas

Almost no one outside the medical profession seems to know what the pancreas does, except those who have a problem with this important organ.

The pancreas is a pink-white, tube-shaped organ whose appearance is somewhat like that of a salivary gland, so much so that doctors sometimes refer to it as the "abdominal salivary gland." The small minority of diners who eat sweetbreads often do not know that this is in fact the pancreas.

Plastered up against the back wall of the abdomen, this structure measures six inches in length and is divided into the three portions: the head, the body, and the tail. The head of the pancreas nestles within the C-shaped loop formed by the duodenum (the upper part of the small intestine). The body of the pancreas comprises the main mass of the organ; the tail is that portion that is quite close to the *spleen,* a lymph organ that disposes of used-up red blood cells.

Most of the pancreas consists of cells that secrete digestive juices that are poured out through a major duct connected to the bile duct. The pancreas is much like the salivary glands in the mouth in that pancreatic secretion contains an enzyme capable of breaking down starchy materials. In addition, this organ contains other potent enzymes capable of breaking down proteins (this enzyme is known as *trypsin*) and fat (the enzyme pancreatic lipase).

The term *pancreatitis* is applied to both acute inflammatory processes in the organ and burnt-out states, termed *chronic pancreatitis*. One of the serious consequences of acute inflammation of the pancreas is that its potent enzymes may be poured out into the abdominal cavity. They can then produce a great deal of local damage, including the breakdown of fat, or *fat necrosis*. Pancreatitis may erupt explosively as an abdominal catastrophe, with evidence of a great deal of inflammation. Chronic pancreatitis, when it leads to sufficient destruction of the pancreatic tissue, may result in serious impairment of digestion.

Recently a patient came in complaining of marked weight loss, diarrhea, and large, bulky, greasy stools: all of which were the result of a serious pancreatitis. As is often true, he was a heavy drinker; this disease is far more common in alcoholics. Fortunately, we were able to control the digestive problem with medical treatments that supplied the missing enzymes. The pills cleared the fats from the stool, and he regained all the lost weight. He also completely eliminated his alcohol consumption, a must in pancreatitis.

On the other hand, pancreatitis also occurs in people who *never* drink. Here are some other factors that can trigger the problem:

- Use of certain drugs (such as thiazides, furosemide, and cimetidine)
- Gallstones
- Hypercalcemia (excess of calcium in the blood)
- Diabetes mellitus
- Tumors
- Hypothermia (exposure to excessive cold)
- Various disorders of the duodenum, such as development of diverticula (pouches)

Removing or correcting any of these precipitating causes can eliminate pancreatitis in many situations.

Acute pancreatitis always appears to be a hospital emergency. Furthermore, a very sick patient with severe abdominal pain is often initially thought to have a perforated ulcer. Occasionally, a perforated ulcer may involve the pancreas, so it may be that both diagnoses can apply in some situations. To treat this problem, a tube is usually placed into the stomach, acid suppressants are used, and the patient is fed intravenously.

Another result of pancreatitis may be diabetes, a disease that has far-reaching implications for those over fifty.

The Dangers of Diabetes

I have already discussed diabetes mellitus, including its nutritional aspects, in some detail in Chapter 4. But more should be said about other aspects of this problem in our discussion of the pancreas.

A word about how the pancreas becomes involved in diabetes is necessary: Scattered throughout the pancreas are tiny little islands known as the *islets of Langerhans.* These secrete insulin. Insulin, the hormone that regulates the glucose (sugar) level in the blood, then passes directly into the bloodstream. As it moves about in the body via the bloodstream, insulin plays an important role in regulating the entrance of sugar into the tissues.

NOTE: In some, but not all, diabetics, an examination of the pancreas may reveal abnormalities or degenerative changes in the little islets. In the minority in whom diabetes is the result of pancreatitis, it is due to the physical destruction the islets of Langerhans have undergone.

Now, let me go into a little more depth with a short "refresher course" in diabetes: *Diabetes mellitus* is a disease in which the body cannot properly assimilate carbohydrates into the energy needed for ordinary activity. In a healthy person, the body changes various sugars and starches into the simple sugar glucose. This energy-producing substance circulates in the blood and can be used immediately for bodily activities or stored in the liver for future use.

One problem with diabetes is that it involves a malfunction in the process that controls the level of available glucose because the body does not have enough insulin, or because the insulin is not working properly on the body's tissues. The blood glucose increases, and as it builds up to dangerous levels, major symptoms and medical problems may emerge.

Typical symptoms of unrecognized or poorly treated diabetes include feelings of fatigue, thirstiness, blurred vision, frequent urination, loss of weight, itching or infections of the skin, and cuts and bruises that are slow to heal.

It is especially important to diagnose and treat diabetes early and well because of the possibility of serious long-term medical complications, including vision losses, stroke, heart disease, kidney failure, and damage to the nerves.

Diabetes often has a hereditary component, but environmental factors may also cause or aggravate the problem. Older adults may suffer from one of two types of the disease:

1. Type I, or *insulin-dependent,* diabetes, which usually starts in childhood or adolescence. This variety usually necessitates insulin treatments throughout life.

2. Type II, or *non-insulin-dependent,* diabetes (also called adult-onset diabetes). More than 85 percent of all cases involve this form, according to the National Institutes of Health. Most people in this category do not need insulin injections. But they do have to take steps to keep their blood glucose levels downs, usually by watching their weight, exercising, and following an appropriate diet. (See Chapter 4.)

Who is at risk for diabetes? Using information provided by the American Diabetes Association and other sources, I have devised the following list of risk indicators so that my patients can get some idea of their level of risk.

This list is divided into major, moderate, and minor categories. You should see your physician if you have one or more of the following characteristics: the major risk indicators, two or more of the moderate indicators, one moderate and one minor risk indicator, or three or more of the minor indicators.

MAJOR DIABETES RISK FACTOR
Identical twin with diabetes

MODERATE DIABETES RISK FACTORS AND SYMPTOMS
Brother or sister with diabetes
Mother with more than one baby weighing more than nine
  pounds at birth.
Weight 20 percent above ideal weight
Periodic blurry vision
Unexplained loss of weight
Frequent urination
Excessive thirst on a regular basis

MINOR DIABETES RISK FACTORS AND SYMPTOMS
Over forty years of age
Frequently very tired
Mother or father with diabetes
Hispanic or black descent
Native American descent

If you think you may have a problem with diabetes, see your doctor, and also consider contacting the American Diabetes Association, 2 Park Avenue, Box AP, New York, New York 10016.

The Liver Lifeline

When one of my patients came in with jaundice (a yellow complexion), fever, unexplained weight loss, and complaints of tiredness, it did not take long to diagnose a liver problem. The sound-wave study revealed he had a *pyogenic abscess* (pus-forming infection) of the liver, a problem that has an 80 percent mortality rate if not treated promptly.

Fortunately, I was able to get him into the hospital in time and begin drainage of the abscess and administration of antibiotics. But this experience pointed up to me once again what a key organ, a veritable frontline organ, the liver is for us.

The liver far and away outperforms all other organs in the body, in terms of its total number of basic tasks. It is also the largest organ in the body, representing about 2 percent of our body weight. After we pass age fifty, the weight of the liver slowly begins to decrease. Despite this weight loss, though, we can usually depend on the liver to operate efficiently throughout the entire life, so long as we refrain from abusing it.

Where Is the Liver and How Does It Function?

Most of the liver can be found in a space hollowed out at the arch of the diaphragm and the lower loop of the ribs. Although most of the liver is in the right upper portion of the abdomen, a large part does extend past the midline of the body and well toward the left side.

Because of its relationship to the diaphragm, the liver descends when you take a deep breath. As a result, your doctor will often asks you to take a deep breath as he *palpates,* or feels, for the liver.

As he probes, he tries to determine whether your liver is firm or hard, smooth or nodular to the touch; whether it is enlarged; or whether other distinguishing characteristics call for further tests. For example, possible cancer involving the liver may be indicated by such symptoms as an enlarged, hard liver; an accompanying weight loss; and perhaps a pain in the upper right part of the abdomen.

The degree of enlargement of the liver is expressed in terms of the number of fingers' breadth that the organ can be felt below the rib edge. A liver that can be felt four fingers' breadth below the rib margin, for instance, is very enlarged.

What important functions does the liver perform? Here is a partial list:

• The liver helps to detoxify the ammonia and various other potential toxins formed in the large intestines during digestion.

• It inactivates the female hormone estrogen, thus setting an upper limit on the amount of this substance that circulates in the body.

NOTE: Small amounts of the female hormone are also manufactured in the male body and are deactivated by the liver. So if a man starts to show feminine characteristics such as enlargement of breasts or loss of body hair, as occasional patients of mine have, these characteristics may indicate the presence of liver disease.

• The liver stores sugar and regulates sugar levels in the blood.

• It manufactures substances necessary for clotting of blood.

• It manufactures many of the proteins found in the blood-stream.

• It manufactures, stores, and regulates many of the bodily fats and lipids, including the all-important cholesterol and its various subcomponents such as high-density lipoprotein (HDL) and low-density lipoprotein (LDL). As you know from our previous discussion of cholesterol, HDL seems to be protective against cardiovascular disease, whereas LDL promotes it.

• It manufactures or stores many important vitamins, ranging from vitamins A and D to K and B_{12}.

• It sets up important defenses against bacteria.

With all of the things the liver has to confront, it is not surprising that it may become inflamed, a condition known as *hepatitis.* This can be caused by a variety of drugs, chemicals, or alcohol. Perhaps the most common cause of hepatitis, however, is viral inflammation, hence, the term *viral hepatitis.*

A number of viruses are capable of causing severe inflammation of the liver. The most common, dubbed *hepatitis A,* is spread mostly via contaminated foods. It can occur in epidemics: I saw hundreds of cases when I was in the army, where it seriously eroded our manpower. Oddly enough, the attack rate among officers exceeded that among enlisted men. This turned out to be due to poorer sanitization of the dishes in the officers' mess. The enlisted men, in contrast, washed their messkits in boiling water.

Because this virus is excreted in the stool, it can be recycled through contaminated water. Thus, epidemics have been traced to contaminated shellfish, which poses an increasing hazard to those who like raw clams.

Travelers are at increased risk because in many parts of the world poor sanitary practices favor spread of the virus. It's customary to give such travelers a shot of gamma globulin (GG), a substance that contains protective antibodies that are pooled from a large population of people and are protective for some weeks. The extra antibodies provide an added line of defense against such diseases as hepatitis.

It is important to know that many of us have protective antibodies, even though we have no history of the disease. The reason is that viral hepatitis can be a silent infection and may not produce jaundice. Often, its onslaught is attributed to a "flu bug" or a "stomach upset." It has been estimated that for every case in which the diagnosis is made—usually because the person turns yellow—there are ten cases or more in which the full-fledged disease does not come forth. But protective antibodies are formed even in the mild or inapparent cases.

It is easy to test the blood for such protective antibodies and comforting to know that one does indeed possess them. I advise my patients who travel to countries with poor sanitation to get such a test. This may eliminate the need for GG shots for each trip, and people are generally happy to know they are resistant.

KEY FACTS

DRUGS THAT MAY INJURE THE LIVER

Some common drugs that may cause jaundice or otherwise damage the liver in a small percentage of persons include the following:

Allopurinol

Many nonsteroidal anti-inflammatory agents, such as ibuprofen, naproxen, indomethacin, sulindac, and phenylbutazone

Anesthetics such as halothane and methoxyflurane

Antibiotics, erythromycin estolate, nitrofurantoin, the penicillins, and sulfonamide

Antineoplastic agents, such as azathioprine, 6-mercaptopurine, and methotrexate

Isoniazid

Rifampicin

Methyldopa

Procainamide

Quinidine

Chlorpromazine (Thorazine)

Niacin (or nicotinic acid, one of the nonprescription B-complex group of vitamins, discussed in Chapter 14)

Chlorpropamide

Tolbutamide

When I found I had these antibodies some years ago, I knew why I had not had the disease during my army experience. And I felt less threatened by clams!

We ordinarily expect patients who have hepatitis A to make an uncomplicated recovery within a few weeks. Not so with type B hepatitis: This variety is more serious, has a higher mortality rate, and can lead to a chronic, ongoing disease.

Type B is spread by blood and blood products, not by mouth. It used to be a predictable consequence of some blood transfusions. Fortunately, with newer screening procedures, the incidence of posttransfusion hepatitis is rare. As one might expect, however, the disease is more common among health professionals, with their constant exposure to blood products. For those at risk, a B hepatitis vaccine is available, and very efficacious.

Injury to the liver, with accompanying jaundice, fever, and pain in the upper right abdomen, may also be produced by a variety of drugs. (See the list on page 411.)

Liver problems caused by drugs usually disappear after the drugs are discontinued. In a few cases, it takes about two to three months for the symptoms to subside, though experts in this field report that full recovery may be possible even when they continue for as long as six months.

In some cases a kind of "desensitization" may take place with the drugs: In other words, the patient may experience symptoms such as jaundice for a time. But then, the problem subsides, apparently because the body has adjusted to the presence of the medication.

In any event, it is important for the process of diagnosis and treatment of drug-induced liver problems to be conducted and monitored closely by a physician.

The Link Between Your Liver and Alcohol

A sixty-six-year-old patient of mine came in complaining about pains in the upper abdomen, pale stools, and weight loss. Even as he walked into my office, I noticed the distinctly yellowish cast to his face, the jaundice that signals a gallbladder or liver problem.

After performing a blood test and conducting other examinations, I concluded that the problem was *cirrhosis* of the liver, a scarring of the organ that arises from chronic inflammation. I suspected, from what I had heard in the past from this man's wife, that alcohol abuse was the underlying cause. After years of being assaulted by alcohol, the liver may become so damaged that it cannot secrete bile normally. The bile pigments then may accumulate in the bloodstream and produce the yellow staining that I had seen in this man's face.

At first, he seemed reluctant to talk about his alcohol abuse. When presented with general questions such as "How about your alcohol use?" he volunteered almost nothing, except such generalities as this: "I drink a moderate amount, but no more than most other people I know."

So I began to put more direct questions to him from the well-known CAGE* questionnaire ("CAGE" is an acronym for key letters in each question). Studies have demonstrated that if a person answers two or more of the following questions with a yes, alcoholism is probably present.

1. Have you ever felt you ought to CUT down on your drinking?

2. Have people ANNOYED you by criticizing your drinking?

3. Have you ever felt bad or GUILTY about your drinking?

4. Have you ever had a drink—an EYE-OPENER—first thing in the morning to steady your nerves or get rid of a hangover?

In this case, my patient answered all of the questions with a yes, so I knew that he had a real problem with his drinking. But I wanted to be sure, so I plied him with other key questions to ascertain the extent of his problem. As we talked, he opened up more and seemed almost proud about an ability to "hold his liquor." During our conversation, I learned the following:

• This man frequently drank to forget his problems or to put himself to sleep.

• He often "swigged" his drinks quickly and was inclined to forget to eat after a drinking bout.

• He drank alone a great deal.

*See John A. Ewing, M.D., "Detecting Alcoholism—The CAGE Questionnaire," *The Journal of the American Medical Association* 252, no. 14 (1984): 1905–1907; J. A. Ewing and B. A. Rouse, "Identifying the Hidden Alcoholic," paper presented at the Twenty-ninth International Congress on Alcohol and Drug Dependence, Sydney, Australia, February 3, 1970; and D. G. Mayfield, G. McLeod, and P. Hall, "The CAGE Questionnaire: Validation of a New Alcoholism Screening Instrument," *American Journal of Psychiatry* 131 (1974): 1121–23.

• He had had three minor car accidents while drinking, though he had never been arrested for drunken driving.

• He freely admitted that he typically got "roaring drunk" more than four times a year, an outside limit that indicates definite problem drinking.

• His tolerance for alcohol had increased greatly over the years: He needed more than half a fifth of scotch to begin to feel the effects.

• He had regular arguments with his wife, usually about their finances and his drinking.

Any one of these characteristics might point to the presence of alcoholism, yet this man incorporated *all* of them in his life! Clearly, he was an alcoholic, and his habit had surfaced in a particularly advanced form of cirrhosis.

Unfortunately, cirrhosis of the liver is often a silent disease: It can progress quite far before symptoms, such as jaundice or abdominal pain, appear. By then, it may be too late. Among other significant findings, sometimes X rays reveal thinned-out bones: Osteoporosis, not common in men, is found in some alcoholics.

In the case of my patient, it might not be too late *if* he stopped drinking. He did take the medications and supplements, including extra amounts of calcium and multiple vitamins, I prescribed to compensate for his failing liver functions. But he wouldn't join Alcoholics Anonymous or take other steps to break his alcohol habit. Within a year, he was admitted to the hospital, and shortly afterward, he died from gastrointestinal bleeding.

Alcohol and the Aging Process

Alcohol abuse among older people is a more serious problem than the public generally recognizes, according to reports by the National Institutes of Health and other agencies. More than 61 percent of those over age fifty drink alcohol, and about 9 million Americans, many in the older age groups, can be classified as alcohol-dependent.

It is hard to identify precisely how many older people have serious alcohol problems. But I can testify, after observing thousands of older patients over five decades of medical practice, that the number of older alcoholics is alarming.

HEALTH REPORT

THE ELDERLY ALCOHOLIC

Elderly alcoholics often are not identified and do not fit the stereotypes of problem drinkers. But the impact of alcohol on the older body seems more serious than on the younger person.

The same dose of alcohol reaches higher levels in the elderly than in the young. Thus, the peak levels of alcohol that linger in the blood increase by 20 percent between ages forty and eighty.

Progressive use of alcohol can contribute to poor nutrition because the calories in alcoholic beverages lack essential nutrients and are consequently no substitute for regular food. Alcohol may also damage the liver's albumin manufacture, thus altering the levels of many medications that bind to the albumin. The alteration may produce serious adverse effects.

Alcohol use can also aggravate other tendencies in aging: The person's gait, speech, dexterity, and mental performance may worsen. Alcoholic drinks also increase the incidence of cancer of the mouth, esophagus, and stomach and may damage the liver and pancreas.

The diagnosis of alcoholism may be difficult in older people, and symptoms of alcoholism may be ascribed to aging. Some of the symptoms are similar: confusion resembling dementia, depression, and various other psychiatric symptoms. Alcoholism should always be suspected when the patient reports mental confusion, falling, injuries from traumatic events such as falls, changes in appetite, or disturbances in gait.

Treatment may require hospitalization, especially because the drugs commonly used for withdrawal from alcohol such as Librium (chlordiazepoxide) and Valium (diazepam) may aggravate confusion or drops in blood pressure. Counseling, support, and abstinence from alcohol are the watchwords. But the outlook in this regard is grim: Only 3 percent of Alcoholics Anonymous participants are over sixty-five, and

as few as 15 percent of elderly alcoholics ever receive psycho-
therapeutic services.

B. C. Scanlan, "The Elderly Alcoholic," *Drug Therapy* 18 (1988): 63–67.

One of the main problems with drinking at an older age is that
your body can no longer process the alcohol as well as when you
were younger. Various scientific reports show that alcohol stays in
the body at higher levels, and for longer periods, when you are
older. (See the preceding Health Report.)

Alcohol and Drug Use

Because older people are more likely to be taking medications than
younger ones, it is important to understand that alcohol should
never be taken with a drug unless your physician gives you explicit
permission. Certainly, alcohol should never be taken under any
circumstances if you plan to drive. *Remember:* The pathologic effect
of alcohol tends to be greater in older than in younger people.

Here are a few guidelines for specific drugs, which have been
derived from my own practice, from the National Institutes of
Health, and from Dr. Philip T. Gerbino, a pharmacologic expert
in this area:

• *The central nervous system depressants.* If an average-size man
has two 1-ounce drinks of 100-proof whiskey (which is 50 percent
alcohol), he can expect significant, possibly dangerous interactions
with the following drugs:

BENZODIAZEPINES. Alcohol should not be used when a patient
is taking diazepam, flurazepam, chlordiazepoxide, oxazepam,
lorazepam.

BARBITURATES AND MEPROBAMATE. Alcohol can impair the effectiveness of these drugs or, in some cases, may increase the drug
effects and produce serious central nervous system depression.

CHLORAL HYDRATE. Combined with alcohol, this drug has dangerous results in older people, including serious central nervous
system depression or death.

ANTIHISTAMINES. Various cold remedies and sleep aids fall into
this category. Alcohol taken with them may produce significant
depression of the central nervous system.

• *Other drugs.* Alcohol may interact with many other drugs and lead to impairments in driving and other psychomotor activities. These medications include the following:

PHENOTHIAZINES. These include chlorpromazine and thioridazine.

ASPIRIN. Although millions of older people take aspirin tablets every day, it is important to remember that aspirin may cause bleeding in the stomach and intestines. Alcohol, when taken with the aspirin, may aggravate this bleeding.

NARCOTIC DRUGS. Prescription drugs such as morphine, codeine, meperidine, and other narcotic analgesics depress the central nervous system and sedate the patient. When alcohol is used with these drugs, the depression and sedation may be increased to dangerous levels.

DRUGS FOR DIABETES. Alcohol may interfere with the functioning of the liver and promote low blood sugar in the blood. In some cases, diabetics who consume excessive quantities of alcohol have had to be hospitalized.

Clearly, the problem of alcohol use and alcoholism extends well beyond the liver, though for many people, the problem may well end with the liver. If you think you have a problem with alcohol or you want more information on this subject, you should contact the following organizations for additional information:

Alcoholics Anonymous (AA), P.O. Box 459, Grand Central Station, New York, New York 10163

National Clearinghouse for Alcohol Information, P.O. Box 2345, Rockville, Maryland 20852

National Council on Alcoholism, 12 West Twenty-first Street, New York, New York 10010.

21

PREVENTING THE ONSET, AND PAIN, OF OSTEOPOROSIS

Osteoporosis, the disease that involves a loss of bone mass so that fractures occur after minimal trauma or injury, can be a devastating, painful experience for older people. Yet with our current knowledge, this pervasive problem, which afflicts an estimated 20 to 25 million Americans and is responsible for an estimated 1.2 million fractures each year, can be prevented. This body of knowledge, which has mostly come to light only in recent years, constitutes a triumph for preventive medicine.

Witness, for instance, the stark contrast between the health of two of my patients, Esther and Alice.

Esther, a small, thin, fair-complexioned woman, was sixty-seven years old when she first came to me for help. She had already suffered two fractures, both of which seemed odd and unexpected in light of the circumstances: One involved her wrist; she had broken it when she had slipped back against her arm when she was

HEALTH REPORT

WHAT ARE THE RISK FACTORS FOR OSTEOPOROSIS?

Some factors tend to put a person at relatively high risk for osteoporosis. These include the following:

HIGH-RISK FACTORS
Aging
Female sex
Light body build
Thinness
Fair complexion
Inadequate calcium intake
Early menopause
Premenopausal oophorectomy (surgical removal of ovaries)
No exercise
Little work activity
Extreme immobility
Cigarette smoking
Significant to heavy alcohol intake
Prolonged cortisone-type drug use
Family history of osteoporosis

Other factors make a person *less* likely to develop osteoporosis. Here are a few of these:

LOW-RISK FACTORS
Male gender
Muscular body build
Some degree of overweight or obesity
Black ethnic background
Menopause estrogen use for women
Good lifetime calcium intake
Regular exercise program, with an emphasis on weight-bearing or gravity-involving activity
Muscle-using work
Nonsmoker

trying to pull herself out of a low chair. The other time, she had fractured a bone in her ankle after what seemed a slight twist while walking. Her back had a typical thoracic (chest-height) bowing.

"What's happening to me, Dr. Rossman?" she asked. "Am I falling apart?"

No, I reassured her, she was not falling apart. But further tests with sophisticated *dual-photon absorptiometry* techniques revealed that she had an advanced case of osteoporosis. This diagnostic tool, which we shall discuss in more detail later, involves shooting subatomic particles through an area of the body to determine the level of bone density.

HEALTH REPORT

ESTROGEN THERAPY: AN ADDITIONAL BENEFIT
FOR THE HEART

A 1988 report in the *Annals of Internal Medicine* evaluated 2,188 postmenopausal women whose coronary circulation was studied by catheterization.

The findings: The likelihood of significant narrowing of the coronary arteries was reduced by more than half in women taking estrogens. The independent beneficial effect of estrogen was apparent after adjustments for age, cigarette smoking, diabetes, elevated blood cholesterol, and high blood pressure.

The authors also review the various other studies that have dealt with this topic, and they note that an overwhelming majority of the investigators have concluded that estrogens confer a significant protective effect against coronary artery disease. In addition, it is well known that estrogens have a protective effect against osteoporosis.

But patients must also be aware of possible side effects: For example, estrogen use has been associated in some cases with increased gallbladder disease and cancer of the lining of the uterus.

J. M. Sullivan, R. V. Zwaag, G. F. Lemp, et al., "Postmenopausal Estrogen Use and Coronary Atherosclerosis," *Annals of Internal Medicine* 108 (1988): 358.

Esther had many of the classic risk factors for osteoporosis: She was small, thin, and fair-complexioned, characteristics that predispose a woman toward this problem. Furthermore, she consumed only about 450 mg of calcium per day in her diet, and she was rather sedentary. Again, these traits tend to promote bone loss.

Finally—and perhaps most important—after going through menopause at age fifty, she had not begun estrogen-replacement therapy. These treatments can be decisive in preventing the development of osteoporosis in postmenopausal women.

Unfortunately, given Esther's age, there were limits to the extent to which I could help her. She was too old now for estrogen therapy to be really effective. Ideally, estrogen treatment should be started immediately after menopause. She had already lost a considerable amount of bone mass, and once lost, bone density generally can't be replaced. About all we could hope for was halting any further loss.

HEALTH REPORT

WHAT IS THE CONSENSUS ON ESTROGEN AND OSTEOPOROSIS?

A conference of Europe's top authorities on prevention and treatment of osteoporosis reached the following conclusions:

• Estrogen (and progesterone) treatment is the only well-established measure that reduces the frequency of fractures due to osteoporosis. A further favorable side effect of this might be the reduction in heart disease.

• Treatment should be started as soon as possible after menopause.

• Appropriate duration of estrogen treatment is unknown, but a minimum of ten years seems reasonable.

• Dietary calcium does not substitute for estrogen in preventing postmenopausal bone loss.

"European Consensus Conference on Osteoporosis," *British Medical Journal* 295 (1987): 914.

HEALTH REPORT

THE IMPACT OF EXERCISE AND DIET ON BONE LOSS

Here are a few highlights from a 1987 survey on exercise, diet, and bone loss in the *Journal of the American Geriatrics Society:*

- On average men lose 10 percent and women 42 percent of mineral from the lumbar spine over a lifetime.
- Healthy young men prescribed bed rest lose 200 to 300 mg of calcium per day by urinary excretion. Sitting for eight hours per day did not improve this rate, whereas *standing* for three hours per day returned the calcium excretion to normal.
- Patients on bed rest lose 1 percent of mineral from the lumbar spine per week. When they resume walking the mineral is restored to its former level over a four-month period.
- Professional tennis players have 35 percent more cortical (long) bone in the dominant arm than in the nonplaying one.
- Male marathon runners have 7 percent more muscle and 11 percent more bone than normally active control subjects.
- Sedentary nursing home residents in their eighties experienced more than a 4 percent increase in density of forearm bone when they performed mild exercises three times a week for three years. A group of nonexercisers underwent a 2.5 percent decline in the bone density over the same period.
- After exercising one hour three times a week for one year, a group of postmenopausal women experienced a positive calcium retention of 42 mg per day. The controls (who were not on the exercise program) experienced a negative calcium balance of 42 mg per day.
- The recommended daily allowance of 800 mg per day of calcium appears to be inadequate to maintain calcium balance.

B. Dawson-Hughes and X. F. Li, "Preventing Osteoporosis: Evidence for Diet and Exercise," *Journal of the American Geriatrics Society* 42 (1987): 76.

In an attempt to improve her condition, I prescribed for Esther a much higher calcium intake. But because she had trouble tolerating milk or dairy products (that is, she had a lactose intolerance), I prescribed a calcium carbonate supplement. In this way, she increased her daily intake of calcium to about 1,500 mg.

In addition to adjusting her diet, I recommended that she become more active physically because exercise has been shown to stimulate the growth of bone. Specifically, I put her on a walking program like the one described in the cardiovascular section of this book (Chapter 13).

I also arranged to enroll her in an experimental sodium fluoride treatment program. In many patients, sodium fluoride helps to increase bone mass, though the bone may not be quite as strong as normal bone. This approach has not been approved for general public use yet by the Food and Drug Administration (FDA) partly because of unpleasant side effects such as stomach irritation. But Esther managed to tolerate the treatments quite well, and the manifestations of her osteoporosis, the fractures she had been experiencing, did not recur over the next few years.

NOTE: I would not want to leave the impression that Esther had been cured of her osteoporosis, because that is not really possible for someone in her position at our present stage of medical advancement. But later absorptiometry tests showed that her bone loss had ceased, and the density even seemed to be increasing slightly, apparently as a consequence of the sodium fluoride treatments.

Alice was also sixty-seven years old when she came in for treatment. She had suffered a bruise and laceration on her leg during a fairly heavy fall. Alice was a lot like Esther in her appearance: small, light-skinned, and thin. But the similarities between the two women ended there.

Alice had been my patient for more than twenty years, and I had kept close watch on her as she moved through menopause, again, like Esther, at about age fifty. In contrast to Esther, however, Alice began estrogen-replacement therapy as she was going through menopause. (I also prescribed progesterone to minimize the possibility of her developing endometrial cancer, a danger if estrogen is used alone.)

In addition to the estrogen, I made sure that Alice was getting plenty of calcium: a minimum of 1,000 to 1,500 mg daily, which she reached by taking a calcium carbonate supplement. I also emphasized the importance of not engaging in weight-bearing exercise, activities that would require her to work against resistance or gravity. As it happened, this was not a problem for Alice because she was an avid hiker and jogger.

The fall that Alice had taken had necessitated a few stitches, but otherwise she was unharmed. But I could not help but reflect on what might have happened if the same injury had happened to Esther. I was virtually certain that she would have broken her thigh bone or hip, a common injury for those who suffer from osteoporosis. Yet Alice's bones were obviously strong enough to sustain a severe blow without snapping.

It is important to keep in mind the distinctions between Alice and Esther as we move through this discussion of osteoporosis for a couple of reasons: First, it is absolutely essential for you to act as soon as possible to prevent or slow the development of osteoporosis. Second, if you already have the disease, you should move fast to get treatment that will slow or stop its progress in your body. The byword here is *speed*. The faster you act, the better your chances of maintaining or recovering your health.

Now, let's go into more detail about what osteoporosis is and what can be done about it.

How Osteoporosis Does Its Damage

I always emphasize the importance of acting quickly to counter bone loss because the groundwork for osteoporosis, the bone-loss disease that strikes so many older people, begins early in life. We reach our maximum bone mass in various parts of our skeletal structure between our late twenties and late thirties. Then, by the time we reach our midforties, our bone mass starts to decline steadily.

Clearly, it is important for younger people to concentrate on building up their bone mass to the highest level possible through such means as weight-bearing exercise and adequate calcium intake. In this way, when bone loss begins, they have a safety margin:

Their bones are dense enough that they can afford to lose more mass than those with a lighter skeletal structure.

Still, bone does inevitably lose its mass as we get older. So it is essential that you do all you can to slow the process of loss. The longer you wait to do something about the problem, the more bone that you will lose irretrievably.

For women who have just gone through menopause, the loss of bone density can proceed at an alarming rate. If some women at high risk fail to embark on an estrogen-replacement therapy program, they can lose 2 to 3 percent of their bone mass a year, between the onset of menopause and about age sixty-five to seventy, according to some estimates, as Esther did.

After about age seventy, bone loss continues at a slower pace in both men and women. Although women tend to be at the highest risk in the decade or so after menopause, in the later years, both males and females can be in danger.

And the danger is significant: One-third of women over age sixty-five eventually have fractures of the vertebrae (spinal column). As they get older, one-third of all women and one-sixth of men will suffer a hip fracture. These hip fractures are fatal in 12 to 20 percent of cases, according to osteoporosis experts B. Lawrence Riggs and L. Joseph Melton.*

Osteoporosis is a particularly insidious disease, because it is almost impossible to detect until the first symptom occurs, and the typical symptom is the fracture of a bone. Because of the silent nature of this maimer and killer, we have to rely heavily on the risk factors listed on page 419 to forewarn those who are in greatest danger.

The causes of osteoporosis are uncertain, but as I have indicated in the list of risk factors, a number of mechanisms may be at work in any given individual:

• Relatively low bone mass in some people may mean that a dangerously low level of density is reached sooner in them than in other, heavier-boned individuals.

• A lack of the female hormone estrogen removes a significant protective barrier.

*See their landmark article, "Involutional Osteoporosis," *The New England Journal of Medicine,* June 26, 1986, 1676.

- A family history may predispose certain individuals to the disease.
- A sedentary life-style will cause bone to become less dense.
- The aging process involves a change in the body's physiology so that more bone is likely to be *resorbed* (lost) than built.

Specifically, concerning this last point, there are two important sets of cells in the body's bone-building process: osteoblasts and osteoclasts. The *osteoclasts* break down bone, leaving little holes and pores throughout the skeletal structure. Then, *osteoblasts* move in and rebuild the lost bone.

In most younger people, there is a balance in the work of the osteoblasts and osteoclasts, with the work of tearing down and rebuilding a piece of bone occurring in approximately four-month cycles. But as we grow older, the balance begins to deteriorate. More and more bone is resorbed without being replaced. Consequently, bone mass decreases, and the foundation for osteoporosis is laid.

How to Fight Osteoporosis

Prevention and treatment of osteoporosis tend to merge because the means of prevention are also often the means of treatment. Here are a few considerations you should keep in mind as you strengthen your defenses against this disease.

Calcium Intake

As I have already indicated, every man and woman over age fifty should be taking in 1,000 to 1,500 mg of calcium daily. I realize that this amount is considerably higher than the Recommended Dietary Allowance (RDA) of 800. But the latest thinking on this subject affirms the higher recommended dosage.

The best way to consume calcium is through your diet. Milk and dairy products such as cheese, yogurt, and ice cream are the best sources of this mineral, though if you're oriented toward low-fat, low-cholesterol foods to lower your risk of cardiovascular disease, you can already see a problem with this approach.

HEALTH REPORT

WILL CALCIUM WORK ALONE?

Using a sophisticated nuclear technology, Danish investigators examined bone density and its maintenance in early menopausal women.

Their findings: Over a two-year period, supplemental calcium (2,000 mg daily) did *not* slow the decline in bone density when compared to that of an untreated group.

In contrast, with estrogen therapy bone was maintained over the period of study.

B. Riis, K. Thomsen, and C. Christiansen, "Does Calcium Supplementation Prevent Postmenopausal Bone Loss?" *The New England Journal of Medicine* 316 (1987): 173.

Still, a careful choice of dairy foods can give you the calcium you need *and* keep your saturated fat and cholesterol consumption at low levels. For example, there are a number of low-fat and no-fat yogurt products on the market now. And skim milk actually contains slightly *more* calcium than an equal amount of whole milk. Specifically, one cup of skim milk contains just over 300 mg of calcium; one cup of whole milk contains about 290 mg.

Other sources of calcium include dark green, leafy vegetables, such as collards, turnip greens, spinach, and broccoli. But the calcium in some of these foods, especially spinach, has been found to be less *bioavailable,* or usable by the body, than that in dairy products. In addition, calcium can be found in salmon, sardines, oysters, and tofu (curd from soybeans).

One problem with relying on dairy products for calcium can be the lactose (milk sugar) intolerance mentioned in Chapter 19. A number of my patients have complained of uncomfortable gas pains and loose stools as a result of this problem, which stems from a deficiency in the enzyme lactase, the substance that breaks down milk sugar. But there is a fairly easy solution I frequently fall back on, taking one of the many calcium supplements now available. The most common is calcium carbonate (for example, Tums or Os-Cal), and that works quite well for many people. Another possibility that is growing in popularity is calcium citrate.

HEALTH REPORT

HOW EXERCISE CAN HELP PREVENT BONE LOSS IN POSTMENOPAUSAL WOMEN

In a 1988 report in the *Annals of Internal Medicine,* thirty-five healthy but sedentary women, aged fifty-five to seventy, were studied for bone mineral content. Nineteen of them then took part in an exercise program, which involved walking, jogging, and stair climbing for fifty to sixty minutes, three times a week.

At nine months into the program, the exercisers had increased their bone mineral by 5.2 percent. Those who continued to be sedentary showed a slight decline of 1.4 percent.

At twenty-two months, the exercisers were up to a 6.1 percent increase in their bone mineral content.

Finally, the exercisers were taken off their training regimen. The result? They reverted to their previous sedentary patterns, and their bone mineral decreased to 1.1 percent above the original baseline readings.

Throughout the study, all the participants had a 1,500-mg calcium intake per day.

Conclusion: Postmenopausal women can add significantly to their bone mineral content by exercise, but this increase in density reverses when exercise stops.

G. P. Dalsky, K. S. Stocke, A. A. Ehsari, et al., "Weight-Bearing Exercise Training and Lumbar Bone Mineral Content in Postmenopausal Women," *Annals of Internal Medicine* 108 (1988): 824.

As you take in calcium, also be sure that you are getting adequate amounts of vitamin D each day. Most scientists recommend that the average person take 400 IUs daily. A balanced diet, with vitamin-fortified milk and cereals and saltwater fish, will provide enough of this vitamin. Egg yolks and liver also have it, but they also contain high amounts of cholesterol.

Apart from diet, perhaps another way to get vitamin D into

your system is to spend some time outdoors. Fifteen minutes to one hour of midday sunshine will fulfill your daily requirement. But be sure to avoid damage to the skin as stressed elsewhere (Chapter 17), and remember that sunning should "start low and go slow."

WARNING: Large amounts of vitamin D (that is, more than 1,000 IU per day) can be harmful, so it is important that you use this supplement only under the guidance of your physician.

Exercise

There has been a great deal of discussion about the role of exercise in helping build bone mass and preventing or lessening the effect of osteoporosis. The emerging consensus is that weight-bearing exercise, or exercise done against the force of gravity, is helpful. The more weight your bones have to support, the more the bone-building osteoblasts will be stimulated to work.

I recommend that my own patients who are at risk for osteoporosis engage in walking or other such exercises that put pressure on the bones. The exercise program described in the cardiovascular section of this book (Chapter 13) is quite appropriate for those who want to use exercise in this way to combat osteoporosis.

Estrogen-Replacement Therapy

When women go through menopause, the amount of estrogen declines markedly. Problems that may result from this loss of estrogen are varied and include the following:

- Vaginal dryness
- Hot flashes
- Decrease in the "good cholesterol" (HDLs) and increase in the "bad cholesterol" (LDLs)
- Increased loss of bone mass

Because of health problems that often arise with the loss of estrogen at menopause, many physicians, including me, have elected to prescribe for their female patients a program of "estrogen-replacement therapy."

What exactly is this therapy, which is often called "ERT" for short?

It is the intake by a woman of estrogen, usually in pill or tablet form, to replace the natural estrogen lost during and after menopause. The hormone may also be applied as a vaginal cream, injection, or skin patch. A skin patch is a transparent adhesive patch that releases estrogen while attached to the skin.

Your doctor will keep your particular health needs in mind as he chooses the manner in which the estrogen is to be administered. For example, he may select a topical cream if you have severe vaginal symptoms. But if bone loss is the only consideration, he will probably prescribe a pill or patch.

The patch is an interesting recent advance in therapy. Because of the capacity of the skin to absorb estrogen, the hormone can be applied to the skin. It is given in relatively small doses and taken up directly into the circulation.

The estrogen thus avoids the familiar intestine-liver route, with the advantage that certain interactions between the hormone and the liver are prevented. One beneficial result is a decrease in the risk of high blood pressure; another is a decrease in the tendency for the blood to clot. The patch does not eliminate the need for progestin (progesterone), however, which experts now agree should always be given when the woman has an intact uterus.

What are the risks of ERT?

For the large majority of women, the risks seem to be minimal. But scientific studies have shown that about 10 percent of women who undergo this therapy have side effects such as headaches, nausea, vaginal discharge, fluid retention, swollen breasts, or weight gain.

A more serious problem for some women is endometrial cancer (cancer of the lining of the uterus), a condition that studies have revealed occurs more often in women on ERT alone. But when estrogen treatment is combined with progestin (progesterone), another female hormone, the risk of this type of cancer is usually reduced or completely eliminated. NOTE: Women who have had a hysterectomy (the operation that involves removal of the uterus) have *no* risk of endometrial cancer.

Although the presence of estrogen in a woman's body has been associated with higher HDLs and lower LDLs, there is some disagreement about whether or not estrogen really protects a woman from heart disease. A number of excellent recent studies report that estrogen may reduce the risk of heart disease. The initial report from the Framingham Study indicated that heart attack was more common in people using estrogen. But a recent reanalysis of the data has reversed this conclusion.

The other bugaboo is breast cancer, but again, the recent studies show that if anything, there is somewhat *less*, not more, breast cancer in estrogen users. As I review the total picture of significant benefits in cardiovascular disease and bone problems, I increasingly lean toward prescribing the patch. I also give progestin to virtually all my menopause patients. Estrogen plus progestin makes for successful aging.

Studies are continuing on this subject, including the altered picture presented by the patch. One point is certainly clear: I would unhesitatingly recommend immediate estrogen replacement for women undergoing early menopause. Early menopause is a biological catastrophe. One of my patients with a menopause at age thirty-eight started to have fractures in her early fifties.

On the other hand, some women who should exercise caution before using estrogen therapy include those with the following conditions: high blood pressure, diabetes, obesity, liver disease, thrombophlebitis (blood clots in a vein), seizure disorders, migraine headaches, history of cancer or gallbladder disease. To what extent these pros and cons will alter with the estrogen patch is still being evaluated.

Other Therapies for Osteoporosis

The drugs currently approved by the FDA include calcium, estrogen, and calcitonin. I have already devoted some space to the first two, but calcitonin deserves further explanation.

Calcitonin is a hormone that decreases bone resorption, or the breakdown of bone by the osteoclasts. In fact, scientists suspect that this hormone acts directly on the osteoclasts, which have calcitonin receptors, or "hooks," that involve the hormone in modification of the bone-breakdown process.

Many patients can use calcitonin without side effects, but in some there may be problems: The hormone is expensive to produce; it has to be given through an injection; and some patients develop resistance to its effect.

Other, more experimental approaches to treatment include the sodium fluoride treatment, which I recommended in the case of Esther. This substance stimulates bone formation and increase of bone mass. As a result, those who respond well to this therapy may find that they can greatly reduce or eliminate the possibility of bone fractures.

How well does sodium fluoride work? In doses of 40 to 80 mg a day, this drug can increase the density of the soft, spongy bone of the spine and other parts of the *axial,* or central, skeleton. However, it apparently does not affect the long bones of the arms and legs.

About one-half of patients treated with sodium fluoride have shown substantial increases in their bone density, according to a number of studies. One-fourth showed "incomplete responses," and one-fourth had no response.

As I mentioned earlier, there are also possible side effects: About 30 percent of patients on sodium fluoride have stomach irritation, and about 10 percent have severe pain in their legs and lower extremities. Whether dose reduction may decrease this effect and still have some benefits remains to be studied.

NOTE: As of this writing, sodium fluoride has *not* been approved by the FDA, though many patients are participating in experimental programs.

Finally, as an alternative to estrogen as a means of controlling the symptoms of menopause, some patients have had success with large doses of vitamin E (600 to 800 IU daily) to reduce flushing and sweats. The drug clonidine, which acts on the vasomotor center in the brain, has been used to achieve the same purpose. However, these two substances *do not* help with osteoporosis.

How Is Osteoporosis Diagnosed?

By definition, according to many physicians, osteoporosis can only be osteoporosis if there is a broken bone of some sort. To confirm the diagnosis after the fracture has occurred, a doctor will usually order one of two tests:

• *Dual-photon absorptiometry.* In dual-photon absorptiometry the patient lies on her back on an examining table, with the lower legs elevated on a block. Then, a radioactive source emitting two beams of photons is sent through the body (with no discomfort or sensation). By measuring the way the photon beams pass through the bone, the specialist can determine the bone density. This method is especially helpful for determining the density of the soft bone in the spine and other soft-bone areas of the skeleton.

HEALTH REPORT

THE OUTLOOK FOR PREDICTING "FAST BONE LOSERS"

A team of Danish investigators devised a system for evaluating postmenopausal women for rate of bone loss.

They used a radioactive tracer to study the decline in the bone mineral of the forearm with repeat measurements every three months. The body fat mass was also determined, and the urine was checked for its calcium and hydroxyproline content (the latter is derived from the protein matrix of the bone).

Using these data, they were able to predict the "fast bone losers," those who lost more than 3 percent of bone mass annually, correctly.

Determining who is a fast bone loser by combining several simple measurements might well favor earlier or more aggressive treatment. A demonstration of a slow rate of bone loss would conversely lessen the need for using more troublesome interventions. One example of this latter determination might be a decision, based on these data, not to prescribe estrogen for a women with a strong family history of breast cancer.

C. Christiansen, B. J. Riis, and P. Redbro, "Prediction of Rapid Bone Loss in Postmenopausal Women," *Lancet* 1 (1987): 1105.

A related method, *single-beam absorptiometry*, may be used for the long bones in the arm. But generally, this technique is less useful in evaluating bone mass than the dual-beam approach.

● *Quantitative computerized tomography (CT).* In quantitative CT the patient lies with knees and hips bent, to flatten out the lower spine against an examining table. The table is fitted inside with containers of potassium phosphate, ethanol, and water. Then, the patient is moved into a tubelike structure, where the lower spine is scanned with radiation. Although this method is generally available, it is not regarded as particularly accurate.

Because there are drawbacks to all the current methods of diagnosing osteoporosis, physicians are limited in their effectiveness in predicting the onset of the disease. As a result, both doctors and patients now have to rely primarily on an evaluation of osteoporosis risk factors.

22

WHAT IS ARTHRITIS, AND WHAT CAN YOU DO ABOUT IT?

Every so often, I get up in the morning, stand up beside my bed, stretch a little—and feel that familiar stiffness in the finger joints.

The slightly sore "creakiness," a symptom of mild osteoarthritis, began about fifteen or twenty years ago, when I was in my fifties. Ever since, year by year, decade by decade, it has gradually become a little worse. To counter the discomfort, I may treat my hands to a warm soak in the bathroom sink for a few minutes, just to loosen and warm them. If the pain persists, I take a couple of aspirins.

I have used my hands a lot throughout my life in my work. After all, a doctor does a lot of pressing, squeezing, and manipulating in examining patients and employing various instruments. I have also had my hands banged up and bruised pretty badly a few times. Like most people, I have suffered an occasional door slam against a finger and the odd bump or twist when shifting furniture or trying some athletic movement I was not prepared to make. The

435

result of these traumas and the overuse of my hands has been the appearance of some relatively mild wear-and-tear arthritis, known as *osteoarthritis.*

HEALTH REPORT

GUIDELINES FOR DETERMINING PHYSICAL INCAPACITY

In a study originating at the Duke Center for the Study of Aging, an attempt was made to reduce more extensive questionnaires to a simple, rapid assessment of the capability of the elderly in the activities of daily living. The five key tests that emerged to determine physical incapacity or physical independence were presented in the form of these questions:
1. Can you get to places out of walking distance?
2. Can you go shopping for groceries or clothes?
3. Can you prepare your own meals?
4. Can you do your housework?
5. Can you handle your own money?

NOTE: If a person can answer all of these questions "yes—without help," then independence and adequate physical capacity have been established. If any of the questions is answered "no" or "yes—with help," the person, his family, and his physician should evaluate whether it is appropriate for him to continue living alone, without someone else to assist in the activities of daily living.

G. G. Fillenbaum, "Screening the Elderly," *Journal of the American Geriatrics Society* 33 (1985): 698.

Arthritis is a problem that many people over fifty face, but sometimes the symptoms are not so mild. The frequent complaints of my own patients confirm for me that it is essential that we spread our knowledge about the various forms of this disease.

What Is Arthritis?

Arthritis is, by almost any measure, an epidemic disorder. An estimated 15 percent of our population, or about 30 million people, suffer from some form of arthritis, with women more likely to be stricken than men. There are different degrees of the disease, from mild discomfort in the morning to constant excruciating pain and disability.

But despite the scope of the disease, there is hope on several fronts, including recently developed drugs, as well as the relatively new area of "natural" treatments, such as exercise and life-style adjustments. In this chapter and Chapter 23, I want to introduce you to a very wide spectrum of helpful measures. But first, what exactly is arthritis?

If you have it, you know all too well the nature and symptoms of the disease. The word *arthritis* comes from the Greek word *arthron,* meaning "joint," and the suffix *-itis,* which means "inflammation." In other words, arthritis refers to all the diseases that affect the joints, with such effects and symptoms as inflammation, pain, stiffness, swelling, and even crippling and disability.

Practically every day of the year, I see a patient who has a pain in the knee, shoulder, or neck. He or she complains of the disability and inquires anxiously, "What kind of arthritis have I got?"

Frequently I say, "It's not arthritis, definitely not arthritis—the joint is okay." With that response, there is typically total relief of anxiety and often 50 percent relief of pain. Arthritis tends to be more feared than any disease, other than those that imminently threaten one's very life.

By definition, arthritis has to be in the joint, not in a tendon (the tendon problem is *tendinitis*), or a bursa *(bursitis),* or a muscle *(myositis).* But arthritis may cause problems with muscles, tendons, and ligaments, all of which are in close relation to joints.

There are many types of arthritis, and it is important to discriminate among them, something that even those with the disease often fail to do. Thus, the joint changes in rheumatoid arthritis as against osteoarthritis, and the outlooks for each, are almost as dissimilar as the differences between night and day. What further confuses people is the similarity of the treatments: Both forms may be helped by similar drugs, heat treatments, or exercise.

Here, then, is an overview of the major forms of adult-onset arthritic disease:

Rheumatoid Arthritis

Rheumatoid arthritis is the most serious and most difficult to control, and it can do some of the worst damage to joints.

KEY FACTS

A CHECKLIST OF SYMPTOMS OF RHEUMATOID ARTHRITIS

- Morning stiffness
- Pain on motion or tenderness in at least one joint
- Swelling of at least one joint
- Swelling of at least one other joint
- Symmetrical joint swelling
- Subcutaneous nodules (bumps under the skin)
- Typical X-ray changes
- Positive blood test result for the "rheumatoid factor"

SOURCE: American Rheumatism Association, Diagnostic Criteria for Rheumatoid Arthritis

---

About 6.5 million people in the United States suffer from this malady, and that includes twice as many women as men according to the Arthritis Foundation. In general, rheumatoid arthritis hits people between the ages of twenty and fifty. First attacks, sometimes explosive ones, after age sixty-five are not infrequent, however. Although the effects may be felt in many joints, the most commonly stricken are the small joints of the hands.

The progressive destruction of this form of arthritis is often insidious: Inflammation and thickening of the tissue that lines the joints cause the person to experience pain and swelling. If the process continues uncontrolled, destruction of the bones may result, with deformities and eventually severe disability. Rheumatoid arthritis is also a general disease, which may affect the lungs, blood vessels, skin, or even the salivary glands.

Osteoarthritis

Osteoarthritis is the most common form of the disease and seems to arise from excessive wear and tear on the joints. Generally speaking, this variation is less damaging than rheumatoid arthritis, and older people tend to be the most frequent victims.

HEALTH REPORT

DRY MOUTH: A COMMON SYMPTOM OF RHEUMATOID ARTHRITIS

Half of all patients with rheumatoid arthritis complain of dry mouth. This condition, known as *xerostomia,* is generally due to a low rate of secretion of saliva, and it can be a relatively common problem in older people, including those with or without rheumatoid arthritis. In one study of 1,148 aged persons, 16 percent of the men and 25 percent of the women complained of dry mouth.

In the most serious cases, symptoms include burning tongue; difficulty in chewing, swallowing, and talking; impaired taste; ulcers of the mouth; and increased dental decay.

The disorder may also follow irradiation to the head area, and it is associated with some four hundred drugs, especially antidepressants and antihistamines. Stopping or reducing these treatments may help the dry mouth condition.

Chewing seems to stimulate the impaired salivary glands, but sips of water with the meal may also be necessary to lubricate the mouth.

NOTE: One of my patients with severe xerostomia tried a variety of liquids to relieve the condition and decided that apple juice was best!

L. M. Sreebny and A. Valdimi, "Xerostomia: A Neglected Symptom," *Archives of Internal Medicine* 147 (1987): 1333.

This disease is so common that it is often referred to as an aging change in the joint. Thus, in the spinal column, an experienced observer can give a good guess as to the age of the person simply by looking at X rays of the neck and back. At what point one can say that aging changes are severe enough to justify a separate diagnosis of osteoarthritis is often hard to say: These are, indeed, *universal* changes.

Typically, osteoarthritis involves the degeneration of joint cartilages that cushion the ends of bones, where the bones move against one another. The cartilage develops small cracks and begins to wear unevenly—in fact, sometimes the cartilage may wear away completely. During the progression of this disease, inflammation occurs and the joint appears to become warm and red.

The most common symptoms are pain and stiffness, especially in finger joints, which are used frequently. Problems may also develop in those joints that bear much of the body's weight. About 10.5 million women and about 3 million men suffer from significant osteoarthritis. But they may have no systemic symptoms, such as fever or lung or skin complications.

KEY FACTS

CHECKLIST TO EVALUATE IMPROVEMENT IN OSTEOARTHRITIS AFTER MEDICATION

- Reduced swelling of joints.
- Reduction in joint redness.
- Less tenderness on pressure.
- Less pain at rest or in motion.
- Increased range of motion of limbs and appendages.
- Improved performance in fifty-foot walking time.
- Doctor's overall assessment of improvement is positive.
- Patient's overall assessment of improvement is positive.

SOURCE: Federal Drug Administration Guidelines to Drug Evaluation.

In addition to these two most common forms of arthritis, several other types of rheumatic disease are a frequent source of pain and concern to many people.

Gout

Gout, perhaps the easiest form of arthritis to detect and treat, usually hits the joints of the feet, especially the big toe (in about half the cases). Still, other joints may also be affected by this form of the disease. Gout is somewhat unusual in that, unlike other forms of arthritis, it typically strikes men and has a hereditary component.

Although this problem can appear in young adults, attacks tend to become more frequent with the passage of the years. Some of the diuretic drugs that are more likely to be used by aging persons may aggravate a mild gout or produce an attack for the first time.

What causes gout? The deposit of a body chemical, uric acid, in the tissues. As crystals of this acid appear in the joints, inflammation and severe pain typically result. The diagnosis is easily confirmed by running a blood test to determine whether there are elevated levels of uric acid.

Sometimes, attacks of gout may occur for no obvious reason and, untreated, can last for weeks. But in most cases, this type of arthritis is triggered by excessive eating and drinking, stress, too much exercise, or, sometimes, surgery.

If a victim treats his gout early enough, treatment tends to be more effective. But if the disease is allowed to progress too long without treatment, kidney disease and high blood pressure may develop. Large amounts of uric acid also may be deposited in and around the joints, a process that can lead to hard lumps on the fingers, the back of the elbows, and the ears.

We are primarily concerned here with arthritis among those who are middle-aged or older. But it is also important to be able to understand and distinguish the types of arthritis that are more likely to strike the young. After all, even at a relatively advanced age, some people may still be suffering from the vestiges of an earlier arthritic problem. So here is an overview of the major kinds of "youthful" arthritis:

Juvenile Arthritis

Juvenile arthritis has stricken about a quarter of a million young people in the United States. Typical manifestations include high fevers, skin rashes, and problems with growth. Although about 30 percent of juvenile arthritis patients suffer permanent joint damage, the majority of the cases can be helped with proper treatment.

Systemic Lupus Erythematosus (SLE)

Although this inflammatory disease of the connective tissues in the body is found most often in people fifteen to thirty-five years of age it also occurs in the middle years. This condition produces changes in the skin, joints, and internal organs and strikes many more women than men.

Nobody knows the exact cause of lupus, but the source of the problem may be a malfunction in the body's immune system, with the presence of *autoantibodies,* destructive substances turned loose against normal body constituents.

What are the specific symptoms? A rash may develop on the face in the form of an "open butterfly" and spread over the nose onto the cheeks. Typical arthritic symptoms, such as inflammation, swelling, and soreness of the joints, also occur. The victim may also experience a lack of energy, weight loss, and suppression of appetite.

Ankylosing Spondylitis

Ankylosing spondylitis, an inflammatory arthritis of the spine, tends to hit young men more often than young women. The usual symptoms are back pain, loss of mobility of the spine, and stiffness. The vertebral joints may eventually become fused and rigid, and the hips and shoulders may also become stiff and inflamed.

Unlike many other forms of arthritis, this spinal disorder rarely causes people to become seriously disabled. In fact, in milder cases those with the disorder may simply think that they have an ongoing strain or back problem.

Reiter's Syndrome

Reiter's syndrome is a combination disease that includes arthritis along with several other maladies, such as inflammation of the eyelids and of the urethra. The arthritis in this disease tends to focus on the spine and related joints. Again, young men tend to be affected more frequently.

The initial attack usually lasts only a few weeks or months, and sexual contact with an infected person is often the cause. In addition, Reiter's syndrome may occur after a bout of diarrhea, and in a number of cases patients who contract this disease seem to have inherited a genetic predisposition to it.

The ongoing symptoms of the disease are varied. Sometimes, a person has only one episode; in others, the patient may have chronic arthritis over a period of months or years.

There are also some other common rheumatic disorders that should be distinguished from arthritis:

Bursitis

Bursitis is an inflammation of a small sac containing fluid located between a tendon and the bone. The sac is called a *bursa,* hence *bursitis.*

Typical symptoms include severe localized shoulder, arm, or knee pain. Bursitis may be caused by abuse or overuse of a joint, damage from pressure on a particular area, or injury.

Usually, bursitis improves after a few days or weeks, especially after an appropriate application of heat and sufficient rest. Aspirin or similar drugs may also help.

HEALTH REPORT

FIBROMYALGIA (FIBROSITIS): A SNEAKY RELATIVE OF ARTHRITIS

Many times, fibrositis (fibromyalgia) occurs in older people along with other disorders of the muscles and skeleton, such as various forms of arthritis. As a result, this problem may be undetected and untreated.

Major symptoms of fibromyalgia include the following:
- Chronic, generalized aches, pains, or stiffness (involving three or more body sites for three or more months)
- Absence of other medical conditions that can account for these symptoms
- Several tender points at typical locations, such as the knees, elbows, and back of the neck

Minor symptoms include the following:
- Disturbed sleep patterns
- Generalized fatigue or tiredness
- Subjective swelling, numbness
- Pains in the neck and shoulders
- Chronic headaches
- Irritable bowels

What are the most effective treatments for fibromyalgia? The medications amitriptyline and cyclobenzaprine are often prescribed. Aerobic exercise also helps many patients.

F. Wolfe, "Fibromyalgia in the Elderly: Differential Diagnosis and Treatment," *Geriatrics* 43, no. 6 (1988): 57–68.

Fibrositis

Fibrositis, also known as *fibromyalgia,* is harder to recognize and diagnose. It produces pain and stiffness, and often small, tender nodules can be felt in the coverings of the muscles. The cause is unknown; it may be exacerbated by muscle strains, injuries, or chronic stress or depression.

Treatment approaches include massage, local injections, heat, and various antirheumatic drugs. Antidepressant drugs, which may contribute to better sleep, are also reported to be helpful by some patients.

Polymyalgia Rheumatica

Polymyalgia rheumatica, literally meaning "rheumatic pains in many muscles," is abbreviated to PMR among doctors. It is little known to the general public and insufficiently diagnosed, even by physicians.

Some authorities believe there are millions of cases; if there are, it should be ranked high on the list of rheumatic disorders. Its cause is unknown, its course somewhat unpredictable, and its treatment potentially spectacular. But the treatment is also somewhat hazardous, as is generally true of the diseases treated by the cortisone group of drugs.

These are a few tipoffs to the presence of PMR, which I have found most helpful:

- The illness is virtually unknown before age fifty.
- It begins abruptly in most cases. People have reported going to bed well and getting up in the morning disabled.
- Often, there is excruciating pain in the trunk muscles, such that patients are almost unable to turn over in bed or get up in the usual manner in the morning. They may have to use their arms to roll out of bed or to get up out of a chair.
- Despite these problems, there are no findings revealed by an ordinary medical examination, for example, no joint swelling or warmth in the joints. Only rarely have I seen a joint swelling in the knees.

PMR does not respond well to the usual drugs, such as aspirin or the "superaspirins" such as ibuprofen (Motrin, Advil, and Nuprin). But the effects of the cortisone group of drugs, of which prednisone is a well-known example, are both spectacular and confirmatory of the diagnosis.

Within twelve to twenty-four hours after starting on prednisone, the disease may seemingly be abolished, to everyone's delight. There is also a simple lab test indicating the *erythrocyte sedimentation rate* (ESR), which is sometimes elevated to extreme levels in PMR. On prednisone, this rate rapidly normalizes. The ESR can then be used to follow the course of the disease.

Apparently, wiping out the illness with prednisone is only a first step, however. PMR continues to lurk and may require months of treatment. Over this time, the doctor will work out the lowest dosage of prednisone that gives control. He will also from time to time decrease the dosage to see whether the original symptoms return.

In most cases, it is possible to taper patients off the medications slowly without a recurrence. A caution for those with PMR: The inflammation may sometimes affect arteries and produce arteritis, most commonly in the head. A frequent target is the temporal artery in the temple area, where the condition produces pain and tenderness. The thickened artery may be clearly visible under the skin.

Another possible target is more serious: the ophthalmic artery that nourishes the eye. In this case, vision may be affected or even lost. So arteritis is the most feared complication and one to be watchful for. The percentage of patients with PMR who develop arteritis is low, but the potential danger should still be kept in mind.

Beware of Quack Cures!

Clearly, the arthritis problem, along with related illness, is massive. But anyone with rheumatic symptoms has to take one essential step before any other: Get a medical examination so that the illness can be diagnosed precisely.

Sometimes a specialist in arthritic problems is needed. He may direct a patient into surgery, drug therapy, or some other such treatment because accumulated medical wisdom indicates that it is precisely the approach that is needed.

On the other hand, in other situations, drug-free, surgery-free options may be available. The possibility of "natural" treatments for arthritis and related ailments has opened the door to some new and rather creative concepts in arthritis treatment.

But at the same time, the so-called natural approach has also introduced some serious problems.

Because arthritis is such a pervasive disease and appears in so many different forms, a great search for a medical panacea—a kind of quest for an arthritis "Holy Grail"—has been conducted for many years. The resulting "answers" that have been offered for the chronic burden of arthritis have sometimes been rather bizarre.

Arthritis is one of the oldest known diseases suffered by human beings. Advanced arthritic changes have been found in the mummies of Egypt and in the skeletons of those who lived in other ancient civilizations.

For example, one of the oldest archaeological sites in North America, located on the California coast just forty-five miles north of San Francisco, dates back to perhaps the sixth to third centuries B.C. Of the forty-four skeletons found at this site, twenty-seven showed signs of arthritis. Specifically, the erosions of the bones' surfaces indicate that these ancient Indians had osteoarthritis, the wear-and-tear variety of the disease.

So the problem has existed for millennia, and so have the efforts to find a cure. Some of the snake oil and other panaceas that have appeared at various times over the centuries include the following:

• Snake venom, such as a combination of cobra and krait venom, which became popular among some sufferers from arthritis in the late 1970s.

• "Perkins Tractors," invented by a man named Elisha Perkins and popularized in the late eighteenth century. Perkins used two pointed rods about three inches long, one gold-colored and the other silver, in an effort to release "harmful" electricity from the body.

• Copper and magnetic bracelets. (Experts say that all the bracelets do is to leave an unsightly green mark on the wrist!)

• Vibrating chairs and mattresses.

• A swiveling exercise stand designed to allow arthritis sufferers to relieve their symptoms by dancing the Twist.

• A pressurized enema device, which unfortunately could spread infection and maybe even puncture the wall of the large intestine!

• Various dietary cure-alls, such as cod-liver oil, alfalfa, poke berries, blackstrap molasses, and a mixture of honey, vinegar, iodine, and kelp.

• Bee stings.

• An "inductoscope," which supposedly cured arthritis through magnetic induction.

• A "Congo kit," which involved the use of two hemp gloves.

• Submersion in cow manure.

• A powder made of black-bear gallbladders, designed to be sprinkled on food.

Advocates of this last treatment—and also a number of the others that have been listed—claim that more than arthritis may be cured by their method. Those choosing the black-bear route will allegedly find their sex lives improved as well. Other arthritis remedies are supposed to have a bonus effect on violent insanity, tumors, yellow fever, and multiple sclerosis.

Of course, this is all complete nonsense. There is no likelihood of the eventual appearance of one "natural" wonder cure that will eradicate arthritis. If there were such a remedy, every legitimate doctor in the country would be prescribing this panacea, and we could all move on to another serious illness.

There Is No Cure-All

Unfortunately, even some members of the medical community have become involved in the questionable arthritis cure business. For example, a few have prescribed the powerful drug Leifcort, though not authorized by the FDA for arthritis treatment. Actually a combination of several approved drugs used for purposes other than arthritis, this drug can result in thinning of bones, reduced resistance to infection, high blood pressure, cataracts, glaucoma, and peptic ulcers.

No drug, diet, exercise, or other special treatment is going to relieve you of all your symptoms. So if a representative of any particular system or treatment *claims* to have the ultimate answer for everybody, you should run quickly in the opposite direction!

There are a number of reasons that finding a panacea for arthritis is probably impossible. For one thing, the disease has a variety of guises:

- *Rheumatoid arthritis* may have a genetic basis, and some believe it may result from a slow, noninheritable virus infection.
- *Osteo-* (or wear-and-tear) *arthritis* occurs after extensive joint use and primarily strikes older people.
- *Gout* is a manifestation of too much of the body chemical uric acid, with resulting deposition in the joints and other structures.

The numerous types of arthritis have their own peculiar causes and characteristics, so it is logical to assume that a cure for one type, if it could be found, would not necessarily apply to another.

There are also strong indications that many types of arthritis may arise from imbalances or deficiencies in the immune system and may be of genetic origin. In other words, one person may have a body makeup that is susceptible to arthritis, and another may not. As a result of these individual peculiarities, it is necessary to approach each person on a case-by-case basis.

On the other hand, there are certain basic considerations that apply to almost everyone with joint disease, and especially to those with milder forms of the disease. I have summed up these basics in the form of several simple strategies that anyone, with almost any form of arthritis, may want to employ.

Seven Basic Strategies for Combating Arthritic Symptoms

Some of these strategies are truly drug-free; others make use of the latest advances in modern medicine. In any event, you should be aware of *all* the options before you and your physician settle on the special approach that is right for you and your condition. NOTE: In Chapter 23 I will deal with the specific treatments that underlie many of these strategies.

1. *Consult medical authorities first.* The very first thing you should do if you notice any of the symptoms I describe in these pages is to seek out a medical specialist who can interpret them properly for you.

Furthermore, you should embark on drug-free or nonprescription approaches to dealing with your arthritis *only* after you have placed yourself in the care of a knowledgeable physician. It may very well be that the best avenue to relief for you will be some form of exercise or life-style change.

But then again, it may be that these "natural" approaches are not what you need at all. Your condition may dictate immediate surgery or use of drugs, and the only way you will find out is to explore the matter with a trained specialist.

2. *Embark on a proper exercise program.* Appropriate exercise is a well-recognized drug-free alternative to relieve arthritis symptoms. Consequently, special exercise programs are used by leading hospitals, therapists, and exercise physiologists for arthritic patients.

It is true, of course, that excessive amounts of exercise can aggravate arthritis. In fact, the wear-and-tear type of arthritis may be caused by overuse of certain joints and certain types of exercises.

On the other hand, moderate, properly executed exercises can help build up your bones, muscles, and ligaments and help support those joints that have been damaged by arthritis. Exercise is also a means of burning up calories and keeping down weight, a useful property in reducing the pressure on diseased joints. To explain how this works, I have included some specific exercise guidelines in Chapter 23.

3. *Get plenty of rest and sleep.* The body's energy levels and immune mechanisms always operate better when you are well rested. As a result, a good night's sleep—and perhaps a nap or rest period in the middle of the day—is extremely important in your efforts to find relief from arthritic discomfort and pain.

4. *Practice proper posture.* Sitting or standing in unnatural ways can put excessive pressure on your joints. So, as you will learn in Chapter 23, it is important to enhance your posture through

proper exercises and to practice good posture as much as possible in your daily activities.

5. *Apply heat to ailing joints.* Through the ages, the use of hot compresses has been a common prescription for relieving the discomforts of arthritis. Use of natural hot springs and muds was once referred to as "taking the cure." In more recent times, hot electric pads have been used to do this job.

There are also definite indications that exposure to excessive cold may aggravate arthritis and even cause it to progress more rapidly. For example, people who work outdoors for extended periods of time in very cold weather tend to have a higher incidence.

This point may have some historical support. In one study of pre-Columbian North American Indians, researchers found that skeletal remains thousands of years old showed a much higher incidence of joint disease than in our own day. The arthritis also occurred among much younger people.

The researchers speculated that poor diet may have been a cause. But it is also possible that relatively scanty dress in cold weather may have been a contributing factor.

6. *Make use of massage.* The work of an expert masseur or masseuse can be quite helpful in relieving muscle and ligament tensions and loosening pressure on certain bones, joints, and tendons. But it is absolutely necessary for arthritic patients to find professionals who know how to be gentle and still do the job!

7. *Establish wise life-style habits.* There are many practical ways that arthritic patients can relieve the pressure on their joints in daily life. These include certain lifting and twisting techniques and use of special kitchen devices to open jars and prepare food more easily.

Finally, as you explore different ways to combat your arthritis, it will be important to monitor your progress. To this end, I suggest that you keep a daily journal or diary.

With this journal, you can document the way you feel each day, both emotionally and physically. Specifically, you should note emotions and activities such as these: (1) the exercise you have had on that day, (2) the weather, (3) your mood, (4) your physical activities such as housework or yard work, (5) the kind and degree of pressures you have experienced on that particular day, and (6) the kind and dosages of any medicines, either prescription or nonprescription, you are taking.

After you have evaluated your activities and your general emotional and physical state, you should rate the way you feel each day according to the following five-point scale:

5—You have no arthritic symptoms.

4—You have mild arthritic discomfort, but you are able to function fairly well.

3—You are experiencing pain but are still able to function physically.

2—You experience severe arthritic pain, with only minimal physical functioning.

1—You have severe pain and are unable to function physically.

If you keep this journal faithfully and rate yourself each day, you will be in a position to evaluate how well you have done over a one-month period on a particular drug or nondrug regimen.

You may notice, for example, that the weather was particularly cold or rainy during one of the months when you were feeling "under the weather" physically. In that case, the weather, rather than lack of drugs or exercise, may have been your main problem. On the other hand, you may find that you can counter the cold weather quite effectively by using more hot pads and compresses at various times during the day.

Finally, be sure to keep your personal arthritis program fairly steady and constant during any given month. In that way, you will minimize the variables and be in a better position to judge your own system's reactions.

And remember this: You are *not* involved in a personal search for a complete cure to your arthritis! If you begin with unrealistic expectations, you are sure to be disappointed. In fact, you may become so discouraged that you quit before you experience the degree of relief from pain that may be possible for you.

In short, if you experience *some* relief from your arthritic symptoms, that's good. If you experience considerable relief, that's even better. Any relief, no matter how slight, is better than none at all.

Now, to investigate in more detail how a particular treatment may apply to your situation, let's turn to the specifics of various drug, surgery, exercise, and life-style responses to the discomfort of arthritis.

23

SOME SPECIFIC SOLUTIONS TO THE DISCOMFORTS OF ARTHRITIS

From the hundreds of patients I have seen who have sought relief from arthritic symptoms, I have learned this for a fact: Each form of arthritis has its own insidious personality. Consequently, there are a variety of types of treatments and drugs to deal with the multiple ways that this epidemic is plaguing us.

Unfortunately, sometimes a long-term drug program is the only way that an arthritis sufferer can find relief. In the best of all possible worlds, there would be a drug-free "natural" answer to every illness. But as I tell my patients, we do not live in that sort of medically perfect world. In the imperfect world of the arthritic, it is often necessary to consult a rheumatologist to see whether it is feasible, given your condition, to decrease or avoid use of drugs entirely.

After investigating this matter thoroughly, you and your physician may determine that drug treatment is desirable, but it is still important that you, as an informed patient, know the limits and likely side effects of those drugs.

To this end, let's take a brief look at the drugs that are most often used to treat various types of arthritis and related rheumatic diseases.

The Drug Solution

Aspirin and Its Kin

Ordinary aspirin tends to inhibit the synthesis in joints and tissues of certain chemicals that may cause inflammation. Among the varieties of this drug, you will find the following:

- Common aspirin
- Time-released aspirin (specially treated so as to dissolve over a longer period)
- Enteric-coated aspirin (a form with special covering that passes unchanged through the stomach and then into the intestine, where it does dissolve)
- Buffered aspirin (contains an alkalinizing agent)
- Other types of salicylates (medications that help relieve pains in the muscles and joints; aspirin is a salicylate)

Some patients may have trouble with aspirin because the stomach becomes upset. Timed-release or coated aspirins may help them to tolerate the medication. Your doctor can also help minimize the negative effects of aspirin by adjusting the dosage or the times it is to be administered.

Despite its great usefulness in relieving arthritic symptoms, aspirin has associated dangers. In particular, problems such as gastritis, ulcer formation, and even symptoms of aspirin poisoning may occur, particularly with high dosages. Thus, some patients may note a ringing in their ears.

To minimize these problems, coated aspirins can help. Informative British studies show that blood levels are just as high on coated as on uncoated aspirin. Direct examinations through the gastroscope show far less irritation and no ulceration in the stomach. If you are still wedded to ordinary aspirin, be sure to take plenty of fluid with it. Otherwise, it can be caustic.

How many aspirins do you have to take to get relief from the symptoms of arthritis?

Differing severities of the disease, of course, require different amounts. But it may be necessary to take up to sixteen aspirin tablets per day to derive the full anti-inflammatory relief.

To be sure that you are not experiencing negative effects from the higher dosages of aspirin, it is important to keep in touch with your doctor when you use it. It may also be necessary to have regular checks of your stool for blood to be sure that no occult bleeding has resulted from aspirin therapy.

The Newer Aspirin Alternatives

In the following listings of drugs, the generic name of the substance is given first; the brand name, if relevant, is included in parenthesis.

Another group of drugs, the nonsteroidal anti-inflammatory drugs, are similar to aspirin in many ways but are more potent. One major way in which they are different is that they often cost more. They are certainly a great deal more convenient for the patient because they may have to be taken only once or twice a day, instead of in the more frequent dosages required of aspirin.

These drugs include

- piroxicam (Feldene),
- tolmetin (Tolectin),
- ibuprofen (Motrin),
- phenylbutazone (Butazolidin),
- naproxen (Naprosyn),
- oxyphenbutazone (Tandearil),
- fenoprofen (Nalfon),
- sulindac (Clinoril),
- indomethacin (Indocin),
- diclofenac (Voltaren).

Although these medications may be more convenient to take, patients on a limited budget may be quite willing to deal with more frequent dosages in order to use cheaper aspirin products. They do vary in their impact on the stomach and possible risk of bleeding. In any case, it is important to consult your doctor before you choose any of these drugs. Some have higher risks than others.

The Corticosteroids

The corticosteroids are chemically related to the hormones made in the cortex (outer shell) of your adrenal gland. They include

- dexamethasone (Decadron),
- triamcinolone hexacetonide (Aristocort),
- hydrocortisone,
- prednisone,
- methylprednisolone (Medrol and many others).

These agents are very effective in diminishing inflammation, but they may have hazardous long-term effects on the body. As a result, only doctors should administer or monitor them.

These substances can rapidly make a patient feel better, even producing a euphoric effect, and they may dramatically reduce pain and inflammation. As a result, they provide considerable benefits for those with severe types of arthritis.

But cortisone and its relatives are two-edged swords: They may interfere with the way that the body metabolizes fat, protein, calcium, and sugar and may even lead to a diabetic disorder.

Common side effects include a puffy, swollen face and neck. Hypertension may also develop. And there may be weakening and softening of the bones because of osteoporosis. In addition, these drugs can suppress the immune system and impair the healing of wounds and the ability of the body to resist infection. In fact, these substances may even help cause other types of arthritis through their side effects!

So it is obvious—if you have to use one of these drugs—why you should do so only under strict supervision. All this is not to say that the corticosteroids should be avoided at all costs, just that it is important to exercise care. I have some patients with arthritis, asthma, and allergies who self-treat flareups of their condition, as if the corticosteroids were on the same, almost innocuous level as aspirin. They are not! For one thing, persons on steroids should taper the doses, not quit abruptly. Otherwise, because of suppression of one's adrenal glands, severe weakness may result.

The Antimalarial Drugs and Gold

Gold salts were once used to treat arthritis because people used to think that rheumatoid arthritis was an infectious disease and salts of heavy metals were thought to have anti-infective power. Interestingly, the gold salts did work in some cases, even though it is now known that rheumatoid arthritis is not caused by bacterial or viral invasion. Newer forms of gold are being used for difficult cases of rheumatoid arthritis. Some are taken by mouth, others by injection. Gold salts include Myochrysine, Solganal, and Ridaura, which are to be taken by mouth.

Considerable investigation has been done with the group of antimalarial drugs. These are still prescribed on some occasions because they work with certain patients. Two of the antimalarial medications now used include the following:

- chloroquine,
- hydroxychloroquine (Plaquenil, Sulfate),
- penicillamine (Depen, Cuprimine) (an agent that removes copper from the body; its effectiveness against rheumatoid arthritis is not understood, but it is a fall-back drug).

As do many potent medications, these antiarthritic drugs may have major side effects. Take them only under the supervision of your physician, and maintain contact with him.

The Folic Acid Answer

There is a so-called folic acid antagonist called *methotrexate,* which has long been used in patients undergoing cancer chemotherapy. Somehow, this anti–folic acid medication interferes with the abnormal immune response that has occurred in patients with rheumatoid arthritis. The substance seems to prevent the body from reacting against itself and helps reduce the inflammation of the joint tissue.

Again, this is a drug that requires concerned guidance from a physician.

The Antigout Drugs

Drugs most often used to treat gout include

- allopurinol (Zyloprim),
- sulfinpyrazone (Anturane),
- colchicine,
- probenecid (Benemid).

Major objectives in treating gout include reduction of uric acid levels in the body and, of course, prevention of gouty attacks. Drugs like probenecid promote excretion, and allopurinol inhibits manufacture of uric acid. Either treatment can contribute to a reduction in the frequency and severity of attacks of gout.

The drug colchicine is also often prescribed by physicians to help relieve the pain of gout attacks and to decrease their frequency.

The Ultimate Drugs

The drugs known as *cytotoxic agents* are designed to kill or otherwise inhibit cells whose activities may cause the major problems in some of the arthritic diseases. These include

- chlorambucil (Leukeran),
- azathioprine (Imuran),
- cyclophosphamide (Cytoxan).

Usually, these drugs are used only for patients suffering from overwhelming pain and disability. The risks with these agents are particularly great because they tend to suppress the immune system and thus make the patient susceptible to infection. They may help to break down some of the normal tissues in the body, such as the lining cells in the stomach and intestines.

From this brief overview, you can see that drugs may sometimes be necessary, but that they are not to be taken lightly. In most cases, it is probably wisest for a patient who must use such drugs to do so in a step-by-step fashion, perhaps from the least serious medications like aspirin up through the more potent drugs that have to be so closely monitored.

Of course, it is impossible in a book written for a general audience to tell you, as an individual, what approach, if any, you should take to drugs. This is why it is important for each person who suffers from arthritis to stay in close touch with his or her own physician.

In any case, it is always wise to ask plenty of questions about just how necessary a given drug may be in your case. You should also question your physician about possible side effects and about alternative drugs that may be less hazardous. Finally, there is nothing wrong with getting a second opinion, especially if your physician prescribes a serious medication without answering your questions satisfactorily.

Drugs, then, are definitely a double-edged sword. Sometimes, though, even the most serious drugs *are* necessary, and in a number of cases, an even more serious step must be taken: surgery.

When Surgery Becomes Necessary

Osteoarthritis produces proliferation of bone. The resultant thickening may press on other structures, especially nerves and tendons, and lead to pain and disability. Rheumatoid arthritis may go through stages of inflammation, joint destruction, and finally loss of joint motion. Some older persons may have both conditions. Sometimes, it becomes apparent that joints have become so damaged and useless that only a radical solution is possible. Drugs, heat, and physical therapy will be inadequate. In such cases, a surgical solution may be the best means of attacking your problems with arthritis. And sometimes, it is also the most effective.

What exactly can surgery do?

The best way to answer this question is to look at a specific, real-life case, one that was handled at one of the major hospitals on the East Coast. A woman in her midfifties came in for treatment in a condition that might best be described as completely handicapped. She was wheelchair-bound, unable to stand or even lie down comfortably in bed. Her hips and knees were both constantly contracted in a painful, sitting-type posture.

A victim of rheumatoid arthritis, she was completely unable to care for herself. This woman's typical emotional state, as you might guess, was depression. She had begun to question seriously whether she would ever have any chance of getting better.

Such a severe case of rheumatoid arthritis leaves open only one possible avenue of significant hope: surgery. And that is the route we led this woman along, with tremendous success.

She underwent complete hip and knee replacements in both legs, involving a series of surgical procedures that took about a year. Four operations were required, one for each knee and one for each hip, with two to three months of recuperation between each. She underwent the operations with a spinal anesthetic, so that she was awake during all the procedures, though under some sedation.

Undergoing four such operations, each of which takes between two and a half and three hours, is certainly a serious matter. But nowadays, if the health of the patient is generally good, the ordeal of the operations is well worth it. The worst part for most patients is anticipating the surgery rather than actually experiencing it.

And what a tremendous difference it made for this woman when her operations were completed! With new artificial joints, consisting of stainless steel and high-density polyethylene, she was transformed into a new woman.

Of course, no prosthetic joint can ever equal the low-friction, streamlined operation of a normal joint. But still, with the new surgical technology now available, people who once believed that they would be confined to a wheelchair or a bed for life now find that they can resume a normal existence.

And this is exactly what happened with this particular woman. Within a year, even before all the operations had been completed, she was on her feet, moving about. This is particularly amazing when you consider that she had not walked a step for about ten years before the surgery.

Within a year of therapy, she was moving about unaided. After another year, her muscle mass had increased so dramatically that she was able to walk about almost normally.

Not every surgical story has this happy ending. But many do.

So if your arthritis is so far advanced that you really cannot move about easily, this may be the way you should go.

Still, surgery is always a last resort, after changes in life-style and reasonable drug therapies have failed. So how can you tell when surgery may be in order for you?

In general, there are two major indications that you should watch for in your own body:

1. *Pain.* Pain in your joints may be one of the most important signals that surgery is appropriate for you. This is especially true if the pain is severe and constant and recurs on a daily basis. For example, according to the scale described previously, if you find that you are regularly rating yourself 1 or 2 out of 5—that is, in quite severe pain—then you should definitely see your doctor and discuss a surgical alternative.

2. *Limitation of activity.* People who are pain-free but also dysfunctional may still need surgery. In other words, you may not hurt that much, but if you find that you used to be able to walk five blocks to the store without any problem, and now you can go only two blocks, that is a sign that your joints may be deteriorating significantly, even though little or no pain may be involved. By the same token, if you find that your ability to walk longer and longer distances increases, that may be an indication that you should postpone surgery. In any case, check with your doctor so that he can monitor your progress.

But now, let's suppose that you are in close touch with your doctor, and he begins to urge a surgical alternative. He may very well be precisely on the mark in making this suggestion. On the other hand, you have a responsibility as an intelligent patient to ask him and your prospective surgeon some key questions before you embark on such a procedure.

Q: *Are there any acceptable alternatives to surgery?*

A: In other words, you should consider that, in light of your progress in recent weeks and months, it is possible that some drug or change in your life-style might be worth trying before you head for the operating table. The main idea here is that every acceptable alternative should be exhausted before surgery comes into play.

Q: *What are the potential risks or complications of surgery for me?*

A: Some types of surgery tend to be very successful these days, including hip joint replacements, finger joint implants, and wrist implants. On the other hand, there was a procedure that was quite popular in the past that involved replacing ankle joints; it was much less successful. These joints became quite loose, and very few of them are used in operations now.

There are certain high-risk operations, for example, neck surgery. In addition, hip and knee surgery with strong, active patients who are involved in heavy physical labor may yield a poor result because of the extra stresses of their work.

So it is very important for you to understand in detail the exact inherent risks of the operation that you are considering and the risk that the operation may entail to your life-style.

Q: *What will be the benefits of the operation?*

A: Many patients often have the wrong idea of what they will gain from an operation for their arthritis problems. Many think that they will be restored to a completely normal status in every case, and this expectation can be quite unrealistic.

For example, surgeons may choose to use fusion on certain joints, such as a hip or ankle. But this procedure will limit the mobility of a patient and may very well cause him to walk with a stiff-gaited limp. Certainly, this result is better than not walking at all. But the benefits from the operation must always be weighed against the condition before surgery.

Q: *What will be the consequences if I do have surgery?*

A: It may be that surgery will make only a slight difference in the way you conduct your life. But more often, if the medical advice you are getting is sound, surgery has the potential of making a dramatic difference. Witness the case of the wheelchair-bound woman just discussed. With certain arthritic problems, surgery can truly mean a new lease on life for the patient.

Q: *What is the durability of the operation?*

A: In particular, will the effect of the operation last for the rest of your life, or will the procedure have to be repeated after several years? In most cases, surgery eventually has to be repeated because artificial joints tend to become loose. Typically these days, both hip and knee replacements may last from ten to fifteen years, but then both may become loose and require a new procedure.

As we have seen, a fusion operation should last forever, but this procedure will limit the mobility of the patient much more than most joint replacements.

Q: *What are my doctor's background and track record?*

A: It is quite fair for a patient to investigate the type of training that his potential surgeon has had, as well as the extent of the physician's experience. Feel free to ask some very direct questions of your doctor: How many operations of this type have you done? How many years have you been in practice? Where did you have your medical training?

Finally, a word about insurance companies: Many insurance companies require that patients get a second opinion before they have surgery, and that policy can certainly be a safety factor that operates to the patient's advantage. On the other hand, you should be cautious when you go to a doctor of the insurance company's choosing, because it is possible that he might be biased against surgery. After all, he wants to save the insurance company money.

So, if you do seek a second opinion from the insurance company's doctor, and his view seems to be radically different from that of the original physician, it is a reasonable idea to check with a third physician before you make your final decision.

Clearly, there are many factors to consider before you decide to undergo a surgical procedure. For most people, arthritis has not become so serious that surgery is appropriate. But still, it is important for any intelligent patient these days to understand exactly what surgery for arthritis may involve and what circumstances or conditions may justify the surgical alternative. Only with this sort of information can you make a reasonable decision about pursuing a drug-free program to relieve your arthritis symptoms.

The "Natural" Way to Arthritis Relief

The Exercise Alternative

Exercise is an absolutely essential activity for every arthritis patient. Why is exercise so important? Here are just a few of the reasons:

• Physical activity will improve your psychological as well as your physical well-being.

• Exercise will improve your muscle tone and thereby improve the capability of your joints. In general, joints that are under attack by arthritis can begin to tolerate the stresses placed on them better as they receive additional support from surrounding muscles.

• Almost any comprehensive exercise program will help improve your posture. And as you will recall from those Seven Basic Strategies described in Chapter 22, good posture is an important factor in fighting arthritis symptoms.

• Morning exercise encourages the loosening-up phenomenon that makes most people's joints work better during the day. Most of us, when we first wake up, have joints that are stiff to one degree or another. But as the day goes on and we move about, that movement helps loosen the joints so that they can be worked more easily.

But despite the many benefits of exercise, those suffering from arthritis must carefully monitor their activity. One important basic principle is that no exercise should cause abnormal stresses on joints and cause pain. Pain is one of the key warning systems in our bodies, especially as far as arthritis is concerned. Those with arthritis *must* exercise in some way if they hope to hold the line or even improve with their disease, but once the line between discomfort and pain is crossed, the exercise may be doing more harm than good.

That is the test: the difference between discomfort and pain. Only you, as an individual, can make the final judgment of what is pain for you and what is merely discomfort. But it is important to push yourself into the discomfort zone. In physical therapy, patients are encouraged to improve their muscle strength and range of motion by exercising until they become somewhat uncomfortable. But once those joints begin to hurt or swell, that is the limit: You have reached the point where it's time to hold off.

What kind of exercise should you choose? That depends entirely on your physical condition and the severity of your disease.

In general, the best endurance exercises for arthritic patients tend to be walking, swimming, and perhaps bicycling. With all these activities, the stress on joints tends to be minimal. At the same time, they can offer considerable conditioning potential. Of course, you have to choose your exercise in light of your particular problem. It may be that you have a problem with one or both of your knees, so much so that walking and bicycling are out of the question. They may simply put too much stress on those joints and cause pain or damage.

But if you are suffering from only moderate levels of arthritis and no diseased joints are put at risk, keeping active with walking, cycling, or swimming can only help you.

How much endurance exercise of this type should you engage in? In general, it is important to have a complete medical examination, including a stress test with electrocardiogram, before embarking on any sort of exercise program. This requirement of a medical examination becomes especially important if you are forty years of age or older. It is only through such a complete checkup that you can be certain that your heart and other key systems in your body are healthy enough to engage in rigorous aerobic activity.

If you pass your physical exams, then, under your doctor's guidance, you may want to begin a regular aerobics conditioning program. In most cases, this will involve twenty to thirty minutes of continuous, moderately rigorous exercise three to four times a week. Then, as your physical condition improves, you may want to increase the time you spend in such exercise.

But again, it is important to monitor your body. Always be alert to the way it—especially your affected joints—responds. If you detect swelling or experience pain during your workout, that is the signal to stop. You have pushed beyond the limit of normal physical development and discomfort into a danger zone that may aggravate your arthritic condition.

For patients with a much more severe disease, vigorous, aerobic exercise may be out of the question. On the other hand, gentle walking or other movement about the house can help a great deal to reduce immobility and stiffness.

There are also a number of simple exercises that can help you maintain or improve the range over which your joints can move as well as your muscle strength. Here are some examples for different parts of the body. You should do each of the exercises five times, and you can repeat them once or twice daily, or even more often, depending on your ability.

The hands

1. Make a circle by touching your thumb to each of your fingertips one at a time.

2. Place your palms flat on a table or over the edge of a table or a book and then lower each of your fingers, one at a time.

3. Pick up a pencil and roll it between your thumb and each of your fingers, one at a time.

4. Pick up coins and buttons of various sizes.

5. Crumple up a sheet of newspaper into a small, tight ball, using only one hand.

6. Rest one hand on a table, spread all the fingers far apart, and then bring them all together again. Repeat with the other hand.

7. Flip balls of paper back and forth with each of your fingers.

8. Loop a rubber band around one thumb and finger. Then spread the thumb and finger as far apart as possible. Repeat with each finger on that hand, and then go through the procedure again with the other hand.

The wrist

1. Lay a folded newspaper or a thin magazine across your hand. Then flip it away from your hand.

2. With your palms together and your arms stretched in front of your chest, draw your hands in toward your body. Your palms should be kept together during the whole motion, with your elbows pointing outward as they bend.

3. Place your forearm on a table, with the hand hanging over the edge. Then, bend your wrist up and down and around in circles in both directions.

The elbows

1. With your elbows next to your body and your forearms parallel to the ground, bent at a ninety-degree angle, turn your palms up and down.

2. Raise your right hand to your right shoulder and then

return it to a hanging position at your side. Repeat with the other hand.

3. Roll out a slab of dough with a rolling pin, all the while straightening your arms out as far as possible.

4. Sit facing a table, with your arms extended forward and your hands on the table. Bend your upper body down toward the table, and then push away from the table with your arms, but without moving your hands.

The shoulders

1. Swing your arms forward and upward and then downward and backward.

2. Shrug your shoulders around and around in a circular motion.

3. Hold your arms straight out at your sides and then move them around so that your hands trace circles in the air.

4. Keeping your elbows bent, place your hands alternately behind your neck and your lower back.

5. "Walk" up a wall in your home with your fingers. Try to reach a higher point on the wall each day.

6. With your arms at your sides and your palms turned toward the front, grasp a broomstick in your hands. Raise the stick up to the front of your shoulders in a "curling" motion. Next, push the broomstick up over your head and then bring it back down to the back of your shoulders. Reverse each of these movements until the broomstick is resting in front of you in the starting position.

7. Repeat the motions in the previous exercise, but this time grasp the broomstick so that your palms are facing backward.

These exercises, obviously, are designed for patients with rather severe arthritic problems. Most likely, people in this condition will not be able to pursue the aerobic activities mentioned previously. But whatever your particular physical condition or whatever the degree of severity of your disease, it is essential that you select *some* exercise program that will allow you to push your body a bit and perhaps improve your overall condition.

No drug-free arthritis program—in fact, no arthritis program at all—can succeed without exercise. The goal in rehabilitation for arthritis patients is to improve the range of motion of diseased joints and to push back those zones of pain that are limiting activities and enjoyment of life.

Exercise may be only a part of the answer for your improvement. But it is an extremely important part, and it goes hand-in-hand with another important answer to arthritis relief: the need to make changes in your life-style.

Changing Your Life-Style

We live in an age when stress and pressure have become bywords for the kind of lives we lead. But for a person suffering from arthritis, that has to change.

"Instead of pressure and stress," I tell my arthritis patients, "the slogans of your life must become ease and relaxation."

Sound impossible in our high-powered, fast-moving society? It does take a little prior planning and a determination to change certain ingrained habits. And let's face it: If you are currently an arthritis sufferer who faces steady physical deterioration unless you take steps to head off the disease, you really have no choice. You have to act—and act now!—to make your life begin to move along in an easier flow, which will help to heal rather than hurt those ailing joints and tissues.

So what can you do to change your way of life?

First of all, you should learn some basic life-style principles of taking care of your joints, no matter how severe your arthritis may be or what particular type of the disease you have. Here are some of the most important principles that experts in the field of arthritis treatment have formulated over the years.

As you read through these principles, you will see that not all of them apply to you or your particular situation. For example, if you do not have any problems with your knees, you may not need to worry about the suggestions about knee postures. On the other hand, it is important to focus closely on those life-style principles that seem to apply to you personally.

1. *Avoid body positions that mimic deformity.* Generally speaking, joints tend to become deformed in a flexed or bent position, so you should do everything you can to keep your joints *out* of that position. As a matter of fact, normal joints that are held in awkward or pressure-prone positions may be affected by inflammation, swelling, or other arthritic changes and may actually eventually become

deformed. So it is extremely important to concentrate on maintaining a good posture and good positions for joints that may be vulnerable.

If you are already experiencing some arthritic signs in certain parts of your body, it is even more imperative to watch the way you hold those parts of the body. Here are some examples:

• *The knees.* If you have trouble making your knees completely straight, try to sleep in a position that keeps them as straight as possible. In any case, do not sleep with a pillow under your knees at night, even though that may seem more comfortable. The flexing of the knees caused by the pillow can cause trouble for you in the future.

• *The hips.* If you have problems with soreness or swelling in the hip region, it is important to straighten those hips out for a short period each day. You might lie on your stomach for a while each day, perhaps up to a half hour, to encourage the hips to fall in a straighter position.

• *The elbows.* If it is hard to straighten your elbows, avoid leaning on your elbows in a bent position for lengthy periods. Instead, rest your arms in a straighter position.

• *The hands.* Many people, when they are sitting in a seemingly relaxed position, prop their head on the back of one or both hands or sometimes rest the chin on the bent finger knuckles. Such posture encourages bending the joints in a position of deformity and should be avoided. Instead, it is best to rest your head or chin in the palm of your hand, with your fingers and wrist in an extended or straight position.

2. *Do not put unnecessary pressure on your finger joints.* From a very early age, we acquire the habit of performing certain common daily tasks in ways that may cause serious problems with our hands in later life. If you are experiencing any problems with inflammation or swelling in your fingers or finger joints, you might try some of these techniques:

• Lift plates and bowls with the palm of your hand, not just your fingers.

• When you cut your food, hold your knife like a dagger, instead of in the normal manner.

● In turning a doorknob, shift your entire body around so that you can grasp the knob with the side of your hand and use a wrist motion to open it.

● Avoid lifting cups by slipping one finger through a handle. Instead, try to slip several fingers through the handle or pick up the cup—preferably an insulated mug—between the palms of both your hands.

● When you lift a hot oven pan, put on two oven mittens and then lift it by using both your hands, one on each side of the pan.

● When washing food that is caked on pans or dishes, use a scouring brush or pad that is attached to a handle, rather than one that you have to hold directly against the dish with your hand. The handle can help reduce harmful pressures that often occur when you are wielding an ordinary scouring pad.

● Screw lids on jars and bottles as loosely as possible. When you have to open a relatively tight lid, press down against it with the palm of your hand, and then, as much as possible, use the motion of your shoulder to turn your hand and the lid on which it rests.

● When closing a drawer, use your rear end!

● When raising a window, use the palm rather than the side of your hand.

● Avoid gripping objects any more tightly than necessary.

● When wringing out wet clothing or other articles, look for creative ways to do the job without putting pressure on your fingers and wrists. For example, you might push against a cloth, rather than twist it, or you might wrap a piece of clothing around a broom or faucet and use this as a base to twist the article.

3. *Avoid staying in one position for lengthy periods.* In general, it is best to keep on the move as much as possible. If you allow yourself to maintain one position for twenty minutes or longer, it is likely that any vulnerable joints or muscles will begin to tighten up or get tired.

Here are a few practical suggestions:

● Alternate sitting and standing while you are doing your work.

● Type, rather than write longhand.

● Avoid knitting if your arthritis is bothering your hands.

• While you are reading, support your book or newspaper on something, so that your hands are left free.

• If you have to hold on to anything for a long period of time, relax your fingers regularly.

• Do activities that require repetitive actions for short periods of time. When your muscles begin to feel tired or your joints start to ache or swell, you have gone too far.

4. *Use your strongest joints when you engage in various activities.* Again, it is necessary to relearn some basic tasks and habits if you find you are beginning to experience problems of discomfort, pain, or swelling in certain joints. For example, you may be accustomed to carrying your pocketbook or shopping bag dangling from your fingers. But if your fingers are bothering you, you should shift that parcel so that it hangs from your forearm. In this way, you will be using your stronger elbow muscles rather than your fingers.

Whenever possible, avoid using scissors if you have any problem with your fingers. Electric scissors will do the job if it is absolutely necessary for you to do cutting.

Even a simple action such as dialing a telephone can put excessive pressure on hands that are afflicted by arthritis, so it is important to find an alternative method. Instead of using one finger, get a pencil, insert it into the appropriate holes, and dial by using a shoulder motion. Better yet, get a push-button phone!

If you have to lift a heavy object from the floor, bend with your knees, not with your back. When you lift the object, be sure to keep your back straight and allow the pressure to be taken care of by your legs. Of course, if you have a problem with your knees, ankles, or back, you really should not lift heavy objects at all.

When you push an object of any type, put your entire body weight behind it whenever possible. In this way, you spread out any pressure that may be exerted on particular joints.

5. *Do not start an activity unless you are sure you can stop it at will.* This is just good common sense. If you become involved in a strenuous activity, and find, for some reason, that you cannot stop, you may overexert yourself. Obviously, this particular principle may require some forethought and prior planning.

For example, you may have planned an extensive shopping expedition with some friends. But before you go, think about it for a moment. Will your legs and arms hold out in most cases when you are walking around, standing, and carrying parcels for several hours? If not, you should probably convey your regrets, or perhaps plan a shorter outing with plenty of rest periods.

6. *Always respect pain.* As we have already seen, pain is one of the most important danger signals that your body can give. If you place yourself under too much pressure or stress and pain results, then it is time to back off. Remember the distinction between pain and discomfort: Pain indicates that you have gone too far. Discomfort may just mean that you're stretching those joints and muscles in such a way that you are likely to get better use out of them.

7. *Rest regularly.* This is one of the most important principles in taking care of yourself if you have any sort of arthritic condition. Exercise and reasonable movement are equally essential. But if you move around or exercise too much without interspersing adequate rest periods, all the activity will become counterproductive.

First, be sure that you get your full complement of sleep at night. If you need nine hours, get it. If your optimum sleep time is eight hours or seven, then get that. Second, it is advisable to set aside a short time during the day, say a half hour or so, to take a nap or just lie down quietly.

Third, take regular breaks in your activities. You may not lie down on a bed or drop off to sleep, but it helps just to sit back and take a few deep breaths after you have been working intensely for a while. During these breaks, it is helpful to concentrate on sitting or standing in positions of good posture, with all your muscles and joints in proper alignment. You might also try certain relaxation techniques, such as a period of regular breathing or intermittent tensing and conscious relaxing of your muscles.

8. *Conserve your energy.* Arthritis is a disease, and any disease makes extra demands on your body. As a result, you may have less energy than those without the disease, so keep this in mind as you plan and pursue your various daily activities.

For example, it helps to plan your activities so that you have to make only one trip to the same place or part of the house instead of two or three. Also, if you are the member of the family who prepares the meals, have a store of prepared foods set aside so that you can use it if you are having a bad day and do not feel like cooking. As far as washing dishes is concerned, try to plan your meals so that you use a limited number of dishes and eating utensils.

Ironing tends to put extra pressure on those who have arthritis problems with their hands and wrists. As a result, you might encourage your family to select fabrics that do not require much ironing.

9. *Get equipment that can make your life easier.* Although certain types of mechanical devices can be quite expensive, these aids can do wonders in making the everyday tasks of life much easier for arthritis patients. Depending on your particular problem, you might want to investigate:

- devices that raise the heights of chairs, toilet seats, or beds;
- handrails, which can reduce strain on your knee joints when you are climbing the stairs;
- splints, which can protect vulnerable wrists and hands;
- long-handled brushes and utensils;
- various types of electrical devices, such as mixers, washing machines, and automatic can openers;
- aids to help you open car doors and jars and assist with turning automobile ignition keys.

10. *Be creative when you are dressing or grooming yourself.* So often, we twist, turn, and strain our bodies and joints without thinking when we are getting ready to meet the world in the morning or preparing for some sort of evening entertainment. But if you have any sort of a problem with arthritis or one of the related joint diseases, you *have* to think when you are engaged in these activitiess. Here are a few suggestions to flesh out this principle:

- Wear lightweight coats and jackets.
- Choose clothing that closes in front, with zippers, Velcro fasteners, and buttons. Avoid tight-fitting pullovers. In general, loose-fitting clothes will put less stress and strain on your hands and upper body.
- Replace hard-to-reach buttons and snaps with Velcro fasteners. You might also try affixing cuff buttons with elastic thread, so that you can slip your hands through them without unbuttoning the shirt.
- Use garter belts and pantyhose, rather than girdles. If you have to use a girdle, choose one with zippers rather than hook-and-eye fasteners.

• If possible, choose a brassiere that you can fasten in the front of your body. If you have to use one with a rear fastener, fasten the bra as it is hanging around the front of your waist. Then, turn it around and pull it up into place. Generally speaking, a bra with elastic straps is the easiest to pull up.

• Arrange your dressing procedures so that you do not have to use excessive pressure or force when you grasp objects between your thumb and your index finger. For example, when you are zipping a zipper, you might tie a piece of string into the zipper tap so that you can pull the zipper up by the string instead of pinching the tap.

• When you are putting on a girdle, roll it down from the top to the bottom, then step into it, and finally pull it up onto your hips and unroll it. Dusting your thighs with talcum powder will make pulling the girdle up into place easier.

If you have had arthritis for a while and you have already explored some of these labor-saving techniques, they may have already become second nature to you. On the other hand, if you are just getting started, you may be overwhelmed with the thought that you will have to change your way of life completely. But really, it is not as unpleasant or radical as all that.

The main idea underlying all these principles is that you should think ahead and plan an overall life-style strategy that will make your daily activities easier. Above all, you want to put as little pressure as possible on your diseased joints and yet at the same time maintain as normal a life-style as possible.

By planning in advance and taking these and other steps to relieve the pressures on your body, you will most likely find greater relief from your disease. Your most vulnerable joints, ligaments, and muscles will become tired and painful less frequently and you will move closer to your ultimate objective: to retard the deterioration of your afflicted joints.

REMEMBER: The more tension, pressure, and stress you put on those bones, joints, ligaments, and muscles, the more problems you will have with them and the more quickly they will be likely to deteriorate. On the other hand, if you are thoughtful and careful, you may very well find you can live a life that is almost normal, and your overall condition may actually begin to improve.

24

A TROUBLE-SHOOTER'S GUIDE

Patients come to me with a variety of health concerns that are not explicitly discussed in the other chapters of this book. Yet these problems are often extremely important and may pose a serious threat to health or even life.

In an effort to cover some of these issues, I have formulated this "troubleshooter's guide." Like other sections of the book, this medical manual is designed to help you collaborate with your doctor in conducting a preliminary evaluation of your own health, and then deal more intelligently and effectively with him during treatment.

The Urinary Tract

The Question of Incontinence

A patient of mine, who was in his late seventies, was embarrassed at first to describe his problem because he felt that it indicated in some way that he was reverting to childhood.

"I just can't always seem to get to the bathroom fast enough!" he finally blurted. "I sometimes wet my pants!"

HEALTH REPORT

A PROFILE OF PROBLEMS WITH URINATION

A 1988 study reported on the extent of urinary problems in a group of over 1,000 community-living persons, all over seventy-five years of age. Some of the symptoms that the investigators looked for and judged significant were:

- urgency: for example, an inability to suppress the urge long enough for an occupied toilet to become available;
- daytime frequency: a frequency of once in less than two hours;
- nighttime frequency: three or more times per night;
- painful urination: significant current discomfort.

The prevalence of such symptoms was highest in men over eighty-five: 12.5 percent. This figure doubtless reflected the prostate problem. For all ages, 7.8 percent of both sexes had some of these symptoms. Some degree of wetting was reported by 5.3 percent of men and 6.5 percent of women. In addition, 3.5 percent wore daytime protective aids.

C. W. McGrother, C. M. Castleden, H. Duffin, and M. Clarke, "A Profile of Disordered Micturition in the Elderly at Home," *Age and Ageing* 16 (1987): 105.

I explained to him that this problem, which is known appropriately as "urgency," is a common complaint among older people. For one thing, the control signals from our brain centers to our bladders do not work quite as reliably as we get older; also, the bladder may suddenly go into heightened contractions, especially if a person waits too long to head for the bathroom. When the individual finally does get on his feet, he may be a little slower than he once was. This combination can precipitate a crisis, and the bladder may begin to empty before the person reaches the toilet.

In this man's case, the problem was easily solved. At my suggestion, he began to make more frequent trips to the bathroom, even when he did not feel the need to urinate. In that way, he prevented distention and sudden, urgent contraction of his bladder and avoided emergency situations.

HEALTH REPORT

A NONSURGICAL APPROACH TO ENLARGEMENT OF THE PROSTATE

Prostatic enlargement produces obstruction to urination in 75 percent of men past fifty. Each year more than 350,000 prostatectomies (surgery to remove the prostate) are performed. Consequently, there has long been a search for a nonsurgical treatment.

In this 1987 study, nine men with bladder-outlet obstruction were given daily injections of nafarelin, an agent that leads to a decline in male hormone production by the testicles.

The results: The prostate shrank by 25 percent with considerable relief of the symptoms in most of the men. Side effects over the six-month trial included hot flashes and loss of libido and potency.

When the injections were stopped, the prostate gradually grew back to its original size and the complaints returned. This medical treatment has obvious limitations, but it may be applicable to men for whom prostatic surgery cannot be performed.

C. A. Peters and P. C. Walsh, "The Effect of Nafarelin Acetate, a Luteinizing Hormone-Releasing Hormone Agonist, on Benign Prostatic Hyperplasia," *The New England Journal of Medicine* 37 (1987): 599.

To prevent accidents at night, he made it a point to urinate immediately before he went to bed. As an added safety precaution, he placed a portable urinal next to his bed. With these measures, his problems with the embarrassments of urgency were over.

Urgency is just one contributor to urinary incontinence: Another, quite common factor that promotes incontinence can be an overly sedentary life-style. At the extreme, those who are bedridden may become completely incontinent. But if they can get back on their feet and become more physically active, the incontinence often disappears.

A number of forms of damage to the nerve supply controlling urination may also produce incontinence. Hence, this problem may emerge after spinal cord injuries, as a result of nerve degeneration due to diabetes (though this is rare), after operations on the prostate or pelvis, or as an effect of strokes.

A special form of incontinence may be caused by conditions that obstruct and distend the bladder. For example, in men an enlarged prostate gland may press against the opening of the bladder. This means that the bladder needs to exert more pressure to push out the urine. As a result, the bladder may fill up more than it should. If this happens often enough, the bladder may lose its tone and become permanently distended. On occasion, bladders weakened in this way may fill up so much that the urine chronically overflows and incontinence results.

Even more serious, if urine is retained in a distended bladder for too long, infections and damage may occur both to the bladder and to the kidneys. This problem may cause a disease of the kidneys called *hydronephrosis,* a result of obstruction to flow of urine from the kidney. The kidney distention may lead to damage or destruction of kidney tissue. If the underlying cause of this problem is an enlarged prostate—which often is the culprit—the difficulty may be solved by a prostate operation.

A significant number of older people may also experience incontinence when they they become sick, feverish, or overly sedated with drugs. Some of these forms of incontinence disappear entirely after remedial measures are taken, such as changing medications.

In other cases, effective bladder control programs can be established. For example, I have had a great deal of success helping teach paraplegics to evacuate the bladder at regular intervals by pressing with their hands on the lower abdomen. This same technique may be helpful for an older person who has a weak urine stream.

HEALTH REPORT

MORE ON MEDICAL TREATMENT OF THE ENLARGED PROSTATE

Enlargement of the prostate occurs in 30 percent of men in their sixties, and the figure rises to 100 percent of men in their nineties. There are 350,000 prostatectomies (surgical removal of the prostate) each year in the United States, and a medical, nonsurgical alternative to treatment is badly needed.

A new group of drugs, known as *luteinizing hormone-releasing hormone* (LHRH) *agonists,* given by daily injection, produce a 24 percent decrease in prostatic size and also improve urine flow rates. On stopping treatment, the prostate returns to its previous size.

Another approach is the use of drugs that act on nerve endings in the bladder opening and improve urinary flow. One example is the drug prazosin, better known for its use in treatment of high blood pressure. This medication could be used for short-term relief and for those patients not suited for surgery. But how it would work out over the long term remains to be studied.

"Medical Treatment of Benign Prostatic Hyperplasia," *Lancet* 1 (1988): 1083.

The incontinence of other older people may result from alterations in the brain centers that recognize full sensations of the bladder. This is not uncommon after strokes and in Alzheimer's disease or other neurological disorders. But what is often impressive is the reversibility of incontinence, even in these conditions. The individual's motivation can help: Even impaired adults dislike incontinence and want to be helped.

Certainly, the problem of incontinence is annoying and embarrassing, and it does strike many people as they age. But there are simple responses that can often mitigate the problem if patient

and physician can work together to find and apply them. On the
whole, I believe that most people can avoid serious problems and
embarrassments with incontinence if they follow these guidelines:

- Remain physically active
- Know where bathroom facilities are and how to get to them
quickly
- Try to urinate at regular intervals, say every one to two
hours, even if they do not feel a need to do so
- Take medications that control bladder contractions, as prescribed by the physician.

When all else fails, diaperlike devices, disposable pads, and
other devices for urine collection are available.

The Challenge of Cystitis

One of my female patients called to complain about these symptoms:

- Blood in her urine
- A need to get up several times at night to urinate
- Pain or a burning sensation during urination

When she came into the office, a urine examination revealed
that she had *cystitis,* an infection of the urinary bladder. This condition may occur when certain bacteria that are normally limited to
the bowel move into the vaginal area and work their way into the
urinary opening. Sexual intercourse may often be a precipitating
factor. Other common symptoms include a constant need to urinate, a feeling of straining at the end of urination, and a sense that
you cannot completely empty your bladder, no matter how hard
you try.

This problem can be caused when the patient wipes with toilet
paper from the back to the front of the body after a bowel movement or urination. The bacteria from the bowel are then introduced into the opening of the urinary tract.

In my patient's case, I conducted treatment in the classic fashion for cystitis:

- We identified the bacteria involved in the infection by cul-
turing (or growing) a sample of her urine.

- I then prescribed an antibiotic to kill the bacteria.
- I also checked her urine after she had taken the antibiotic for a week or so to be certain that the medication was working.
- Because this patient took the antibiotic for the fully prescribed time period, we soon succeeded in "knocking out the infection."

NOTE: A related disorder, the *urethral syndrome,* also occurs in some women. This syndrome has cystitislike symptoms, though there is no bacterial inflammation of the bladder. The problem typically is due to varying degreees of irritation to the *urethra,* the small channel leading from the bladder to the exterior of the body.

The irritation may arise from the presence of an organism, such as yeast, that invades the urethra only. In some cases, the event that triggers the syndrome is the trauma of sexual intercourse. The usual treatment is to prescribe cortisone for the irritation and an antiyeast medication, such as mycostatin, when yeast is present.

The Pain of Kidney Stones

On many occasions, patients have come to me complaining of terrible, almost unbearable pain in their flank and pelvic regions. Many times, I finally find that the correct diagnosis is a kidney stone.

Stones in the urinary tract are generally referred to as "kidney stones," though actually they may lodge in the bladder and other parts of the urinary tract. Movement of stones is called *renal colic,* which is usually marked by severe pain in the flank, radiating down into the pelvic area. Other symptoms may include some blood in the urine, formed as the painful stone migrates. The pain, as my patients can attest, can be one of the most excruciating experienced by any man or woman. But if you confront this problem, do not despair! With proper treatment, be assured that it will pass.

Of kidney stones, one of my old professors, C. M. Huggins, later to become a Nobel Prize winner, used to say, "The real wonder is why we don't all get kidney stones." He would then note the fact that urine is often a completely saturated solution whose mineral constituents would precipitate out of an equal amount of pure water. The key question is what constituents of the urine prevent this from happening. Unfortunately, the answer to this question is not completely understood, as sufferers from stones well know.

Of course, increasing the dilution of urine helps to prevent precipitation, so doctors typically advocate increased water consumption for those who have ever had an episode of stone formation.

Sometimes, we also find that increased amounts of certain substances are being excreted in the urine. When these are thrown out of solution, they may initiate stone formation. For example, increased amounts of uric acid tend to be formed in gout. The body deals with this by pushing out more uric acid by way of the urine. A frequent outcome is the formation of uric acid stones.

A good treatment response to this uric acid problem is to encourage the patient to take alkalinizing agents such as sodium bicarbonate. As the urine becomes more alkaline, its ability to hold uric acid is greatly increased.

The most frequent constituent of stones is calcium. Calcium in urine is increased by glandular disorders of the thyroid and parathyroid. Interestingly, however, the calcium is reduced by the thiazide group of diuretics. Some of my patients who used to have bouts of kidney stone colic several times a year have gone on diuretics and as a result have been free of the colic for one to two decades.

As a general rule, then, different types of kidney stones require different treatments. Therefore, it is important that anyone who has stone symptoms try to capture the stone when it passes out of the body for a chemical analysis. We often advise patients to pass their urine through cheesecloth with this in mind. The stone is then submitted to a laboratory through the doctor so that its chemistry can be determined.

The big breakthrough in this field most recently has been the discovery of *lithotripsy,* a method of pulverizing stones that has largely replaced the need for an operation. After the doctor locates the site of the stone, the patient is then treated with a machine that generates shock waves focused on the stone. The dissolved stone is then passed out with the urine.

The Lungs

Living with Your Lungs

The health and capacity of your lungs change as you grow older:
With age, lungs typically become less elastic; the total airflow into
and out of the lung (vital capacity) diminishes; and the rate of
oxygen consumption, a key factor in physical endurance, declines.
With these and other changes, there may be an increased tendency
for those over fifty to develop age-related lung problems.

KEY FACTS

SOME CAUSES OF CHRONIC (LONG-LASTING) SHORTNESS OF BREATH

- *Chronic congestive heart failure.*
- *Emphysema,* due to distended, inelastic air sacs of the
lungs.
- *Chronic bronchitis,* often associated with emphysema,
due to obstruction by mucus and inflammation of smaller
bronchi (*bronchioles,* the final tubes in the lungs that lead to the
air cells).
- *Tumors* may obstruct or encroach on the lungs or produce fluid accumulations.
- *Scarring* and *inflammation* in lung tissue, asbestosis (a
chronic inflammation of the lungs often seen in those who
work around asbestos dust), interstitial fibrosis (the growth of
fibrous tissue in the spaces between lung tissue), extensive
tuberculosis.
- *Chronic anemia.*

A patient told me that he had been experiencing episodes of
shortness of breath while he was walking. I examined him thoroughly, including a test with a *spirometer,* a pulmonary function
machine that requires that the patient blow into a container to
demonstrate lung capacity.

After the the results of the checkup came back, it was obvious that in comparison with previous exams, the man had a decline in his lung capacity. The cause was what we doctors classify under the broad general category of *chronic obstructive pulmonary disease* (COPD), a lung impairment that can include components such as emphysema, bronchitis, and variable bronchial spasm, sometimes minimal, other times like those that occur in asthma.

KEY FACTS

SOME CAUSES OF ACUTE (SHORT-TERM) SHORTNESS OF BREATH

● Most common form produced by *exertion* and made worse by poor conditioning, that is, climbing stairs, walking up a grade. Prompt relief comes from resting.

● Due to *bronchoconstriction,* as in asthma. An exercise-induced bronchospasm may be brought on in those with asthmatic tendency. Prompt relief from various inhalers or pills. On the other hand, controlled asthmatics may experience bronchoconstriction with certain medications (for example, beta-blockers).

● *Cardiac origin.* May be produced by an *arrhythmia* (irregular, inefficient heart rate). Also, *congestive heart failure,* leading to lung congestion, may produce acute shortness of breath. A more severe form, which awakens the sleeper at night, is called *paroxysmal nocturnal dyspnea.* Heart-rate regularizers and diuretics often give good relief.

● *Embolus* to lungs. Involves breaking off of a portion of a clot, most often from lower extremities (for example, legs), which then migrates to the lungs and cuts off some of circulation to the lungs.

● *Severe hemorrhage.*

● *Rapid ascent to high altitude.*

● *Nervous stress,* sometimes with hyperventilation. A common complaint: "I can't get a satisfactory breath."

● *Pneumonia.*

The varying shortness of breath this man experienced suggested an important constriction in his *bronchioles,* the small tubes in the lungs that lead to the air cells. To ascertain whether or not this was really his problem, I gave him an inhalant, albuterol (Ventolin), in the office. Almost immediately, his bronchioles opened considerably, and he could breathe more freely. His lung capacity increased in an immediate follow-up test with the spirometer. It was clear that he had an exercise-induced bronchospasm as a prominent cause of his shortness of breath. This is generally more marked in cold weather.

As we age, a number of different kinds of lung problems become increasingly common, and in some cases, they overlap with one another. That is why doctors often lump a person's problem under the COPD label: It is just not clear where one component such as emphysema ends and another begins.

At this point, let me list a few of the possibilities; then I'll give you an overview of the approaches to treatment, which may apply to several of the different lung diseases.

Emphysema

Emphysema is a lung disease that involves obstruction of the airways, characterized by an increase in size of the *alveoli,* the terminal airspaces. As a result, the chest seems overexpanded, but less air is able to flow in and out. Typically, people with emphysema are in the fifty- to seventy-year age range and have symptoms that include shortness of breath, difficulty in breathing, and perhaps a cough. They also may develop heart problems.

The specific cause of this disease is not clear, but factors that contribute to it include the following: cigarette smoking, air pollution, childhood lung infections, and family history of emphysema. (For an idea of the treatments available for emphysema, see the section "More on Prevention and Treatment of Lung Problems," page 491.)

Chronic Bronchitis

Chronic bronchitis, which may become apparent in middle age, results from chronic inflammation of the varied-size bronchial tubes of the lungs.

By medical definition, the chronic form includes these possible signs and symptoms:

• a regular cough on most days at least three months of the year, for more than two consecutive years;

• excessive production of mucus;

• overgrowth and enlargement of the mucous glands in the lung's large airways;

• moderate levels of shortness of breath (dyspnea), especially with physical activity;

• history of recurrent lung infections;

• obesity;

• bloated appearance;

• wheezing.

(For treatments available for bronchitis, see the section "More on Prevention and Treatment of Lung Problems," page 491.)

Pulmonary Embolism

Pulmonary embolism often involves the formation of a clot in a blood vessel, often one in the leg. Then, part of the clot breaks off and travels through the bloodstream until it finally lodges in the lung. There, the clot blocks off blood flow to one degree or another to the lung, and damage of the lung tissue results.

There are an estimated half million occurrences of pulmonary (lung) embolisms each year, and about 10 percent are fatal; that means that about fifty thousand people a year die from this problem.

Conditions that are often associated with pulmonary embolism and may trigger its onset include the following:

• Thrombophlebitis
• Varicose veins
• Extended bed rest or physical immobilization
• Recent surgery
• Heart attack
• Congestive heart failure
• Irregular heartbeats (arrhythmia)

Typical symptoms, which may lead to a diagnosis of pulmonary embolism, involve these possibilities: chest pain, sweating, coughing up of blood, and shortness of breath.

HEALTH REPORT

THE DANGER OF BLOOD CLOTS DURING AIR TRAVEL

This 1988 study in the British medical journal *Lancet* focuses on several cases of clotting in leg veins. The problem is ascribed to sitting for lengthy periods on long airplane trips (three to four hours and sometimes much longer).

Clotting occurs in the relatively immobile legs. Often, the travelers have been in a cramped sitting position and have done little or no moving or walking. A major complication is movement of the clot upstream, where it is finally arrested in the lung. This is known as a *pulmonary embolus* and results in chest pain with difficulty in breathing. Occasionally, such an embolus may prove fatal.

Two of the physician-authors detail their own experiences with thrombosis and embolization associated with air travel. They note that the embolus may occur days or even weeks after the initial leg clotting. To prevent the problem, they advise leg and body exercises, walking, prophylactic aspirin, and avoidance of smoking and alcohol.

[NOTE: Exercises that have worked for me and my patients include wiggling the feet at the ankles, bending the knees, crossing the legs back and forth, and doing light stretching and one-quarter kneebends in the open areas near the exits.]

J. M. Cruickshank, R. Gorlin, and B. Jennet, "Air Travel and Thrombotic Episodes: The Economy Class Syndrome," *Lancet* 2 (1988): 497.

The best approach to this problem is to prevent it. That involves keeping your legs in motion as much as possible, because the legs are a common site for formation of the clots, which can eventually move to the lungs. Common preventive techniques in such settings as long trips involve walking about, or at least moving the legs; avoiding sitting immobilized in one spot more than about fifteen or twenty minutes at a time; wearing elastic stockings; and, when possible, elevating the legs. It can be helpful—under your physician's direction—to take certain drugs if there is a past history or immediate threat of thrombosis (clotting). These include anticoagulants such as warfarin and heparin; antithrombotic agents such as dextran; and antiplatelet drugs, such as aspirin and dipyridamole.

HEALTH REPORT

DOES THE PNEUMONIA VACCINE WORK FOR OLDER PERSONS?

There has been some debate over the years about the effectiveness of pneumonia vaccination. As a result, in an effort to enhance the shot's effectiveness, the number of strains of the pneumonia organism was upped some years ago from fourteen to twenty-three.

There have also been questions as to whether older people react as well as other age groups in the populations to the vaccinations. Some studies have been hampered by the presence of debility and lowered competence in warding off disease in general.

In the present study, all these factors and questions were taken into consideration. The authors concluded that in the normal older person, the pneumonia vaccine has a 70 percent effectiveness, which is at the same level as that seen in younger groups. They also note that the infection is less serious in those with a history of pneumonia vaccination.

R. V. Sims, W. C. Steinmann, J. H. McConville, et al., "The Clinical Effectiveness of Pneumococcal Vaccine in the Elderly," *Annals of Internal Medicine* 108 (1988): 653.

If a clot has already lodged in the lungs, more aggressive therapy may be required. Such therapy may involve the medication streptokinase or urokinase to break up the clots. In addition, when there is a massive pulmonary embolism with hypotension (very low blood pressure), the best response may be an *embolectomy,* or removal of the clot by surgery.

The Threat of Pneumonia

Every year, I treat a number of older patients with pneumonia. Those who are hospitalized, or who are undergoing treatments for chronic diseases in institutions, may contract an especially resistant strain of pneumonia as a secondary disease to their primary health problems. The pneumonia may then become even more of a threat than the original disorder.

Pneumonia is an inflammation of the lungs that may be caused by the *Pneumococcus* organism, or by other bacteria, such as the *Staphylococcus* or *Streptococcus*. This disease may be more frequent in chronic obstructive pulmonary disease (COPD), cancer, alcoholism, or diabetes mellitus or may be a complication of viral respiratory illnesses. So I always keep the possibility of pneumonia in mind when I deal with patients who have these problems. The inflammation may be patchy (bronchopneumonia) or involve a whole segment (lobar pneumonia).

Pneumonia and influenza, taken together, are the leading cause of death by infectious disease and are the fourth most common cause of death overall. As is well known, they often strike in epidemic form.

Symptoms that a number or my patients experience each year include chills, sweating, chest pains, and excessive production of sputum. Those with this disease may experience changes in their mental state varying from mild confusion to outright delirium. There may also be a worsening of other chronic illnesses, such as congestive heart failure or COPD. Rapid breathing and speeded-up heart rate are also signs that point to pneumonia, and a fever, sometimes high or spiking, is fairly common. Less often, in the old and debilitated, there may be virtually no fever.

Treatment of pneumonia is ideally based on the knowledge of the strain of bacteria causing the disease. Several lab tests, including sputum stains, can make that determination. It is customary to start antibiotics at once while awaiting lab test results. Frequently used antibiotics include penicillin, ampicillin, cephalosporin, tetracycline, and erythromycin. For life-threatening pneumonia, other medications and combinations may be given, such as an aminoglycoside, metronidazole or trimethoprim-sulfamethoxazone, perhaps intravenously.

HOW PROTECTIVE IS INFLUENZA IMMUNIZATION?

All patients in an institutional facility were offered influenza immunization. Of these, 181 chose vaccination; 124 refused but were kept under close surveillance.

The results: The overall mortality was 7.2 percent in the vaccinated participants, versus 17.7 percent in the unvaccinated group. In those with positive evidence of influenza infection by blood testing, significant illness was more common in the unvaccinated than the vaccinated.

The researchers concluded that influenza vaccination reduced mortality by 59 percent.

Reference was also made to a previous study in the same facility of deaths from pneumonia during the winter season. This investigation found mortality to be three times higher in the unvaccinated group.

P. A. Gross, G. V. Quinnan, M. Rodstein, et al., "Association of Influenza Immunization with Reduction in Mortality in an Elderly Population," *Archives of Internal Medicine* 148 (1988): 562.

Asthma

Asthma is a disorder characterized by an abnormal response of airways in the lungs to certain forms of stimulation. Specifically, the smooth muscles of the airways constrict and the bronchial tubes narrow. This is often followed by production of mucus and swelling in the bronchial lining, and to further obstruction of airflow.

For many years, asthma has been classified into two groups: (1) *Extrinsic* asthma is associated with external agents, such as pollen, molds, or animal hair, which trigger the attack. Frequently, the person has known nasal hypersensitivity (hay fever) and the asthma is clearly one of a number of allergic reactions. (2) *Intrinsic* asthma, which may come on for the first time in older people, is regarded as a nonallergic condition and may be triggered by such events as a viral infection. Asthma has also been linked to sinusitis (inflammation in the hollow cavities connected to the nose) and nasal polyps, a common late finding in nasal allergies.

Associations, and possible triggering mechanisms, have also

related asthma to other factors. One of these is aspirin. Aspirin sensitivity is a more frequent problem in asthmatics over the age of thirty than it is in younger people. Furthermore, an estimated 4 percent of those with chronic asthma have a history of aspirin sensitivity.

Symptoms of asthma may include wheezing, chronic cough, and shortness of breath on physical exertion. The latest thinking on this subject divides a typical asthmatic attack into two distinct phases, the early and the late.

● *Early phase:* This first stage of an asthma attack begins minutes after an exposure to certain triggering factors. Common factors include pollen, house dust, animal dander, cold air, and infection. The early phase reaches a peak within ten to fifteen minutes and may last for one to two hours. The outward manifestations of the early phase include rapid and readily apparent *bronchospasm,* or contraction of the passageways of the bronchial tubes. There may also be an increased sensitivity of the airways, which produces coughing and sputum.

● *Late phase:* This second asthma-attack phase follows about three to four hours after the first phase. It reaches a peak after five to twelve hours and may continue for hours or even days. The findings in the late phase are swelling of the lining of the bronchial tubes; increased mucous secretions; accumulation of celluar debris, which may show up as particles in the mucus; and even greater sensitivity of the breathing apparatus, with coughing, rough breathing, and worsening discomfort.

The most common treatment for asthma is first to give medications, such as the theophylline group, that open the airways and promote easier breathing. Then, medications from the corticosteroid group, such as cortisone, may be administered to reduce lung inflammation.

More on Prevention and Treatment of Lung Problems

Many times, the severity of various lung diseases can be reduced by simply watching how you conduct your life during times of relatively high risk.

For example, those with any lung problems should stay indoors or otherwise escape during periods when outdoor pollution is high. If you know you have a bad reaction to certain animals, such as cats or horses, take no chances. Stay away from them!

Smoking, as I have already indicated, is unwise for anyone, and doubly unwise for those with any lung problems.

With many chronic obstructive pulmonary diseases, such as emphysema, the use of oxygen at home can be very beneficial. It may promptly relieve shortness of breath. In severe cases when oxygen is necessary, it should usually be administered for a minimum of eighteen hours a day and in some cases should be taken continuously. Although oxygen is regarded as relatively benign, some individuals may find that their respiratory problems actually worsen with it. As a result, it is necessary that the physician monitor the patient's progress regularly.

As for other medications, here are some further thoughts and guidelines:

• *Antibiotics.* To use antibiotics for lung problems, or not? That's a tough question with many facets, a few of which I want to discuss with you now.

As you may have noted, bacterial infection and nonbacterial inflammation (for example, allergic or viral) are variable components of many lung diseases. It is often difficult to decide how much of each is going on in an asthmatic or in an individual who has chronic obstructive pulmonary disease. It is also sometimes hard to know what to do about the "chronic bronchitis" found in many of these disorders.

Another facet of this problem is illustrated by the various viral respiratory disorders, such as the common cold or the "influenza syndrome." So long as the inflammation is ascribed to the virus, our usual antibiotics—which attack bacteria, not viruses—will make no contribution.

HEALTH REPORT

MANAGEMENT OF THE COMMON COLD

A 1987 survey of the common cold in *Advances in Internal Medicine* made these points, which are worth keeping in mind as you are dealing with your own colds:

Colds, along with flu, allergies, and other respiratory illnesses, account for almost one-half of all acute illnesses. Flu is distinguished by higher fever, muscle aches, and weakness.

Allergic illnesses are marked by a personal history of allergy, itchy eyes, profuse nasal dripping, seasonality of onset (for example, summer), and eosinophile cells on a nasal smear.

"Cold preparations are as commonly found in the American home as bread and milk," the authors observe.

Will there ever be a "cure" for the common cold? Colds may be caused by one or more of two hundred virus strains from six virus families: too many viruses make the development of one universally successful vaccine impossible.

How do you catch a cold? Even when an infected patient sneezes directly into a dish, little of the virus can be recovered. So even kissing is unlikely to transmit a common cold! In fact, most transmission is by hand-to-hand transmission of nasal secretions. The virus is recoverable from the hands of 40 to 50 percent of those with colds.

Most colds are mild and uncomplicated, but acute sinusitis occurs in 0.5 percent, and middle ear problems in 2 percent of the general population.

Most cold and cough preparations contain an antihistamine, plus one or more sympathomimetics (decongestants). Antihistamines are effective with allergy, but there is no allergy in the common cold. Still, antihistamines may help by other mechanisms to dry up cold secretions. The sympathomimetics, taken by mouth, provide marginal improvement of cold symptoms. Dextromethorphan and codeine preparations reduce the amount of coughing.

Most folk remedies, including laxatives, are of no value. Possibly garlic will provide some help, as will hot soups and steam vaporizers. One study of zinc lozenges indicated that they have some value.

The majority of colds are self-treated and seldom get to the physician. Perhaps this is why William Osler, father of American medicine, once stated, "There is just one way to treat a cold and that is with contempt."

Osler was also famous for his "hat-trick" remedy: "Go to bed. Hang your hat on a bedpost. Drink whiskey until you see two hats."

T. A. Parino, "Management of the Common Cold," *Advances in Internal Medicine* **32** (1987): 207.

There are probably hundreds of research reports testifying to the fact that courses of antibiotics given to groups such as college students have no impact on the common cold. In fact, some authorities frown on any such use, insisting that prescribing them means that the patients are put at risk for the side effects of the antibiotics, without any gain against the presumed viral infection.

But the matter is not so simple, and one must consider the complexities confronting actual patients. For example, I have had many a reasonably healthy person come in complaining of an obviously serious bacterial sinusitis that was associated with a viral respiratory illness. At some point the simple viral infection had blazed the path for a secondary bacterial invasion.

It may be difficult to determine when the transition to such a sinusitis—or, for that matter, to a bacterial bronchitis—takes place. But there are certain signals: I usually warn my patients that if nasal mucus or phlegm turns from clear or white to yellow or green, a bacterial infection is taking place. At such a point, antibiotics may be advisable. This is especially true if the person has a past history suggesting an ongoing pattern.

An example: A middle-aged woman who consulted me told me that one or more times a year during the respiratory season, she would come down with the common cold. After about a week, she would note increased coughing up of thicker yellow sputum, associated with wheezing. She said, "What's so terrible is that the coughing and wheezing go on for weeks! I just have the most awful colds."

I suggested to her that we might try some prophylactic antibiotics. "Start them early in the course of the cold and we'll see what happens," I advised.

She reported more than once thereafter that "the antibiotics have nipped the whole process in the bud. I don't go on to the bronchitis and the wheezing!"

It was apparent that she suffered from an asthmatoid bronchitis and that the usual sequence from an upper respiratory infection (the familiar URI) to a lower respiratory disorder had been interrupted by the antibiotics.

Many experiences of this kind have made me freer in my use of antibiotics than some others. My notions about the prophylactic use of antibiotics years ago have now become standard practice in surgical services: They are given often as one or two shots prior to the surgery, with demonstrable reduction in postoperative infections.

Not that this point of view is all that new: Studies in Britain more than thirty years ago showed that prophylactic administration of penicillin or other antibiotics to persons with chronic lung disorders through the winter season led to a reduction in hospitalizations for the treated group. Chiefly, this involved the control of pneumonia. So if you run to frequent bacterial complications in your respiratory tract, you may want to discuss with your doctor the applicability of such use of antibiotics.

● *Aerosols,* which dilate the bronchial tubes, can be quite helpful for asthmatics. But very old people sometimes have trouble using them because they require a certain degree of hand strength and coordination. Oral tablets, such as metaproterenol, may then be preferable. Terbutaline is a stronger medication that helps open the tubes, but it may produce tremor in older people.

I would also advise most older patients to avoid ephedrine, another asthma drug, because it may have side effects on the cardiovascular and nervous systems. Furthermore, for men with prostate problems, ephedrine may cause urinary retention.

● *Theophylline* is the most popular drug in the United States for the treatment of asthma. Slow-release products are especially attractive because they can produce their effect over an eight- to twelve-hour period instead of requiring dosages at more frequent intervals.

As might be expected, there are possible side effects: irregular heartbeats, nervousness, changes in blood pressure, and gastrointestinal discomforts. On the whole, it is best to use progressively lower dosages of this drug for each decade after age fifty. Blood levels of theophylline can be checked in evaluating dosage.

● *Steroids* can help with many forms of chronic obstructive pulmonary disease, including asthma. But for older people, the well-known major risks increase: osteoporosis, worsening of cataracts or diabetes, psychiatric disorders, possible peptic ulcers, and aggravation of hypertension. Steroids are preferably given as inhalations, or as single larger doses every forty-eight hours with considerable lessening of the risks.

● *Expectorants* are useful to treat lung problems that involve production of mucus. Hot drinks, and especially herbal teas and broths, can often do as much good as any prescription drug. In addition, potassium iodide may help, though this drug should be avoided by patients who have thyroid disease or a history of iodide intolerance.

• *Over-the-counter cough and cold remedies* can pose risks for older people, and they often help less than advertisers claim.

Antihistamines, for example, should not be used routinely for most viral or bacterial infections in which there is nasal congestion or coughing. True, they have a drying effect on the nasal area, but they may dry out the throat as well and increase the problems in getting rid of sputum. They also tend to produce drowsiness, diminished alertness, retention of urine, and constipation. These drugs may even cause slower heart rates and trigger glaucoma.

Drugs such as phenylephrine, pseudoephedrine, and phenyl-propanolamine—which reduce mucus production—may work in limited doses. But if used regularly, they may lessen appetite or promote addiction. Older people with hypertension, vascular disease, or prostate problems should avoid these drugs.

Cough suppressants should be used only sparingly, under a physician's guidance, by older people who have chronic lung obstruction problems. These drugs may decrease ease of breathing and may also cause dizziness, constipation, and drowsiness.

Infectious Diseases

Shingles

After infections of the respiratory tract, the second most important viral infection among older people is *Herpes zoster,* or shingles.

When one of my savvy patients came in with symptoms of this disease, and I told him what he had, he immediately responded, "You mean at my age I've got chickenpox!" I was surprised because most people do not know there is a connection between shingles and chickenpox. But in fact, it is quite true that the diseases are produced by indistinguishable viruses.

Shingles, though, has different manifestations. Sensory nerves come under attack in shingles to produce pain and inflammation along the course of the nerve. On the other hand, about one-third of patients with this disease experience little or no pain.

When the pain—which my patient described in a classic fashion—does occur, it has a stabbing, burning, or boring-in quality and can be excruciating. Sometimes, the pain is felt even before the typical shingles eruption on the skin occurs.

HEALTH REPORT

AN EFFECTIVE TREATMENT FOR SHINGLES

In a study reported in 1986 in the *British Medical Journal,* 100 patients over sixty with shingles (herpes zoster) were treated with acyclovir (Zovirax), administered in dosages of 800 mg five times a day. Another 105 patients received a placebo (inert) medicine.

When treatment was started within forty-eight hours, acyclovir led to a more rapid healing of the rash, and a more rapid diminution in pain. The lessening of pain was more noteworthy in those with the most severe pain. In this latter group, 40 percent had no pain, or only mild pain, at the end of treatment. In the placebo group, all had residual moderate or severe pain.

M. W. McKendrick, J. I. McGill, J. E. White, and M. J. Wood, "Oral Acyclovir in Acute Herpes Zoster," *British Medical Journal* 293 (1986): 1529.

The skin eruption is limited to the course of the underlying nerve. As a result, there is a stripelike appearance to the eruption, characterized by angry red patches covered with tiny blisters. The involved skin may be so sensitive that even the pressure of clothing is intolerable.

The pain and duration of shingles vary from patient to patient. When severe and protracted, the disease may interfere with sleep and sap the patient's morale. Generally, however, it runs its course in a couple of weeks, though strong medications may be required during this period to diminish pain and allow sleep. Most people who have had shingles agree with my patient: "There's nothing quite like it, and I never want to have it again!"

In about 20 percent of cases involving older people—but fortunately, not my patient—the eyelids and eye are involved. When they are, it is essential to consult an eye specialist as well as the family doctor. One severe complication after the disease is a *neuralgia,* or pain along the nerve lasting more than a month after the outbreak of the disease.

The usual treatment for simple shingles is the use of wet compresses (such as Burow's solution) on the affected area and also mild analgesics. Some physicians prescribe the antiviral drug acyclovir, and others favor corticosteroids as a first-line drug. Both have been shown to shorten the course of the disease and reduce the complications. Sometimes, oral narcotics may be required to reduce pain. With more complex cases, including the neuralgia that may follow as a complication, corticosteroid drugs, such as prednisone, may be necessary.

Overall, the outlook, with treatment, is fairly good: About 70 percent of older people diagnosed or treated at a medical center return to their original good health after eight weeks. About 90 percent of those under sixty return to their original state of health. Others may experience lingering complications of various degrees and types, such as neuralgia.

There are no immunizations currently available for this disease, and most older people are susceptible to it because of their previous chickenpox infections. Because immune responses begin to decline with age, at a critical point those who had chickenpox in childhood suffer a recurrence: The long-latent virus flares up from its hiding place in nerve cells. Yet it does not seem to be terribly "catching," and most adults need have no fear of contracting shingles from an infected person at any stage.

25

THE PROSPECTS FOR SEX AFTER FIFTY

As we get older, our sexual powers decline, but a loving spouse can do wonders to maintain an exciting emotional *and* physical relationship. I have seen many married couples who, as they age, make marvelous adaptations to the changes in their sexuality. Others, like Charlie and Sue, may need a little help.

During a counseling session, this couple, who were in their early sixties, told me, in a somewhat embarrassed way, that they were running into some problems in their sex life. Specifically, Charlie had been experiencing difficulty getting an erection. And Sue's vagina tended to remain dry much longer than it had when she was younger.

I first asked Charlie whether he ever noticed that he had an erection when he got up to go to the bathroom at night or when he woke up in the morning. He replied, "Many times," a response, as I explained to him, that indicated that he had no organic problem with impotence. Then I questioned Sue and learned that her

HEALTH REPORT

THE NATURE OF SEXUAL RELATIONSHIPS AFTER FIFTY

Sexual feelings for many elderly men and women endure despite all the family and cultural negatives and may continue into the nursing home.

The oldest couple treated at the Masters & Johnson Institute was a ninety-three-year-old man and his eighty-eight-year-old wife. At the author's clinic (Loyola of Chicago) 20 percent of the couples were over fifty and 20 percent over sixty-five.

After age fifty changes that may be expected in women are reduced lubrication and lessened vaginal elasticity. Men may expect delayed and partial (less high) erections, reduced fluid and force of ejaculation, more rapid detumescence after orgasm, and longer refractory period before the next capability.

In the Duke University study 70 percent of sixty-eight-year-old men and 25 percent of octogenarian men regularly had intercourse. So did the majority of women in their seventies, if they had an active partner.

The normal sexual decline in the male can be helped with more prolonged foreplay and genital caressing. Women with reduced lubrication may benefit from hormones or bland vaginal lubricants.

There are also a variety of constructive approaches that can help with sexual performance in the presence of arthritis, alcoholism, cardiac disease, and stroke. Even in the presence of diabetes and its organic changes, sexual therapy has helped reverse impotence.

Finally, drugs may be an obstacle to sexual performance: Some tranquilizers and hypnotics cause partial erections, delayed ejaculations, or impotence.

D. C. Renshaw, "Sex, Age, and Values," *Journal of the American Geriatrics Society* 33 (1985): 635.

vagina did eventually become lubricated in some sexual encounters, but it took a long time. "Also, I just don't get turned on like I once did," she said.

My treatment suggestions for these two were rather simple: I told Charlie that he probably could not expect to be as sexually active as he was when he was younger, because male sexual performance does tend to decline with age, but that did not mean he could not have a good sex life. The best solution for his problem emerged in our discussions: His wife would try manual massage with a lubricant to encourage an erection, an approach they had not attempted as yet.

As for Sue, I prescribed a vaginal cream containing estrogen, which she had been taking orally since menopause. This would serve as a lubricant for her dry vagina. I also prescribed a brief course of quite small doses of the hormone testosterone, which has proved beneficial in increasing the sexual drive of many older women.

The final report I received from them a couple of weeks later was total success. Both were enjoying their relationship and their sex life more than ever.

Be Realistic

The keys to a happy and successful sex life in the later years are realistic expectations and a sound personal philosophy of the sexual relationship.

It is most important to think preeminently of *quality,* not quantity. I see very little merit in the man who is a sexual acrobat, capable of considerable sexual feats, especially when his wife tells me he wears her out or, worse, is not loving. Men who have intercourse with their wives at far less frequent intervals but who are warm and affectionate, both in and out of bed, have a far better sex life, at least to my mind.

At any age sex is an interaction that mirrors the underlying relation, not an isolated event occurring without any context. Great sex can occur once a week—or even far less often—yet be full of tenderness and sweetness. Routine sex, on the other hand, though performed more often, may remain devoid of the necessary emotional charge.

A word of caution is in order at this point: The following facts and figures relating to the quantitative decline of sex with aging will not always be accompanied by those additional qualities that infuse good sexuality. For example, the erections reported in a scientific sleep laboratory—where responses during sleep are observed and analyzed—are biological facts, not necessarily related to affection and love. What the sleep laboratory cannot measure is the psychologic energy of a human sexual relationship. This is the higher sexual pathway that originates in the brain in response to all the meanings of a good relationship.

Interestingly, the emotional component as reported by many couples may make for better erections and much more satisfactory intercourse, even when the sleep lab reports an overt aging decline! The reason for this discrepancy is fairly obvious: Life, living, and sex are not conducted in a lab. The sexuality of the real world flows from a hug, a kiss, a flood of memories and feelings. These are the essence of love at all ages. They charge up the sexual act, and they transcend the confines of the laboratory.

With this perspective in mind, let's turn now to some specifics about sexual performance in the later years:

The Sexual Changes in Women

The menopause, of course, is clear-cut and unmistakable. Monthly periods cease, and there may be a succession of uncomfortable associated changes, such as the familiar hot flushes, sweats, and sometimes minor depression and nervousness.

Because the female hormones tend to plump up the skin and produce some water retention in it, loss of the hormones following menopause may make some women's skin look older. Another quite common complaint is of increasing vaginal dryness and a decreased capacity to lubricate with sexual stimulation.

In addition, the passage of the years may produce some atrophy of the vaginal lining, as it becomes thinner and more delicate. Where hormone deprivation in the vagina is great, all the structures, including the vaginal outlet, seem to shrink and contract. Fortunately, however, we have a quick and reliable answer to all this: The female sexual hormones, available in a variety of pills and in various combinations, prevent all these changes.

HEALTH REPORT

SEXUAL PROBLEMS AND SOLUTIONS IN THE LATER YEARS

According to a 1987 study of a group of women aged forty-five to sixty-nine, 7 percent of the younger women and 31 percent of the older women reported lack of sexual interest.

Several studies agree that there is a decline, sometimes dramatic, in sexual interest in the years after menopause. In one novel investigation, for example, a researcher studied a group of 250 women in Lagos, Nigeria. By nine years after menopause, almost 70 percent were sexually inactive, and they reported that about 50 percent of their sexual partners were experiencing difficulties.

Women past menopause report decreased lubrication and lessened sexual responsiveness and orgasm. They may also experience pain during intercourse. These results arise from declining blood supply and shrinkage in the genital area, but they can be reversed by hormone administration.

Painful uterine contractions sometimes lasting for hours after orgasm are experienced by some postmenopausal women, especially in the sixty- to seventy-year group. This may leave women with a fear of sexual intercourse, but the pain responds well to hormone treatment.

P. M. Sarrel, "Sexuality in the Middle Years," *Obstetric and Gynecology Clinics of North America* 14 (1987): 49.

The Sexual Changes in Men

In men there is no change comparable to the menopause, though there once was talk about a "male menopause." Cases of aging men with diminished sexual drive and capacity, which allegedly could be helped by injections of the male hormones, were described.

Probably most of thse cases were really cases of depression. Some aging men find themselves facing a loss of their original

HEALTH REPORT

THE EFFECTS OF AGE ON MALE POTENCY

The original Kinsey report noted that male sexual capacity, as determined by the number of ejaculations over a defined time period, peaks in the mid to late teens. This ability starts declining in the twenties and thirties and goes down to virtually zero in the eighties and nineties.

One of this group of investigators later reported impotence increases to 8 percent by fifty-five, 20 percent by sixty-five, and 40 percent by seventy-five. The increases in impotence did not necessarily result in a loss of self-esteem or feelings of sexual failure.

There is no decline in blood levels of testosterone (male hormone) over this time period. However, a few other studies have shown some decline with aging, though probably this is of no relevance to the marked age-related decline in sexual activity.

There are slight changes in the semen from youth to old age, but these are not major, and old men are therefore capable of becoming fathers.

The manufacture of testosterone and of sperm is governed by the pituitary gland at the base of the brain. Though there have been slightly variable results reported by different investigators, there seem to be no significant changes in the hormone from the pituitary, which governs the making of testosterone, or in the follicle stimulating hormone (FSH), which governs sperm production.

These findings may be contrasted with those for females who experience ovarian failure that leads to the menopause. This event produces a large rise in the FSH, which soars to fifteen times normal levels and which is associated with the characteristic hot flush.

P. D. Tsitouras, "Effects of Age on Testicular Function," *Endocrinology and Metabolism Clinics* 16 (1987): 1045.

hope for their careers, of their anticipated achievement of economic security, of their expectations of marriage, or of what their offspring will produce. When these hopes are dashed, that can lead to depression. And certainly, one of the major impacts of depression is a decline in sexuality.

Virtually all of the men I see in the older age brackets have sufficient male hormones, as judged by blood tests. They may be statistically at a somewhat lower level than those of younger men, especially past age seventy. But it is exceptionally rare to find an aging man whose testosterone levels are really low and for whom shots of male hormone might be appropriate.

On the contrary, many older men still possess at least an average amount of the hormone. Indeed, it can be readily demonstrated in many of them that they are still making sperm. In short, as far as the function of the testes is concerned, there is no cutoff as there is with the women's ovaries in menopause.

On the other hand, there is a decline in male sexual performance with age. As was pointed out by Kinsey and his co-workers in their classic work of forty years ago, male sexual performance seems to peak at around age twenty. Then, slowly but surely, it tends to decline in the following decades.

When I hear about some older man with an alleged fountain-of-youth sex life, I often respond this way: "Show me a man of fifty or sixty who claims to have the same sexual powers as he did when he was twenty, and I'll show you a man who is not telling the truth, the whole truth, and nothing but the truth!" This is not to say that he may not be enjoying sex as much, or even more, then he did in youth. But all the evidence from various surveys repeatedly emphasizes that performance capability slowly runs down with age.

Students of the subject—mostly males—stress that sexual performance in the male is much more complicated and more taxing than in the female. The fact is that an erection involves bodily machinery that is far from completely understood. The automatic responsiveness that one sees in the male of such species as the dog, the cat, the horse, the bull, or other familiar animals simply is not present in the human.

What are the differences? Not only do psychologic factors such as depression, worry, and boredom operate in crucial ways in humans, but important unknown factors may enter the scene as well.

The fact is that we still do not understand all the neurovascular (nerve and blood flow) mechanisms that are involved. During an erection, the smaller arteries have to open up, and outflow through the veins has to shut down. This complex mechanism may not always work quite right, and even a slight malfunction can leave some men fuming over erections that are not rigid enough, or are not maintained long enough, or are not frequent enough to satisfy them and their partner.

The celebrated team of Masters and Johnson made other observations on male sexual function as related to aging. Some of the characteristic declines that they found with aging were the following:

- The male requires a longer time to reach erection and may require greater stimulation, such as manual stimulation.
- Once response to stimuli has occurred, the erection may be somewhat less rigid.
- The erection may start to wilt earlier than has been customary with that individual.
- The spurts of semen produced in the orgasm diminish.
- The latency period, which is the time from orgasm to the next erection, may be much prolonged in the aging male. Younger males may have multiple erections and orgasms in a single sexual encounter; there may perhaps be only minutes during which they cannot achieve an erection. But with aging, many hours may go by in which even maximum stimulation will not produce an erection.

It is obvious when you look over these data that a lot of other basic changes are occurring in the erection mechanism with aging. To some extent, psychologic factors will always be at work. Men of almost any age who have experienced a failure to have an erection often find that at the next sexual opportunity, their fears hamper their ability to perform.

Still, it is quite clear that the increasing decline in potency that occurs with age is far too widespread to be explainable simply on a psychological basis. After all, many men perform perfectly and competently over a long period of time, and they may not experience any unusual stresses or emotional pressures. Yet they find as they get older that they cannot perform at their former frequency.

What May Cause Impotence?

Here is a checklist of some of the factors that I have discovered in my practice as possible causes of impotence in men. Some have already been mentioned; others have not yet been touched on; all should be kept in mind as possible sources of declining sexual performance.

• *Aging.* As we have already seen, one of the major accompanying changes of aging is a decline in sexual capacity. According to Kinsey, there is a 2 percent impotence rate at forty, 18 percent at sixty, and 25 percent at sixty-five. Another study has reported a 31 percent incidence of impotency in the fifty-five- to fifty-nine-year age group.

• *Depression.* In a highly competitive materialistic society, where the rules of the game ensure failure for a majority, it is common for depression to plague many men who are middle-aged or older. Depression erodes libido, and there is evidence that it may do so via diminished testosterone and even thyroid secretions.

Psychotherapy and antidepressants may be required to relieve this situation. Testosterone may act both as a supplement and as a powerful placebo (inert substance) in some clinical situations.

• *Drugs.* A variety of drugs impair sexual performance. There are well-known ones, such as the ganglionic blocking agents used to treat hypertension. Impotence may be a side effect of many other drugs as well, including the following: barbiturates, tranquilizers, reserpine, narcotics, and excessive alcohol. One of my patients regularly complained of impotence when he was prescribed standard doses of amphetamines.

The solution to this problem: If your health permits and your doctor agrees, suspect drugs should be temporarily withdrawn or alternatives found.

• *Diabetes.* This is the classic metabolic disorder that can produce impotence. The nerves may be involved, for example, with demonstrative degenerative changes in the nerve terminals in the penis. Usually, this diagnosis becomes even clearer if the impotence is accompanied by nerve-related bladder disturbances or disease of the nerves in the legs or peripheral areas. The usual prescriptions here include regulation of diabetes and high vitamin intakes.

KEY FACTS

NOCTURNAL ERECTIONS IN LATER LIFE

Erections during sleep, known medically as *nocturnal penile tumescence* (NPT), occur repeatedly during the night throughout the life cycle of the sleeping healthy male. Generally, the erection occurs in association with dreaming, as manifested by rapid eye movement (REM). Changes in the erections in various age groups of normal men are reported in a 1988 article based on observations in a sleep laboratory:

• Total episodes of NPT decreased progressively over the decades and were about half as frequent in the oldest (age sixty to seventy-three) as compared with the youngest (twenty-three to twenty-nine) men. The two groups had 2.4 and 4.3 episodes, respectively.

• Total duration of erection in sleep was on the order of 195 minutes in the youngest, versus 94 minutes in the oldest.

• The fullness of the erection diminished progressively, from the oldest to youngest group.

• The rigidity of the erection was judged by visual inspection and photographs. These observations revealed that 96.7 percent of the men under sixty had full erections. In contrast, five of the nine men in the sixty- to seventy-three-year-old age group did not have full erections, though they reported having intercourse on a regular basis. (Interviews with the subjects and their wives accounted for the apparent discrepancy in these last findings: Manual stimulation enabled the older men, with less than satisfactory erections, to achieve penetration and satisfactory ejaculation.)

R. C. Schiavi and P. Schreiner-Engel, "Nocturnal Penile Tumescence in Healthy Aging Men," *Journal of Gerontology* 43 (1988): M146.

HEALTH REPORT

DIABETES AND IMPOTENCE

One of the troublesome complaints of diabetics is the early onset of impotence. This appears to be due to a combination of blood vessel changes and disorders involving the nerves to the penis.

Failure to have erections during the night, on awakening, or on masturbation indicates that the impotence has an organic, not a psychologic, basis.

To correct the problem, drug therapy is being investigated: One possibility is papaverine, which, when injected into the base of the penis, may produce a prompt and durable erection. But this medication has a number of complications over the long term.

An old drug, yohimbine, has been found helpful in 30 to 40 percent of cases.

There are also a number of vacuum devices that produce penile engorgement; a rubber band may also have to be applied to the penis.

The most widely used devices are implants into the penis, which have at least 90 percent success rate. Approximately 50,000 diabetics have been given implants.

E. D. Whitehead, "Diabetes-Related Impotence and Its Treatment in the Middle-Aged and Elderly," *Journal of the American Geriatrics Society* 42 (1987): 77.

● *Endocrine disorders.* Possible gland-related causes of impotence include hypothyroidism, hyperthyroidism, hypoadrenalism, hyperadrenalism, and hypopituitarism. As a rule of thumb, it seems that any endocrine disorder that produces menstrual disturbances in the female may adversely affect male sexual performance.

● *Vascular (blood vessel) and neural (nerve) impairments.* Impairment in the neurovascular pathways concerned in erection is not always easy for a doctor to detect. In one impotence-producing condition, *Leriche's syndrome,* patients have a history of intermittent claudication (periodic pains and cramps) in the thigh or other muscles. Or neural (nerve) pathways may be destroyed in pelvic surgery, including colectomy (removal of the colon) and perineal prostatectomy (prostate operation). Accidents involving the vessels in the head, multiple sclerosis, and other degenerative nerve disorders may also produce impotence.

• *Chronic progressive, or wasting diseases.* Impotence is often a by-product of other serious diseases. Successful treatment of those diseases frequently cures the impotence.

Age-Related Sex Problems

During my years of practice, I have encountered a wide variety of sexual problems and complaints. Some of them have been quite serious, such as those rooted in physical incapacity. Others have been relatively easy to handle with practical advice.

When impotence is relatively advanced, and perhaps accompanied by nerve damage, it still may be possible for a man to have an erection by using certain assisting devices.

One of these is the *vacuum assistive device,* a simple mechanism placed over the penis so that a vacuum is produced. The result is a slow, progressive filling of the penis with blood, so that the organ can then attain an acceptably rigid state. A couple of rubber bands at the base of the device are usually slipped over the penis and secured at its base. The bands prevent a runoff from the engorged penis, and satisfactory intercourse becomes possible.

A more familiar device is the permanently implanted *prosthesis,* a rigid or flexible rod inserted into the penis in an operative procedure. This has the drawback of producing a permanent rigidity, which some consider obtrusive. The most popular version permits the device to be bent down or up, as needed. It is thus less likely to be noticeable.

Many times, though, it is not necessary to resort to these artificial devices. For many men, the most important point to remember is the fundamental fact that the male erection is not an all-or-nothing phenomenon, so less drastic means may be used to produce an erection.

For example, manual stimulation, as Charlie and Sue practiced it, may do wonders to firm up a less than total erection. Here, again, love and affection are the bywords.

From a purely mechanical viewpoint, a lubricant is usually necessary for effective manual stimulation of the penis. And remember: It almost always takes longer for the aging male to attain a full erection than it does for a youth.

Another important consideration is timing. Things may be much smoother—and sexier—in the morning after a refreshing sleep, than at night, when the day has been long, frustrating, and tiresome. Relaxation is extremely important to successful sexual performance. I have even known a few businessmen whose sexual interest and activity were almost entirely limited to their vacations. Naturally, I advised more frequent vacations!

Of course, relaxation and a little playfulness are important, and a mutual shower may help in this regard. Other couples like to engage in mutual massage. I have found that women, in particular, are more responsive when their husbands give them a little rubdown before beginning to engage in sex.

Older women also tend to find that arousal and lubrication of the vagina are slower, especially if they are not taking estrogen. There are exceptions, of course: One sixty-five-year-old, who had come in to see me with her husband, surprised me when I began to talk to them about their sex life: "I'm an instant lubricator!" she said. I thought she might be boasting, but her husband immediately confirmed her statement.

When an older woman is not taking hormones, there tends to be shrinkage in the entire vaginal area. This, together with diminished lubrication, may make for some difficulty and even pain in intercourse. As I recommended to Sue, lubricants are very useful to correct this problem, and they may also be desirable for women who are having estrogen therapy. Sometimes I prescribe a vaginal cream containing a hormone.

If a woman complains of a lack of sexual drive in the later years, I may prescribe small doses of the male hormone testosterone. Interestingly, this approach can restore sexual interest and response, though the doses have to be kept well below the level at which a masculine effect, such as increased body hair, can be observed. Furthermore, the increase in libido often persists after the medication is discontinued. The male hormone can also be given in an ointment locally, if desired.

To sum up, then, sexuality, like other basic functioning of the body, undergoes changes over the life span. Understanding what is normal about these transformations is important: Too often, people panic and say, "It's over, all over! I'm old before my time!" But for most people, that is simply not true! Rather, some adaptations and perhaps a few visits to the doctor may be all that is needed to open the door to a satisfying and successful sex life in the later years.

HEALTH REPORT

BRIDGING THE GAP BETWEEN SEXUAL INTEREST AND PERFORMANCE

The authors of a 1988 article in the *Journal of the American Geriatrics Society* note that "the frequency of sexual intercourse declines dramatically with aging." But even though less than 15 percent of men of eighty report having sexual intercourse, more than 50 percent retain sexual interest.

The progressive gap between ability and desire has been referred to as the "libido-potency gap." Numerous studies indicate that it is not a male hormone decline that is responsible for this phenomenon, but complex factors involving the nerve and blood supply.

Expert observers note a decline in rigidity that gradually progresses to an inability to have an erection, even during sleep, dreaming, or masturbation. On the other hand, the psychologic factors that may inhibit a young male are seldom prominent in the elderly.

An encouraging development has been the prompt erectile response produced by certain agents injected into the penis. A number of externally applied devices and penile implants also make successful intercourse possible for many elderly couples.

T. Mulligan and P. G. Katz, "Erectile Failure in the Aged: Evaluation and Treatment," *Journal of the American Geriatrics Society* 36 (1988): 54.

Above all, if you see you have a problem, do not let it go unresolved. You should realize by now that a lot of progress has been made in this area. There are more answers around than you probably dreamed existed, so take advantage of them!

The Prostate

When a sixty-eight-year-old patient told me he had been experiencing a weak stream when he was urinating, I immediately suspected he had a prostate problem. Dribbling or difficulty in urinating in an older man is a characteristic symptom of an enlarged *prostate,* which is a small, pecan-size organ situated next to the bladder, where urine is stored.

The majority of older men eventually have prostate problems, and about 350,000 a year have to undergo prostate surgery. Eventually, my patient had to have this operation too.

The prostate wraps around the urethra, the channel for the passage of urine from the body. During sexual activity, the prostate secretes a fluid that helps transport sperm. When the prostate becomes enlarged with age, urination may become difficult and a variety of infections and other disorders may make it necessary to operate or otherwise treat the problem. Your doctor will usually check for a prostate enlargement when you come in for a regular exam by probing your rectum with a glove-encased finger.

Some of the health problems that arise in the prostate include the following:

• *Enlarged prostate.* This condition, which is called *benign prostatic hypertrophy* (BPH), results from the development of benign (noncancerous) tumors that grow inside the prostate. Eventually, the enlargement may obstruct the flow of urine, and surgery may become necessary.

Recently, progress has been made in the medical treatment of this condition with the drugs nafarelin acetate and leuprolide (see the box on p. 477). Given in daily injections in experimental treatments, these drugs shrank the prostate gland significantly over a six-month period. During the treatment, all the participants who were sexually active became impotent, and some also had hot flashes. But their sexual functioning returned to normal when the drug was discontinued.

• *Acute prostatitis.* This refers to a bacterial infection of the gland. Symptoms include chills, fever, painful or difficult urination, and pain in the lower back and between the legs. Antibiotics usually clear up this condition quite well.

• *Chronic prostatitis.* This recurring infection generally has less severe symptoms than the acute type. The symptoms resemble those of acute prostatitis: bladder inflammation, frequency of urination, and discomfort in urinating. There may be aching in the perineum, the area between the scrotum and the rectum. Because of the innumerable tubules that the prostate comprises, the infection may persist despite extensive use of antibiotics.

It is hard to treat some forms of chronic prostatitis because the problem may not be due to obvious bacteria, which can be eliminated with an antibiotic. Sometimes, a physician massages the prostate to release fluids that build up with the infection. The so-called prostatic regimen consists of daily hot sitz baths and avoidance of alcohol, spices, and sexual overstimulation.

• *Cancer of the prostate.* This subject has been dealt with in chapters 17 and 18. A malignancy of the prostate generally stays localized in the early stages and is not life-threatening. The cancer tends to spread rather slowly. It is important to have a rectal exam during your regular annual checkups because the hard nodule of prostatic cancer can be felt fairly early. Despite slow growth, cancer of the prostate can eventually spread to other parts of the body.

What impact does a prostate problem, including prostate surgery, have on a person's sex life?

As I have already indicated, sexuality can be interrupted with certain drugs that may be used to treat an enlarged prostate, but this result is temporary. Radical surgery on the prostate may damage nerves in the pelvis that are involved in producing erections. This damage may result in impotence.

In the most common operative procedure for prostatic hypertrophy, that performed through the penis and known as a *transurethral resection* (TUR), there is no risk of damage to crucial nerves. Nonetheless, some men complain of decline in sexual capacity afterward.

Perhaps the major cause of such reduced sexual drive and desire is psychological: A man may feel inadequate because he assumes that somehow he is not "a complete man" or that an important part of him is "missing."

But in general, without this psychological component, the usual surgery on the prostate does not interfere with sexual functioning or potency.

Menopause and the Estrogen Issue

There are several schools of thought, both in lay and medical circles, regarding the use of estrogens in the menopause.

One school is the *reluctant* one: If the flushes and sweats and other discomforts that may accompany this transition time of life are very trying, then perhaps you should use estrogens. The idea of those who advocate this viewpoint is to use the lowest efficacious doses, and as soon as the symptoms are controlled, to begin tapering and then discontinuing the hormones.

Another school is the *all-natural* one: The cessation of ovarian activity at around age fifty is a "natural" occurrence, and conversely, it is "unnatural" to tamper with the body at this time. By definition, any reintroduction of female hormones after they have been lost is a "tampering" with nature's decree. So one should tolerate the flushes and sweats: They will eventually pass. Or if it is really necessary, a woman might use a "natural" substance, such as vitamin E, which in larger doses (perhaps 800 IU or so per day) seems to be helpful.

A third school is the *watch-out-for-danger* one: Continued use of estrogens raises the possibility of cancer of the lining of the uterus (endometrium) and thus illustrates the dangerous side of hormonal administration. We know that malignant conditions did occur some twenty years ago when estrogens alone (without progestin) were freely prescribed for control of menopause symptoms.

What is my position? I believe it is now thoroughly clear that the benefits of hormone administration are considerable. Furthermore, the so-called risks vanish when *both* the female hormones, estrogen *and* progestin, are correctly used. As I discuss the pros and cons with my patients who are entering menopause, I generally advise that it is well worth their while to use estrogen-progestin therapy.

Those who oppose this type of therapy may simply be overlooking the fact that all sorts of problems and dangers can arise from our given physical makeup. Many people, for example, have a terrible predisposition to collect cholesterol deposits in their arteries. This disorder causes half of the deaths in our society through heart attacks and strokes. Yet every physician dealing with human disease knows that such natural developments must often be fought off, and that the earlier the fight is joined through appropriate drugs and other means, the better.

The loss of estrogen during menopause is another natural development that is frequently best dealt with through medical means. Osteoporosis is a prime example of how many women need extranatural help to compensate for their loss of this hormone. As soon as women enter the menopause, calcium starts to drain from their bones, a process that cannot be corrected by taking calcium tablets. Indeed, the only known natural agent that prevents this is the female hormone. Is there any logical reason why physicians and patients should stand by while a woman's skeletal structure is being irreparably damaged?

It is also now amply clear that women possess a great natural advantage up until the menopause that reduces their risk of heart attacks and strokes, in comparison with men. This advantage, which disappears with menopause, can be restored through the administration of estrogen. Women so treated will have less life-threatening vascular events than women not so treated.

As for the cancer problem associated with estrogen use, the best studies reveal that endometrial cancer does not increase—and indeed, may be reduced—when estrogen and progestin are given in cyclic fashion. The same can be said of breast cancer, with the possible exception of that in women whose families have a very high incidence of this disease. In women with the usual family background, however, it now seems likely that breast cancer may even be slightly less prevalent when there is proper hormone treatment.

Other advantages of estrogen therapy also have to be considered: Atrophy of the genital tract through a lack of estrogen in women may lead not only to sexual difficulties but to an increase in the unpleasant condition known as *stress* incontinence. In this situation, laughing, coughing, or rises in pressure within the abdomen lead to the forcing out of urine, a potentially embarrassing and annoying event. Other hormone treatments can help correct this tendency.

Finally, many women notice that they "feel better" when they use the female hormone, a vague description that may nevertheless describe a very true happening. In some women, there may even be a lifting of depression.

I freely admit that not all doctors agree with my point of view. Furthermore, I certainly agree that any choice in this area must be the individual's decision, made in consultation with her doctor. I do not deny that there are some drawbacks to estrogen-progestin therapy, including the nuisance of continued menstrual cycles and a tendency toward spotting and staining. Your doctor may also decide that if you have large fibroids or fibrocystic breast disease, you are not a candidate for continued hormonal therapy. Finally, there will always be a need for ongoing medical supervision with estrogen therapy.

In any event, whatever you decide about the estrogen issue, when you enter the menopause, you automatically have a medical problem. As a result, your response to this necessary, inevitable transition time of life should be discussed thoroughly with your doctor.

26
THE MATURING OF THE MIND AND EMOTIONS

When one of my female patients consulted me one day, she was obviously upset. She said that at breakfast that morning, she had thought of something that was in the bedroom. She then got up and went into the bedroom, but when she got there, she realized she had forgotten what it was she had gone there for. Try as she might, the reason kept eluding her.

Soon she became annoyed and unsettled because this sort of forgetfulness seemed to be increasing in her life, even though she had never experienced anything quite like it when she was younger.

"That's some hours ago now," she told me. "And I *still* don't know why I walked over to the bedroom."

In addition to these forgetful episodes, she said that in recent months she had been harboring a feeling that her "mind might be going," though she could not tell me exactly why she felt that way. One of her worries, she said, was that she might be developing

Alzheimer's disease, the mental deterioration that had already stricken another member of her family.

In examining her, I evaluated some basic points, including her reflexes and her blood pressure. I also checked her recent and remote memory. I asked her some basic-intelligence questions, such as whether she could subtract sevens from a hundred serially. And I checked whether she could state the meaning of statements like "A rolling stone gathers no moss" or "A bird in the hand is worth two in the bush."

When she had passed all these tests with flying colors, I assured her that she was not suffering from Alzheimer's. In fact, I said, "You've experienced a common event, a kind of forgetfulness often first noted in the forties or fifties. Of course, this kind of absentmindedness may occur at a much younger age for some people. But in any case, it's not a forerunner to a decline in either memory or other brain functions."

Twenty years have passed since I examined this woman, and we can still joke about her worries. Her age at the time of the memory lapse? She was only forty-six.

How Can We Expect Our Minds to Mature?

I think a majority of those I meet, in or out of my offices, believe that personality change, memory loss, and severe declines in other intellectual functions are inevitable with aging. Yet these expectations are not in accord with the facts.

For example, at the National Institute of Mental Health, a group of older males, of an average age of seventy, was studied with a battery of mental tests. They were then reexamined eleven years later at an average age of eighty-one. In this study, vocabulary and picture arrangement testing improved over time. On the standard tests for information, comprehension, recognition of similarities, block designs, and completion of pictures, there was no significant change.

There were a few declines, but none of them very dramatic. Scores for addition rates declined from 0.93 to 0.80. The speed of copying words went down from 34.95 to 29.11; and the draw-a-person test score declined from 24.2 to 21.4. Clearly these eighty-one-year-olds were not intellectually battered by age.

HEALTH REPORT

HOW MUCH OF A MENTAL DECLINE OCCURS WITH NORMAL AGING?

The author of a 1988 review of studies on decline in mental functioning with age concludes that the decline is real, but it is variable and not due to a slowing in reaction time or educational disadvantage.

He notes the evidence for shrinkage in the brain and the decreases in brain blood flow in many older people. However, much of the mental decline can be related to disease processes, he says. These include high blood pressure, elevated blood cholesterol, diabetes, sleep disturbances, and alcohol abuse. In the absence of such disorders, older subjects in unusually good health show much less evidence of mental decline.

He observes, "Most elderly persons have some medical disorder, whether they know it or not, that is compromising their mental functioning and causing a 'normal age-related' decline."

W. E. Rinn, "Mental Decline in Normal Aging: A Review," *Journal of Geriatric Psychiatry and Neurology* 1 (1988): 144.

A number of similar studies have confirmed that the verbal measurements of intelligence and mental functions, based on stored information, show little or no decline with aging. What *do* decline, however, are the performance subtests that involve perception and performance, such as the speed in copying words.

A study of thousands of members of one health maintenance organization threw some light on previous studies, which had reported major declines in intelligence with aging. In this study, younger members scored higher on certain parts of the intelligence test than older members because of better educational background! It was this previously overlooked finding about education that had led in the past to the notion that intellect declines with aging.

Ongoing studies continue to refute the notion of a serious intellectual decline with normal aging. A number of sophisticated evaluations of the testing process itself have also uncovered factors that may affect exam results. These include motivation, tenseness, and the person's response to time restrictions.

HEALTH REPORT

HOW HEALTHY ARE NINETY-YEAR-OLDS?

In this 1987 study, thirty-three men aged ninety to ninety-seven years were compared to a similar group sixty-five to seventy-five years of age living in the same facility, a California veterans' home.

The results: The nonagenarians were more physically active, had more family contacts, consumed less alcohol, smoked less, used fewer major medications, and (as might be expected) had more cardiac, visual, and hearing problems.

There were also fewer psychiatric problems and depressions in the older group.

There are various ways to interpret the findings, but some of the differences noted (less smoking, less alcoholism, more contact, and so on) may represent favorable longevity factors.

G. D. Jensen and P. Bellecci, "The Physical and Mental Health of Nonagenarians," *Age and Ageing* 16 (1987): 19.

On some of the time tests, older subjects perform less well. But if the time permitted for responding is extended, older people may show marked improvement in their scores. The conclusion that researchers have now reached is that timed tests discriminate against older subjects.

Another conclusion that has emerged from the many recent investigations is the recognition that two types of intelligence are involved in the aging process. One, called *crystallized intelligence,* represents the individual's native endowment, as it has developed after exposure to education and other life experiences. Crystallized intelligence undergoes virtually no change up until very old age.

In contrast, *fluid intelligence* involves the speed of processing, comprehending, and utilizing information. This type of intelligence does decline with aging: a decline that begins in the thirties and progresses rather uniformly right on past age seventy-five.

Thus, much intelligence testing measures two components, only one of which declines with aging. What all this comes down to is that on many, though not all, tests for intelligence, a bright individual at age thirty will be just about as bright at age seventy, in the absence of an adverse disease, of course.

NOTE: All the investigations point up individual variability. Some of us show much less of the predicted decline, and others actually outperform younger people.

Most people are aware that as they get older, it is harder to take in new information. We know also we are less likely to recall things as easily as we once did. Psychologists now recognize various depths of memory function: Sometimes memorizing may be shallow; other times, it may be "deep" so that information sticks with us.

A common example: We look up a telephone number in the directory and then walk over to the telephone and dial it successfully. This feat may not be repeatable an hour later, and we have to look the number up again. This is an example of short-term and shallow memory. It has been argued that this tendency to lose such information has a valuable function in that it prevents our accumulating too much clutter in our brains. If you remembered every single item, minor or major, the brain burden would be staggering, or so the argument goes.

On the other hand, if there is a major reason for retaining a bit of information, you may process it more deeply and its durability will be greater. To illustrate: If you are introduced to someone who may be important to you at some future date, you are more likely to retain his name and recall his face. Motivation is important to memorization.

Children seem to have few problems with either superficial or deep memory. But it has been pointed out that children do not have much to remember. An adult, on the other hand, who has met thousands of people, read millions of words, and gone through decades of living, has been presented with countless bits of information. Small wonder, then, that the memory function occasionally balks, so that perhaps you cannot recall a name or remember where you put something.

How Can You Maintain Your Memory as You Age?

Despite the tendency of memory ability to decline with age, there are ways of combating the deterioration through certain practical techniques that I have recommended to many of my patients.

One example of a memory aid familiar to young as well as older people is *mnemonics*. This term, from the Greek word for memory, refers to a line, letter, poem, or other aid that helps fix facts in one's mind. One that I learned and have never forgotten is a poem I heard when living in England forty-five years ago. It was designed to give the stages of progression in diet for someone recovering from a severe illness or major gastrointestinal upset: "Fluid, farinaceous, fish. / Then a chicken in a dish. / Thence to veal and on to beef. / When from all rules there is relief."

I am often surprised that older people sometimes show so much resistance to using little tricks like this to help their memories, as if pride prevents them from relying on such practical memory helps.

Take the making of lists as an example. There are some who feel it is a sign of strength to go to the supermarket with six or eight items in mind, but without a written list. Yet even younger people frequently find they forget one or two of the needed items, and realize that it is safer to put them down on paper. As I tell my patients, "He who does not keep a list, will not dine on what he missed!"

I also advise older people who are frustrated about their memory problems to keep a written daily itinerary. As I get older, I sometimes arrive home at the end of the day and find a message about a promised house call I had forgotten to make, or I remember, too late, a book I forgot to pick up from the library. A reminder list always helps.

Another practical memory tip has been suggested by the celebrated American psychologist B. F. Skinner. He found himself increasingly annoyed by declines in his short-term memory, and so he worked out various maneuvers for compensation.

One example might involve the following situation: You are eating at the breakfast table. There is an announcement on the radio of probable showers today. Your response: Stop eating, get your umbrella, and put it on the door handle. Then, resume eating.

Skinner had found from a number of frustrating experiences that this was the only reliable way to ensure that he would actually leave his house with an umbrella. NOTE: Skinner's book *Enjoy Old Age* has other helpful memory ideas, as does *The Memory Book* by Harry Lorayne and Jerry Lucas.

Here are some other dodges or tricks that I have found helpful in overcoming my own memory problems, as well as those of my patients:

• *Combine the visual with the auditory.* We remember things that we see, and we remember things that we hear. Combining the two can improve performance.

For example, when looking up a phone number, reading out loud the numbers you see will improve your recall when you finally walk over to the phone and start dialing. The same multimodal approach will help with trying to remember names, addresses, dates, and the like.

• *Plan ahead—and write your appointments and other engagements in a schedule book.* In January, you might put down the important dates on your new calendar and add any special notes. For example, you may have trouble recalling at the appropriate time that on June 15 or September 15 quarterly tax payments are due unless you adopt some such system. The same applies to anniversaries, birthdays, and other important aspects of family life. The birthday issue can be a special problem if the number of your grandchildren is increasing!

• *Lean on memory aids to help you recall when to take your medications.* It is perilous to rely only on your unaided memory when it is necessary for you to take drugs. To protect yourself, you may want to keep the medications in plain sight on the dining room table. This way, you will be more likely to take them with meals.

Or perhaps you might write a reminder and attach it to the refrigerator. Another helpful technique is to tie pill-taking and other important routine events to familiar parts of your daily pattern, such as brushing your teeth or drinking your morning cup of coffee. It may also be helpful to keep your medications in special time-labeled dispensing containers, which can be loaded once a day, or even once a week.

• *Remember that short-term memory is sharper and more accurate than longer-term memory.* If your doctor tells you how to do something on your office visit, write it down then and there, not after you get home. After a few hours, his instructions are much more likely to become cloudy.

• *Know that there are medications that can impair the memory.* Among the common medications that may impede memory are some of the tranquilizers and sleeping pills. Medications used for cardiac conditions and high blood pressure may hurt your recall ability.

If it seems that your memory has become worse in association with taking a given pill, tell your physician about this. An alternative medicine may be available.

Does Age Affect Problem-Solving and Decision-Making Ability?

Psychologists have done extensive research into the relationship between age and problem-solving ability, but many questions remain unanswered.

One of the difficulties here is that solving a new problem also requires a person to call on his memory. For example, the retention of instructions, some quite complex, may be a part of problem-solving tests.

It is generally agreed that at the same intelligence level, younger people perform better than older ones on certain problem-solving tests. The more complex the problem, the more often older persons have to consult the directions or ask questions of the examiner. Sometimes they ask the same question over and over, thus indicating a failure to incorporate and act on the information supplied. But older people who are given some preliminary training in how to approach a test are able to increase their scores.

Unfortunately, problem solving in a test-taking situation has often been linked to decision making and problem solving in the real world. However, the two do not necessarily go together. Still, the misconception persists that somehow judgment, decision-making ability, and related qualities deteriorate with age.

I was surprised years ago to be told by a high-level executive of one of our great corporations that his company had a long-standing policy of not promoting anyone over fifty-five to a major decision-making position. Although this was before antidiscrimination rules were established, my first reaction was that this was a silly policy. As I told him, the company might well be depriving itself of a source of highly talented individuals by such blanket "agism."

It is true that some older persons may be more cautious than young ones and thus be less likely to take big risks. But are caution and prudence bad in human affairs? Is it not possible that one may learn some valuable lessons about caution and good judgment and other qualities that may still be applied after age fifty-five?

I think the answer to this last question is yes. I used to take hill-and-dale walks with an older friend (eighty-plus) who had owned two steel companies, one of which he still ran. The other had been turned over to younger executives for management.

My friend kept telling me that the younger executives had still not mastered the great secret that the steel business was inherently cyclic, and that one had to read the trends correctly to be successful. A down cycle could be a long one, and as we talked, we were in the middle of the slump in retail auto sales and building in the 1970s. Yet the younger executives had failed to realize the duration and intensity of the slump. As a result, the old man had had to bail them out of some tough situations.

It is not at all unusual to read in the financial pages, or even on page one of your daily newspaper, about a large corporation's recalling a retired officer to remedy imprudent decisions by younger replacements. In short, most of us, no matter what age, recognize the value of "accumulated experience," of "maturity," and of "wisdom." These are not catchwords, but real qualities in the real world. They have been recognized over the centuries as having real value. Moreover, in many societies, they are the prized qualities needed by those who aspire to be in leadership positions. Hence, on the world scene, older people are often chosen to be president, prime minister, cabinet minister, supreme court justice, special negotiator, and the like.

Clearly, then, there are attributes of the aging mind that cannot be adequately tested by our current intelligence tests. As for me, give me a wise old man over a quicker young one!

Other Factors That May Impair Mental Performance

Although aging per se should not put an individual at an overall intellectual disadvantage, certain health problems that accompany aging may. Here are a few possibilities:

- *A traumatic event* such as a stroke may impair brain function.
- The *narrowing of the arteries,* even small arteries such as those seen in advanced diabetes, may lead to mental deterioration.
- Sustained *high blood pressure* may do the same.
- The *thyroid,* a master gland that controls the basic processes going on in all cells, may wreak havoc on brain performance. Even mild deficiencies in the thyroid may produce many complaints of mental slowing and memory loss.
- *Anemia* and especially pernicious anemia, disturbance of blood salts, or vitamin deficiencies may produce impaired intellectual functioning.
- *Taking alcohol to excess* is a familiar cause for memory impairment, the most dramatic illustration of this being the alcoholic blackout.
- I suspect that *cigarette smoking,* which has been shown to decrease blood flow to the brain by about 7 percent, may be harmful to mental performance as one becomes older.
- *Fatigue* is another well-recognized factor in the impairment of the intellectual process. Tired people are more forgetful. In fact, the level of competence at which one's memory functions is not

fixed, but may vary up and down, depending on a host of recognized and unrecognized factors.

- *Depression* in older people may lead to what seems a loss of one's faculties. Depressed older people may show more or less severe memory loss and apparently major declines in intelligence. This form of depression may be confused with a senile impairment, but there is an important basic difference: The apparent major loss of function is completely reversible with an antidepressant. (For more on depression and the mind, see Chapter 27.)

What About the "Crusty Old Curmudgeon"?

Periodically I see a patient who fits the classic stereotype of the short-tempered, irascible, suspicious old man or woman. This is sometimes referred to as the "old curmudgeon personality." With these people, suspicion gets completely out of hand and becomes irrational.

One of my patients recently brought in his father, saying the older man had become increasingly accusatory toward his spouse. They had had their golden anniversary that year, and up to a year or so ago, the marriage had appeared to be satisfactory and durable.

But now, the relationship seemed to be deteriorating: The story I was told was that the old man used to keep his cash secreted in several books for use for home deliveries or for shopping. Now, he was no longer replenishing the cash as usual, though somehow, he *thought* he was.

On going to his favorite "cash books" and finding no money after an increasingly agitated search, he had taken to accusing his wife of taking the money. Nothing that she could say would disabuse him of the notion that she was stealing from him.

Coincidentally, the very same day at lunch, a lifelong friend told me of a troubling visit back to his hometown in rural Pennsylvania. It seemed that his mother, age eighty-three, was telling her neighbors that her eighty-seven-year-old husband was having daily sexual relations with a much younger woman during his shopping visits to a nearby town.

Accusatory behavior of this kind, referred to as *paranoia,* may become highly charged and even violent. Considering the importance of sex and money, it is not surprising that these two topics are high on the list of the usual accusations.

Furthermore, there is no doubt about the intensity of the accuser's belief in his accusations. These people may go into a rage and repeatedly call up friends and offspring to recite complaints.

Sometimes, psychological testing of paranoid patients reveals other impairments, such as those involving memory and judgment. Considering the age-group involved, these results are not surprising. In any event, the distortion in thinking seems to be limited to a small area with delusional content.

Occasionally, an underlying illness may be responsible for the paranoid behavior. One of my patients with severe underfunctioning of the thyroid gland became paranoid when she failed to take medication. Yet all the paranoid delusions disappeared with even minimal doses of thyroid.

Episodes of paranoia may also follow general anesthesia and surgery. This mental problem is quite common after open heart surgery, for instance, and has been ascribed to the shakeup in brain cells associated with the procedures. Such episodes can be expected to pass with time.

Finally, it has been frequently noted that there is a higher incidence of paranoia in people with hearing impairments. Seeing other people's lips move and yet not hearing them may stimulate negative or hostile thinking, which is the basis of paranoia. Unfortunately, even under the best of circumstances—with proper explanation, hearing aids, and drugs—some older people may never give up their paranoid beliefs.

Other Age-Related Mental Developments

Other psychiatric disorders, which begin in the younger years, may recur or intensify in older age. One of these is manic-depressive disorders: When the person is not depressed, he may engage in manic behavior, such as wild spending, grandiose beliefs, and shopping and traveling sprees.

Preoccupation with bodily symptoms and concerns about the possibility of illness are termed *hypochondriasis.* Some people with these tendencies, whom we popularly call hypochondriacs, act that way all their lives, though the behavior may be exaggerated in old age. The elderly are often known to focus on their digestive tract. They are especially likely to be bitter about their bowels' not functioning well and may engage in many anticonstipation maneuvers.

Over recent years, a distinct branch of psychiatry, called *geropsychiatry,* has emerged to handle these problems. The geropsychiatrist has special training in the psychiatric complaints of older people. He also has an enhanced knowledge of how the physical illnesses and health peculiarities common in old age, such as drug sensitivity, relate to the evaluation and treatment of mental disorders.

Numerous studies reveal that older people are undertreated for their psychiatric complaints. With an equal severity of symptoms and an equal extent of disability, a younger person is definitely more likely to get psychiatric evaluation and care than an older one. Older people may be less tuned in to the concept of seeking psychiatric help, but it is equally true that many medical practitioners seem less motivated to urge or persuade their older patients to seek psychiatric help.

It has often been shown that older people are amenable to psychotherapy and are responsive to drugs at less than the usual dosages. So neither drugs nor psychiatric help should be denied them.

Dementia and Alzheimer's Disease

A few days before the scheduled appointment of one of my male patients, an appointment that had been made by his wife, I received a letter from the wife:

> My husband would be embarrassed if I told you some of these facts in his presence. Yet I thought you might like to know them. He used to be very handy, very good at repairs. Today he can take something apart but cannot put it together again.
> At times he cannot express himself. He is at a loss for the name of a simple object. He is nervous about going out socially. Tries to find excuses not to go.

This week he poured orange juice into his cereal, instead of milk. At times he finds it difficult to coordinate his clothes for dressing.

His family history: His mother and two sisters died at 65–70 years of age in senile stages.

He cries frequently during the night. Frustration and depression, I believe.

I hope you can help him.

In this brief letter, a concerned spouse has listed almost all of the relevant observations that would clinch the diagnosis of Alzheimer's disease. She succinctly describes the loss of previous capacities, the difficulty in memory, and the tendency to fumble for the names of familiar objects in speech.

HEALTH REPORT

RISK FACTORS FOR ALZHEIMER'S DISEASE

The cause of Alzheimer's disease is not known. Among the approaches to solving the riddle have been studies in which possible risk factors are elicited for patients with the disease and compared to normal controls in the population.

In this 1986 study the researchers looked at some eighty factors, such as head injury, allergies, alcohol, anesthesia, animal exposure (dogs, cats, and so on), thyroid disorders, and various social factors.

No factor showed a positive correlation with the presence of Alzheimer's disease, except two: (1) a history of probable Alzheimer's disease in other members of the family (with the risk being greater the closer the relationship), (2) a history of the mother's being over forty when she gave birth to the child under study (a risk factor similar to that for a Down's syndrome baby).

L. A. Amaducci, L. Fratiglioni, W. A. Rocca, et al., "Risk Factors for Clinically Diagnosed Alzheimer's Disease: A Case-Control Study of an Italian Population," *Neurology* 36 (1986): 922.

She also notes confusion, problems in getting dressed, difficulty in socializing, and depression, also common findings with

Alzheimer's. In addition, the letter notes the important hereditary factor: the presence of similar disorders in several members of the man's family.

In general, there are two major types of dementia, or deterioration of the brain function:

• *Alzheimer's disease* is marked by insidious onset and slow, progressive destruction of the brain cells. Memory declines; ability to process information diminishes; social skills and sensitivities disappear; personality changes, often with fearful, hostile, or other negative manifestations. Total mental incapacity may finally result, with the individual unable to recognize family members or perform the simplest functions.

HEALTH REPORT

HOW PERSONALITY CHANGES IN ALZHEIMER'S PATIENTS

Two of the highly variable aspects of Alzheimer's disease are the extent of personality change and the rate at which it occurs. This question of personality alteration is a key as to how difficult life may become for caretakers, and how long the person may remain in a home or community setting.

The investigators in this 1987 report studied forty-four patients over a period of years. The disorder was mild but unmistakable at first examination. Three common personality changes were found initially:
1. PASSIVE BEHAVIOR (found in 66 percent)
   • Diminished initiative
   • Diminished emotional responsiveness
   • Hobbies relinquished
   • Less cheerful
   • Withdrawn
   • Fearful
   • Inappropriate hilarity
2. AGITATED BEHAVIOR (found in 30 percent)
   • Irritable
   • Sexual misdemeanor
   • Purposeless hyperactivity

3. SELF-CENTERED BEHAVIOR (found in 34 percent)
- Impairment of emotional control
- Coarsening of affect
- Loss of concern for feelings of others

Of the twenty-four patients followed for fifty months, five remained at the same mild level. Two progressed to moderate dementia, and seventeen progressed to severe dementia. With progression, two-thirds developed agitated and self-centered behavior, and almost 90 percent also exhibited passive behavior. It was impossible to predict at initial examination who would deteriorate and what behavior they would exhibit.

E. H. Rubin, J. C. Morris, and L. Berg, "The Progression of Personality Changes in Senile Dementia of the Alzheimer's Type," *Journal of the American Geriatrics Society* 35 (1987): 721.

- *Multi-infarct dementia* (MID) is expressed in episodes resulting from vascular damage through small strokes. Usually, this form of dementia comes on more rapidly than Alzheimer's, but the result is similar.

There are also a number of other variations of dementia, but these two are the most common, and Alzheimer's remains the greatest threat of all. There are several reasons why Alzheimer's disease has reached a high level of awareness, and why it appears to be on an increase. Up until relatively recent times, both the public and the medical profession lacked clear concepts regarding the disorder.

The public, on the one hand, often seemed to think that the loss of some faculties with aging was fairly common. Significant losses in memory or in judgment with aging seemed to be regarded as normal, perhaps akin to such normal aging losses as decrease in muscle mass and loss of hair.

In medical circles, there was confusion as to what was occurring in the brain. It was widely believed that the impairments were due to diminished circulation caused by hardening of the arteries, that is to say, atherosclerosis and the cholesterol problem. True, it had long been recognized that small strokes in an individual could produce a considerable loss of faculties and ultimately lead to a dementia. This is still known to be the case with MID.

The original case described by Dr. Alzheimer in 1907 was that of a woman in her early fifties who showed a fairly rapid and progressive decline in her mental functioning over the course of a year or two. Alzheimer observed certain characteristic changes in the brain cells clearly unrelated to the circulation or to arteriosclerosis. For decades this condition was referred to as *presenile dementia.*

It is in only recent years that we have come to realize that the dementia of older people is the same in at least 50 percent of the cases. As a result it is sometimes referred to as *senile dementia of the Alzheimer's type* (SDAT).

HEALTH REPORT

ARE ALZHEIMER'S DISEASE PATIENTS HEALTHIER?

In this 1988 report, 348 patients in a geriatric clinic were studied. Of these, 143 had normal mental status, 75 Alzheimer's disease, and 139 mental abnormalities not due to Alzheimer's disease.

The number of significant medical disorders averaged 5.0 in males, 5.4 in females of normal status. In the non-Alzheimer's, mentally abnormal group, the figures were 5.5 in males, 4.6 in females. But in the Alzheimer's group the other medical disorders averaged only 2.9 in males, 2.8 in females.

In the Alzheimer's group there was significantly less hypertension, heart disease, and stroke. There was also strikingly less diabetes in the Alzheimer's patients, a fact that has been noted by other investigations.

The one exception to the trend was an apparent higher incidence of prostatectomies (prostate removal operations) in elderly males with Alzheimer's disease.

G. P. Wolf-Klein, F. A. Silverstone, M. S. Brod, et al., "Are Alzheimer Patients Healthier?" *Journal of the American Geriatrics Society* 36 (1988): 219.

Despite all of the study—and there have been millions of cases to study, so common is the disease—we still do not know exactly why this brain cell deterioration takes place. But one fact has emerged quite clearly: Alzheimer's disease is in fact a disease and can be distinguished from normal aging.

Whatever declines in brain functioning occur in normal aging, Alzheimer's disease is distinct from these processes. The majority of us will grow old and even older and escape this disease. Still, there is no doubt that it is age-related, in the sense that the number of cases does rise after age fifty. Thus, Alzheimer's disease falls into the group of degenerative diseases that somehow require many decades of living before their effects become manifest.

We also know that there is a genetic component and that the disorder is far more frequent in some families than in others. In fact, in such families the genes responsible for the disease have been identified. What this remarkable discovery tells us is that there may be a transmitted vulnerability. Yet the mystery remains why the vulnerability may not show up until the seventies or eighties or even later.

In any age-related disease, the number of cases rises as the numbers of the elderly increase. Further, everyone has become sensitized to this disorder: not only is it recognized earlier but it is also being overdiagnosed. Major reasons for this overdiagnosis are the problems and the confusion that may be inherent in trying to decide the extent to which the difficulties of certain older people exceed the changes associated with normal aging.

Even the experts cannot always be sure. Suppose I were to see in my office an eighty-year-old man who has memory impairment, some slowing down in his ability to do simple arithmetical problems, and an experience of becoming lost recently in what should have been a familiar neighborhood. These *might* be an indication of Alzheimer's, but I could just as well determine that the family's suspicion of early Alzheimer's disease was unfounded.

In one recent case, for instance, the chief problem for the symptoms described turned out to be eye problems: cataracts and deterioration in the macular portion of the retina. These conditions led to a visual impairment of sufficient magnitude to account for most of the man's difficulties.

One of the critical challenges in making a proper diagnosis arises because a major manifestation in early Alzheimer's disease is memory loss. But as we have seen, memory impairment is one of the more common complaints of the perfectly normal older person. One might suppose that any degree of memory loss might

be crucial, but normal elderly people with some memory impairment say that on those days when they are tired or have not slept
well, their memory is definitely less acute. So memory is a particularly vulnerable faculty.

HEALTH REPORT

WHAT IF YOU FEEL CONFUSED?

Confusion is a symptom or finding, not a disease. A sudden
appearance or sudden aggravation of confusion in an older
person may have many causes that may be *outside* the brain.
These include:
   1. A decline in circulation to the brain, as a result of
      • a heart attack, which may be painless in old age,
      • a change in heart rhythm,
      • a drop in blood pressure,
      • a hemorrhage somewhere in the body.
   2. A metabolic change, as a result of
      • a drop in blood sugar, usually from an overreaction
        to insulin or a drug in a diabetic, that may appear
        to indicate a stroke,
      • excessive changes in the salts of the blood, as with
        high or very low sodium, dehydration, overly pow-
        erful diuretics, or diarrhea may contribute to this
        condition.
   3. An infection, as a result of
      • pneumonia (a quite common cause of confusion),
      • urinary tract infections,
      • any febrile (fever-associated) disease, such as the
        flu.
   4. Drug effects—many drugs, but especially tranquilizers, sedatives, and sleeping pills—may be responsible for confusion.
   5. Environmental changes—going from the familiarity of
the home to a hospital or other institution—are common
circumstances that may lead to confusion.

   Memory may be impaired by many drugs commonly used, to
the point where people seem to be quite confused. Yet they

become unscrambled when the drug is stopped. Depression is also notorious for interfering with memory function in the elderly. Hence, memory improves when an antidepressant medication is administered.

Perhaps the major problem that memory impairment presents to physicians trying to make a diagnosis of Alzheimer's disease or organic dementia is that much of intelligent behavior depends on good memory function. Consider this competency test, which is typical of many such short questionnaires that I use in my office practice:

MENTAL COMPETENCY TEST

1. What is today's date?
   Month _____ Day _____ Year _____
2. What is your birthday?
   Month _____ Day _____ Year _____
3. How old are you?
4. Who is president of the United States?
5. Who was president before him?
6. Name four insects.
7. Name four vegetables.
8. Subtract 7 from 100, 7 from that, and continue on down.
9. Name some of the colors in the rainbow.
10. Draw the face of a clock showing the time at 3:20.

As you can see, many of these questions rely upon memory. Some involve recent memory: What is today's date? Who is president of the United States? Some refer to more distant events: Who was the president before him? What is your birthday?

Naming four insects and four vegetables requires the capacity to do categorization as well as memory. Question number 8, a subtraction problem, tests the ability to do arithmetical calculation. And the last question, number 10, asking the person to draw a clock face, is a performance as well as a memory test.

The first five questions in this test are easier than the last five. But speaking generally, failing five or more questions certainly points to significant impairment.

Moderately advanced Alzheimer's patients show confusion on this simple test. For example, they may include some fruits with vegetables. Or they may mention the correct current president but think the one before him was Roosevelt. Even though they may be told that this year is 1989, and recall correctly that they were born in 1905, they may still be unable to figure out that their present age is eighty-four.

HEALTH REPORT

HOME OR INSTITUTIONAL CARE FOR THE DEMENTED PATIENT?

A 1985 report concludes that home care rather than institutional care is beneficial to a demented patient and family. The mortality rate of such patients who are relocated is increased. On the other hand, home care can be stressful, and the burden may force the family toward the institutional solution.

This study reports on the outcome of supportive measures in these situations, primarily group therapy for the caretakers. Information on Alzheimer's disease, behavioral problems and their management, medical and legal concerns, and development of a helping network were considered in eight weekly two-hour meetings. At the end of this time reevaluation of those in the program revealed decreases in stress and depression and improvement in knowledge of the disease, all to a significant degree. All the participants judged the program to be moderately to markedly helpful.

[NOTE: Similar reduction in the family burden has been shown for other supportive services such as home help, respite care, and organized home care programs.]

J. Lahan, B. Kemp, F. R. Staples, and K. Brummel-Smith, "Decreasing the Burden in Families Caring for a Relative with a Dementing Illness," *Journal of the American Geriatrics Society* 33 (1985): 664.

To sum up, then, *dementia,* the gradual loss of one's mental faculties to the point where social and occupational functioning is impaired, is a terrible scourge that to one degree or another afflicts about 15 percent of people sixty-five years old and older. Alzheimer's disease is the most common form of this group of brain disorders. As of now, there is no cure for Alzheimer's, and in the worst cases, the disease results in death.

HEALTH REPORT

SOME PRACTICAL TIPS ON CARING FOR THE DEMENTED PATIENT

The following are a few highlights from a renowned expert in this field, addressed to doctors but of general interest:

- Skilled care is a form of scientifically informed common sense. A first principle is to find out what is wrong (not always easy with some patients and families).

- A second principle is to treat disability, not abnormality. Treat what bothers the patient or family. Do not treat statistical abnormalities that primarily bother health care professionals.

- Care of demented patients rests on a triad of considerations: Treat curable illness, gently but effectively; limit symptoms; and continue support, until the end.

- All sedatives and hypnotics are suspect. The rule is to inspect every medicine in the house carefully.

- Illness that increases disability should be treated even in demented patients. Someone trying to remember to be continent is not helped by urgency and frequency from an untreated bladder infection.

- In prescribing drugs, doses should be low initially: Old brains, damaged brains, and particularly damaged old brains are typically sensitive to drugs that act on the brain.

- Depression should be treated vigorously not only when patients are misdiagnosed as demented but also when depression complicates dementia.

- Sleep disturbances can bother patients and exhaust caretakers. Hypnotic drugs that induce sleep "all night" frequently induce unacceptable hangovers. A small dose of an antihistamine when the patient awakes during the night often allows a relatively full night's sleep for all concerned.

- So-called violence in demented patients is more often disorganized and frustrated behavior.

- Robert Loeb taught a generation of Columbia University medical students that "when things are going well, change nothing; when things are going badly, reevaluate."

J. P. Blass, "Pragmatic Pointers on Managing the Demented Patient," *Journal of the American Geriatrics Society* 34 (1986): 548.

But because many of the early symptoms of Alzheimer's and other forms of dementia mimic normal memory loss and intellectual changes, there is no reason to panic when you forget an appointment or your housekeys. In any case, if you are worried about your symptoms, see your doctor for a professional evaluation—and for reassurance.

Parkinson's Disease

Parkinsonism is characterized by weakness and slowness of movement, immobility of the face, rigidity of the body, and tremor. It affects about one in one hundred people over age fifty-five. In fact, this disease is the second most common disorder of the nervous system among older people, after strokes.

KEY FACTS

SOME TYPES OF TREMOR: CHARACTERISTICS AND CAUSES

EXAGGERATED "NORMAL" TREMOR
- Large amounts of coffee
- Drugs: amphetamines, alcohol (especially in withdrawal), antidepressants, some asthma preparations
- Anxiety and fatigue
- Thyroid disturbances

ESSENTIAL (FAMILIAL) TREMOR
- Often present over lifetime, worsening with aging
- Runs in families
- Relieved by alcohol or propranolol

RESTING TREMOR
- Parkinson's disease ("pill rolling" tremor of fingers) at rest, worsened by emotions, disappears on sleep
- Psychotropic drugs

CEREBELLAR (HINDBRAIN) TREMORS
- Large tremulous or jerky movements on attempted motion; subsides on reaching target; may be found in stroke or head injury cases

---

A few indicators of possible presence of early Parkinson's disease that I have found useful are the following:

- *Loss of associative movements.* A good example is the loss of arm movements on walking, which may be present only on one side in some persons.
- *Micrographia* (literally, "small writing"). Patients complain that their handwriting is getting smaller. Sometimes the letters are normal size as they start to write but fairly rapidly become smaller.
- *Increasingly stooped posture.*
- *Trouble turning over in bed* at night and increased backache.

The consensus now seems to be that the most effective treatment for older people is a combination of the drugs levodopa and carbidopa, or levodopa and benserazide. Recommended dosages are low, beginning with 100 mg of levodopa combined with 10 mg of carbidopa, or 25 mg of benserazide. The medications are initially taken once daily and are increased in frequency and amount every third day until the disease is under control or side effects become too disabling.

Possible side effects include nausea, vomiting, postural hypo-

---

HEALTH REPORT

IS IT NORMAL TO HAVE HALLUCINATIONS?

Visual hallucinations may be experienced by normal elderly persons who have decreased visual acuity, and they become even more frequent as vision deteriorates.

Persons with such hallucinations may see people and other objects; if the observed people are talking, lip movements but no sounds are noted. If vision improves, as by cataract extraction, the hallucinations disappear.

One theory is that these events represent spontaneous activity in the visual part of the brain when normal visual input is cut off by the decline in sight. The phenomenon was first described by Charles Bonnet in 1769.

F. Rosenbaum, Y. Harati, L. Rolak, and M. Freedman, "Visual Hallucinations in Sane People: Charles Bonnet Syndrome," *Journal of the American Geriatrics Society* 35 (1987): 66.

HEALTH REPORT

HOW WIDOWS HALLUCINATE

Widows and widowers may be subject to a little-known phenomenon in which they experience the presence of the dead spouse.

In a 1985 review of the subject, the authors found references to this type of "hallucination" going back to at least one 1892 study of 1,689 persons, 10 percent of whom reported sensory contact with an absent person.

In a 1977 Welsh study 47 percent of the entire widowed population (293 women) of an isolated medical practice reported the experience to be common. The experience was rarely disclosed to friends or relatives and never to the physician. A majority felt the experience was normal and helpful.

In the present study 46 widows residing in two nursing homes and oriented for time, place, and person were interviewed. Average age was eighty, and all reported their marriages as mostly happy.

To the question "Have you ever experienced your husband with you in any way since his death?" 29 (61 percent) responded yes. In addition, 22 reported a visual experience, 14 an auditory experience, 6 a tactile one, 5 a conversation with the deceased, 13 reported combinations of these experiences. Twenty-three of the widows also reported hallucinatory experiences of other deceased relatives. The researchers also found that 54 percent of those with hallucinatory experiences had never discussed the experience with anyone prior to the interview.

P. R. Olson, J. A. Suddeth, P. J. Peterson, and C. Egelhoff, "Hallucinations of Widowhood," *Journal of the American Geriatrics Society* 33 (1985): 543.

tension, hallucinations, irregular heartbeats, and involuntary movement.

Improvement usually takes places in stages: First, the rigidity lessens, body movements speed up, and improvements are manifested in gait, posture, and balance. Weaknesses in speech and tremor may show improvement later.

There also appears to be a somewhat higher incidence of dementia in individuals who have Parkinson's disease, though the two disorders have entirely different brain changes. There is also more depression: 40 percent or more of individuals having Parkinsonism have significant depression. Oddly, the depression may even worsen somewhat after the motor improvement produced by antiparkinsonian drugs.

Thus, evaluating the mental functioning of Parkinson's disease patients and sorting out causes may be quite difficult. Early parkinsonism is hard to diagnose, and so questions as to whether

---

HEALTH REPORT

DEALING WITH PARKINSON'S DISEASE

Any combination of tremor, rigidity, diminished movement, and postural instability may be found in Parkinson's disease.

Of the various medications available, some are more useful for a symptom such as tremor, others more applicable to complaints of stiffness and rigidity. Some in the class of anticholinergic drugs help with tremor: Artane, Parsidol, Cogentin, Kemadrin, and Akineton. Of these, Parsidol is perhaps the most effective.

Amantadine is a useful agent (also used for the treatment of influenza A strain), but it may lose its impact after a time.

Tricyclic antidepressants are of value for the tremor and for the frequent associated depression.

The mainstay of therapy is levodopa, which compensates for the decline in dopamine in the portion of the brain whose cells disappear in parkinsonism. Sinemet is the usual agent for this purpose.

Parkinsonism, even when well treated and responsive, tends to progress with time. One manifestation is the "off-on" phenomenon, in which a usual dose of the drug seems to wear off suddenly, with reappearance of symptoms. An apparently useful drug available in Europe, Deprenze, is currently under investigation in the United States.

M. J. Aminoff, "Parkinson's Disease in the Elderly: Current Management Strategies," *Journal of the American Geriatrics Society* 42 (1987): 31.

the disorder is present keep popping up in many older persons. Even experts cannot be sure sometimes.

For more on this disease, see the box on page 543.

Transient Global Amnesia

A number of my patients, often feeling greatly disconcerted and even agitated, have described these symptoms to me:

Without warning, there is a sudden short-term loss of memory: Patients cannot recall most recent events that happened before the attack began. During the attack, they are often unable to take in or process new information; their learning ability is impaired. Within a few hours, however, they begin to improve without any medical treatment. Usually, by the following day, they have returned to normal, except that they may not be able to remember the episode.

This problem typically affects people who are fifty or older, and men and women are affected approximately equally. Many times, the attacks begin in the morning. One-third are triggered by changes in temperature, stress, or some strong emotional impact. Specific triggering events include sexual intercourse, a hot shower, a swim in cold water, or a painful injury.

Probably, transient global amnesia is caused by a temporary cutoff of blood flow to the brain as a result of the triggering event. But there are apparently no permanent effects of these attacks. Unlike transient ischemic attacks (TIAs), which may include paralysis and other strokelike symptoms, transient global amnesia does not signal a later stroke. Nor is there any evidence that these occurrences may eventually lead to permanent amnesia or other mental impairment.

As one physician, Dr. Mark Kritchevsky, has said, a single, isolated attack should probably be treated "with reassurance only." Recurrent attacks may warrant a CT scan and aspirin therapy.

27

HOW TO DEAL WITH DEPRESSION

"Doctor Rossman, I've really been down in the dumps lately," one of my patients reported.

When I asked her how long she had been feeling this way, she responded, "About a month." So I knew I was not dealing with a passing, overnight problem. Her appetite was also decreased, and her sleep had been unusually fitful. In the ensuing conversation, I learned that she had been feeling "old" and "useless." She was about to turn sixty-five and would be retiring shortly from a job she had held for nearly twenty years.

To begin with, I recommended some professional counseling to help her make the transition to retirement. In addition, I prescribed a small dose of the drug methylphenidate, also known by the brand name Ritalin. When I checked with her about a week later, her mood and outlook on life had already become more upbeat. It was apparent that she had undergone a common emotional malady among many older people: mild depression.

What Is Depression?

Everyone gets depressed at one time or another. Perhaps you've felt "down" or "blue" when you

- failed to get a promotion,
- lost your job,
- had a falling-out with a friend,
- lost money on the stock market, or
- grieved over the death of a loved one.

More often than not these downcast feelings pass reasonably quickly, and soon, you are back to your normal self. But sometimes, bouts of depression can turn into what is often called *clinical depression,* or a longer-lasting emotional oppression that requires medical intervention.

How can you tell the difference between ordinary "down" feelings and clinical depression? One helpful approach is to evaluate yourself by answering the questions on the Depression Scale (pp. 547–48), which I have assembled especially for this book.

First read through all the statements under question 1, and decide which statement best describes you. You should have experienced a feeling or condition for at least two weeks before you say it applies to you.

Finally, on a separate sheet of paper, write down the number of points assigned to that statement. Continue in the same way with each of the other questions, and when you finish, add up the total number of points you have accumulated.

What do your answers to these questions suggest about your emotional state?

First, you should consider the meaning of the total number of "depression points" that you have accumulated. I find that the following guidelines are reasonably accurate in pinpointing a person's level of depression:

0–4   points: normal
5–8   points: borderline depression

DEPRESSION SCALE

	POINTS
QUESTION 1:	
I feel my mood is about the same as usual.	0
I feel a bit more "down" than I used to.	1
I feel sad much of the time.	2
I feel very sad just about all of the time.	3
QUESTION 2:	
My appetite is about the same as usual.	0
My appetite is down some of the time.	1
My appetite is down much of the time.	2
I really never have any appetite.	3
QUESTION 3:	
I sleep about the same as always.	0
I have trouble falling asleep, or I wake up early.	1
I like to get into bed earlier and sleep later.	2
I like to stay in bed just about all the time.	3
QUESTION 4:	
On the whole, I think life is worthwhile.	0
I sometimes think life may not be worth living.	1
I often think life just isn't worth living.	2
Life isn't worth living.	3
QUESTION 5:	
I weigh about the same as usual.	0
I think my weight may be down a few pounds.	1
I've lost 5–10 pounds in weight.	2
I've lost more than 10 pounds in weight.	3
QUESTION 6:	
My daily activities are pretty much the same as always.	0
I've cut down on some activities.	1
There's very little I care to do.	2
I feel too "down" to do anything.	3

DEPRESSION SCALE (continued)

	POINTS

QUESTION 7:

I like getting together with other people.	0
I don't care whether or not I see other people.	1
It's a great effort to get together with other people.	2
I just don't want to see other people.	3

QUESTION 8:

I like sexual activity the same as ever.	0
My interest in sex is down some.	1
I'd prefer not to have anything to do with sex.	2
I don't want sex at all.	3

9–16 points: mild-to-moderate depression; will probably require some medical help

17–24 points: severe depression; requires immediate medical attention.

For most people, questions 1 and 4 will probably be the most important "leading indicators" of serious depression. In contrast, question 8 may assume less importance, especially if you became relatively uninterested in sex or stopped sex long before your depression began.

In any event, it is best to monitor yourself in light of all these statements because each of us has individual needs and idiosyncrasies that one or two of the questions cannot describe completely. In general, the main signs to watch for with more serious forms of depression are abrupt and major changes for the worse in your physical or emotional condition, and, as I have already indicated, those changes should have lingered for at least a two-week period.

A Brief Profile of Depression in Older Persons

Men and women of every age, occupation, and social position may wrestle with depression, but how many older people have this problem? Some studies have shown that a full 15 percent of the elderly population have depressive symptoms, with the affliction equally distributed among men and women. Other community studies indicate that as many as 30 percent of their elderly population have some depressive symptoms.

Even so, older people seem to be freer of major depressions than those who are younger. The Eastern Baltimore Mental Health Survey of 1981 reported that people in the eighteen- to sixty-four-year-old age-group had considerably more major depressive disorders than older people. Specifically, the younger people had more than three times the incidence of major depressions of those in the sixty-five to seventy-four-year-old group, and nearly twice as many such disorders as those seventy-five years old and older.

But still, depression remains a big problem for older people, and unfortunately, it is often not easy to distinguish depression from other medical problems, or even from ordinary aging.

The Depression Masquerade

Other maladies may masquerade as depression. I find I sometimes have trouble identifying this problem, even after I have followed a patient for decades and have become quite familiar with his appearance, gestures, activities, and values.

One of the impersonators of depression is ordinary aging. Many people, for instance, experience fatigue and lack of energy as they get older. Advancing age may also usher in sleep problems, declining sexual interest, and other characteristics of depression. These and other changes may—or may not—signal the onset of depression. So do not assume, if you recognize some traits of depression in yourself, that you are suffering from a clinical form of depression. In fact, you are probably just showing some of the normal signs of getting older

- *if* these characteristics have arisen over a long period of time,
- *if* you are generally satisfied with life, and
- *if* you do not exhibit the more serious signs of depression, such as abrupt, major weight loss; constant and deep sadness; or a sense that "life isn't worth living."

HEALTH REPORT

DEPRESSION IN THOSE WITH DEMENTIA

A study published in 1987 in the *American Journal of Psychiatry* compared the incidence and severity of depression in 44 patients suffering from Alzheimer's disease with age-matched normal persons in the community. The researchers used a number of objective scales to determine the presence of depression, and they also arranged for two forty-five-minute interviews with the participants by geriatric psychiatrists.

The results: Of the patients with Alzheimer's, nine had mild depression, four had moderate depression, and five had severe depression. Only five of the elderly non-Alzheimer's subjects had significant depression.

The depression in those with dementia was marked by anxiety, as well as feelings of helplessness, hopelessness, and worthlessness. They did not have such frequent somatic (physical) symptoms of depression as weight loss and sleep disturbances.

L. W. Lazarus, N. Newton, R. B. Cohle, et al., "Frequency and Presentation of Depressive Symptoms in Patients with Primary Degenerative Dementia," *American Journal of Psychiatry* 144 (1987): 41.

Depression itself may be masked under the guise of what seems to be serious mental illness, or dementia, especially if the depressive symptoms suggest a decline in mental powers, such as a loss of memory or an inability to concentrate. But an astute medical observer can usually tell the difference between dementia and true depression. Here are a few guidelines:

• Dementia usually comes upon a person slowly, whereas depression typically descends so rapidly that its date of onset can be fixed.

• With dementia, the patient often tries to cover up his mental problems, whereas the depressed person emphasizes or highlights his difficulties.

HEALTH REPORT

DEPRESSION IN DISGUISE

Sometimes, depression may in effect disguise itself as dementia, but this "pseudodementia" should be diagnosed as early as possible for what it is, because it is eminently treatable and generally reversible.

The authors of a 1988 report in *Geriatrics* point out important characteristics that may be present in pseudodementia:

- Rapid onset of symptoms
- Usually short duration
- History of depression of the patient or family members
- Depressed moods
- Unresponsive moods
- Unresponsive behavior
- Fatigue
- Appetite disturbances
- Variable and inconsistent intellectual performance
- Complaints about deficiencies in memory, though memory tests may show no problems

Pseudodementia can be treated with either medications or *electroconvulsive therapy* (ECT), which is sometimes referred to as "shock treatments." Clinical experience has shown that ECT may have some advantages.

The authors also note that some medications and some illnesses may produce a severe depression. For such depressions, stopping the medications or treating the medical illness is basic.

J. J. Haggerty, R. N. Golden, D. L. Evans, and D. S. Janovsky, "Differential Diagnosis of Pseudodementia in the Elderly," *Geriatrics* 43 (1988): 61.

- Dementia is characterized by relatively stable mental deficiencies; depression produces fluctuations in mental abilities.
- The moods of a person with dementia often vary; while the mood of a depressed person is consistently "down."
- When a person with dementia takes an exam designed to

evaluate his mental status, frequently he evades the answers or gets them wrong. In contrast, when a depressed person takes such an exam, he often responds, "I don't know."

The symptoms of depression may also appear with other conditions or emotional states, such as grief over the loss of a loved one, various physical illnesses, and certain types of drug use. Furthermore, some of these conditions and states may trigger the onset of a true major depression that requires medical intervention. But more must be said about this as we delve into some of the causes of depression.

What Causes Depression?

Depressions may be caused by a variety of factors that can easily be identified, such as bereavement, drugs, or illness. Sometimes a depression descends without any warning and for no obvious reason, as it did with one typical patient of mine.

The Unknown Cause

For no apparent reason, one seventy-five-year-old woman, who had been quite an energetic person in the past, passed the line into depression during an identifiable two-week period. Before the problem struck, she frequently spent time on the telephone with her friends and relatives, she loved to go out visiting and shopping, and she was a good eater.

But then, over that two-week period, all this changed. She lost her energy, she stayed at home most of the time unless she was prodded to go out, and she lost her appetite. She also scored a relatively high 20 on the Depression Scale included earlier in this chapter on pages 547–48.

Clearly, this woman had fallen into a major depression, and she had to be treated medically for it over a period of several months.

Certainly, it can be quite helpful to find the cause of a bout of depression because if you know the cause, you are in a better position to counteract it. But do not despair if you cannot identify the source of your "down" feelings. It is not necessary to try to trace down the precise cause of the depression before taking corrective action. The important thing is to recognize the symptoms and respond quickly to them.

From Bereavement to Depression

Old age is a season of losses. The more of a survivor you are, the more you have to be prepared to face the loss of valued friends and relatives. The reaction to the deaths of loved ones is often indistinguishable from a spontaneous depression, and the symptoms are much the same.

HEALTH REPORT

BEREAVEMENT AND DEPRESSION

Some 15 percent of bereaved spouses are still significantly depressed a year after their loss, according to a 1987 report in *Psychiatric Clinics of North America.*

In a study reported by the authors, eight widows and two widowers with obvious depression were treated with antidepressants. The depressive symptoms improved in seven of the patients within a few weeks. Four had a 60 to 80 percent reduction in their depressions, and three more were much improved.

S. C. Jacobs, J. C. Nelson, and S. Zisook, "Treating Depressions of Bereavements with Antidepressants," *Psychiatric Clinics of North America* 10 (1987): 501.

Generally speaking, feeling "down in the dumps" after you have lost a spouse, sibling, or close friend is quite normal. Almost everybody has this reaction. But if serious mourning continues for weeks, or certainly for months, a genuine depression may have taken over. In such a case, your doctor may treat your extended bereavement in the same way that he would treat any depression.

Big Changes May Breed Big Depressions

Symptoms of depression may also follow other major adjustments or disruptions in your life, such as retirement, divorce, or change of residence. Most of the time, these symptoms are a predictable part of living, and usually they pass. As with bereavement, though, if the "down" symptoms continue for longer than a few weeks, you may be in the throes of a longer-term depression, and medical assistance may be required.

Depression Resulting from Illness

Some symptoms of depression may also arise from physical illness or from the medications used to treat various illnesses. For instance, stroke may precipitate a depression. I have even seen very mild strokes temporarily pass unnoticed because of the depth of the resulting depression.

Similarly, some depressions may arise after a heart attack. Depressions are also rather common in patients with Parkinson's disease, and they may also follow major surgery, especially heart-lung surgery, in which the patient must be hooked up to life-sustaining machinery.

Alzheimer's disease and other brain disorders often are accompanied by depression. In addition, depression may be traced to hypothyroidism, Cushing's disease (malfunction of the adrenal gland that may lead to such problems as high blood pressure and obesity), various cancers, and vitamin B_{12} deficiencies.

Depression Due to Drugs

You should also keep in mind the possibility of drug-induced depressions. Sometimes, the down-in-the-dumps feelings may come on within a few weeks of the administration of certain drugs. Among the more common are medications used to treat hypertension, such as those in the beta-blocker group, including clonidine (Catapres), propranolol (Inderal), reserpine (Serpasil), and some diuretics.

Tranquilizers may also produce apathy and depression, even when the dosages are carefully monitored. In addition, certain disorders such as hypothyroidism, in which there is an under-functioning of the thyroid gland, may produce a mild to severe depression. Oddly enough—and only in the elderly—the reverse action of the thyroid, in which it overproduces its secretions, may have the same result. If you want to have some medicalese to help you communicate better with your doctor, you should know that this reverse-thyroid problem is known technically as *apathetic hyper-thyroidism.*

Changes in the Older Brain May Trigger Depression

Recent medical investigations have revealed that the brain contains an important enzyme called monoamine oxidase (MAO). MAO is essential in the formation-destruction cycle of certain chemicals in the brain called *catecholamines.* These catecholamine chemicals, which are part of a group called *neurotransmitters,* pass messages from one brain cell to another.

MAO breaks down the neurotransmitters after they have stimulated a particular cell so that the chemical environment of the cell reverts to its normal, steady state. Otherwise, a cell would constantly be in a highly stimulated condition, a kind of twitchiness, such as you may experience when you drink excessive amounts of coffee.

The investigators have shown that MAO increases in some aging brains, though why this happens, no one knows. In any case, with increased MAO, there are fewer catecholamine neurotransmitters moving between the cells. This condition mimics the changes known to take place in depressions that have been induced experimentally.

Consequently, it seems quite likely that this biochemical change in the aging brain, this increase in the presence of MAO, may contribute to the increased fatigue and lethargy experienced by some older people. Excessive MAO may also be a factor in the tendency toward depression.

What Can You Do?

If you suspect that you or someone you care for is suffering from depression, it is best to approach the problem systematically. Find out whether the depression is just a normal, short-term "down" reaction to bereavement or some other identifiable cause. If this is the case—and if the symptoms of the depression seem rather mild—it may be best just to wait and see whether the problem will run its course and disappear on its own.

You might also check whether the depression could be caused by medications. Your physician can guide you and help you make any necessary adjustments in your prescriptions.

On the other hand, some depressions simply do not go away by themselves and cannot be eliminated by changing a drug. If you have felt mildly depressed for more than two weeks and you scored between 9 and 16 on the Depression Scale, you should probably take some definite steps to deal with your mild depression. Here's how to get started:

Mild Depression

Mild depressions, in which you feel somewhat "down" but your attitude does not interfere substantially with the way you function, can often be treated through counseling by a physician, pastor, rabbi, or therapist. Sometimes, just talking seriously with an experienced person about your problem can give you a sense of perspective and help lift the cloud of gloom that has been plaguing you.

This approach may work best for people who constantly feel tired, do not sleep well, or feel generally negative about life. But if you have lost a great deal of weight, feel that life is not worth living, or possess similarly serious symptoms—and if you scored 17 or higher on the Depression Scale—you may well be plagued by a major, not a mild, depression. In this case, you should skip ahead to the discussion of major depressive illness.

Drugs for mild depression. If counseling fails to work for people suffering from mild depression, I often feel justified in trying small doses of antidepressant drugs. These may be especially helpful for people with sleep problems because the antidepressants typically improve the quality of sleep.

A doctor can sometimes get an inkling of what the outcome of treatment with drugs may be by first trying out small doses of psychostimulants, such as the amphetamines or the drug methylphenidate, marketed as Ritalin.

It's a pity that these drugs have a bad name as a result of their being abused by some people. Even medical professionals tend to be wary of using them because of the public furor that has sometimes surrounded them.

But actually, in small and well-regulated doses, these drugs can be of value in correcting chemical imbalances in the brain. They are entirely safe when used properly. In fact—in contrast to their use with the elderly—Ritalin is often used to calm hyperactive children! For some unknown reason, this drug helps to quiet such children and increases their ability to concentrate in classroom situations.

KEY FACTS

TIPS ON USING STIMULANTS TO TREAT DEPRESSION

In a review of a number of studies, an article in a *Massachusetts General Hospital Newsletter* cites these facts about stimulants and depression:

- Stimulants help some depressed patients.
- Stimulants may be helpful when they are added to the patient's usual antidepressant drug programs.
- Apathetic older patients respond better to stimulants than do those who are agitated.
- Dexedrine may contribute to agitation and confusion.
- Methylphenidate (Ritalin) is a better choice than dexedrine for the elderly.

D. C. Goff, "Stimulants in Depression," Biological Therapies in Psychiatry, *Massachusetts General Hospital Newsletter* 10 (1987): 36.

It is my experience that a small morning dose of Ritalin or a similar drug can help many mildly depressed older people "get going." Typically, they tell me they feel much better and livelier after the medication. Furthermore, I have encountered no problems with those who have taken Ritalin under a doctor's supervision over a fairly long period of time.

Major Depressions and the Need for More Extensive Drug Treatment

Those who exhibit the signs of major depressive illness—such as large weight losses, incapacitating fatigue, desire to stay in bed much of the time, frequent crying spells, or life-is-worthless feelings—are definitely candidates for drug treatment. Generally, people in this category score between 17 and 24 on the Depression Scale.

Because physical and mental decline may occur rapidly in severely depressed older people, physicians often move quickly with medications to prevent a person's emotional state from degenerating into a danger zone. The danger is usually quite apparent to the trained observer. As one of my colleagues said in referring to one very seriously depressed person, "It almost seems as if someone has suddenly poured glue in between his brain cells so that messages can no longer go from one cell to another!"

This description may in some ways be medically quite accurate. We now can think of depression as a disturbance in the balance of the neurotransmitters, including a marked decrease of the catecholamines that leads to a slowing down or grinding to a halt of the brain cells' ability to communicate with one another. Many experiments suggest that antidepressants can increase the level of chemical message transmission between cells.

Antidepressant drugs for major depression. Before the advent of antidepressant drugs, medical specialists used to teach that all depressions were *self-limiting*: That is, they generally ran their course and ended in about six months or so.

Although this may be true for some depressions, it is not the case for many others. For the elderly in particular, a major depression may produce a chronically cloudy outlook, with little hope for a happy ending just around the corner. In one recent British study, one-third of the elderly with serious depressions were found to be no better off after a year, despite the use of all sorts of drugs and even ECT.

Fortunately, though, many depressions do respond well to treatment, and there are now a wide variety of antidepressant drugs to choose from. Some psychiatrists still like the older ones, such as imipramine (Tofranil) and amitriptyline (Elavil). But I feel that more recent antidepressants may be superior. The new drugs, such as trazodone, produce fewer side effects, such as slowing of urination in older men who have prostate enlargement, dry mouth, or extreme sedation.

Recently, medical researchers have discovered that smaller doses than are prescribed for middle-aged or younger people can work quite well on depression in the older population. Your doctor will most likely select the drug and the dosage in part on the basis of both your age and the severity of your depression.

HEALTH REPORT

LOW DOSES OF ANTIDEPRESSANTS WORK AGAINST DEPRESSION!

An antidepressant drug (doxepin) in low dosages improved the depressive symptoms of a small group of patients in a rehabilitation setting, according to a report in the *Journal of the American Geriatrics Society*.

The average age of the patients who were treated was over seventy-five, and a majority had suffered strokes. Although the medication dose used was small by the standards employed for young and middle-aged people, it clearly had an impact.

Most older patients tend to complain about the side effects of medicines, including antidepressants, which may result in dry mouth, urinary problems, or dizziness. Furthermore, older people with these reactions tend to abandon the drugs that are giving them so much trouble. So it is good news that a low-dose approach, which involves fewer side effects, may work.

M. Lakshmanan, L. C. Mion, and J. D. Frengley, "Effective Low Dose Tricyclic Antidepressant Treatment for Depressed Geriatric Rehabilitation Patients: A Double-Blind Study," *Journal of the American Geriatrics Society* 34 (1986): 421.

Common side effects of these drugs include blurring of vision, dryness of the mouth, speeding up of the pulse, and tendency of the blood pressure to drop when the person is standing. The antidepressant drug may take two to three weeks to begin to work well.

Unless the patient's situation involves an emergency, I usually recommend that he begin with lower doses, generally as a single dose before going to bed at night. If extra medication is needed, the drug can then be increased slowly. "Start low and go slow" is a good guideline for all drug treatment of the elderly. In most cases, some safe level of an antidepressant will begin to relieve a serious depression after the first several weeks.

After a period of several months of improved mental health, your physician may feel that it is desirable for you to start tapering the dosage of the antidepressant drug. Some feel, however, that even with great improvement, a drug dose at some level should be maintained for a long time, and perhaps even indefinitely.

The Next Step

When the antidepressant drugs fail, this may be an indication we are dealing with a *refractory depression,* a more severe condition that does not respond to the usual medication. The next step in this case is to turn to a class of drugs called the *monoamine oxidase inhibitors* (MAOIs).

These drugs may reverse the effect of the MAO, which you will recall is the enzyme that breaks down the neurotransmitters, or chemicals that carry messages around in your brain. Researchers believe that these drugs help overcome the MAO, help raise the level of neurotransmitters, and thus relieve the depression.

HEALTH REPORT

IS DEPRESSION UNDERTREATED?

A 1988 review in the *British Medical Journal* argues that depression in the elderly is underdiagnosed and undertreated.

In some cases, the patient may conceal or minimize the impact of the depression. Friends and loved ones who have a chance to observe a depressed person should therefore be as alert as the patient to the most obvious symptoms of depression. These include helplessness, hopelessness, low self-esteem, and loss of pleasure.

At least three-fourths of depressed patients recover or show major improvement with appropriate medications or electroconvulsive therapy (ECT). Some patients may need indefinite maintenance treatment, however.

G. Baldwin, "Late Life Depression: Undertreated?" *British Medical Journal* 296 (1988): 519.

But there are some characteristic side effects. Patients using this class of drugs have to avoid foods that contain certain fermentation products. These include some of the cheeses, beer, wine, chicken liver, and yeast. These foods contain substances known as *pressor amines,* which the body can usually break down quite easily. But people who are on the MAOIs may not be able to break them down, and sudden and severe rises in blood pressure may result.

When Drugs Fail

When no drug seems to be effective, the fall-back position is electroconvulsive therapy (ECT), known as "shock treatment." There is probably no medical treatment or medicine that has received a worse press or been more irrationally denounced than ECT. So what exactly does this treatment involve, and what are the results that can be expected?

KEY FACTS

SOME MAJOR CAUSES OF WEIGHT LOSS

- Diabetes
- Depression
- Cancer
- Malnutrition and malabsorption of foods or nutrients
- Drugs
- Parkinsonism
- Kidney failure (uremia)
- Thyroid malfunction
- Pancreatic disorders
- Dietary changes and anorexia

Superficially, ECT resembles a common epileptic seizure. The major difference is that the ECT experience takes place under highly controlled conditions, with extensive protective measures. For example, those undergoing ECT receive a medication to relax the muscles just prior to treatment. This drug prevents any violent contraction of the muscles that can produce severe stresses on bones and even put the person in danger of fracture.

Nobody knows just how ECT works, but the fact is that it *does* work on those with the most serious cases of depression. Indeed, sometimes the effect can be dramatic.

I recall one wholly incapacitated, weeping anorexic woman who was certain that her own death was imminent. She was actually starving herself, she thought she was totally worthless, and she blamed herself for everything that went wrong in her life. She was convinced that there was no point to living any longer, and I feared that she might take her own life if she were not watched quite closely.

HEALTH REPORT

THE OLDER YOU GET, THE LESS DEPRESSED YOU MAY BE!

In a California veterans' home, thirty-three men aged ninety to ninety-seven years were compared with a similar group sixty-five to seventy-five years of age. All the participants lived in the same facility.

The older men came out on top in several respects: The nonagenarians were more physically active, had more family contacts, consumed less alcohol, smoked less, and used fewer major medications. On the other hand, as might be expected in light of their advanced age, the ninety-plus people had more cardiac, visual, and hearing problems.

But the older people were, according to certain measures, in better shape emotionally: They experienced fewer psychiatric problems *and depressions* than the younger participants.

How should we interpret the findings? There are a number of possibilities, but some of the differences in the older people—notably less smoking, less alcoholism, and more family contacts—may represent favorable factors promoting greater longevity.

G. D. Jensen and P. Bellecci, "The Physical and Mental Health of Nonagenarians," *Age and Ageing* 16 (1987): 19.

In part because of the life-threatening malnutrition, she had ECT treatment. Typically, a course of ECT involves eight to twelve sessions, administered three times a week until the course is completed. By the time she was finished, this woman's personality had returned to its cheerful, outgoing predepression outlook.

What are the negative side effects of ECT? There is often a temporary memory loss or sense of confusion, which improves after the treatment. After the course of treatment has been finished, patients may complain for some weeks or months that they cannot remember certain events in their lives. But as a general rule, memory keeps steadily improving.

Many physicians familiar with severe depressions in the elderly feel that ECT may be the treatment of first choice, rather than the one to fall back on after drugs failed. Why do they take this position? For one thing, improvement occurs more rapidly after ECT than after drugs. The various side effects of drugs may also make drug treatment less desirable than ECT. There are also a few studies indicating that giving an antidepressant drug *after* a course of ECT may have merit in preventing a relapse.

To sum up, then, there are a considerable number of possible causes for depression, and many other problems or conditions may be disguised as depression. As a result, depression is often not diagnosed properly. Consequently, making a proper diagnosis may require several trials by the doctors and additional evaluations.

In the last analysis, however, depression is a highly treatable illness, and when the right treatment has been found, you can expect significant improvement.

28

USING MEDICINES WISELY

When I first hung out my shingle, there were no antibiotics and therefore, no treatments for pneumonia, peritonitis, urinary tract infections, or even spreading skin infections.

There was no polio vaccine, and every summer carried a polio dread: Many mothers hung cloves of garlic around their offsprings' necks to ward off the virus.

There were no diuretics or other antihypertensive drugs. Seriously elevated blood pressure often progressed to stroke, and there was virtually nothing that could be done about it.

There were not even antihistamines to control hay fever and allergies. I often wonder how we had the courage to practice medicine in those days. What happened was that we became resigned to the fates. The man who was perhaps the greatest of American physicians, William Osler, remarked with resignation of pneumonia that it was the "old man's friend," by which he meant that it was a quiet and painless way of dying. Nowadays, however, we see pneumonia as a defeated enemy, and we are perturbed when it fails to respond to the appropriate antibiotic.

So remarkable has been progress in treatment in recent years that we are literally flooded with tablets and capsules. Early in this development, most doctors could identify medications by their characteristic appearance. For example, the widely used antibiotic tetracycline was a yellow and orange capsule. But as the flood of medications increased, manufacturers ran out of identifying characteristics such as color. Now, a yellow and orange capsule may be an antibiotic, a sleeping pill, a drug for lowering blood pressure, or a number of other things.

Perhaps the first point to keep in mind as you try to formulate a wise approach to drug use is always to remember the proliferation and potential of medications. Specifically, it is best not to rely on appearances in identifying a less-than-familiar pill.

It was my practice for many years to insist that the pharmacist put the name of the drug on the label. Not only that, I urged him to add a word or two about its action. As I mentioned at the beginning of this book, I arranged to have "WATER PILL" written on diuretics, or "HEART PILL" on digoxin, a medication used for slowing certain rapid heart rates and for strengthening the heart's contraction. In this practice, I was just following the example of my intelligent patients who took to labeling the drugs themselves: SLEEPING PILL, HEADACHE PILL, GOUT PILL, and so forth.

We have already considered many different types of drugs in this book. But in this chapter, I want to provide a final overview and give you some practical strategies for dealing with your pills intelligently and wisely.

Effects and Side Effects of Medications

However wonderful and lifesaving our new medications are, they are far from perfect. Perfection would mean that a drug would act only on the target, such as a certain bacterial strain, and produce no effect whatsoever on anything else. That is to say, the pill would have no *side effect*.

HEALTH REPORT

OVERMEDICATION OF LOW-WEIGHT OLDER PEOPLE

The impact of a drug varies, depending on a variety of factors; weight and age are two such important factors.

The authors studied the prescribed dosage of three drugs: cimetidine (Tagamet), a preparation used to decrease stomach acid secretion; flurazepam (Dalmane), a sleeping pill; and digoxin (Lanoxin), a widely used heart medicine.

Analysis revealed that physicians generally did not reduce dosage for older patients. Thus, some lightweight older persons received these drugs at 31 to 46 percent higher levels than the average in the group, and at 70 to 88 percent higher dosages, in relation to their body weight levels, than the heavier persons (who were 198 or more pounds in weight).

To prevent the problem of overdosage the authors advocate reducing medication dose on the basis of lessened weight and age, much as pediatricians have traditionally dosed children.

E. W. Campion, J. Avorn, V. A. Reder, and N. J. Olins, "Overmedication of the Low-Weight Elderly," *Archives of Internal Medicine* 147 (1987): 945.

It is true that as we begin to perfect a given class of drugs, very often the side effects can be diminished. Take some of our newer sleeping pills. One may fall asleep quite promptly after taking one, sleep soundly for six to seven hours, but then awake heavy-headed and even a little dopey. In other words, some degree of dizziness in the morning is not an uncommon side effect of sleeping pills. Others that have been noted are hangover, with bouts of sleepiness during the day; confusion on awakening; and memory impairment.

A major problem that aggravates side effects is the fact that many drugs are only slowly broken down in the body. This is especially the case with the widely used sleeping medication flurazepam (Dalmane). Half of the original dose may still be present in the body four days later, a result that makes for an unusually long-lasting effect until a *steady state,* or proper drug balance, is reached. An accumulation of the drug can occur in the body, producing more side effects, chiefly dizziness and overtranquilization, in some people.

Newer drugs that are much more rapidly broken down and excreted from the body have been produced. They may also carry a lessened likelihood of hangover and dizziness. Indeed, some are now so short-acting that they are less useful in some cases. For example, with certain sleeping medications, patients may complain that they fall asleep promptly but wake up at 4:00 A.M. For those who experience such an effect, a somewhat longer-acting medication may be used.

The side effects of drugs attest to the difficulties in making medications that hit the target only, without any additional ripples or splatters. One of the original antihistamine drugs, diphenhydramine, much better known under its trade name, Benadryl, provides a good illustration. The antihistamines were very welcome when they appeared. For a hay fever victim suffering from a runny nose and much sneezing and tearing, these medications represented a real boon. They dry the secretions and make waking and sleeping much more pleasant.

In addition, antihistamines may have side effects. They may produce variable degrees of sleepiness, and after they appeared, there were many tales of professors dozing in the middle of a lecture and of businessmen falling asleep at conferences. So warnings not to use them when working with machinery or when driving appeared.

In an effort to reduce the side effects of antihistamines, physicians and researchers took a number of steps. Doctors decreased the dose of the drug, and this adjustment helped diminish the side effect of sleepiness, while the desired drying effect remained. Ingenious combinations were also concocted, such as pairing the antihistamine with other drying drugs that had a mildly stimulating effect. The combination cancelled out the sleepiness, more or less.

Finally, newer antihistamines that have little or no tendency to produce sleepiness arrived. Still, Benadryl may be a very good medication for a hay fever sufferer who has a tendency to insomnia. For such a patient, a night dose has both a desired effect and a desirable side effect.

Other side effects of drugs become well known to patients who

have to take them repeatedly. Some antibiotics, for instance, may produce gastrointestinal upsets, varying from a little nausea to a mild diarrhea. Some tranquilizers and some of the drugs used for Parkinson's disease and depression may produce considerable dryness of the mouth or some blurring of near vision. Too large a dose of aspirin may produce ringing in the ear, and some other drugs may diminish kidney function in certain people.

Some side effects may also be indications of the strength and efficacy of a drug. As many a woman has found out when on an antibiotic, the wiping out of bacteria leads to an overgrowth of other organisms such as the yeasts. The result may be a yeast vaginitis, a condition that necessitates treatment with an antiyeast medicine.

In addition to side effects, there are also *allergies* that arise from drugs. These are more likely to occur in people who have known allergies, but some do occur in individuals with no known history of past allergy. Common manifestations are fever and rashes. In rather rare instances, some people have also had asthmatic reactions.

It is sometimes difficult to distinguish between an allergic reaction to a drug and manifestations of the underlying illness itself. *Drug fever,* for instance, is an allergic reaction to a medication, in which fever occurs. It is apparent that at some points in some illnesses, the continuation of fever may be due to the original cause. Sometimes, however, the fever is a response to the medications that are being used. Where there is doubt, the physician usually stops administration of the drug and observes the result: Generally within forty-eight hours or so, any fever due to the drug diminishes or disappears.

Many drugs have also been accused of the side effect of hindering sexual drive. This may be an unfair accusation in some cases, because many ill people have very little sexual urge. But some high blood pressure drugs, tranquilizers, and sleeping medications *can* impair sexual urge or performance. Sometimes, as far as sex is concerned, the issue can be settled only by shifting from the suspect drug to another or even withdrawing medications temporarily.

One of my patients whose libido was easily diminished because of his age and his diabetes once grumbled to me that he did not understand why *all* the side effects of drugs tended to diminish, rather than enhance, his sex life. I agreed with him that this was so, and at the time, it was. But then, along came a new antidepressant (Desyrel), which in rare instances has been reported to produce prolonged erections in some men!

The Placebo Response

A reaction to an inert substance is called a *placebo response,* and it is a response that is of great importance in the evaluation of drugs, and in the practice of medicine in general.

With a placebo response, many people, when given the inert substance, have a clearly negative or positive reaction. A positive response might be the disappearance of a headache, an improvement in joint pain, or perhaps even an increase in energy or appetite. Negative responses are very often complaints of headache, nausea, dizziness, or perhaps a gastrointestinal upset.

Some of the complaints that arise from a placebo may have no relation to the placebo: They may be due to other factors affecting the patient, such as stress, improper food, or work problems. But some of them *are* simply responses to the fact that a medication has been given.

A genuine placebo response is a far more common event than one would anticipate: It occurs in about one-third of all patients given any pill.

Because there are so many responses to placebos, both good and bad, all good trials with medicines are generally conducted with both a drug and a placebo. The manufacturer may make up an inert pill that looks exactly like the active one. Then, the trial of the drug is conducted with neither the patients nor the doctors knowing which pill is which (this is called a *double-blind study*). Such a trial is a powerful research tool to determine whether a pill really has the desired or supposed effect.

Those Amazing Drug Interactions

One day, one of my bright—and somewhat critical—patients said, "Dr. Rossman, something has to be done about your pill-pushing. Do you know how many medications I took yesterday? Nineteen!"

I said that seemed awfully high and went over her list with her, but I soon found that her count was accurate: She was taking a pill for diabetes, a female hormone pill, a diuretic for her high blood pressure, another pill three times a day for high blood pressure, a mild tranquilizer three times a day for her jitteriness, an antihistamine for her hay fever, potassium supplements to correct a low potassium level, and a calcium tablet three times a day.

When I reviewed this list, item for item, it was obvious to me that every one of those pills was absolutely necessary. And when I explained the situation to her, my patient agreed that she could not give up a single one of those medications without incurring a further problem.

Unfortunately, with aging it is easy to accumulate a number of illnesses for which long-term or indefinite treatment may be necessary. Thus, one set of pills is piled onto another set of pills, a sequence that is termed *polypharmacy.* This accumulation attests to the fact that with so many illnesses around, we have no panacea, no once-and-for-all cure. We simply have ongoing control measures with our daily medications.

One potential complication of all this is the possibility that some drugs may adversely interact with other drugs. This is much less common than one might presume: My patients periodically ask whether it is okay to take drug B and drug C together with their breakfast. The answer: Sometimes it is. But in other cases, drugs may interact with one another or with the food and produce an undesirable result.

HEALTH REPORT

DRUG INTERACTIONS: ORAL ANTIBIOTICS AND COMMON CHRONIC MEDICATIONS

Those over sixty-five are the largest consumers of medications, and 10.7 prescriptions are written annually per person in this group. Often they may use a given drug for long periods or indefinitely.

Examples might be digoxin, a heart medicine; theophylline, a drug prescribed for keeping the bronchial tubes open; and warfarin (Coumadin), an anticoagulant used for diminishing clotting of blood.

If an acute infection pops up, how might a prescribed antibiotic interact with the other medications the patient is using?

An example might be digoxin, whose level in the blood should be kept within a given range: the *therapeutic range*. A certain amount of digoxin is destroyed by the bacteria of the intestine. If an antibiotic such as tetracycline or erythromycin is administered, the gut bacteria are partly destroyed, and the digoxin now available for absorption is increased. Consequently, the level of the digoxin in the blood may rise, sometimes to the point of digoxin toxicity.

Another example: Warfarin (Coumadin) is broken down in the liver at a certain rate. Administered erythromycin or sulfa drugs, when they reach the liver, compete for the same breakdown process. The result is a rise in the blood level of the Coumadin with an increased possibility of bruising and bleeding.

Some of the fluctuations in drug levels may not be significant (that is, they may still be within the therapeutic range), but others may be. One should ask the doctor about such possibilities, because an alternative drug may not exhibit the sme degree of interaction.

[NOTE: One might remember also that tetracycline interacts with foods such as milk, with calcium tablets, and with other antacids. This interaction produces a consequent decline in its availability as an antibiotic.]

R. H. Raasch, "Interactions of Oral Antibiotics and Common Chronic Medications," *Journal of the American Geriatrics Society* 42 (1987): 69.

For example, the widely prescribed antibiotic tetracycline should *not* be taken with milk or at the same time as calcium tablets. The reason: Calcium binds to the tetracycline and partly inactivates it. Apart from diminishing the effectiveness of the tetracycline, this interaction will not produce any harm. But there are some interactions that are potentially dangerous.

Among commonly prescribed cardiac drugs, for instance, you will find digoxin, which is used for congestive heart failure and for slowing of certain irregular heart rhythms. Another medication is a drug called Quinidine, which is used for particular disorders of heart rhythm.

Now, here is the problem: With any given patient, the daily dosage of digoxin has to be very carefully determined and monitored for various effects and side effects. One way of keeping track of the correct dose is by watching the levels of the digoxin in the blood.

But suppose there is a heart rhythm disorder and a need for Quinidine arises. With the Quinidine added, the amount of digoxin in the blood may abruptly rise, and symptoms of overdosage may occur. The lesson here: As with any other drug, keep in close touch with your physician, who should be monitoring the impact of any change in medication.

Tips for the Wise Consumer

When you are buying drugs, you should work with your doctor to become a wise consumer, a person who can buy an effective and, if possible, inexpensive medication. In this regard, there are two major considerations I tell my patients to keep in mind: (1) Understand the difference between brand-name and generic drugs and (2) be careful about old or expired medications.

Brand Name Versus Generic

Generally, the manufacturer who discovers and develops a medication gives it a proprietary or trade name, such as *Valium*. This has the commercial advantage of identifying it on behalf of the company. Even after the patent expires, prescriptions using the brand name continue to reward the company for its original research and development.

But once a patent has expired, other manufacturers may make the drug and distribute it under its chemical name. For example, the chemical name of Valium is *diazepam*. Drugs such as diazepam are called generic drugs, and they are usually marketed at a lower price.

The Food and Drug Administration (FDA) has taken the general position that most of these medications, though manufactured by companies other than the original, are essentially equivalent in dose and effect. Some state departments of health have distributed to physicians long lists of equivalent drugs and have attempted to increase use of the cheaper generics.

For example, a widely used alternative to aspirin, which has been around for more than fifty years, is known chemically as *acetaminophen*. This drug has been much more widely recognized by both professionals and the public under the brand name *Tylenol*. There is no reason to believe, however, that Tylenol is significantly different from a generic drug company's cheaper acetaminophen.

Still, generic drugs are not always the best. There are some medications that, because of special steps in their manufacture or quirky aspects in the formulation of the pill or capsule, are better if taken as the branded product rather than the generic one.

Perhaps the best-known illustration of this type of pill is the product known as *Lanoxin*. This is digoxin, the well-known heart pill formulated and manufactured by the Burroughs Wellcome Company. An important study many years ago, one of the first of its kind, demonstrated that Lanoxin was better absorbed and yielded better blood levels than the similar amount of the generic digoxin. Hence, doctors using this group of drugs prefer to prescribe Lanoxin, despite the increased cost.

Somewhat the same advantage has been shown for a few other brand-name drugs. But on the whole, these are exceptions. By and large, if the FDA says generics are equivalent, both physician and patient can accept that evaluation. For someone who is on multiple drugs, the annual savings with generics can be impressive, running into many hundreds of dollars.

Unfortunately, however, from the point of view of medication expense, some of our very best and effective drugs are still under patent. This means that the prices continue to be quite high.

Old and Expired Drugs

Manufacturers stamp an expiration date on the label of the medications they sell to the pharmacist. When making up your prescription, the pharmacist generally copies the expiration date onto the prescription label. The manufacturer's expiration date is essentially a warranty that the drug will be stable and measure up to expectations until the stated date.

This does not mean that if the expiration is marked, say, March 1990, its ability to be curative or useful suddenly expires when that month rolls around. What it may mean is that the potency may possibly change by that time. In any event, the manufacturer cannot be certain enough to guarantee maintenance of drug potency for so long a period, though a therapeutic effect may continue weeks or months after the date of original purchase.

An example of a drug that *does* slowly undergo degradation with the passage of time is aspirin. This wonderful drug goes back to the turn of the century and is basically a simple synthesis of acetic acid (the chief ingredient of vinegar) and a somewhat more complicated compound, salicylic acid. If you smell aspirin pills that have been around for some time—and especially if the weather has been damp—you may be able to detect the odor of vinegar. This is an indication that some of the aspirin is beginning to break down into its components.

Many other compounds are extremely stable, however. For example, you can expect old calcium carbonate tablets to give a reliable dosage of calcium, even years after the manufacture.

On the other hand, some medications are more complex and more unstable. This makes them more likely to undergo change after exposure to air or after passage of time. Penicillin tablets, for example, may slowly lose some potency with the passage of a month. Some antibiotics, especially in a solution, may also lose potency in days. For this reason, I counsel patients to keep penicillin and some other drugs in the refrigerator if a period of storage is contemplated. Obviously, when drugs have gone well past their stamped time of expiration, it is time to get rid of them.

How to Prevent Medication Errors

Because there is such a potential for confusion in the administration of medicines, doctors and patients alike have shown a great deal of concern about this issue. Many patients have grumbled to me that when it comes to dispensing and administering drugs, neither drug companies nor pharmacists have spent enough effort on being "user-friendly." So let me give you a few tips on how to use your drugs more wisely and prevent potential drug-related errors.

KEY FACTS

HOW HARD IS IT FOR OLDER PEOPLE TO OPEN MEDICATION CONTAINERS?

In a 1988 report, fifty noninstitutionalized persons over sixty years of age were observed and timed opening fifteen containers.

The results: Only 50 to 70 percent of the group were able to open certain child-resistant containers (that is, align arrows, align tab with notch, or depress tab and turn).

Only 40 to 60 percent were able to open certain types of nitroglycerin skin patches.

Some subjects needed as much as thirty-six to thirty-nine seconds to open some of the child-resistant containers.

Conclusion: If there is no need for childproofing, the simple nonresistant containers are more suitable for the elderly.

S. Keram and M. E. Williams, "Quantifying the Ease or Difficulty Older Persons Experience in Opening Medication Containers," *Journal of the American Geriatrics Society* 36 (1988): 199.

• *Do not keep medications that are no longer being used or have expired indefinitely.* Also be wary of medications that have changed in appearance or color. If you are in doubt, take the drug to your doctor or pharmacist and ask him or her about it.

• *Make sure all your medications are labeled,* either with their name or purpose, in capital letters. If you have visual problems with labels, you might think of color coding. Just put a piece of colored tape on the container so that you can identify it more easily.

• *The use of dispensing containers may help you keep things straight.* One version is labeled from Sunday through Saturday and can be loaded with the appropriate medications for dosages up to four times a day. It is simple and easy to place the one-a-day pill, the four-times-a-day pill, and so forth, in the appropriate compart-ments. A further advantage is that this method allows you to plan your medication schedule for the week.

● *Ascertain from your doctor when a pill should be taken:* before or after or between meals, if this is not clear from the drug label.

In general, you get higher drug levels in your bloodstream if medications are taken on an empty stomach. Taken after a meal, a medicine has a slower absorption and a longer duration of action. In addition, drugs sometimes have to be taken so as to prevent interactions.

● *If you miss a dose of your medication,* there are several possible courses of action: Double up on the next dose, *if* your doctor agrees; simply let the dose pass; or decrease the remaining inter-vals between drug use so as to make up for the lost dose. Which-ever approach you choose should only be used in consultation with your physician.

● *Do not rely on your memory* to recall what the doctor told you about the medicine. Write it down or ask him to write it down, so that when you get home, the instructions are there for you to see in black and white.

● *Be a good observer of the impact that the medication has on your mind and body.* Watch for side effects, and notify your doctor if you notice anything unusual. A rash, itching, significant bowel upset, or other such change may indicate an adverse or even allergic reaction to the drug.

Use your head if your health or circumstances change while you are taking the medication. For example, if you are taking a pill labeled a diuretic, you probably know that it increases the flow of urine and draws fluid from your body. So if a day comes along when you are losing fluids because of vomiting or diarrhea, it may not be desirable to promote more fluid loss through the diuretic. Similarly, if you enter an excessively hot area and perspire a great deal, use of a diuretic may be inadvisable.

Medications represent wonderful advances in our scientific efforts, but to take full advantage of them, we have to play by the rules formulated by physicians and pharmacists.

If you are supposed to take a pill in a certain dose several times a day, then do it! Noncompliance is a big problem that physicians face: It is estimated that 10 to 20 percent of patients do not comply even with written instructions. Yet if you don't follow instructions, at the very least you may not be helped by the medication. And at the worst, you may be placing yourself in jeopardy.

Just use good common sense as you and your physician plan your drug strategy, and you will most likely find that you will enjoy the maximum benefits from your medications.

29

SOME SECRETS TO A FINE APPEARANCE AFTER FIFTY

I have never had a face-lift or any other type of cosmetic surgery, but I certainly have a positive attitude toward my patients who feel a need to give nature a boost by smoothing out some wrinkles or otherwise adjusting their appearance with the help of a medical specialist.

The job of the cosmetic surgeon is to give you a new lease on life, but not to turn you into a twenty-year-old. The best of these specialists can remove some of that tired, drooping look in your face, with a touch here and a tuck there. As long as your expectations are realistic, you may find that cosmetic surgery is a way to become rejuvenated, both physically and emotionally.

To assist you in understanding some of the possibilities of cosmetic surgery—or "aesthetic" surgery as it is often called by physicians in this field—I have consulted my colleague Dr. Arthur Ship, a skilled plastic surgeon. Some of the following information is based on an interchange with him.

But let me caution you once more: It is important to realize that you cannot recapture your youth with surgery. You may be able to *look* somewhat younger, but you cannot turn back the clock.

On the other hand, it is understandable that many people may want to take more initiative in improving their appearance. The first question that you may ask if you decide to explore cosmetic surgery, is, Who should perform the operation?

Who Should Perform the Operation?

There is a great controversy these days about how cosmetic surgery should be done and who should do it. The most obvious specialist to perform cosmetic surgery is a *plastic surgeon,* who is trained first as a general surgeon, then as a specialist in plastic surgery. But there are also three other categories of physicians who can now perform the operations:

• *Otolaryngologists,* who are ear, nose, and throat specialists. They perform only facial surgery and have one year of general surgery training.
• *Ophthalmologists,* who specialize in the eyes.
• *Dermatologists,* who are primarily skin doctors, with limited or no training in general surgery.

Representatives of these four disciplines have traded criticisms and charges on various levels. The otolaryngologists, for example, say they are best suited for facial plastic surgery because they concentrate on that area. The plastic surgeons, in contrast, argue that they have far more training in surgery than any of the other specialists, and therefore they should be preferred.

Here is a checklist of what I think you should look for in a cosmetic surgeon:

• He or she should be affiliated with a major teaching hospital or a major community hospital. This affiliation tells you whether or not his or her peers approve of his work.
• He or she should be board-certified in plastic surgery or in otolaryngology (ear-nose-throat).

• His or her credentials, including all medical training, should be thoroughly checked and you should be referred by your own physician or a physician whom you respect.

• He or she should have a significant, successful track record over a period of several years in performing the type of operation you want.

• He or she should inspire confidence in you after you have had *several* consultations before any operation. You should never have just one meeting with a cosmetic surgeon and then have the operation. There is a strong emotional component to these procedures, and it is essential that you be absolutely certain about your attitude and the implications of the step you are taking.

But even before you choose a surgeon, you have to know what kind of cosmetic surgery you want, or need. What are the options?

The Options for Aesthetic Surgery

Eyelids

An eyelid operation offers the most for the least investment of time and expense. The procedure takes away sleepy eyes by removing the bags and re-creates natural folds, though it does not remove wrinkles. Wrinkles can be handled by other procedures, which we will discuss shortly.

This is a very successful operation, but extremely delicate, with little room for error.

What are the possible dangers? If the surgeon removes excessive amounts of skin, he may uncover too much of the white of the eye, and this can lead to dry eyes and irritation. There are even an extremely small number of cases of blindness (a total of eleven in the entire body of world medical literature), but this is not a worry with a top-level plastic surgeon.

There are medical and not just cosmetic reasons to have this operation. The upper lids of some older people begin to hang down and may actually interfere with vision. This is called *ptosis* and is a normal sagging that occurs with aging. Other conditions that may necessitate corrective surgery are a turning-in or turning-out of the lower lids, which may produce irritation. These operations are often covered by health insurance, whereas ordinary cosmetic surgery is not.

How long will the effect of this operation last? The lower lids should last at least ten years; the upper lids generally hold up for at least five years.

Face-Lift

The fat under the skin begins to disappear as we get older, and the skin also becomes less elastic. Exposure to the ultraviolet rays of the sun may contribute as well to sagging of the face and skin. This operation opens the face and gives a fresher look.

The surgery is performed by making an incision in front of the ear and then up into the hair-bearing area in the scalp. If the patient is a man who is partially or totally bald, and the hairline is not adequate to hide the scar, the physician makes his incision over an area next to the ear where the scar can be covered up by beard or sideburns.

The surgeon literally peels the skin off the face down to the smile lines at the mouth. Then, he redrapes the tissues more firmly over the skull. New procedures include surgery on the supporting tissues, the *fascia*, underneath the skin. The specialist may perform extensive muscle surgery on the face as he redrapes the skin. The skin is then drawn firmly back up onto the scalp. The excess skin is cut away and discarded. Plastic surgeons try to avoid pulling the skin too tightly over the skull because that may produce broader scars and make the face nearly immobile.

Certain parts of the face-lift last longer than others, and the durability of the operation is a very individual matter. The shortest period of time that a face-lift lasts is about a year, and the longest time, on average, is about four years. Some sort of periodic lesser operation is necessary to supplement the original face-lift if the patient wants to maintain a continuing cosmetic effect.

Dangers with this procedure include possible nerve damage. When the doctor operates on tissues below the skin, there is a risk that a nerve will be sliced or severed, an injury that can result in a lopsided smile or paralysis in part of the face, especially at the jawline.

There may also be a great deal of *liposuction* (fat suction) performed during face-lifts these days. If this procedure is not done properly, damage may result, including possibly serious damage to the blood vessels, along with the promotion of blood clots.

Another possibility, which is quite remote with a good surgeon, is a slough of the skin. This means that the skin dies, and as the underlying tissue grows back to replace it, serious scars may develop.

When the procedure is performed by a competent specialist, however, these dangers are minimal or practically nonexistent. But what a person who has this operation can expect in almost every case is a feeling of mild or heavier depression a week or so after the operation. At first, there may be euphoria. But then, the patient begins to see that not all signs of aging have been removed. So he or she wonders, "Why did I pay all this money to have this operation done? It wasn't worth it."

Then, after about three to four weeks, a more realistic attitude typically sets in, and many are quite satisfied with the results of the surgery. They feel they look better, and they even sense they have more energy and confidence in relating to others.

Finally, it is important how the patient displays his or her new façade. Some plastic surgeons who perform many face-lifts actually have cosmetics experts on staff to show their female patients how to apply makeup properly to their new faces.

The Chemical Peel for Wrinkles

The smile lines and purse lines around the eyes and mouth can be eliminated by a procedure called a "chemical peel," done with carbolic acid. The solution is painted on, and then a wet dressing is placed on the face to *macerate,* or take off, the dead skin. This can be done on the entire face and can be particularly helpful for those with sun damage. The peel removes all the fine lines and fine wrinkles (but *not* the heavy wrinkles).

Because this procedure creates a biochemical change in the *collagen,* the supportive structure of the skin, the direction of the fibers in the skin, under the epidermis, changes. You in effect really do get a new face.

Many times a patient wants this procedure *and* a face-lift, but the operations cannot be done together. The best approach seems to be to perform the face-lift first, to establish the underlying foundation of the face. Then, the specialist performs the chemical peel to smooth out the fine lines and wrinkles.

The operation can be expected to last for ten years or longer.

Coronal Brow Lift

The coronal brow lift procedure eliminates the heavy wrinkles on the forehead. The surgery is performed by making an incision at the top of the head and pulling the skin up to smooth out the deep wrinkles. The underlying muscles are softened, or made weaker, so that the face relaxes.

This operation lasts almost indefinitely.

Rhinoplasty

Rhinoplasty is the "nose job," the most common plastic surgery operation in the country. The operation has a high degree of success, and older people turn to this procedure to alter some of the changes that accompany aging. Specifically, the tip of the nose tends to grow downward, so the surgeon may shorten the tip and restore some of the original youthful look of the nose.

A rhinoplasty will last indefinitely and may be included in a face-lift procedure.

Neck

The standard face-lift does not eliminate wrinkles on the neck. It is possible, however, to alter the two thin bands of muscle that begin to droop with age just to the sides of the larynx (voice box).

Here is the way it works: The surgeon can tie together the two stringy muscles in the front of the neck, to eliminate some of the droopiness. It is also possible to notch those drooping muscles in the neck during the face-lift and eliminate the sagging look in the neck that way.

How about injections into the skin during face-lifts or other procedures? The use of silicone injections has not been approved by the FDA, and it can be quite dangerous. There can be sloughs, due to a dying of skin and other problems. So stay away from this approach. Fat injections into the skin may also lead to calcification and other problems. Consequently, it is best to avoid this procedure as well.

Breast Surgery

There are three types of women in the older age groups who can benefit from plastic surgery on the breasts:

1. Those with very large, pendulous breasts. These women often experience serious back pain, irritation of the skin where the breasts rub against the chest and abdomen, and other ailments. So a breast reduction would be appropriate here. Dangers include fat *necrosis,* or death of the tissues.

This operation, when performed successfully, is a very durable procedure and probably will not have to be repeated.

2. Another problem for older women is having breasts of different sizes. When one is quite large and the other small, the back may even become twisted, and *scoliosis,* or curvature of the spine, may result. The chest and rib cage can become twisted as well.

3. A third breast procedure involves the correction of sagging breasts. An older woman's breasts may be the right size, but not in the right place, if they have sagged.

There are a couple of possible procedures here. The newest technique is to resuspend the breast from the chest wall from a higher spot. At the same time, the nipples are repositioned higher. This is a procedure that has been pioneered by Dr. Ship. Another surgical approach, which has been more common in the past, is to move up the nipple on the breast and fill in the breasts with tissue or perhaps even silicone bags.

The durability of these operations may vary from a relatively short period of time to ten or more years.

Abdominal Skin Apron

A woman who has been quite heavy and has lost a lot of weight may have a loose-skin "apron" hanging down from her navel. She probably hates the way it looks because as much as she diets and exercises, she cannot get rid of that unsightly drooping skin fold. So she may have a "tummy tuck," or a surgical removal of that extra skin around the abdomen.

Fat Suction

In the liposuction procedure, a small hose, called a *cannula,* is placed into a fatty part of the body through a half-inch slit. Then, the surgeon rotates the hose and tries to shake free as much fat as he can. The fat is then suctioned out through the hose. This procedure has become the most common form of cosmetic surgery in the United States and is performed on thighs, buttocks, abdomen, and face.

Many people are having this operation, but I would advise you to stay away from it, except as it is done in a limited way with face-lifts or other procedures. It should be an adjunct to other surgery. A massive liposuction (fat suction) is probably never appropriate, especially for the older patient. The dangers? There is a relatively high risk that blood vessels will be torn, and blood clots may develop. So avoid this procedure!

Other Cosmetic Considerations

Much mythology and questionable advice surround the subject of improving your looks. So let me give you a few short opinions on two appearance-related topics:

• *Retin-A,* a synthetic relative of vitamin A, is becoming a highly touted wrinkle remover. Applied as a topical cream or gel, it is claimed to be able to reverse some aging changes in skin, according to its proponents. They say it also diminishes wrinkling and reverses some skin damage. But there are also negatives, which are still being explored: Retin-A produces a lot of redness in some people. It also increases sun sensitivity, so it has to be regarded with some caution. Consult your doctor about its use.

• *Minoxidil,* the high blood pressure medication, has enjoyed some success as a temporary hair restorer for some younger men with a slight to moderate baldness problem. But for older people, and especially those with considerable hair loss, the prospects are not good.

When you are exploring these cosmetic possibilities, do not allow yourself to be sold on a certain cosmetic operation without checking its pros and cons quite thoroughly. Reasonable expectations are the best course for a patient considering cosmetic surgery.

You may very well be pleased with what you see after your operation. But then, after you think about it and examine yourself more closely, you may not be so pleased. Plastic surgeons do not work miracles in the operating room. But if they do their job, they can inject a breath of new life and youthful feeling into their patients.

30

LOOKING FORWARD

One of my most respected medical teachers used to say, "Listen to your patients; listen to your patients! They'll give you the diagnosis."

I have always taken that advice to heart because I believe the doctor-patient relationship should be reciprocally educational. I know I have a lot to give those who need help with their health, but I *also* know they have a lot to give me.

The doctor who underestimates or ignores the intelligence and capacities of patients to contribute to their own physical and emotional well-being is a doctor who is disregarding one of the best possible sources of information and guidance. After all, your body is, in a sense, a business of which you are the sole proprietor. Who knows that body's peculiarities, reactions, and personal history better than you?

To be sure, a physician, in dealing with a particular complaint or disorder, has special training and a degree of objectivity that enhance sound medical judgment and decision making. But a physician, unaided, can go only so far. One who proceeds without the assistance of the patient's personal understanding of a problem is a limited care giver indeed.

Throughout this book, I have encouraged you to enter into the prevention and treatment process. You have been provided with a variety of practical tips, warning signals, and background materials on everything from heart attacks to constipation to Alzheimer's disease to cosmetic surgery. This information should alert you to possible problems in your body and mind as you age and also should put you in a strong position to work hand-in-hand with your doctor.

Furthermore, I want to encourage you to expand the boundaries of your knowledge about your body beyond the covers of this book. For example, it is helpful to monitor newspapers and magazines for late-breaking medical developments and to ask your doctor about them. In a similar vein, you might keep a clipping file on these articles and reports for further reference.

Some of my patients go even further: They like to explore the latest reports in professional medical journals, many of which I've cited in the Key Facts and Health Report boxes throughout this book. For those with such ambitions, I recommend publications that can be found in many local libraries, such as *The New England Journal of Medicine, The Journal of the American Medical Association, Lancet,* and the *Journal of the American Geriatrics Society.*

Of course, many of the articles in these publications will not be entirely understandable to those without medical training. But many other articles *will* be reasonably clear, especially if they deal with a special health problem of the patient. In general, I suggest that those who delve into the professional literature focus on the summary abstracts, which can often be found in boldface at the beginning of the main article.

It is also important that those who do additional reading *not* assume that they can now "play doctor" themselves and ignore trained medical experts. The extra study is only intended to make you a better informed patient who can work more effectively with a personal physician—not to transform you into a doctor.

Finally, learning more about your health, and where your current health practices may be taking you, is somewhat like taking a trip into the future. By exploring various diseases and disorders, you can see where others have been and where you may be going as well.

The advantage that you have is that, after looking forward into the future and examining what might be, you can focus on the present and begin to change your possibilities for the better. With your doctor, you can develop an overall personal health plan, along with specific strategies to prevent or mitigate problems that you may face in later years. Above all, you can maximize your chances to enjoy a long and fruitful life in the decades to come.

INDEX

Stomach acids, 357
Stomach cancer, 56, 309, 319, 340, 415
Stomach disorders, 376–84
Stools: black, 382; blood in, 455; color of, 390–91; loose, 372, 357
Streptococcus, 489
Streptokinase, 488
Stress, 91, 113, 373, 468, 484
Stress incontinence, 516–17
Stress test, 176, 226, 250; before exercise program, 232–33, 465
Stroke(s), 9, 30, 133, 290–303, 534; aspirin in prevention of, 249–53, 254; defined, 291–92; and depression, 554; diabetes and, 58, 407; effect on memory, 527; and epileptic attacks, 131; estrogen and risk of, 516; family history of, 278; hypertension and, 270, 271, 272, 296, 297; and incontinence, 478, 479; mild, 125, 144, 533 (see also Transient ischemic attack [TIA]); personal history of, 297; rehabilitation following, 302–303; risk of, 185, 295–301; and sexual performance, 500; surgery in prevention/treatment of, 301–302; TIAs and, 167; types of, 292–93; warning signs of, 293–95
Sublinqual glands, 364
Submaxillary glands, 364, 365
Subnutrition, 36, 199–203
Sucrose, 59, 372
Sugar metabolism, 105, 106
Sulfate (hydroxychloroquine), 457
Sulfinpyrazone (Anturane), 458
Sulindac (Clinoril), 411, 455
Sun exposure, 20, 429; risk factor in cancer, 317, 337–39, 347
Sunscreen, 337, 346, 347
Surgeon(s), 301, 302, 463, 580
Surgery, 39, 41, 144, 486; depression following, 554; eye, 154, 157, 159–61, 165–67; fusion, 462, 463; high-risk, 462; and incontinence, 478; overuse of, 260–61; paranoia following, 529; pelvic, 510; prostate, 345, 513, 514–15; in relief of cancer pain, 352–54
Surgical treatment: arthritis, 459–63; back pain, 98; breast cancer, 327–28; cancer, 326–31; cardiovascular disease, 260–62; colon disease, 395, 396, 398; esophageal cancer, 374; foot problems, 109; gallbladder disease, 402, 403, 404; hearing loss, 150; hemorrhoids, 53; oral cancer, 346; pulmonary embolism, 488; PVD, 185; salivary gland problems, 365; skin cancer, 348; sleep apnea, 85; stroke, 301–302
Swallowing, 366–69; difficulties, 39–42, 373–74, 378, 382; mechanism, 40–41, 366–67, 368, 369

Sweating (sweats), 177, 244; mechanism, 102; with menopause, 432, 502, 515
Swelling: in arthritis, 437, 438; in feet, 31–33
Sympathetic nervous system inhibitors, 286
Sympathomimetics, 493
Symptoms: Alzheimer's disease, 530–32; AMD, 162–63; arthritis, 437; asthma, 491; breast cancer, 342; bursitis, 443; cataracts, 156–57; colonic ischemia, 398; colorectal cancer, 340–41; common, in elderly men, 115; common, in elderly women, 114–15; cystitis, 480; dementia, 540; depression, 560; diabetes, 407; esophageal cancer, 373–74; eye problems, 168; fibromyalgia, 443; glaucoma, 158; heart attack, 175; heart disease, 176; heat exhaustion, 103; heatstroke, 102; hypertension, 270; hypotension, 276; hypothermia, 101; indigestion, 356; kidney stones, 481; lupus, 442; major depressive illness, 557–58; malabsorption, 388; mistakenly attributed to hypertension, 273; oral cancer, 346; osteoarthritis, 440; Parkinson's disease, 543; peptic ulcer, 381–83; peripheral vascular disease, 184–85; pernicious anemia, 389; pneumonia, 489; prostate cancer, 345; prostate problems, 514; pulmonary embolism, 486; rheumatoid arthritis, 438, 439; TIA, 294, 295; uterine cancer, 343; warning, in exercise, 242
Syncope. See Fainting
Systemic lupus erythematosus (SLE), 441–42

Tagamet (cimetidine), 382, 384, 405, 566
Tandearil (oxyphenbutazone), 455
Taste (sense), 10, 43, 357, 365–66
Taste buds, 363–64; deterioration of, 36–37, 43, 357, 361, 362
Teeth, 358–59, 360–61, 363, 364; and appetite, 37; brushing, flossing, 360
Tendinitis, 437
Tendons, 437, 459
Terbutaline, 495
"Terminal-reservoir" phenomenon, 49
Testes, 505
Testosterone, 16, 501, 507, 511; levels of, 504, 505
Tetany. See Muscle spasm (tetany)
Tetracycline, 359, 388, 391, 489, 565, 571
Thallium scan, 250
Theophylline, 371, 495, 570
Theophylline group, 491
Thiazide, 285, 405
Thioridazine, 417